PRAISE FOR *THE CRESCENT STONE*

Matt Mikalatos has built a compelling fantasy world with humor and heart.

GENE LUEN YANG, creator of *American Born Chinese* and *Boxers & Saints*

Matt Mikalatos has penned a tale straight out of today's headlines that will tug at your heartstrings. *The Crescent Stone* is a compelling story that will get under your skin and worm its way into your heart.

TOSCA LEE, *New York Times* bestselling author of *Iscariot* and *The Legend of Sheba*

The Crescent Stone hooked me from the first page! With the rich characterization of John Green and the magical escapism of Narnia, this book is a must read for all fantasy fans!

LORIE LANGDON, author of *Olivia Twist* and the Doon series

This is what sets Mikalatos's epic world apart from so many other fantasy realms: the characters feel real, their lives are genuine and complicated, and their choices are far from binary. Mikalatos's creativity and originality are on full display in this epic tale for adults and young readers alike.

SHAWN SMUCKER, author of *The Day the Angels Fell*

The Crescent Stone blends . . . glitter unicorns, powerful healing tattoos, and an engaging cast of characters into a funny and thoughtful story that examines the true costs of magic and privilege.

TINA CONNOLLY, author of *Seriously Wicked*

The twists keep coming in *The Crescent Stone*, a fabulous young adult fantasy with a great cast of characters. I particularly loved Jason, whose humor, logic, and honesty will make readers eager to follow him into a sequel. I found the Sunlit Lands a fantastically engaging place to visit and grew ever more delighted as I discovered more about each culture, their knotted histories, and how the magic worked. Fantasy fans will devour it and ask for seconds.

JILL WILLIAMSON, Christy Award–winning author of *By Darkness Hid* and *Captives*

From C. S. Lewis to J. K. Rowling, the secret magical place that lives alongside our own mundane world has a rich history in fantasy literature, and *The Crescent Stone* is a delightful tale that is a more-than-worthy continuation of that tradition. Matt Mikalatos weaves a rich tapestry that is equal parts wonder, thoughtfulness, and excitement, while being that most wonderful of things—a joyful and fun story. From the first page, you can't help but root for Madeline as she stumbles about trying to navigate a future that is uncertain and fraught with pain. The beauty of Madeline as a character is that her journey is both all too familiar and yet entirely contemporary—the magical land that is her salvation is so much more. I don't know where this series will go. All I know is that I don't ever want it to end.

JAKE KERR, author of the Tommy Black series and a nominee for the Nebula Award, the Theodore Sturgeon Memorial Award, and the storySouth Million Writers Award

The Crescent Stone inspires thought on matters of compassion and privilege in a breathtaking and fun fantasy setting. This is a book that will leave readers empowered—not by magic, but by the potential within their own hearts.

BETH CATO, author of *The Clockwork Dagger*

PRAISE FROM READERS

Jason's personality throughout the whole book brought a smile to my face the entire time.

✦

[The book is about] injustice. The rich taking advantage of the poor. The powerful taking advantage of the weak. How desperate people will do desperate things for their loved ones. That all of our actions affect others around us. Change starts within.

✦

I thought the story itself was very compelling and left me with the excitement of wanting to get to and through the next chapter so I could see what would happen next. . . . I thoroughly enjoyed reading the story and the cultural commentary that was throughout the book.

✦

I love the parallel world aspect of this book. It was unexpected and kept the discussion of privilege and race a fresh perspective.

✦

Overall, I loved the book. I thought the characters and the alternate universe were interesting. I loved the struggles of each character and the surprises within the Sunlit Lands.

✦

Lewis wrote Narnia as a fun story that provided thinly veiled allegory and life lessons. Mikalatos does the same thing here for today's generation. Tackling issues that divide the most rational of adults, Mikalatos shows all these issues with honesty, a story that keeps you engaged, and characters that keep you smiling.

✦

The Crescent Stone is a rare book that shows incredible depth that is matched only by its fun and whimsy.

✦

One of the most engaging stories I have ever read. Nonstop fun meets a conversation-starting masterpiece.

THE SUNLIT LANDS

No one ever talks about this island

PASTISIA
NECROMANCERS.
HARD PASS

SAFE
(MORE OR LESS)

NOPE.
NOPE!
KAKRI
TERRITORIES
NOPE!!

COURT OF
FAR SEEING

TOLMIN PASS

CINIAN SEA

WASTED
LANDS
GROSS

SHARK PEOPLE?!
NO THANKS

TREES? UH-PROBABLY FINE?

YUCK!
LIZARDS

N

THE
SOUTHERN
COURT

ALUVOREA

THE SUNLIT LANDS

BOOK ONE

THE
CRESCENT STONE

MATT MIKALATOS

wander
An imprint of
Tyndale House
Publishers, Inc.

Visit Tyndale online at www.tyndale.com.

Visit the author's website at www.thesunlitlands.com.

TYNDALE and Tyndale's quill logo are registered trademarks of Tyndale House Publishers, Inc. *Wander* and the Wander logo are trademarks of Tyndale House Publishers, Inc. Wander is an imprint of Tyndale House Publishers, Inc., Carol Stream, Illinois.

The Crescent Stone

Designed by Dean H. Renninger

Edited by Sarah Rubio

The author is represented by Ambassador Literary Agency, Nashville, TN.

The Crescent Stone is a work of fiction. Where real people, events, establishments, organizations, or locales appear, they are used fictitiously. All other elements of the novel are drawn from the author's imagination.

For information about special discounts for bulk purchases, please contact Tyndale House Publishers at csresponse@tyndale.com, or call 1-800-323-9400.

Library of Congress Cataloging-in-Publication Data
Names: Mikalatos, Matt, author.
Title: The Crescent Stone / Matt Mikalatos.
Description: Carol Stream, Illinois : Tyndale House Publishers, Inc., [2018]
| Series: The sunlit lands ; book 1 | Summary: When Madeline, a teen with terminal lung disease, accepts healing in exchange for a year of service in the Sunlit Lands, she and her friend Jason enjoy being privileged members of Elenil society, until they learn that magic carries a high price.
Identifiers: LCCN 2018007553 | ISBN 9781496431707 (hc) | ISBN 9781496431714 (sc)
Subjects: | CYAC: Fantasy. | Sick—Fiction. | Friendship—Fiction. | Magic—Fiction.
Classification: LCC PZ7.1.M5535 Cre 2018 | DDC [Fic]—dc23 LC record available at https://lccn.loc.gov/2018007553

Printed in the United States of America

24	23	22	21	20	19	18
7	6	5	4	3	2	1

To Shasta

CAST OF CHARACTERS

ARCHON THENODY—the chief magistrate; supreme ruler of the Elenil

BAILEYA—Kakri warrior who has come to Far Seeing to make her fortune; daughter of Willow, granddaughter of Abronia

BASILEUS PRINEL—one of the Elenil magistrates; in charge of celebrations, rituals, and communal events

BLACK SKULLS—elite fighting force of the Scim; there are three known members

BREAK BONES—a Scim warrior imprisoned by the Elenil

BRIGHT PRISM—a "civilized" Scim man who works in the archon's palace

CROOKED BACK—spokesperson of the Scim army

DARIUS WALKER—American human; Madeline's ex-boyfriend

DAVID GLENN—American human in service to the Elenil

DAY SONG—a "civilized" Scim man who serves Gilenyia

DELIGHTFUL GLITTER LADY [DEE, DGL]—a unicorn

DIEGO FERNÁNDEZ—Colombian human in service to the Elenil; has the power of flight

EVERNU—gallant white stag who works alongside Rondelo

FERA—Scim woman; wife of Inrif and mother of Yenil

FERNANDA ISABELA FLORES DE CASTILLA—Lady of Westwind; human woman; older than most humans in the Sunlit Lands

GARDEN LADY—mysterious old woman who has taken an interest in Madeline

GILENYIA—an influential Elenil lady; Hanali's cousin; has the power of healing

HANALI—Elenil recruiter who invites Madeline to the Sunlit Lands

INRIF—Scim man; husband of Fera and father of Yenil

JASON WU [WU SONG]—American human who follows Madeline into the Sunlit Lands

JASPER—American human in the service of the Elenil; in charge of the armory

JENNY WU—Jason's sister

KEKOA KAHANANUI—American human in service to the Elenil

KNIGHT OF THE MIRROR—human in his mid-forties; fights the Scim without magic

MADELINE OLIVER—American human in the service of the Elenil

MAGISTRATES—the rulers of the Elenil. There are nine of them, including the archon.

MAJESTIC ONE—the Elenil name for the magician who founded the Sunlit Lands

MALGWIN—half fish, half woman; harbinger of chaos and suffering; lives in the dark waterways surrounding the Sunlit Lands

MALIK—Darius's cousin

MOTHER CROW—a Kakri matriarch

MR. GARCÍA—the gardener at Madeline's home on Earth

MRS. RAYMOND—English human woman who runs the Transition House for humans in the Sunlit Lands; fifty years old

MUD—Scim child who lives on the streets of the Court of Far Seeing

NEW DAWN—a "civilized" Scim woman who works for Gilenyia

NIGHT'S BREATH—a Scim warrior

POLEMARCH TIRIUS—one of the Elenil magistrates; the commander of the Elenil army

PEASANT KING—the figure from Scim legend who founded the Sunlit Lands

RAYO—the Knight of the Mirror's silver stallion

RESCA—Hanali's mother

RICARDO SÁNCHEZ—American human in service to the Elenil; healed by Gilenyia

RONDELO—Elenil "captain of the guard" in the Court of Far Seeing

RUTH MBEWE—Zambian eight-year-old who lives in the Knight of the Mirror's household

SHULA BISHARA—Syrian human in the service of the Elenil; has the power to burst into flame

SOCHAR—a member of the city guard; Elenil

SOFÍA—the housekeeper in Madeline's home on Earth

SUN'S DANCE—a "civilized" Scim man; advisor to the Elenil magistrates

THUY NGUYEN—Vietnamese human guard in Westwind

VIVI—father of Hanali, son of Gelintel

YENIL—a young Scim girl; daughter of Inrif and Fera

PART 1

There must be something better,
I know it in my heart.

FROM *THE GRYPHON UNDER THE STAIRS*
BY MARY PATRICIA WALL

1

THE GARDEN LADY

The king's gardener spoke the secret language of all growing things.
She knew the songs of the morning flowers and spoke the poems
of the weeds. She spent long afternoons in conversation with the trees.

FROM "THE TRIUMPH OF THE PEASANT KING," A SCIM LEGEND

✦

The bench stood twenty feet away. Such a short distance. Such an impossible one. Madeline clung to the trellis of ivy that bordered her mother's garden path as she tried to force air into her ruined lungs. Every gasp felt like pushing sludge through broken glass.

It was late morning on a Sunday, and she'd taken her inhaler an hour before—a quick, sharp breath of cold that disappeared much too quickly. She should have been in bed, flat on her back—not sitting, not standing, much less walking. But if the doctors were to be believed, it was one of the last spring Sundays she would ever see. Her chest and back hurt from the coughing.

The sunlight caressed her face. She couldn't stand at the trellis forever, and the return path to the house was longer. A few steps set off the coughing again. She pushed her fist hard into her ribs. She had dislocated them coughing three days ago, and they still didn't feel right. Three steps brought her to the maple tree which crowded the path. Her vision dimmed, and her knees softened. She slid down the trunk, and when the coughing fit passed she dropped her head against the rough bark.

A hummingbird spun into the air beside her, its shining green body hanging to the right of her face. It chirped three times, then zipped to her left, its small, dark eyes studying her before disappearing toward the pineapple sage. The citrusy fragrance of the roses hung heavy across this part of the path. She took little half breaths, and it felt close to natural. The bees hummed as they visited the flowers. A squirrel hung off a sunflower by its hind legs, plucking seeds out of the wide circle of the flower's face with its forepaws. This garden never quite seemed to follow the seasons . . . sunflowers blooming in spring instead of summer, roses year-round, frogs singing in the evenings no matter the weather. It was an oasis of near-magic in their suburban lot. Madeline used to build fairy houses along the "shore" of the fountain when she was a kid, using bark, leaves, and flowers to make tiny homes for make-believe friends.

Her mother had never cared for those little homes. She had planned the garden, a full acre of wandering paths, stone bridges, and small fountains. It was eclectic and a bit overgrown in places. Mr. García had done the planting and did the upkeep, too. Mom liked it a bit unkempt, and he worked to give it the impression of slight wildness. It didn't look manicured, but there weren't weeds, either. The fairy houses, Mom had said, looked like someone had forgotten to clean up after doing yard work.

Everything in its place, Mom always said.

Then again, Mom also wanted her house to "look lived in." That meant strange habits like telling their housekeeper, Sofía, that she couldn't immediately put an abandoned glass in the dishwasher. Once Madeline had come home and smelled fresh cookies, only to discover it was an air freshener her mother had bought from a Realtor. "To make it smell like home," Mom had said, seemingly oblivious to the reality that she was, indeed, home, and that actually baking cookies would have been simpler.

A few more steps, Madeline decided, but halfway to the bench a racking army of coughs marched across her chest. She touched her lips, then wiped the blood in the grass. With her eyes closed and the little half breaths coming again, she counted to twelve. When the jagged feeling in her chest passed, she lay flat and watched the clouds drifting in some high, distant wind. Air moved so easily for everyone but her.

It may have been a mistake, sneaking into the garden without telling anyone, with no way to call for help. She had chosen the perfect moment. Mom and Sofía had gone upstairs, something about washing the curtains. Dad was at the golf course, or work, or both. Her phone sat inside, turned off. The constant texts from Darius were making her feel guilty, but she had made a decision, and it was final. He couldn't waste his life waiting for her. There wasn't a cure. He needed to live his life. She needed to live what remained of hers.

Birds chirped in the maple. The warmer air made it easier to breathe. Going outside in the winter had been nearly impossible. And the sun felt nice. She closed her eyes. The tree shaded her face, but her hands and feet baked in the sunshine. Last week the doctor had said, "If there are things you want to do, you should do them." He was trying to be encouraging, she knew that, but it sounded too much like "enjoy your last spring." Her mom didn't think she should sit out in the backyard because "she might catch cold," as if that would change anything now.

And here Madeline was on her back, stranded and straining to breathe. So much for doing whatever she wanted.

The hummingbird wheeled overhead. It zipped back and forth over her, then shot off again, chirping incessantly.

"I see her, I see her."

Madeline struggled to prop herself onto her elbow, looking for the source of the unfamiliar voice. It sounded like the voice of an old woman, but there was no wavering in it, no sense of weakness. It sounded, in fact, almost musical . . . as if the woman had been a professional singer once upon a time and the music had never left her. Still, she was trespassing in their backyard. A small thrill of adrenaline coursed through Madeline.

A woman made her way toward Madeline, hunched low, as if carrying a heavy load on her back. She wore a broad hat with pale violet flowers along the brim, and her grey hair stuck out like the straws of an overworked broom. Her patched and dirty skirt trailed the ground, and she carried a canvas sack. Madeline couldn't imagine how she'd gotten in through the hedge that ran around the garden.

Another coughing fit overcame Madeline. Her vision blurred at the edges, and she pressed hard against her chest.

"Don't get up, dear, rest yourself. It's the hummingbird who's in such a hurry, but I saw you, don't worry, I already saw."

"Does my mom know you're . . ." Madeline couldn't finish the question.

"Of course not," the old woman said. She settled next to Madeline with a great deal of groaning. She looked at the house, her eyes sparkling, a smile tugging at the edges of her lips. Her face was weathered and wrinkled, but her eyes shone like black stones in a clear river.

"You shouldn't be here," Madeline said. "My mom won't . . ." She stopped to catch her breath. "She won't like it."

The old woman nodded thoughtfully, then smoothed her skirt. "Mothers rarely do, dear. Now, to business." She reached into her sack and pulled out a small white button, crusted in dirt, then a recently unearthed bottle cap and a small roll of twine. "I would like to borrow these."

"Borrow them?" Madeline pushed her hand against her chest again, trying to get a deeper breath. "I don't understand."

"They are yours," the woman said. She raised her hand. "Don't deny it. I found them in your garden. The birds brought me the twine, and the squirrel mentioned the button, but I dug it out with my own hands. The bottle cap—well, I've had my eye on that for several seasons."

Madeline tried to call her mother, but she couldn't shout loud enough. She coughed and coughed, and the old woman put a fleshy arm around her shoulders. "My mom," Madeline managed between coughs.

"I won't cheat you," the woman said. "I only want to borrow them. In exchange, I'll give you three favors and one piece of advice." The hummingbird zipped in front of them again and chirped twice. The old woman made a shooing motion. "I know what time it is, go on with you."

Maybe the old woman would go if Madeline gave her what she wanted, and it was only a few pieces of trash from the backyard. "Take them," Madeline said.

The woman beamed at her and collected the bits of junk, scooping them into her bag. "Thank you, dear. Thank you, thank you—and that's three thanks for three items, so all has been done proper."

Madeline wheezed a you're welcome. She took a shallow breath. "Could you . . . Do you think you could ask someone to come out for me?"

The old woman looked to the house again, and her face crumpled. "Not for the wide world, dear."

"For one of my favors?" She took the woman's hand. "I can't breathe."

"The flowers sent word of that, they did. That's why I came. But have they come to you? Have they offered you a bargain?"

Madeline gasped for breath. What was wrong with this woman—couldn't she see that Madeline couldn't breathe? The old woman stared at her with a steady gaze, waiting for an answer. Hoping the woman might help after she answered, Madeline shook her head. "Who? The flowers?"

"No, of course they haven't. Not yet. I can't get involved until then. Not much."

Madeline lay back, coughing. The bright green leaves were waving in the branches. Clouds scudded in from the west, much too fast, covering the sun. She shivered and thought she could see the cloud of her breath when she exhaled. But it was too warm for that on this spring day. "Call my mother," she said. "Or Sofía."

The old woman's face appeared over her. "No favors yet, my sweet seedling. But I can give you the advice now."

Madeline closed her eyes. "Okay."

The old woman squeezed her hand and whispered in her ear. But Madeline could scarcely hear her over her own racking cough, and when she could breathe enough to roll on her side, the sun was shining brightly again, and the old woman was stepping into the hedge, like a rabbit running into a thicket of thorns. She was gone.

Her mother's cry of horror came from the direction of the house, and feet pounded along the garden path toward the shady space beneath the maple.

2
DARIUS

Love comes hand in hand with Joy.

FROM "RENALDO THE WISE," A SCIM LEGEND

✦

Madeline used to sing. In fact, she was lead soprano in the school choir last year, her junior year. She used to dance—ballet, contemporary, hip-hop, swing. She used to drive down the road with her friends, all of them shouting over one another, laughing at each other. She used to run track, her specialty being the marathon runs, where she could pace herself and feel her legs moving like pistons, her arms like pendulums, her whole body like the gears of a clock, ticking off the seconds to the finish line with precision. She had gone to State last year. She used to drive herself to school. She used to walk upstairs to her bedroom without stopping to catch her breath, clinging to the banister like a sea star suction cupped to a black rock.

She used to be able to breathe.

"I arranged your ride to school today," Mom said, her voice making it clear this was a final decision. Madeline had used a similar tone of voice when her parents tried to get her to stop going to class. Stay home, they said. You're too sick, they said. But when she did stay home, her parents didn't. Dad had work, Mom had activities, and Madeline ended up in bed, hacking her lungs out, sweating through her sheets, lonely and miserable.

Her mom took a cup of steaming coffee from Sofía and leaned against the kitchen counter, brushing an invisible speck of lint from her ice-blue athletic top.

"I thought you would take me," Madeline said. She had taken her inhaler fifteen minutes before, and for the next thirty minutes or so she should be able to breathe with relative ease. It was like pushing water in and out of her lungs, but at least the air moved. Sofía had made pancakes this morning, Madeline's favorite. Madeline had barely touched them. Like it or not, she wasn't well, and the thought of trying to rally the energy to pretend she was while her friends drove her to school, blaring music and trying to cheer her up . . . She didn't want that today. A silent, uncomfortable ride with her mom would be better.

"I have badminton this morning." Of course. Mom wore her pleated white badminton skirt, her platinum hair pushed back just so with a white headband.

"I can set up my own rides, then. It's not far for Ruby."

Her mother raised her eyebrows. "It's fifteen minutes out of her way. I texted Darius."

"Mom!"

"It's not right, the way you've been avoiding him."

"Why the sudden concern for Darius?"

Mom tapped her nails against her mug, taking another sip before saying, "You dated the boy for over a year and then dropped him without an explanation. He deserves better than that."

"Without an explanation? Who told you that?"

"People talk, Madeline. Your friends were worried, and they mentioned it to me. Poor boy. He was always good for you. You should spend more time with him."

"You don't even *like* him."

Mom shook her head. "Not true."

"Oh yeah, then why the big sit-down in the living room before prom?"

Mom's lips pressed together, making fine lines branch along her mouth. She always did that when she was done with a conversation. "He'll be here in ten minutes." She blew on her coffee and shook her head. "I'll see you after school."

As her mother walked from the room, Madeline shouted, "Dad's exact words were, 'He won't provide for you the way you're accustomed to.' If that was meant to convey approval, I missed it." She hadn't raised her voice like that in a while, and it cracked, followed by a deep-chested cough. She put her hands flat on the counter and tried to relax.

Sofía put a hot mug in front of Madeline. Steam infused with lemon and honey wafted to her. Sofía's gentle hand brushed her shoulder. "For your breathing," she said, and then she was off, cleaning the breakfast dishes.

"Thank you," Madeline muttered. Sofía had a way of smoothing everything over in this house. The drink was warm and soothing, and Madeline told herself it worked, but reflecting on the conversation with her mom made her angry. There was no way one of her friends had told her mom anything about the breakup. Most of her friends barely checked on her now. It was hard to be friends with the dying girl. Oh, they responded to texts. Most of them did, anyway. But she couldn't imagine any of them sitting down with her mom to talk about Madeline's dating life. Or lack thereof. What did her mom know about Darius, anyway? Next to nothing. Madeline had dated him for over a year, and her mom hadn't shown a moment's interest. Now she was setting up a car pool with him? Whatever she was up to, it was infuriating.

Madeline's backpack was by the door. Probably also Sofía's doing. Everyone treated her like an invalid, which she basically was, but it still made her angry. Her mom made her angry. Embracing reality made her angry. She should stay home—that was reality. She shouldn't wander in the garden alone—that was reality. She shouldn't have a boyfriend—that was reality. It wasn't fair to Darius to ask him to walk this road with her, wasn't fair to keep him tied to her, like an anchor. Breaking up with him had been an act of love, a way to set him free from her illness, and now her mom was trying to undo that.

She waited by the door so Darius wouldn't have an excuse to come in. His beat-up black Mustang pulled into the driveway, and he jumped out to come get her at the door. He moved like an ice skater, the ground rolling away beneath him like a moving walkway. Today he wore jeans and a button-down shirt, with his letterman's jacket tossed over it. She knew the buttoned shirt was for her. She had told him on their first date that wearing something other than a T-shirt might show he was at least a little bit excited.

She had met Darius in track. He was beautiful, with dark skin and an angular face. He kept his hair short—she could tell he had probably shaved it the night before—and when he smiled it was like the sun rising. That wasn't the reason she had started dating him, though. It was because of the day she'd turned her ankle during track and he had noticed and turned back for her. She'd told him to keep running, it was no big deal, she was alright. He'd told her they were a team and he needed a breather anyway. He'd walked beside her, gotten her back to the coach, stayed there while they put on the ice, made sure she was okay, and checked in with her the next day. After that, he was checking in on her every day. It started with the ankle, but from there he wanted to know how she was doing in class, with her parents, her friends, with life in general, and pretty soon they were texting, calling, laughing, deep into each other's lives. She asked him about his cousin Malik, who was away at college. Darius helped her think through how to respond to her parents when they were being difficult.

And when her breathing trouble started, and her mom took her to the doctor, Darius offered to come. Madeline's mom said no, that it wasn't right for "a stranger" to come to a doctor's appointment, and anyway, it was probably just a little infection. But when she and her mom came out into the hospital parking lot after the appointment, Darius was leaning against his car, reading a book, his cell phone in hand. He grinned and put the phone to his ear. *Call me.*

Saying good-bye had been hard. It was the right thing to do, but it was impossible, and now here he was, on her front porch, beaming. He reached for her backpack.

Madeline flinched away. "I'm not broken." She winced. She hadn't meant to come across like that, but seeing him here . . . There was a gravity there, a desire to come back together, and she couldn't allow that. It would be too hard on him, too painful for her.

"I know," he said, and bowed with a flourish. "But I . . . am a gentleman."

She smiled despite herself. She debated for a moment, then unslung her bag and let him carry it. "How's your breathing?" he asked, once they were settled in the Mustang and he was backing toward the road.

"Terrible. How did Mom get your number?"

He shrugged. "How does your mom always get whatever she wants? Called the principal maybe." He tapped his hands against the driver's wheel. "Listen, has your mom told you she's been calling me the last month or so?"

"What?! No!"

He raised a hand. "Don't be mad, she's just worried. Ever since you . . . uh . . . Since *we* broke up." He glanced at her, then back to the road. "Worried that you've given up."

Madeline watched the neighborhood spin past. Her parents had made it clear they didn't like Darius. What they hadn't made clear was why. Dad said he wouldn't make enough money, but that was years away, and what did he know? She and Darius were getting the same education, after all. He had grades nearly as good as hers, and if she wasn't in honors classes, his GPA might even be higher than hers. She didn't know if it was because they were both seventeen, or because Darius was black, or because he was at her private high school on a scholarship, but something about him didn't meet Mom and Dad's approval. And now Mom was texting him to check up on her? She gritted her teeth. Mom would hear about this when she got home.

And "*worried that she had given up*"? She hadn't given up—she was embracing reality. That was part of the stages of terminal disease, right? She had gone through denial. Through anger (well, maybe not all the way through). Now she was approaching acceptance. There was nothing more to be done. No more treatments, no miracle cures. She was walking a path her parents couldn't go down, not really. She was alone, and no one else needed to suffer this with her: not her parents, not her friends, and certainly not Darius.

She turned his radio up and kept it loud until they got to school. Darius, without even asking, pulled up alongside her classroom instead of parking in the lot. So she wouldn't have to walk so far, of course. She didn't know how to explain to him how infuriating she found his thoughtfulness. Especially when she was already mad at him. She knew it wasn't his fault—everything made her angry—and she knew he wouldn't understand if she tried to explain.

The car chugged to a stop, and the radio fell silent. Darius stared out the windshield. She knew that look. He was gathering his thoughts, trying to find words. She put her hand on the door handle, but despite herself, she paused. She missed hearing his voice. Missed talking about life, about things that mattered. "Maddie," he said. She melted a little at that. She had missed hearing the way he said her name. "I got you something."

He held a package wrapped in brown paper. He'd never been great at wrapping gifts, and this one was no exception: too much paper crookedly cut, with tape all over it and an attempt at a bow made with twine. It was obviously a book. She couldn't take a gift, though. It wasn't fair to him. Or to her, really. "Darius—"

"I bought it before we broke up, but it just got here. Shipped from England." She didn't say anything. "I know you're going to love this, and I want you to have it." He held it out. When she took it, their fingers brushed against each other.

Madeline pulled the tape loose and slid the book out. "Darius. I can't believe this."

It was a copy of her favorite book, *The Gryphon under the Stairs* by Mary Patricia Wall. It was the first of the Tales of Meselia, a series of children's fantasy novels. The final novel had never come out, so it wasn't as popular as other series, and not as easy to find, but Madeline loved it best. Darius had never read the Meselia books until she got sick. He had come to her house, sat on the floor while she curled on the couch, and read aloud the whole series, a couple chapters at a time. It had taken months to get to the end. She had loved seeing the books through his eyes, listening to him talk about them, hearing his thoughts and questions and insights.

"First edition," Darius said proudly. "Hardback, too."

She ran her hand over the cover. It had been released in 1974, and the picture on the front was of a gryphon crouched under a stairway, two children standing to the sides, stepping back in surprise. Ivy grew up around the outside of the picture, and the whole illustration had the look of a wood-block print.

Her anger drained away. She couldn't believe it. She had always wanted a first edition, though she had never mentioned it to anyone, not even Darius. Holding it in her hand now, feeling the texture of the cover, the weight of the book, seemed almost miraculous . . . like maybe things that were impossible could happen. She didn't know what to say. She settled for "Darius, thank you so much." Then, before the emotion choked off her words, she asked, "Where did you find this?"

He grinned. "I started calling bookshops in the UK. Little places that didn't put their books online."

She flipped open the book, shocked by the crispness of the pages. "It looks like no one has ever read this copy," she said. "Like it's untouched by human hands."

"Nah," Darius said. "Look at the title page."

She looked from him to the book, then back at him. It couldn't be. She turned the first page, a blank one, and there it was. The name Mary Patricia Wall was written in a neat, curved script in black ink, just beneath her typeset name. Mary Patricia Wall had held this book in her hands, had put her fingers on these pages to keep them open.

Tears cascaded down her face, and she couldn't keep away from Darius anymore, couldn't pretend, even for his own good, that she didn't want to be with him. She let his gravity pull her in, leaning into his embrace, and he didn't say anything, didn't ask for anything, just wrapped his arms around her and let her cry. She cried for his thoughtfulness, for thankfulness to have someone who knew her so well, for fear of what was to come. She cried because she was angry and sad and afraid and loved and so, so tired. There was no way out, no solution to her illness, but at least there was this, a moment of loving human touch, a gift from someone who knew her well.

The warning bell for first period rang.

The crying set off a minor coughing fit. She sat up, bracing herself on the dashboard. Darius put a comforting hand on her shoulder. When it passed, she wiped her eyes with her sleeve and slipped the book into her backpack.

"'There must be something better, I know it in my heart,'" Darius said, quoting a line from the book. The main characters, siblings Lily and Samuel, are standing at the space beneath the stairs, and the wall has fallen away, and there is a swirling of color in the space. The gryphon has disappeared into it, and beckons Lily and Samuel to follow. "'And the only impossible thing is that I would leave you.'"

Madeline wiped her eyes again, then replied with Samuel's words, "'If we're together, I won't be afraid.'"

Lily's next line was, "Then take my hand, Samuel, and let us see what beautiful things await," but before Darius could say it, Madeline took his hand and squeezed, and before she could stop herself or think about what it meant or what the consequences might be, she leaned toward him and kissed his cheek.

She pulled away, the heat from Darius's hand familiar and comfortable. She looked into those dark-brown eyes, so deep they were nearly black. It was like looking into the night sky if all the stars blinked at once. It had been weeks since she had looked at him like this, and she wanted him to reach out, to touch her cheek.

Instead, he opened his door and came to get her. He walked her to class, her backpack on his shoulder, his hand on the small of her back, ready to catch her if she fell. Did she look as weak as that?

"If you need to go home early, text me," he said. His words were so gently delivered that she didn't get angry at the suggestion she couldn't make it through the day.

"You're going to be late for class," she said.

He grinned. "Impossible." Then he ran toward his classroom in that loping, long-legged stride of his, leaping like a deer over a planter, so full of life and joy and breath.

"Your car," she gasp-shouted.

He changed directions immediately, sprinting, a sheepish look on his face. "I might be late to class!" he yelled back, just as the bell rang again.

3
PARTNERS

Humans! Ye shall live upon another earth,
a people of science and dust.

FROM "THE ORDERING OF THE WORLD," AN ELENIL STORY

✦

After what had happened to his sister, Jason Wu had made a decision. He would never keep quiet about what he saw again, and he would never lie. No matter the cost, he would speak up and speak truth.

Sure, he'd gotten detention over the whole Principal Krugel fiasco, but his toupee *was* on backward. Maybe Jason shouldn't have mentioned it in front of the football team. He almost certainly should not have repeated it over the school intercom. He could still hear the principal's shrill voice shouting, "JASON WU!" from his office. That could have been the end of it, but when Jason refused to apologize or retract his statement, the principal had taken to the intercom to explain he did not wear a toupee.

That didn't excuse what Jason had done next. He saw that now.

Seeing Principal Krugel in front of the whole school at the football rally the next day, his ridiculous fake hair sitting on top of his head like a shag car-pet, had driven Jason right to the edge of madness. Then Darius Walker had shouted to Jason, "Krugel's hair looks real to me! What are you going to do?"

Jason had said, "Pull his toupee off," meaning it as a joke.

But then he thought, *I promised never to tell a lie.*

Taking off the man's toupee wouldn't be good.

But if he didn't, he was a liar. Again.

It was a moral conundrum.

Anyway, it had earned Jason detention and earned Principal Krugel the nickname Principal Cue Ball.

He had received a second detention when the principal called his parents, put them on speakerphone, and made Jason explain what he had done. When the principal said there had been a mini riot at the assembly, Jason's mom asked if it was true. Of course Dad didn't say anything. He hadn't spoken—well, hadn't spoken to Jason—since things had happened with Jenny. Before he could stop himself, Jason said, "Yes, everyone was wigging out." Even that didn't get Dad to speak up. It had, on the other hand, turned Principal Krugel's face a shade of red Jason had never seen before, so it wasn't a complete loss.

So he wasn't trying to be insensitive when his chemistry partner, Madeline Oliver, came in to class looking like someone had given her a swirly. "You look terrible," he said. "Your mascara is running everywhere. Your eyes are red." All true.

Madeline choked out a sarcastic thanks, then started coughing. She coughed a lot. He knew she was sick. She didn't talk about it, ever. Everyone at school acted like it was a big secret, but he noticed that meant they couldn't take care of her, either. Couldn't ask how she was doing, couldn't make sure she was taking care of herself. That's why he'd asked to be her chem partner. She didn't know that—she had been at the doctor the day they picked partners. Besides, she was better at chemistry than he was. So they were watching out for each other, in a way. That's what partners do.

"You sound terrible too. Should you even be in class?" Jason spun a pencil in one hand, twirling it like a baton.

"I can't skip school all the time." She slammed her bag down and slid onto a stool, leaning against the counter.

"You already skip half the time," Jason said. "You're the worst lab partner I've had. Besides, it's a sub today. We're probably doing some idiotic worksheet."

"You just described half of high school," Madeline said. "Who are you to say I look terrible, anyway? Your clothes look like they're on day three of being picked up from your floor."

"Day four," Jason said. He hadn't combed his hair, either, and he knew it went five directions at once. Only one of his shoes was tied. The other one he had overknotted yesterday and couldn't get it undone. He had actually worn his left shoe to bed last night. He watched Madeline coughing and digging through her backpack for her textbook. She really shouldn't be here. She didn't even notice the substitute call her name. "Here," he said.

The substitute looked at Jason over the top of his glasses. "Your name is Madeline Oliver?"

"Nah, it's my partner, but she's busy coughing up a lung. She needs to go to the office."

The sub regarded Madeline skeptically. He had a big nose and a wreath of brown hair that stuck up on the sides. He looked like an angry koala bear. "It's not my first time as a substitute," he said.

"I'm fine," Madeline said, still coughing.

"Try not to distract the class," he said, and continued calling roll.

Jason spun on his stool. He knew what was coming. He leaned over and whispered to Madeline, "He's going to read my Chinese name, I can feel it. And he's gonna say it wrong. I hate this guy already. Maybe you should take your inhaler."

"Already took it," she said, gasping for air between words.

He opened her purse—she tried to stop him, and yes, he knew you shouldn't dig in a girl's purse—and pulled out her inhaler. He shook it three times and handed it to her. She took a deep puff, her eyes shut. She leaned on the counter, panting.

"Song Wuh," the substitute said.

"Jason," he called. "It's Jason."

"Says Song Wuh here."

Jason sighed. Should he correct the guy? He got so tired of correcting people when they said his name wrong. "With Jason in parentheses, right? And it's pronounced *woo*, and the *o* in Song is long, like in *hope*. Wu Song, that's how you say it—family name first. It's not that hard. Seriously."

The substitute wrote something on his paper. "Ah. Jason. Yes, the principal mentioned you."

The principal *mentioned* him? It made him sound like some sort of troublemaker. One little incident with a man's fake hair and you're branded for life. Was it in his personal record? Would it follow him to college? *Make sure this boy never gets near a toupee—he will take it and run around the gym, waving it like a hairy flag.* Oh yeah. He had done that, too. He hadn't run it up the flagpole, though. That had been someone else.

"Is my name so hard?" Jason asked Madeline. "Wu Song is famous, too. Killed a man-eating tiger with his bare hands. Doesn't seem like it's asking too much to get my name right, especially when I'm named after a famous guy."

"Your life is hard," Madeline gasped. She had her phone out and was texting someone.

"It's like mispronouncing Robin Hood."

"Jason." Her body listed to one side, like a sinking ship. She grasped at the counter, trying to keep herself upright. Jason grabbed her sleeve, pulling her toward him, pulling her upright, and then she was slipping, falling. Her arm slid out of her jacket, and she half rolled, half fell onto the floor, her head knocking against the polished cement.

Jason jumped off his stool, knocking it over with a clang. He threw Madeline's stool out of the way and knelt over her. He asked if she was okay, but she didn't answer.

"Mr. Substitute," Jason shouted. "Call an ambulance."

"You two stop messing around."

"She's actually sick," Jason shouted, and other kids in the class chimed in, telling the sub it was true, that she had some lung sickness or something.

"I'll call the office," he said, but he was still standing there, staring.

Madeline's eyes rolled back into her head, and her skin went pale. Jason put his hand on her face. Cold and clammy. She wasn't breathing. A knot of panic sat in his chest, small and cold as her skin. For a second he was looking at Jenny's face, still and pale, but he shoved the image out of his mind, hard. He needed to think about right now. He tilted Madeline's head back and got ready to do chest compressions.

One of the other kids said, "Dude, you're not going to—"

"Shut up," Jason said, and started chest compressions.

He pinched her nose shut, sealed his mouth over hers, and breathed two quick breaths into her mouth. Her chest rose, she coughed, and she started to breathe again.

"Her color is coming back," one of the kids said.

The substitute stood there at the end of the row, the stack of worksheets in his hand. His mouth was open, and his glasses had slid down his nose. He cleared his throat. "Calm down, class. We'll—"

Jason interrupted him. "Mr. Koala Bear. Snap out of it. Call the office. Right. Now."

This was taking too long. The sub was in shock or something. Jason pointed at a kid in the row in front of him. "You. Kid with the braces. Call 911. Tell them we're headed to the hospital."

He leaned over Madeline. "It's gonna be okay. Keep breathing." He slipped one hand under her neck, grabbed the belt loop on her jeans with the other, and lifted.

The classroom door slammed open, and Darius stood on the other side, panting. "What happened? She just texted me."

"Help me get her to the car," Jason said.

The security guard in the parking lot said something to them, but Jason rushed past. Darius shouted an explanation, and then he helped sling Madeline into Jason's sports car and put her seat belt on.

"Where are you taking her?"

"She can't breathe, Darius, where do you think? The hospital. Get in the car or step back." Why were people such idiots during times of pressure?

The car settled under Darius's weight as he got in the back. "Drive," he said.

Jason peeled out of the parking lot and screeched onto the road.

"Red light!" Darius yelled.

Jason punched it through the intersection.

"An accident won't get us there faster," Darius said.

"This isn't driver's ed," Jason said. "I know what I'm doing." He glanced at Madeline. She was coughing up blood now. There's no way he was going to stay quiet, no way he was going to wait for an ambulance. No way. "Hang in there, partner."

She coughed until she fainted. Jason laid on the horn and sped toward the hospital.

4

THE STRANGER

And he placed a tower in the center
of the Sunlit Lands and called it Far Seeing.

FROM "THE ORDERING OF THE WORLD," AN ELENIL STORY

✛

I t felt like someone had put cinder blocks on her chest. Transparent tubes snaked into her nostrils. A red plastic band clung to her wrist. Sensors were stuck to her chest, an IV line dripped into her left arm, and a clip on the finger of her right hand monitored oxygen levels. Her lips were dried and cracked.

The hospital again. More and more of her life found its way here. Appointments, tests, paperwork, treatments. Meetings to talk about tests and treatments. The harsh lights, the antiseptic smell that came even through her oxygen tube, the incessant beeping and nurses checking in and noise. She hated finding herself here. Hated that she couldn't make it through one day of school, hated the reminder yet again that she should just stay home like a good girl, hidden away and waiting, alone, for the end to come.

Darius was in a chair beside the bed. Jason was sitting in a windowsill to Darius's left, half an arm's length away. Even with only two visitors, the room felt crowded.

Darius touched her hand gently. "You're awake."

Madeline looked at her hospital gown. "How—?"

"They cut off your clothes," Jason said. "Don't worry, they kicked us out until you were dressed."

"Are my parents here?"

"Not yet," Jason said. "The hospital called."

"I texted your mom," Darius said.

Jason was chomping on an apple. "When I said you looked terrible, I didn't realize how low the scale goes, you know? You looked pretty good earlier, all things considered."

Darius punched him in the arm.

"What was that for?"

Madeline asked, "What did the doctor say?"

Darius's brow furrowed. "You don't remember?"

"Was I awake?"

"You told them we could stay," Jason said. "And that it was okay for us to hear, um, your diagnosis."

Madeline blushed. She hadn't really told the other kids at school what was going on. Darius knew the basics. Jason, weirdly, seemed to have figured it out, but they never talked about it. She didn't want to talk about it at school, didn't want to answer the endless questions. What's interstitial lung disease? Is it common in teens? Will it kill you?

Scarring in the lungs. Not really. Probably, yes.

Madeline's scarring was advancing. Every hour, every minute, it progressed through her lungs, like an army gaining a few yards each day. Where the lungs scarred, they didn't process oxygen. Eventually she'd run out of usable lung tissue, and she'd asphyxiate. It was only a question of how long. All the doctors' appointments and medications and oxygen tanks were to prolong her life, not save it. She was on the list for a lung transplant, high on the list, actually—no previous illness, a fatal disease that wasn't responding to treatment, she was young. But every time a donation came up, something got in the way. The tissue went bad. Another donor somehow jumped in line. Her application was mysteriously deleted. It was like an unseen hand kept intervening, frustrating any chance of her getting better. And now she was getting so weak, the doctor wasn't sure she'd survive the surgery. She cleared her throat, which felt raspy and raw.

"Could I get a drink?" Madeline asked. "Maybe some ice chips."

"I'm on it," Jason said, stepping away from the window.

Darius said, "Could you bring her something soft to eat, too, like some applesauce?" Jason nodded and scooted out of the room.

The oxygen tubes in her nose rubbed, and her arm felt stiff and uncomfortable where the IV entered. Darius leaned in close and squeezed her hand.

A blinding light hit her full in the face. Her first thought was that it was the kind of light they put in an operating room, the bright white light surgeons use, but it wasn't in one place, it seemed to come from all over. Her second thought was that she was passing out or something, but she knew what that felt like, had experienced the light-headed, rolling blackness more than once, and this wasn't that.

Then the light started to burn, and she could feel it searing her skin. It seemed to be coming from the end of the bed, so she turned away, but even with her eyes shut, that white light pierced her eyes, as if her eyelids weren't even there.

The light disappeared as quickly as it had come, leaving the room dim and Madeline shivering in the sudden cold. Darius's hand still held hers, but it was rigid, though still warm. He was leaning toward Madeline but not moving or blinking. She slipped her hand away from his, and he didn't move, didn't so much as breathe.

"Darius?" What was happening? Was this a hallucination brought on by lack of oxygen? She felt coherent, but her brain couldn't process what she was seeing. Her own heart ratcheted up, beating faster. She took a deep breath, ready to call for help, and instead gave an involuntary shout when she looked toward the door.

At the foot of her bed stood a tall, slender man. He had the palest skin she had ever seen, almost the color of platinum, with a bluish undertone. His silver-white hair was fine and long, falling to his shoulders. He wore a brocade jacket with pale-pink roses worked into the silk and veins of gold shooting through the design. Stiff lace blossomed from his sleeves, nearly covering his gloved hands, and more lace covered his neck, where a white cravat was tied with perfect grace. He inclined his head to her.

"It is customary you should bow," the man said. "But there will be time to learn such pleasantries. I am called Hanali, and I have come as a representative of the Sunlit Lands."

Madeline tried to speak but found herself choking instead. It was like a dream, but in a dream she wouldn't be in so much pain, would she? Darius still hadn't moved. She managed to get a breath and said, "What did you do to him?"

The slim man looked at Darius as if seeing him for the first time. "Ah. Your friend is unaware of our conversation. After our business concludes, he will continue about his day."

Something about the strange man reminded her of the lady in the garden. Madeline didn't know if these were hallucinations or fever dreams or real, but the woman had gone away when Madeline gave her what she wanted. Maybe the same would be true for this strange man. "What do you want?" she asked.

"More importantly, child, what do *you* want?"

Annoyance flared up in Madeline. She gestured to the tubes coming out of her body. "Nothing you can give me."

Hanali reached into Darius's jacket pocket, slid out his cell phone, and dangled it in front of Darius's face. With a flourish he released the phone, and it stayed there, unmoving, floating in the air. "Which is easier? To stop time or heal lungs?" Hanali asked.

Jason walked through the door. "Stop time? Huh. Is that what happened?" He had a cup of ice in one hand, and his arms were full of pudding cups. "The nurses stopped talking all at once. I thought it was performance art."

"Starless night," Hanali said. The way he said it, it sounded like a curse. "How are you unaffected by my spell?"

Jason dumped all the pudding cups on Madeline's bed and handed her the cup of ice. He shrugged. "The world is full of mysteries. Why are you cosplaying at a hospital?"

Hanali gaped at him. "You can see and hear me and move about."

Jason tore open a pudding. "I forgot spoons."

"This has never happened in my lifetime."

"Wait!" Jason dug around in his pockets. "Here they are!" He held one out to Madeline. She shook her head, popping an ice chip in her mouth and sucking it.

Hanali's eyes narrowed. "Did an old woman speak to you? Did a stranger approach you in a garden?"

Madeline's ears perked up. He knew her, then, the Garden Lady. Had she spoken to Jason, too?

Jason shoveled some pudding into his mouth. "I don't know what you're talking about, dude."

"Remarkable." Hanali turned reluctantly away from Jason. He tugged on the frilled cuffs of his sleeves, straightening them. "I am here, Madeline Oliver, to offer a bargain. In exchange for one human year of service to the Elenil, lords of the Sunlit Lands, we will cast a magic spell that will heal your lungs. You will be able to dance and run and sing again."

Madeline's chest ached. She didn't understand everything the strange man was saying, but she had caught the basics. A year of work in exchange for healing. "I won't last a year," she said. She glanced at Jason. He had paused, another spoonful halfway to his mouth. "The doctor said three months. Maybe a little more."

"We would, of course, give you the magic as soon as our terms were agreed upon. You can have your breath returned to you this very day. You will come to the Sunlit Lands, and in one human year we will return you to this place, permanently healed."

Jason said, "Wait, why are you going to school if you only have three months to live?"

"My friends are there," Madeline said. And then, to Hanali, "Explain this again. You want me to serve . . . the Alelni?"

"Elenil. They are the lords of the Sunlit Lands."

"Hawai'i, I'm guessing," Jason said.

The strange man scowled. "The Sunlit Lands are not part of Earth— they are another world. Smaller than Earth, but full of magic. No doubt you've read of such places. Faerie lands."

Faerie lands. Something about the way he said it set off all the associations in her mind, all the places she knew and loved: Meselia in the books of Mary Patricia Wall. Narnia. Hogwarts. Earthsea. How many times had she pushed her hand against the back wall of a wardrobe or stood in front of a painting wishing she could jump into it? How often had she wished for a magic ring or button, a hidden passageway, a garden gate grown over in ivy that would transport her to some magical land? She thought of the hobbit Samwise Gamgee and his aching desire to meet the Elves, and she, too, felt a piercing longing to walk among a strange and beautiful people. She thought of Lily and Samuel standing at the portal beneath their stairs, watching the color-swirled space where the gryphon had gone. They had been afraid and just scarcely believing. She remembered Lily's words in *The Gryphon under the Stairs.* "There must be something better, I know it in my heart," Madeline whispered, and for the first time in many months she felt a flutter of hope. Every book she had read in her entire childhood, every book she still cherished, had prepared her to believe in a moment like this.

Jason spoke up, his mouth still full of pudding. "Sounds like Harry Potter–land. Which means more school. If you want to learn magic, it apparently involves a lot of school."

"It is more like Mount Penglai," Hanali said. "Or Tír na nÓg."

Madeline tried to mask her excitement. She wanted to leap up and take Hanali's hand and do whatever was necessary to go to these Sunlit Lands, but she needed more information. "Why do the Elenil need people like me?"

Hanali smiled, and his teeth were white as seashells. "The Elenil scour the world for people in need—people without food, or in the midst of a crisis, or dying. If the magic of the Elenil can help, we make an exchange. Some small token of their lives in exchange for a bit of magic. Your world has precious little magic, so our help is keenly felt."

"Sounds too good to be true," Jason said, opening a second pudding cup.

Madeline shushed him. "What is it like? The Sunlit Lands?"

A smile spread over Hanali's face. "In the heart of the Sunlit Lands lies the capital city of the Elenil. The Court of Far Seeing is bright and beautiful. All things fair and wonderful are there. There is music in the city squares and art upon the streets. No one is hungry, and the white towers fly crimson flags in the warm breeze from the Ginian Sea. Above the city stands the Crescent Stone, bright beacon of our magic, a reminder of the good things available to those who inhabit the blessed city."

"If this place is so great," Jason said, "why do you need us? You need janitors or something?"

Hanali glared at Jason. He yanked on the lace at his cuffs, pulling them down over his hands. "A corrupted people called the Scim live to our south. They call themselves servants of darkness, of shadow, and they wish to tear down the Court of Far Seeing. We are in need of your help in this conflict."

Madeline coughed for a minute, holding up a finger to pause the conversation. "So . . . what exactly is the agreement? What do I have to do?"

"You agree to serve the Elenil in our war against the Scim for one human year. In exchange we will heal you. You must leave your friends and family behind. You will not be able to say good-bye or explain your absence."

Another coughing fit overcame her. When a coughing attack came, she couldn't think about her mother or father, her friends, Darius, school, the way she liked to wake in the morning and lean her head on her windowsill, listening to the birds in the garden. She could only think about the way her chest constricted and squeezed every molecule of oxygen out of her body, of the blackness that pressed in against her eyes, and the burning pain that burst through her every cell. She knew how her life would end . . . like this, a million minuscule knives in her chest. One day, she would inhale, pull as hard as she could with her ruined lungs, and there would be nothing. Just thrashing and panic and death. There would be no peaceful final smile, no gentle bedside farewells. Wouldn't this deal be better than that? No good-byes, but she wasn't going to get good-byes when she coughed herself to death, either, not really. And she'd be back in a year. Panting after the coughing fit, she tried to wheeze out an answer, but Jason spoke up first.

"No offense," he said, "but this is one of those candy-and-strangers situations."

"Not having candy and not being able to breathe are quite different," Hanali said.

Jason said, "You're recruiting desperate people who won't ask questions. What's your angle?"

Hanali's smile remained on his face, but his eyes bored into Jason. His words came out clipped and perfectly enunciated. "A human year of assisting in the war against the Scim in exchange for healthy lungs for the rest of her life. The conditions are plain."

Jason sat at the foot of Madeline's bed, putting himself between her and Hanali. "It's a bad idea, Madeline. You could die in the war. You won't be able to say good-bye to your friends and family. Also, I don't trust this guy."

Madeline shook her head. Jason didn't understand. She didn't expect him to. How could he know what it was like to stand on the precipice of death, never knowing if this was the last time you'd pull a breath? Sometimes she was terrified she'd go faster than the doctor said, but if she was being honest, there were also days when she was afraid she'd last longer than the doctor said. She couldn't take this pain, this slow descent. If there was a way out of this sickness, what price would be too much? "What's the worst that could happen, Jason?"

"You could be eaten by a dragon." He looked at Hanali. "Are there dragons?"

Hanali raised an eyebrow. "Dragons?"

"Giant lizards that breathe fire? They have wings. Hoard gold. Eat people."

"No, we do not have 'dragons' in the Sunlit Lands."

Jason shrugged and looked back at Madeline. "You could get gored to death by a unicorn."

She almost laughed at that. "Better than suffocating."

"It's a high price," Jason said, and for a moment she saw his genuine concern. No bravado, no jokes, just a sweet, almost brotherly desire to protect her. He seemed to think that she didn't understand the cost, but it was Jason who didn't understand. She knew the cost. She had been paying it every day since her diagnosis. She was on a journey of saying good-bye, of leaving everything behind. Jason didn't understand that Hanali wasn't asking for anything that wouldn't be taken from her anyway. But he was offering a chance—maybe it was a gamble, maybe it was a bad deal in some way she couldn't see, but it was a chance at least, which was more than she had now—a chance at life. No one else was offering her that.

"I'll be able to breathe the entire year?"

Hanali nodded gravely. "So long as you follow the agreement, yes. With the exception of the Festival of the Turning—an Elenil festival day without magic. Other than that, you will breathe freely."

"So long as I follow the agreement," Madeline repeated. "How does it work? What do I have to sign?"

Hanali pulled a thin bracelet from his jacket. It had a tiny, clouded jewel set in it and intricate patterns etched into the silver. "No signature. Only slip this onto your left wrist, and we shall be on our way. The power of the Crescent Stone will seal our bargain."

She turned the bracelet over in her hands. It was lighter than she expected, and delicate. Was she hallucinating? The whole thing was so surreal. But if it was real—and it did *seem* real—she could be healed. She'd have to leave her life behind for a year, but that was worth it, right? She imagined Darius waking from this strange moment of frozen time to find her gone. Her parents. Her father would sue the hospital into the Stone Age. Her mom would weep and scream and yell and never be the same.

She wished Darius could move. He still sat beside her, frozen and unseeing. She wanted to talk it through with him, ask his opinion. In these last couple years, even before they were dating, he had been there for her so many times, had talked about everything with her. She had been trying to say good-bye, trying to make some distance, but now she wanted to hear his steady, reasoned voice weigh the pros and cons. He would understand, she thought, the excitement of this magical land. He had often said, "If only there was magic, if only there was some way out of this . . ."

So maybe Jason was right. She should think about it. Consider it. For a few minutes at least. She shouldn't just take this deal and jump headfirst into some world, some war, she didn't understand.

"I want to think about it," she said, choking it out before another bout of painful coughing.

Hanali shook his head. "Do not contemplate too long," he said. "There are others who are suffering, and we can take our offer to them should you reject it."

"If I decide to . . . to come to the Sunlit Lands, how do I let you know?"

Hanali looked at her carefully. "The Sunlit Lands exist alongside your

Earth. Not below or above, but beside. Parallel. You have but to leave this life behind and follow the narrow road that opens before you."

"Second star to the right," Madeline said, her coughing growing worse. "And straight on till . . . till morning."

The stranger crossed his arms, plucking at the lace at his wrists. He reached out and took the bracelet, tucking it into some concealed pocket in his sleeve. "Send your strange friend to find me should you change your mind."

"Yeah, yeah, we got it," Jason said. "Now you heard the lady, get out of here. I'm allergic to all that lace."

"Beware," Hanali said. "When time crashes in on you again, you will be reminded of your weakness. The shock of reentering normal time can cause great stress on the human body."

Hanali spun and walked from the room, and the world came to life again. Darius's phone clattered to the floor and he shouted in surprise, looking down in confusion to find Madeline's hand no longer entwined with his.

Madeline's breath left her completely, and her heart rate spiked. She fought to stay conscious. The machines attached to her blared shrill alarms.

"Maddie?"

It's okay, she tried to say. It's going to be okay. But she couldn't speak, couldn't draw a breath. Her eyes met Jason's.

"She's turning blue," Darius said, pushing Jason back. "Give her room."

A doctor hurried in, close behind the nurse. "You kids get out," the doctor said. "Right now."

"We don't have time to argue," the nurse said, speaking over their objections. "If you want us to save your friend, get out now."

"Jason," she managed to wheeze. "Bracelet." She didn't have any choice, did she? She didn't have time to think this out, to weigh the consequences. She was drowning. Hanali hadn't offered her a choice, he had offered her a life vest.

She *needed* the bracelet. There was no guarantee the doctors could do anything for her in this moment. Tears squeezed out of her eyes, her hands clutched the bedsheets, her back arched up as her body cast about desperately, trying to find breath. Jason paused in the doorway and looked back at her. Had he heard her? Why wasn't he running to get Hanali? Did he understand how serious this was? She tried to lift her hand, tried to show him her wrist, but then a nurse shut the door, and there was only the shriek of the alarms and the struggle to breathe.

5

HAMBURGER

Bereft of magic, short lived and passionate,
there shall still be beauty and wonder among you.
FROM "THE ORDERING OF THE WORLD," AN ELENIL STORY

✛

The door shut, and Jason put his hand against the hallway wall. Madeline was dying. He didn't have any question. So he needed to find that magic man, and there wasn't much time. He started down the hall, but a viselike hand grabbed his arm.

Darius said, "What was Madeline talking about when she said 'bracelet'?"

Jason debated whether to explain. Darius didn't seem like the kind of guy to go in with dragons and unicorns, but Jason didn't know him well. But then again, he had promised to tell the truth. How much of the truth was the question. "This Renaissance faire reject came in the room and offered her a magic bracelet to help her breathe. She's telling me to go find him and get it."

Dairus's face clouded over. "What are you talking about? Nobody came into the room. I was there the whole time."

"You were frozen," Jason said.

Darius's gaze sharpened, and he looked at Jason critically. "But you weren't frozen?" His grip on Jason's arm tightened.

Jason peeled Darius's fingers off. "Listen, man, I don't have time to explain. You saw Madeline in there."

Darius's hands relaxed a fraction. "Okay. Right. How do I help?"

Jason's mouth fell open. "You believe me?"

Darius shrugged. "I don't know. But if Maddie wants this bracelet, let's go get it. Whatever's going on, Madeline gets what she wants. Got it?"

"Okay," Jason said. "I have to figure out where this magic guy went. You want to help look for him?"

Darius looked back at the closed hospital room door. Jason could practically see the relational connection between the two of them, like a glowing string. "I'll wait here," he said. "If the guy comes, I'll grab him. What does he look like?"

Jason was already trotting down the hallway. "You'll recognize him, believe me."

Now. Where would a magic person go in a hospital?

Not the waiting room. Everyone hates waiting rooms. The other direction was just more rooms, another hallway. Jason ran full speed through the maze of hospital hallways, keeping an eye out for the long, whitish hair of the stranger. He collided full force with a priest, sending them both sprawling to the floor.

The priest picked up his fallen glasses and put them on. Jason helped him to his feet. "Sorry."

"What's the rush, young man?"

"I'm looking for this magic guy. Looks like he fell in a closet full of lace. Long white hair. You know him?"

"A magic guy," the priest said, his eyes widening. He looked more carefully into Jason's eyes. Jason knew that look, too. It was the are-you-on-drugs look. "No. Not in recent years, anyway."

Of course not. Jason tossed a half wave at the priest and started down the hallway. Then he stopped, turned around, and trotted back. "Hey, uh, Mr. Priest. In past years or whatever . . . Do you know how to find a magic guy?"

The priest shook his head slowly. "It's dangerous, my lad, to invoke powers you don't understand."

Invoke. He knew that word. *Invocation.* It meant, like, to speak an invitation to someone. "He's a person, don't worry. He's not a demon or anything."

The priest grabbed his forearm. "Son, I'm not talking about demons. There are such creatures, and they are dangerous. But I am talking about the people of the Sunlit Lands."

Wait. "You know them? Creepy guys who want to trade a year of your life in exchange for letting someone breathe again?"

The priest nodded. "When I was a boy, I was orphaned in a fire. I lived on the streets, and a man came to me and said that in exchange for a few years in the Sunlit Lands fighting the accursed Scim, I could have wealth and a family."

Whoa. So the bargain . . . it was real. This guy had taken a deal, and here he was, alive and back in the real world. But the old man didn't seem exactly happy about it, either. And he said he had made the deal when he was a boy. How long had this war been going on, anyway?

Everything in Jason told him there was more to the story than the lacy stranger was saying, that somehow—and he couldn't see how—the deal was rigged. But then again, here was this priest, alive and well, as far as Jason could see. His bargain had been different, though . . . "wealth and a family." There was a big difference between wealth and a miraculous healing. And also, so far as Jason knew, priests weren't known for being wealthy. Or for having family. At least, not a wife and kids.

"They're trying to make a deal with my friend. She's dying, and they said they can make her well."

The priest's eyes softened. "Perhaps they can. But enter into agreements with them carefully, and—" He looked into Jason's eyes, as if studying his soul. "Don't send her alone, young man. It's a hard road to walk, but without a friend . . ."

"It won't matter if I can't find the guy. My friend's not going to last long."

The old man's lips began to tremble. "What was his name? This magic man?"

"I can't remember. Starts with an *h*. Hamburger? Something like that."

The old man echoed the name. "Hamburger?"

"Hamburglar? Hambutcher? Hamolee? I don't know."

"Hanali?" the old man asked, tears welling up in his eyes. "Listen to me very closely—"

And then Hanali stood in the hallway, leaning against the wall, plucking at the lace around his sleeves. "You only had to say my name," he said nonchalantly. "I was listening for it." Hanali looked at the priest, whose tears had frozen on his cheeks. Time had stopped again. Hanali studied the old man's face, and his eyes darted to Jason, then back to the priest. "You are fortunate this old man said my name," he said slowly.

"I said Hamburger like five times."

"But my name is Hanali," the thin man said, standing up straight. "Though I suspect you knew that already."

How long had it been now? Three minutes? Five? Was it too late already? Jason knew about bargaining, knew that you can't show how badly you need something. Everything in him wanted to grab the guy by his oversized lapels and shake the bracelet loose, run down the hallway, and slide it onto Madeline's wrist. Instead, Jason shrugged. "Madeline is thinking about taking the bracelet."

Hanali produced it from his sleeve. "And the bargain which accompanies it?"

"Yeah. Except I'm going to go with her."

Hanali hesitated. "I did not come to bargain with you."

"On the other hand," Jason said, "your weird magic doesn't affect me, which must mean something."

"Indeed." Hanali's expression clouded just for a moment, and then his face smoothed, as if he had put on a mask. He pulled out a second silver bracelet and showed it to Jason. "If you are to join her, you must agree to a year of service to the Elenil in exchange for your heart's desire."

"No. I'd make a terrible servant and a worse soldier. How about I agree to come to the Sunlit Lands, but no guarantees on any service or allegiance or anything like that. In exchange I get a unicorn."

The stranger shook his head. "Of what use is that pledge? We give you entrance to utopia in exchange for a unicorn? They are war beasts, in any case, and not given to civilians."

"Aha! So you admit you have unicorns! Okay. New deal. I get to ride a unicorn. And in exchange I live among you for a year."

"It won't do. You asked to own a unicorn, so clearly to ride one is less than your heart's desire. The archon and the magistrates would punish me for such a bargain. Though I must admit many would find you entertaining, and perhaps you are meant to join us. Still, it is a frivolous vow to make. Especially when sealed with the power of the Crescent Stone."

It hadn't occurred to Jason that Hanali might not take him. The thought of Madeline going alone made him feel sick. He thought of his sister, Jenny. He thought of his failure. He needed to go with Madeline. To make sure there was someone with her, whatever happened. "Final offer. I pledge allegiance to Madeline. Whatever she tells me to do, I do. In exchange, I get my non-unicorn-related heart's desire."

Hanali touched his fingers to his mouth. "It might suffice. For if Madeline is pledged to the Elenil, and you to her, then are you not in some sense pledged to them?" Hanali stepped closer, peering into Jason's face. "And I sense in you a deep sorrow. Perhaps it is sufficient to meet the conditions necessary to come to the Sunlit Lands. So be it. What shall your payment be?"

Jason paused. It felt dangerous to share anything real. And the things he wanted most, well, honestly, even if it was in this weirdo's power, he didn't think it would end well. "I really like those hospital pudding cups."

Hanali's eyes widened. "A pudding cup?"

"One pudding cup a day," Jason said. "In the morning, at breakfast, when God intended pudding to be eaten."

Hanali looked at Jason warily, as if sensing a trap. "One pudding cup a day, in the morning, for the duration of your human year in the Sunlit Lands."

Jason looked at Hanali as if he had said something insane. "For the rest of my life," he said.

Confusion flitted across Hanali's face. He didn't understand the request, didn't know if he was being played in some way. Good. Let him wonder.

Hanali weighed the bracelets in his gloved hand.

"Now or never," Jason said. "I know it's a lot of pudding—"

Hanali grimaced and held out the bracelets. "The deal is struck," he said.

Jason reached for the bracelets, then paused.

Hanali raised an eyebrow.

"*Chocolate* pudding," Jason said. "Don't try to pull a fast one with that fake vanilla stuff."

"Yes, yes, infuriating child, chocolate pudding. The deal is struck. Will you make me say it thrice?"

Jason shook the bracelets together. They were cold, like they had been in a freezer. "Deal."

Hanali scowled and lightly touched Jason's arm. He leaned close to the priest. "What is this man's name?" Hanali examined his face. "He has a familiar look." He sniffed experimentally. "There's a whiff of smoke to his life, don't you think?"

"I don't know. I randomly bumped into him."

Hanali studied Jason's face, looking for a lie. "Randomly. Hmm. What a strange creature you are." He straightened and put his arms behind his back. "Once your friend has her bracelet, you must follow the way to the Sunlit Lands. She won't be permanently healed right away. The magic responds to intention. So long as she is moving toward fulfilling her promise, her breathing will improve."

"How will we know the way? Is it over on Fifth Street? There's weird stuff over there."

"The way will open if you follow," Hanali said. "It is a narrow path. You may need to leave certain things behind." He hesitated. "Or certain people."

A jolt went through Jason. He had forgotten Darius. He would want to go too, Jason knew. He would insist on it. "Wait—"

"The deal is struck," Hanali said. "The bargain final." Then the Elenil man disappeared, and time flowed in around Jason like water in a tide pool.

"—you must not make a deal with Hanali under any circumstances," the priest finished.

Jason pulled away and flashed the two bracelets at the priest. "Too late."

The priest's mouth gaped open. "He was here? Hanali?"

"Yeah," Jason said, and he slid one of the cold bracelets over his left hand. It constricted like a snake around his wrist, digging in deep until it felt like it would break his bones. Jason gasped and leaned on the old priest for support. Then there was a sound, a pop, and it disappeared into his skin, leaving only a silver-looking tattoo with a glowing circle where the clouded gem had been.

"Oh no. My child. What have you done?" Tears slid down the old man's cheeks. He helped Jason straighten, and the left sleeve of his black jacket pulled up, revealing a shiny mess of old scars. The scars crisscrossed and spun around his wrist in a pattern similar to the silver tattoo on Jason's own wrist.

"She can't *breathe*," Jason said. "There wasn't another choice."

The priest looked at him sadly. "There is always a choice."

But Jason was already running toward her room. "She'll die without this!"

The priest shouted something, but Jason couldn't hear. The words kept ringing in his ears: *There is always a choice.* But if it ends in death, is that really a choice? Can that even be on the table as a possibility?

No.

Blood rushed to Jason's face.

Definitely not. Not if he was making the call.

Darius was leaning against the wall outside the room. He straightened when he saw Jason. "They won't let me back in," Darius said.

"She needs this," Jason said, panting. He couldn't breathe now, either.

Darius looked skeptical. "This is the bracelet?"

Jason didn't have time to keep explaining everything to Darius, and in the end, did it matter? Darius wasn't going with them. Jason's stomach clenched with guilt. He hadn't meant to make that decision for them, but he had. "Yes, Darius, this is it," he snapped, much more curtly than he had intended. "This is magic jewelry from Hamburger, and it's gonna make Madeline better as soon as we stick it on her left wrist. Then we're going on an adventure to Narnia or whatever, and when she gets back you can figure out if you're going to date. But in the meantime, she can't breathe, so first things first, yeah?"

Darius searched Jason's face. "Narnia?" he asked, with a sort of quiet reverence. He looked at the bracelet, turning it over in his hands. "It's cold."

"Magic," Jason said and showed Darius his wrist.

Darius nodded. "Okay. You open the door. I'll do the rest." Jason yanked the door open, and a nurse came flying over to close it, but Darius dodged the nurse, and then he was soaring toward Madeline like a rocket, the bracelet stretched out in front of him, the silver designs shining in the artificial light.

6
TO THE ENDS OF THE EARTH

How can I be loyal to the king and disloyal to my beloved friends?
I will never leave you. I will follow you to the ends of the earth.

PRINCE IAN, IN *THE GOLD FIRETHORNS* BY MARY PATRICIA WALL

✦

Darius saved her. Whatever came later, that was something to remember. It was Darius who saved her life.

The room was crowded with people in scrubs and the blaring screams of the machines, the clipped orders from the doctor, the quick replies of the nurses. Darius burst in, spinning past the nurse who stepped in front of him. He danced through the crowd of medical people until he arrived on the left side of her bed and slipped the bracelet onto her wrist.

The bracelet did nothing for a terrifying three seconds.

Then it tightened.

It kept tightening until it was cutting into her skin. She gasped, and then the burning started. The bracelet seared her like it had been in an oven. It glowed furnace bright. Just when she thought she couldn't bear it, the bracelet cooled. On her left wrist was the latticework of a silver tattoo, and the clouded jewel had grown to the size of a watch's face, glowing beneath her skin.

And she could breathe.

The sudden burst of oxygen rushed to her head, and a dizzy wave of giddiness washed over her. She was breathing again, gulping in the sterile, cool hospital air. She wrapped her arms around Darius and felt his strong arms encircle her, almost lifting her from the bed.

The doctors pulled him away. Someone called for security, and Madeline tried to object, but she was so shocked she couldn't speak. She just kept breathing, and for the first time in a long time it felt like she could keep breathing forever, like a normal person, breathe for ten, twenty, seventy years without thinking about it.

A security guard had Darius by the arm and was pulling him out of the room. "Can you breathe?" Darius shouted.

"Yes! Thank you," she said, but it was more whisper than words, and she wasn't sure he heard. She wanted to tell the guard to let him stay, she wanted to explain to the doctors that she was okay now, but she was over-whelmed, confused, and *breathing*. There was scarcely room in her head for anything but that.

A smile like sunlight spread across his face. "I'll wait for you down-stairs," he called. "I won't leave."

Tears welled up in her eyes. Darius always said that. *I won't leave.* She knew it was true. He had already stuck with her through some terrible things, and there was no evidence he would stop. It was what Prince Ian said to Lily in *The Gold Firethorns*, the third Meselia book: "I will never leave you. I will follow you to the ends of the earth." That's what Darius always said to her. When she first started to get sick. When the diagnosis came. When she couldn't stand the thought of seeing another doctor's face. *To the ends of the earth.*

She heard Darius scuffling with the security guard until the door closed, muffling the sound. She laid her head on the stiff hospital pillow.

Madeline's head throbbed where it had hit the classroom floor, but her lungs felt brand new. She could run a marathon. She could do jumping jacks or swim or dance or sing at the top of her lungs or yell at someone and still she could breathe!

The doctors ran tests. Tested her oxygen levels. Listened to her lungs. They didn't have much to say. They weren't sure what had happened, but in the past her lung capacity had seemed to come and go. They wanted to keep her for observation. Given what had happened with Darius barging in, they said no one else could come in until her parents arrived. No one mentioned the bracelet. They didn't comment on the tattoo. It's like they hadn't seen that part, had only noticed a high school boy bursting into the room, hugging her, and being dragged away.

But between nurse visits, Jason slipped in. He had a pudding cup in one hand and a silver tattoo on his other wrist. "People say tattoos hurt, but I barely felt this one."

"You have one too?" Relief flooded her. She wouldn't have to go alone.

"Your friend Handy gave it to me. I figured I'd put mine on today to guarantee we'd go together to the Sunshine Place."

Madeline looked at Jason. "What did you promise to him? What are you giving up?"

Jason shrugged. "I get to go with you, and they give me snacks."

Madeline's stomach dropped. "Jason . . . you're leaving behind your life for a year. You don't . . . You don't have to do that."

The edges of Jason's lips twitched up. "I would have flunked chemistry without a partner anyway. Might as well take a gap year."

"But your parents—"

Jason didn't let her finish. "Are going to be fine, if not happy to see me gone."

Madeline couldn't imagine that was true. Picturing Jason's parents and their grief somehow made it more real. Her parents would be going through the same trauma.

"Are my parents here yet?"

Jason shook his head. "Darius texted them, though."

If her dad was in a meeting, he wouldn't look at his phone for hours at a time, and her mom often left hers in the car. "I guess we can wait to leave until they get here? Do you want to say good-bye to your parents?"

Jason shook his head. "Hanali said that unless we 'start our journey' the magic stops working. Like, if the magic thinks you're not going to follow through, it takes away your breathing. We should get going soon."

Now that he mentioned it, she did notice a hitch in her breathing. So slight, and so small compared to what she had been living with up until now, but definitely there. She took a deep breath—amazing that she could do that again—and reflected on leaving home. This was going to be hard. She couldn't imagine missing her birthday, missing Christmas and Thanksgiving and a hundred other little family traditions. But, she reminded herself, she probably wouldn't have made it to Christmas anyway. She needed to set aside the chaotic mess of excitement and fear and sadness and confusion and loss, and get ready. Maybe she could send a message to her parents, although she didn't think they'd believe it for a second. Still. It was time to go. "Close the curtain," she said to Jason.

He pulled the curtain shut around the bed.

"With you on the other side, dummy," she said. "I'm going to get dressed."

Jason blushed and disappeared through the curtain.

Her shoes and socks were in a bag hanging on the end of her bed, but the rest of her clothes were gone. Right. They had cut her out of her clothes. It had been an emergency, they had been moving fast. She put on her socks and sneakers. "You can come back in," she said.

Jason looked at her hospital gown. "Bold fashion statement," he said. "I like the shoes."

Madeline wrapped a blanket around her back. She slipped the oxygen tube out of her nose, something she had done a hundred times before. Hopefully this would be the last time. "I'll need help getting the IV out."

Jason looked at her arm, his face pale. "Maybe I should go find some clothes for you."

He disappeared, and the sound of the door clicking shut echoed in the small room.

Fine. She didn't need his help. She peeled up the edges of the tape on her inner elbow and pulled both sides toward the center. The needle bit deep. She wasn't sure how to turn off the drip or if there was some special way to pull out the needle. She grabbed the base of it, her hand shaking, and with the smoothest motion she could muster, pulled the needle away from her arm.

She gasped. It was out, still drooling liquid onto the floor. A pinprick of blood welled up. A quick rifle through the bedside drawers produced a small piece of cotton, which she put over the wound. She found a roll of colored Coban to wrap around her arm and bit the edge to tear it.

Jason ducked under the curtain with some folded green scrubs. His shirt had brown stains dripping down the front.

"What happened?" she asked.

"I spilled chocolate pudding all over my shirt and went in the waiting room and started shouting that I was covered in blood and needed a change of clothes." He looked down at his jeans, which were also covered in pudding. "I got you some pants, too. I'll wait outside."

She tugged the pants on. They tied at the waist, so although they were baggy, they would stay up. The top slid on easily. She found a rubber band in the drawers and pulled her hair back, wincing at the tender spot on the back of her head. The strange silver markings of her bracelet tattoo glimmered even under the fake light in the hospital room. The jewel glowed under her skin, but it didn't hurt.

They slipped out of her room and into the elevator. Darius was downstairs in the waiting room. Darius gave Jason a funny look when they came out of the elevator together, but then he was wrapping Madeline in his arms. She leaned into the hug, thankful for him, thankful he was here and had brought her the bracelet, and glad that, for a moment at least, this seemed uncomplicated and normal.

"Did they release you already?" he asked. "Shouldn't they do some more tests?"

Madeline squeezed his hand. "Darius. There aren't more tests. We know everything there is to know."

He lowered his head, a look she had seen too often on his face since her diagnosis. "Okay," he said. "I know that. Can I give you a ride home?"

A sharp pain came from the bracelet. "I can't go home." The whole story came pouring out. Darius held her hand loosely, his eyes on hers the entire time she spoke, but he didn't speak until she was done.

"So the magic works?"

She lifted her left hand so he could see the silver network of tattoos. "A hundred percent."

Darius's face filled with wonder. "Madeline, it's everything we dreamed about. It's just like *The Gryphon under the Stairs*."

She nodded, smiling. "Finally something is working. There really is magic."

"So we're going to fight these—what are they called again?"

"Scim."

"We're going to fight the Scim, and in a year we're coming back."

Madeline pulled her hand away when he said "we." Of course he would say that. But there was no guarantee he could come . . . He hadn't made a deal. He hadn't seen Hanali.

Jason said, "I don't think you have a ticket." He held up the silver tattoo on his wrist.

"I'm coming," Darius said, glaring at Jason.

"Darius," Madeline said. "Your parents—"

"We'll be back in a year," Darius said.

Jason was getting nervous. "Can we take this outside before someone comes looking for the kid who checked herself out of the hospital?"

Madeline led them out to the street. She walked with purpose, away from the automatic doors and toward 23rd Street. Darius paced beside her, and Jason brought up the rear, his hands in his pockets, his shirt and jeans still covered in pudding. She knew Darius wouldn't be able to go. She felt it, as deep and certain as the magic moving through her. That was how it worked. She had read all the books. Darius didn't see Hanali, Darius didn't make a deal, Darius wouldn't be able to cross into the Sunlit Lands. That didn't mean they couldn't try, but . . . She tried to think of a way to make it noble, make it helpful for him to stay.

"I need someone to explain all of this to my parents," she said.

Darius laughed. "Your parents will call the cops if I tell them this."

"I could leave a note with you. Or send them a text." But her phone was still at the school, in her backpack. Her tattoo twinged, and Jason gave a yelp at the same moment. She knew which way to go, sort of—it seemed to be almost pulling her off the main street, down a narrow alley. "You're right," Madeline said, stepping around a dank puddle. "Don't tell them anything. I don't want you to get in trouble."

"How about I just come with you? Then this won't be an issue at all."

"Okay," Madeline said, exhausted. "Come with us." Darius winced when she said "us."

The bracelet was guiding them into an old neighborhood. If she went too slow, her breath started to go ragged. She moved quickly, following it toward the end of a long cul-de-sac.

A chain-link fence surrounded a low spot where long grass grew in a slight depression. All the neighborhood's runoff water eventually came through here. No one stirred in the neighborhood. No one opened a door or looked out a window. A hummingbird sat on the fence, chirping. That was weird. She hadn't noticed a hummingbird doing that before, and it seemed larger than usual. She thought back to the bird that had been talking to the woman in her garden. Could it be the same one? Could the Garden Lady have sent it?

Madeline rubbed her chin. "I think . . . we're supposed to climb this fence."

Jason groaned. "Tell me we're not about to crawl through a drainage ditch." He wrapped his fingers through the chain-link fence and pressed his face against it. "Ugh, I can smell it from here."

"I'll go first," Darius said, but when he put his hands on the fence, a brilliant flash of light knocked him backward. He lay on the ground, smoke rising from his clothes.

Madeline's heart leapt into her throat. She ran to Darius and knelt beside him. She helped him sit up. "Are you okay?"

"Electric fence?" Darius asked, still dazed.

"I'm still holding onto it," Jason said.

The hummingbird chirped and flew to the other side of the fence, zipping back and forth in a strange, almost hypnotic pattern.

"We should come back with a ladder," Darius said.

Madeline considered this, but her breath went immediately ragged. "I can't wait."

Darius frowned. "I always told you I'd follow you to the ends of the earth."

Madeline smiled and pulled him into a warm embrace. In *The Gold Firethorns*, Lily betrays the Eagle King. Ian, Prince of the North, escorts her to the edge of Meselia after she is banished. In one of Madeline's favorite moments of the whole series, he lays his crown down at the border and steps across with her. He says, "How can I be loyal to the king and disloyal to my beloved friends? I will never leave you. I will follow you to the ends of the earth."

Madeline leaned back so she could see Darius's face. "But do you remember what happens in the story?"

Darius nodded, a frown returning to his face. "Lily sends Ian back to serve King Kartal, and she heads into the wilderness alone. He watches her disappear into the mist, and the people call him Prince Ian the Sorrowful in the years to come."

"Except I'll only be gone a year," Madeline said. "And when I come back . . . things will be normal again."

Darius squeezed her shoulder. "That's not how it works, Maddie. You don't go away for a year and come home to 'normal.' You come back and . . . you come back and everything has changed."

She didn't answer him, because she knew he was right. She stood, and he stood beside her. "So I guess this is the ends of the earth," she said.

"On the bright side," Jason said, still at the fence, "she'll be fighting evil monsters during that year. So. There's that."

Darius frowned. "How is that a bright side?"

Jason shrugged. "Monsters are bad. Somebody's gotta fight 'em."

"Ignore him," Madeline said. She pulled Darius's forehead against hers. "I'll miss you," she said. "But a year from now I'll be able to breathe. I'll be able to live life again."

Darius sighed. A deep, resigned sound. "It's only a year," he said.

"Tell my parents . . . Tell them something. Tell them I'm okay." She shook her head. "Or don't tell them anything, I don't know what's best. Do what you think is right, Darius."

"I know the right thing to do already. I'm going to find a way to come to you," Darius said, and she knew it was true that he would try.

One more hug for Darius, as long as she dared, until her breathing started to go ragged. When she stepped away from him and toward the fence, her breath returned.

Jason stood near the fence. He cupped his hands into a stirrup. "I'll boost you."

Madeline laughed and leapt onto the fence. She slung herself over and dropped to the ground on the other side. She could breathe. She'd never need help to jump or run or scale a fence again.

Jason, on the other hand, appeared to have never climbed a fence in his life. She tried to coach him, and he fell off twice. Eventually Madeline leapt back over the fence and cupped *her* hands into a stirrup. She boosted Jason to the top, and he made his way to the other side with the help of a missed rung and gravity.

"I did it!" he shouted. "King of the world!"

They grinned at each other. Madeline looked back to Darius, but the world on the other side of the fence looked grey and sluggish, like a video in slow motion, covered with a thick fog.

"Magic?" she asked.

"No turning back now, I guess," Jason said, but that had never been a real possibility. Madeline shouted good-bye to Darius and told him they were safe, but he moved so slowly she couldn't tell if he heard. She wrapped her fingers in the chain-link fence, trying to see him more clearly, but the fog only grew thicker. She could barely see him now. Madeline whispered another good-bye. The space between them had already begun to grow.

The hummingbird zipped in front of her face, and she spun to watch it, but she couldn't see where it had gone. She didn't think the bird had crossed outside the fence. The drainage area wasn't huge, but it was clear of fog, and there wasn't another way out that they could see. A cement pipe protruded from the ground, just big enough that Madeline could crawl in on her hands and knees. A sludge of accumulated mud coated the bottom. A flicker of light came from far down the pipe.

"Do you think this . . . ?"

"I absolutely do not," Jason said, but she knew this was the way. Of course it was.

They stared at it for a full five minutes, neither of them speaking. Her breathing didn't change, but she knew. "I have to," she said at last.

Jason shook his head. "There's no way Hanali crawled through there."

The hummingbird appeared between them, then darted into the pipe. A chirp echoed back. Madeline glanced at Jason. "You saw that, right?"

"I did not see that," Jason said, crossing his arms.

Madeline put her hand on the lip of the pipe. She wrinkled her nose. A dank smell of ancient, decayed leaves and old mud came from the darkness. But there was light farther down. She could see it now for sure. She took a deep breath, thankful once more that she could breathe at all, and crawled into the tunnel. The mud squished beneath her hands and knees, but she moved steadily forward. She felt a lightness, a relief to be moving in the right direction. She would miss Darius, and her family, and her friends, but she was glad to be moving, to be breathing, to be headed toward health and freedom. If only Darius could have come.

From somewhere behind her Jason said, "Seriously. Hanali would never get his costume dirty like this."

She smiled, glad for Jason's company, and crawled steadily toward the dim light ahead.

7

UNDERGROUND

In great need may ye return to the Sunlit Lands,
for ye are our cousins and neighbors.

FROM "THE ORDERING OF THE WORLD," AN ELENIL STORY

✦

Jason had never followed a hummingbird into a disgusting sewer before, and so far he did not like it. He suspected he would pass on future opportunities. It stank like something had died, then been eaten, digested, and expelled, and then died again. The stench climbed right up into your nose and just lay there.

The pipe narrowed. Crawling became difficult. "I feel like a snake," Jason said and immediately regretted it. *Please let there not be snakes in here.* His arms were folded under his chest, and he moved himself along with his fingers and toes. He felt like he was having trouble breathing, but it was just good old-fashioned panic.

"You'll be okay," Madeline said. "Pretend it's a waterslide."

"I'm afraid of waterslides," Jason said.

Madeline scooted ahead of him, also on her belly. All he could see were her sneakers as she pushed forward bit by bit with her toes. All he could hear were Madeline's muffled sounds of exertion and the sucking sound of their bodies moving through the sludge. He bumped into her now and then, or even gave her a push, a process which involved putting his forehead on her heels and wedging forward. She didn't seem to mind. His arms and legs felt like gelatin. He wished someone was shoving him from behind. He wished he wasn't in a pipe at all.

He hoped the name Sunlit Lands was not a euphemism. If they popped out of this tube into a giant sewage factory and Hanali expected them to fight giant sludge monsters or something, he would . . . Well, he didn't know what he would do. Throw a mud ball at Hanali, maybe.

The stench got worse.

"I don't know what you're doing up there," he said. "But it stinks."

Madeline didn't answer. No doubt keeping her mouth shut to prevent anything getting in there. Smart. With every hard-earned inch forward the light intensified, as did the smell of the mud.

"There's a turn in the pipe here," Madeline said. "It's a little tight. Wait—don't push yet."

Jason stopped. He lay his head down at the bottom of the pipe, trying to conserve his strength. Bad choice—now he had mud on his face. *Great. C'mon, Madeline. Keep moving.* He didn't think he could go back the way they'd come. He hoped the pipe didn't narrow any farther, or their year in the Sunlit Lands might be spent in this pipe. Stupid hummingbird.

"I can see the exit," Madeline said. "The pipe slopes down from here. I'm going to lie sideways, and when I say to push, push."

The mud slurped as she wiggled around trying to find a better angle to get herself through the kink in the pipe. "Okay," she said. "Push, but not very—"

Jason pushed with everything he could, his muddy forehead connecting with her muddy sneakers, and there was a slurping pop followed by a high-pitched scream of terror or maybe joy from Madeline. Jason reached for her, but he missed, and he stuck his head around the corner in time to see a blazing circle of light and Madeline sloshing toward it in a river of mud and water.

The pipe widened below (finally!), and Madeline managed to get her arms and legs against the sides of the pipe and stop herself from shooting out the end. "It's the exit!" she called. Her head was silhouetted against the light. "It's a big cave," she said. "Really big, with lots of pipes everywhere. They're all gushing water into a pool below. I can't tell how deep it is, but it looks like it's maybe twenty-five feet down."

Desperately worried he wouldn't be able to get himself around the corner without Madeline's help, and certain that she couldn't get back up the pipe, Jason twisted once, violently, and found himself careening down the pipe on his back, screaming and—as the pipe widened—flailing his limbs. He slid down at roughly the speed of a bowling ball covered in olive oil. He had time to shout half of Madeline's name before knocking into her and carrying them both flying out of the pipe and into the cavern in a confused tangle of limbs.

This is the end of our adventure, he thought. He was glad no one else was there to see him die by barreling down a mudslide out a sewage pipe and into a runoff pond. He felt sorry for the coroner because they both stank so bad.

The water clapped shut over them, and they sank, fast. The water was half mud and revealed little when he opened his eyes. In the thick darkness he saw a white shape nearby—Madeline? He kicked over to her.

What turned its face toward him was not Madeline.

It was a face he might have said was a woman's if not for the sickly white color and the sharp, protruding teeth. The flat, black, pupil-less eyes were another giveaway. She reached for him as he tried to swim away, kicking with all his might.

Her hands were webbed, with black claws where fingernails should be.

His head broke the surface just as the creature's hands closed around his ankle. He shouted for Madeline, who was pulling herself up onto a long metal walkway, then he descended, struggling, toward the bottom of the murky pool. He heard a distant splash, but all he could see was the mermaid thing pulling his face toward its gleaming shark's teeth.

Madeline's fists barreled into the creature with the full force of her dive behind them. It shrieked and lost its grip on him. Jason thrashed, trying to get away, then Madeline kicked off from the creature's midsection, grabbing Jason under the arms as she rocketed upward.

They broke into the air, and Jason drew an enormous, gasping breath. Madeline dragged him out of the water onto the walkway.

"Mermaids," Jason gasped. "I am now afraid of mermaids."

"We should get away from the water as quickly as we can," Madeline said and started across the narrow walkway.

"That was a scary mermaid," Jason said. "Not the nice kind who sings to sailors and then murders them. The mean kind that gets murdery without the music."

Madeline shivered. "Maybe that was a Scim."

"We should have brought some dynamite to throw in all the lakes, then," Jason said. He imagined telling his parents about this when he got home, not that they would want to talk to him. He could practically see the skepticism on his father's face. One thing Jason never understood was how often people assumed he was lying. Since he had started telling the truth about everything, he felt like people should always believe him. Which was funny, because when he'd told lies in the old days, he had always assumed he had to convince people things were true. Now he just expected them to recognize it. But whatever. People were slow to believe in scary mermaids. Fine.

"I don't think we're going to be able to get back up to that pipe," Madeline said. "So I guess we follow this walkway."

The walkway wound through a tunnel large enough for a car. It was a relief not to crawl. No obvious source of light lit the tunnel, but it wasn't dark. After a while the tunnel walls changed from concrete to brick and then from brick to very old brick: hand mortared and brown with age, half the size of a regular brick, thin and long.

Madeline walked in front, her fingers running along the bricks.

"Hey," Jason said. "Something's written on there."

They paused to look. Chinese characters were scratched into some of the bricks. "That's strange," Madeline said. "Can you read them?"

"Well, it's complex characters, not the simplified ones. But yeah, I can read a lot of them. It's people's names. Maybe the people who laid the bricks?"

Madeline ran her fingers across one of the names. "How old do you think these are?"

Jason grinned. "I'd say these come from sometime between 1850 and 1882."

Madeline's eyes widened. "How can you be so certain?"

They started to walk again, side by side now. "Chinese immigration to the US started mostly in the 1850s . . . people trying to get in on the gold rush. Then they stuck around to do whatever made money: farming, construction, stuff like that. Chinese Americans built most of the railroads, you know."

"I knew that, more or less," Madeline said. "But why 1882?"

"You never heard this before? That's the year of the Chinese Exclusion Act, when the US government made it illegal for Chinese people to immigrate to the United States."

Madeline stopped. "When they *what*?"

Jason shrugged. "Yeah. It was a mess. My great-grandpa, he got separated from his family. They couldn't come to the United States . . . They thought the ban would lift and they could get back together, but, well, it didn't."

"That doesn't make any sense," Madeline said. "So it was only the Chinese—"

"People were worried they were taking jobs away. You know, like laying steel for the railroads or laying bricks in creepy underground magical sewers. The kind of work no one else wanted anyway."

Madeline stopped, hands on her hips. "Maybe you heard the story wrong. It's just . . . it's un-American. What about the poem on the Statue of Liberty about the—how does it go? Bring the weary to me?"

Jason kicked a stone, and it went skittering ahead of them down the tunnel. "The Chinese didn't come in past the Statue of Liberty. Or not many of them. Most of them came in through Angel Island, in California. It was a different experience."

"I'm sure Ellis Island wasn't exactly fun," Madeline said. "Lots of people came through with their names misspelled, or had harsh things said to them."

"That's actually a myth about the name-change thing," Jason said. "But anyway, the average person made it through Ellis in a few hours. A quick physical exam, a couple questions, and you were on your way. People were commonly at Angel Island at least a few days. The longest recorded time someone was held there was twenty-two months. Only direct family members of US citizens were allowed in. And unlike all the English and Polish and Irish and whoever coming in through Ellis, they actually checked the answers of the Chinese and other Asian immigrants against the answers given by their family in the US. If they couldn't track them down, you had to stay until they could. If your answer looked like it might not be quite the same, they'd send you back. People were packed into small barracks with no mattresses, or kept in cells, while they waited to find out if they'd be allowed entry. I'm not saying everyone who went through Ellis had an amazing time, but on average they had it better than anyone going through Angel Island."

"I've never heard of this."

Jason shrugged. "A lot of people haven't."

Madeline started to say something, then closed her mouth. It was fine. He didn't expect her to know this sort of thing. It's not like they talked about it at school. Where would she learn about it? He wondered if he would have learned about it if it hadn't affected his own family, once upon a time. He wasn't surprised she didn't believe it at first, either. He remembered the day he had learned that it had been illegal for Chinese people to come into the United States all the way until 1943, and they changed that only because of World War II, and then it was only like a hundred Chinese people a year. That didn't change until the sixties . . . Eighty years of few or no Chinese people allowed into the States.

"Hopefully the immigration rules in the Sunlit Lands are a little nicer to Chinese Americans," Jason said, trying for a joke.

But Madeline didn't laugh. She seemed troubled.

Eventually the old bricks gave way to natural stone, as if someone had carved the tunnel through a mountain. Madeline stopped and put her hand on the last of the carved names. "I'm glad they came," she said.

Jason grinned at her. "Yeah, otherwise you'd be covered in stinky mud and walking through a tunnel alone."

She punched him in the arm, and they kept walking. *It's fine she didn't know*, he said to himself again. It was fine, but it made him sad.

The tunnel spilled out into a forest. Green light filtered through the trees, but they could still see patches of the cavern ceiling above them, a bright-grey sky illuminated by some unseen source. "Impossible," Madeline said, turning to take in all of this underground forest. A dark canopy of leaves overhead blocked most of the ceiling. Vines snaked up the trees, enormous leaves turned toward the canopy. Thick brush obscured the ground. A narrow path forced its way forward, making a round tunnel through the branches which arced over the packed dirt. Roots burst through the soil, piling over each other, wrapping each other, intertwining across the dirt path.

"They're making it hard enough to get to the Sunlit Lands," Madeline said. "I thought we'd just step into a magic painting or something."

"Instead we have to go *hiking*."

"I hope Darius is okay."

Jason snorted. "At least there aren't any evil mermaids where he is."

She stepped onto the path. "I don't think we should wander off the trail," she said.

"Me neither," Jason said. The sudden change from tunnel to underground forest creeped him out. He was standing much too close to Madeline. She gave him a look. He shrugged. "I get clingy when I'm scared, so sue me."

"Come on, you big baby," she said, holding out her hand. He took it without comment, and they stepped onto the trail.

Soon the path got too narrow for them to hold hands. They hiked in silence for an hour. At one point, something crashed through the underbrush to their left.

"That sounded big," Madeline said.

"Probably just an old refrigerator," Jason said. That was the safest big thing that jumped to mind. Yup, just an old refrigerator, wandering the underground forest, looking for someone to open it so they could have some refreshments. That's the kind of magical creature Jason could get on board with. Whatever it was, they never saw it. No birds sang in this forest, though once or twice Jason thought he saw the hummingbird ahead of them, flitting among the branches.

By the time they came to the clearing, the forest had begun to darken. A bonfire burned in the center of the open space, casting strange shadows on the enormous trees. Trails radiated out into the forest, like spokes centered around the fire, trees lining them like columns.

Madeline gasped and grabbed Jason's forearm, pointing to some people near the fire. She gestured for him to be silent. Made sense to Jason. Might be wise to check these people out, in case they were crazy land mermaids or something. They crouched behind a bush and studied the clearing.

Five people hunched around the fire, three adults and two children. Humans, as far as Jason could tell. All five of them had tan skin, with blonde hair that hung in greasy knots from their heads. The man wore only a pair of jeans. He held a long hand-cut walking stick. The women wore shorts and loose sleeveless shirts. One of the women wore shoes, a pair of muddy white sneakers, but none of the others did.

As for the children, the girl's hair was combed down over her face. The boy wore nothing but filthy shorts and a featureless wooden mask made of bark. Two small holes had been cut out for his eyes. He carried a long stick in one hand. Jason shuddered. Something about the kid was unsettling. Probably the bark mask. Definitely the bark mask.

The girl didn't look up or uncover her face, but in a dull monotone she asked, "What are your names?"

Jason winced. "Maybe they're not talking to us," he whispered.

Madeline hesitated, then said, "I'm Madeline Oliver."

"Stand here beside the fire," the girl said, still in a monotone.

Madeline stood and stepped into the clearing. Jason stayed at her elbow. His gaze flickered among the strange collection of people around the fire. "I think I'd rather fight the mermaid."

The man's attention snapped onto Jason. "You fought Malgwin?"

"*Fight* is a strong word," Jason said. "More like . . . let her try to drown me? Madeline punched her, though."

The man glanced at the boy in the mask. The boy said, "Go." The man jumped to his feet, staff in hand, and hurried back the way Madeline and Jason had come.

"Your name," the girl said again.

"Jason Wu."

The girl nodded. "Madeline is expected. The boy must stay with us."

Jason balled his hands into fists. "The boy?! I'm older than you." He took two steps toward the fire. The women pulled small, silver knives from their belts. "Uh. I mean. You can call me boy if you want."

"We go together," Madeline said. "Hanali sent for us."

One of the women spit into the fire. The girl shook her head. "Jason Wu is not a name we have been given. You must go ahead alone, or turn back together."

Jason thought back to the Chinese names on the bricks. No one ever got his name right. Never. That's the whole reason he went by Jason. So he said his real name. "I'm Wu Song."

The women watched Jason carefully. "Why did you try to pass with a false name? Are you a Scim spy? This passage is only for allies of the Elenil."

"Peace, Sister, he doesn't have the look of the Scim."

"There are magics for such things," the first woman said.

"No matter," said the girl, and they both fell silent. "Wu Song is expected. They may pass. My brother will show you the path you must take."

The boy stood, his bark mask regarding them for a long moment. Then, without a word, he turned and walked into the forest. Madeline followed, with Jason close behind. One of the women took the final position in their procession. Jason wondered if she was there to keep them from running the other way.

The masked boy led them on a winding path that ended at a ten-foot-tall round metal door, which hung in front of them with no visible means of support. A spinner, like the wheel on a bank vault, jutted from the middle. "You have agreed to the terms," the boy said. "One human year of service in exchange for what has been promised you. Do you enter into this agreement willingly and without coercion?"

"It's too late to turn back," Madeline said.

The bark mask tilted. "It is not too late. With this staff I can smash the jewel of your bracelet, undoing the agreement. If you wish to be free, only say the word."

There wasn't much choice here. Without the magic, Madeline wouldn't be able to breathe. Part of Jason wanted to go back, because of the forest and especially because of this kid with the creepy mask. Madeline was looking at him, and he thought of his sister. If he walked away, he wouldn't ever forgive himself. Again.

"I'm willing," he said.

Madeline echoed him, a profoundly grateful look on her face.

Jason tapped the kid with the mask on the shoulder. Best way to hide your fear was a joke. At least, he always thought so. "I should have mentioned that I like my pudding cups slightly chilled. Is it too late to add that to the agreement?" The boy just stared at him from behind the bark mask. "Never mind," Jason said.

The boy wedged his stick high into the wheel, jumped, and yanked it toward the ground. The wheel turned, and the metal door opened. "You have come to the Sunlit Lands," the boy said.

A series of bright, slender trees greeted them. They had yellow, almost golden, leaves and shining white bark. Jason held up his hand to shield his eyes from the dazzling sunshine. Hanali stood there in resplendent white embroidered clothes shot through with gold thread, his hands covered in lace and resting on a small walking cane. The color of the roses in his clothes had changed—they were now a deep crimson. His walking cane had roses on it too, but these appeared to be actual roses, their vines curving in on themselves to form his cane.

Jason and Madeline stepped through the doorway and into the Sunlit Lands.

At Hanali's feet was a gilded birdcage with two bright-plumed birds inside. They almost looked like parrots. Hanali motioned to the boy with the bark mask. "Two have entered, two may leave. If you wish."

The boy with the mask turned and looked at the woman. She shook her head. "Together, or not at all. We have told you this many times."

Hanali tipped open the door of the cage, and the two birds flew out joyously, through the round door and into the woods beneath the sewer. "So be it," Hanali said. "Spin the wheel well when you lock the door." The boy and the woman pulled the door, both of them leaning backward. It closed with a monstrous boom. Hanali took hold of the birdcage and shook it once, and it collapsed to the size of a matchbook. He slipped it into his coat pocket and looked them over. "You are both filthy, though you have all your limbs. All in all, a pleasant passage, it seems."

Jason's mouth fell open. "Was that mermaid going to *eat our arms*?"

Hanali cocked his head. "Mermaid?"

"Scary lady who lives underwater with green hair and shark teeth."

The Elenil raised one eyebrow. "You can't mean Malgwin, certainly."

"That's what they called her, yes," Madeline said.

Hanali tapped his cane in the dirt. He didn't look at them and spoke almost to himself, as if lost in thought. "Strange. She rarely leaves the Sea Beneath. She is not, however, a mermaid. She is half woman and half fish. It is strange indeed that she would show interest in the two of you."

"Where we come from, a half-woman, half-fish person is called a mermaid," Jason said.

Hanali pulled at the lace on his sleeves. "Is that so? An interesting bit of trivia from your world."

"Why do you play with that lace all the time? Maybe you should trim it off."

"A nervous habit," Hanali said, dropping his hands. "Perhaps it was the mention of Malgwin that set me to arranging my cuffs."

"Madeline punched her in the face and kicked her in the stomach," Jason said.

A slight smile tugged at the edges of Hanali's mouth. "I would have liked to have seen that. But no matter. You are both here now, and safe. Step over here, and I will show you something wonderful."

Hanali walked through a small grove of trees which led to the edge of a cliff. He leaned against a white-barked tree and gestured with his gloved hand. Jason and Madeline came up to the edge, and Madeline gasped. Jason looked at her, then Hanali. Both of them were staring into the distance, smiling. He looked straight down and saw stones and bush scrub and a long fall. From there a wide, flat plain stretched away from the cliff. In the distance, Jason saw what had captivated Madeline.

It was a city unlike any Jason had ever seen. Tall white towers rose from the corners, with crimson flags flying in the breeze. A low wall, smooth and white, encircled the city, and behind the wall trees grew and fountains splashed and pastel-colored houses leaned together in unstudied camaraderie. A hill rose gently in the center of the city, streets festooned it like flowers, and beautiful alabaster buildings wound alongside the streets like precious jewels. A wide river flowed from the city and toward them, and Jason could see its clear, babbling water as it passed them and watered the wood. The central tower held a massive purple stone, easily visible from this distance, which radiated energy like a lighthouse.

"I'm awake," Jason said. "I'm awake." His whole life he had been told what the limits of possibility were, and he had just discovered that everything he had been told was a lie. This city, white and glorious, made him believe that there was good in the world. If this was the home of the Elenil, he didn't need to make a deal to serve them. He wanted to protect a people who could make something so beautiful. He wanted to know about their art, their politics, their social structures, their belief systems. Because if they could make a city like this, they could do anything. He couldn't wait to walk down those streets, to see those fountains, to put his hands against the white walls.

"It's gorgeous," Madeline said. Tears were running down her face. "It's everything I ever imagined, in all the books I read, all the fantasy paintings, all the movies. It's the most beautiful city I've ever seen."

Hanali smiled. "The Court of Far Seeing. It is the capital and greatest work of the Elenil. It will be your home during your time with us. Within a fortnight it will be so deeply in your heart that you may not wish to leave. Do you see the symbol of our power atop the main tower? All that we have accomplished these several centuries has been made possible because of the Crescent Stone. Come. My carriage awaits. I will take you to your housing." He took a deep breath, enjoying the view. "Truly, it is an unparalleled place."

Jason cleared his throat. Things were getting a little too emotional. "Does it have indoor plumbing, though?" Hanali glared at him. "What? It's a legitimate question." They walked back toward the door that had brought them into the Sunlit Lands. A rounded carriage, pure white and carved with intricate patterns, arrived beside them. A human teen wearing a white wig drove the coach, and white horses pulled it, four of them, with not a spot of another color, not a single hair out of place.

The coachman opened the door and, with a flourish, invited them to climb aboard. "But the mud," Madeline said, looking at the perfect white silk on the pillowed interior, then to her own disgusting hospital scrubs.

"The smell is unfortunate," Hanali admitted, "but the mud itself is easily cleaned. Climb aboard and be at ease. I would usually have clothes and a bath waiting for you here, but we have been on an accelerated schedule. I didn't expect to invite you so soon, but with your delicate health . . . In any case, my apologies for not being properly prepared to receive you."

Jason shrugged. The worst of the mud had washed away when they fell into the water under the pipe, and their clothes were dry after the long walk through the forest.

"It's okay," Madeline said. She stepped in first, facing forward, and Hanali sat beside her. Jason flopped onto the opposite side.

"Don't you want to watch the city?" Madeline asked. She stuck her head out the window. "The trees! It's like the sunshine is coming out through their leaves. It's so beautiful!" She took a deep, deep breath.

A sudden fatigue washed over Jason. Was it only this morning he had carried her into the hospital? He looked down and saw that his hands were shaking. She could have died. She could have died right there on the floor of their chemistry room, and now here she was, her face kissed by the golden sun of another world. He shivered. If he hadn't carried her to the car, if he hadn't spoken up, if he hadn't driven like a maniac bank robber, she would be—well, he knew how a story like that ended. He knew it all too well. A heavy cold seeped into his limbs, and he closed his eyes. "Wake me when we get there," he said.

"Welcome to the Sunlit Lands," Hanali said, but Jason pretended not to hear.

8
ROOMMATES

Your arrival—how like the sunrise!
When the cool eastern light shimmers
upon the morning waves.

FROM "THE PARTING," A TRADITIONAL ZHANIN SONG

✦

Hanali had ordered Madeline to stay in the coach, but his argument with the woman in the courtyard seemed to be about her. They had made easy time to the beautiful city of Far Seeing (properly called the Court of Far Seeing, according to Hanali). They traveled more than an hour, first down from the mountain and then through wide farmland. Farmers walked through the fields behind strange purplish beasts of burden, shaggy things with four long, curved horns. Their coach passed long citrus groves and orderly rows of some sort of berry—purple, plump, and round.

Madeline's heart felt like a helium balloon on an enormous tether. She floated above everything, taking it in, loving it all. She didn't know if it was the increase in oxygen or the fantastical world that matched every book she had ever read, but she felt almost giddy, like a kid waiting in line for a favorite roller coaster. She leaned out the window, taking deep breaths of the air and trying not to giggle uncontrollably at every wonderful thing.

At last they had come to the city walls. Everything about the place was amazing, even the traffic. Not ten minutes ago a woman in a bright-red dress and an enormous floppy hat had ridden by on a gigantic ostrich. Elephants decorated in long silks carried people in curtained rooms upon their backs. They had passed a fountain near the main gate where the falling water landed in crystal bowls that played different tones as the water struck them. The fountain sang a tune Hanali called "The Triumph of Ele and Nala." It was a beautiful, soaring thing, but he wouldn't allow the coach to stop for her to listen. She had reached out her hand, though, and when a bit of the water sprayed her fingers she had whooped so loud it woke Jason momentarily.

She knew she should miss Darius. She should be worried about her parents. She should be afraid of what was to come, of fighting the Scim and learning to live in a new world. But she didn't feel any of those things. She felt *happy*. All her life she had wanted something like this: horses and fantastical beasts and elves and mermaids and evil monsters to battle . . . and here she was, and how could she be anything but deliriously, uncontrollably happy?

In time they had come to a smaller wall surrounding a large country estate. It was on the outskirts of the city, just inside the wall. A human woman had come out to greet them, dressed as a kitchen maid, but now she was clearly giving Hanali a rough time.

Jason still snored on the opposite side of the carriage.

Madeline stepped lightly out of the carriage and walked toward Hanali and the woman, hiding behind a hedge which was covered in beautiful orange flowers. She couldn't just sit there in the carriage, not when there was an entire new world to explore. A fresh scent floated in the air, as if someone had scraped the skin of a ripe tangerine. She took a deep whiff, delighted.

"—telling you this is the girl who will bring justice for the people of the Sunlit Lands. Multiple far-seers have said so. She's going to save us, do you understand?" Hanali's voice had taken on an almost pleading tone. Surprising, coming from him.

The woman crossed her arms. When she spoke, Madeline noticed her British accent. "Oh, fine then. I suppose I'll have Scim trying to break into my place to murder her."

Hanali hesitated. "That may be."

Madeline gasped. This was not the story she had been told. This was the first she had heard about any prophecy, and definitely the first she had heard about the Scim trying to assassinate her. Her good mood deflated. Something about seeing this woman, who seemed solid and dependable and, well, ordinary . . . Something about seeing her and hearing her concerns about the Scim reminded Madeline of the seriousness of her situation. And listening to Hanali's story, a story she did not recognize, made her realize she may have come here in the company of someone who had a completely different agenda than the one he claimed.

"—ask the magistrates to provide protection, but I tell you this, Mrs. Raymond, that I won't be treated with this sort of disrespect. You didn't even wear gloves for my arrival, and now you are disparaging my deliveries."

The woman—Mrs. Raymond—scowled. "I've told you more than once, Hanali, son of Vivi, that in the Transition House we go by human rules. I can't teach the children all at once to follow the way of the Elenil. It takes time. I'll put gloves on when you invite me to visit at the palace."

"Now, Mary—"

"*Mrs. Raymond,*" she said firmly.

Hanali flinched, as if slapped. "*Mrs. Raymond,* then. You know I cannot invite—"

"What's that? You're not planning to invite me to the palace? What a surprise. What a surprise."

Hanali slumped, deflated. "How do you do this to me? Here I am, five hundred years old to your fifty, and you make me feel like a child."

"You act like a child," Mrs. Raymond snapped. "Most people are just too polite to point it out. Now the girl I can see was in dire straits. You were right to bring her here. But the boy . . . What are you playing at, Hanali? The boy doesn't fit the pattern."

Hanali glanced back at the carriage. He didn't seem to notice Madeline wasn't there. Maybe he thought she had slouched down and closed her eyes.

"The boy," Hanali said, "is infuriating. But he belongs here, make no mistake."

"He's a wild card."

Hanali smirked. "A wild card can be a good thing. It depends on the game you are playing."

"What was his tragedy that allows him to come into our lands?"

Hanali fell silent.

Mrs. Raymond shook her head. "I'll not break the rules, Hanali. Not for you nor anyone else. I'll not be sent back to my lot on Earth, thank you very much. You know as much as I that only a child in dire need can enter the Sunlit Lands."

"There's a sorrow to him, Mrs. Raymond. It runs deep. Perhaps not as deep as the girl's, I will grant you that. I cannot see it clearly, but he is meant to be here."

Mrs. Raymond ran her hands over her hair, tucking away any loose strands. "A wild card is unpredictable. You of all people with your prophecies and prognosticating should be nervous about that. No matter the game, the wild card is only to your advantage if it's in your hand. You didn't even bind him to you, or to the Elenil for that matter."

Hanali inclined his head. "But he is bound to the girl, and she to the Elenil, on pain of eventual death."

"You know my feelings about this."

Hanali nodded. "I have no other choice, Mary."

She didn't correct him about the name this time, she only said, "Be careful, Hanali. Be careful."

"Any punishment that comes upon you because of these two," Hanali said, "I'll take it on myself."

"You'll bind yourself to that?"

"By sun and bone, moon and flesh, I'll bind myself."

"Humph. Well then. No special treatment, though. I don't care if she's the savior of the world and he's her servant. We split them up, and you take the girl to the storyteller tomorrow yourself. After the orientation they go to their assigned duties, just like any other human who comes to the Court."

Hanali bowed low. "Of course, Mrs. Raymond."

"Enough with your foolishness. If someone saw you bowing to a human woman . . . the trouble! The scandal, sir."

Hanali grinned. "But we're on Transition House land. Such behavior is allowed outside the Court of Far Seeing."

"No wonder you're a recruiter. No doubt your churlish behavior seems charming to the humans."

"No doubt," Hanali said. "But what's this? I see one of your new charges has hidden behind an addleberry bush."

Madeline straightened and brushed herself off. It didn't do much, given the amount of mud caked onto her scrubs. But she walked to Hanali regardless and stretched out a hand to Mrs. Raymond.

Mrs. Raymond's grip was strong. "What's your name, young lady?"

"Madeline Oliver."

The older woman's eyes dropped and rose again, taking in Madeline's filthy clothing. "You need a change of clothes and a bath. We're a good three hours from dusk, and I suppose you've had a long day."

Madeline nodded. "A bath would be wonderful. But I couldn't help but overhear that you were worried someone might try to kill me."

Hanali's eyes flickered from Mrs. Raymond to Madeline. She could tell he was worried about what she might have heard. He covered it well, though, with a bright laugh and a wave of his gloved hand. "You are a terrible eavesdropper, my dear. Actually, she was worried assassins would damage her house while trying to kill you."

"You Elenil never know when to stop talking," Mrs. Raymond said. She took Madeline's hand. "We're all at risk from the Scim here, Miss Oliver. Hanali and I have some old ongoing arguments, and one is about how much risk is acceptable." She turned to Hanali. "You take the boy to meet his roommates, and I'll take Miss Oliver here to meet hers."

Madeline didn't get to say good-bye to Jason because Mrs. Raymond took her arm and guided her toward the house. The carriage, along with Hanali and Jason, headed for the back of the house while she and Mrs. Raymond went in the front. She noticed that neither Hanali nor Mrs. Raymond had answered her question about whether someone was trying to kill her. Not really.

Mrs. Raymond ran a finger over the tattoo on Madeline's wrist. "A word of advice, Miss Oliver. The other young people will ask you for details of your agreement with the Elenil. I'd suggest keeping it to yourself. Such gossip always leads to distress, one way or another."

She guided Madeline through a wide white door. The polished wood floors smelled of lemon, and a heavy red carpet runner ascended the stairway. Something seemed strange at first, and it took Madeline a moment to realize that there were no lights in the house. No switches, no chandeliers or fixtures, no candles, nothing but windows letting in the pure sunshine.

Several flights of stairs later, they walked down a long hallway, coming at last to a simple wooden door. "Your roommate will help you find your feet," Mrs. Raymond said. "She's . . . formidable. Should there be trouble." A sharp rap on the door brought an annoyed shout from inside.

Mrs. Raymond pushed the door open. "In here," she said, "you will find a change of clothing and a hot bath."

A young woman, close to Madeline's age, lay sprawled on one of the two beds in the room. An unruly mane of black hair surrounded her like a halo. She wore a loose-fitting T-shirt and a pair of jeans. She was barefoot. Her eyes glittered with determined ferocity, and a shining scar ran from the outside of her left eye down to the corner of her lip.

"Why knock if you're only going to let yourself in?"

"I'm with your roommate," Mrs. Raymond said.

"Another one?" The girl sighed and dropped her head back on her pillow.

Madeline held her hand out and said her name. The girl stared at the ceiling.

"The bath is through there," Mrs. Raymond said. "There are clothes in the chest at the end of your bed. You'll stay in your room the rest of tonight. I'll send food up."

"What about Jason?"

"You'll see him tomorrow," Mrs. Raymond said. "After you visit the storyteller."

"I don't—"

"Take a bath. Put on clean clothes. Sleep. Answers are for tomorrow. Good night, Miss Oliver." She paused halfway out of the room. "And good night to you, Miss Bishara."

"Lock the door," the girl said, as soon as Mrs. Raymond left the room. Madeline did as she was told. "The locks don't do much," the girl admitted. "Mrs. Raymond can still get in." She sat up. "I'm Shula."

"Madeline."

Shula pushed her massive mane of hair back, then let it fall around her face again. "What deal did you make with the Elenil?"

"Mrs. Raymond said not to tell anyone."

"Ha. Of course she did. Well, I can wait. You'll tell me when you're ready." Shula jumped to her feet and opened the bathroom door. She turned the tap and steaming water fell into the tub. "There's chocolate by my bed," she said. "Take some if you want."

Some chocolate sounded wonderful. Madeline broke off a square and set it on her tongue. She sucked on it until it was gone. Shula handed her a towel and told her to come back when she was clean. A long nightgown lay on her bed when she returned, clean and relaxed, her skin glowing with heat from the bath. She put the nightgown on and crawled under her covers. Light still streamed through the window, but her eyes wouldn't stay open.

Shula said, "Good night, and may you wake to good things in the morning."

"You're being so nice," Madeline said.

Shula laughed. "We stick together, you and me. But Mrs. Raymond isn't one of us."

"So we're friends."

"In this place, our lives depend on trusting each other. So we're going to have to watch each other's back whether we like each other or not."

Madeline yawned and tried to keep her eyes open. "I like you," she said, her eyes falling shut. "And I'll watch your back." A wave of thankfulness washed over her. A bath. Chocolate. A new friend.

"You are a funny one," Shula said. "So quick to trust." She patted Madeline's hand. "Tomorrow we'll go to the storyteller."

"What kind of stories does he tell?" Madeline asked, without opening her eyes.

"Different stories at different times," Shula said. "Don't worry, I'll go with you. Then we'll fight the Scim."

9

BREAK BONES

The Scim in deep darkness accursed.

FROM "THE ORDERING OF THE WORLD," AN ELENIL STORY

✦

When you're done looking at the toilet, we can do something more interesting."

It wasn't a toilet, though, not exactly. It was a bowl with a lid, but it didn't have any pipes or a water tank or a lever to flush or even a hole in the bottom of the bowl. No water, either—it was just a dry white porcelain bowl sitting in what looked more or less like a bathroom. "Hand me that apple," Jason said, kneeling in front of the bowl.

His two roommates exchanged a glance. They were both thin and muscular. Their names were Kekoa Kahananui and David Glenn. Kekoa's short hair had bleached tips, and he had an angular, handsome face. David had dark hair swept back into a ponytail, and so far Jason hadn't seen him get worked up or excited about much. His default expression was mild but friendly.

"I was gonna eat that apple," David said.

"This is for science!" Jason snapped. "Now give!"

Kekoa slapped it into his palm. "It's not science, brah. It's magic."

Jason slammed the apple into the bowl. He peered down at it. A perfectly normal apple, with no place to go. He closed the lid slowly, keeping his head level with the rim, trying to see inside the bowl as long as he could. As soon as the lid touched the rim of the bowl, he flipped it up. The apple was gone. The bowl was pristine. "Where does it go?"

"Man, I'm hungry," David said. "I could have had a couple bites if that's all you were doing. You could have experimented on the core."

"Magic plumbing," Jason said. "Hmm."

Kekoa crossed his arms. "Jason, why don't you take a bath and get all that mud off you, and then we'll take you to see the armory."

Jason perked up. "Is the shower magic?"

David shook his head. "I don't think so. No showers, either—they only got baths."

"Hmm." Jason looked around the bathroom for something else to "flush." Besides the apple, he'd already done away with a pillow, a bowl they had served him some sort of gruel in, and a baseball cap that had apparently belonged to Kekoa. He hadn't made the strongest first impression.

"I miss showers," Kekoa said. "But I really miss toilet paper."

Jason jumped to his feet. He hadn't even noticed the lack of toilet paper. "What do we use?"

David tipped his head toward a folded pile of thin washcloths. "I like the cloths, man. They smell good."

Jason sniffed one. The scent was similar to lilies, strong and sweet. He threw one in the toilet and closed the lid. When he opened it again, the bowl was empty. "Seriously. Where do they go?"

Kekoa sighed. "Listen, brah. I know you love toilets, but you can visit this one every day. Can we go to the armory now? We need a third in our Three Musketeers, and you're our roommate, so it's gotta be you."

"War Party," David said. "I'm telling you, we should be called the War Party. Three Musketeers is, like, French dudes."

"Yeah, yeah," Kekoa said, swinging the door to their room open. "Let's go pick out weapons first, though, okay?"

"I want to check in on Madeline, too."

"You're not allowed to see her until after you hear the story of the Sunlit Lands. Them's the rules," David said. "C'mon."

They walked down the hallway. Transition House was enormous, bigger than any place Jason had been in before. It reminded him of a boarding house or military dorm from olden times, like he had seen in movies. He followed the guys down a long flight of stairs, which had a red carpet held in place by fasteners along the stairway edge. "Don't let Mrs. Raymond see you walking around all muddy," Kekoa said.

"C'mon," David said, pulling Jason along a narrow hallway that doubled around under the stairway. He opened a door, and a cool breeze washed over them. A wide stone staircase led downward, and torches lit the path.

"That shouldn't fit in this house," Jason said.

"More magic," Kekoa said. "Technically it's not in this house, it's some castle somewhere."

A wooden door with an enormous black iron lock stood at the bottom of the stairs. Kekoa unlocked it. Inside was a brightly lit white room, and much like the forest path, the illumination had no obvious source. Weapons of all kinds hung on racks and from hooks on the walls.

Kekoa threw his arms wide. "Welcome! Here is where we choose our weapons for fighting the Scim!"

"I'm not fighting anybody," Jason said. "I didn't sign up for that."

Kekoa and David exchanged glances. David said, "Yeah, but when you see the Scim you'll want to."

Kekoa ran to the far wall and came back holding a weapon that looked like a large, distended Ping-Pong paddle with a hole through the middle, sharp teeth jutting out from the edges, and a hooked handle. "This is my leiomanō," he said. "This is an old one. It's made from kauila wood. That stuff's endangered now! You're not allowed to cut it down anymore. Those teeth are shark's teeth, and the lashings that hold the teeth are handmade."

He offered it to Jason, who turned it over in his hands. It was beautifully made. "What kind of shark's teeth are they?"

"Tiger shark," Kekoa said. "My people made this. Me and David, we like to use traditional weapons when we fight. It's pretty epic when we're out there, smashing those Scim."

"What do you use?" Jason asked. "What's traditional for you?"

"I'm Apsáalooke, from southeastern Montana," David said. When Jason looked at him blankly, David said, "Crow tribe." He picked up a long hatchet. "I'll probably use this one in the next battle. Sometimes I use knives." He spun the hatchet in his hand. "I like this one because it's part hatchet and part ax."

"What's it called?"

David shrugged. "I call it a hatchet ax. I don't know. I never used one before coming here."

Kekoa slapped Jason on the shoulder. "David and I saw some stuff the other day that would be good as ancestral weapons for you, too. In fact, there's a whole outfit. It's lit. Come check it out."

Kekoa and David both seemed thrilled to show him. They took him around one of the standing racks, and there was a full set of samurai armor. The flared helmet, the breastplate, the katana, everything. It was clearly old, and the polished, dark breastplate seemed to simultaneously reflect and hoard the light. Kekoa grabbed the katana and held it out to Jason, hilt first. "What do you think?"

The katana was beautiful. He studied the sheath for a long moment before using it to whack Kekoa in the legs. "I think that it's Japanese and I'm Chinese, you idiot."

"What? So what do Chinese soldiers use?"

"Armored tanks, I hope," Jason said. "Besides, I already told you, I'm not fighting. And before you say another word, no! Ninja are a Japanese thing too."

"Chill, brah. It's not that big a deal, is it?"

"Dude," David said. "You want him to call you Samoan?"

"Nothing wrong with Samoans," Kekoa said. "But I'm kānaka maoli."

"Yeah. Hawaiian. China versus Japan, that's a big difference." David made a mock jab at Kekoa with his hatchet ax. Kekoa made a face and stepped out of the way. "So what should we be looking for? What's a Chinese dude use?"

Jason picked up a silver broadsword. It was heavier than he expected, and the tip hit the floor with a clang. "I have no idea. Weapons have never been my thing. There's a double-edged straight sword called the jian. But like I said, I'm not fighting anybody."

"It's fun, though," David said. "Seriously. I get all my war paint on to terrify the enemy. We get ourselves to look as scary as possible, and then we take those things out."

"Yeah," Kekoa said. "And so long as you don't get decapitated or something, the Elenil fix all your battle wounds, so you're good to go the next day."

So that's why it sounded "fun" to them. There wasn't much risk if there were magic cure-alls at the end of the fight. Why would they even need to fight if everyone was magically better at the end? They might as well be playing checkers for dominance. He liked his roommates, but their laid-back attitude toward war creeped him out a little. They acted like it was a video game, and granted, if they could just "respawn" after every battle, maybe it kind of was. But he was here for Madeline, not to crush skulls with a shark-toothed Ping-Pong paddle. "I'd need a crazy good reason to fight anybody. It's not my style."

Kekoa gasped like he had been punched in the stomach. "Oh," he said. "Ahhhh ha ha ha."

"Oh no," David said. "He starts making weird sounds when he has a big idea."

Jason hefted the sword back into place. "Do you hear that sound often?"

Kekoa swung his leiomanō, a whoop of joy coming out of his lips. "Let's take him to see the prisoner."

"No way, Kekoa. Humans aren't allowed to talk to him."

"Come on. There's a door right near here that goes straight into the dungeon."

"No."

"Five minutes, David! Then Jason'll fight for sure. Besides, what will the Elenil do if they catch us? Send us home?"

"I said no way, Kekoa!"

"David Glenn. We're the ones who captured him. The least they can do is let us talk to him."

"I still say no."

Kekoa's eyes flickered toward Jason. "Tiebreaker."

David folded his arms. "Fine. Jason decides."

Jason had the samurai helmet on his head and a throwing star in one hand. He had also picked up an ancient pistol that looked like it had a harmonica sticking through the middle of it. "What kind of prisoner? Who is it?"

"It's a Scim warrior," David said.

Jason rolled back on his heels. So far he had only seen an Elenil, and he hadn't been much impressed. The toilets were way more interesting. He sort of wanted to see one of these evil Scim things. "Let's take a look," he said.

David's eyelids closed halfway. "Alright, then." He set his hatchet ax down.

Kekoa bounced from foot to foot and led the way out the door. He locked the armory, then grabbed a torch off the wall and led them through a much narrower, darker corridor. "No lock on this door," he said. "We don't know where it takes you, exactly. I think maybe the palace. David thinks outside of Elenil territory. We're not sure. So you have to come back through *this door*. Don't go up the steps in the dungeon, because we're not sure where they go. You could be on the other side of the world if you do that." He cracked the door open. "All clear."

The dungeon matched every description Jason had ever heard. Dank, dark, and smelling nearly as putrid as the dried mud on him. There was a pile of hay in a corner and massive chained manacles hanging from the walls. Attached to one wall was a heavily muscled, brutish creature. Its arms were too long, like an ape's. Its skin was the color of old concrete, though a swirl of black tattoos covered most of its chest and arms. It had totally black eyes—no whites—and a heavy brow. Its mouth jutted forward, full of crooked, yellowed teeth. A small wreath of neglected black hair encircled its grey brow. It wore a ragged cloth around its waist. Its fingernails were wide as quarters, ragged and split. Its ears were tiny and round, flat against the side of its head. Scars crossed much of its torso.

Jason's heart revved up immediately. This thing was clearly powerful, and if it got its hands on Jason he wouldn't last a second. Jason's lips curled back in disgust and terror. And yet . . . there was something intriguing about it too. It was the most alien thing he had seen in the Sunlit Lands, and there was a strange sort of grace to the monstrous form. He imagined an army of these things and shuddered.

"Not too close, brah."

Jason calculated the distance from the wall to himself, studying the length of the chains. The Scim turned its wide grey head toward him.

"This is Jason," David said. "A friend of ours from the human lands."

"I'm Wu Song," Jason said. "That's my real name."

The Scim chortled. "Truth teller, are you?" Its voice was like gravel spilled on concrete.

Jason's eyebrows rose. "Yes."

"We Scim say only three tell the truth: prophets, storytellers, and fools. Which are you?"

Jason considered this question. "Probably fool."

"Ha!" The Scim straightened, seeming suddenly interested. "I will trade you, truth for truth. I am called Break Bones."

Hmm. Interesting. "I am called Jason."

Break Bones smiled, opening his wide, frog-like mouth to display jagged and uneven teeth that were each the size of Jason's pinky. "Why do you come to the Sunlit Lands?"

"To protect my friend," Jason said. He thought about his answer for a moment. "And to lay to rest old ghosts. And you?"

The Scim stood and shook its chains. "To shatter the sun and bring a thousand years of darkness and terror to the Elenil and all who befriend them. To crush skulls and break necks. To build a temple of bleached bones that reaches to the great dome of the heavens. To humiliate every Elenil before their death, then tear down the works of their hands, stone by stone, beam by beam, brick by brick. Only then shall I rest."

"Huh," Jason said. "I guess that's why they call you Break Bones."

"The fountains will run with blood. The city walls will be shelves for their heads."

"Better make a priority list, because if you tear down all their bricks and *then* try to use the walls as shelves, you're going to have to rebuild the walls again. It's a lot of work."

"You mock me," Break Bones said, his voice low. "The Scim are not fond of mockery, Wu Song."

Jason cocked his head. "Is anyone fond of mockery?"

"I think you're ticking him off," David said.

"It's a legitimate question," Jason replied, watching the Scim.

Break Bones's chest was heaving, his breath coming in staccato pants. "Humans. Are you even allowed in this prison?"

"We should go," Kekoa said. "I think you get the point. The Scim are terrible monsters."

"No," Jason said, answering the Scim. "We snuck in."

Break Bones laughed, and the horrible sound of it filled the dungeon. "I like you, Wu Song. When I am free from this place, I will honor you with a violent death. I will not humiliate you with captivity."

"That's nice," Jason said. "Though I might prefer humiliation."

Break Bones grunted, flashing his broken yellow smile. "What is the name of your friend? The one who is under your protection?"

"Don't tell him," David said.

Kekoa grabbed Jason's arm and pulled him toward the door.

"Madeline," Jason said. "Madeline Oliver."

Break Bones wrapped his right arm into the chains holding him fast. "On the night I bring the darkness to you, I will come with her lifeless body, so you will know." He slammed his arm forward, and dust puffed out of the wall where the chain was anchored. He yanked again, and the chain rattled, starting to come free. "So you will know you failed!" Break Bones roared, pulling the chain nearly all the way out. A distant trumpet sounded, and there was the sound of feet on the stone stairway.

Kekoa pushed Jason toward the exit, David close behind. They squeezed out the door, and David slammed it shut, leaning hard against it. The three of them stood there, panting. "Should we look?" David asked.

"Nah," Kekoa said. "The Elenil will have him chained back up by now. No need to show our faces."

"You're crazy," David said to Jason.

Jason scratched his head. "I guess." He thought about Break Bones's insane violence. He hadn't even tried to disguise his desire to rain destruction on the Elenil, and he had threatened Jason—and Madeline—for little more than teasing him. The intensity of the creature's violence and his certainty that he could smash Jason to bits terrified him. "Are all the Scim like that?"

"More or less," Kekoa said.

David shrugged and nodded.

"Then I'll be beside you in the next battle," Jason said. He regretted his words the moment they came out of his mouth. He didn't know how to use a sword, and the biggest fight he had ever been in was in fifth grade when Maurice Mandrell had made fun of another kid for reading too much. Jason had gone after him with the book, determined to beat Maurice over the head with it. He had woken up in the nurse's office. His friends said it seemed like Maurice had been tired after beating Jason unconscious, so he counted that as a victory. It didn't matter, though. Now he had said he was going to fight the Scim, and that meant there was no turning back. Not if he was going to be completely honest in everything from now on. He had to keep his word.

"Welcome to the War Party," David said, smiling.

"Brah," Kekoa said. "We have not settled on that name."

They argued about it all the way back to their room. Jason tried to put Break Bones out of his mind, but he kept seeing those heavy chains shuddering under the creature's massive strength. In retrospect, he probably shouldn't have shared Madeline's name. Or his own.

10
THE STONE FLOWER

Thus the Aluvoreans left in peace to populate the woods of the world.
They are a gentle race, though some say they have come to
love their trees more than people, a great misfortune.

FROM "THE ORDERING OF THE WORLD," AN ELENIL STORY

✦

P ut these on," Shula said, handing Madeline a pair of thin white gloves. Madeline had already put on the white dress with its high neck, long sleeves, and low hemline.

She spun for Shula. "I'm not getting married, am I?"

The gloves fit perfectly, just like the dress. She hoped there wouldn't be a veil.

"Every newcomer wears white for twenty-eight days. So the citizens know to be patient when you don't know the culture."

Sunlight filtered in through their open window. A trellis of a mint-like plant grew outside, and the scent wafted to them. The temperature was perfect, and Madeline hated to cover herself completely when she could be baking in the sun.

Mrs. Raymond brought them breakfast: a warm cereal, similar to oatmeal, with tart purple berries on the side. In the future they'd be eating in the "common room," but since she hadn't had the basic orientation, Madeline wasn't supposed to be with the others. She sat on the windowsill and took a deep breath, marveling again at her return to health.

"How did you come to be here, Shula?"

Shula pulled on a pair of long leather boots. "Like everyone else. The Elenil offered me my heart's desire in exchange for fighting the Scim." She frowned. "Those monsters. I would have fought them for nothing."

"What did you get in exchange?"

Shula sighed. "I'll share when you do." She held up her left wrist, and the silver tattoo glittered on her arm. "As you can see, some of the bargain must be the same as yours."

Madeline's own tattoo shone in the morning light. "When do I start to fight?" Her heart pounded in her chest. Fighting scared her. She didn't want to hurt anyone, let alone kill them, and it seemed clear people were talking about full-out war. Then again, from what Hanali said, the Scim were trying to kill *her*. So maybe it would be self-defense.

"They won't make you fight until you want to fight," Shula said, shrugging into a light jacket. "Today we'll talk to the storyteller. The Elenil will give you a sort of history lesson to show you how unique and wonderful the Court of Far Seeing is before they ask you to defend it. When your first month is done, they'll know you well enough to give you your job for the rest of your stay here. You'll probably get some local work in the city until then . . . Maybe guard duty, or running messages, something like that."

Shula wore jeans and a T-shirt under her jacket.

"When do I get to wear normal clothes?" Madeline asked.

Shula grinned. "In twenty-eight days or so. Though plenty of humans wear local clothes even once their month is up. Easier to blend in." She slipped on a thin pair of leather gloves and pulled the door open. They made their way down the stairs and out the front door.

"Should we tell Mrs. Raymond we're leaving?"

"We're not prisoners, Madeline. We can come and go whenever we like."

Then why wasn't she allowed to see Jason?

There was no carriage waiting. Shula shrugged and said maybe Hanali was meeting them at the storyteller's. "Not a big deal. It's not far to walk."

They made their way toward the city center. Madeline couldn't get over the sights and sounds of the place. They walked through a market full of silk, strange fruits, and food cooking over coals in metal troughs. The different types of people amazed her also. She saw what she could only assume were more Elenil, dressed in elaborate clothes that covered them almost completely. They were all tall and painfully thin.

She saw guards and soldiers walking along the cobbled street. They had swords on their belts. Most of them were human. Apparently there were only a handful of Elenil soldiers.

"There are no street signs," Madeline said.

Shula nodded. "The Elenil don't have a written language."

"They're illiterate?"

"Most of them, yeah. Why would you need to write when you can just speak your message to a bird and have it delivered? Most everything we accomplish through reading, they do with magic, and without all the trouble of learning to read."

Madeline felt a small disappointment at that. She had hoped to read some Elenil fiction. She wondered what magical people would write about, and what their fantastical stories would hold. Then again, she was on her way to a storyteller, wasn't she? And no doubt she could scavenge the occasional book this year or ask Hanali for some. The humans must have some hidden away.

All colors and sizes of people moved in and out of the shops. Short, hairy men and women with dark, almost grey, skin wove through the crowd. She saw one man wrapped in a series of cloths so that only his eyes could be seen—eyes which seemed to glow from within the shade of the cloths. She even saw a woman whose skin appeared to be blue darting beneath the shadows of a rounded trellis. The blue woman stopped to talk to two human guards.

"Are all these people Elenil?"

Shula laughed. "Those shorter people, those are the Maegrom. Did you see the man wrapped in cloths?"

"With the glowing eyes?"

"Kakri. Desert people. They love stories even more than the Elenil.

For the Elenil, stories are almost sacred. For the Kakri, they are life. They use story as a form of currency. The greatest storytellers are considered the wealthiest among them."

"What about the blue woman?"

Shula stopped in her tracks. "Oh, probably an Aluvorean. Where?"

Madeline scanned the crowd. "Over by the trellis there. Talking to the two guards."

The two human guards waved to Shula, and one of them called her over.

Shula sighed. "Stay here for a second. Technically I shouldn't introduce you until you've met a storyteller. I'm sure it's just a quick bit of business." She stripped off her coat. "Hold this, please."

Shula strode into the crowd toward the guards and the blue woman. The four of them had an animated conversation. Shula clearly was unhappy with the guards. One of them gave a shrill whistle, and a small bird darted down to rest on his finger. He spoke to it. The bird tweeted twice, then zipped into the air and sped past Madeline, toward the city center.

Madeline watched the bird go, reminded of the hummingbird she and Jason had followed into the Sunlit Lands and the birds Hanali had released when they arrived. She studied the square, dazzled by the riot of colors, the sounds of the people calling out about their wares, and the sweet smells coming from the food stalls.

A hummingbird whirred by. Madeline watched it as it flew through the crowd, flitting around, hovering by a Maegrom here, an Elenil there, and then finally zipping across the crowded square to linger beside an old, bent woman in a straw hat festooned in flowers, standing in what appeared to be a tiny garden built into the side of a building. The Garden Lady. Her back was to Madeline. The hummingbird hovered by the lady for a moment, then burst off in a straight line along the main avenue.

Madeline stole a quick glance at Shula, who didn't seem any closer to ending her conversation. Shula had told her to stay put, but it wasn't that far to walk over to the Garden Lady. Madeline would keep an eye out for Shula and come back as soon as she was done with her business.

The Garden Lady, still in the small garden built along the city path, stood talking to a woman whose skin was a slightly green color, like some-one who was standing under a sunlit canopy of trees. In fact, on closer inspection, her skin was multiple shades of green, as if a pattern of leaves was cast upon it, and the darker spots moved, like leaves in a breeze. Her hair was thick, short, and deep green, like a healthy moss, and she wore a nut-brown robe with silver trim.

The two women stood in front of a wall thick with ivy. Madeline came closer, feeling foolish for not knowing the Garden Lady's name. She didn't know how to call out to her. She moved closer. She came around so she could see the Garden Lady's face and gasped. It wasn't her. She had a gourd instead of a head, berries for eyes, and a mouth made of trailing ivy.

Madeline stumbled backward, trying to put distance between herself and the strange scarecrow version of the Garden Lady, but green fingers wrapped around her bicep. They felt almost sticky, like a plant with tiny barbs on it. They didn't hurt, just felt like they would cling if she pulled away.

"I am sorry," the green woman whispered. She came barely to Madeline's shoulder. "We did not know how else to get you away from them."

Madeline cast a hurried look at Shula. She still hadn't noticed that Madeline had wandered off. Which was . . . good? She wasn't sure now. She didn't want Shula to know she had immediately disobeyed her, but she also felt nervous that Shula didn't know where she was.

"Away from who? From my friends?"

"Yes. And from the Elenil," the woman said. "My sister is distracting them for a moment, but soon they will see. My people need your help."

"*My* help? I just got here."

The woman's teeth were white as birch bark. "Which is why you are wearing the white, we know. But there is trouble in Aluvorea and—it is tangled—but the Eldest believes you are the one we must grow alongside."

Madeline's head swam. "Who told you that? How can I help when I have to serve the Elenil for the next year? And what does 'grow alongside' even mean?"

The woman's grip tightened. "It is a simple question—will you help my people?"

Madeline could barely help herself. She was obligated to the Elenil for a year, and then she needed to go home. She couldn't stay here forever in this fantasyland, even though it was something she had always dreamed of. But the idea of a quest, a goal, a good deed to be done, rang in her like a bell.

Tears formed in the woman's eyes and slipped down her green cheeks. "Please."

Madeline took both the woman's hands in her own. "Of course I will," she said.

"It is a promise then," the woman said, with a desperate intensity. Her eyes widened, looking at something over Madeline's shoulder.

She turned around to see the Garden Lady—the real one—pushing her way through the crowd, still a good distance away but headed straight toward them, her face flushed, her eyebrows low, her jaw jutting out, and a monstrous frown on her face.

"I must go," the green woman said.

At the same moment the Garden Lady bellowed, "Make a dummy of me, will you, child? And a gourd for my head? Oh, you and I will have words, yes we will!" Humans and Elenil pushed to get out of her way. A Maegrom scurried from under her feet, and every eye in the square was turned toward her.

Madeline looked at Shula, whose eyes moved from the Garden Lady toward the object of the old woman's wrath. When Shula saw Madeline, her eyebrows rose as if to say, *That is not where I left you.*

"Our time is at an end," the Aluvorean woman said. She held up her hand. "For you." In her tiny palm was a flower, bright red, as red as a spot of blood on a handkerchief. It was the size of a fifty-cent piece, delicate and lovely.

"Thank you," Madeline said and reached for it, moved by the woman's generosity and kindness.

Green tendrils unfolded from beneath the flower and grasped hold of Madeline's hand, climbing onto her and settling on her right wrist. "Don't be startled," the woman said. "It's a stone flower. They grow on the stumps of dead trees, only in Aluvorea. They glow in the dark. It likes the warmth of your arm, that's why it's wrapping onto you."

"Thank you," Madeline said again. It was beautiful and like nothing she had seen before, though the crawling tendrils reminded her unpleasantly of spider's legs.

"Come to us in Aluvorea," the green woman said, then gave a yelp at the sight of the Garden Lady barreling ever closer, and turned and ran straight into the wall of ivy. There was a shaking and rattling of leaves, and the woman disappeared completely. The blue woman came sprinting from a different direction, running full speed into the wall of ivy and, like her sister, disappearing somehow into the leaves.

The Garden Lady huffed up to the wall, studied it for a moment, then paused to look at Madeline. "So you made it," she said, "and not a moment too soon."

"I don't even know your name," Madeline said, blurting out the first thing she thought.

"Well, child, that was never part of the bargain, was it? What did those two want with you?"

"She asked me to come to Aluvorea and help her people."

The Garden Lady turned her head, as if trying to see Madeline in a different light or at a different angle. "Interesting," she said. "Interesting, yes. But not any time soon, dear." She shook her head. "No, no, it will be too late by then. You have adventures and duties to perform for the Elenil first."

"But what should I—"

The lady held her palm up toward Madeline. "I gave you free advice once already, dear, and not another word until you've heeded the first." She paused. "Now what's that on your wrist, child? Did those two give you that flower?"

The flower's petals moved on their own, as if an unseen breeze ruffled them. "Yes."

"Of all the addlepated—why, those little—didn't they think for a minute—" The old woman's scowl deepened, and her face turned nearly scarlet. "I'll pull them up by the roots," she snapped, and without another word she put one arm in front of her and pushed through the ivy, grumbling as she went.

Madeline put her hands into the ivy and pushed as well, but there was a stone wall behind the vines. Nowhere to go, no way to follow.

Shula made her way over to Madeline. "Who was that green woman?"

"I don't know. An Aluvorean. She asked me to come to Aluvorea."

"That's strange," Shula said. "There aren't many Aluvoreans in the city, but one was just telling those guards she had heard a Scim plotting to sneak in."

"She said that was her sister," Madeline said. "They both ran as soon as they saw the Garden Lady."

Shula gave her a quizzical look. "The who?"

"The old lady I was talking to . . . I don't know her name. I call her the Garden Lady."

Shula gave her the sort of look you give a confused child. "I didn't see her. We sent word for one of the Elenil to come look into the supposed Scim invasion, but the woman slipped away while we were waiting. Ah! Here's Rondelo now."

An Elenil on a white stag came bounding through the crowd, the alarm bird tweeting and flitting around his head. The Elenil dismounted in an easy leap to the ground. He moved like a dancer—smooth and graceful and precise. There was never a person so beautiful in all of human memory, Madeline thought.

"This is Rondelo," Shula said. "He's a . . . well, it's hard to explain before you know how things work."

"A captain of the guard," Rondelo said, and he smiled, like a sunrise on a cold morning.

Madeline couldn't think of a single thing to say. She wanted to tell him all about the Garden Lady, the Aluvoreans, her journey to the Sunlit Lands, her friend Jason, Hanali's crazy fashion sense, Darius. She blushed, remembering that she sort of had a boyfriend. She opened her mouth, not sure what was about to come out. "I'm holding Shula's jacket," she said.

"I was going to say 'prince,'" Shula said, grinning. "I forgot what an effect you have on people when they first meet you, Rondelo."

"She asked me to hold it," Madeline said. Her face felt even hotter.

Rondelo grinned. The lopsided smile made him even more charming. He looked more human than the other Elenil. He looked like a statue breathed to life. "Miss Madeline, welcome to the Sunlit Lands. This is my companion, Evernu." The white stag inclined its head, its antlers tilting toward the ground.

"A pleasure to meet you," she said. The surreal experience of greeting a stag broke her out of Rondelo's spell.

"Where is this Aluvorean?" Rondelo asked.

"My apologies," Shula said. "She slipped away. I thought it would be best to call for you when she said she had heard some Scim plotting a way into the city, though."

"You did the right and responsible thing," Rondelo said. "I have heard rumors of the Black Skulls trying to find a shadow entrance to the city."

Shula spit on the ground. "Those three. They're not the sort to sneak around, it seems to me."

"They're after something," Rondelo said. "And their battle tactics lately are . . . different. New."

"Nothing we can't handle for a few hours each dusk," Shula said.

"Still, it troubles me that the Aluvorean would appear and then slip away so quickly. As if trying to distract us, almost. I should get back," Rondelo said, swinging onto Evernu's bare back. "Ah. What's this?"

Madeline followed his gaze. "Oh." She lifted her hand. "It's a stone flower. Another Aluvorean gave it to me."

Shula stepped back, a look of horror on her face. "Don't move, Madeline."

"It's just a flower."

The tendrils tightened on her arm. "Don't! Move!"

Madeline froze.

"It's triggered," Rondelo said.

"You're fast," Shula said to Rondelo. "You can do it."

"It's *triggered*," he repeated. "She has to do it herself. It's no longer about speed but precision."

"Okay," Shula said. "Madeline. Stone flowers are . . . they're poisonous."

Madeline relaxed. She wasn't going to eat it.

"Not poisonous," Rondelo said. "Venomous."

Shula shook her head. "They sting. Like a bee. They're carnivorous. If it stings you, you're going to be paralyzed. In Aluvorea, they swarm you and they . . . Well, there's only one, so you'll just be paralyzed. But there's no cure. They're called stone flowers because people who are stung are frozen, like statues." She snapped her fingers, and Madeline looked back up from the flower to Shula. "The stinger, it's on the bottom, between the tendrils. It extends the stinger by lifting its petals. So long as those petals stay flat, you're safe. If you put your finger slowly in the center so it can't close its petals, it can't sting. Then we can pull it off."

"Like grabbing a snake behind the head."

"Exactly. Only slow, Madeline."

Why would that green woman try to hurt her? It didn't make any sense.

Madeline realized with a distant disappointment that she had forgotten to ask for her name, too. But now she needed to focus. There was a venomous plant on her wrist.

Being careful not to move the arm with her deadly corsage, Madeline took one finger and reached slowly across. The flower tensed, like a spider getting ready to leap. She paused, waiting for it to relax, but it didn't. The petals quivered, then started to close.

No way would her finger get there in time if she stuck with the "slow and steady" plan. One sharp breath in. Here she was, day two in fantasyland, about to be stung by a flower and put out of commission. She would be able to breathe but not move . . . No more running or walking or health. She wasn't about to let that happen. She exhaled, hard, and at the same instant struck like a snake for the center of the flower.

Her finger wedged partway in, but the petals closed halfway. She pressed down until she managed to pry the petals apart. The tendrils of the flower gyrated crazily, slapping at her free hand. It snagged hold of her left hand, released her right wrist, and swung to her other arm. She shook, but it didn't come off. It tightened down hard, and before she could get her finger in, the petals snapped closed and a monstrous cracking sound echoed from her wrist.

The plant shuddered, and the tendrils loosened. The bright red flower faded and fell to the ground. Madeline examined her wrist. A pinprick of blood stood out precisely in the center of the bracelet's glowing face beneath her skin.

Rondelo's gloved hands were on Madeline's arm. He pushed her sleeve up. "Apologies," he said. "The Majestic One protect her. The stinger implanted."

Shula stabbed the flower through the center with a sword. Bending down beside it, she said, "It's spent, Rondelo. Dead."

Madeline felt the whole market fall away from her. She could only see the tiny mark where the flower had struck. "What happens now?" she asked.

Shula hugged her. "Lie down, Madeline," she said, trying to be gentle.

"I'm okay, Shula, honestly."

"It will be easier to move you when the paralysis sets in if you're lying down."

Madeline lay down, waiting for the venom to take effect, trying not to cry. Rondelo sent a bird for help.

"Why is someone trying to kill a newcomer?" he asked. "Who is she?"

Madeline felt a little annoyed that he was talking to Shula as if she wasn't lying at their feet.

Shula said, "I don't know why, but the Aluvoreans went to a lot of trouble to do this. One distracted me with the guards, the other pulled Madeline away."

Rondelo's frown deepened. "The Aluvoreans are the most peaceful people in the Sunlit Lands. What drove them to this?"

"I don't think they were trying to kill me," Madeline said, wiggling her fingers so they could see she wasn't paralyzed. After a few minutes of being ignored, she stood up and put her hands on her hips. "Obviously, whatever happened, the poison didn't take. So can we get on with our day?"

Shula and Rondelo exchanged looks.

"Should we take her back to the dorms?" Shula asked.

Rondelo scratched Evernu behind the ears, watching Madeline with careful interest. "No. But I'll join you wherever you're headed. A little extra company today can only be good."

Three times he made Madeline repeat the description of the woman who had given her the flower: once to him and Shula, once to the guards, and a third time to a bird, which he released. "They will search for her," he told Madeline. "Though since she escaped through magical means, I fear it is unlikely they will find her. Come, let us walk together."

Shula walked on one side of Madeline, with Rondelo on the other. The stag walked behind them. Shula's hand kept moving to Madeline's arm, as if to steady her. "I feel fine," Madeline said.

"Sometimes," Shula said, "when a snake bites, it doesn't release venom. Maybe it was like that." Madeline shuddered. She hated to think she had avoided paralysis by a quirk of fate. She made a mental note not to accept any more flowers. She rubbed her hand where the flower had stung her. There was an irritated red mark on her skin but nothing more.

11
LESSONS

And so the Majestic One sent away the Kakri,
and they live in the desert to the east, beyond the Tolmin Pass.
They build no houses and plant no crops.

FROM "THE ORDERING OF THE WORLD," AN ELENIL STORY

✦

After the terrifying interview with Break Bones, Jason took a bath. He still couldn't get his left sneaker off, which meant he couldn't get his jeans off, so he took a bath in his jeans with one shoe on. The level of filthiness in the bathroom afterward couldn't be exaggerated, partly because Jason was fascinated with how the tub magically filled with the correct amount of perfectly hot water. He had a splash war with the tub, seeing if he could empty it before it refilled. The mud on him seemed to cloud into the water and then disappear, so he experimented with slinging the freshly remoistened muck out of the tub as well. When he was done, he was clean, but the bathroom looked as if a gigantic muddy dog had shaken itself off in the middle of the floor.

He sloshed into the room he shared with Kekoa and David. "I'm afraid to look at the bathroom," David said, "if this is you all cleaned up."

Kekoa had a book in his hands, but he dropped it onto his bed, his mouth open wide. "Did you bathe in your jeans, brah?"

"I couldn't get my shoe off," Jason said.

Kekoa reached into his waistband and pulled out a small, sharp knife. "Come here then."

Jason stepped backward, but David grabbed him and threw him onto the floor. Kekoa cut his shoelaces, then scooped up both of Jason's shoes, walked into the bathroom, threw them into the toilet basin, and closed the lid. The shoes were gone.

"Aw, man," Jason said.

"You don't have to keep messed-up stuff like that," David said. "We can order up fresh ones."

It was time for bed after that. There were three beds, one on each wall except the one with the door to the hallway. They gave Jason the bed beneath the window, so he could "smell the night rain." It wasn't night, though, not really, even though it was late. There was a sort of dimming but no true night. Out the window Jason could see the short wall around their gigantic house, and beyond that a few scattered buildings, and then the much taller city wall. It wasn't even dark enough to see any stars.

Kekoa and David had an evening ritual. They each shared a thing they were thankful for from the day. This surprised Jason. He made a joke about them being "so sensitive," and they gave him a lecture about it. "A true warrior has to be thankful for the people and places and world they are protecting," Kekoa said.

"Yeah," David said. "You have to respect the land and the people in it. If you don't take the time for gratitude, you miss your everyday blessings."

"Also if you don't participate, we will beat you up."

"It's true, dude."

"Fine," Jason said. "I'm sure I can think of something." But honestly, since what happened with Jenny, he had struggled to find things to be thankful for. Some of the rawness had begun to pass, but he still couldn't make it through a day without thinking of her. Of course he had also ditched his entire life to come to the Sunlit Lands with Madeline and had been immediately separated from her. On the other hand, he hadn't been eaten by a mermaid, which was a new category of things to be thankful for.

Kekoa said, "I'm thankful for the weather today. Clear skies, blue and deep."

David said, "Yeah, man. For me, I'm glad there's a night off from the fighting to welcome our new roomie."

Jason didn't say anything for a while, and he could tell they were waiting. "I'm glad Break Bones didn't yank his chains out of the wall and kill us," he said finally.

They laughed at that for a while. "Now one thing we hope for the new day," Kekoa said. But Jason didn't hear those, because he was sound asleep.

He woke to full, bright sunlight streaming through the window. His roommates were already up and dressed. David laughed when he saw Jason's eyes flutter open.

"Breakfast!" he said and slapped a warm bowl of porridge with purple berries into Jason's hands. The porridge was bland and the berries too sour. Then he saw the pudding cup sitting on the end of his bed.

He scooped the pudding into his porridge and mixed it in, which created a sort of chocolate-flavored chunky puddle that was somewhere between edible and delicious. Kekoa grabbed the empty pudding container and ran a finger around the inside.

"What is this? Pudding?"

"Yeah," Jason said. "My deal with Hanali was a cup of pudding every day for the rest of my life, and in exchange I'd hang out here for a year." He smacked his lips. "Magic pudding tastes exactly like hospital pudding."

Kekoa and David laughed until Jason grinned too, even though he didn't know what was so funny. "I'd love to have seen Hanali's face," David said. "Some guy who didn't ask for money or fame or anything, just a cup of pudding. Ha ha ha."

"What did you guys get in your deals? Or are we not supposed to tell each other?"

"Ah, that's poho, man. Everybody knows everybody's business around here," Kekoa said. "For me, some haole stole my family's land. I do my time here, and when I go back the Elenil give me back the land, and they said they'd take care of the haole, too."

Jason took another bite of his strange breakfast. "What does that mean, they'll take care of him?"

"I don't ask, they don't say. Maybe they'll bring him back here, I don't know."

"Me, I stay until I'm twenty-one," David said. "My parents died. Well, my mom. My dad, I can't live with him. So when I'm twenty-one, I go home, the Elenil give me a hundred grand, and I'm on my way."

Jason looked at his empty pudding cup. "A hundred grand. That's a lot of pudding."

"Yeah," David said. "But I didn't think of that 'for the rest of my life' thing. I should have just said a thousand bucks a day."

Kekoa threw Jason a pile of white clothes with a pair of white sneakers on top. "Pudding cups, that's a new one around here. There's some real interesting ones, you'll see."

Jason got dressed, though he hesitated when he got to the white gloves.

"You have to wear those," David said. "It's an Elenil thing. Hands are private—you only show them to people who are close to you."

They asked if Jason planned to fight the Scim that night, and he said he wanted to go with them, at least. See what it was all about. He wasn't sure he wanted to fight. They talked about it while David led them to a long, grassy field where they could practice. "We have to get him to a storyteller, though, yeah? They're not going to let him fight tonight if he hasn't heard the story."

A table the length of a limo had been set out, and on the table there were weapons. Bows, scimitars, maces, knives, staffs, and a variety of others, mostly hand-to-hand stuff. No guns or any sort of firearm or explosive. Kekoa sorted through them, setting aside different options he thought Jason might like. "Hmm, maybe a mace? Oh! These are cool, this is called a katar. Or what about this? What's this called again, David?"

"Tonfa."

"Yeah. Tonfa." He held it up to Jason. It looked like a night stick.

Jason picked up a bow. He didn't want to stab or smash anyone, and if he did get involved in the fight that evening he'd rather be as far away from it as possible. Kekoa pointed out a hay bale with a target draped on it. Jason grabbed an arrow and tried to put it up against the bow, but he kept fumbling and dropping it.

The fifth time it fell off the drawstring, he threw the bow on the ground. "Why do the Elenil want inexperienced teenage fighters again?"

Kekoa and David burst out laughing. David showed him a smooth oval on the bow, near the grip. "Put your bracelet tattoo right next to that," he said.

A warm sensation traveled through the lattice of Jason's tattoo. He picked up the arrow, expertly nocked it, found himself standing in the proper position, and straightened one arm, the fletching of the arrow now near his ear. He corrected slightly for the wind, loosed the string, and watched the arrow fly. It thunked comfortably into the outer edge of the target. Not a bull's-eye, but a moment before he hadn't even been able to get the arrow onto the bow.

Jason looked at his hands in wonder. A thrill of adrenaline went through him. It felt like that perfect moment when you're an expert and everything is going right and you're on top of your game. It came so naturally, so easily. "How?"

"Magic, brah. We don't learn how to fight—we learn how to channel the magic. Takes an afternoon to become the best fighter ever."

David juggled an ax and two knives, spinning them easily over his head. "The Elenil loan us their fighting skills. Most of them are hundreds of years old. So it's their skills, but we do the fighting."

Jason frowned. "Our bodies, our risk."

"Nah," Kekoa said. "You get wounded, they fix you with magic. Just don't get killed dead. They can't do anything about that. But lose an arm or get a crushed rib cage, boom! They'll fix you right up."

"That's not cool, man," David said. "Bringing up the arm thing."

Kekoa laughed and handed Jason another arrow. "One of the Black Skulls cut David's arm off a couple weeks ago. Should've seen him running for the wall with one arm, the Black Skulls chasing him. Pretty hilarious."

David gave him a fake, sarcastic laugh. "Yeah, hilarious. They would have killed me if not for Shula."

"Black Skulls?" Jason had the bow up again, the arrow nocked and ready to loose. A minor adjustment to his fingering, and the arrow sailed to the target, lodging a bit closer to the center this time. Amazing. He felt a swell of pride at his skill, at how easy it was to launch an arrow into the target from this distance.

Kekoa picked up a bow, held his tattoo against it, and started firing arrows. Three shots, three bull's-eyes. "They're like the best Scim fighters. Pretty creepy looking too. There's three of them, and they wear long white robes and black-painted animal skulls over their faces. Nothing hurts them. They're not like us, where they need to go somewhere to heal—it's like an arrow to the heart doesn't do anything other than slow them down."

"They're dead already," David said. "I'm telling you, they're dead. They don't even bleed."

"Stupid," Kekoa said. "There's no such thing as zombies."

"Man, you don't know. You're shooting magic arrows for a war between monsters and angels. How do you know there aren't zombies?"

Kekoa put a hand on Jason's bow and pushed it toward the ground. "Okay, quick tutorial. The oval on the bow, that's a magical receptor. Think of it like a permission slip. Some Elenil has given the bow permission to borrow their skill. While you have it, they don't."

"It's like your tattoo," David said. "It's the permission slip that tells the magic you're allowed to be in the Sunlit Lands and allows your pudding to be delivered in the morning."

"So," Jason said slowly, "I'm stealing someone else's skills to do this."

Kekoa shook his head emphatically. "They've given permission, remember? But when you aim, you reach out through the magic and *take* the skill. Some of it's coming through without trying, but you have to—" Kekoa struggled to find the right words, finally ending with "—you have to reach for it."

"It's like a waterway," David said. "You have to open it all the way to get the full skill. You're leaving some of the skill with the owner. You're taking enough magic that there are two mediocre archers right now, instead of one terrible one and one amazing one."

"Does it . . . does it bother them when I take their archery skills?"

"They don't even know unless they're trying to use those skills at the same moment."

Jason took a deep breath. Okay. He could do this. He concentrated on the archery skills he would need. Balance. Steady hands. Clear vision. The smooth movement of the drawstring, the careful release. A confidence came over him, the sort of confidence you feel when you've done something a million times and it's not even that it's easy, it's automatic. When he opened his eyes, his silver tattoo was shining with a white light.

"Look at how much magic is flowing through!" David said. "Good job. Shoot an arrow!"

The arrow fell effortlessly into place, and raising the bow was like taking a breath. Jason could see the precise place he wanted the arrow to go, could feel himself correcting for the slight breeze and the distance, and when he released, the arrow flew in a graceful arc, beautiful and perfect and dead into the center of the target. He raised his bow in the air and let out an enormous whoop of joy, and he and David and Kekoa danced and jumped around, shouting and cheering.

"You almost sound proud. As if you have done something worthwhile," said a voice, low and skeptical.

They stopped celebrating. Kekoa made a face. "Hey, Baileya," David said.

She was a full head taller than Jason and wore loose-fitting cream pants tied at her waist with a red sash. Her blouse was also loose, but a deep-blue color like clear water, billowing out wide at the sleeves then tapering to a tight cuff on her wrists. Her smooth skin was the tan color of sunbaked sand. Her hair was pulled back but flowed as easily as her clothing, a dark-brown wave moving around her face and past her shoulders. The color of her hair was echoed in a spray of freckles across her cheekbones. But her eyes were easily the most striking thing about her. Jason had never seen eyes that color. They seemed almost to emanate a pale silver light. He couldn't look away. If not for the eyes, he would have almost thought she was human.

He reached out to shake hands. "I'm Jason," he said.

She held his gaze, as if waiting for something, but he didn't know what.

She turned to his roommates. "Have you taught him nothing?"

David shrugged. "He can shoot a bow."

"We did cut him out of his shoes," Kekoa said helpfully.

Baileya sighed. "In the Sunlit Lands, especially among the Elenil, to touch bare hands is a great intimacy. It's deeply offensive to offer such a thing when announcing one's name. It is wise to keep your hands covered and, in most cases, to keep them out of sight altogether."

"I'm not Elenil, though," Jason said. "And neither are you."

Her eyes sparkled. Or maybe it's just that they were glowing, Jason couldn't tell. "It is a compliment that you noticed," she said. "I am of the Kakri people, beyond the Tolmin Pass. My mother is called Willow, and my grandmother Abronia. I have come to make my fortune and fight the Scim."

David flopped down on the grass. "She fights the old-fashioned way. Her own skill—no magic—and she keeps her wounds."

Baileya nodded curtly. "Which is why I come here to my practice area. A practice area I assume you are finished with, as you are taking the hard-earned skills and abilities of others rather than honing your own."

"Yeah, yeah," Kekoa said. "We're done." He paused. "Hey, Baileya, we're supposed to take Jason to a storyteller to get the whole 'why we fight the Scim' story. Any chance you'd want to tell him?"

"Tell him yourself," Baileya said, studying the weapons in front of her. She picked up a medium-sized hatchet.

"It can't be a human telling the story," David said. "You know the rules. It has to be a citizen of the Sunlit Lands."

Baileya gave him a sour look. "I came to make a fortune, not spend it."

"What does that mean?" Jason asked.

Kekoa laughed. "The Kakri don't use money, they use stories. It's their only currency. So when she says she came here to make her fortune, it's like she came here to live some adventures, or learn stories their community doesn't have."

David rearranged the weapons on the table, putting everything he and his roommates had messed around with back in their places. "Please, Baileya? We'll have to hike into the city center and find a storyteller, then come all the way back before dusk, and then fight. We'll be exhausted."

Baileya shook her head, then looked at the far-off target, hefting the hatchet. With a sinewy grace, she stretched back with her entire body, then sprang forward, like an Olympian throwing a javelin. The hatchet flew in a high arc, its spinning blade catching the sunlight over and over. It descended to the target and buried itself deep into the center, shattering the arrows there and sending up a plume of hay.

Jason dropped his bow. "Whoa."

Baileya smiled at him. "You fight for the Elenil and against the Scim.

That is all the story you need to know." She looked him over carefully. "If you wish to exchange stories another time, I will consider it. You look to be from a different clan than other humans I have spoken to."

Without another word, she turned, marched toward the target, and yanked out her hatchet and what remained of the arrows. Jason just stared. David picked up Jason's bow and put it away, and Kekoa grabbed his arm and pulled him backward until he started to walk, half in a daze.

"She's amazing," Jason said.

"I don't know if that counted as you hearing the story," David said. "I hope we don't get in trouble at roll call."

Kekoa said, "Jason didn't even agree to fight in his contract with the Elenil. He can do what he wants."

"She's so amazing," Jason said.

Kekoa said, "You heard the bit about not waving bare hands at the Elenil, right?"

"Did you see that ax-throwing thing?" Jason asked.

"No handshakes," David said.

"And no high fives!" Kekoa said. "Super insulting."

"How did she even throw that far?" Jason turned back to look, but David grabbed him and pulled him toward the house.

"She'll be at the wall tonight," David said. "Let's eat lunch."

Jason's feet skimmed along the ground. *She'll be there tonight.* "She's amazing," he said.

Kekoa snickered. "First girl he sees who's good with a hatchet and he's head over heels."

David didn't laugh. "Don't tell Baileya. She'll want you to fight on the front lines with her."

Kekoa threw his arms around both of their shoulders. "Not tonight, though. Because tonight the Three Musketeers fight again!"

"Dude. The War Party," David said.

Jason had a sudden, worrisome thought that pulled him out of his reverie of Baileya. What had happened to the previous third of their Three Musketeers? Where was Kekoa's and David's previous roommate?

"Don't get beheaded" they kept saying to him. Gulp. Maybe he wouldn't be riding out to battle with them tonight after all.

12

THE STORYTELLER

O Keeper of Stories!

FROM "THE DESERTED CITY," A KAKRI LAMENT

✦

Madeline and Shula found Hanali standing outside a bakery talking to a squat grey-skinned person in a dun-brown robe. The smell of fresh bread and pastries hung in the air.

"Strange," Shula said. "I've never seen Hanali talking to a Maegrom before."

Hanali's eyes rose lazily toward them, and with a charming smile, he spoke again to the Maegrom, and it scurried off into the crowd. By the time Madeline and Shula reached him, Hanali had something that looked a great deal like an apple turnover neatly balanced on his gloved fingers.

"Someone tried to kill Madeline," Shula said.

Hanali raised an eyebrow at Shula. "You?"

Rondelo bowed. "Your Excellency. It was, in fact, an Aluvorean. She gave the child a stone flower."

Hanali sniffed. "Are those poisonous to humans?" He grinned at Madeline. "I jest. Stone flowers are quite deadly to everyone."

Trumpets blared deep in the city center. Rondelo leapt onto his stag's back and begged to be pardoned, and Evernu bounded away through the crowd.

"That was a security alarm," Shula said. "But it's full sun. The Scim couldn't possibly have broken through the walls."

Dusting the sugar from his gloved fingers, Hanali said, "Yes, and knowing it was a drill, it was rather rude of Rondelo to leap off like that."

"I should go check in with the guards too," Shula said.

"Nonsense," Hanali said. "And miss the storyteller? My dear human child, don't prattle on so."

Madeline crossed her arms. With some time to think as they walked, she had come to realize the seriousness of being offered a deadly flower. "Seems to me there should be a little more concern about the attempted murder."

"Bah. You're safe with Shula," Hanali said. "Did you die? No. Now come along."

"But—"

"*Did you die?*"

"No."

"Then *come along*."

When Madeline didn't move, Hanali let out a great theatrical sigh. "Do you have the flower?" he asked.

Shula handed it to him. It had wilted nearly completely and lost most of its crimson color.

Hanali hemmed and hawed, then asked to see Madeline's arm. She showed him where it had stung her, and he studied it carefully. "Do you see this tiny dot?" he asked.

She hadn't noticed it until he pointed it out, but there was a black spot, oblong and half the size of a grain of rice. She licked her lips. "I see it."

"That, my dear, is a seed. Stone flowers can inject poison in their youth or, before they die, a seed." He straightened and threw the flower to the ground, crushing it beneath the heel of his boot. "Typically they inject it into a rotting log, but I suppose this one became confused."

Madeline rubbed at the spot where the seed was. "What will happen to me?"

Hanali grimaced. "Are you a rotting log?"

"No," she said, annoyed.

"Then, I suppose, nothing. Do let me know if a flower bursts from your skin. Now. May we get to the business at hand?"

Madeline frowned at him. He didn't seem to be taking the whole thing seriously. Then again, maybe that was a good sign. "Fine," she said.

The Elenil practically danced up a clay stairway that climbed the side of a two-story house. There were no railings or handholds, just simple stairs. At the top, he bent low and entered a dark room.

The woman was hard to see in the dim light. She sat against the wall, which was covered in ivy. The ivy had snaked across the woman, too, so only her face could be seen. The lines on her face branched and split like climbing vines, and her hair was tangled in the leaves. She looked almost like one of the Aluvoreans, what with all the ivy, but her skin wasn't green. Madeline couldn't tell if she was human or something else.

"I brought your fee," Hanali said and placed a small pewter spoon in front of the woman. A vine curled around it and lifted it to the woman's eyes. She nodded, and the spoon disappeared into the ivy.

"What . . . what happened to you?" Madeline asked.

The woman's dark eyes rested on her for a moment. "I'll not tell you that without a spoon, or a pair of bone dice, or a rusted knife from a knight's traveling chest."

The recitation of junk reminded Madeline of the Garden Lady. Bending closer, she tried to see the woman's eyes. The ivy shifted, and the leaves shuddered. The woman looked away. Madeline tried to put her hand into the ivy to see if the wall behind it was solid, but the ivy curled from her touch, revealing the wall.

Standing against the doorjamb, Hanali said, "Tell them of the Sunlit Lands."

The leaves spun and waved, as if in a gentle breeze. "Which story would you have, Lord Hanali?"

"Why, the story of its founding, and the seven peoples. The story of the beginning."

"As the Elenil have told it?"

"Of course!"

The storyteller nodded curtly. She glanced at Madeline and said, almost under her breath, "Listen well. The Elenil share this story, without cost, so that you may know how the world is meant to be."

Then she began the story. It was a story about a great magician whom the Elenil called the Majestic One, who saw the rebellious nature of all the people of the land and decided he would "repair the world." But most of the people refused to listen to him and continued on in their various violent ways.

The first people to agree to help the magician were named Ele and Nala, who would become the mother and father of the Elenil race. The Majestic One set out to tame the whole world, with Ele and Nala and their children at his side, and in time all the people were brought under his rule.

Much of the story was actually a long poem that Madeline had a hard time following, with all the unfamiliar names. It was about the rewards and blessings that the magician gave to the different people after the war had ended. He made the Elenil the guardians of the world, and according to the story he himself founded the Court of Far Seeing and put the Elenil in charge of the entire Sunlit Lands.

The wizard sent all the other people to different lands, giving them their places in the world. The Aluvoreans made their home among the trees in the southlands. Madeline shuddered. She wouldn't be taking any unfamiliar flowers in the future. She rubbed the small dark mark on her arm, but she couldn't see it as clearly now. Had it already faded? Maybe it would come out on its own, like a splinter. There was a parade of unfamiliar names and people: the Kakri, who lived in the desert; the Maegrom, who lived in the caves beneath the world; the Zhanin ("Shark people," Shula whispered. "We rarely see them this far from the sea."); and the Scim, who were the last people to surrender, and so were cursed to eternal darkness. The Majestic One even cursed their appearance, making them frightening monsters. The Elenil, of course, were rewarded for their loyalty and were made the guardians and caretakers of the Sunlit Lands.

There was even a stanza about human beings, a detail Madeline found surprising. She listened closely to it, interested in how the Elenil saw humans.

According to the leaf woman, the Majestic One said this to the humans:

Humans! Ye shall live upon another earth,
a people of science and dust.
Bereft of magic, short lived and passionate.
There shall still be beauty and wonder among you.
In great need may ye return to the Sunlit Lands,
for ye are our cousins and neighbors.

Madeline listened, fascinated. In the Elenil legends of that long-ago time, humans were considered just another magical race of beings, but magic (and apparently long life) had been taken from them, and they were sent to Earth. Interesting. They could only come to the Sunlit Lands in "great need." The story wrapped up with a poem about the rightful place for each type of person to live. Humans on Earth, Zhanin in the sea, Kakri in the desert, and so on.

The woman shuddered when the story was done, and the leaves around her trembled. Her eyes closed for a long moment, and when she opened them she said, "Now my story is done, the truth unspooled. Listen well or be a fool."

"You didn't tell her about the Kharobem," Shula said.

"They were not people made at that time. Not then."

"Or the Southern Court," Hanali said. "What of them?"

"Monsters and animals," the storyteller said. "Nor did I mention the Pastisians, for they are human. Who is the teller of tales here? Do I tell you how to fight a war, Shula Bishara? Do I tell Hanali, son of Vivi, how to choose fine clothing?"

The woman in the ivy shuddered again, and long tendrils of plant life cascaded over her face. It cleared again in a moment. Wet streaks ran down her face.

Without thinking, Madeline stepped closer. The ivy recoiled, making a path for her. Madeline bent down and kissed the storyteller's cheek. "Thank you for the story."

The look in the storyteller's eyes was one of wonder and dismay. She stared at Madeline for the longest time. "It's you," she said. "After all these years."

Madeline didn't know what to say. She whispered, "You're not . . . trapped, are you? In the ivy?"

"Not in the way you think," the storyteller said. "No more than you."

Hanali pulled Madeline back and knelt in front of the storyteller, studying her carefully. "What did you see, old woman?"

"I'm younger than you, Elenil."

Hanali's mouth snapped shut. The muscles in his face flexed. "Show some respect, storyteller. What did you see?"

A long sigh came from the woman, like air escaping a balloon. "Her blade shall bring justice at long last to the Scim."

Hanali did not move for a long time. He only stared at the woman, unblinking. He mumbled, almost to himself, "I know there's more to it than that. The Aluvoreans have taken an interest in her as well. Why would your people show interest in her?"

The woman said nothing at first, but when Hanali continued to glare at her she finally said, reluctantly, "There is trouble in Aluvorea. She may be a seed of hope. But I fear it is still a long way off, Hanali. Another time, another tale."

He studied Madeline. Then to Shula he said, "At dusk, take Madeline to the battlements to see the Scim and watch the battle."

"It's only her first full day, and she's not ready to—"

Hanali's eyes narrowed, and Shula stopped speaking. "She need not fight, but she will watch."

Shula bent her head. "Of course, Excellency."

Madeline found herself surprised by Hanali. He was kind and hospitable one moment and dismissive the next. He seemed foppish and ridiculous most of the time. But he had these moments of decisive command, and no one dared cross him then—not Shula, and not the storyteller. He was a strange person.

Hanali guided them outside, bowed deeply, and begged their leave. He wandered off into the crowd. Shula watched him go, a concerned look on her face.

"What's wrong?" Madeline touched Shula's arm.

Shula looked up, startled. "Hanali is not usually so polite to humans.

Asking permission to leave us. And *bowing* to us? It's very strange. He must think there's something to these prophecies."

They strolled along the street, arm in arm. There were so many wonderful things to see here. "Why did it seem like Hanali didn't know the story the ivy woman was telling? And why were the details different than what you both expected?"

Shula shrugged. "Storytellers tell their stories differently depending on the time of day, the audience, and their whim. That's why she asked if he wanted the story as the Elenil tell it—she likely knows the same story from different peoples, different tribes, different times. I've heard that story five or six times, and each time with different nuances."

That was interesting. Madeline wondered about that while they walked. So the woman in the ivy may very well have been tailoring that story just for her. She wanted to think about that more. She glanced at her arm. She couldn't see the seed at all now.

She didn't want to think about that anymore. She was alive. She could breathe. She had been stung by a deadly flower, and it hadn't bothered her a bit. She wanted to do something fun, to celebrate, to run and dance. She asked Shula if they could walk past the singing fountains she had seen from the coach, and Shula, delighted, agreed.

"Don't worry about those prophecies," Shula said. "The Elenil love prophecies. They use them constantly. Hanali uses them to learn what people will wear to parties so he can make sure his outfit is unique."

"You're kidding." They laughed.

"They have a low tolerance for not knowing or understanding things. They—" Shula hesitated. "They go to extremes to learn about the future. They're plotters and planners. They hold prophecies over each other's heads to get people to behave the way they want. They'll lie about a prophecy if they think it gives them an advantage."

"So the thing about me bringing justice to the Scim with my sword?"

Shula patted her hand. "Could have been invented by Hanali to advance his social standing among the other Elenil."

Madeline felt a mix of relief and disappointment wash over her. So much had changed in the last twenty-four hours. She was still getting used to the fact that she could breathe. She didn't want to be some Elenil hero.

At the same time, there was something exciting about being someone special, someone with a fate that would change the world. "Why would the storyteller say the same thing, then?"

Shula didn't respond, a troubled look crossing her face.

At the fountain, they listened to the music as the water leapt from bowl to bowl. Shula explained how the bowls represented the Sunlit Lands cosmology: a series of crystal spheres that turned like clockwork over the world. Madeline had a vague memory of learning something like it in an advanced English class when they were reading Shakespeare. It was another reminder that they were not on Earth. The people, the clothing, the architecture, even the astronomy, all looked different.

On the way home Shula bought her a snack using a few wooden coins she fished from her pocket. The fruit had a hard, purplish exterior, which the merchant (a surly Maegrom) cut deftly in two with a curved knife. She and Shula each took half, and the merchant gave them each their own wooden spoon, more like a tiny paddle. The soft, white interior of the fruit was both sweet and tangy and left her tongue tingling with pleasure. When they finished, Shula took the "bowl" of the fruit and threw it straight into the air. A large green bird sailed out of nowhere, snatched the peel from the sky, and disappeared, fighting off two smaller birds. Madeline threw hers into the air, and another bird snatched it.

By the time they were nearly home, most of the shops along the street were closing, with merchants pulling in their wares and folding up their canopies. "The market is closing for a time of rest before nightfall. We should rest also," Shula said. "Tonight you'll watch from the city wall . . . You won't get much sleep before tomorrow."

Madeline's heart began to pound. The thought of being in a battle, of being in a fight at all, made her nervous. Her palms began to sweat. Shula squeezed Madeline's shoulder. "Do not fear. You made an agreement to serve the Elenil, but there is no guarantee they will assign you to fight. They may put you on guard duty, or have you serve food in the archon's palace. You agreed to serve them, not necessarily to fight."

"But the prophecy Hanali keeps mentioning—it sure sounds like fighting."

Shula sighed. "Six months ago, Hanali was invited to a party for someone in the Elenil elite. It was a big deal. He went to sixteen prophets, four soothsayers, and three party planners. He chose his outfit and bought new gloves and obsessed about this party for more than two months. One of the prophets told him I would ruin the party. I was supposed to go as his 'bodyguard' . . . The Elenil like ridiculous shows of luxury, and that was one of his. But he was so terrified that he switched me out for someone else. The party came, and he attended, and he even spoke to some of the most influential Elenil, the magistrates. The whole city was talking about it the next day, and Hanali's name came up more than once in the gossip chains."

"So you didn't ruin it?"

"No," Shula said. "But the next time I saw him, he cornered me and said, 'You ruined the party. I spent the entire night worried about how you were going to ruin it, so I didn't enjoy it for a moment.'"

Madeline laughed.

It was definitely getting darker now, but there was still plenty of light to see. They had walked past Mrs. Raymond's house and were now at the base of the city wall. "So just because my sword will bring justice, that doesn't necessarily mean I'm fighting a war?"

Shula shook her head. In the dim light, the scar on her face stood out more clearly. "Maybe you drop a sword on someone's toe, and they get so angry they destroy the Scim once and for all. Or maybe you work in the kitchens and make a sword cake that gives all the Scim a stomachache at the signing of a peace treaty. Or—" Shula up held a finger. "—and this is the most likely one of all—Hanali is trying to get some attention and has made up a prophecy. The whole city would be looking for you if the prophets pronounced you as some sort of chosen one."

Madeline thanked Shula, then gave her a hug. Madeline's muscles unknotted, and her fists unclenched. She took a deep breath, something she would never, never get tired of doing. "I've been worried," she said, "that I would come all the way here to get away from—from the thing that was killing me back home—and that I would get killed by the Scim instead." She felt weird not telling Shula about her deal with Hanali, but Mrs. Raymond had seemed to feel so strongly about it. Maybe she would wait a few days until she better understood how everything worked.

But she already knew she could trust Shula. She felt it to the core of her being.

"The Scim can't kill you if you kill them first," Shula said. "Climb to the top of this stairway and tell them your name. I have to get ready to fight. But it's time for you to see the Scim."

13
WAR PARTY

None could stand for long against the might
of the Majestic One or his servants, the Elenil.

FROM "THE ORDERING OF THE WORLD," AN ELENIL STORY

✦

Jason debated whether to go into battle with his friends. He debated right until the moment when another teen said to him, "You're the guy who gets the unicorn, right?"

"I'm the—" Jason looked around, bewildered. David, Kekoa, and Jason had just walked outside the city wall, into a sort of staging area where the army of the Elenil was preparing for war.

The other guy, an African American kid with a military buzz cut and green fatigues, looked him over. "Listen, kid, I know you're new here, but I gotta get everyone outfitted. Are you the guy who gets the unicorn or not?"

David elbowed him. "Speak up, Jason. Sorry, Jasper, he's new."

Jasper rolled his eyes. "I could tell by the white clothes, Glenn."

"Yeah, I'm the one who gets a unicorn." He couldn't stop the enormous smile from growing across his face. "Jason Wu." He held his hand out.

"Gloves, Wu. Where are your gloves?" Jasper sighed. "Come here." He led Jason to a stand that held what looked like traditional Chinese armor, but all white. "Hanali sent this over. Said you didn't like the Japanese stuff in the armory. You know how to put this on? It's a Song dynasty replica, pretty typical mountain pattern armor. Leg plates, chest plate . . . You tie this all together with the silk cords. And the helmet is there on top."

Jason had no idea how to put it on. And how did this guy Jasper know so much about ancient Chinese armor? *I guess that's how you get put in charge of the armory.* "I'll figure it out," he said. Why would he need armor anyway? He would be on a unicorn.

Jasper looked at him skeptically. "When you're fitted out, meet us outside the wall, and we'll get you mounted." Jasper moved off into the crowd.

The crowd was strange. Human teenagers, mostly. In fact, almost all of the people here looked to be about the same age. There weren't a lot of Elenil ("They watch sometimes, from the wall," David had said), and he hadn't seen Baileya, or any other Kakri for that matter. It was weird that the humans did all the fighting . . . On the other hand, they were the ones who had made deals to fight the Scim. Except him. He was fighting because . . . well, because Break Bones seemed pretty awful, and David and Kekoa had made the whole thing sound more like a sporting event than anything dangerous, and also there was a unicorn.

"We've never had a unicorn," David said. David wore an open buckskin jacket and a looping necklace of some sort that looked like a ladder of beads hanging in front. His hair was swept up in a sort of pompadour in the middle, with two thick braids on either side of his face, and he had worked a few feathers into his hair. He had two white lines on the front of his face, coming down like tears. He and Kekoa had been the ones to tell Hanali there was nothing appropriate for Jason in the armory. It wasn't mandatory to wear a traditional war outfit, it was just his roommates' preference. You could request whatever you wanted. A lot of people wore some sort of military gear from modern times or earlier. A medieval European knight's armor just seemed right to a lot of people who had grown up watching fantasy movies.

"What do you usually have instead of a unicorn?" Jason asked, trying to figure out how to put his breastplate on.

"Horses, mostly. Elephants, too. These big birds called rocs sometimes, but I think those are seasonal or something. I tried riding a giant cat once, but it went crazy and started pouncing on our own people, so we shrank it again. Lives in Mrs. Raymond's kitchen now, but I think it might have gotten a taste for human blood. I try to stay far away from it. Name is Fluffywoogins."

"Terrifying," Jason said. He had the breastplate on, he thought, more or less correctly. The other pieces tied on with silk cords that ran through holes in the armor.

"Howzit?" Kekoa called. He was barefoot and bare chested, wearing what looked like a red towel around his waist. He had his leiomanō in one hand.

"Dude got his unicorn," David said.

"What? That's epic, brah."

The leg guards fell off again. "Do unicorns talk, you think?"

Kekoa laughed. "One day I was practicing slinging stones at a bird, and it came over and asked me to stop. It's always hard to say in the Sunlit Lands."

"Help me tie these," Jason said, and the three of them set to work knotting the armor together. In the end, David and Kekoa said he looked fierce, but Jason was almost certain it wasn't on correctly. He settled the helmet on his head. The boys clapped.

"Man, you're unrecognizable," David said. "Pretty awesome."

The armor was heavy. Jason started sweating after a few steps. David slung a quiver of arrows on Jason's back and gave him a bow. "Use your magic, and you should be able to hit a Scim even while riding a giant white stallion with a horn."

They walked toward the wall, debating if the unicorn would gore people with its horn. It seemed likely, and Jason didn't think that would make for a comfortable ride. Not that war was about comfort, but still.

"Now we all line up," Kekoa said. "Not much organization to it—we sort of pick our own places."

"Some kids tried to organize us last week because they had grown up playing strategy games or something, but the Elenil don't care, so we do what we want. That's why we're the War Party," David said, and he and Kekoa tapped their weapons together like toasting someone at a party.

"Three Musketeers," Kekoa said.

"Speaking of which," Jason said. "What happened to your previous roommate, anyway? Did he, um, you know, get horribly beheaded?"

David and Kekoa burst out laughing. "No, man, he finished his service and went home. He was from Ohio, I think. Hanging out in Cincinnati right now, I bet."

"The Scim will line up over there," Kekoa said. There was a long ridge to the west of the city. "When it's dark enough—they always wait for the darkest moment—we fight. Not for long, usually. Our job is to keep them out of the city. Their job is to . . . Well, I never listen to their whole thing. You know, bring a thousand years of darkness and so on."

"I'm surprised they don't burn the farmlands and everything outside the city, or put it under siege."

"They're not the smartest," David said.

A horn sounded, and an entourage came out of the city gates. A fully armored knight led the way, his helmet under one arm. His horse was a silvery color, wide chested and powerful. The knight's armor flashed brilliantly even in the low light, and he wore an emerald-green sash across his chest, and on his flag was a stylized silver horse prancing on an emerald field. His face was weathered and scarred, and Jason realized he was the oldest human he had seen since coming to the Sunlit Lands. Ancient. Maybe in his mid-forties.

"The Knight of the Mirror," Kekoa said. A large group of warriors surrounded him, a few on horses but many of them on foot.

"He won't use magic," David said. "None of his people will, either."

"Like Baileya," Jason said, and as the words came from his mouth he saw her, taller than most of the men around her. She hadn't changed from earlier, other than to use a long white scarf to tie her loose clothing closer to her body. Probably to keep it from getting in her way during the battle. She carried something like a long spear with a pointed metal head on one side and a curved blade on the other. Red feathers hung from the base of each blade. "She's amazing," Jason said.

Kekoa rapped him, hard, on the breastplate. "Pull it together. You're going into battle, not on a date."

"Uh." Jason tried to snap out of it. "Why do they call him the Knight of the Mirror?"

"He's vain," David said, jumping from foot to foot, warming up. "Always looking in mirrors. He usually brings one out to—yup, there he goes."

The knight pulled a mirror from the inside of his sash and held it up, looking intently into it. He didn't seem to see or hear anything else going on around him, even when a monstrous cheer rose from the western ridge and a nightmare army crested the top.

David shoved Jason back toward the wall. "Go get your unicorn, dude, and meet us in the middle of the fight."

Kekoa shouted, "Some of the Scim, they target the newbies, so be careful. The white armor gives it away!"

"And stay away from the Black Skulls," David said. "Just . . . don't even go near them. Focus on the regular Scim."

Jasper stood near the wall, next to an enormous tent. Elephants came lumbering from inside, small decks built on top of them, warriors at the ready looking out the sides. Jason paused and shouted back to his friends, "How will I know which ones are the Black Skulls?" but they were already gone, pushing their way to the front of the lineup.

Jason ran to the tent—well, as close to running as he could get in his armor—and stopped in front of Jasper. He gave him a quick salute. "Jason Wu, Unicorn Captain First Class, reporting for duty."

"Unicorn Cap—" Jasper looked disgusted. "Get in here, Wu. I'll introduce you to your animal."

"Does she have a name already?" Jason asked as Jasper led him past partitioned stalls in the monstrous tent.

"You get to name your own war beast, that's tradition around here," Jasper said.

Jason stood up straight. "Then I shall name her . . . Delightful Glitter Lady!" He grinned. Now *that* was a good unicorn name. "My sister, she would have wanted Sparkling Ruby Rainbow, but I'm thinking it's too many *r*'s."

Jasper rolled his eyes. Outside there was a roaring sound, and then the muffled sounds of a gravelly voice shouting. Jasper said, "The Scim are making their declaration of battle. You have maybe three minutes. Okay, listen, kid. You ever ridden a unicorn before?"

"I've never even *seen* one. Unless you count dreams."

"Focus, Wu, I'm trying to train you. You know how to connect your magic to your weapon?"

"Sure." Connect through his tattoo, and reach out to take the skill he needed.

"Same thing, only you use the saddle. *Not* the unicorn, okay? The saddle." He glared until Jason nodded. Jasper stopped in front of a fifteen-foot-tall curtain. "If you're losing your concentration and can't focus on both your weapon and the saddle, then you should—"

"Stay focused on my weapon," Jason said, nodding.

"On the *saddle*," Jasper said, exasperated. "Better to lose control of your weapon than to fall off your mount. I'm not sure you're ready to go out." He rubbed his eyes. "Okay, look. If you get in trouble, you find one of the big magic users, okay? There's a woman named Shula Bishara, she's the one who'll be shooting fire everywhere. Or find Diego Fernández, he's the one who can fly. Or that kid—what's his name?—Alex, I think, who can make rocks move. And if you can't find them, or they're too far, you stick to the Knight of the Mirror. You know that guy, the old one?"

"I saw him, sure."

"And *stay away from the Black Skulls*."

Jason nodded sagely. He paused for a long moment, waiting for Jasper to say more. When it was clear Jasper wasn't going to volunteer the information, Jason asked, "I'll be able to recognize the Black Skulls . . . how, exactly?"

Jasper looked at him in complete amazement. "They are wearing black skulls. Seriously, who briefed you for tonight?"

"Aaaaanyway," Jason said, "Can I see Delightful Glitter Lady now?"

Jasper waved a hand at the curtain. "Go ahead."

Jason took a deep breath and leaned his face up against the curtain. He heard a snort. He imagined her beautiful white mane and pearlescent horn. He threw the curtain aside. Delightful Glitter Lady lifted her thick neck and snorted again.

Jason cocked his head to one side. He turned to Jasper. "That's a rhinoceros," he said. "A really, really huge one."

"The Elenil are a little sketchy on zoological classifications," Jasper said. "But, yeah, I think you're right."

Not only was it a rhinoceros, it was about twice as large as a regular Earth rhino, easily as large as an elephant. It had deep-grey skin, wrinkled and tough, and a horn three times as big around as Jason's arm. "Just the one horn," Jason said. "So I guess, technically . . ." He walked carefully in front of the rhino. It turned its head sideways, watching him with a tiny black eye.

A multicolored cloth had been thrown across the rhino's swayed back, with a massive saddle on top of that. Jason kept his distance as he made his way around the rhino's side. There was a stepladder. He climbed it slowly. Jasper was nowhere to be seen. *A wise man*, Jason thought.

Before getting into the saddle, Jason looked for the spot to connect his tattoo. It was just close enough that he could touch it before climbing on. He let the magic flow through his tattoo and reached out to find the skills of some Sunlit Lands unicorn rider. A feeling of certainty came over him, and he vaulted onto the rhino's back. He leaned close and patted the thick folds of skin on the creature's neck. The rhino's ears turned back toward him.

He nocked an arrow. Then he shouted, "ONWARD TO VICTORY, DELIGHTFUL GLITTER LADY!" and jabbed the rhino hard in the sides. She made a sound that was a cross between ten untalented trumpet players and an enormous balloon shrieking as air was being forced out of it, and charged.

She went straight through the side of the tent, pulling it down around them. The tent billowed up and covered their faces, tearing away in time for Jason to see Delightful Glitter Lady trampling their own soldiers as she galloped through the front lines.

"Sorry!" he shouted back at the trampled humans. "Still getting the hang of my rhinocorn!"

He burst through the enemy front lines. Terrible beasts hacked at him with axes and fired arrows at Delightful Glitter Lady. Terror coursed through his body like electricity, and he wanted to shout at the top of his lungs. But then his leg plates came off, thrown from the side of the rhino, and Jason saw them get trampled into splinters. *That could have been me*, he thought, and all desire to shout disappeared. He frantically checked his breastplate and helmet—they, at least, seemed to be secure.

The Scim looked more frightening and terrible than Break Bones, if such a thing was possible—long limbed, with too-large heads and protruding, tusklike teeth set in wide mouths. Some of them rode enormous rats, and one streaked by flying on the wide, leathery wings of a bat. It would have seemed like a video game, except that instead of a carefully created entertainment experience, the sounds around him clashed together into one muddy roar, the smells of the creatures and the chaotic movements of the enemy spinning past him faster than he could process. He needed to focus, to try to remove the dizzy confusion of the battlefield. He chose the bat because the sight of the giant thing gave him a sick feeling in the pit of his stomach.

Jason focused on the magic of the bow in his hand, reached out, and borrowed the skill necessary to let an arrow fly. He tracked the bat as it flitted and flapped across the field until he felt the magic take hold, and then he released the bowstring. The arrow soared, straight and true, and lodged in the bat's rider. He toppled from the beast and fell into the battle below. A cheer rose from the forces of Far Seeing. Jason was cheering too. The sheer amount of adrenaline coursing through his body made him feel strong, powerful, invincible. The bat wheeled away and flew off into the dusk. A few more shots like that might make this whole experience almost enjoyable.

In the distance, Jason saw the Knight of the Mirror hacking his way through the Scim, his magic-less warriors following behind and to the sides of him. It was almost beautiful, the smoothness of their motion as they scythed through the crowd. Jason caught sight of Baileya for a moment, her strange spear spinning through the enemy.

Out of nowhere, a monstrous wolf, nearly the size of a compact car, leapt onto Jason's rhinocorn. "Gah!" he shouted, recoiling from the terrifying sight of its enormous maw and rolling backward off his mount, the wolf pouncing just behind him, missing only because Jason continued to roll when he hit the ground.

Jason scrambled to his feet, his bow and arrows scattered on the ground between him and the wolf. He tried not to hyperventilate at the sight of the mangy, drooling monster. He hadn't brought a knife. Not even a small one. The wolf advanced, and Jason stepped backward. "Is there a pause button?" Jason asked nervously as the wolf took another step forward. "Um. Time out?"

An ear-shattering war cry filled the air, followed by David Glenn's lean body leaping onto the wolf's back, hacking into its neck with his ax. Kekoa ran in from the side, slicing at the monster's legs with his leiomanō. The wolf collapsed, and the boys kicked and stabbed at it. It shook once, violently, and knocked David from its back before slinking away into the battle.

"Hi," Jason said, panting. "What was that?"

"We call those giant wolves," Kekoa said nonchalantly.

"But we liked that name you used," David said.

Then they both shouted together, looks of mock horror on their faces, "GAH!"

"Har, har," Jason said, gathering his bow and arrows, his hands shaking. "Giant wolves are scary. I do not like them."

"Nice shot with the bat," Kekoa said. "They'll be talking about that one tomorrow!"

David shouted, "Split up or stick together?"

"I wanna get that big spider they brought tonight! Did you see it?"

"Gross," David said. "Hard pass. I'm going after that wolf. Jason?"

Kekoa put his hands on Jason's. "You're shaking, brah. That's just adrenaline. It's okay. Remember, you got nothing to be afraid of. The Elenil will fix you right up if something happens, and we're keeping an eye on you. You want to go hunt a giant spider with me?"

Jason shuddered. He did not want to see a giant spider.

"Think of the positives," David said. "What are the good things happening right now?"

"I have a unicorn," Jason said reflexively.

"No one else has a unicorn," Kekoa said. "Right?"

"I gotta go find her!"

The three exchanged grins, and David shouted, "WAR PARTY, TO WAR!"

David gave Jason a thumbs-up and ran after the wolf, and Kekoa let out a whoop and dove back into the fray. Jason watched them go, his hands on his hips. He scooped up his arrows and put them back in the quiver. He had no idea how to find Delightful Glitter Lady. "Uh," he said, then cleared his throat. "Here, unicorn! Over here! Uuuuunicooorn!"

✦

Madeline watched Shula leave before climbing the stairs toward the top of the wall. The more she thought about it, the more Madeline realized she had no intention of lifting a sword against anyone, Scim or Elenil or human. War was not her thing. She couldn't imagine that a night on the wall would change that, not for an instant. She might be in service to the Elenil, but she didn't have to kill anyone. Her breath went ragged for a moment. Surprised, she pushed up her sleeve to see the bracelet tattoo pulsing in time to her breathing. Maybe it could sense her wavering in her commitment to the Elenil. Okay, okay, she was going up the stairs like she was supposed to.

It was a wide stone stairway. At the top, a shimmering golden haze prevented her from stepping onto the wall. A voice came from the haze as Madeline approached it. "Declare your race and enter."

"My *race?*" Madeline looked back down the stairway, as if for help. She wasn't sure what to say. "White?" She paused. "Caucasian?"

Nothing happened.

She waited for a minute, unsure what to do. "French? Scottish."

Hanali descended the stairs, the shimmering curtain gently making way for him. "My sweet child," he said. "Is this so difficult? It is a simple security measure—it should not be so vexing."

"I don't understand what it's asking, I guess," Madeline said.

"Observe," Hanali said, and started up the stairs.

The shimmering golden haze's voice said, "Declare your race and enter."

"Elenil," Hanali said, and the curtain parted. He walked through, glancing over his shoulder at Madeline with a look of pity.

"Declare your race and enter."

"Human," Madeline said, and the curtain parted. She stepped onto the wall. She felt a vague sense of unease at the security magic. Was being a human sufficient reason to trust someone for entry? She wondered what happened if the curtain determined you were Scim . . . or something else.

Hanali waited, impatient, one gloved hand held out to her. He wore a new emerald-green outfit and a ridiculous floppy hat. "We use the same magic at the city gates, to keep the Scim out. The only real danger on this side of the wall is that they could tear down the gate itself."

The wall was wider than she had expected. ("Wide enough for six carriages to race side by side—though who would enter such a foolish race?" Hanali said.) Below them the Elenil army gathered. Madeline noted that not many of them were Elenil, something that, again, struck her as strange. They were, in fact, nearly all humans, or at least seemed to be. She had thought maybe that was just the city guard, but it appeared to be true of their entire army.

The atmosphere at the top of the wall was not one of war. Merchants strode down the center selling snacks, and seating areas festooned with flowers and banners bedecked the outer edges, where the view would be best. Musicians gathered at the inner edge, playing jaunty tunes on stringed instruments. The musicians, the merchants, the dancers, the security guards: all humans. Elenil, taller and far more elegant, walked among them or sat on the edge chatting amiably with one another as they waited for the battle to start.

"I have someone to introduce you to," Hanali said, his face aglow with excitement beneath the ridiculous wide brim of his hat. While the other Elenil tended toward elegance, Hanali often looked like the most outrageous model at an experimental fashion show. Madeline wondered if he did this on purpose. "She's well known to the archon, and if all goes well she may bring you into the court in her service after your training. Her name is Gilenyia."

Madeline didn't know much about who the archon was, and she didn't know why it was good to be taken into the court after her training, or even how long it would be (when she got to stop wearing white?), but this seemed important to Hanali, and whatever came, she continued to be thankful to him for providing her a way to breathe.

Hanali fussed over her gloves, making sure they covered her wrists where they met the long sleeves of her dress. He told her twice not to offer to shake hands and not to curtsy and certainly not to draw attention to herself. "Be your usual charming self," Hanali said, "only more charming."

Hanali threaded the crowd, past the jugglers and actors, the poets and puppeteers, until they came to a cream-colored tent shot through with gold and silver thread. Two humans stood on guard outside, wearing a strange mishmash of medieval European armor and fantastic Elenil designs. One of them lifted a chin to Hanali, which delighted him to no end. "I brought those two into the Sunlit Lands," he whispered as they entered the tent.

The tent was lit by floating glass balls, each of which held a spark of light. "An extravagant use of magic," Hanali murmured. "Especially when the dark so rarely comes to the Court of Far Seeing."

An Elenil woman lay stretched on a divan in the center of the tent, her long dress draped carefully to cover her completely. Her laced collar crept so far up her neck that it caressed her chin. The skin of her face was pale as milk on marble, her hair like tame sunlight. Her eyes were a deep blue, almost purple, that Madeline had only seen while on an airplane, looking at the distant sky above the clouds.

"Ah," the Elenil woman said. "This must be Madeline Oliver."

Hanali had told her not to shake hands or curtsy but hadn't explained what she *should* do. Madeline allowed herself a slight smile and forced herself to look away from Gilenyia. Out of the corner of her eye she saw Hanali bow deeply.

Gilenyia laughed, and her laugh built on itself, like a handbell choir playing a particularly merry tune. "So polite, Hanali! Even your human charge did not curtsy, so why should you be so formal? Come, friends, and sit. Let us enjoy this evening together."

Two chairs waited on either side of her. Madeline hadn't seen them appear. Hanali escorted her to a chair, then sat on the other side of the divan. Why did Hanali tell her not to curtsy, and then bow himself? He was so frustrating. Her cheeks flushed with embarrassment.

Gilenyia smiled at Madeline. "He scared you, didn't he? Told you not to curtsy or shake hands?"

Madeline glanced at Hanali, who shook his head.

"Yes," Madeline said.

Gilenyia burst into laughter, and Madeline couldn't keep from smiling in return. "He's my cousin," Gilenyia said. "Or at least, that's the closest concept among your people. We grew up in the same household, like brother and sister. We are young for Elenil, born in the same year. I am not easily offended, even by the strange manners of humans."

Madeline wasn't sure if she should respond, but she said, "He acted like you were a celebrity."

"She is," Hanali said, "in her way."

Gilenyia slapped his shoulder. "You never treated me thus when we were children." She leaned toward Madeline and whispered, "He uses his youth as an excuse when he violates good manners. The Elenil at the Court talk about him incessantly. He is well known as a rogue."

"Please," Hanali said, fastidiously pulling the fingers of his gloves to fit more perfectly. "I spend so much time among the humans, I occasionally forget the ins and outs of Elenil society."

"Nonsense," Gilenyia said, laughing again, her gloved hands covering her mouth. "Ah, you have always been a rogue."

"What changed?" Madeline asked. "Why did he start treating you differently?"

Gilenyia's face darkened, and Hanali's paled. Madeline couldn't see why her question might be rude, but she hastily apologized. Gilenyia didn't respond, didn't seem to have heard her.

"In other news," Hanali said brightly, "my new haberdasher assures me this hat will be the talk of Far Seeing."

Gilenyia spoke over him. "It is a fair question, Cousin, and if she is here to fight the Scim, why not tell her all? You did not bring her to Far Seeing for her insights on hats and silk jackets."

Hanali inclined his head. "As you wish, Cousin. But I would rather she see the Scim first, and know of your work."

Gilenyia sighed. "At last fair Hanali speaks his mind. So be it then. Far be it from me to discourage you when you get the courage to speak as family and not some sycophant." She leaned her head to the side and whispered something, and three waiters appeared with drinks. Or . . . something like waiters. Again, humans, and they did not meet Madeline's eye.

The drink was sweet, like some combination of strawberry and peach, and cold, though it had no ice. It was, like many things among the Elenil, the most delightful drink Madeline could recall. She drank it faster than she intended, and a second drink appeared in her hand at the same moment the empty glass was whisked away.

"Take off your glove," Gilenyia said.

Without thinking, Madeline pulled her hand away from the Elenil woman. It was a request she wouldn't have thought twice about at home, but here it was a matter of propriety, perhaps even modesty. She knew it was the height of rudeness to show one's naked hand to the Elenil, and she assumed to ask someone to remove their glove was rude as well.

"I don't want to offend you," Madeline said.

But Gilenyia took a firm hold of Madeline's left wrist and slipped the glove from her hand. The action shocked Madeline. She looked to Hanali for guidance, but he appeared almost queasy. He gave her a look she thought was intended to seem reassuring.

"Fascinating," Gilenyia said, studying the silver loops and swirls of Madeline's tattoo. It almost pulsed in the light of the hovering glass orbs. She traced one of the leafing branches. "This is a healing spell." She turned to Hanali. "Who wrought this? Did you learn so much in the household of our childhood?"

Hanali inclined his head slightly. "Indeed. It was I who struck the deal, Cousin."

Gilenyia looked into Madeline's eyes. "So young to be at death's door. You cannot breathe?"

"I can now."

"Because—" Gilenyia traced the silver tattoo, puzzling through its knots and cords. "Because you agreed to fight the Scim. For a human year." She looked to Hanali again, "A canny bargain, Cousin."

"A canny bargain?" Madeline asked. "Isn't everyone's about the same?"

Gilenyia gave her a pitying look. A horn sounded, distracting her. Madeline pulled her glove over her hand and moved away from the woman.

"The Knight of the Mirror," Gilenyia said, sounding pleased. She made a motion, and one curtained wall opened, revealing the edge of the city wall and the battlefield beyond. Madeline bit her lip, watching the massive scale of the army preparing itself for battle. "Do not worry, child. Before this night is through I will show you the power of Elenil healing magic."

"It is a great honor," Hanali said. "So few are able to heal, even among the Elenil."

Below them, a knight and his entourage moved toward the front lines. It wasn't night yet—it would never be night here. But a sort of twilight had fallen over the field. Madeline could still see the army below with amazing clarity, and she wondered if there was some magical enhancement improving the view. Rondelo, one of only a handful of Elenil on the field, rode out on his white stag, Evernu. Madeline found it hard to imagine herself on the field of battle, wearing extravagant armor. What weapon would she use? Who would be her commander? The whole idea was odd. She wondered for a moment if she could ride Evernu behind Rondelo, her arms around his waist, then felt the heat in her face. How would she fight if her arms were full of the Elenil warrior? Madeline's heart beat faster, and she was suddenly glad Darius wasn't here to see her face. Besides, Rondelo was Elenil. She didn't think that would work, and she would be gone in a year. Darius was waiting for her.

"Rondelo has become well respected," Hanali said, as if reading Madeline's thoughts. "His insistence on joining the field of battle has drawn attention."

Gilenyia made a noncommittal noise. "I have heard his name spoken among the magistrates."

"He is young to be mentioned for polemarch," Hanali said. "And yet I, too, have heard his name among the prophets and soothsayers in the market. And he is plain for an Elenil. He could almost pass for human."

Gilenyia sipped her drink. "If he were to become commander of the Elenil army, it would give the current polemarch more time to attend to social matters. It could come to pass."

"So that Tirius can attend more parties? You have a wicked tongue, Cousin."

Gilenyia smiled slyly. "I know we are family, Hanali. You need not call me Cousin every time you speak."

Hanali said nothing.

A great cheer came up from the west, and the Scim army appeared over the ridge. A spider the size of a semi crested the hill first, followed by enormous creatures of various disgusting types: wolves, rats, bats, and even a monstrous, scabby possum.

"Now they will list their supposed grievances," Gilenyia said.

Madeline knelt at the wall's edge so she could see better. Hanali handed her a brass spyglass. Madeline held it to her eye, and the distant Scim appeared, more disgusting than she could have imagined. The Scim spokesman had massive teeth, tusks nearly, jutting from behind his bottom lip. Grey skin, ears like wads of chewed gum, and a heavy shelf of a brow over small, angry black eyes. The rags that covered his heavily muscled frame were stained and no doubt stank. His hands were too large, the wide fingernails yellowed and broken.

The Scim began to speak, his gravelly voice rolling over the field of battle and to the wall. It must have been magically amplified, because he wasn't shouting, but every word was crystal clear.

"I am Crooked Back, spokesman for the Scim. We see you tremble in fear at our approach." The Elenil forces jeered. Crooked Back continued, "We do not come seeking war but only a return of what is ours. The Elenil have stolen what rightfully belongs to the Scim. They have taken certain artifacts which are of our heritage. Five magical artifacts, made by Scim, empowered by Scim, belonging to the Scim. Stolen by the Elenil. If these five artifacts are returned to our people, we will leave in peace."

Gilenyia put her hand lightly on Madeline's shoulder. "What would they ask for tomorrow if we gave in to such demands today? Those artifacts are dangerous and were taken from the Scim for their own safety after the War of the Waste. No, we won't be returning those."

Hanali grunted. "Nor do we have them, for the magistrates turned them over to a human, did they not?"

"An excellent point," Gilenyia said.

"But . . . if they belong to the Scim?" Madeline looked at Gilenyia.

"They are weapons of unimaginable magic. The Scim cannot be trusted with such things."

The Scim spokesman had continued talking, little caring about the conversation happening on the wall. "—then we shall bring a thousand years of darkness and tear every white stone of this city down. We shall salt your fields and burn your homes, and the great darkness shall reign. Flame and darkness, death and suffering await you. What say you, Elenil army?"

In response, the Elenil army shouted jeers, and several arrows were loosed toward the Scim front lines.

"So be it," Crooked Back roared. "May darkness rain down upon you!" With that, the Scim army raced down the hill to battle. The terrible screaming and shrieks of the Scim sent shivers down Madeline's spine. The Elenil army met them, and the sounds of metal on metal resounded over the field.

It was terrible to watch, like hundreds of car accidents happening at once. The sounds of horses screaming, the shouts of humans and Scim, the bellowing of war animals . . . And yet here, upon the wall, someone was playing a stringed instrument and singing with a clear, sweet voice, and Madeline could smell the remnants of the sweet juice in her cup and someone cooking a delicious meal farther along the wall's edge.

The contrast turned her stomach. It was like a Roman coliseum, and she had a box seat with the rich and powerful. Below them, humans—kids like her who had come here because of injustice and trouble and problems in their world—risked their lives so the Elenil could sip fruit juice and discuss politics and hats. It wasn't a war, it was an entertainment. She set her glass down and waved the servant aside when he offered another.

Still, they watched.

The Knight of the Mirror and his people carved a swath through the Scim. None seemed able to stop him. Hanali pointed out an explosion of flame and explained that it was Shula, that she had the power to burn like a torch without being harmed. "It was what she asked for when I invited her to the Sunlit Lands," Hanali said.

Gilenyia smiled. "She is a fierce one."

The battle continued. An Elenil soldier in white armor rampaged through their own lines on an enormous rhinoceros.

Gilenyia winced. "Who is responsible for that soldier?"

Hanali cleared his throat. "I will make inquiries."

A gigantic spider stalked through the armies. Madeline shivered at the thought of being out there among them. The Scim moved with barbaric efficiency, tearing Elenil soldiers to bits where they were most vulnerable.

Hanali leapt to his feet and strode closer to the battle, his hands clenching the balustrade.

"What is it, Cousin?"

He stared at the field with a sudden intensity. He pointed out a strange Scim soldier in a black helmet shaped like a horned skull who was dragging a flaming woman across the field. "They're targeting the magic users."

Madeline jumped up and stood beside him. "Is that . . . is that *Shula*?"

"I am afraid so," Hanali said grimly. "And there." He pointed to their right. A monstrous bat plucked a flying man out of the sky. "They're stealing our magic."

"We have to get out there," Madeline said. "We have to do something!"

"There is nothing to be done," Hanali said. "If those upon the field cannot prevent it, we will not arrive in time to do any different."

Madeline watched in horror as the Scim in the black skull dragged her new friend away from the city walls and toward the Scim army.

14
NIGHT'S BREATH

*[The Scim] were evil things, their hearts filled
with wickedness and foul deeds.*

FROM "THE ORDERING OF THE WORLD," AN ELENIL STORY

✦

Jason couldn't find Delightful Glitter Lady, though he did occasionally hear what sounded like someone playing a bagpipe half underwater, which he assumed was her. He did, however, catch sight of
the Knight of the Mirror again. The battle was so thick that if he
kept an eye out for any unengaged Scim and avoided them, he
didn't have to fight much to make it through the crowd. He was getting the
hang of it. His fear and worry sluiced off him, his muscles relaxed, and his
ability to focus came back. His hands weren't shaking anymore.

He was glad his helmet was still on, though, as one Scim warrior
knocked him pretty well with a broadsword. The Sunlit Lands guy who
could fly (Jason couldn't remember his name) swooped down and took
the Scim away. The Scim roared the horrible things he would do to Jason
when he got back on the ground. Jason knew he was getting targeted by

the Scim for his white armor, but the armor also made it easier for his side to keep an eye on him. They were watching out for him.

A quick count of his arrows showed he only had nine more. He looked for a discarded weapon, but slowing down was an easy way to become a target. He ran toward the Knight of the Mirror. After a moment, he noticed Baileya running alongside him, her Kakri spear tucked beneath her right arm.

"Head back toward the city wall," she shouted. "Now!"

"What's happening?"

"The Scim are targeting the more heavily magical soldiers tonight. They are trying to not even engage with the Knight of the Mirror. There is an evil plan in motion, and I cannot see the shape of it. The Knight has ordered the less experienced to fall back to the city gates."

"But I can help—"

The flying teen dropped down beside them. "The Black Skulls! You can't see it from the ground, but they're triangulating on Shula. I think they're trying to kill her! Permanently!"

"Who's Shula?"

"The burning girl," he said. "Baileya, try to slow down one of the Skulls. I'll see if I can distract the second one. Shula should have a chance against one instead of three."

Baileya's eyes grew wide. Jason followed her gaze. She had sighted one of the Black Skulls. The Skull was riding a possum the size of a horse—its long rodent snout covered in blood, its red eyes filled with bloodlust, its bald tail whipping the air. The Skull itself wore a white robe, the hem of which was filthy with mud and ichor. It wore black gloves and boots, and on its head was an antelope skull painted a shining black, the curved horns rising several feet. In its right hand it held aloft a sickle.

"Run, Jason!"

Baileya sprinted, leaping like a deer over soldiers from both sides. Jason knew she meant for him to run for the gate. Everyone had warned him to stay away from the Black Skulls, and his own brain was screaming at him to do as he was told and run for the wall, but something else—a deeper voice—said this was the whole reason he was here. To protect people. What if Madeline was out here somewhere?

He tightened his grip on his bow and ran after Baileya.

Baileya ran full speed at the Black Skull, sliding to the ground in front of the charging possum. Jason opened his mouth to scream a warning, but she crouched calmly in the beast's path, and at the last possible moment jabbed the curved, bladed side of her spear into the mud, dropped to her knees, and tilted the blade forward.

The possum slammed into the spear. The blade sank into the possum's chest, and it let out a horrible scream as it collapsed, crushing Baileya beneath its heavy corpse before skidding to a stop.

The Black Skull stood slowly, apparently unharmed, its towering horns rising to their full height with a slow implacability, the blade of its sickle glinting in its hand. It turned, the black cavities of its eyes regarding Baileya. Distracted from its mission, it stepped toward the woman who had dared impede its path.

Baileya shoved the possum's head to one side. But to Jason's horror, she didn't stand. She scrambled backward until she found her spear, broken in half now, and used what remained of it to get to her feet. Her left leg hung limply, twisted at an angle that made Jason sick. She dropped her spear, reached behind her back with both hands, and pulled two curved daggers out of her sash.

Why am I standing here, doing nothing? A distant buzzing echoed in Jason's ears. His thoughts came thick and slow. The Black Skull had crossed nearly half the distance to Baileya. *Shake out of it!*

Jason, still a solid twenty feet behind Baileya, slipped an arrow from his quiver and onto his bow. His heart beat so hard against his chest he thought it might break through. He felt the magic, clear and strong, and opened the conduit through his tattoo as wide as he knew how. The confidence of an expert archer flooded him, and the sounds of battle fell away until he saw only one thing: his target. The heart of the Black Skull. He wouldn't allow that thing near Baileya, wouldn't let it hurt her. He breathed once, twice, then held his breath and loosed the arrow. It flew past Baileya, so close the fletching could have brushed her cheek. It sank into its mark, and the Skull stumbled backward.

It did not fall.

It righted itself, snapped the arrow from its chest, and stepped forward again, sickle raised.

"No!" Jason shouted and shot another arrow, then another and another. Five, six, seven arrows, and still the Black Skull walked, its robe an explosion of arrows but not stained with a single drop of blood. Two more arrows, and then Jason was out, and the thing still stalked toward Baileya.

Jason ran between them. "Stay away from her!"

The Skull laughed, and a chill ran down Jason's spine.

He balled his fists, ready to fight the thing to the death. He heard Baileya shouting at him to get back, but it barely registered in the face of those horrible empty eye sockets and the towering horns of the skull.

A meteor streaked between them, and its supercharged air blew Jason back. He stumbled into Baileya, and they fell to the ground. From the center of the fire, a girl's face turned toward them.

"Shula!" Baileya shouted. "It's a trap!"

"Run," the flaming woman said. "I'll take care of him."

Another bright, cascading explosion of fire came from Shula, the hot air singeing Jason and Baileya. Jason helped Baileya move farther from the flames, but the Black Skull advanced despite the heat.

The Black Skull caught on fire, its robes alight, the arrows like torches in its chest. The sickle fell from its hand, the blade red from the flames. It grabbed hold of Shula with both hands. She kicked at the Skull, but it didn't respond to the blows any more than it had responded to the arrows or the fire. The Skull's laughter came rolling over the battlefield again, and it called out in a loud voice, "Victory!"

The Scim roared and echoed the Black Skull's cry, smashing weapons against their shields and helmets as they stopped fighting and began a sudden retreat. "Victory!" they shouted. "Victory, victory, O People of the Shadow!" The Black Skull, still aflame, ran, dragging a struggling Shula. A wolf loped up alongside the Skull, and the Skull pulled itself onto the wolf's back.

Baileya grabbed Jason's arm so hard it bruised him. "Jason. If tonight's battle was only to capture Shula, then we must frustrate their plan." She pushed a curved dagger into his hand. "Slow them however you can. The Knight of the Mirror will come to your aid."

There was no time for instructions or second thoughts. Jason strengthened his grip on the dagger and ran as fast as he could, passing wounded

Scim warriors and monstrous limping creatures. A desperate need to stop the Black Skull washed over Jason. He'd been telling himself that this wasn't his battle, but now this horrible magical creature had grabbed some Earth girl and was dragging her across the field—headed to a terrible end, no doubt. And sure, the girl could light on fire, but that didn't mean she wasn't a human being, and it didn't mean Jason wasn't going to do everything in his power to help her. He tried to run faster, but he kept stumbling on the broken bits of weapons and bodies on the field. If something didn't give soon, he would lose them. He couldn't keep up with the wolf.

Then, as if in answer, the wolf caught fire. It let out a long, plaintive howl and collapsed beneath the Skull. Jason didn't lose a step, just kept running straight ahead. The Black Skull paused for a moment, getting a better grip on the nape of Shula's neck, then strode forward through the battlefield, dragging Shula behind him.

Jason was close now, close enough he thought he had a chance if Shula could slow the Skull down just a minute longer. Thirty seconds and he would be there. His skin hurt from his burns, and he could feel Shula's heat growing as he got closer. He settled his grip on Baileya's dagger and got ready to use it.

A body slammed into him from the side.

It was a Scim warrior, one grey fist holding a club nearly as tall as Jason. It growled, and its foul breath struck him like a blow just before the club did.

Knocked off his feet, Jason landed on another fallen soldier, whether human or Scim he couldn't say, but the Scim warrior was in front of him already, the club swinging toward Jason's chest. He tried to roll away, but he was too slow. He felt his rib cage go, and a cold breeze settled onto him—Shula's heat moving away. So this is how it was going to end. Jason felt a distant regret, cushioned by the thought that he could rest now. He wouldn't have to worry about his parents anymore, wouldn't have to carry his grief about Jenny. He didn't need to save Shula or Madeline or anyone . . . He could just let it all go.

A horn sounded in the distance, and the Scim's head snapped up. It gave Jason a quick sideways glance, but the horn sounded again. The Scim grunted, kicked him once, and loped after the other Scim.

Jason still had Baileya's knife. It was loose in his hand, but he couldn't tighten his grip. He had lost his . . . what was it? Unicorn? And the burning girl. But he still had other things. Like this. The knife. But someone would need to come get it, because his legs weren't working. In fact, his arm wasn't moving either. His thoughts seemed to be coming slow too. Like in a dream, or being half awake. Where was his unicorn again? He thought he heard her trumpet in the distance.

He closed his eyes, and the darkness swept him away.

✦

Madeline watched in mute horror as Shula was dragged across the battlefield by a black-skulled warrior.

"No doubt a message," Gilenyia said. "They begin the battle saying we've stolen their artifacts, and they end by stealing ours."

Hearing Gilenyia call the humans "artifacts" sent a chill down Madeline's spine. The Scim sounded retreat with a series of shouts about their victory and then a thin, shrieking blast from something like a trumpet. The battle shifted as the Elenil army targeted the Scim who carried the Elenil's magic users with them.

Gilenyia stood, and one of her attendants immediately draped a thin satin stole over her shoulders. It nearly touched the ground. "Come," she said. "We shall walk awhile among the corpses."

Madeline shivered. The thought of walking out on the battlefield among the broken dead filled her with horror, but Gilenyia said it with a complete lack of passion, like she was inviting someone to take a stroll around her neighborhood.

Madeline shot a look at Hanali, hoping for a reprieve. Instead he said, "I must speak to Rondelo. Gilenyia will return you home." So. Madeline would go and walk among the corpses with Gilenyia.

Two human attendants flanked them as they descended the stairs and followed the wide avenue through the gate. A ragtag stream of wounded soldiers headed the opposite way, entering the city. Two people held up a third person. A woman helped a man—no, not a man, he looked to be twelve or thirteen—hobble inside.

"We'll help them directly," Gilenyia said. "But first, the more heavily wounded."

She strode straight toward the center of the battlefield where the fighting had been most vicious. They passed broken spears and crushed pieces of armor, people sprawled on their backs, groaning, trampled in the mud. There was a metallic tang in the air and an underlying smell of smoke. The sound of the Scim's retreat came to them like distant waves beating on stone.

Gilenyia stopped in the center of the field, her satin stole stained where it had dragged along the ground. A teenage boy lay at her feet, the shaft of a spear jutting from his chest. His dark hair was plastered to his brown skin, his eyes closed but moving rapidly beneath the eyelids. He was breathing: a slow, irregular rasping sound. Gilenyia knelt beside him and put one gloved hand lightly on his chest. "We start here." To her attendants she said, "You know what to bring me."

Madeline's heart climbed into her throat. The entire field looked like a trash heap, only it was people and creatures strewn across it. To her left was some sort of wooden wagon, arrows stuck in the sides like porcupine quills. There were hands reaching out from beneath it, and a tall, heavily muscled beast, neither human nor Scim, collapsed beside it.

"Come here, girl," Gilenyia said.

Madeline could barely respond. Her mind felt distant and slow, but when Gilenyia snapped her name, she made her way to the Elenil woman's side. The attendants had returned, working together to drag a Scim warrior beside the broken boy at Madeline's feet. One of the Scim's jagged tusks was broken off, and black tattoos crisscrossed its skin. It was unconscious. A great gash from a sword had parted its filthy tunic and torn across its chest.

"Take hold of the spear in the boy's chest," Gilenyia said. "I have broken the blade from the other side."

Madeline goggled. "What?"

But Gilenyia did not repeat herself. She was demurely removing her gloves. The attendants looked away, and Gilenyia snapped at them to find more wounded. "There are some we can save," she said, tucking her gloves into a small pocket inside her stole, "and some who can save others. Now take hold of the spear. Good. When I say, pull it out. It will require some strength."

The wood of the spear was rough and thicker than Madeline had imagined. Something with large hands must have held this weapon. She accidentally jostled the spear, and the boy groaned. Gilenyia gave her a sharp look then put one hand on the boy's chest and one on the Scim warrior's chest.

Gilenyia's hands were not flawless white like her face. A network of golden tattoos covered each hand like spiderwebs. Her palms, fingers, and even fingernails were laced with intricate patterns and intersections and partings. A glowing pulse branched out through the tattoos, and a small wave of heat touched Madeline's face.

"Pull," Gilenyia said.

The spear did not budge.

"Harder!"

Madeline felt the spear give. The boy arched his back and screamed.

"No need to be gentle, girl—tear it out of him."

Angered by her inability to pull the spear free and the string of instructions from Gilenyia, Madeline snapped. She put one foot on the boy's chest, leaned back, and pulled with all her might, stumbling backward with a bloody spear shaft dripping in her hands.

The wound in the boy's chest closed like water over a stone. The Scim's wound simultaneously widened. The grey-skinned warrior thrashed for a moment, Gilenyia's hand still resting on its chest, and then it fell still.

The boy opened his eyes, which widened upon seeing the luxuriously dressed Elenil woman leaning over him. "Lady Gilenyia," he gasped. He leapt up and knelt before her. "Thank you, lady."

"Your name, sir?"

"Ricardo Sánchez, lady."

"You have served us well, Ricardo," she said. "Now join my attendants and gather more wounded. Start with those with the most grievous wounds."

"Yes, my lady," he said. He bounded into the junkyard of the battle.

The Scim soldier did not move, did not breathe. "Did you—" Madeline cleared her throat. "Did you kill him?"

Gilenyia gave her a curious look. "His people abandoned him. He would have died in a few hours. I sped his death and healed one of our soldiers. It was a mercy twice over. Does it displease you?"

Did it displease her? What a strange question. Of course it displeased her. It seemed unjust in every possible way to heal a human warrior by killing a Scim. But Gilenyia was right—the Scim hadn't looked like it would last long. Madeline didn't know much about punctured chests, but the boy hadn't looked like he would last long either. So maybe instead of letting two people die, she had helped one live?

"I help the Scim wounded as well," Gilenyia said. "Their people have abandoned them. We take them into the Court of Far Seeing and rehabilitate them, give them meaningful roles in the Sunlit Lands. It's more than their foul kinfolk have ever done for them."

"It seems . . . something seems wrong about it." Madeline couldn't figure out how to say it, but a sick feeling in the pit of her stomach threatened to spread to her whole body.

"I am a healer," Gilenyia said. "I had hoped you might assist me during your allotted time. To find someone with healing potential is rare among the Elenil, and I see that potential in you. But perhaps you do not have the stomach for it. No matter. Today you shall at least go among the wounded and find those I may help."

"You want me to . . . to find the wounded for you?"

Gilenyia nodded once, impatiently. "Even if I don't heal them, we must take them within the city walls, agreed? Look for the most egregiously wounded first. I cannot save them once they pass death's gate."

Okay. Okay, she could do this. She was only pointing people out, people Gilenyia would find eventually anyway. Or maybe she should run. Maybe she should look for a way home out of this crazy place. Her breathing went ragged just thinking about it. Somewhere there was a gate or portal or closet or painting that would open and land her back with her mom and dad, where Sofía would make her hot chocolate in the morning and pack her lunches, and where Mr. García would smile at her in the sunlit garden as he placed new plants in the black soil. Darius would pick her up and take her to school, and in the afternoon he would read to her.

She stumbled, her chest tightening. Her breathing was coming ragged and uneven. The tattoo on her wrist stung. She whipped off her glove. Maybe it was her imagination, but the tattoo looked wider than before. Not by much, but a tiny bit, like it had swollen.

Were these thoughts enough to invalidate her agreement? Was the magic removing her ability to breathe because she wasn't serving the Elenil with her entire heart? She tugged her glove back on. She didn't want to touch anything out here with her bare hands.

She found a wounded Scim warrior. He was pinned beneath some beast she did not recognize—like an oversize ox. She couldn't tell if the pungent stench came from the animal or the Scim's bloodied and stained rags. The warrior's eyes fluttered open, and when his eyes met hers, his lip curled up in disgust, revealing a scarcity of crooked yellow teeth.

"Can you hear me?"

The Scim licked his lips. "I . . . hear you . . . Elenil."

"I'm human. My name is Madeline."

He grunted or maybe laughed.

"We're going to heal you." She stood and called for Gilenyia.

Gilenyia arrived with five humans—her two attendants and three soldiers she had patched up. She regarded the broken Scim coolly, but she didn't critique Madeline's choice. Instead, she bent over the warrior and said, so quietly that only he and Madeline could hear, "What will you do, brave warrior, if I use Elenil magic to save you?"

"A pox . . . on your magic," he wheezed. "Darkness . . . a thousand years . . . darkness. For you and your . . ." His face contorted in pain, and his hands scratched at the hide of the ox.

"Pull him out," Gilenyia barked, and Ricardo immediately took hold of one arm, an attendant the other. The other two humans put their backs against the ox and pushed. It wasn't enough to get much movement, and the Scim roared in pain.

Madeline said, "We could dig him out," and that's what they did. The mud moved easily enough, and with a combination of hands and broken weapons they managed to get his legs loose enough to tear him away from the dead ox.

"His legs and pelvis are broken," Gilenyia said. "Some minor internal damage. Have you found someone who will balance these wounds?"

One of her attendants brushed the hair out of his eyes with a muddied hand. "I have one." They dragged another Scim warrior, much worse for wear, through the mud. Madeline couldn't believe she was still alive. She had been cut neatly from the shoulder down, and the wound already stank.

Gilenyia looked the Scim over carefully, then motioned to Madeline to join her. "This one won't last long. It is a mercy to her and to the one with broken legs. Do you approve?"

"Do you need me to . . . to approve?"

"Before we leave this battlefield I hope to see you understand the work I do. You have chosen this Scim soldier to be healed. You must have some compassion for him."

The Scim had snarled at Madeline. But still. It was right to heal him. Wasn't it? "Will it kill her? To fix him?"

"She will die regardless. My magic, remember, cannot pass the gates of death. She will die in an hour if we let her or in a few minutes if she gives her legs to her countryman."

Madeline couldn't decide. Gilenyia waited, then asked again, "Do you approve?"

She couldn't say the words. The groans and cries of the two Scim warriors were too much for her. Gilenyia grew tired of waiting and put her bare hands upon their foreheads. The male Scim arched his back and screamed, while the female exhaled once, sharply, and lay still. The black swirls of her tattoos faded then disappeared completely.

The male Scim sat up on his knees, his legs and pelvis miraculously whole, and cradled the female's body, weeping bitterly.

"Ungrateful creature," Gilenyia said, disgusted.

"May the Peasant King welcome you into his court," the Scim said soft and low into the dead Scim's ear.

"Better the Majestic One than the Peasant King," Gilenyia said.

The Scim scowled at her.

"Do not run," Gilenyia said, "unless you would have your sister's sacrifice be in vain."

The Scim stayed near them after that as they combed the field for more survivors. The sun had risen in earnest, and they had wandered far from the center of the battlefield now. The Scim soldier winced in the sunshine, which seemed to be physically hurting him. After a couple hours, Gilenyia had healed perhaps twenty human soldiers and three Scim, some with broken limbs and a few with more serious wounds. The serious wounds were the most troubling, as Madeline watched the nearly dead succumb because of Gilenyia's magic. Once Gilenyia used a badly broken human to fix a

Scim warrior, but Madeline noticed dark looks exchanged by the human soldiers when she did. Madeline wondered if this was part of a show meant for her, to try to convince her that Gilenyia gave everyone an equal chance.

Some of the soldiers were sent back into the city with the Scim warriors, but Gilenyia kept the first one she had healed, the one Madeline had chosen, there in the crowd, finding bodies. Madeline worked her way over to him. His thick, grey muscles were covered in black tattoos that whirled in loops up both arms and over his shoulders. His hair, greasy and limp, hung past his shoulders. He had the smell of someone who hadn't washed in weeks, maybe longer.

"I told you my name," Madeline said. "What's yours?"

He scowled at her. "Call me Night's Breath."

"Is that a common name among your people?"

He drew himself up to his full height and hit his chest with one massive fist. "It is my war-skin name, given in my first battle. For when the enemy feels my breath upon his neck, already night has come for him."

She helped him move a splintered battering ram off a large, hairy creature that looked almost like a goat with human arms and legs. It had wide, staring eyes. There was nothing to be done for it. "Why do you want to bring darkness to the Elenil? Why do you hate the light?"

Night's Breath spit. He mumbled something to himself, then said, "A thousand years of darkness is a mercy to the Elenil. I would crush their skulls. I would grind their bones."

"But why do you hate them? Look at the Court of Far Seeing. Isn't the Crescent Stone beautiful in the sunlight, there on the highest tower? Look at the white walls and the colored flags and the bright river winding through. Do you see the palace on the central hill? I've never seen anything so beautiful." It reminded her of the descriptions from the Tales of Meselia—the beautiful, magical cities she had longed to see her entire life. She stopped for a minute and looked at the city, reminding herself of the beauty here, of the good things, of the magic and wonder.

"Hold, little human," Night's Breath replied. "Look again at those fair walls. Do you think they would be a thing of beauty to one such as me? What awaits Night's Breath behind the walls of Far Seeing?" He snorted. "Death is a better end for one such as I."

It was a good question. What would be done with the Scim soldiers? They were prisoners, certainly, but the Elenil would be kind to them, she was sure. Thinking about it, she hadn't seen any Scim in the city proper. She hadn't been here long, though, and no doubt they were in a prison or jail cell. Or maybe they were bargained back to the Scim in exchange for Elenil prisoners? She didn't know. It was a question worth pursuing, she thought, and she promised herself she would not forget to look in on Night's Breath after they returned to the city.

The Scim grunted. "Look here. Another fallen human." It was a boy in white armor, his chest caved in. "Ground to dust beneath the wheels of war. The Elenil could return what they have stolen from the Scim, and the bones of such little fools need not be grist. But until that time comes, I will kill as many as I have opportunity."

This one looked to be too far gone. Madeline dreaded the thought of touching another dead body. Her heart beat faster. She didn't know how many nightmares she would have in the weeks to come. "Let's take off his helmet," Madeline said. She steeled herself. If she was going to walk the battlefield looking for survivors, she was going to make absolutely sure who had survived and who had not.

Night's Breath removed the boy's helmet. His black hair was plastered to his face, but she recognized Jason immediately. *Oh no. No, no!* She fell to her knees at his side. He had come here because of her, and why was he on the battlefield already? He didn't even agree to fight when he came—he shouldn't be here, broken and bleeding. Madeline put her face near Jason's. A faint stirring of breath touched her. He was alive. Barely. She leapt to her feet and screamed for Gilenyia, who made her way toward them with infuriating slowness.

Gilenyia's bright eyes flicked between Jason and Madeline, and she seemed to know immediately who he was. "Ah. Your friend. He is grievously wounded. We would need someone in full health, or near enough, to recover him."

Madeline's mind raced. Someone healthy who could take Jason's place? "Take me," she said. It would be worth it, and she didn't have long anyway.

Gilenyia shook her head. "Would that it were so simple, child. You are healthy only because of our magic. And you have a contract to fulfill to the Elenil. No, it will not work, though it is noble that such would be your first thought."

"Okay, so could we help him enough that he could heal naturally? Is there another person on the field like the last one, who is going to die either way?"

Gilenyia shook her head. "He is too far gone for that, human child. But there are ways." She turned her head slightly, enough that Madeline followed her gaze to see Night's Breath, hunched just beyond the circle of human soldiers and attendants who had followed Gilenyia. *Oh no.* Could Madeline agree to that? She licked her lips, thinking hard.

Night's Breath tightened his hands into fists. One of the soldiers, realizing what Gilenyia meant to do, turned, his ax at the ready. Night's Breath swung one massive arm in a punishing blow, and the soldier flew backward, his helmet toppling from his head. Another soldier moved toward him, but Night's Breath shattered his knee, then broke into a desperate gallop over the battlefield.

"His life for your friend's," Gilenyia said.

Jason's face was almost white. She couldn't tell if he was still breathing. "That's not fair," Madeline said. It wasn't fair at all. Who was she to make this decision? She knew Jason, knew him to be a loyal and kind person, and she barely knew this Scim soldier at all, but every indication was that he was a terrible creature, bent on destroying every good thing in this beautiful city. Look at this disgusting field, for instance. Dead bodies, ruined war machines, trampled grass and stinking mud. The Scim had done this, not the Elenil. But could she agree to kill him? Her head spun, and her stomach turned over. She couldn't make this decision. She couldn't be the judge, the executioner, even if it meant saving her only friend from home.

"It is precisely fair. What did the beast say to you? No doubt that he would kill us all. That he would rather die than join the Elenil?"

Blood rushed into her face. "He said both those things."

"They are an irredeemable race, Madeline. Violence and shadow are their meat and drink. They choose death over life, darkness over light, filth over food. And your friend—is he a good man?"

Madeline brushed the hair from Jason's face. A breath rattled out of him, as if in reply. Her hands shook. She waited for him to take another breath. *Please take another breath!* He gasped, pulling in another long drag of air. Madeline slumped against him, relieved. There wasn't time for this, wasn't time to make this decision. "He took me to the hospital when no one else would help. He came to the Sunlit Lands with me just because he is my friend." She didn't know if this was a eulogy or if she was convincing herself to do this thing. All she had to do was say yes to Gilenyia. One simple word and Jason would live.

"A noble soul," Gilenyia said. "And you would let him die so that beast can escape and kill yet more noble souls?" She clucked her tongue. "The human morality is so muddied, I cannot make sense of it."

Jason's body began to shake. "Are you going to save him?" Madeline cried.

Gilenyia smiled, but it was a sad smile that didn't touch her eyes. "With your approval, child, I will."

Jason's body trembled, and his breath seemed to be all exhalation now, a single sigh coming out for an eternity with no sign he would ever breathe in again. His hands were cold, and she tried to unbuckle his breastplate, but it was caved into his body. She couldn't tell where it ended and Jason began. "Can't you just—?"

"Quickly, child, the beast is nearly away."

Night's Breath was so far now that Madeline didn't think they could catch him if they tried, and every second that passed he moved farther away. Then Jason's body went strangely limp, and Madeline shouted, "Yes, yes, do it!"

Gilenyia whirled and grabbed a spear from a soldier. She hurled it, and it flew across the field, impossibly far and fast. Madeline didn't know if it was the angle of the light, or if the sun glinted off the shard of metal at the tip, but for a moment the spear flashed like a bolt of lightning. It struck Night's Breath in the back of the thigh. He cried out and fell.

Gilenyia's people scurried across the field toward the Scim, their weapons at the ready. Gilenyia herself scooped Jason up from the ground, paying no attention to the blood that spread across her gown. She leapt across the field with the grace of Rondelo's stag, overtaking her own people and arriving beside Night's Breath before anyone else. Madeline ran as fast as she could, choosing her footing carefully so she wouldn't fall on any of the broken remnants of the day's battle.

Gilenyia knelt between the two figures, a bridge between the too-still form of the crushed human boy and the writhing, furious Scim. "Let me live!" Night's Breath shouted. "Lady, let me live!"

Gilenyia pushed the Scim down with her left hand and placed her right palm on Jason's face. A horrible sound, half scream and half defiant shout, echoed across the field. Night's Breath's face went slack. The tattooed whorls on his arms and shoulders faded as Madeline watched, and his chest fell still. He looked even more like a beast now that he was dead, his waxy lips falling back from the jutting yellow fangs, the skin of his face sagging toward the ground.

It made it worse, almost, to see Night's Breath like that. Like he was an animal and didn't know any better. That maybe the horrible things he'd said had all been brute instinct. Madeline's stomach dropped away beneath her, and she fell on her knees beside him. She leaned down beside the Scim. She whispered in his ear, "May the Peasant King welcome you today." Isn't that what he had said to the dead Scim woman? She couldn't remember the exact words.

A stinging slap knocked her face to one side. Her own hand flew to her cheek, which burned with the imprint of Gilenyia's palm. "The Majestic One gives you back your friend, and you speak the Peasant King's name? Such small decencies should be common sense."

"I didn't know," Madeline said.

Gilenyia's gaze did not waver. "Now you do."

Jason coughed, and his eyes fluttered. Madeline rushed to him. Gilenyia removed her gloves from her cloak and meticulously pulled them on, straightening each finger.

Jason opened his eyes, and they focused in on Gilenyia, who now stood a few feet away, the sunlight catching her pale hair. She looked glamorous and perfect despite the smoke and ash of the battle, despite Jason's blood on her gown. "I knew it," he said. "I've died and gone to Hollywood."

Madeline, beside herself with joy, threw herself onto him and hugged him, long and hard. "You're not dead!"

Jason frowned. "Madeline?"

She laughed and helped him to his feet.

He leaned on her for a moment while he got his balance. "I didn't even know you were one of my groupies."

"It has been a long day," Gilenyia said. "Return to your homes, all of you."

Jason seemed slow, almost dreamy, most of the way back to the city. He kept talking about his unicorn, needing to find his unicorn. Then he stopped, agitated. "Where's Baileya?" he asked. "Did you see her?"

"I don't know who that is," Madeline said.

"Baileya. And the burning girl. I can't remember her name . . . Schoola? Something like that."

"*Shula?*"

"Yes! They took her, Mads. They took her, and we have to get her back."

"They're long gone by now, Jason. It's been hours since they retreated."

Gilenyia looked back at them. "The Knight of the Mirror has given chase," she said. "He will not fail. They will soon be returned to us."

Madeline didn't answer. She looked away, pretended not to hear, though she desperately hoped it was true that the Knight would bring Shula home.

Jason's face darkened when he saw a group of people carrying a Scim body between them, throwing it into a large pile. "Something isn't right," he said.

Madeline squeezed his arm. "Let's get home."

"Something's wrong." He stopped short. He stared out across the field, toward the ridge the Scim had appeared on hours ago. "Does the name Night's Breath mean anything to you?"

"Night's Breath?" she asked, her heart beating so hard she could feel it in her throat. "Nothing," she said. *Nothing, nothing, nothing,* she said to herself, and kept saying it all the way back to the city walls. She promised herself never to tell Jason this one thing. To spare him, at least, knowing that he owed his life to a fallen Scim warrior.

There was a strange squeaking sound from somewhere behind them, like a balloon the size of a van squealing as air forced its way out. Jason perked up, a glint of light returning to his eyes. "My unicorn," he said. "I hear my unicorn."

Madeline turned to see a rhinoceros barreling toward them over the battlefield. She thought it was farther away than it was, because it was so small. It was about the size of a golden retriever, and it leapt up onto Jason, knocking him over and leaning against him like an overly affectionate dog.

"They shrank you!" Jason shouted. "This crazy magical battle. I can't believe they shrank you. It's good to see you, girl, good to see you." He scratched her ears and patted her belly. She wouldn't leave his side, practically tripping him as they walked the rest of the way to the city.

They passed through the shimmering golden curtain that awaited them at the city's gates. Hanali met them there with a jovial shout and a promise of a ride back to their homes. He clapped Jason on the shoulder and laughed along with him as he described discovering his unicorn was actually a rhinoceros, saying, "We have always called such beasts unicorns." His carriage came, and Madeline scarcely remembered climbing into it— rhinoceros and all—or the journey to Mrs. Raymond's house. She barely said good-bye to Jason. She didn't think he noticed, because two bloodied human boys came rushing up to him, cheering and jumping around and admiring his unicorn and congratulating him on his first battle.

Her room was empty. Shula's bed was perfectly made, like in a hotel room, like no one had ever been there. Mrs. Raymond brought Madeline a steaming wooden bowl filled with stew. Madeline set it on the wooden table under the window and sat in front of it for a long time. She kept thinking of the grey-skinned corpse that had been Night's Breath. *I did the right thing. I did the right thing*, she said to herself again. He was a monster, bent on destroying the world. He wanted only darkness and pain and death.

Which is what she had given him.

Outside the birds sang, and the sun shone as bright and clear as ever.

PART 2

In the desert, there are no paths.
In the desert, the way is made by walking.

A KAKRI PROVERB

15

SCARS

*Three things we cannot live without: clear water,
deep stories, a heart that is loved.*

A KAKRI PROVERB

✣

Jason woke up with his legs pinned to the bed by Delightful Glitter Lady. The affectionate rhinoceros had gotten into the habit of sleeping at his feet. He reached over and rubbed between her huge, rabbit-like ears, and she let out a contented squeak. He had learned in the aftermath of the first battle, twenty-seven days ago, that she hadn't been shrunk by the enemy but by their own side. The Elenil didn't see much use in keeping their giant animals huge except in battle. They were easier to feed and care for if they were smaller. Jason had been given a dial—a small, round, black device with a red piece of shell set in the center—that when turned to the left shrank Delightful Glitter Lady to about the size of a full-grown golden retriever. Mini Delightful Glitter Lady weighed about seventy pounds, and she loved to climb onto his lap and get her ears scratched.

The same dial, turned to the right, made her normal rhinoceros size, and then gigantic war-rhino size. This was the reason Jason's bed had been replaced the first time Delightful Glitter Lady had fallen asleep on it. The dial was turned too easily. According to Mrs. Raymond, war beasts were not allowed in the dorm rooms. But Jason figured, what were they gonna do, kick him out? Mrs. Raymond had told him multiple times this was a possibility, but he doubted it.

David Glenn had already left the room. He got up early. He said he liked to watch the sunrise, which was ridiculous because the sun never set, not really, in the Court of Far Seeing. But David said he could feel the change as the sun came up over the horizon, if not for the Sunlit Lands, for everyone else.

Kekoa, on the other hand, would sleep until forced out of bed. Jason leaned close to Delightful Glitter Lady. "Hey, Dee," he whispered. "Dee! Where's Kekoa?"

Dee's long ears perked up, and her eyes opened.

"Where's Kekoa? Where is he?" Jason mimed looking around, like he couldn't see his roommate sleeping twelve feet away.

Dee sat up, her thick, ropelike tail thumping against the blanket. "Where's Kekoa? Go get 'im!"

Dee gave a delighted snort, scrambled from Jason's bed, and flung herself across the room, flying up to land full force on Kekoa's back. She trumpeted in triumph, and Kekoa yowled in pain. "Ay, Dee! C'mon, tita, I was sleeping!"

"I got one," Jason said. He, Kekoa, and David had been playing a game. These first twenty-eight days, Jason was supposed to be learning all about the Sunlit Lands. In this game, Jason would mention something weird about the Sunlit Lands, and his roommates had to either (a) explain it, (b) trick Jason into thinking a fake explanation was a real one, or (c) admit they didn't know the answer. Jason got a point if he stumped them, and they got a point if they tricked him.

Kekoa pulled his pillow over his head. "It's too early, brah!"

Jason ignored him. "Why aren't there any Elenil kids?"

Kekoa pulled the pillow off his head. His hair was pointing in every direction. "Man, are you serious? You just now noticed that? You've been here a whole month."

"It's weird, though," Jason said. "No babies. No pregnant ladies. No toddlers or even teenagers. They act like Rondelo is a kid, but he's—what did he tell us?—three hundred years old."

David slammed the door open and shouted, "Good morning, roomies! The sun is shining!"

"It's always shining," Kekoa grumbled, then yelped when Delightful Glitter Lady jumped off him and ran, panting, to David.

David crouched down and scratched her behind the ears. "Hey there, DGL! I brought you something. I brought you—settle down now, it's right here, behind my back. Look!" David pulled out a gigantic handful of long yellow grass that the Elenil called sweetsword. It was Dee's favorite food. She leaned against David while she chomped on it.

Kekoa sat up. "Wu Song's got one."

Jason put his hands behind his head and waited for David to look at him. He paused for dramatic effect. "Why aren't there any Elenil kids?"

David snorted. "You just notice that?"

"He's slow," Kekoa said. "I noticed that my first week."

David grinned. "That Jason's slow? Or about the kids?"

"I did see a creepy kid in a mask my first day," Jason said.

"Ugh," Kekoa said. "That kid is the worst."

"Human," David said, nodding his head. "Been in the Sunlit Lands too long. He's all twisted around with magic."

"So why no kids?" Jason asked.

Kekoa and David exchanged looks. "The Scim took them," David said. "Sixty years ago, the Scim kidnapped all the children, and they put a curse on the Elenil so they can't have any more."

Kekoa rubbed his jaw. "It's why they're such terrible enemies. Scim took all their kids, brah. No way the Elenil can forgive that. Not only did they take them away, they wouldn't let them celebrate Elenil holidays, or learn the culture at all. They made them into Scim, too."

David flopped onto his own bed. "Pretty terrible."

"So the Elenil are going to keep fighting the Scim forever, you know. There's no way out of that one. No path to forgiveness."

"Whoa," Jason said. "That makes sense. That's gotta be true."

Kekoa and David burst into laughter, jumped off their beds, and high-fived each other. "That's a point for us, Wu!"

"What do we have now, seventeen points?"

"Sixteen," Jason mumbled. "I thought for sure that was the real story. It sounded so convincing."

David picked up a ball from beside his bed and threw it against the wall. It bounced back to him, and he threw it again. "Happened often enough to the Native people. My grandpa got taken off the reservation, sent to a missionary school, and whipped if he spoke Crow. They cut his hair, wouldn't let people do the traditional dances, and wouldn't let them wear their regalia. Couldn't be any religion other than Christian, either. They even had a saying, 'Kill the Indian, save the man.'"

Jason sat up and grabbed the pudding cup by his bed. It was always within reach when he woke up. He should have put spoons in the deal too, because there wasn't ever one nearby. He saw a dirty one from yesterday on the floor, so he rubbed it clean on his blanket and started eating. "Yeah, right. You don't get points for tricking me about Earth history, only Elenil history."

David caught the ball he'd been throwing and sat still. He didn't say anything at first, and a weird silence fell in the room. Kekoa didn't move except to turn his eyes toward Jason. Even Delightful Glitter Lady stopped, as if she sensed danger, her ears perked up, her eyes still. Jason paused, a bite of chocolate pudding halfway to his mouth. A pit opened up in his stomach. He didn't know any stories like David's, but he should have realized it was in the realm of possibility. Was it really any different than what had happened to his own family not so long ago? "Uh-oh," Jason said. "I assume that actually happened."

"Man, you should know that's not a joke," Kekoa said. "Didn't they teach you anything in history class?"

Before Jason could reply, David spoke. "My grandfather," he said, "was of the Apsáalooke. The Crow people. He was whipped for speaking our language. When I was a kid, I didn't want to learn it. I heard the elders speaking it, and a lot of the other kids even, but I always liked English, you know? My cartoons were in English. School was in English. But my grandfather, even when I was little, he would point at the sun in the morning, and he would say áxxaashe. He would wake me at night and show me the bilítaachiia. He would cup his hands in the river and hold it up to me and say bilé. Some of the other elders, they didn't feel right speaking our language. Grandfather said they still 'felt the whip' when they spoke. They'd speak it sometimes, but they felt pale eyes watching them. When I was eight years old, Grandfather called me into his room, and I helped him take off his shirt. He showed me his back, and he said, 'When I was your age, I earned these scars.' That's what he said, he *earned* them. 'I earned these scars,' he said, 'so you could learn the tongue of your elders and ancestors.'" David stared out the window, and the strange atmosphere in the room slowly lifted, like a fog evaporating. "My grandfather fought to keep our language alive. After that I never complained."

"Whoa," Jason said. "That's intense."

David shrugged. He pointed to a tiny scar in his left eyebrow. "See this?"

"Yeah."

"Kid named Billy skimmed a rock at me across a pond, and it sailed up and clipped me. I always thought he did it on purpose. Point is, though, I wouldn't remember Billy skipping rocks that day without a mark on my skin. Scars help us remember. I remember the missionary schools because of my grandfather's scars. That's an important thing, Jason. That's something to ask yourself. One of your weird questions. *Why don't the Elenil have any scars?*"

The answer flew into Jason's mouth. It was so simple as to be self-explanatory. "Because they heal all their wounds right away with magic."

David got up, threw his ball to Kekoa, and opened the door to their room. "Nah, man. It's because there's something they're trying to forget."

The door slammed. Delightful Glitter Lady jumped and snorted. She watched the door for a few moments, and when David didn't come back in she trotted over to Jason and leaned against his legs.

"We better get dressed," Kekoa said.

"I feel bad, man. I didn't mean to upset David." Today was Jason's last day to wear white. At the ceremony tonight, the Bidding, they called it, he would be able to wear clothes with color in them again.

Kekoa rolled out of bed, already in a pair of jeans and a T-shirt. He had a habit of going a couple days in a row in the same clothes, even though there was a magic laundry hamper. You threw your clothes into the hamper, and they returned, cleaned and folded, to your drawer within forty-eight hours. Jason had no right to judge Kekoa's clothing choices, though. It looked like someone had been using white clothes to build a nest around his bed. He scooped them up and shoved them all into the clothes hamper, forcing the lid down over the top until he heard the tiny pop that told him they had disappeared.

"He's not mad at you, brah," Kekoa said, doing a quick smell check on his T-shirt. "It's just . . . Man, you know the teachers at his grandfather's school? They didn't have any scars, either. You know what I mean?"

Scars. Jason's entire chest had been crushed. That's what they told him, anyway. He barely remembered it. There wasn't a scar or any other indication he had been hurt. There was a sort of echoing memory of something called Night's Breath. He wasn't sure what it meant. Madeline wouldn't talk about it, and Kekoa and David both said they didn't know what it was. It sounded almost like one of the Elenil names for a plant. He wondered what it was, what it looked like, and why he couldn't get those two words out of his head. Another nagging theory kept trying to make room in his head too, but he didn't want to think about it. He was curious, yeah, but he felt conflicted, too. Maybe it would be better if he didn't know exactly what had happened. Still, he lay in bed at night and turned the words over and over in his head, trying to find a new way of hearing them, some unattainable insight.

Kekoa said, "Why didn't you believe David when he told you about his grandfather?"

Jason paused, considering this. Since his vow to be completely honest, he had found questions about his own motivations difficult to answer. Sometimes he didn't understand his own decisions, and it took time to think them through. Other times the motivations were too complicated—ten different reasons, all intertwined. Some more important than others, yes, but he hated to give an incomplete answer. So why hadn't he believed David? One, he was tired of being fooled by Kekoa and David's answers about the Sunlit Lands. He felt like a fool, guessing at weird trivia about a magical and sometimes illogical place. They had just tricked him with their fiction about the Elenil's children being stolen by the Scim, and something about that rubbed him the wrong way. He was sick of the lies and exaggerations. He worked hard to be truthful, and he didn't understand why other people couldn't do the same thing. Second, he had to be honest, in some way the idea that the United States of America would systematically and purposefully destroy another culture seemed unlikely. Which was so ironic, so hilarious, because he had evidence of it in his own life, in his own family. But somehow he had bought into the lie that things must be different for everyone else, that his experience was the exception, not the norm. There was this voice in his head saying, *That can't be true, that's not the American way!* And that voice was keeping him from seeing what was true. But Jason wasn't letting lies stand in his life anymore. He was rooting them out, replacing them with the truth.

Jason finally said, "I didn't want it to be true."

Kekoa nodded. "I get that. David told me once that some Native Americans didn't get the right to vote in the US until—I can't remember—the 1950s or 60s. I told him there was no way that was true. I mean, black people had the right to vote a hundred years before that almost. But he explained that the Native people weren't even allowed to become US citizens until the 1920s."

Jason didn't know why it surprised him. He knew the history of the Chinese immigrants to the United States. It was only a month ago that he had lectured Madeline about it, and the Chinese hadn't been allowed to become citizens until the 1940s. He shouldn't be surprised by these things, but the honest truth is that he was. These sorts of facts went against his cultural narrative, the story he'd been told about the land of the free and the home of the brave. The stories had an almost fantastical quality to them, as if they had happened long ago and far away in some fantasy world, not decades ago to their great-grandparents. And, yeah, black people—or black men, anyway—got the right to vote a hundred years before Native people, but then a whole system built up around preventing that, which was part of the point in the Civil Rights movement in the 60s.

So of course David's story was true. Even a moment's reflection should have told him that. The problem was that he hadn't taken a moment to reflect before opening his big mouth. "I'll apologize," Jason said.

He stood at their window. Baileya was on the grassy field outside the dorms, running. Her leg was healing. The guys said the Kakri healed faster than humans, but still, it had only been a few weeks, and she was out there with a walking stick, practicing a strange lope that allowed her to move fast by using the stick as a crutch. He didn't know how she kept going when she had been hurt so badly, or why she refused to use the Elenil healing magic. It had completely restored him, after all, and in a matter of moments. But there she was, a month after breaking her leg, trying to stay in fighting shape and overcome the battle effects of just one night in the war. *The scars help us remember*, that's what David had said. Jason put his hand against his unmarked chest. No scars, but he still remembered. *Night's Breath.* What did that mean? He couldn't shake it. He knew, from his own bitter experience, that not every scar was visible. What happened with Jenny—that hadn't left a mark. No physical mark, anyway. But it had changed his life forever. Nothing could be the same, not ever.

Which reminded him of Madeline. He was supposed to meet her in the market to prepare for the ceremony tonight. Now that they had been here a full Sunlit Lands month, they were supposed to be inducted into Elenil society. They would get an assignment of where they would live, what their roles would be. They'd be allowed to wear whatever clothing they pleased. Jason hoped to be put back here with Kekoa and David, but that meant joining the Elenil army. He had enjoyed his one night in the war, and he loved the way some people still called him the Bat Slayer. But he had almost died. According to Madeline, almost died in the not-coming-back-even-with-magic kind of way. He wasn't sure he wanted to do that again. And Madeline had made it clear she was not planning to fight. Jason had come here to keep an eye on her. To watch over and protect her in the way he had failed to do with his sister.

"I have to meet Madeline," he said to Kekoa.

Kekoa grinned at him. "Hold up, man. David is gonna be back in a minute with a present."

"A . . . present?"

"Yeah, we planned ahead and—"

The door opened. David stood there, holding a flat white box.

"I'm sorry—" Jason started, but David interrupted him.

"You believe me now?"

"Yeah."

"We're good then. But you have to learn to listen when someone speaks their heart."

"Right," Jason said. "Sorry." Relief washed over him. He realized that he had been worried, on some level, that David would stay angry at him, that he had somehow permanently messed up their relationship. But they were better friends than that. There was room to mess things up and still be friends.

"Kekoa and I had something made for you," David said. "An outfit for the ceremony tonight."

Jason took the box, laid it on the bed, and pulled off the lid.

The first sight of the outfit assaulted Jason's eyes. It was garish. Awful. Ridiculous. "It's horrible," he said, pulling it out of the box. "I love it."

16
THE BIDDING

"Has your boon brought you happiness?"
the Peasant King asked.

FROM "RENALDO THE WISE," A SCIM LEGEND

+

The tattoo on her wrist was growing. There were times Madeline could see it pulsing on the edges, small tendrils curling outward, moving farther along her wrist, snaking toward her palm. It was nearly two inches wide now. She kept it covered, a surprisingly easy thing to do here in the Sunlit Lands. She hadn't mentioned it to Jason. She had been about to, and then he had whipped his gloves off to share some theory of his that the designs in the tattoo reflected the magic one used it for, and she saw how thin and delicate his tattoo still was. For some reason it gave her pause. It made her nervous to share with him.

Every day, Madeline woke up alone, staring at Shula's perfectly made bed. They still hadn't found Shula or the guy who could fly, Diego. The Scim hadn't returned to battle since the night they took Shula, and although the Elenil knew where the Scim lived, knew where the army had gone, there was no sign of her. The Knight of the Mirror had ridden out two weeks ago looking for her and had returned yesterday, empty handed and grim. It made it difficult to celebrate today, which is what she was supposed to be doing.

She had chosen a sky-blue dress. The collar came just to the hollow of her neck, and the skirt fell nearly to the floor. It had half-length sleeves, but she had matching gloves to pull over her arms. It was a relief not to wear all white, but she was nervous about the day. She had been told what to expect by Mrs. Raymond. There was a sort of market, and Elenil citizens would mill around, meeting the new arrivals. People would propose to take humans like her and Jason into their households. This was called the Bidding, though no money exchanged hands. This would define what their role would be in the Elenil city and where they would live. Mrs. Raymond's dorms served as home only to new arrivals and human soldiers.

If she was taken into an Elenil house, she might be changing linens, serving food, or caring for gardens. Or helping the Elenil with their own duties, which could be a position of high status. If Gilenyia, for instance, took Madeline into her household, people would treat Madeline with enormous respect. Gilenyia had implied more than once that she was considering it, which caused Hanali to hyperventilate, imagining all the wonderful balls and parties they would be invited to attend. He would get a great deal of honor as a result of having been the one who chose Madeline and brought her to the Sunlit Lands.

However, the idea of living with Gilenyia distressed Madeline. Every time Madeline was with her, she couldn't help but remember what had happened with Night's Breath and Jason. She couldn't help but remember that she had been the one who made the decision—the Scim's life for her friend's. She hadn't told Jason, but he knew something was wrong. She didn't think he knew how the healing magic worked, or at least not when someone had been mortally wounded, but he suspected something. Because the Scim had not returned since the first battle, there hadn't been any need for more major healings.

Instead, she and Jason had been thrown headlong into a sort of training curriculum from Hanali. History, manners, and fashion. Mostly manners, with a strong running commentary on fashion. Hanali seemed particularly concerned about Jason's performance on all three topics and how that would reflect on him. They had time for other things too. She and Jason had spent some time with his roommates when their schedules matched up, which wasn't often. She had been "loaned" to Gilenyia more than once for an afternoon, to "assist" in healings of illnesses and minor injuries, which largely meant doing precisely what she was told. A few afternoons had been spent walking in the market or standing on the city walls with Jason, but mostly they had been kept busy, focused, and overwhelmed with fatigue. She fell asleep as soon as she touched her bed at night.

"Pay attention," Hanali said.

The coach had stopped. Madeline had been staring out the window, blankly ignoring the wonders of the Court of Far Seeing. A crowd of coaches lined the avenue. Some were pulled by horses, some by strange, hairless beasts with round faces. An elephant lumbered past with what looked like an entire house on its back. Some strange creature with legs longer than a lamppost walked by, carefully lifting its legs and setting them down between the coaches, wagons, and people making their way. "I'm sorry," she said earnestly. "I know this is a big day for you."

"Yes," Hanali said haughtily. "As you know, you're not the only new arrival I have brought to the Court. I need to look after my other graduates as well."

"Like Jason," Madeline said helpfully.

Hanali's face clouded, and he sniffed at a handkerchief from his sleeve. He mumbled to himself, "Where is that boy?"

"He'll show up."

"That is precisely my fear, dear girl." Hanali stepped out of the coach and handed Madeline down. "As for you, be sure to remember what I have taught you regarding manners."

This is where Jason would have said something rude and funny, Madeline thought. She wished he was here. Despite Hanali's constant assurances otherwise, Madeline was nervous something terrible was about to happen. *Only eleven months to go*, she told herself. Eleven months and she would be back in the real world. Back with her family, back with Darius, back in her own house. She would be able to breathe, and she could pick up her life where she'd left off. Yes, she'd probably have to start her senior year of high school over, but it would be worth it. It would be worth all of this.

They ascended a wide marble stairway along with a thousand other people. No one noticed her at first, but then, to Hanali's delight, a human saw her, gave a little cry of alarm, and scurried off into the crowd. "Someone has sent their people to keep watch for you," Hanali said. "An excellent sign of what is to come."

The building at the top of the stairs was set on a broad marble square. There was plenty of room for people and creatures to mill about, and that is what they did. One large creature, at least twelve feet tall, turned and looked at Madeline with yellow eyes the size of saucers. It had wide, pointed ears, and greenish-brown hair, like moss, covered its entire body. The hair was longer on its arms and legs and moved softly in the breeze. Madeline had no idea if this was another magical race of Sunlit Lands people or someone's pet. She still had a lot to learn.

Most people in the crowd were Elenil dressed for a party. Strange oversize hats, shining gowns, and canes seemed to be the prevalent style. Hanali wore a long red jacket that buttoned to the waist, then opened in an inverted V, the tails dragging on the ground. He wore black pants beneath that and tall black boots. He didn't wear a hat. ("A calculated choice to draw attention in this era of overgrown haberdashery.") Humans and colorful birds flitted among the Elenil, delivering messages and running errands.

Hanali led Madeline toward the building beyond the square, a rectangular marble edifice with Greek-style columns on the outside. The building seemed almost pedestrian compared to other things she had seen in Far Seeing. Until they passed the columns.

The ceiling disappeared, replaced by the vault of the sky. A river wended through the building, surrounded by graceful white trees with golden leaves. Living tables, made by cleverly interweaving the branches of some sort of bush, grew up from the ground. Matching chairs grew next to them. Birds darted back and forth among the people, occasionally flying off to the dark woods in the distance. There was no evidence they were inside a building. "This is the Meadow at World's End," Hanali said. "Historians tell us it was here that humans first made the choice to leave the Sunlit Lands. Between those dark trees in the distance lies a way back to your world. The humans gathered here, their belongings packed upon their backs, and made their final farewell to the world of magic, becoming the powerless, dry people you have known. It pleases the archon and the magistrates to welcome our newest citizens here, as a reminder that you have chosen to come home to us."

All told, there were about thirty other human teenagers who were there. They all wore clothing like Madeline's, covered from head to toe in the style of the Elenil, the women wearing ball gowns and the men in formal wear of various kinds.

"Ah, a fair one," said a voice to their left. An Elenil woman stared at Madeline through a monocle held up to her face. "It would be diverting to have her in one's home. She looks nearly Elenil."

Hanali bowed deeply. "Were she not so young, lady, I daresay she might be mistaken for one of us."

"Indeed," said the woman. "Well done, Hanali, that you found such a child and brought her here."

Hanali bowed his head slightly. "It is an honor that you would consider bidding upon her, lady."

"She's a package deal, though," Jason said, strolling casually into the clearing. To say his outfit was an assault on the eyes would be generous. He wore a tuxedo with a frilled shirt, but the shirt was sunshine yellow. His pants had one bright-red leg and one bright-green leg. The jacket was baby blue on one side and pale green on the other. He had an orange top hat, and the whole ensemble was overlaid with sequins. The brim of his top hat had bells sewn into it, so when he cocked his head, it jingled.

The Elenil woman smiled politely at Hanali and moved along.

"What is this monstrosity?" Hanali hissed. He rubbed the material between his fingers. "What is this cheap cloth? I have never seen the like."

Jason twirled. The back panels of the jacket were still more colors. He looked like the place where rainbows go to die. "In my homeland we call this a tuxedo," Jason said. "They are very popular for weddings and prom dates."

Madeline laughed so hard her ribs ached. The astonishing garishness of the tuxedo went beyond anything she could have imagined. "I think you look dashing," she said, wiping tears from her eyes.

Jason swept the hat from his head and bowed low. "Thank you, my lady. And as you can see, your dress matches my jacket." He looked seriously at his jacket for a moment, as if trying to find something he had lost. "Riiiiight . . . *here*." He pointed to a pocket square on his chest. It was, indeed, the identical color of her dress.

"It does not even match itself," Hanali said. "You will change at once or suffer the consequences."

"What consequences? Our deal was that I had to come for a year and stay devoted to Madeline. If she wants me to change, I will." He turned toward her and adjusted his pink-and-green paisley bow tie with his gloved hands—one glove white, the other purple.

She took his hand, a wave of affection coming over her. "You look delightful."

Jason grinned. Hanali, unable to contain his despair, stalked off into the crowd.

Jason leaned close and said, "You know, I don't think that Elenil lady even needed a monocle. She was putting on airs."

Madeline put her arm through Jason's. "Putting on airs, huh?"

He nodded with great solemnity. "I heard that in a movie once."

A bird about the size of a parrot settled on Jason's head. Black feathers radiated out around its eyes, and emerald-green ones made a ridge down its back. "Your presence is requested," the bird said, "at the seat of the magistrates."

Madeline curtsied. "It would be our pleasure."

The bird turned its head sideways. "Only you are invited, lady."

Jason reached up with his hands, feeling the bird. "Is this a monkey or a cat or what? I can't see it past my hat."

"A bird, sir!" The bird ruffled its feathers. "A cat! How impertinent."

"More impertinent than sitting on someone's head?" Jason wondered aloud.

"Follow me," the bird said and, with a great deal of flapping and fluttering, leapt from Jason's head, knocking his top hat so aggressively Jason had to use his hands to keep it on.

Madeline gathered her skirts and did her best to follow the bird's path, but between the uneven ground, the other people in the crowd, and the trees they had to weave between, it was hard going. Jason helped as best as he was able, giving her his hand when necessary.

The bird sat on a branch and called back to Jason, "You are not invited, sir!"

Jason snorted. "I doubt a bird is in charge of the invitations."

The bird ruffled its feathers. "On your own head be it if you should anger the magistrates."

The magistrates were the rulers of the Court of Far Seeing. This had been drilled into Madeline and Jason during their lessons, so that they would not make a social faux pas in the presence of the leaders. There were nine of them, with three who were considered "first among equals." One, the chief magistrate, was known simply as the archon. The archon was named Thenody. Another magistrate was called the polemarch: Tirius, who was in charge of the army of Elenil. Then, lastly, there was the basileus, Prinel, who oversaw celebrations, rituals, and remembrances. Another six magistrates, equal but lesser, oversaw day-to-day matters, problems, and difficulties within the Court of Far Seeing.

The bird led them along a forested path that descended into a ravine. A stream ran through the center. Madeline had a dizzying moment when she tried to think about whether they were still inside a building or if they had somehow been transported outside. Ahead of them lay a tower, tall and stark white, with a stairway that grew along the outside edge like ivy. There was no railing. The bird perched on a stone at the bottom of the stairs. "They await you on the highest observation deck," it said.

The thought of climbing those stairs in this dress did not sit well with Madeline. The stairway was narrow enough that her dress would brush against the wall on one side and hang over the precipice on the other.

Madeline said, "I don't think I can climb in this dress without falling. Maybe they could come down here and talk."

The bird studied the tower. "It is not so high."

"We don't have wings," Jason said. "What we do have is a rather distressing relationship with gravity."

"Very well," the bird said. It paused and looked at Jason. "You carry a magical artifact with you?"

Jason, surprised, said, "You mean my pudding bracelet?"

"No," the bird said. "A dial. For animals."

Madeline furrowed her brow. Jason had mentioned the dial, but

Madeline had tried to convince him not to carry it around after he had accidentally enlarged Delightful Glitter Lady in the marketplace and crushed
a vendor's stall. Delightful Glitter Lady had been trying to get her mouth
around a pink fruit of some kind. She had eaten about forty of them before
Jason had gotten her shrunk down again.

"It's for my unicorn," he said, pulling it from a multicolored pocket. "It
doesn't work on birds."

"Nonsense," the bird said. "Only touch it to my beak."

Jason did so. The bird told him to turn the dial to the right, and he did.
The bird was now the size of a two-person glider. "Hold my tail," it said,
"but do not let go until your feet are on the ground."

"Maybe I'll take the stairs," Jason said, but he put his hand on the tail
next to Madeline's.

The bird flapped three, four, times and then lifted slowly. It swept up
and around the tower, and the ground fell away. They were over the trees
in a moment, then making their way in lazy, looping circles toward the top.
Something magical was at work—holding the bird's tail seemed to require
no effort at all. Madeline's hand didn't ache, her arm didn't feel like it was
holding any weight. She felt only exhilaration at flying and excitement to
see the world stretched out below her.

"Your hat!" Madeline called. The horrible top hat had been swept away
by the wind, its bells chiming merrily as it spun toward the ground.

"We'll get it later if we survive!" Jason shouted, but by then they had
landed, the bird making a windstorm that swept over the assembled Elenil
on the tower's top. The view from here was astounding. Distant mountain
ranges rose out of a misty sea of evergreen trees. Madeline couldn't imagine
they were still inside a building, but distant, wispy clouds, on second look,
appeared to be enormous columns, larger and taller than the tower they
stood upon. It was as if an entire nation had been shoehorned into a single
enormous room.

Arranged before them were eight Elenil: the magistrates. Madeline
hadn't met or even seen them before this moment. They wore, if it was
possible, more clothing than the typical Elenil. More layers, certainly, and
their collars crept up the back of their necks and furled out into giant fins
behind their heads. In the center sat a ninth magistrate who was completely

covered in a thin gold cloth, draped as though over a piece of furniture. Even the face was obscured. This figure stood when they let go of the bird's tail.

There was a strange Scim standing near them, his hair in a ponytail. He wore Elenil clothing: long sleeves, gloves, a waistcoat, and trousers. He didn't have tusks like many Scim, but instead had small, regular, white teeth. He stood straighter than other Scim Madeline had seen, and his small black eyes watched her with something like mirth.

On the floor in front of him was a second Scim. This one was in chains. His greasy hair fell around his face, and black swirls of tattoos covered his bare chest and arms. He grinned, and his yellow, crooked teeth and jutting tusks made Madeline shiver. His eyes fell on Jason and a low, guttural laugh came from his wide mouth. "Wu Song," the chained Scim said. "Then this must be your friend Madeline Oliver. A pleasure to make your acquaintance."

Something about the way he said it conveyed a different message. The words were polite, but Madeline could see from his face that he meant her harm.

"Uh-oh," Jason said. He grabbed Madeline's hand, then snatched hold of the bird's tail again. "Fly, fly!" he shouted.

But the bird didn't move, and the Scim's booming laugh shook Madeline to the bones.

17

THE MAGISTRATES

Elenil rule from Far Seeing,
in lands by our master bequeathed.
The Majestic One keeps all in his sight,
Elenil first in the warmth of his light.

FROM "THE ORDERING OF THE WORLD," AN ELENIL STORY

✦

Jason yanked on the bird's tail feathers several times. "Stop," the bird said and knocked him backward with a well-placed wing stroke. Grumbling to himself, Jason pulled out his dial (which apparently worked on birds, too!) and shrank the bird to parrot size. He paused, then turned the dial all the way to the left and the bird shrank again, to the size of a sparrow.

"Now try to knock me over with your wings," Jason said.

Madeline's hand was on his arm. He straightened his jacket and tie.

"You were neither invited nor summoned," one of the magistrates said. He wore a blue robe and a small gold circlet on his forehead. "You may leave us now."

Jason crossed his arms. "Yeah, well, the magic bird says no. Besides, were *you* invited or summoned?"

The Elenil stiffened. "Magistrates are not summoned!"

Jason shrugged. "Invited, then?"

"Certainly not. A time was set, and I was made aware of it. I arrived at the appointed time."

"That's how I got here," Jason said. "I heard about the meeting, then I came to the meeting."

"Enough," the archon said. At least, Jason assumed he was the archon. The guy in charge. The boss of the Elenil. He was completely covered by a gold sheet. He looked like a ghost from a poorly done Halloween costume, minus the eye holes. Only fancier, because he was golden. In Jason's experience, the guy with the goofiest outfit might just be in charge.

The archon continued, "We have gathered with a specific purpose, and it is not to banter with children or our lessers."

Break Bones sneered at those words.

"Let us do this quickly, that I may return to the festivities," said another Elenil, this one in a close-fitting silver sheath, his blond hair braided, a wide hat on his head.

"We shall take the necessary time," the archon said. "Do not worry, Basileus Prinel. Your party will await you when you are finished here."

"What's the deal with the weird Scim?" Jason asked.

Prinel bristled. "You forget yourself, human. Show the proper respect. Would you care to be sent back to the human lands?"

Madeline gave him a warning look, but Jason put his hands in his pockets and said, "I've lived up to my end of the agreement. It never said I had to be respectful of the Elenil."

"You agreed to be in service to us," one of the magistrates hissed. "Respect is demanded as part of your service."

"Nope," Jason said. "I never agreed to that. I'm here in service to Madeline." He bowed his head in her direction. "All respect to you, milady."

A moment of furious whispering broke out among the magistrates. "Show us your bracelet," one of them said.

Jason pulled up his sleeve, and a magistrate studied his tattoo carefully.

"The boy speaks the truth. No pattern here suggests the Elenil are even mentioned in his terms."

Break Bones laughed heartily. "Oh, how I like you, Wu Song. It pains me that I have promised to deliver your friend's corpse and utterly destroy you."

"Promised to what?" Madeline cried.

"Long story," Jason said.

"Hanali will face brave punishments for this unorthodox recruiting," Prinel said. "Thenody, what say you?"

Jason racked his brain. He remembered the name Thenody. Hanali had specifically said to remember that one because . . . Oh yeah. Because that was the archon's name.

"Enough," Archon Thenody said from beneath his golden sheet. "I have said it once, will you make me say it again?"

All fell silent.

Thenody sat down in a high-backed chair. "Bring Hanali forward."

A door opened in the floor of the tower, and Hanali ascended to the platform, followed by the Knight of the Mirror. Jason got the idea that the knight's presence was some sort of threat. The knight's sword was buckled to his belt . . . No one else in this place carried a weapon. Hanali wore a slight, peaceful smile on his face. Beside them came a small girl, no more than eight years old, who wore a ragged dress and a long swath of cloth wrapped around her eyes.

Hanali turned his face toward Jason so the other Elenil could not see him, gave a fierce, furious scowl, and mouthed, *Say nothing*.

Hanali bowed. "Your most august Excellencies."

"You are young," Thenody said. "But surely not so young that you would bring a human into the Sunlit Lands without professions of loyalty."

Hanali's gaze flicked to Jason. "An oversight, Excellency. It shall not happen again. It must be admitted that he is, at least, entertaining?"

Thenody sighed. "Perhaps he does bring the frustrations of childhood into our presence once again, after all these centuries."

Prinel spoke up again. "We have heard rumors among the people that this girl, Madeline Oliver, has been prophesied to bring justice at last to the Scim. Is this true?"

"True that you heard it, my lord? I can only assume yes."

"Do not play games, Hanali. It is well known that you invent prophecies for your recruits."

Hanali flinched as if struck.

"Please," Prinel said. "Spare us the theater. How many girls have you brought to us saying they were messiahs or saviors, warriors or soldiers, who would bring justice to the Sunlit Lands?"

Hanali studied his gloved hands. "No more than ten." An outraged gasp came from the magistrates. "Ah, wait. I've forgotten the twins from the Congo. Twelve, then."

Jason said, "What, only girls can save the Sunlit Lands?"

Hanali's eyes bugged wide, his scowl sharp enough to slice a cement block in half. He mouthed, *Be silent.*

Prinel, sarcasm dripping from his voice, said, "Hanali. Twelve is the full number, I assume. You did not do the same thing with your male recruits?"

"In my defense, Your Grace, you did ask how many girls . . ."

"Very well, how many boys have you brought and done the same? Said they were the ones who would save the world? Or bring justice to it?"

Hanali cleared his throat. "Thirty-eight."

"That's fifty," Jason said.

Hanali gave him an exasperated glare.

Madeline said, "So there's not a prophecy about me?" She looked relieved. Almost ecstatic. But Madeline had told Jason the storyteller had prophesied the same thing.

The magistrates clumped together in a tight group, murmuring among themselves. The strange Scim stood to the side, keeping a careful eye on Break Bones. Hanali folded his hands across his stomach. The magic bird fluttered over to the girl with the blindfold and whispered in her ear. The Knight of the Mirror produced a small handheld mirror from somewhere and gazed at himself with rapt attention. Wow. He really was conceited.

"If there's no prophecy," Madeline whispered, "maybe they'll let us go home. Maybe they'll still let me breathe and send us home."

Hanali raised an eyebrow. "The Elenil follow their agreements to the letter, miss. They will not return you before the human year passes."

"Are you in trouble, Hanali?" she whispered.

Jason snorted. "These people can't get dressed for a party without talking to a prophet. Hanali will be fine."

Madeline punched him in the arm. "Show a little compassion. He could really be in danger."

The magistrates straightened and resumed their places. Archon Thenody spoke first. "Before the magistrates take further action, Hanali, son of Vivi, we shall consult with an oracle."

Jason felt smug. "Told you."

"However, we will not allow Madeline Oliver to be bid upon tonight. We have . . . certain concerns that our friend Sun's Dance has brought to us."

Hanali inclined his head. "I eagerly anticipate hearing his thoughts."

The strange Scim took hold of his lapels with two massive grey hands. "I have heard a rumbling among my people—the Scim in this city. It is said the Black Skulls seek a human girl who cannot breathe. It is said they wish to remove her from the Court of Far Seeing."

Break Bones spit at Sun's Dance. "Traitor."

Prinel sneered at Break Bones. "Traitor? Because he has walked out of the darkness and into the light? Because he has left behind a life of poverty? He rejected the foolish excuses of your kind and became something better. Do not judge him for it."

The girl with the blindfold spoke. "Did I hear Break Bones threaten Madeline Oliver? Is that sufficient evidence the Scim seek her death?"

Break Bones laughed. "That is a promise I made to Wu Song and has nothing to do with my people."

Madeline raised her eyebrows and looked to Jason. He laughed nervously. "Long story," he said again.

"A story we must needs hear," Prinel said.

Jason sighed. This whole not-telling-lies thing was getting him in a lot of trouble. "I snuck in through a magic door and talked to Break Bones. He said he would kill Madeline before he came to kill me."

"How did he know of Madeline at all?" Hanali said, his voice high and tight. His eye twitched. Jason hadn't seen that before, and he thought he had angered Hanali in every way possible.

Jason blushed. "I told him I'd come to the Sunlit Lands to protect someone. He asked her name, and I told him."

Break Bones roared with laughter. "He is a strange little beast, is he not? I shall raise a glass in his honor when he is no longer in the world."

Madeline's hands curled into fists. "Wasn't your promise that you would kill me first?"

Break Bones grinned. "Indeed. I told him I would bring your lifeless body as a warning that his own time had come."

Madeline put her arm around Jason. "Then he doesn't have much to worry about, because a miserable, sad little ogre like you won't stand a chance against me."

Break Bones roared with laughter, rattling his chains. Sun's Dance yanked on the metal collar around Break Bones's neck, choking him into silence. "You see, my lords. We cannot trust my countrymen to behave like civilized people. They do not know any better. They are uncouth and vile. They know only darkness, and is it their fault? No, for they do not know the Majestic One, having heard only the corrupted tales of our kind."

Archon Thenody raised his arms, lifting his golden sheets as if he were a kid on Halloween trying to scare his friends. "It seems clear we cannot risk the girl in the Bidding. What if the prophecy is true? No, even Gilenyia would not protect her well enough for my peace of mind. I think she must come to the Seat of High Seeing and serve in my household."

Hanali swooned with excitement, and Jason grabbed him by his jacket to hold him up. Hanali said, breathlessly, "Of course, Your Greatness, if you think it best for her to serve in your estate, we would be only too happy. She is quite fair for a human and could even pass for an Elenil. More than one Elenil has mistaken her for one of us. See how pale her skin is? And her hair, like gold. She's quite lovely for a human."

Madeline was watching Hanali as if he were a refugee from a mental hospital. "What if I prefer not to go with Archon Thenody?"

Hanali's eyes flew wide. "A joke!" He laughed uncomfortably. "A joke, Highness. Ha ha."

"I am serious. What if I prefer to enter the Bidding? I would rather go with Gilenyia and learn the art of healing."

"An art that could be learned in the house of the archon as well as in Gilenyia's," Hanali hissed.

Thenody stood. From the look of things, he was trembling beneath his robes. Jason guessed it was a big insult to reject his offer of living at his palace. *Some people are so sensitive.*

"You will do as you are told," Thenody said, his voice shaking nearly as badly as his robes. "Or you will face the consequences of breaking your contract!"

He made a twisting motion beneath his robes and reached out to Madeline. She gasped and took a wheezing breath. She fell to her knees, struggling to breathe.

"What is wrong with you?" Jason shouted. "Let her breathe!"

"It's her own fault," Thenody said. "Disrespecting me, the leader and head of the Elenil! Speaking back to the archon! She has forfeited her agreement! She cannot treat me thus and expect our magic to treat her well."

Jason knocked Hanali aside and advanced on the archon. The Knight of the Mirror did not move to intervene. His eyes flickered toward Jason but then returned to his mirror. Jason grabbed hold of the golden sheet with one hand and swung his other fist at the general location of the archon's head.

Thenody stepped back, pulling his sheet out of Jason's hand. He pointed at Jason, twisted his arm, and said, "I will remove your magic as well!"

Jason punched Archon Thenody in the midsection, and he flew backward, landing in a heap on the ground. "Now you're stealing my chocolate pudding?" Jason shouted, and leapt toward the pile of golden sheets.

But a stunningly fast Elenil in light armor intervened. He threw his arm in front of Jason, catching him just below the neck, and drove him onto the stone floor of the tower. With a two-handed shove he threw him back against Break Bones. "If you strike the archon again," the Elenil said, "I will run the girl through with my own sword. I swear this on my name, Tirius, and on my title as polemarch and commander of the armies of the Elenil!"

Archon Thenody rose, his golden robes disheveled, and moved toward Madeline, who was gasping, her face bright red.

Hanali fell to his knees and bowed his head. "My lord. Surely she has learned her lesson."

"Not yet," the archon said, his voice expressionless. He turned toward the knight. "What of you? You did not move to protect my person?"

The knight didn't look up from his mirror. "I am sworn to fight the Scim. I do not fight my own kind."

The archon drew a furious breath and unleashed a torrent of abuse on the impassive knight. Madeline lay on her back now. Jason had to do something. The archon was going to let her die like a fish, flopping around on the ground, breathless. He couldn't attack Archon Thenody, not directly, because Tirius claimed he would kill Madeline himself if Jason made a move.

He heard the guttural laughing of Break Bones close behind him. He turned away from the furious monologue of the archon. "What are you laughing at, Break Bones?"

"Your friend dies, and the Elenil war amongst themselves. They brought me here to show you the terrors of the evil Scim, and instead they entertain me."

A way out, or at least a chance at a way out, opened up to Jason. He would have to play it just right, though. "I took you to be a person of honor. How disappointing to be proved wrong."

Break Bones stopped laughing and leaned his wide face closer. His rotten breath, hot and foul, washed over Jason's face. "What mean you by this brave insult, Wu Song?"

"You told me you were going to kill Madeline and bring me her body. But here you sit, letting the Elenil make a liar of you."

The smile faded from Break Bones's face. He glanced at Madeline with sudden concern, then to the archon. He shook the chains on his wrists. "These chains prevent me from my oath."

Jason frowned. "I didn't realize the word of a Scim was worth so little." He pulled the dial out of his pocket. "I'm wondering if this magic dial works on people."

Break Bones grinned. "Ah, boy, I will rue the day I feast upon your bones. But do not use the magic upon my flesh, but rather these chains. I will save the girl, so that I may slay her later."

"It only works on animals, you know, not on chains," Jason said. But he touched the dial's casing against the chains and turned the dial to the right. The chains grew larger, and Break Bones slipped his hands free. Jason looked at the dial and the newly gigantic chains. "Huh. What do you know?"

Before standing, Break Bones slammed one massive fist into Sun's Dance's knee, sending him sprawling to the ground. He leapt to his feet with astonishing speed, and bounded to Thenody's side, wrapping his great, tattooed hands around the archon's neck. The sheet bunched above the archon's head, then flared out over his body, making him look a lot like a badminton shuttlecock. The archon's tirade cut off mid-word.

The Knight of the Mirror drew his sword.

"Ah, have a care, Sir Knight, lest I squeeze the archon in fright," Break Bones said. He shook the body beneath its golden sheet. "Release thou the girl, O valiant soul."

The archon, trembling, twisted his hands. Madeline gasped as air flooded her lungs again.

"Leave the magistrates unharmed, and I will allow you a five-minute lead," the Knight of the Mirror said. "Then I must follow and destroy you."

"Sporting, sir," Break Bones said. "Sporting indeed. In five minutes I could not even exit this grand building. No, I think another plan will be necessary. First, throw your sword from the tower."

The knight hesitated, then did as he was told. The sound of metal clanking against stone echoed up to them as the sword bounced against the tower, and then silence. "Nothing can be taken from my hand unless I allow it," the knight said. "It is a boon granted me some years ago."

Break Bones nodded. "I have heard tales of that magic."

"I give my word I will escort you safely to Scim territory. I will put my hand upon your arm. Your life will be in my hands, and none but I could take it. Only release Archon Thenody."

Break Bones grinned. "*Your* word I trust, sir. And Wu Song's. Perhaps the girl, should Wu Song vouch for her. The rest of these here—I would sooner trust a hungry wolf to guard my pigs. No, I have a plan in mind that will serve me better." He pulled the archon close against his chest, and there was a distressed yelp from beneath the golden sheets.

Madeline, still gasping and on her knees, looked up. "What are you going to do, Break Bones?"

Break Bones looked to the knight. "Give me your word that neither you nor any here shall leave this tower until I am safely outside the city walls."

"You have it," the knight said. "So long as you promise, on your honor, not to murder any citizen of the Elenil nor any human on your exit."

"Done," the Scim said triumphantly. "Now, Wu Song, lend me that bird you have shrunk, that I might send word when I am safe."

"It's not my bird," Jason said. Jason noticed Tirius shake his head, fast, when Break Bones wasn't watching. Tirius was meant to be the head of the Elenil army, but he hadn't done anything to help so far.

The bird said, "I will not help you, Break Bones. Indeed, as soon as you leave this place, I will fly to find the guardians of the city, and we will fight you from here to the city wall. If all goes well, you will be in chains again in an hour's time."

"I feared you would make some foolish speech," Break Bones said. "So I am forced to make a hard choice." He looked around at the gathered magistrates, the archon struggling weakly in his massive hands. "Are there no healers here on this tower top?"

The girl in the blindfold spoke. "None, save Madeline, and she has not been trained."

Break Bones turned his back to the Elenil, and with swift motions he folded Archon Thenody in unnatural directions, snapping appendages and collapsing ribs. He dropped the magistrate's still form in front of Tirius.

Jason's stomach lurched. He was thankful, suddenly, for the sheet, but even so he could tell what lay beneath was piled in a horrible shape. A keening cry came from beneath the golden covering.

"He will not die," Break Bones said, "so long as the bird goes for a healer rather than for the army. So I have kept my word." He bowed to Madeline. "You I shall see again." Then to Jason, "You have the heart of a Scim warrior. I give you humble thanks for my release."

He leapt from the side. Jason ran to the edge in time to see Break Bones grab the tower, his thick arms straining as they arrested his descent. He climbed down with unbelievable speed then loped across the plain below.

"Fly and warn the army," Tirius shouted to the bird.

"Shame," the knight said. "Shame on you and all the magistrates if the life of one Scim is worth more than the life of the archon, first among equals. The city will hear of this. They will speak of it for decades to come."

Prinel put his hand on Tirius's arm. "It is true, Tirius. The archon must come first."

Tirius shouted in rage. Break Bones was nearly to the exit now. "A healer first, and then the army. Fly with all speed, bird!"

The bird fell like lightning from the tower, then extended its wings and flew.

"Now there is nothing to do but wait," Prinel said, crouching beside the archon. He reached out a hand toward the golden cloth, then withdrew it.

Hanali cleared his throat. "If I may be so bold, it makes a great deal of sense to me that Madeline Oliver go to live with one of the nine magistrates."

Tirius barked a laugh. "Will you send the human traitor with her too? He released a Scim upon us!"

"He was killing my friend!" Jason shouted. He wasn't going to let that happen. He wasn't going to stand by and wring his hands when Madeline was in danger. If that meant folding the archon down small enough to fit in a suitcase, so be it. If that meant unleashing Break Bones on the world, that's what he would do. He didn't regret it for a moment.

"He is the lord of the Elenil and thus, your master. He can do as he pleases," Prinel snapped.

"My *master*?" Jason stalked over to the pile of golden sheets and, before anyone could stop him, grabbed hold of the fabric and prepared to yank it off. "I'm not anyone's slave! I'll throw him off this tower before I'll—"

"Jason, stop!" Madeline shouted.

Her voice stunned him. Her face was pale and creased with worry. He wouldn't really have thrown the archon off the tower. At least, he didn't think so. He had been doing the right thing, protecting Madeline. It infuriated him to have that questioned. He wouldn't have thrown him off the tower, though. They shouldn't have said the archon was his *master*. He wasn't some slave. He wasn't here to serve the Elenil. He was here for Madeline, pure and simple. But it was Madeline telling him to stop now.

He dropped the sheet. "He's not my master," Jason said. "Also, he better turn my pudding delivery back on, or I *will* drop him off a tower."

"Well," Prinel said mildly. "It seems clear the archon's estate will not be a safe home for these humans."

Tirius watched Jason closely. "He could not have harmed Thenody much. He has the anger of a warrior. Perhaps I will take him on, train him together with Rondelo."

The girl in the blindfold spoke. "The Scim will target Madeline, this much seems clear. To put her with the magistrates increases the risk to her and to them. The Knight of the Mirror should take her. Nothing can be taken from his hand unless he wills it. She will be safe in his household."

Tirius rubbed his chin. "An elegant solution, and delivered by a seer. What say you, Sir Knight?"

The knight gazed into his mirror, murmuring to himself. After a long moment he turned his attention to the Elenil. "I will take the girl under my protection. She will serve out her contract with me, in obedience to the Elenil and according to the terms of her bargain."

"And me," Jason blurted.

The knight shook his head. "You are too unpredictable and unwise. I cannot take you into my home."

The blindfolded girl tugged on his sleeve. He leaned down, and she whispered in his ear. His face, stony and impassive, did not change when he straightened. "I will take the girl," he said, "and also the fool."

Jason sputtered. "The *fool*?!"

Hanali whispered in his ear, "Bow, fool, if you wish to stay with Madeline."

So Jason bowed, and Madeline curtsied, and just then a healer came rushing up the stairs, and the bird told them the Scim warrior had left the city much faster than the city guard could be alerted. Released from the knight's agreement with Break Bones, Hanali grabbed Jason and Madeline by the arms and pulled them to the winding stairwell that led down alongside the outer wall of the tower. Hanali went first. Madeline descended holding her skirts with one hand and Hanali's shoulder with the other to keep herself from being pushed off the stairs by her voluminous dress. Jason followed.

"That could have gone worse," Hanali said when they were at the bottom, mopping his brow with a handkerchief. He gave Jason a dark glare. "It also could have gone much better."

That seemed like a fitting motto for Jason's entire time in the Sunlit Lands so far.

18
WESTWIND

Look at the walls, so bright and fair,
each stone placed by a master builder.

FROM "THE DESERTED CITY," A KAKRI LAMENT

✦

Mirrors stared at Madeline from every room in the knight's castle. A full-length one stood in her bedroom—a room with a flagstone floor, a fireplace large enough to stand in, and a wide, stone-framed window open to the world outside. A meticulously woven carpet covered the floor beneath her bed and spread out several feet beyond on all sides. The bed itself wore a silk canopy and stood on sturdy legs made of a dark wood unlike any she had seen at home.

To Madeline's chagrin and, for some reason, Jason's unending delight, there was no magic bathroom. Instead, they used something called a garderobe. The garderobe, a room scarcely larger than a closet, sat perched over the moat around the castle. A wooden bench with a hole in the middle sat atop a stone floor with a hole in the middle and—well, she missed the magic toilets.

No magic was allowed in Westwind. That's what the Knight of the Mirror had named the castle, though Madeline wasn't sure why, because it stood on the eastern edge of the Court of Far Seeing. Out Madeline's window towered proud, distant mountains, the deep green of a forest at their feet. The blindfolded girl had told her that the break in the mountain range was called the Tolmin Pass. The pass led to the Kakri territories. The Kakri came through once a year to trade stories, if you dared to sit with them. They were a violent and unpredictable people, according to the girl.

The blindfolded girl was named Ruth Mbewe. She had come to the Sunlit Lands four years ago, when she was only four years old. She was the youngest human Madeline had seen in Far Seeing. She wouldn't answer questions about her eyes, but almost any other thing she would gladly talk about at length. Why wasn't there magic in Westwind? Because the Knight of the Mirror forbade it. Why? He did not like magic. It had done great harm to his family. Why was there a castle inside the walled city of Far Seeing? The knight had brought it with him. The answers to her questions, delivered so matter-of-factly, often made less sense than the thing being questioned.

No magic meant Madeline did her laundry by hand, with hot water brought up from the kitchen fires. Filling a bathtub with hot water took more work than Madeline cared to do, so she had taken to sneaking out of the castle every few days and bathing in her old room at Mrs. Raymond's house. Jason had apparently given up bathing, which was doubly unfortunate since the Knight of the Mirror would not allow Delightful Glitter Lady in the house. No magic meant no shrinking Dee, so she had to be kept in the stables at regular rhino size. Jason bunked in the straw beside her.

Their host, the knight, haunted the halls. He often rode out on his silver stallion, Rayo, in the early mornings, through the eastern gate. He never went as far as the Tolmin Pass, not that she had seen, and she had watched from her window more than once. Sometimes he rode through the heart of Far Seeing. When he rode west, he might not return for several days. He would not answer where he had been, but Ruth said he rode into Scim territories, seeking the captured human soldiers. Seeking Shula.

More than once, Madeline came across the knight in some dark hallway of the castle, standing in front of a full-length mirror and muttering to himself. He carried a hand mirror on his person at all times. For all the time he spent in front of the mirror, he seemed to care little for his appearance. He wore his dark hair long, usually tied into a ponytail, thick streaks of grey painting the sides. The dirt and mud from his long rides sometimes caked his gaunt, lined face for days at a time, as if he couldn't be bothered to wash with a hot rag. Yet he stared into the mirrors at all hours.

Madeline wanted to escape the mirrors. They followed her like flat silver eyes watching everywhere she went in the castle. Sometimes she would catch movement out of the corner of her eye and turn to find only another mirror, another image of herself staring back. Sometimes she thought she saw reproach on her own face . . . and she knew she must have been thinking about Night's Breath.

She asked Ruth if she could cover the mirror in her room with a sheet. It was a strange moment, watching the little girl with the blindfold standing in front of the mirror, a sheet in her hands. Her head was tilted to one side, as if listening intently to someone speaking in a far room. Then with one swift motion, she threw the sheet over the tall mirror. "He won't come into your solar," Ruth said.

"What?"

"Your solar. That's what a room like this is called. Here, on top of the tower, your own room."

"Oh, I've heard others say that. I meant, what do you mean, he won't come in here?"

"The knight," Ruth said. "But if he does, you must pull the sheet off the mirror."

"Why so many mirrors? He seems almost afraid to be without one."

For once, Ruth did not answer. She hesitated. "It is not my story to tell."

Ruth talked like someone who had been born in the Sunlit Lands, taking on the peculiar formality of the Elenil. It shouldn't be a surprise, with her having arrived here so young. Madeline had asked Ruth once what she had agreed to in coming here, and she'd said, "A year's service in exchange for being saved from a massacre in my town." Madeline had asked what happened at the end of the year. Why was she still here? Ruth had simply put her tiny hand on Madeline's and said nothing. The knight, she assumed, had taken Ruth in after that.

Madeline couldn't imagine electing to stay here when her year was up. It was an amazing place, yes, full of strange beauty and terrifying dangers. She missed her parents, though. She missed her parents, and Sofía, and Mr. García. She missed Darius, and now that she could breathe again, she wanted so badly to see him, to be with him. She hoped after she and Jason jumped the fence to go into the drainage pipe that Darius had decided to wait for her. It was only a year, after all. But he had no way to know what was happening here, and she had no way to tell him. She hoped he still felt the same . . . And of course, she had broken up with him, so there was no reason for him to wait. No reason other than maybe he loved her.

She yanked the sheet off her mirror. A flicker of movement caught her eye, but when she focused on it there was nothing there. Since coming to Westwind she had been allowed to wear whatever she liked. But it wasn't the T-shirt and jeans or her pale hair she noticed. The silver glint of her magic tattoo held her complete attention. In the last few weeks it had spread further. It grew from her wrist nearly to her elbow in a looping, tangled design like ivy. The tattoo snaked across her palm and curled around the base of her fingers. She wore gloves even when she was alone with other humans now. Jason didn't know, hadn't seen yet, what was happening. She had tried, ten days ago, to ask Hanali about it, but when she started to tug her glove off, he had averted his eyes and firmly pulled it tighter onto her hand. Her only thought now was to ask Gilenyia, but she didn't completely trust her, and she wasn't sure the Elenil woman would answer honestly if it was to her advantage to lie.

In the aftermath of Break Bones's escape, she and Jason had been more or less under house arrest. They could wander the hallways, the kitchen, the great hall, and the grounds of Westwind, but they couldn't leave the castle walls without permission. There were chores to be done, of course. Stone floors to wash. Tapestries and rugs to beat with a broom, trying to get the dust out. Laundry. Dishes. Stalls in the stable to be mucked (a task left most often to Jason because of his insistence on remaining with Dee). But when she had a free moment, what she loved to do was climb one of the towers and watch the city outside Westwind's walls.

Someone knocked on her door, loud and insistent. Madeline threw the sheet over the mirror and pulled on a jacket to cover the spread of the bracelet on her forearm. She kept her gloves in her pocket when she wasn't wearing them, now. She slipped them on before opening the door.

Jason stood outside, panting. "Let's go," he said.

"What is it? What's wrong?"

"The knight just came in through the eastern gate. He's headed this way. He sent a messenger bird ahead." Jason shouted this over his shoulder, already running down the winding tower staircase.

"What's happening?"

Jason stopped, gasping for breath. She was in much better shape than him—she had taken to running every morning along Westwind's walls, early, before everyone else got up—and he had just run up the stairs too. "Shula. He found Shula."

"What?" She ran past him, taking the stairs two at a time. Jason yelled for her to wait, but she couldn't, she just couldn't stop. She burst out the bottom door of the tower and raced through the great hall before speeding across the courtyard and toward Westwind's front gate. Although the knight had come in through the eastern gate of Far Seeing, there was only one gate into the castle compound, on the western side. So he would be riding around the entire property to get in.

Ruth was at the gate, a somber expression on her face. A ten-foot-tall mirror stood at the entrance. She held her palm up as Madeline came rushing forward. "You cannot leave Westwind."

"Is Shula okay?"

Ruth raised her face toward the sunlight. "I have seen a path for you, Madeline. It is narrow and treacherous, and on every side the possibility of injustice, pain, and heartache. Remember the advice given you by the lady in the garden."

How could Ruth possibly know about that? "I passed out as she said it. I didn't . . . I don't remember her exact words." It was something about changing the world. *Change the world, change the . . .* She couldn't quite remember.

"I walked in the garden beside Archon Thenody's palace today. The Garden Lady came to me through a grove of trees. I could smell the citrus on her skin. She asked me to remind you. She said, *To change the world, change first a heart.*"

Yes! That was it. To change the world, change first a heart. She had no idea what it meant, but she remembered it now. She wouldn't forget again.

The Knight of the Mirror appeared, galloping across the cobblestones, a blanket-wrapped form in his arms. He dismounted at the gate's threshold, placing Shula gently on the ground. Madeline dropped to her knees beside her old roommate. Shula's hair was tangled around her face. The scar on her face looked pale, and her cheeks sank under her black-rimmed eyes. A sizeable bruise bloomed beneath her left eye. She shivered as the blanket fell from her shoulder, and Madeline quickly covered it again. "Help me get her inside," she said.

"I fear she will need a healer," the knight said.

Madeline, confused, shouted, "Let's get her to a bed while we're waiting for the healer."

Ruth said softly, "The Knight of the Mirror does not allow magic within the walls of his castle, Madeline."

Jason arrived and flopped on the ground, gasping for breath. "Made it," he said.

"Jason, I need you to run for a healer," Madeline said.

"But—"

"*Look at her, Jason!*"

"Okay, okay," he said, climbing painfully to his feet. He stepped across the threshold of the gate, but the Knight of the Mirror blocked his path.

"Sir Knight, you have to let him go," Madeline said. "Unless—have you already sent word?"

"I cannot entrust you—either of you—to the streets of Far Seeing. There are too many Scim here as servants or even as reformed citizens. I do not know which can be trusted and which may wish you harm. You see what they have done to your friend."

"No offense," Madeline said, "but the only way you're going to stop us is if you harm us yourself."

"Gilenyia comes," Ruth called.

The Elenil woman swept up the street, resplendent in a red dress and white elbow-length gloves. Two Scim flanked her, looking a great deal like the strange one they had seen on the tower on the night of the Bidding.

A "civilized Scim," as Hanali called them. One carried a leather satchel, and the other two carried long sticks wrapped together with cloth.

The Knight of the Mirror did not greet Gilenyia. He stood before the gate mirror, speaking under his breath, his fingers running through his hair. He seemed unconcerned now for Shula or Madeline or Jason or anything at all.

Gilenyia surveyed the scene. "Ah. The burning girl has returned to us. Day Song, set up my work space. New Dawn, prepare yourself." She spared a glance at the knight. "Gone into some other world," she said. "Madeline, I require your assistance."

The Scim rolled the cloth out from between the two long sticks, forming a sort of wall. He looked behind himself, as if gauging the amount of room, and drew the cloth out further. He took a ninety-degree turn, then another, then another, and formed a sort of square out of the cloth, which seemed to keep coming no matter how far he pulled it. In a matter of moments he had made a ten-by-ten room, complete with a cloth roof and a folding door. Madeline followed Gilenyia inside. Two long, flat beds had somehow been set inside already. Day Song entered, carrying Shula. He set her down on one of the beds. New Dawn lay on the other and closed her eyes, breathing deeply.

Shula moaned. Her skin burned, and she flinched when Madeline touched her.

"You are not to live with me," Gilenyia said. "And yet I wish to teach you as much as I may about healing. You know how this process works, do you not?"

Jason had followed them in. "What is going on? Is this place sanitary? Did you people even wash your hands?" He was rubbing his hands, bouncing from foot to foot. She hadn't seen him so nervous before.

Madeline nodded. "I know how it works."

"Then remove your gloves," Gilenyia said, her voice even and calm. "It is time for you to try your own hand at healing."

Madeline hesitated, then looked at Jason. "Maybe you could wait outside."

"Ha," he said. "I've seen your naked hands about a million times. They might not understand it here in the Sunlit Lands, but you and I were *chemistry partners* back in the real world. That's a pretty tight bond, you know. Covalent, even."

Fine. There was nothing to be done about it then. At least she wouldn't have to hide it from him anymore. She pulled her right glove off, and then the left. Jason gasped when he saw the silver tracings curling up over her fingers.

"Whoa," Jason said. "How did you get—"

"Hush," Gilenyia said. "Let her concentrate. Sit in the corner."

Madeline put one hand on Shula's chest. Her heart beat distant but strong, and her body felt feverish but otherwise normal. She put her right hand on New Dawn, who convulsed lightly at the touch, then fell still. She almost asked if New Dawn was doing this willingly, but what difference would it make? For Shula, she would do this again, just like she'd done for Jason with Night's Breath on the battlefield. And, yes, she would allow Gilenyia to teach her how. In this strange world of Scim and Elenil and masked children and giant wolves, she needed to be able to protect herself and her friends without relying on knights or Elenil or anyone. The sight of Shula's broken body told her that much. She couldn't go along with the flow, trusting everything was going to be okay. She was going to take care of her own friends.

"Now," Gilenyia said, "reach out through your bracelet. Find Shula's bracelet and use that to guide you to where she is broken."

Her bracelet. It was more than that now, though, wasn't it? It was a sleeve. A glove. She felt power rush through her, like hot liquid into the veins of her tattoo. The magic reached into Shula but found only flesh. No magic, no connection. "It's not working."

"Take hold of her bracelet," Gilenyia said. "Perhaps that will make it easier."

She moved her hand to take Shula's wrist, and instantly, like water pouring from a bucket, felt her power move into a flow with Shula's magic. She felt the branching, slow growth of her magic join in with the sudden bonfire of Shula's. Shula's felt jagged, bright, terrifying, and dangerous, where Madeline's was slow, consistent, building to something.

Moving past the magic, a deeper connection eased into place. Madeline's face ached from Shula's bruises. She felt the fever, the cracked dryness of her lips and tongue, the skin of her face. She was badly dehydrated. Her legs hurt so much she could scarcely keep from crying out. Taking a single breath took a week's energy. It hurt to move her eyes.

Then, somehow, an even deeper well. Shula Bishara. She didn't know anymore if that was her name or someone else's. She remembered her baba and mama, her little sister, her big brother. She saw a building collapsed into rubble and people pulled from the wreckage, the color of dust and blood, some still breathing, others laid out in a careful line. A tank sat outside their home, firing shells at the other side of the city. She remembered the little Christian church her family attended, and how crowded it became as the refugees flooded from one side of the country to the other, and how even Muslims filled the pews, desperate for a bag of rice, a roll of toilet paper, a place to lay a sleeping bag. The soldier's knife which had cut her face flashed beneath the streetlight. Her neighbors in the fire leapt out of the flames, towels and scarves covering their faces.

"You've gone too deep," Gilenyia said softly. "Come back. Now take New Dawn's wrist."

Gilenyia's voice came from so far away, and untangling her own hands and arms and thoughts from Shula's took a moment. She reached her right hand over, taking New Dawn's wrist. The moment she touched the inky tattoo of the Scim, it sucked her in. A gravity pulled at her, taking her deeper into the Scim woman's world.

New Dawn's body pulsed with strength. It had been bridled, controlled, and channeled by the Elenil, but she had strength enough to tear a person into pieces. Nothing hurt. Nothing ached. Her heart beat steady, regular, in perfect time. That strength reached through Madeline, questing. It touched on Shula's pain, her aches, her broken places, and latched onto them, urging them to flow back through Madeline's body and into the Scim woman.

Madeline pinched the connection. She didn't want to do that, not yet.

She wondered if she could go deeper, like she had with Shula. It might be good to know the Scim better. She pushed on the link to New Dawn, but instead of a deeper connection she found a wall—long, thick, and impenetrable. Gilenyia was saying something to her in the world outside, but she could not make out the words, nor was she trying. A weak spot in the wall caught her attention. She couldn't break it, but she could squeeze into it, she thought.

Her name was not New Dawn. That was her "civilized" name. Her Elenil name, so they would know she bowed the knee to them. Nor was it Shatter Stone. That was her war-skin name. Her true name she would not share, not even here. It was not right that the human asked for this, too, when she was giving so much already. In time she would heal . . . faster than a human. Gilenyia would credit her, and she could help her family in the Wasted Lands. One more humiliation, one more burden to carry so the human children could frolic and live without consequence. So give her the pain. Did Madeline think she could not shoulder pain? Did she not know the Scim? This exploration, this hesitancy was more painful than the healing itself. She would not wait any longer.

The sucking gravity from New Dawn increased. It pushed through Madeline and felt for the pain. Felt for broken places and fear, touched on fever and aches. Madeline's own pain increased. The bruise under her eye, hot and swollen, pierced her with blinding pain, then slid to New Dawn. The fever crept through her. The aches and throbbing, the brokenness passed through their connection like swallowing glass, leaving behind only a bone-deep exhaustion.

New Dawn tried to take even that.

Let me keep at least the tiredness, Madeline thought. *Let me carry that one small piece.*

Another presence glided into their shared space. Cold and ancient as a shark, unblinking, and revealing nothing of itself. Madeline's connection to New Dawn broke in a terrified moment, as if a magnet which had been attracting another magnet had flipped and now pushed her away.

Madeline gasped, her eyes flying open, just as Shula sat up, also gasping. Gilenyia's bare hand covered Madeline's. New Dawn lay on her back, her face bruised, one eye swollen shut, glaring at Madeline with the other.

"Do not go so deep," Gilenyia said. "Not with your friends if you can help it, and never with a Scim." She leaned toward New Dawn. "Did she harm you?"

New Dawn closed her eyes. "She shouldn't have gone so deep, mistress."

"Indeed not. Are you well?"

"Of course, mistress."

Gilenyia gave Madeline an appraising look. "Well then, take your friends and run along to the knight."

Madeline stood halfway before her legs gave out. Jason rushed to her and helped her to her feet. "I can help," Shula said. She stood, obviously shaky herself, and pulled Madeline's other arm over her shoulder.

Gilenyia tapped her fingers to her lips, then pulled her gloves on. "New Dawn. Did you neglect to take the exhaustion from the girl? To heal someone is quite taxing, and this was her first time."

New Dawn's eyes flew open. "Mistress, she would not give it to me."

"Hmph. Very well. I will adjust your credits accordingly."

New Dawn glared at Madeline again, but she could scarcely keep her own eyes open. Jason pulled back the flap on the tent, and the three of them made their way out, a hodgepodge of legs and arms, like people in a three-legged race. The Knight of the Mirror stood at the gate, still looking at himself. He dragged his gaze away unwillingly, but when he saw Madeline's state, he came to them and scooped her into his arms like a drowsy kitten.

"One more thing," Gilenyia said. "I happened along here because I was sent by the archon. He desires to see you both again. He requests your presence tomorrow night at the palace. I trust you will be rested by then, Madeline. Next time, do not be so foolish as to shoulder a Scim's burden. They are able to carry more than a human."

Perhaps Gilenyia was right. The knight carried her through the castle grounds and the castle itself, and then up the long stone stairway to her solar, where he laid her on her bed. He noticed the sheet over the mirror, frowned, and pulled it off.

Shula, who had just returned from captivity and a hard desert journey, sat by Madeline's bed. Jason sat outside the door and could not be persuaded even to go to the stable, and Ruth fell asleep curled beside him on the stone floor.

"A human can carry quite a lot when they must," the knight said before leaving her room, as if correcting Gilenyia, or maybe praising Madeline. It was the last thing she heard before she slept.

In her dreams that night, Madeline shuddered at the memory of the cold-eyed presence of Gilenyia during the healing connection. She shuddered and pulled her covers close. She cried out, and only the gentle reminder of Shula sitting beside her bed calmed her. She slept again, and remembered it only as a vague unease when she woke.

19
MUD

If truth is not your companion,
death walks beside you.

A KAKRI PROVERB

✦

Jason was not an idiot. He'd watched Madeline perform the healing and seen the bruises go from Shula to Madeline to the Scim. Which meant his own wounds, which Madeline had described as near fatal, had been transferred to someone else. He suspected the words Night's Breath were significant in this regard. His chest had been caved in, that's what Madeline had said. Could a Scim survive that? He knew they healed faster than humans. He suspected that Night's Breath was a name. He wondered if there was a way to meet him, the Scim who'd saved his life. The other possibility—that Night's Breath had died as a result of Jason's wounds—filled him with unimaginable dread. Madeline wouldn't do that to him.

"Pay attention," Ruth said.

He shook himself aware. Ruth Mbewe, the weird kid with the blindfold, held his arm with one tiny hand. He had stepped into a puddle on the road. Ruth, despite having her eyes covered, had stepped around it.

"It's amazing how not being able to see makes your other senses sharper," Jason said.

"Don't be ridiculous," Ruth snapped. "I have average smell, taste, and hearing. I just use them. Unlike you."

Jason closed his eyes and took a deep breath. He tried to sort through the smells of the Court of Far Seeing. He didn't smell anything disgusting, now that they had left Westwind behind. The toilets at Westwind were just holes in the floor that fell several stories into the moat, which smelled like something hairy had exercised vigorously before falling in and dying. It backed up Jason's First Rule of Magic: poop has to go somewhere. Those magic toilets in Mrs. Raymond's place weren't eradicating whatever went in them, they were transporting it. He didn't know how (that's what made it magic), but he suspected it wasn't going to the archon's palace.

The First Rule had a corollary as well: if it ain't here, it must be somewhere else.

He had been thinking about Delightful Glitter Lady. To magically make her huge required a stone or some other object to become small at the same time. He remembered this from physics class: conservation of matter. Mass and energy were constant in the universe. Or something. Maybe that was the Pythagorean theorem. Whatever. The point being there must be something, somewhere, that allowed Dee to get larger or smaller by taking on the opposite. So his magic dial wasn't an embiggenator so much as a transference device.

"Ow!"

Ruth had pinched him. "Pay attention, I said, and you immediately stopped in the street, closed your eyes, and let your brain wander."

"It's creepy how you talk like an adult. What are you, eight?"

Ruth frowned. "Meanwhile, you behave like a five-year-old."

Jason gasped. "How dare you? A six-year-old, at least!"

"Charming," Ruth said. "Walk us to the cloth merchant over there. The one to your right."

The knight didn't usually let him or Madeline wander the city unattended, but the archon had sent specific directions that Jason was not allowed to wear his multicolored tuxedo to the palace. He had been informed that the tuxedo clashed "with everything." So Jason had been sent into the city to buy new clothes. Ruth was his babysitter. She had a tiny leather pouch tied at her waist with the money, or whatever passed for money here in the Sunlit Lands. Being watched by an eight-year-old—a blindfolded one, at that— did not do much for his self-esteem. He didn't even get to hold the money. He stared at the heavy little coin purse. He could keep track of something like that if they gave him a chance.

A small, quick hand snatched Ruth's money satchel. Jason stepped away from Ruth and grabbed the little thief by the neck before he could escape. An unkempt Scim kid wriggled in his grasp. The kid screamed and thrashed, but Jason had a solid grip. "See? I was paying attention," he said to Ruth. Except she couldn't see, of course. Ugh. "I caught a pickpocket," he said.

"I hear him," Ruth said. "What is your name?" she asked the kid.

The ugly little thing scowled at her. He peeled his grey lips back, show-ing them his protruding yellow teeth. "Mud."

"Why are you stealing from me, Mud?"

"I'm hungry," he said. "We're going to buy some fruit."

Ruth took the leather satchel from Jason, slipped it open, and dropped a large metal coin in Mud's hand. His eyes widened, and he looked quickly at the blindfolded girl in a way that made it clear he suspected she didn't real-ize how much money she had dropped in his palm. "Thank you, mistress," he said, ducked his head, and ran across the street, where a small knot of Scim kids enveloped him. They disappeared into a nearby alley.

"That better not have been my top hat money," Jason said.

"Top hats have specifically been vetoed."

"Outrageous! Who does the archon think he is! This is a free country, and I can wear a top hat if I want!" He realized with a strange little shock that the Sunlit Lands were not the United States, and he was still fuzzy on the political setup. "Wait. *Is* this a free country?"

"It was Madeline who vetoed the hat," Ruth said. "She described your previous hat in great detail. All the girls in the castle were laughing. One girl nearly fainted."

"All the girls?" Jason asked. "Who's that besides you and Shula and Madeline?"

Ruth smirked. "That's who I was talking about."

"Philistines," he muttered under his breath. "Still. You shouldn't give little thieves like that money. You're just contributing to the problem."

Ruth's face went still. "You have never been poor, have you, Jason?"

"Who, me? No way. My parents worked hard. There's a reason I hardly ever saw them. But we had money."

"So what would you suggest that little ruffian do? How would he eat if I did not give him money?"

Jason sighed. "You could give him a job or something, I guess. Can we go buy my suit now, please?"

"You don't have any money," Ruth said. "How will you get a suit?"

"Why are you acting like this? Are you—?" Oh. Ruth had been poor. Maybe here, maybe back on Earth. But she had lived without money. Maybe she had stolen fruit to survive herself. Maybe she had been a pickpocket on the street. "I'm sorry," Jason said. "I am. But stealing is wrong."

"Of course it is," Ruth said, as if it was the most obvious thing in the world. "But can honesty fill a rumbling stomach?"

"I suppose not."

"No," Ruth said. "Now walk over to the fruit stand and steal a piece of fruit."

There was a fruit stand across the road from them, on the right-hand side. Jason could smell it from here, the rich, pungent smell of ripe citrus baking in the sun.

"Um," Jason said, "as your elder, I feel like I should set a good example by *not* stealing a piece of fruit." The stand had stacks of beautiful fruit carefully arranged. A human girl stood behind it. There were other stands too, selling other things—carpets, buttons, vegetables, and so on.

"You have never worked for your money," Ruth said, her head cocked to one side. It was more statement than question.

"I did chores at home."

"Chores." She rearranged the cloth covering her eyes. "I also did chores." She tapped her fingers against her lips. "That street thief has worked harder in the last month than you have in your entire life."

Jason laughed. "Okay, okay, I get it. Feed the street kids. That's fine."

"Bring me a piece of fruit," Ruth said. She faced forward, waiting for an answer.

She wasn't going to drop it. This whole thing was ridiculous. He took a quick look around and didn't see any of the city guards. A lot of them were humans, anyway, and he had met them when they all lived together at Mrs. Raymond's. Anyway, he lived with the Knight of the Mirror now. That should give him an out if he got caught. "What kind of fruit should I get?"

"Whatever kind you want," Ruth said.

"Fine, fine," Jason said. He left her standing on the other side of the street. He couldn't avoid the feeling she was watching him, even though he knew that wasn't possible.

The young woman running the stand said, "May the light shine upon you, sir. Can I help you?"

Jason surveyed the fruit. An amazing variety of beautiful fruits were perfectly arranged by color. Oranges. Apples. Pineapples. A few things he had never seen before. "What's that one?"

"Addleberries. They only grow here in the Sunlit Lands."

"Ohh, what's that?"

"Guanábana. From Costa Rica." Huh. That was interesting. They must have some sort of deal set up. Or trained birds that flew fruit back and forth. Or, well, who knew in this place? Maybe they had magic penguins who carried the fruit in little backpacks.

"Is that a durian?"

"Yes, it's an Asian fruit."

Jason knew durian. They were gigantic, almost basketball-sized fruits with hard spikes covering the outside. If a durian fell out of a tree and hit someone, it could absolutely kill them. If you broke one open you would be greeted by a pale, creamy fruit that smelled like a gas leak. It was the worst-smelling edible thing Jason had ever run across. Strangely, the taste was sweet, despite the horrific smell. Most public places in Asia (like the subway) had rules about transporting durian because everyone—even people who loved the fruit—agreed that it smelled like corpses.

Jason debated what to steal. He could take a grape. Technically that would fulfill Ruth's request. The star fruit and the kiwi looked pretty good.

On the other hand, walking across the street with a giant spiky monstrosity of a fruit made a lot of sense. Ruth should be able to smell that thing coming, and it would serve her right.

He picked up a durian, then "accidentally" knocked a few lemons over. When the girl bent to pick them up, he turned his back so she couldn't see the spiky baby he cradled to his body and crossed the street.

"Sir!" the girl called. "You forgot to pay!"

Jason shoved the durian into Ruth's arms, then turned around to look at the produce girl. He shrugged. "I didn't forget!" he shouted. "I stole it!"

The girl put her hands on her waist and shouted back, "Then I'll call the city guard."

"I think you should," Ruth called.

"Hey!" Jason said. "This whole thing was your idea!"

The girl let a small green bird loose from her shop, and it darted into the heart of the market.

"You should run," Ruth whispered, pressing the durian into Jason's hands.

Jason stared at the gigantic thorny fruit. "Doesn't that make it worse?"

A roar came from the crowd, and an Elenil guard riding a tiger appeared. "He's looking for you," Ruth said. "Don't you wish I had given you a coin to pay for it now?"

Um, the police had tigers? He had seen Rondelo's stag more than once, but tigers? That changed everything. Jason ran, hands over his head, the durian bobbing above him, a stinky reminder of his thievery. "Make way!" he shouted, weaving through the crowd. The cries of people startled by a fast-moving tiger grew closer and closer. He ducked into a perfume shop but was immediately ejected. They didn't allow durian.

Ahead of him he saw a familiar shape—Rondelo, the captain of the guard, standing beside his white stag, talking to another citizen. "Rondelo!" he shouted.

Then Jason rolled to the ground, wrapped in a snarling, heavily muscled tiger. When the nausea-inducing spinning ended, he was on his back, the tiger was on his chest, and the durian was still in his hands, extended over his head.

The Elenil guard loomed over him, hand on his sword hilt. "Hello, citizen. What is that in your hands?"

"Where were you when that Scim kid was trying to steal our money?"

The guard narrowed his eyes. "We will come back to that, sir. What is that in your hands?"

"It's not a weapon, if that's what you're asking. I see why you might think that."

"Sir. Did you steal that fruit?" He sniffed twice, taking in the odor wafting off the durian. "Also, why?"

"I did steal it," Jason said earnestly. "Your tiger won't eat me, right?"

The guard grinned. "Not unless I give her permission. She follows the law, do you understand? You would like her to follow the law, right?"

"Yes," Jason said.

At a signal from the city guard, the tiger moved off his chest. "Go back and apologize, and pay for what you've stolen. Do not do that again. You do not wear the white any longer, you should know what is expected of you."

"Yes, sir."

The guard smiled at him, his perfect white teeth gleaming. "Now. What is this about a Scim stealing from you?"

"Oh, we took care of it," Jason said. "Just some kid named Mud, but we worked it out."

The guard snorted. "Mud. He is well known to the guard. I will speak to him." The guard pulled Jason to his feet.

"Like I said, we worked it out."

The guard stared at him, as if he couldn't understand the words coming out of Jason's mouth, then wandered into the crowd with his tiger.

Jason let out a long breath of air. Whew. His hands were shaking. He had almost been mauled by a tiger for stealing a durian.

Rondelo clapped him on the back. "You have run afoul of the city guard. That is Sochar. He is a hundred years my senior, but with a mercurial temper. I keep a close eye on him. You met him in good spirits." He laughed. "He has a soft spot for humans. Be glad you weren't a Scim!"

Jason could smell the tiger still, even over the constant stench of the durian. "What's the worst that could have happened?" Jason asked, doing his best to sound brave, like the whole event had meant nothing to him. "He'd take me to jail?" A memory rose of Break Bones, chained to a dungeon wall. Jail here might be a different experience than on Earth.

"He could have taken your hand," Rondelo said. "Or killed you if he thought you a threat."

Jason's stomach dropped into the soles of his shoes. Ruth was going to get an earful. Well. At least he could introduce everyone back at Westwind to durian. Honestly, it tasted great. It would be funny to watch them gagging on the smell before they tasted it.

He found Ruth in the center of the market, haggling with a merchant over a pair of pants. She had already bought him a shirt, jacket, and gloves. She didn't need his sizes, she told him, because she already knew.

"Did you know I could have died for this durian?"

"Yes. It was foolish to steal it."

"Well, I learned my lesson. No more listening to Ruth Mbewe!"

Ruth gave the merchant some money and handed Jason the pants. "We have your clothes now, so let us return home."

Jason kicked the cobbled street. "I need to go apologize to the fruit-stand lady and pay for my fruit. The guard said I had to."

Ruth's eyebrows raised from behind her blindfold. "But where will you get the money, Wu Song?"

"I was hoping from you."

"Maybe I will offer you a job," she said, her voice grave.

"I get it, I get it," Jason said. "Now give." He held his hand out, and Ruth dropped a coin in his palm.

The girl at the fruit stand smiled when he apologized, and Ruth gave her a handsome tip on top of the cost of the durian.

On their way home, Jason noticed the little gang of Scim kids again. They were gathered at the mouth of an alley, eating oranges. There were peels discarded all around them. Some of them sat on the curb, juice running down their chins as they shoved pieces in their mouths, while others stood against the wall, peeling segments of orange away and popping them in their mouths. "Better keep a hand on your purse," Jason muttered.

Sochar came from the other direction, his tiger at his side. They had a lazy gait to their walk, as if they were out for an afternoon stroll. Jason knew that look. They were about to hassle the Scim kids. Sochar had his hand on the hilt of his sword when he walked up to the kids.

"Where did you get that fruit?" Sochar asked, nudging Mud with the toe of his boot.

Mud gave him a surly look and kept eating.

"It's okay," Jason said. "I already told you, we gave them money."

Sochar grunted. "You buy that fruit?"

Mud didn't answer, and the other kids didn't speak up, either.

"Answer me," Sochar said, nudging Mud harder.

"The lady gave me coin," Mud muttered.

Jason stepped between Mud and the guard. Mud jumped to his feet, and the guard pulled his sword with lightning speed. The other Scim kids disappeared in a frenzied explosion of motion, leaving behind only peels, pulp, and Mud.

"Stay calm," Jason said to Mud. "Stand still and speak respectfully."

Mud stood beside him, trembling. He leaned toward Jason, half hiding behind his leg.

"Did you steal that fruit, sir?" Sochar asked.

"No, sir," Mud said, his voice quavering.

Sochar shook his head. "Do not lie to me."

"There's no need for that sword," Jason said.

"Get on your knees and show me your hands," Sochar said.

Mud bent his knees, and for a moment it appeared he would do as he had been asked, but then he whipped an orange through the air at Sochar's face and dashed away for the alley. Without thinking, Jason grabbed Mud's arm, trying to get him to stand still, but Mud yanked his arm away. He ran.

The tiger pounced, tearing the boy's leg. Sochar, crushed orange on his face, came two steps behind and with one practiced lunge skewered Mud through the side.

Mud fell to the ground, eyes open. An orange rolled from his shirt, coming to rest in a filthy puddle. His eyes flickered toward Jason.

Jason stepped toward them, but the guard threw his hand up. "Stay back!" Sochar rifled through the child's pockets, throwing out pieces of crushed fruit and a short black knife. "A necrotic blade," he said. "Dangerous. Illegal. No doubt meant for you or someone like you, sir."

The black metal of the blade didn't reflect light correctly. Jason felt a small relief to the tidal wave of guilt threatening to engulf him. Perhaps the boy deserved this, if he was carrying that knife. Maybe he was an assassin, a spy, a troublemaker. *He shouldn't have run*, Jason thought. But then he stopped himself. He was committed to the truth, and while it made him feel better to think Mud deserved this . . . Sure, the kid was a pickpocket, but he hadn't gotten away with the money. Ruth had given it to him. He had bought those oranges. Jason had run when he saw that tiger too. And maybe Mud needed the knife to protect himself. Or maybe . . . Jason thought about this carefully. Maybe it wasn't his knife. Sochar's back had been to Jason when he'd pulled the knife from the boy's pocket. Could he be sure the city guard hadn't planted it? He could not.

The boy lay on the ground bleeding because of Jason. Yes, Mud had tried to steal something. Yes, Sochar had wielded the blade that had skewered the boy. But Jason had been the one to speak up, to say that Mud had tried to steal from them. He shouldn't have done that, but he hadn't known, hadn't suspected for a moment this would be the end result. He didn't care what happened—it wasn't worth the kid's life to stop him from stealing a handful of coins.

"Take him to Gilenyia," Sochar said to the tiger.

"Is he alive?" Jason asked, a flutter of relief coming to him at the mention of the Elenil healer.

Sochar ignored him. The tiger lifted Mud's body in her jaws.

Two members of Mud's gang appeared, shouting and mocking Sochar. One threw a piece of fruit, which spattered the tiger's face. She dropped Mud, growling. Sochar, furious, shouted at the tiger, and they split up, each chasing a different Scim.

Jason fell to his knees beside Mud. Was he breathing? Jason couldn't tell. The black tattoos on his arms were fading, turning grey.

Four more Scim children came sliding out of the shadows. "Get away from him," one of them, a girl, snarled.

Two of them lifted Mud, pulling his arms over their shoulders, and a third swiftly gathered up the spilled fruit. The girl stared at Jason, hands clenched. "Why did you hold his arm when he tried to run? He didn't take anything from you. He didn't do you no harm."

Jason opened his mouth to answer and realized he didn't know, not exactly. He thought Mud shouldn't run. He'd thought, on some level, that if they stood there and talked it out, everything would be fine. That may not have been true, because stabbing the kid wasn't a reasonable response, not at all. Maybe he had wanted to teach Mud, to help him do the right thing. He'd wanted to teach him what was right, and only now, mud and blood on his hands, did Jason stop to wonder if he really knew what was right in this moment. What he knew with a deep, burning certainty was this: the boy's life was worth more than a few oranges. More than a whole cart of them.

The children were gone now, all but one. "Well?" she demanded, and he realized he hadn't answered her.

"I'm sorry," he said.

She spit on the ground between them.

"Here," Jason said, holding out the durian. "Take this. If he—*when* Mud wakes up, give it to him."

The girl lifted the durian over her head. Jason covered his face, tried to shield Ruth. The girl hurled the durian to the cobblestones with all her strength, and it burst. The stench of it exploded into the air. The sweet white meat flew up, splashing all over him, covering his new clothes.

He wiped the juice from his eyes.

The girl was gone.

Only the crushed durian remained.

20
PREPARATIONS

I saw a woman who sang as she slopped the pigs, though she had no apron
to cover her dress. A scribe laughed to see his papers blown by the wind.
A man whistled a tune when he saw his wagon wheel had broken.

FROM "THE THREE GIFTS OF THE PEASANT KING," A SCIM LEGEND

✦

Big rhino, little rhino," Jason mumbled to himself.

He stood in the square courtyard near Westwind's stables. Delightful Glitter Lady snorted at him, her ear twitching as a fly landed on her head. She closed her eyes halfway, enjoying the sunshine. She was in battle mode, much larger than a typical rhino. Unicorn. Whatever.

Jason had the embiggenator in his hand. The dial was turned all the way to the right, to get her to full size. He had been studying how the magical debt was paid. It was helping to keep his mind off what had happened in the market. Sort of. Anyway, for Dee to get big, something else had to get small, right? He had figured it out soon after the big battle by switching Dee's size a few times while walking around the stable near where he had first met her. There was a row of large stones near the city wall. He had noticed that one of them shrank when Dee grew, and vice versa. Once he'd figured it out, he had dialed Dee up to giant size and pocketed the corresponding small stone.

He tossed the pebble in his hand. So far he had managed to remember to not slip it into his pocket and then switch her size. He scratched Dee under the chin, and her eyes shut. She made a low, rumbling, contented sound.

Madeline came jogging around the corner of the castle. With the Elenil modesty rules, she had to wear a long-sleeved shirt and thin gloves when she ran. She had a small backpack as well. She stopped by Jason, hands behind her head, and caught her breath.

"You're sweaty," Jason said.

"Well, hello to you, too." Madeline grinned at him.

"Are you having trouble breathing?" he asked, studying the way she gasped for air.

Her grin grew wider. "It's what happens when you exercise, Jason. You should try it."

He tapped his temple. "I'm exercising my *mind*, Mads." He pointed at her backpack. "For instance. My mind is saying, why is Madeline carrying a backpack while exercising?"

"Interesting. My mind is wondering why you're doing magic in the courtyard where the knight might see and kick you out."

Jason nodded. "Fair question. I've been studying how Elenil magic works. For Dee to get big, something else has to get small." He showed Madeline the pebble in his hand. He tossed it by the wall. "Watch." He dialed the embiggenator to the left, and the rock grew to the size of a mailbox and then a trunk.

Dee flicked her ears again, but now she came to Jason's knee. She looked up at him lazily, unconcerned. She prodded him in the leg with her horn. Okay, maybe slightly annoyed.

Madeline knelt down and scratched the little rhino behind the ears. "Can I try it?"

Jason shrugged and handed her the embiggenator. "Turn it to the right to make her bigger and to the left to make her smaller."

Madeline turned the dial to the left. "Like this?"

"No! She can't get any smaller—"

Except apparently she could. Dee trumpeted and rose up on her hind legs, barely the size of a kitten. "Aw!" Madeline said, scooping her up in her arms. Dee cuddled in against her, squeaking and making happy unicorn noises. The stone, meanwhile, had grown still larger, leaning against the castle walls.

"Huh," Jason said. "I didn't think she could go that small."

"You could probably sleep in the castle now," Madeline said. "Just sneak her in your pocket until you get to bed."

"She's a noisy sleeper, though. Now spill, Madeline—what are you doing with that backpack?"

"It's got my clothes in it for our meeting with the archon," Madeline said. "I want to take a hot bath before we go to the palace, so I'm going to sneak over to Mrs. Raymond's."

Jason took Dee from Madeline and set her down. "How are you going to get out?"

"I have my ways," she said. "You should take a bath too."

Jason snorted. "My suit smells like durian. It won't make a difference. I could tag along, though—there's something I want to do too."

"Get your clothes, then, and let's go."

"They're in the stable, hold on." Jason ambled toward the stable, Dee frolicking at his feet. He nearly tripped over her several times. "Okay, girl, in you go." He turned the embiggenator to "normal" and shoveled some grass into her stall. "Don't give me that look. If the knight sees you the size of a stuffed animal, I'm going to get in trouble." He scooped up his suit and headed to catch up with Madeline.

He found her near the front gate, where one of the knight's soldiers stood guard at the drawbridge. She was a human teenager too, and the guarding was largely ceremonial. No one could get into Far Seeing without passing plenty of guards. This guard was supposed to keep the knight informed of who came in and out.

Still, Jason's stomach clenched at the thought of being caught. "How do you get past the guard? We're not supposed to leave the castle unattended."

"Watch," Madeline said. "Hey, Thuy," she called to the guard. Jason had no idea how Madeline knew her name already. She must have been hanging out with the other humans in the castle. He remembered Ruth's comment that "all the girls" had made fun of his hat, and he blushed.

"Hey, Madeline," the guard said. "Sneaking out to get a bath again?"

"Yeah. I hate how there's no magic in the castle."

"Tell me about it. You know we're going to get busted if you get caught out there."

"Don't worry," Madeline said. "We'll be careful."

"We?" Thuy glanced at Jason. "You're not taking him, are you?"

"If it's okay with you," she said.

"I don't know. He's sort of . . . unpredictable."

Jason wasn't sure how he felt about that. He tried to think of something unpredictable that he could do in the moment, but nothing came to him. Maybe that was unpredictable?

"I'll bring you something from the market," Madeline said.

"Not the market," Thuy said. "I want a cinnamon roll from Mrs. Raymond's place. I love the knight, but the food at Mrs. Raymond's is so much better than here."

"Deal."

"Great," Jason said. "That's easy."

The guard glared at Jason. "And a pudding."

"A . . . uh . . . a what now?"

"I want one of your magic puddings. We all know you get them, and I haven't had pudding in a long, long time."

Jason crossed his arms. "That's because pudding is terrible. People only want it when they're in the hospital or think they can't have it."

"Well, I can't have it now, so I want one."

"Fine," Jason said. "I'll give you a magic hospital pudding. Can we go now?"

Thuy looked straight ahead. "I don't know what you're talking about."

Madeline walked over the drawbridge. "Come on," she said, looking back at him still standing next to Thuy. "That's her way of saying she can't see us. Now get moving."

Oh. That made sense. He trotted across the drawbridge, and they headed toward Mrs. Raymond's place. The path they took would pass directly through the market. He told Madeline the story of Mud and that he wanted to check in on him. He felt embarrassed telling Mads about it . . . because, in retrospect, he felt he should have known better and especially because it had ended with such unexpected violence. But Mads took it in stride and didn't seem to think less of him for it. It was a relief to talk with her about it and to have her support.

He didn't tell her about the dreams he had been having . . . weird dreams filled with strange people. People that reminded him of the Scim, but less scary, kinder, and strangely endearing. They had looked more human than Scim, when he thought back on them, but he had known in his dream they were Scim. And there was the house: an old dilapidated mansion with moss hanging from the roof that came into his dreams over and over. He stood in front of it in near complete darkness, and he could feel a small breath of air on his neck. An old Scim woman lived in the house, and he was there to visit her, to check in on her.

"Jason?"

Startled, Jason almost lost his footing. They stood near the fruit stand now, a full minute's walk from the castle, and he had been so deep in his own thoughts he hadn't noticed. He vaguely remembered that Madeline had been talking to him a moment before. "Sorry," he said.

"Are you okay?"

"Yeah. I just . . . I was thinking." He cracked his knuckles. "Okay. The Scim kids ran down that alley."

The alley stank. It wasn't dark . . . There weren't dark places in Far Seeing, but it shouldn't have smelled, either. Apparently magic toilets were not in use wherever the alley took them.

Madeline strode ahead of Jason, who felt unaccountably nervous. He had a deep, unsettled feeling that the little Scim boy had already died. The cobbled alley gave way in places to patches of dirt and mud, as if whatever magic kept the city in perfect repair did not work here.

They found the gang of Scim kids huddled together along the alley pathway, throwing colored stones in a circle. One of the kids looked up at them, grimaced, and looked away. They kept throwing stones.

"Excuse us," Madeline said. They ignored her.

"We're looking for Mud," Jason said.

One of the kids grinned at him and, without warning, slung a handful of mud in his face. "There you are," the kid said, and the rest of their little gang chortled and laughed and continued throwing their stones.

Jason wiped a streak of mud from his face with his fingers. "I just want to make sure he's okay."

One of the kids, a young girl, stood. Her dark hands were closed in fists, her tusklike teeth rubbing against the disgusted curl of her lips. "Is that so? You care what happens to little Scim children? Then why is this the first time we've seen you?" She scooped up her rocks. "Mud is gone."

"Gone like . . . gone? Or like . . . dead?"

But the girl walked down the alley without turning back.

"The human lady took her," one of the boys in the circle said.

Madeline crouched down beside them. "The human? Do you mean the Garden Lady?"

The children laughed. "You don't know nothin', do you?" said the boy. "The Garden Lady, she only appears in a garden, don't she? Not in Scim alleys, huh?"

The children gathered their stones, evidently tired of the obtrusive humans. "What's her name?" Jason asked.

One of the smaller boys lingered back. "What will you give me for it?"

"What do you want?"

The boy licked his lips, looking at Jason's feet. "Your shoes, I think. Or . . . what's in the bag?"

"Fine," Jason said. He couldn't give him the suit—Ruth would kill him. "The shoes for a name." He kicked them off. He could snag another pair from David and Kekoa's room easily enough, and they could just order more.

The boy snatched the shoes up, cackling to himself. He held them against his chest. "She has a tame name."

"Tame name?"

"Like she was Scim once, but instead of being named Darkness Boils or some such she has a tame name, a sunlight name. You know."

The kid started to back away, but Jason grabbed him by the arm. "Don't sneak away, buddy. You haven't given me her name yet."

Another clod of mud came sailing down the alley and again caught Jason in the face. He lost his grip on the kid, who skittered backward with the shoes. "I don't remember it quite," the boy said. "But something about sunbeams. Ray Man. Something like that." Then he scampered off with his friends.

Jason wiped the mud from his face again, then wiped his hand on his pants. "Ray Man. Well. That was worth it, I guess. Mud is alive, at least. Or was."

Madeline looked at him in consternation. "You didn't figure it out? He's talking about Mrs. Raymond. Ray Man—Raymond."

Jason gasped. "Uh. I did not catch that."

Madeline had already turned on her heel and was running for Mrs. Raymond's house. Jason pelted after her, barefoot and embarrassed. By the time they reached Mrs. Raymond's sprawling residence, Jason's feet ached.

Jasper, the kid in charge of the armory, was sitting on the front steps, enjoying the sunshine. "Is Mrs. Raymond here?" Madeline asked.

He shrugged. "Haven't seen her since breakfast." He squinted at Jason. "Hey. Where's that unicorn? You didn't check it out of the armory."

Check it out? Dee wasn't a library book, and besides, no one had told him he was supposed to do that. It wasn't his fault Dee loved him so much that she wanted to be with him at all times. "I can't even keep track of my shoes," he said. "How am I supposed to keep track of a unicorn?" He chased Madeline into the house, ignoring Jasper's shouted instructions.

Madeline held her hand out, slowing him. She looked up the long stairway with the plush carpet. "Should we see if she's in her room?"

"There's no way she brought some Scim kid into her house. The Elenil would go nuts. Even a lot of the human kids here hate the Scim."

"But we can wait for her there, if nothing else."

"Okay," Jason said. They walked up the stairs, and Jason sighed with relief at the feeling of the plush carpet on his bare feet. He didn't know where Mrs. Raymond's room was, but Madeline seemed to. She took them through a series of hallways, twists and turns, and came to a simple wooden door. Madeline knocked, but no one answered.

"I guess we'll wait," Madeline said, and leaned against the wall.

Jason leaned against the door beside her. It gave way, and he stumbled backward into the room. He straightened, taking a quick look to make sure Mrs. Raymond wasn't sitting in the room watching him. He pulled the door shut again.

"What are you doing?" Madeline asked.

"It was an accident!"

She pushed the door open. "No, I meant, why are you closing it again?"

"Bad idea," Jason said, but he followed her in and shut the door behind them.

The room was about twice as large as the one he had shared with Kekoa and David. There was a window directly in front of them and a closet door on the wall to their left. A modest bed sat in the corner, a comfortable-looking chair was placed near the window, and there was even a fireplace, which was so clean he wasn't sure it had ever been used. But Madeline walked with reverent wonder toward the unexpected feature against the far wall: a rustic bookshelf packed with books.

She ran her hand across the spines. "Look at all these. Tolkien, Lewis, L'Engle, MacDonald, Rowling." She pulled one from the shelf, turning it over in her hands. "They're all fantasy novels."

"That's weird," he said. "Seems like you'd just want to enjoy living in your own fantasyland, not dreaming about other ones."

Madeline gasped, shelved the book she had been holding, one by T. H. White, and crouched down to a lower shelf. "I can't believe it," she said. "It's the Tales of Meselia. All of them and all first editions. Jason, these are my favorite books of all time."

It was a little strange, seeing books again after all this time in the Sunlit Lands. Jason picked up one of the books. It was called *The Winter Rogue*. He flipped through the pages.

"That's the second one," Madeline said. "Then comes *The Gold Firethorns* and then *The Skull and the Rose*. Oh, you'd love that one, Jason."

Jason sighed and put his book back on the shelf. He was glad Madeline had found something to distract her for a moment, but he couldn't keep himself from wondering about Mud. Which reminded him of Night's Breath. Which, somehow, reminded him of his sister. He put his hand against the bookshelf to steady himself.

"Are you okay?" Madeline stood and put her hand on his shoulder.

He nodded, just as the closet door swung open and Mrs. Raymond came walking out, drying her hands on a towel and talking as she walked.

"—will be fine, but you can't keep bringing me these orphaned—ah. For instance, these two."

Hanali had been walking close behind her and crashed into her when she stopped. He glanced up, the perplexed expression on his face changing into a look that said, *Oh, of course this is Jason's fault.*

"I do not recall extending invitations or permission to enter my private room," Mrs. Raymond said.

Hanali frowned. "The boy has a way of weaseling into places uninvited."

"The door was open," Jason said, realizing how lame it sounded even as the words left his mouth.

Mrs. Raymond took the books from Madeline and put them back on the shelf. "Nor did I invite you to paw through my library."

"We didn't mean any harm," Madeline said. "It's just that—"

"Your hands are filthy," Mrs. Raymond said. She looked at Jason. "His entire . . . What happened to your face, Mr. Wu?"

Oh yeah. The mud. "Hygiene standards are surprisingly lax here," Jason said.

Hanali rolled his eyes. "This from the boy who took a bath while wearing his shoes." He looked at Jason's feet and then, with a weary sigh, looked back to his eyes. "Where are your shoes?"

"I sold them to a Scim kid."

Hanali scowled. "You should not be fraternizing with the Scim, Wu Song. It reflects poorly on me as your benefactor."

Something in Hanali's voice caught Jason's attention. He knew somehow that Hanali was hiding something. Hanali's eyes flickered, just for a moment, back toward the closet door. "You know," Jason said, "certain doors in this glorified youth hostel go places they shouldn't." He walked toward the closet.

"Keep your hand off that door," Hanali said.

"I have a way of weaseling into places uninvited," Jason said, and swung the door open.

Mud lay sleeping on a narrow bed in a stone room. Day Song, Gilenyia's Scim assistant, looked up from the boy, a washrag in his hand.

Mrs. Raymond pulled the door shut with a firm hand. "Stay away from the boy. You are covered in filth. He's in pain enough without an infection."

Jason locked eyes with Madeline, but she appeared to have as little idea of what was happening as he did. He looked a question to Hanali, who plucked at his sleeves with nonchalance.

"Mrs. Raymond has a way of picking up unfortunate strays," Hanali said. "And should you not be dressing for our audience with the archon?"

"Don't get me wrong," Jason said. "I'm glad Mud is getting medical help, but why do you have him here?"

"Hanali is well known in the Scim community as the Elenil to approach if there are needs," Mrs. Raymond said.

Madeline's eyes widened. "He's *what*?"

"Enough," Hanali said, steel in his voice. "We will talk no further of these things. The boy will be returned to his home when he is well. No one here will mention this again. Not to me, not to one another, and certainly not to the archon."

Mrs. Raymond's face set to stone. "Hanali, son of Vivi," she said. "Have you not shared your plans with these two children, even though they are a central piece of it?"

"Nor would I have shared them with you if you were not so persistent and infernally nosy," Hanali snapped.

"Hey," Jason said, offended. "I'm persistent and nosy too."

Hanali glared at him. "You. To the baths. We leave here in one half of an hour. Every particle of mud must be gone from your face." He turned to Madeline. "And you? Have you more to say? Intrusive questions? Infuriating requests?"

Madeline blushed. When she spoke, her voice was so low Jason almost couldn't hear it. "Mrs. Raymond? Could I maybe borrow some books?"

Mrs. Raymond put her fists on her hips and rounded on Hanali. "These are the children you've staked everything on, and you've not given them so much as a clue as to the deeper game you're playing?"

Hanali gave her a shocked look, his gloved hand on his chest. "Deeper game? My dear Mrs. Raymond, I only desire invitations to more prestigious parties."

She glowered at him a moment more before turning to Madeline and saying, "Of course, dear, so long as none of them leave the house—and don't show them to the Elenil. Since they can't read, they always think we're passing secret knowledge. If they catch you with a book, they'll make you read the entire thing aloud before they let you leave. Now run along and clean up."

Jason hadn't seen Madeline so giddily happy before. She went to hug Mrs. Raymond, who turned her aside with a huff. Still giddy, Madeline grabbed Jason's hand and pulled him into the hallway. "Mud is going to be fine!" Madeline said. "And there are *books*!"

"Yeah. And Hanali has a secret plot. Big surprise, I guess."

As if summoned, Hanali opened the door and stuck his head out. "Mr. Wu."

"Yes?"

"Use soap."

Hanali closed the door again, leaving Jason alone with the laughing Madeline. "Use soap," Jason grumbled. He picked up his bag with the suit in it and tossed Madeline her backpack. He started off down the hallway, then realized he had no idea where they were in the massive maze of Mrs. Raymond's house.

"Your room is the other way," Madeline said, passing him. "Don't be late."

Jason turned back, listened to Madeline's footsteps headed the other direction. When she was gone, he paused by Mrs. Raymond's room. He could hear dim, concerned voices on the other side. He leaned his head close to the door but couldn't hear what they were saying. It sounded like Mrs. Raymond was angry and Hanali was trying to mollify her.

He cracked the door slightly.

Mrs. Raymond was talking. "—too great a risk, letting them in. Not just to you but to all of—"

"We've already discussed this at length, Mary."

"*Mrs. Raymond*, Hanali. You don't get to call me Mary anymore."

Hanali sighed. "It is a risk. A terrible risk. But, my dear Mrs. Raymond, how could the situation become any worse?"

There was a pause, and when Mrs. Raymond spoke again, her voice sounded tired and sad. "There is always a way, Hanali."

"I suppose," he said. "But it is the choice I have made. Now. If you will excuse me, I feel an urgent need to check on Mr. Wu. If I leave him alone for even a few minutes, he makes the worst kinds of trouble."

Jason jumped away from the door and hugged his bag close to his chest. He half ran, half walked to the end of the hallway and turned right, then speed walked until he knew where he was.

If he hurried, he should have just enough time to clean up and get dressed. Hanali had asked how the situation could get any worse. Jason had a sinking feeling that he would be the one to figure that out.

21

THE PALACE
OF A THOUSAND YEARS

*The glory of a king comes from neither wealth nor finery
but from the well-being of his people.*

FROM "THE THREE GIFTS OF THE PEASANT KING," A SCIM LEGEND

✦

The archon's palace stood at the center of Far Seeing. A hill rose gracefully beneath it, pastel-colored houses and buildings lapping up along the sides like waves. Shops and markets splashed beneath those, filled with people from all over the Sunlit Lands seeking a trinket or a necessity from carts and stands festooned with bright flags and flowers.

"None but the Elenil are allowed beyond this point without a host," Hanali said to Madeline as they stepped down from the carriage. "Humans may neither ride a steed nor carry a weapon. Nor may the Scim, the Aluvoreans, emissaries from the Southern Court, the Zhanin . . . all the other races. They must pause here before entering the heart of the Elenil world and the seat of our magic." Hanali paused and stared at the pulsing crescent-shaped stone at the apex of the main tower.

Jason, freshly bathed, straightened his jacket. They had tried to get the durian smell out, but it lingered. Without magic it couldn't be easily cleaned, and Ruth had told him buying another would be a "luxury" and that he could find his own money rather than spend the knight's. Shula had not been invited to the palace. She had business elsewhere, she said, and had wanted to reconnect with some of the other soldiers. Jason had asked her about Baileya, a Kakri woman he mentioned from time to time but whom Madeline had not yet met. Shula knew her and said she would likely see her and asked if Jason had a message. "Tell her—" Jason said, looking like he was thinking carefully, "—tell her, uh . . . I said hi." Shula, grinning, had promised to do so.

For the seventieth time Hanali launched into how to be polite in the archon's presence. Curtsy or bow. Speak when spoken to . . . with the proper restraint. Do not release Scim prisoners to wreak havoc in the court or mention previous instances where one might have done so. Do not touch the archon. Are you listening, Jason, *do not touch the archon*. Not with a fist nor with a fingertip.

Madeline found it painful to hear again, especially since it seemed to be aimed at Jason. The wonders of Elenil architecture distracted her in any case. The main tower of the palace stood in the center: a delicate, slender white column with graceful lines. Nine slightly shorter towers stood at equidistant points around it, with white latticework like lace covering their lower halves. Wide marble stairs arched between the towers, leading to meticulous gardens overflowing with bright, gorgeous flowers. A stunning variety of people and creatures moved up and down those stairs, each of them accompanied by at least one Elenil guide. None of the guards here were human, unlike elsewhere in the city, but only Elenil in splendid royal-blue uniforms with gold trim.

"It's beautiful," Madeline said, almost whispering.

Hanali paused his lecture and stopped, one gloved hand on the elbow of each of his charges. "It is known as the Palace of a Thousand Years. It was built entirely by hand. No machines from your world, no shortcuts or tools other than what can be held in a person's hand. Each stair is a single piece, mined by the Maegrom. The Aluvoreans coaxed the gardens into being. Not a single blade of grass was planted—they encouraged local plants to arrive of their own free will. Even the Zhanin participated, in their way, by not interfering with the amount of magic drawn upon in that century. It would cause a war today to use so much power so quickly."

"That century?" Madeline asked. "Didn't you say it was the Palace of a Thousand Years?"

"Yes," Hanali said, guiding them to the stairs. "It would have taken a thousand years without magic. There is no comparable architecture in any world I've seen. My forefathers built it, I am told, in less than two centuries. A hundred and sixty years, more or less."

Jason asked a question, trying to sound nonchalant, but Madeline could tell he asked with purpose. "I've been studying Elenil magic. So for these buildings to go up more quickly, there must be other places where building happened more slowly?"

Hanali's face lit with delight. "Ah! At last young Jason takes an interest in the culture of the Elenil. Indeed. There are trade-offs. The speed and beauty of this construction means that, by necessity, there is a balance elsewhere. The magic here was carefully wrought, and it is geolocational. Which is to say, the spells made it easier and faster to craft the palace here, on this hill. There is another place elsewhere in the Sunlit Lands, linked to this hill, where it would be immensely difficult—if not impossible—to build. Magic would fight you every step of the way."

Jason wrinkled his nose in distaste. He'd probably caught a whiff of himself again. "Where is that place, Hanali?"

"Somewhere in the Wasted Lands, no doubt. We could ask a storyteller. They keep tales about such things hidden away for curious minds such as yours."

They paused at the top of the stairway to appreciate one of the gardens. It sank away to the left of them like an amphitheater and was filled to the brim with fruit trees, luscious grasses, and exotic animals. Peacocks wandered in the shade, shaking their fanned tails. Birds zipped between the branches, and large cats lounged, uncaring, in the dappled sunshine. Madeline gasped. A white mare, as brilliant as mother-of-pearl in the sunlight, stepped out of the trees. She had a long, silver horn protruding from her forehead.

Jason's hand clenched Hanali's forearm. "What is that?"

Hanali smiled gently. "A rare Earth animal. I believe it is called—what was it now?—ah, yes! A rhinoceros. I'm told they are extinct in old Earth."

Seeing the look of impotent rage on Jason's face gave Madeline the giggles. She tried to keep a straight face, but soon she was leaning against Hanali, wiping tears from her eyes. Jason's face softened, and soon he was laughing too. Hanali asked what was so funny, but they wouldn't answer. A foal emerged from the trees and cavorted at the mare's feet. They both stopped to feed on the sweet grass.

"We can speak to them later if you wish," Hanali said. "Though it is rude to laugh at such noble creatures."

"They can talk?" Madeline asked.

"Of course," Hanali said, as if it were a ridiculous question. "All rhinoceri can speak."

They entered the palace through a gateway arch which soared above their heads, several stories tall. There were no gates or doors because, Hanali explained, most of the defensive capabilities were magical. And if an enemy made it this deep into Far Seeing, the defense of the city had already fallen, and it was better to allow their enemies entrance to the palace than risk its destruction.

The rooms in the tower wound up along the inside of the wall, leaving the center free all the way to the top. Birds glided above them, delivering messages. A series of long ropes hung from different levels of the palace, allowing braver souls to swing across the vast space between the walls. Toward the top of the tower, suspended in a glass room, was a crescent-shaped crystal. Significantly smaller than the one affixed to the exterior of the main tower, it was, like that larger stone, black and glowing with a purple aura. It could be seen even from the bottom of the tower, as the ceiling was made of some sort of glass or transparent crystal.

"The Crescent Stone. Also called the Heart of the Scim," Hanali said, noticing Madeline staring. "At the heart of all our magic is that stone. It is displayed there at the top of the Palace of a Thousand Years in a glass room which can only be accessed through the archon's quarters. It is transparent so all can see if any approach it. I do not know of a person entering that room in a generation or more."

"Don't you mean the Heart of the Elenil?" Madeline asked.

Hanali, surprised, drew away from her, as if trying to get a better look. "Ha! Of course, that would make sense. Many centuries ago, the Elenil and the Scim exchanged stones. The Heart of the Elenil is with them, the Heart of the Scim with us. Some find it distasteful to call the stone after the Scim, and so they call it the Crescent Stone. In those days, though, we were friends, and the name was without controversy. Those were better days. I am told the Heart of the Elenil is a beautiful stone—so transparent one seems to see a delicate blue sky within it and a faint shine of sunlight in a corona around it. More beautiful, most say, than the stone we keep watch over here."

"Wait, wait, wait," Jason said. "If that's the Crescent Stone, what is that big crescent stone that's on top of the tower? The one we can see from outside? The gigantic one?"

"Ah," Hanali said. "Another insightful question. The Crescent Stone itself is smaller than you would think, though great magic flows through it. The stone affixed to the top of the tower is an amplifier, which allows the magic to flow freely into the rest of the Sunlit Lands."

Jason's brow furrowed with concentration. He was working hard to figure this out. "So the true Crescent Stone is not the one on the exterior of the tower."

"Indeed not. As I have just said."

"Got it," Jason said, and it sounded as if he had filed that information away for some reason.

"So where do we meet the archon?" Madeline asked.

Hanali pointed out a gaudy throne, three times the size of what a normal person would fit on. It was on the fourth through sixth floors and could be seen easily from anywhere in the building other than directly above it. "On feast days and during celebrations, the archon sits on the Festival Throne. Today he desires a more intimate setting, so you are to meet him in the Apex Throne Room, near the top of the tower."

Jason groaned. "That's a lot of stairs. Couldn't he meet us down here?"

"We won't climb the stairs," Hanali said. "Step upon these circles."

The circles painted on the floor were about the size of dinner plates and all different colors. Madeline stepped solidly into the outline of two dusky-orange ones and, following instructions from Hanali, imagined herself moving to the 114th floor. The circles lifted from the ground and began to move smoothly upward. No ropes or pulleys, no seat belts, and no nets, air bags, or pillows waiting below. She yelped. Jason screamed.

Jason fell off from about ten feet up, landing in a clutch of Elenil who had the misfortune to be walking below him. They helped him to his feet, clearly unhappy, and sent him floating upward again.

"Stand up straight!" Hanali yelled to Jason. "Stop flailing!" He floated past Madeline, confidently standing on only one of the flying plates, his other foot moving in graceful arcs, toes pointed.

They were about thirty stories up now, and Madeline couldn't bear to look down at Jason. An Elenil swung past her, headed from one side of the wall to the other, his golden hair streaming behind him. "Are you okay, Jason?" she called, still looking toward the top of the tower.

"Jason wants to take the stairs!" Jason yelled.

"Posture," Hanali shouted. "Good posture is paramount, Mr. Wu!"

The Heart of the Scim stood above them, its purple energy crackling with power. The light gleamed against the glass walls, revealing that it rested on a glass pedestal—it was not floating, as Madeline had believed. It was about the size of a manhole cover—there must be some sort of magnification effect that allowed it to be seen so clearly from the bottom. Above it she could see the gigantic crystal crescent that hung over the tower.

Hanali floated up and to the left, disembarking with a careless step onto a wide landing. Relieved to be at the end, Madeline held out her gloved hand as she rose to his level, and he took it, helping her to step more or less gracefully from the floating circles.

Jason came only a moment behind. He panicked, leaning toward the solid edges of the wall, and fell from his circles, his arms grabbing the landing, his legs kicking out into empty space. Hanali dragged him across the floor. "Stand still and stand straight. Are these instructions truly too difficult for you?"

"I don't like hover plates," Jason said.

"They are perfectly safe," Hanali replied. "Only a child would fall from them."

Jason snorted.

A civilized Scim stood nearby, his entire uniform, from boots to gloves, a stark white. Even his dark hair had been caught up in a white tie, and his collar extended even higher than the current style. He had no tusks and small, white, almost human teeth. He bowed gravely. "Sirs and miss, I am called Bright Prism. I will guide you to your audience with the archon."

Madeline helped Jason to his feet. "I'm Madeline, and this is Jason. You probably already know Hanali."

"Indeed," Bright Prism said, politely inclining his head. "Kindly follow me." He led them through an endless series of sumptuous rooms—ballrooms and dining halls, leisure rooms and rooms full of paintings. One room was an indoor garden cunningly made to look as if it were outside by painting on the ceiling and walls and, as near as Madeline could tell, not through the use of magic. They did not pass any kitchens or bathrooms or bedrooms or any evidence that people lived in this section of the tower, though Hanali had assured them these were, in fact, the archon's quarters. Of course there were no televisions or other technology, though there was a room with a variety of musical instruments. There was no library, a reality of the Sunlit Lands that still struck Madeline as strange. No books, no street signs, no grocery lists, no notes to loved ones. Magic allowed them to mimic high technology in some sense, but they were illiterate.

Nevertheless, the tour, she suspected, was intended to awe them. They wandered in and out of strange halls, through parties and balls and choral performances. Madeline found it impossible to believe all these things happened constantly and had not been set in motion merely to impress her, Jason, and Hanali. They arrived, at last, at two large golden doors which met at a point two stories above. Bright Prism stood with his back to the doors. "The Duru Paleis are the only doors in the palace. When one seeking entrance places a hand against this door, it can sense their intention. It grants or refuses access based on what is seen in that person's heart. Archon Thenody has instructed that each of you place your hand upon the handle to request entry."

Hanali nodded brusquely, stepped up to the door, and took hold of the long handle that ran down the middle. In a moment he stepped away. "I have been denied entrance," he said quietly.

Madeline narrowed her eyes. "We can't go in without Hanali," she said.

"You must," Hanali said. "It will be worse for me if you do not."

Madeline strode to the door. Could it be that Hanali had pretended to be denied access? There had been no flash of light, no obvious display of power. She took hold of the door's handle. At once the world around her grew dim. The doors alone held light. She noticed, now, carvings in the door's surface. People moving about, as if in the midst of their day, in a village. One of them, a poor man in ragged clothes, waved to her. She waved back, and a smile spread across his wooden face. He motioned for her to follow him, which she did not understand, but as she concentrated on the man, the scene on the door shifted so that he grew to life size.

"Who are you?" she asked.

He smiled, and she noticed a simple crown upon his forehead. "An ancient king, long since gone from the Sunlit Lands. I reigned before this palace or city came to be, and my throne was a bale of hay, my crown a twist of holly. They called me the Peasant King. In mockery at first and later with respect. More titles came, in time, but the Peasant King is one I have cherished."

"How did you come to be a . . . a door in this palace?"

"Hmm? Oh! I'm not a door. I saw the door open your mind, and I thought I would say hello. I am no longer in the Sunlit Lands, but I think of the people there as . . . well, the closest word for it would be children. They are my children, and I like to look in on them."

"Your children are quite strange."

The Peasant King laughed at that. "As are most children! Now, my friend, a word of advice. There are a great many people who want you to be a great many things to them. A savior or messiah or agent of world change."

Madeline sighed. "You're going to tell me to be true to myself or something like that."

The king's eyebrows raised. "Not at all. You are already a person committed to being true to yourself and your friends. I wanted to say only this: the myth of redemptive violence is just that, a myth. Violence solves a problem in the way gasoline solves a fire. There are other paths. They are, almost always, more difficult. Seek them out." He smiled at her. "The door's magic fades. Farewell."

The king receded into the door, leaving it smooth and untroubled. Madeline jolted back into the real world and found the door had budged under her hand. She pulled, and it swung open. "Come on," she said to Jason.

"He must also put his hand upon the door," Bright Prism said.

"He comes, or I don't. It doesn't matter what the door says." She gestured to Jason again. He stepped ahead, carefully making his way past Bright Prism and through the doorway. The door shut behind them. The last thing they heard was Hanali calling to them, "Be sure to bow or curtsy!" She couldn't keep track of when one was meant to curtsy or not. No doubt that was why Hanali kept reminding them.

The room housed a wide pond with trees growing along the outer edges. A white path wound around the pond to a cottage on the far shore. A fish jumped in the pond. Two moons rose over the cottage. It was, for the first time in many weeks, nighttime. The stars made no noticeable pattern. "We go to the cottage," Madeline said. Without discussing it, Madeline took the lead and folded Jason's hand in hers. Her heart was beating fast, thinking about the encounter with the Peasant King and the upcoming audience with Archon Thenody. She was glad Jason was with her.

"Do we knock?" Jason whispered. They heard nothing but night insects and a brief crashing in the undergrowth.

The door creaked open as if in answer.

Madeline stepped in.

They were in a formal throne room. Archon Thenody sat on a raised throne, several civilized Scim standing near him at attention, two of the blue-clad Elenil soldiers at the base of his dais. "I hate this place," Jason said. "Everything is the wrong size. The outdoors are indoors, the indoors are outdoors. It's terrible."

Archon Thenody, again wearing his strange golden sheet, raised a hand as if acknowledging them. Madeline curtsied. So did Jason, badly, beside her.

"Jason," she hissed.

"Hanali said we could bow or curtsy."

"He meant for you to bow and me to curtsy."

"That makes sense. Curtsying is hard."

She snickered. Did he do these things on purpose? No doubt he had offended Archon Thenody again.

"Leave us," the archon said. The Scim left with crisp, quick steps. "And you," the archon said, and the guards stepped out the door Madeline and Jason had entered. "Come closer."

Madeline walked to the bottom of the dais. The archon stood and flowed down the stairs to her.

Archon Thenody removed his golden sheet with a flourish, letting it slide to the floor. Underneath he wore white-and-gold brocade clothes that covered everything but his head. Golden crisscross lines of magical connections spread across his entire face. If she hadn't seen it so close, she knew his skin would appear golden. Even the whites of his eyes had branching golden tattoos, even the roots of his hair follicles. Every bit of him was traced with magical tattoos. At his neck he wore a choker with a facsimile of the Crescent Stone—a black sliver of rock that sparked with purple energy.

"I thought we should get to know one another, we three. No need to stand on ceremony," the archon said. "You made me look the fool on that tower," he said to Jason. "Fortunately, it was only my closest advisers there. If that had happened on a feast night—the Festival of the Turning is coming, for instance—I would have had to punish you both publicly. Along with that young fool Hanali."

"He had nothing to do with that," Madeline said quickly.

"He invited you to the Sunlit Lands, did he not? There are rules we follow." The archon gestured to the floor, and three chairs appeared. He took one and invited them to take the others, which they did. "When recruiting, we only take children. What you call teenagers or younger. Never adults. Never."

"Why?" Jason asked.

"They lack a certain flexibility," the archon said. He tugged absently on his glove, taking it off, revealing more skin colored gold by his network of magic. "Secondly, they must be in dire need. Perhaps they are victims of war or refugees. Perhaps their parents are cruel and abusive. Some have medical problems, like you, Miss Oliver. There is also the question of whether they can survive the journey. The road to the Sunlit Lands winds through deadly, dire landscapes. If a child cannot cross that road, they cannot come to us." He tugged off his second glove. "Do you meet this requirement, Mr. Wu?"

Jason didn't come back with a joke or a quip for once. He bit his lip, concentrating. "I believe I do, Mr. Archon," he said.

"You may call me Thenody here, in private," the archon said. "May I see your agreement again?"

Jason pulled off his glove and pushed his sleeve up, then leaned over so Thenody could see it. The archon studied Jason's bracelet for a long time, the golden pathways on his fingers pulsing lightly. At last, he said, "Your heart's desire is a dessert. You are a curious creature."

"Do I pass your 'hard life' test?"

"I suspect you do. It is hard to say, for your agreement is scarcely magical at all. The delivery of a single pudding cup every day takes less magic than that necessary to make these chairs appear for a few minutes. There is little to be gleaned from your markings. It does not, however, include a promise of fealty to the Elenil, a third requirement of those who come here. Hanali has broken that rule at the least."

"But Jason promised loyalty to me, and I've promised mine to the Elenil," Madeline said.

Thenody leaned back in his chair, studying her, one fingertip resting on his lower lip. He dropped his hand casually to the side and a goblet appeared. He sipped from it lazily. "You speak with such familiarity to me. If I did not know better, I would suspect you contradicted me in that last statement."

"I didn't mean to," Madeline said. Was he doing this on purpose? Telling them to call him by his name, then accusing them of being too familiar when they disagreed with him? He seemed to be purposely pushing them off balance.

"She completely meant to, you crazy golden psycho," Jason said, and then dropped his own hand, staring at it to see if a drink would appear in it. When none did, he turned back to the archon and said, "Honestly, it feels like you invited us to a private audience so you could make sure we'd treat you with the proper respect in public."

The archon flew from his seat so quickly he knocked his chair backward. A frigid wind blasted Madeline, and when she could open her eyes again, Thenody had Jason by the throat and had lifted him out of his chair. Jason's hands held the archon's forearms, pulling his body up to try to lessen the choking. Thenody stalked across the room as if Jason's weight meant nothing. Madeline scurried after them. The archon moved down a long hallway, pausing in the middle. He muttered something under his breath, and the room expanded. Doors appeared along the hallway.

Thenody kicked one of the doors open. Instead of revealing another room inside the palace, it led onto a mountainous cliff overlooking a raging sea. The archon stepped onto the cliff, holding Jason over the ocean. Madeline rushed at him from behind, but with his other arm the archon easily stopped her by grabbing her forearm and forcing her to the ground.

"I would like to make sure," Thenody said, "that you treat me with the proper respect." He shook Jason over the edge.

Jason tried to speak, choking out his words. "I . . . knew . . . it!"

Disgusted, Thenody threw him aside, leaving him on the ground between the cliff and the door. "You have no natural fear of your betters," he said. "It is a troubling quality."

"He only speaks truth," Madeline shouted. "It's not troubling, it's amazing. I wish I could do that."

Thenody's golden eyes drifted down his arm until he found her face. "But you are bound to the Elenil—to me—through your agreement." He tore off her glove, revealing the silver latticework of her tattoo. He turned her wrist. "This agreement can be canceled," he said slyly. "No more Sunlit Lands. No more Elenil. No more breathing."

"Leave her alone!" Jason shouted.

"Ah. I have your attention at last."

"You already showed us you could do that," Madeline said. "On the tower."

Golden fingers readjusted their grip. The archon touched Madeline's wrist with his index finger. "See there? That's where the gem on your bracelet used to be. It has spread now. Much faster than most. But pay attention." He pushed into her wrist, and a surge of piercing pain spread up her arm and nearly to her shoulder. She screamed. "If I break the gem, the agreement is broken. No breath for you, no oath of fealty to the Elenil." He dropped her arm. It ached like she had just done a thousand push-ups. "Remember that when next you think to insult me in public. Break the gem if you want to be free from our agreement, but do not think to violate it without dire consequences." A bell rang, somewhere back in the palace. "Ah. I believe our tea is ready."

The archon stood by the door like a hotel doorman. Jason got up, then helped Madeline to her feet. They leaned against each other for strength.

The edges of this place were blurry, like a video game where the designers hadn't managed to get all the scenery finished. "We have to get away from him," Madeline whispered to Jason.

They made their way back to Archon Thenody's receiving room. He motioned to their chairs. They sat, and he served them tea from an antique ceramic teapot with delicate flowers. "Sugar?" he asked, holding a lump of sugar in a pair of golden tongs. Madeline shook her head.

"Yeah," Jason said. "Oh, more than that. Yeah. Like, ten of those."

The archon smiled faintly, counting them out. "Eight . . . nine . . . ten."

"Make it eleven."

Thenody frowned, but gave him one more. "Eleven, then. I believe that is all of them."

"I hope you wanted some," Jason said.

Thenody sighed. "Perhaps I have been overly harsh."

"Ya think?"

The archon took a sip from his cup and said to Madeline, "Perhaps this would be smoother if we were alone."

Madeline shot Jason a warning look, terrified they would be separated. "He'll behave."

"Ah, lovely. I suppose he will thank me for the sugar, then."

Jason's face flushed. He clamped his lips tight. "It's okay," Madeline said.

"Thank you," Jason said.

"My pleasure," Thenody said brightly. "Now. I asked you both here because I am concerned about your safety. The Scim—those vile creatures— have expressed an interest in you. I fear it is more than you have heard. The Black Skulls themselves have made it clear that they will not rest until they find you, Madeline. I do not know why they desire you, but they are not so . . . gentle . . . as I am." His eyes rested on her bare hand.

Madeline covered it with her napkin. She had left her glove near the cliff. She couldn't bear to have the archon's eyes on her bare hand, though, not after he had hurt her arm like that. "We'll be safe with the Knight of the Mirror," Madeline said. "Ruth explained his magic to me. Once something is given to him, it can't be taken away again, not without his permission. The magic doesn't allow it."

"Yes." Thenody licked his lips. "It was a clever solution the magistrates came to. A solution they arrived at when I was in great pain and unable to participate in the discussion because of—" his eyes flicked to Jason— "an unfortunate prison break."

"Hey!" Jason said. "I bet the knight's magic means you can't throw me over any cliffs!"

"You would be wise not to test such boundaries," Thenody said.

"In any case," Madeline said, "we're safe."

The archon sipped from his teacup. "It is said you will bring justice to the Scim, Miss Oliver. If that is true and not some outlandish tale of Hanali's, then you are immensely valuable to me. But you should know there are limits to the knight's magic."

"Like what?"

"A clear boundary: should he choose to give you willingly to the Scim, his magic will be no protection to you."

"He wouldn't do that!"

Thenody barked a laugh. "How delightful, the innocence of the young. There are certain precious things the knight might value more than your life. That is only one possibility. Or you could be taken during the Festival of the Turning, when all magic that flows from the Crescent Stone ceases. Or his magic could be neutralized somehow. Countered. Evaded." He raised a hand. "No, I do not know how, only that my seers have said that when the time comes, his magic will not protect you."

"The same seers who said Mads is the one who is going to save the world?"

Thenody sniffed disdainfully. "They have said no such thing. They do not see any special qualities in you or the girl. The other treasures we have given the knight to steward over the decades are of more value. The Sword of Years, perhaps, or the Ascension Robe. Have you heard those names?"

"Never," Madeline said, sipping her own tea.

"The Memory Stone? The Mask of Passing? The Disenthraller? He has mentioned none of these things?"

"No."

Thenody rubbed his smooth jaw. He had not put his gloves back on, and Madeline wondered how such a dainty hand could have so painful a grip. "I am filled with wonder that he has not mentioned those artifacts, since it is only a month past that the Scim came looking for them. To mention them would be no risk, since nothing can be taken from his hand. But perhaps he has been too busy gazing into mirrors. Surely he has not betrayed the Elenil and turned those artifacts over to the Scim. Although— it is strange that they have ceased warring against us."

Jason slurped his tea, loud. "You're saying you think the knight gave them back their stuff in exchange for . . . something he wants. Whatever it might be."

"The opposite," the archon said.

"You're saying he took the artifacts away from the Scim, and in exchange they took something he wants?"

"No, fool, I am saying he would never betray us in such a way."

"Ookaaaay," Jason said slowly. "But we would have never thought that."

"You're trying to plant the idea in our heads," Madeline said.

Thenody spread his hands wide. "Not at all. But if he had traded those artifacts away . . . I would want to know. I would want you to tell me. It could mean that you, my children, are not safe."

Madeline set her teacup on its saucer and, no table being near her, set it at her feet. "I think I've had enough."

The archon's face twisted in rage. "You dare dismiss *me*?"

"Enough *tea*," Madeline said, making an effort to sound calm.

Thenody stood angrily. He clapped, and all three teacups disappeared. Madeline gasped.

"Hey, I wasn't done!" Jason said. "I was just getting to the sugar sludge at the bottom."

"*I* am done, however, and you wait upon my leisure," Archon Thenody said, walking away from them.

Bright Prism appeared again, bowing low, and escorted them from Thenody's quarters. The journey out was not as long as the journey in. They passed a few dank corridors and a blazing hot kitchen. The servants' passageways, probably.

"Those doors," Jason said. "I don't think we actually went anywhere. The magic here doesn't work like that. He'd need to have three people waiting to come through another door into the palace if the three of us wanted to come out of it."

"It was an illusion," Madeline said. "I don't know why, but he's trying to make us see things that aren't there."

Bright Prism led them back through the golden doors, and they stood on a wide landing. They could see the Heart of the Scim glowing in the glass room at the center of the tower, just one floor above them. They could just walk up to it if they wanted. Bright Prism bowed and said, "The master wanted you to have this, miss." He held out a box meticulously wrapped in golden paper, with ribbons spilling off it.

"It's probably socks," Jason said. "He's just the type to give out socks. White ones, probably. Those short athletic ones."

Madeline opened the gift. Inside was one glove. A left glove, like the one she had lost, as golden as the archon's magic-infused skin. It filled her with dread to touch it. Her skin crawled just looking at it.

Bright Prism said, "He asked me to say, 'To remind you of our talk overlooking the sea.'"

Madeline's stomach fell. A burning sensation started in her center and moved up into her face, a boiling, furious heat. "Tell him I hope to repay him one day," Madeline said. "A thousand times over. Tell him that."

The Scim bowed. His small black eyes darted left and right before he spoke. "Lady, you ought not say that."

"Say those exact words," Madeline said. "Now, which way is out?"

Bright Prism pointed a large hand toward a stairway which hugged the outer wall. "That way, lady."

Of course he would make them take the stairs. Hanali was gone, no doubt sent away the moment she and Jason had gone through the golden doors. She balled up the archon's glove and threw it over the side. She watched it float a few stories, crumple, then fall. She didn't see where it landed.

Jason said, "Do you think they have magic toilets here? Because I want to use one before we go back to Westwind."

"Yes," Madeline said. "I'm sure they do."

It was a long walk to the bottom of the tower. Madeline spent the entire time figuring out what to do. It seemed she had somehow made an enemy of the most powerful of the Elenil—the people she was sworn to serve. The Scim army had withdrawn, though it appeared they wanted to kill her.

She couldn't believe it, but today she sort of missed chemistry class.

22

THE KNIGHT'S SOLAR

Where is the fountain which brought joy
to the city, clean and clear at its heart?

FROM "THE DESERTED CITY," A KAKRI LAMENT

✦

Madeline felt thrown off her rhythm. The confrontation with the archon went against everything she had expected. She wouldn't be waiting around anymore, waiting to see what other people told her to do. It was time for action.

Her legs had nearly given out by the time they reached the bottom of the stairs. They found Hanali leaning against an elaborate marble handrail and watching the unicorns munching grass in the garden below.

They started to tell him what had happened, but he shushed them. He smiled broadly, chatting amiably all the way back to the knight's castle. When they crossed the threshold of Westwind, he whispered, "Do not speak negatively of him. Not in this city and certainly not where magic is in use. Do you think he cannot hear?"

He whisked them into the great hall and called for the knight. The two of them listened with furrowed brows as Madeline and Jason told their story. The end result was not, as Madeline had hoped, a promise to keep them away from the archon. Instead, the knight and their benefactor debated which activities were safe for them in the city.

"They are not to leave the city limits, that much is plain," the knight said.

Hanali sniffed. "They have been watched carefully since arriving, just like any of the new arrivals. The one exception was allowing them on the battlefield. Even then I watched Jason from the wall, and Gilenyia accompanied Madeline."

"You are not to leave this castle during the Festival of the Turning, with or without accompaniment," the knight said.

Madeline objected that she didn't know what or when that was, although she did remember the archon mentioning it. Jason objected that a festival sounded like a party, and it hardly seemed fair to be locked away in a castle. "Not a nice Disney castle, either," he said. "No offense."

Furious about the whole thing, Madeline stormed off to her solar. Which, being at the top of one of Westwind's towers, was a long hike, especially after descending hundreds of flights of stairs at the palace. She had run out of anger by the time she made it to her room. She collapsed on her bed.

A half hour later a sheepish knock woke her. She opened the door to find Jason, a goofy smile on his face, a loaf of slightly burned brown bread under his arm, and a cutting board covered with a thick, salty cheese. Shula stood beside him, holding an enormous bowl of a red, juicy citrus fruit called burst. Jason had named it, of course, and failed to remember the common name. When placed on the tongue the skin of the fruit nearly exploded, and the flavor was both tongue-numbingly tart and chocolatey sweet at the same time.

Madeline and Shula tucked their feet up on the bed, and Jason pulled a large chair over, and they descended on the food. Halfway through her second slice of brown bread, Madeline began to feel human again. Partway through her third, she lay back on her bed, one hand under her head, the other on her full belly.

"I'm beginning to wonder," she said, "if the Elenil are the bad guys here.

Something is seriously wrong with the archon, and it doesn't seem like a huge request by the Scim to have their artifacts returned to them."

Shula popped some cheese in her mouth. "Artifacts returned, and you and Jason turned over," she said.

Jason added, "Killed, I think. Not just handed over. Break Bones was very clear about Madeline's 'lifeless body.'"

"Whose fault is that?" Madeline asked, throwing a crust of bread at him.

"I said I was sorry!" Jason protested. "He asked me your name. He didn't say, 'I'm going to murder someone, let's brainstorm names.'"

"The Scim are monsters," Shula said. "The Elenil have their faults, yes, but who threatened to murder you? The Scim."

Jason, his mouth full of food, said, "Break Bones said he wanted to usher in centuries of darkness. I can't even remember how many he said. At least five."

"Maybe you shouldn't have let him go, then," Madeline said.

"Who kidnapped me?" Shula asked. "Who held me prisoner in the wastelands? They gave me rotten meat and filthy water. They left me in public so they could throw garbage at me when they walked by. They beat me trying to get answers about you two, and trying to get me to tell them where their artifacts are." She paused, the muscles in her jaw flexing. "I don't even know what happened to Diego."

That was the boy who could fly. He had escaped the Scim but hadn't returned to Far Seeing. The knight couldn't find him. Madeline put a hand on Shula's knee. "I'm sorry, Shula."

"I don't see how the Scim can be the good guys," Shula said.

"On the other hand," Jason said, "Break Bones wasn't in a day spa. He was chained in a dungeon. So the way the Elenil treat their prisoners isn't much different."

Madeline crossed to the small, arched window in her solar, which looked out toward the city wall. "The city is so beautiful, though. The singing fountains! The palace gardens! Even the marketplaces are colorful and well organized. The Elenil create such beautiful things. The palace! It's amazing."

"It is beautiful," Shula said. "It was the Scim who hurt me, and the Elenil who used their magic to heal me. You, too, Jason. The Elenil are bright, beautiful people. They don't live in squalor and make speeches about destroying the light."

At the mention of Jason's healing, Madeline stiffened and looked straight at him. He stared back, one eyebrow raised. He knew something was wrong but hadn't asked her directly. Not yet.

"The magic," Jason said, "works in an interesting way. If I want to use a sword, I have to take those skills from someone else who earned them. While I have those skills, someone else doesn't. Or Shula, when Madeline healed you, that Scim woman had to take your wounds. Which naturally brings up the question, if I was nearly dead when I was healed by the Elenil—"

"Wait," Madeline said, interrupting him. She wasn't ready for this conversation. She couldn't talk about it, not right now, and she couldn't bear the thought of what Jason would say when she told him that Night's Breath had died so he could live . . . and that neither Jason nor Night's Breath had any choice in the matter. "Shula, what is the Festival of the Turning like?"

"I've only been to it once," Shula said.

"Once more than us," Jason said. Then, his voice bitter, "The knight doesn't want us to go. He says it isn't safe."

"He's right," Shula said. "Did he tell you why?"

Madeline shook her head. "He's not the most talkative."

Shula scraped the scraps of cheese from the cutting board out the window, into the moat below. "For one day, all the magic of the Court of Far Seeing is reversed. It's an entire day without Elenil magic. The Crescent Stone must rest for a day, and all the magic that runs through it must cease. The people of the Sunlit Lands celebrate the day in different ways. They go to their own territories and tell the story of the coming of magic to the Sunlit Lands and how the Majestic One—a magician from centuries ago—made the place. Rich people wear rags, and the poor dress in fine clothing. It's a time of reversals, and people playact that they are something other than what they are. The highest society people take pride in appearing to be impoverished, because it announces their high status at other times."

"I don't see how it puts us in danger," Madeline said, making room for Shula to lean on the windowsill. "The Scim will be in their home territory. Who is going to harm us?"

"There will still be Scim here. If one of them hurt you, there would be no healing magic available. You never told me what your deal with the Elenil is, but you'll lose that for the day too. I won't be able to light myself on fire in battle."

Jason said, "Madeline can't breathe by herself. She's got a terminal illness. So she won't be able to breathe?"

"Jason!" Madeline shouted. It wasn't right for him to share that—it was hers to share or not. People looked at her differently when they knew. It had happened a hundred times with her friends. Her disease wasn't contagious, but people acted as if it were. They made suggestions about how she could take care of herself, even though she was healthier than most. Or they gave her pitying looks . . . as if they were healthy because they were better than her.

But Shula acted as if she had just learned Madeline had asked for a haircut. She didn't make a big deal out of it or look at Madeline with pity. She only rubbed the long scar on her face and said, "That's right. Once the ceremony starts, all magic starts to fail. We could go to the palace for the beginning, but once night falls, she won't be able to breathe."

"Night falls?"

"Of course. Once a year the Elenil experience true night and see the stars. It's their magic that keeps Far Seeing in perpetual day. When the sun sets, magic starts to fail . . . It takes a while, and some magic fails faster than others. But before the night is over, you won't be able to breathe. I won't be able to light on fire."

"I won't get pudding for breakfast," Jason said, but his jovial tone of voice rang hollow, and he looked nervous.

"That's the dumbest thing I've ever heard," Shula said. "Was that your deal? Pudding every morning?"

Jason acted offended. "Every morning for the *rest of my life*. Except festival days, apparently." He deflated a little. "What about you, Shula? You just got healed a few days ago. Will that be undone?"

"Yes," Shula said, "though my Scim counterpart will have healed some by then, so I'll only get a portion of that damage back, and only for the day."

Madeline beat Jason to his question. "What if someone was almost dead and healed?"

Shula shrugged. "It depends. If the counterpart died from the wounds, then the transfer is sealed and permanent. Someone like that would remain healthy. If the counterpart has been recovering, they would get the wounds back for the day."

Jason held Madeline's gaze. She could tell what he was thinking: on the Festival of the Turning, he would know what had happened to Night's Breath. Madeline wouldn't be able to avoid the conversation any longer. She tried to hold his gaze, but she couldn't. He must suspect, because why would she be avoiding the conversation if all was well? A pang struck like a knife in her ribs. The thought that Night's Breath was gone, dead, because of her had been keeping her awake, watching the light on the ceiling of her chambers. *That decision kept Jason alive*, she reminded herself. That ridiculous, overly truthful, loyal, infuriating guy who had gone from chemistry partner to good friend mostly on the strength of picking her up when she had fainted and driving her to the hospital. That had to count for something.

The archon's accusations against the knight lingered in her mind. What if he wanted to keep them in the castle so he could trade them away to the Scim? If he had already given the Scim the artifacts, maybe she and Jason were next. She didn't think the knight would do such a thing, but no one had seen the artifacts in some time, according to the archon.

"We have to search Westwind," she said. "We have to find the Scim artifacts. It might help us figure out what is going on."

"I don't even know what they are," Shula said. "It's not a topic the Elenil share about freely."

"The archon mentioned some of them to us. There was a sword called the Sword of Years, I think. A robe called—what was it, Jason? The Robe of Ascension?"

"Yeah," Jason said. "Plus something called the Socks of Silence. Lets you sneak around all sneaky like. I don't know. I clearly can't remember."

Madeline ignored him. "There was a mask, I think, too."

Jason jumped out of his seat. "Ahhh! That kid with the bark mask was so creepy!"

"Calm down. That was before we even got into the Sunlit Lands."

Shula paced the room. "Could we just ask the knight to show them to us?"

"No way," Jason said. "That's crazy. Let's tromp all over his home opening locked doors and hope he doesn't notice."

"If he's secretly working with the Scim, we don't want to tip him off that we know," Madeline said.

Shula, still looking out the window, said, "He left earlier, going toward the palace. He never tells us what his business is day to day, but he will be gone at least an hour or two. So. Where do we start?"

Madeline had been thinking about this ever since Thenody had suggested the knight might have done away with the artifacts. If the artifacts were well hidden, that might make them as impossible to find as if he had already given them to the Scim. The only way to prove his innocence was to find the actual artifacts, all of them. Not that she needed to prove his innocence, but she needed to know if she and Jason were safe. "Is there an armory?" she asked.

"Yes," Shula said thoughtfully. "I've been in there, though. Not much to see."

"Nothing in the stables," Jason said in a tone of voice that suggested he honestly believed this to be a helpful data point. "Or the kitchen."

"The knight's solar?" She still thought it strange that in a castle a private room was called a solar, but she wanted to use the correct terms.

"It would make sense for the artifacts to be somewhere near where the knight sleeps," Shula said. "If someone broke in, he would want to be nearby."

"We could ask Ruth," Jason said. "She knows an awful lot for a kid."

"She's loyal to the knight," Shula said. "He's like a father to her."

Did that mean that the three of them were disloyal? Madeline didn't like to think that. She wanted to think they were protecting themselves, doing what was best for them and the Elenil, checking in on the knight to make sure he was keeping those Scim artifacts safe. "We'll start at his solar," Madeline said. "We can work our way down the tower from there. If they're not in his tower, we'll regroup and try again."

Jason tucked the cutting board under his arm. "You know I'll tell the knight everything if he asks me."

Shula winced. "Jason also has a bad habit of volunteering information he doesn't need to."

"It's part of my charm," Jason said, batting his eyelashes at Shula.

"Well," said Shula slyly, "Madeline, why don't you and I go look in the solar to see if the knight is there. We can chat with him and ask if it would be okay for you to go to the Festival of the Turning if I go with you. We can take care of all this artifact business later."

Madeline frowned. "But he's—" It dawned on her what Shula was doing. "Riiiight. Jason could stand at the bottom of the stairs and shout up if he finds the knight. If the knight asks what we're doing up there—"

"We'll say we're looking for him."

"You already know he left for the day," Jason said. "This isn't a loophole that will work. I know you're lying to me right now."

"Are we?" Shula asked, and she poked him in the nose with her index finger. "Bring your cutting board and let's go."

A quick stop in the kitchen and then they cut across the great hall toward the knight's tower. A huge mirror was fastened to the wall at the entrance of the stone stairway. "Stay here," Madeline told Jason. "If someone comes, shout up to us."

"You mean if the knight comes," Jason said.

"Anyone who comes might know where he is, so go ahead and shout up the stairs," Shula said.

Jason slumped against the wall. "Uh-huh."

A thick wooden door with iron bands blocked the entrance, but it swung open at a light touch. On the other side Madeline noticed a beam of wood which could be placed in an iron bracket to brace the door from the inside. The door being open at all was a good argument the knight was gone. Unlike the stairs to Madeline's solar, there were no tapestries on the upward climb. There were small gaps in the stone, just wide enough to shoot an arrow from, which let in the pure light of the Sunlit Lands. Across from each gap, right where the sun would hit them full on, were mirrors.

"The Knight of the Mirror earned his name," Madeline said.

"Yeah." Shula paused to look out an arrow slit. "He's a careful man, Madeline. We should be cautious when we enter his room. There may be traps or alarms. Even magic."

"He doesn't allow magic," Madeline said.

"The artifacts are magic," Shula pointed out. "Nothing can be taken from his hand—that's magic too."

They passed a small room that projected out from the tower over the moat. A garderobe, complete with the wooden stool with a hole in it. "No magic toilet, though, as I'm sure Jason would say. I don't know about you, but if I were going to cheat on my no-magic rule, that's where I would do it."

"We should still be careful," Shula said.

A fair amount of shouting came from downstairs. Madeline couldn't understand what Jason was saying. She leaned down the stairs and shouted, "What?"

His words were garbled, but she heard "something in the mirror." Madeline asked Shula if she had caught more than that, but she shook her head.

"Probably making a joke," Shula said.

That could be. They studied the closest mirror, seeing only the backward versions of themselves. Madeline shrugged and started up the stairs again.

"Hmm," Shula said. "I thought I saw something move in the mirror."

"Maybe you saw me."

"Or a bird flying past the window, I guess. Nothing to worry about," Shula said.

They continued their climb. Jason shouted something else, and although they couldn't understand his words, his tone of voice seemed calm. They debated turning back, but at this point turning back didn't mean they wouldn't be caught—there was only one stairway in the tower—it only meant they wouldn't get a chance to check the solar.

The stairway rounded the final loop, and the knight's private room stood ten steps ahead of them. There was no door, which made sense since there was nothing in the tower other than this room, and the door at the bottom of the stairs could be locked. Shula crouched, climbing the last few steps on her hands and knees, peeking over the top of the landing. Madeline joined her, marveling again at how wonderful it was to be able to breathe. Her heart was pounding, adrenaline pumping, but she could take full, quiet breaths without coughing. She felt energized and alive.

The knight's room had open windows in the masonry. Sunlight streamed in. There were no curtains or anything to prevent his room from being essentially in the open other than the fact that it had a roof with a long overhang that would keep rain out. A bed sat more or less in the center of the room, the sheets twisted as if they had fought the knight to keep him from sleep. A sword leaned against the bed on one side. Between the windows stood full-length mirrors, and a simple table was pushed against the wall, empty.

Madeline entered and took in the whole room, turning in a circle. She saw a flash of white in one of the mirrors, maybe caused by the sunlight. She inspected the mirror more closely and saw something strange. "Shula, look at this."

The rumpled, unmade bed was not rumpled in the reflection. It was perfectly made, with tight corners. She looked at the table's reflection in the mirror. She put her hand against the glass. There, on the other side, lay the Scim artifacts.

23
THE KNIGHT'S SECRET

She weeps into the fountain. She lingers at her
window and sobs to hear the silent streets.

FROM "THE DESERTED CITY," A KAKRI LAMENT

✦

The sword caught Madeline's eye first. Nicked, rusted, and
neglected, the sword could have been found in an archaeological
dig or at the bottom of the ocean. Worn leather straps wrapped
the pommel. A pristine black scabbard worked with gold sat
beside it, though it was clear the sword hadn't been cleaned,
sharpened, or put into the scabbard in a long time.

A silver mask lay next to the sword, almost as reflective as the mirrors.
Thick red ribbons spooled from the sides of it, and its empty eyes stared
at the ceiling.

A robe, carefully folded to show off the finery of its design, sat in the
center of the table. It appeared to be handmade and hand dyed. It was blue
with gold trim, and oxen, eagles, humans, and lions danced up the edges
and around the collar.

There was a stone, white and smooth. And a thin key. Madeline tri
to reach through the glass, but of course she couldn't.

"What are you doing?"

Startled, Madeline and Shula jumped. A woman stood in the mirr
her black hair swept out of her face, her olive skin flushed with anger. S
wore a rose in her hair, and her white dress, long and beautiful, press
against the glass where it billowed out from her waist. "You are not to be
this room of Westwind," she said. "Nor should you attempt to touch th
instruments. They are not yours to handle."

Jason stumbled into the room. "There's someone in the mirror!"
shouted. "A woman!"

Madeline pointed to the woman with her eyes.

"Oh," Jason said. "I see you've met."

"Who are you?" Shula asked.

"You break into the knight's solar and demand my name? Who are y
thief?"

Madeline stepped forward. "I'm Madeline Oliver. We didn't mean a
harm."

"We did know we shouldn't be in here, though," Jason added. Not hel
ful, but true. "I'm Wu Song."

"My name is Shula Bishara."

"All of them should have known better." The Knight of the Mirr
stood in the doorway. His long black hair hung in thick curls to h
shoulders, streaks of grey cascading through them. His nose, obvious
broken many times before, drew one's attention more than the piercir
brown eyes, or the white scars on his brown skin. His wide shoulders fill
the doorframe.

"Who, me?" Jason asked.

"Silence," the knight said.

"You can't learn if you don't ask questions," Jason said reasonably.

The knight gave him a withering glare, and Jason fell silent. "I hav
invited you into my home. I have extended protection to you both, an
you repay me by violating my privacy. I should send you back to Archo
Thenody for this." Madeline gasped. Jason's hands tensed. They woul
have to run. They might be safe here in this castle, maybe, but she coul

not go back to the archon's palace. But where would they go? They might be able to return to Mrs. Raymond. Or they could petition to enter the Bidding again. Gilenyia had offered to take Madeline, more or less. Maybe she could be convinced to take Jason, too, if he could keep his mouth shut long enough for Madeline to ask.

The woman in the mirror must have seen the distress written on Madeline's face, because her own face softened and she said, "He speaks from anger. He would not do such a thing."

"Has your anger passed so swiftly?" The knight moved past them and put his palm on the mirror. The woman put her hand on his from the other side.

The woman's lips twitched into a gentle smile. "You of all people should know better."

"Ah," the knight said. "You use my words against me."

"That's not exactly what you said," Jason said, and Madeline elbowed him.

The knight turned to them. "This is Fernanda Isabela Flores de Castilla. She is the greatest lady in the Sunlit Lands or any other—compassionate, kind, and generous even to those who would burst into her chambers uninvited."

"Is she . . . your wife?" Madeline asked gently. The knight's lip turned up in a half snarl, then fell neutral again. His eyes narrowed, softened, then closed. One of his gloved hands rose to hide his face.

"It is not your place to ask such questions," the knight said. "That story is for those I trust and them alone. Today," he said, looking pointedly at each of them, "you have lost what trust you had previously earned."

"We'll go, Sir Knight," Shula said.

"Sir Knight?" Fernanda said softly. "Has he not told you even his name, then?"

The knight turned his face from hers. "They call me the Knight of the Mirror. It is name enough for one such as I."

Fernanda dropped her face toward the ground. "What I would not give to see you in your glory once again."

The knight said nothing.

Shula looked heartbroken. Although she didn't fight in the knight's

company because she was a magic user, she often spoke of her respect for him. "It wasn't Shula's idea," Madeline said.

"Or mine," Jason chimed in.

Madeline continued, "Archon Thenody implied you might have given the Scim back their—well, whatever this stuff is—and that you were going to turn me and Jason over to them also. The easiest way to prove him wrong or right was to find these."

The knight pushed his hair back. He sighed heavily. "Come then, the three of you. Come close to the table." They moved over to the table, each of them on a side. Fernanda moved to the other side of the mirror, sitting down on the reflection of the bed. "Close your eyes," the knight said. Madeline obeyed. When he told them to open their eyes again, the reflected artifacts were now on the table in front of them.

"Whoa," Jason said.

Madeline felt almost light headed. It was such a strange thing to see. But then, why didn't he allow Fernanda out of the mirror if he could pull these tools out of it so easily?

The knight picked up the mask. "This is called the Mask of Passing. It is filled with Scim magic. He who wears the mask appears to be what others expect. You can see why the Elenil fear it."

"A Scim spy could wear it and walk into the city," Madeline said.

"He could walk into the palace," the knight said. "Into Archon Thenody's bedchamber, should he desire. No one would think twice, for the spy would appear to be whatever or whomever made sense." He handed the mask to Madeline. It was shiny on the front side, like a mirror, but dark as space on the other.

The knight took the mask from her and set it back on the table. "My lady cannot leave the mirror. Nothing can be taken from my hand, save her." A sadness washed over his face, and hers, too.

"You can pull swords out of mirrors," Jason said. "This is better than a Las Vegas magic show. Do you do card tricks?"

"Jason," Madeline said, annoyed. When he felt uncomfortable he made jokes. This was not, however, the time.

"Why is this sword in such disrepair?" Shula asked. "Do you want me to clean it?" It was such a clear request for forgiveness it made Madeline wince. Shula wanted to show him she could be a good soldier, to serve him in some way. He ignored her question, though, and instead told them about the Scim artifacts.

"Long ago, the Elenil defeated the Scim in a great battle. They had been long at war, and in response to an attack on Far Seeing, the Elenil rode down upon the homeland of the Scim with great fury. They killed three Scim for every Elenil who had fallen at Far Seeing. When the Scim begged for mercy, the Elenil gave it. The terms of peace included taking away any magical items the Scim might use in war. These are the most significant of them. In time the Elenil grew concerned the Scim might try to take them back. In fact, the Scim have told us more than once they intend to do so. I had been given a certain magical boon which grants me the ability to hold on to anything that is given me. None can take it from my hand unless I allow it. So long as magic reigns in Far Seeing, these things cannot be taken from this room without my permission." He paused. "This same magic protects you two."

"How did Shula get kidnapped?" Jason asked.

"She has not been given to me."

"She was one of your soldiers, though."

"Jason, hush," Madeline said.

"No! He's trying to make Shula feel bad for being a good friend and coming in here with you, and at the same time he doesn't take responsibility for her being kidnapped and gone for weeks while he did nothing about it."

"She was not my soldier—she was a magic user! You say I did nothing? Nothing but ride into Scim territories, seeking for sign of her. Who brought her home at last?" The knight's face flushed red.

"You shouldn't have lost her in the first place!" Jason shouted.

Shula put her hand on his arm. "Peace," she said. "What happens in a battle is not one man's fault."

"I almost died trying to keep the Scim from taking you, Shula," Jason said. He looked at Madeline. "Some people did die. Didn't they?"

Madeline's heart dropped, still beating, into her stomach, falling like a star through her body. Blood rushed to fill every square inch of her skin. She wasn't ready for this conversation, not now.

"No," the knight said. "He is not wrong. I did not realize the Scim were taking our magicked soldiers until too late. It was a bold move, and one that cost them dearly. If not for the Black Skulls, they would not have succeeded. They did, however, succeed. That must fall to me and me alone." He shook his head. "These Black Skulls. Wherever they have come from, may the Majestic One protect us. They fight like old hands but have the strength of youth."

"It's good there are only three," Shula said.

"You will find a way to defeat them," Fernanda said. "You always have."

"So far," the knight said.

Fernanda stood and moved toward the knight's reflection. "It is time to let your anger sink away," she said.

The knight closed his eyes. "As always, my lady, I do as you wish." He took Shula's hand. "Shula Bishara, you must not clean this sword. It, too, is magic. The Sword of Years it is called or the Sword of Tears by some. The Sword of Ten Thousand Sorrows." He lifted the sword. Rust covered the heavily nicked blade. "Some have called it Thirsty, for it thirsts for the blood of those who have wronged its master. It is an old blade and a deadly one. It must not be cleaned, nor must it be placed in its scabbard again, for on the day that happens, its magic will be renewed, and it will seek again to kill those who are on its list."

"So it's a blade of revenge," Shula said quietly.

"Yes. An old magic in response to ancient wrongs. Some who would feel this blade's bite would not know the origin of its fury." He placed it carefully on the table, beside the scabbard. "This is why I do not allow you to clean it, not because of any wrong you have done me."

"We did wrong you, though," Madeline said. "We didn't believe in you when Thenody made it sound like you might betray us."

Fernanda smiled at her, but it was the pitying smile of an adult knowing there is no way to explain to a child how little they understand. "The Elenil are ancient creatures, and they think in craftier paths than we humans. Their thoughts wander in labyrinths, and they rarely reveal their deepest hearts. No doubt the archon expected you to search here and expected the knight to learn of it."

"It may have been a warning," the knight said. "Or merely a reminder that he watches me."

"Or perhaps," said the lady, "it is because these instruments are safe not only from the Scim but from the Elenil, too. Should Archon Thenody ask for one of these tools, who knows what answer he might receive?"

"I know what answer," the knight said. "He would not take them from my hand."

"Thenody wasn't totally wrong, then." Jason said this while sitting on the floor, tying his shoes. "You're not completely loyal to him."

"I am as loyal as he has given cause for me to be," the knight said carefully. "Now. Peace, children. Leave my chamber. Do not come here again without permission."

They said their good-byes to the lady, who inclined her head to them. Madeline realized with a start that she did not wear gloves and that her dress was open around the neck. She did not dress like the Elenil.

The knight escorted them down the spiraling tower stairs. At the wide wooden door he paused.

"I fear you will not obey me regarding the Festival of the Turning," the knight said.

"We will!" Madeline said.

"I'm not making any promises," Jason said, and Shula pinched his arm.

"It is a great deal to ask of you to stay in the castle," the knight said. "Jason has made his frustrations plain."

"Just being honest," he said.

"I will make this agreement with you. You may go to the festival in the day. Walk among the people, hear the stories, eat the food. But when the time comes for the Fall of Dark, you must make all haste back here. Magic will be upended in those hours. Madeline, you will not be able to breathe. Jason, what wounds you had may return. Shula, yours, as well. When night has passed, we will see how you have all recovered. I may allow you to attend the Celebration of the Sun." He paused, looking at each of them in turn. "Do you understand?"

"Yes," Madeline said. "We understand. We can go to the festival, but we must be home before night falls."

"Shula," the knight said. "Bring them here if they disobey me in this."

"I will, Sir Knight."

"Keep a special eye upon the fool."

"Hey!"

With that the knight slammed the door shut. They heard the sound of the heavy wooden bar falling into place.

"That went better than expected," Jason said.

"Are you kidding?" Madeline asked. "We got caught."

Jason shrugged. "I thought we might get killed. Or thrown in a dungeon. Also, what is that delicious smell?"

Madeline sniffed the air. Golden pastry. Beef? Onions, for sure. Some sort of savory pie, maybe. Jason floated toward the kitchen like a fish on a line.

Shula put her hand on Madeline, stopping her. "You can't breathe without magic. It is a difficult situation." Shula hugged her. "We all take hard roads to come to the Sunlit Lands." She traced the scar on her own face. "If your every breath draws on your magic, though . . . that is more magic than any Elenil agreement I've ever heard."

Madeline didn't know what to say to that. "It's keeping me alive." The thought of losing her magic during the Festival of the Turning made her queasy.

Shula took both Madeline's hands in her own. "Your bracelet," she said. "How far has it spread?"

Madeline had been trying not to look at it, not to notice. It had helped to cover her mirror. Still, she could almost feel it, like a burning itch from an infection, spreading across her body. "All the way up my arm and onto my shoulder. It's branching out onto my shoulder blades. It will be on my neck soon, and it's spreading onto my back."

Shula's face fell, and a dark look of determination moved across it, like a cloud. "Your term of service, then, how long was it? A year?"

"Yes."

Shula dropped her hands. "We still have time, then," she said. Then, again, as if reassuring herself, "We have time."

24

THE FESTIVAL OF THE TURNING

When the world was young and foolish, the people burned the cities.
The oceans, enraged with violence, flooded villages and
carried away children. The ground shook, and the sky wept
blood. The people cried out day and night for help.

FROM "THE ORDERING OF THE WORLD," AN ELENIL STORY

✦

I don't need a babysitter," Jason said for the third time.

Baileya stopped in the festival throng and looked down at him with those glowing silver eyes, her brown hair in loose waves around her face. "I do not know this word."

"It's someone who cares for children," Madeline said, grinning. Madeline and Baileya had instantly hit it off, which made Jason nervous. Baileya and Shula were already friends too, from fighting together against the Scim. Jason had been following behind them through the crowd like some sort of fourth wheel. Wait. Third wheel? But there were four of them. Four wheels were good. Whatever. He was following behind them like the fourth, less happy, wheel.

"I do not understand," Baileya said. "There are no children with us. So you are telling us that you do not need someone to watch the children who are not here?" She looked at Madeline and Shula. "Is this a joke among your people?"

"It's a saying," Madeline said. "It means he doesn't think he needs anyone to watch over him. He can take care of himself."

Baileya put her gloved hands on Jason's shoulders. "You are a man who always speaks truth, Wu Song. Do you need someone to watch over you?"

Jason couldn't look into those silver eyes for long. He had a hard time concentrating on her question when her hands were on his shoulders. He tried to ignore the thrill of energy coursing through him and focus. Did he need someone to watch over him? So far he had escaped a weird mermaid thing on the way into the Sunlit Lands (okay, okay, with Madeline's help), made friends with some warriors, adopted a rhinoceros, and fought some nightmare monsters using magic. On the other hand, he had managed to make an enemy of the most powerful Elenil in the city, and he had accidentally told Break Bones about Madeline, then released Break Bones into the world. Those were pretty big mistakes. He cleared his throat. "On second thought, it might not be bad to have someone watch over me."

"I will be that person tonight," Baileya said. "The Knight of the Mirror has ordered this."

"Okay," he said. His knees felt weak.

"Madeline and Shula also will take care of you," she said, dropping her hands. "You will have only three 'babysitters.' Now come, we must get to the palace in time for the story."

Madeline looped her arm through Jason's. "Come on, buddy. I'll take care of you."

The crowd pressed in around them. There were people from all over the Sunlit Lands. You had to be careful not to step on the tiny grey-skinned folks called Maegrom—they were the size of toddlers. He hadn't seen any other Kakri, like Baileya. He wasn't sure there was another person like Baileya in the whole world anyway. A clutch of women with shadowy blue skin passed. "Aluvoreans," Madeline said, rubbing nervously at her wrist. There weren't, he noticed, any Scim. He asked Baileya about it.

She pulled them underneath the awning of a fruit stand and bought a small, hard, yellow fruit for each of them. "The Festival of the Turning is celebrated by many of the people of the Sunlit Lands. The Scim celebrate differently than the Elenil. Some have been given permission to return to their people for a time. Others are gathered in some quarter of the city, no doubt."

"Do you wish you were among your people?" Shula asked.

Baileya took a bite of her fruit. "The Kakri do not celebrate the Turning," she said. "We have a festival close to this time, when the third and fourth spheres meet. I do not think we will hear the music of the spheres' meeting here in Far Seeing. That I will miss. It is a festival where stories are given freely to one another among my people. It is a cherished night."

"If the Scim are all holed up in some other part of the city, we should be able to stay out as long as we like," Jason said.

Madeline stiffened. "I won't be able to breathe, though, Jason."

"Oh yeah."

Shula didn't say anything, but she would have wounds returning to her, too. And Jason . . . well, he'd either be half dead, or he'd be fine. The daylong reversing of magic was going to be a mess for all of them. Jason didn't know if he'd rather be in a hospital bed or completely well, because if he was well that meant Night's Breath, whoever he was, was dead. Dead, and it was Jason's fault. He had told himself he was going to look into it, but he never had. He wasn't sure if that counted as lying to himself.

"The first magic to Turn," Baileya said, "will be the light. Night will come upon Far Seeing. Other magics will begin to Turn soon after. It is unpredictable. But this much is certain . . . whether within a few minutes or many hours, all Elenil magic will Turn by night's end. We should make our way to Westwind during that first hour of darkness, so that you may each be settled safely into your beds."

"I sleep in the stable," Jason said absently.

"We will stay in the outer ring of the crowd, before the stairs leading to the gardens, so that we may leave the festivities early and return you to Westwind. Besides, we have no Elenil to accompany us to the inner courts."

The magistrates, all nine of them, stood upon a massive dais that had been constructed in front of the main entrance to the palace. Jason shivered at the thought of Archon Thenody catching sight of them. He didn't want to be in the same room with that guy ever again. "Where are the guards?" he asked. There were always people milling around with swords or pikes or some sort of weapon. Today he didn't see any.

"Everyone's celebrating," Shula said. "All wars and grievances are set aside for a day. Tonight it will be day in the Wasted Lands and night in Far Seeing. The wealthy will go about in rags, and the poor will feast. It has long been tradition among the Elenil and Scim and all the peoples of the Sunlit Lands that there can be no fighting or war on this day, the most holy of their celebrations."

"They've given everyone the day off," Jason said.

"Yes."

"That's crazy," Jason said. "They don't have any guards on duty?"

Shula shook her head. "A small group of guards remain on duty. But the thought that someone would attack during the Festival of the Turning is inconceivable to them, and all the gates are locked. If someone were to try to break into the city, they would have plenty of warning. They would have to fight, in any case, because the humans would not have any fighting skills. Besides," she said, "the Maegrom have an agreement with the Elenil. They use their earth magic to block the entrances to the city and guard the walls. No one can get into the city during this time."

Baileya said in a low voice, "It is foolish of the Elenil to be so careless. It was only 137 years ago that the Maegrom broke the Treaty of the Turning to attack my people with magic. Even now there is a city hidden among the dunes where some of my people live under their curse."

"Are you saying we're not safe?" Madeline asked.

"My people can celebrate without setting aside caution," Baileya said.

Jason snorted. "They must be fun at parties."

"Yes," Baileya said. "There is much dancing."

A thought occurred to him. "Are you carrying a weapon now?"

Baileya reached into the loose blue folds of her sleeves and pulled out two long wooden shafts with a metal connector on the end of one. "The blades are easily accessible." She nodded, as if confiding to a friend that of course she kept a roll of paper towels in the kitchen in case of spills.

"I only have my fists," he said.

Shula laughed. "I hope there's no trouble, then!"

Madeline laughed, too, but Baileya considered Jason carefully, sizing him up like a football coach weighing a freshman at tryouts. "Do not forget your feet," she said with level sincerity.

"Yeah, okay," Jason said, looking down at his feet. Baileya's taking everything he said with complete seriousness had confused him at first. Now, though . , . he was getting used to it. Baileya treated him like someone worth listening to. She treated him like an equal, even though she was better than him at everything. He looked up from his feet to see her smiling at him. He blushed, and her smile widened.

"They're about to say something," Madeline said. Grateful for the interruption, Jason turned toward the magistrates.

Archon Thenody stepped to the front of the dais. He wore a long robe that was emerald green and gold. The golden sheen of his skin matched the robe precisely. Madeline said, "Jason, look, he's not wearing that covering he usually wears. I wonder why?"

Jason shrugged. "My mom always says you have to wash your sheets once a week. Probably laundry day."

"It is to show the extent of his magic. It will be more dramatic when the magic fails," Baileya said. "Now listen."

The archon raised his arms, waiting for the crowd to quiet, and then he said, "May the light shine upon you." His voice reverberated through the city square, as if the stones of the buildings themselves were speakers. No doubt it was magic, but it made Jason feel like the archon was all around him, beneath his feet, dissolved into the wall beside him, watching and aware of anything Jason might do here, in his city.

The crowd answered in unison, "May it never dim or wane." Oh, that first part was what the woman at the fruit stand had said to him. It must be a traditional or old-fashioned greeting, because he didn't hear it often. Hanali, for instance, had never once used those words.

"The world is about to Turn," Thenody said, and the crowd cheered. "Many centuries ago, before we learned to harness magic, this was a chaotic, dangerous world. Our ancestors lived lives of considerable toil filled with pain and the constant fear of death. Different peoples have used magic in different ways. But we, the Elenil, have wisely made this great city. We have used our magics to bring light to the Sunlit Lands. We have grown beautiful buildings. We have extended our lives in more years and beauty than any people before us." He held his arms up at this, and the people cheered again.

The Crescent Stone, pulsing with purple magics, descended from the top of the palace, floating down toward the archon's hands. The stone was enormous, three or four times the size of the archon, and it floated with a slow but implacable motion. As it came closer to the people below, it began to shrink. It didn't happen all at once. Jason thought at first it was moving down and also away from him. By the time it reached Thenody, it was small enough for the archon to hold it up in two hands. "Our magic is made possible by this great gift: the Crescent Stone."

"I thought it was called the Heart of the Scim?" Jason looked to Baileya for confirmation. He also noticed that Thenody had used the stone from the top of the tower, not the stone in the glass room. It must be for show, he realized. It was more dramatic to have a gigantic crystal fly down from the apex of the tower than to walk a smaller stone down the stairs. And likewise, he must not want to put the real stone in harm's way. Interesting.

"Some do not care for the true name," Baileya said in a low voice. "You would be wise to be cautious when using it."

"Once a year," Thenody said, "we live as our ancestors lived: in a world without magic. In a moment I will silence the stone, and bit by bit magic will leave us. But fear not, my friends! This lesson in darkness will end in light. For tomorrow, our magic will return."

Jason watched the crowd. So many interesting people and creatures wandered through the crowd. Something like an ape, but with ten-foot-long arms and purple-streaked hair, made a whooping sound. A group of the little Maegrom stood on a stand they had constructed, bringing them more or less into Jason's sight line. There was a man dressed in what looked like seaweed leather and a woman in a green robe and a tall hat covered in flowers. Three human-looking people stood about halfway between him and the dais, their backs to him. They wore black clothing, and slung backward over their shoulders were what appeared to be white masks. He couldn't see the masks clearly because they were partially covered by hoods the three people had left hanging down over their backs.

"Do people dress up, like for Halloween?" Jason asked. "Is that a thing during the Turning?"

"No," Shula said.

"Look at those three," he said. As he watched, the middle one shifted, and an arrow's fletching poked up from under his robe. He readjusted, and it disappeared again. "Um. They have weapons. From here it looks like they're dressed like the Black Skulls."

Baileya, without a word, stalked into the crowd, shrugging her weapon from her sleeves and assembling it.

"There's Rondelo," Madeline said, pointing into the sea of people to their right. "Sitting on his white stag. We should tell him."

"It's probably nothing," Jason said, staring at the middle figure, who had moved his robe to put his hand on the hilt of a sword. "Wait, it might be something." Jason pushed his way forward toward Baileya, calling back to Madeline, "Get Rondelo!"

Baileya had her long staff with the blades on either side out now, and the crowd parted before her like water moving aside for a ship. She spun the staff twice, as if reassuring herself of its heft. Jason pushed into her wake and ran to catch up. He didn't have a sword or bow, but he might be able to grab something off one of the Black Skulls if Baileya managed to stop one of them.

Hanali appeared beside him, matching him step for step. "The Sunlit Lands," he said, "are full of things that are not what they appear to be."

"I've seen those Black Skulls in action," Jason said. "Also, nice outfit." Hanali was wearing a tuxedo that looked suspiciously like a toned-down version of the insane riot of clashing colors Jason had worn to the Bidding.

Hanali smiled, his teeth and eyes sparkling. "What color," he asked, "are those skulls again?"

Jason blinked. The Black Skulls were wearing black robes, but their skulls were white. The exact opposite of the Black Skulls he had seen on the battlefield. "Uh-oh," he said.

Baileya grabbed the shoulder of the middle stranger—the White Skull—and spun him around. His face shone with a strange iridescence, almost as if it were covered with small, fine scales. He had no hair—what had appeared to be hair from behind was only more, differently colored scales. His eyes had yellow irises with vertical slits in them, and sharp white teeth crowded his mouth.

Baileya didn't put away her staff, but she no longer held it in a threatening way either. When Jason and Hanali arrived beside her, she was already talking. "—understand why it appears to be a threat to the Elenil."

The first White Skull bowed low. "Now that you explain, Kakri woman, we understand."

A second White Skull spoke, his voice as harsh and unpleasant as the other's. "It is, among our people, considered a comedic statement."

"Your humor is notoriously difficult to understand," Baileya said.

"This is a joke?" Jason studied the three of them carefully. They looked like the Black Skulls, but as if someone had switched all the colors around.

The White Skulls laughed, and the center one said, "We see, and our hearts understand, Kakri woman. This human male does not perceive the joke, and his soul is not lightened with laughter." They ignored Hanali completely. He, for his part, did not seem bothered by this. He turned and waved Rondelo away. Madeline and Shula were making their way to them.

"They are from the Southern Court," Baileya said to Jason. "They thought it would be funny to pretend to be Scim at the Elenil celebration."

All three White Skulls laughed. "Our cousins have appeared as Elenil at the Scim celebration," one of them said. "It is a cause of great merriment, no doubt."

"I'm going to dress up like your worst enemy and come to the Southern Court next time," Jason said.

All three Skulls burst into uproarious laughter. "Yes, friend, do!" They all three clapped their left hand onto his left shoulder, then turned and wandered into the crowd.

Baileya gave him an affectionate look. "They liked you," she said.

Jason wasn't so sure. "I am likeable," he said tentatively.

"It is rare for them to invite someone to their land," Hanali said. "You showed respect by telling them you would come as their enemy, because that means you know there is no enemy who frightens them. It is a great compliment among their people."

"I was trying to insult them."

"They are a strange people. Shape-shifters and tricksters. The Elenil have an uneasy alliance with them. Now come, all of you," Hanali said.

"Thenody's long-winded speech will end soon, and I want you to meet my parents before night falls."

Hanali's parents, Vivi and Resca, looked precisely the same as Hanali. Vivi, his father, had the same ageless face and wore a silken brocade jacket that reminded Jason of what Hanali had worn the first day they met. Long curls of blond hair spilled out of a wide, floppy silk hat. Hanali's mother, Resca, wore a loose, flowing robe that covered her completely and a sheer veil through which could be seen yet another ageless face and a gentle smile.

Jason looked at each of the three of them, baffled that they all looked to be the same age. "You must have had Hanali very young," he said at last, and Hanali's parents burst into delighted laughter.

"We were young," Vivi said, looking lovingly into Resca's eyes. "We were—what? Three hundred years old? Infants!"

Resca put a hand on Hanali's arm. "No one else our age had a child. What a blessing you are, my son."

"Your parents are super nice," Jason said. "That's more nice stuff than I've heard from my dad in my whole life."

Resca smiled again. "It is lovely to meet the children Hanali has ferried into the Sunlit Lands. They are always so delightful and interesting and loyal."

Loyal? Jason glanced at Madeline. "Loyal to who?"

"To Hanali, of course," Vivi said with a delighted laugh.

"Enough, enough," Hanali said. "Unless I am much mistaken, our friend Thenody is finishing his speech."

Friend? Jason gave Hanali a sideways look. Was it just him, or did the Elenil reserve the word *friend* for people they disliked?

Vivi took the arms of Shula and Madeline and turned toward the dais, chatting amiably. Baileya stood nearby, collapsing her war staff. Resca took Jason's arm. "One day Hanali will stand on that dais," she said softly.

"Like . . . as a waiter or something?"

"You are delightful. Perhaps he will be a butler for a magistrate. I doubt a waiter." She smiled at Jason as if they shared a deep secret. He had no idea what she was talking about.

"Okaaaay," he said. "That will be nice."

"Yes," she said, patting Jason's gloved hand. "He is a good son."

Her hand gripped his arm tighter as the audience murmured, then fell silent. The archon held the Heart of the Scim over his head now, and the black color was leeching out of it, leaving only a brilliant white. Without the darkness inside of it, the stone looked like a gigantic diamond or maybe a piece of glass. "Now," the archon said, "darkness falls, and our magics leave us for a time, that we might remember the great sacrifices made by our ancestors who created the Court of Far Seeing, and remain thankful for the light!"

Then, for the first time since they had come to the Sunlit Lands, night fell.

25

A FLIGHT THROUGH DARKNESS

Another turning shall come.

FROM "THE DESERTED CITY," A KAKRI LAMENT

✦

As the archon spoke, night fell on the Court of Far Seeing. Madeline gasped. Her hand tightened reflexively on Vivi's arm. She reached across him, reassuring herself that Shula was still there, and called out for Jason, who bumbled into her, asking if she was okay.

There were no stars. No moon, nothing. No torches or streetlamps, doubtless because the Court of Far Seeing almost never experienced true dark. The crowd, to Madeline's surprise, did not seem panicked. On the contrary, they cheered the darkness.

"Do not worry," Vivi said. "We allow complete darkness for but a moment. It is part of the story of Ele and Nala, when they stopped the sun in the sky and caused darkness to flee. In a moment there will be—ah, there they are—stars."

More stars than Madeline had ever seen. Enough to wash the whole city in pale, blue light. She had seen the Milky Way once on a camping trip with her parents, but this was more than one swath of white spilled across the sky. It looked like someone had scattered a chest of jewels across a dark floor. Yellow, blue, and red stars shone with a purity of color she had never seen on Earth, and they moved just fast enough that she could see their motion if she stared for even a minute.

"Why wouldn't the Elenil want to see this every night?" Madeline asked, but no one answered.

The archon, on the dais, lit a torch. In the new dark that torch was like a bonfire of glaring brightness. "We must not let the light fade," he said. "It is in the darkness that our light shines brightest, and tomorrow we will light the world again." He lit another person's torch near him, and that person lit yet another torch, and soon candles and torches were being passed into the crowd.

Shula leaned across Vivi. It was just bright enough to see her face clearly. "Madeline, we should make our way back to Westwind. Other magics will begin to fail over the next hour, and it's unpredictable which will go first."

Madeline nodded and then, realizing that it might be difficult to see, said, "Okay, Shula. I'll follow you."

They said their good-byes to Hanali and his parents, who tried to encourage them to stay for the festivities. "The feast begins in a few minutes," Vivi said. "The Elenil will eat dry crusts of bread. The Scim servants who remain in the city will come and feast, and the humans will be given food and drink as well."

"We should definitely stay," Jason said. Madeline wanted to remind him that when the magic left, she wouldn't be able to breathe, but she didn't want him to think about Night's Breath or to think about the fact that if he felt well when the magic faded, it was only because she had allowed the murder of a Scim to save him.

Baileya saved her the trouble, though, by looking down at him and saying sternly, "The Knight of the Mirror has ordered me to return you to Westwind, and that is what I will do."

"But the feast!"

"I will bring you a pastry," Baileya said, "if you behave."

Madeline laughed. This amazing, sculpted warrior woman bringing Jason a pastry . . . Something about the image struck her as funny.

Jason hung his head. "I should stick close to Madeline, anyway."

"Then it is settled," Baileya said. "Let us make our way to the castle."

"Should we wait for some torches?" Madeline asked.

Baileya shook her head. "All four of us come from lands where night and day trade places with regularity. We are not afraid of a small spell of darkness."

Jason said, "We do have lightbulbs where we come from, though, Baileya."

A dark shape skimmed the crowd, flapping its wings, and landed on the dais near the archon. "Did you see that? Was that a bird?"

It was a bird. In a few seconds another bird zipped in from the direction of the southern gate, and then another. Then a massive flock of birds, all different sizes, appeared over the crowd in a chaotic swarm of chirping, hooting, cawing messengers. They flew from all places in the city and lit beside different people in the crowd, relaying their messages before flying off on their next errand.

"No one told me about this part of the festival," Madeline said.

Baileya had already pulled her weapon out, swiftly assembling the two bladed ends. "This is not part of the festival," she said. "We must move quickly to Westwind."

Instead of putting her staff together, she held half out to Jason. He took it in his hand, looking uncertain what to do. She snatched it out of his hand and gave it to Shula. "We will flank you," she said. "You must go as quickly as you are able."

Madeline grabbed Jason's hand so they wouldn't lose each other in the dark, and they pushed through the crowd. She could feel a surge of energy in the crowd. She didn't know what message they had received, but it must be something dire, because the people were all moving with a panicked purpose now. Rondelo and Evernu leapt past them, headed south.

"Hurry," Shula said. "I've seen this sort of crowd before. We need to get out of it."

A horn sounded, harsh and discordant, from the square behind them. Madeline didn't stop to look but felt Jason hesitate. Then he ran ahead of her, yanking on her arm. The crowd around them started to run as well. Someone fell to her left, then disappeared beneath the thundering feet of the crowd. Madeline cried out, but Shula pushed the small of her back, urging her forward.

A voice boomed out over the crowd. "Release the girl to us, and you may live. Deny us, and face the consequences."

Panicked, confused cries rose from the crowd. "What girl?" "Who is he speaking about?" "What does he want?"

"The girl who cannot breathe," said the voice again. "Madeline Oliver is her name."

Madeline stopped, turning back to look. Jason yelled at her to move, yanking on her hand, but Shula had stopped too, Baileya's weapon at the ready.

A Black Skull stood on the far end of the crowd, a scythe in his hands. "Very well," he said. "The archon first." He raised his white-clothed arm, then dropped it again.

A volley of arrows flew from the edges of the crowd. The archon tried to run, but an arrow caught him in the calf, and as he fell, several more pierced him. Screams rose from the people, and the stampede began in earnest.

"This way," Baileya hissed and pulled them into the sheltering alcove of a merchant's shop. "Listen closely. Run if you can, hide if you must, fight if there is no other option. I will be with you in the crowd, sometimes ahead and sometimes behind. Shula, you must stay near them in case one gets past me. Do not hesitate, and do not stay your blade. Be it Scim or human or Elenil, let no one hinder our path."

"What if it's a Maegrom?" Jason asked. "Or a . . . a Kakri or something?"

"Pray it will not be a Kakri warrior," Baileya said grimly, "or you will be lost. Follow the path I direct, even if it seems to take us away from Westwind. The desert has no paths, but a city has many. If we cannot find one that leads where we wish to go, we will make our own."

An Elenil couple fell out of the crowd, pushing up against them in the alcove. "It's her," the woman said, her eyes wide. "They're killing Elenil out there. Elenil! We must give them this girl."

Baileya sliced the woman's arm with her blade. She cried out in surprise, covering her arm. "How dare you, desert vermin!"

Baileya's face twisted in disgust. "There is no magic and thus no healing until the festival ends. You had best run for safety, citizen. If you fall on my blade today, you will not rise again."

The woman said, "Our bird told us someone has allowed the Scim entry to the city. A traitor! The Scim bypassed our guards, they found the gates unlocked. No Elenil would do such a thing, and here we find a company of Kakri and humans." She sneered at them.

Baileya moved toward the couple, but Madeline put her hand on the Kakri woman's arm. "We had nothing to do with that," Madeline said. "But you should run. I can't hold her back for long."

The Elenil couple backed away, and the man said, "When the festival passes, we will speak again."

"Hope that I have no blades on that day," Baileya snarled, and the two of them, wide eyed, stepped back.

"Go," Madeline said. "Run! She's not joking."

The couple stepped into the crowd and disappeared.

The crowd swirled and crashed in on itself. Trying to find a stream of people moving in the right direction seemed overwhelming. Madeline wasn't sure the four of them could go the right way and stay together. "It's too crowded," Madeline said. "The roofs?"

Baileya studied the flat roofs on either side of the street. "You must stay low so the Scim do not see us." With one practiced kick she knocked in the merchant's door. "Swiftly now."

They stumbled through the dark shop. Madeline found a narrow stairway that led to the roof. Baileya forced the top door open. The small, flat roof held a few potted plants and a short wooden bench. The buildings huddled together, and the distance from one roof to the next was rarely more than a single step. They hunched down as they ran to keep from making silhouettes on the field of stars. "The torches are going out," Jason said.

It was true. Starting at the dais and rapidly spreading in a wave across the square, the torches were flickering and dying. Screams came from behind them, and guttural war cries. "Scim warriors," Shula said. "They're in the square."

"Why are they after me?" Madeline asked.

Baileya held still on the edge of a roof. "We should cross the street here," she said. "It's a long jump, but going down among that crowd seems foolish."

"No way," Jason said. "We could wait here for sunlight. No one will see us up here."

Baileya looked to Shula. "I know a thing or two about battles in a city," Shula said. "If they can't find you, they'll set a fire. They'll trust the fire to flush you out."

"We should jump," Madeline said. It was a narrow cobblestone street, but the jump was long enough to be intimidating. Baileya jumped first, soaring across with ease, landing on her feet on the other side. Then Jason went, landing clumsily but whole. Madeline would go next, and Shula last. Madeline's heart beat fast, and her breath came in shallow pants. She squeezed Shula's hand, then backed away from the edge. Jason and Baileya crouched low on the opposite side.

A searing pain shot through Madeline's left wrist, traveling in complicated whorls up her forearm and over her bicep, ending with a series of branching swirls on her shoulder. She gasped and stumbled. Shula hurried to her side.

"Are you okay?"

"I—" She stopped, struggling to breathe. Of course. The magic had just given out. Jason was staring at his own wrist. His eyes met Madeline's, cold and hard.

"We have to get you across," Shula said. She inhaled sharply, and Madeline watched bruises bloom on Shula's face. Her wounds had returned as well. "Should we go into the street or—"

"No. I'll . . . jump."

"You can't breathe!"

"I'll . . . hold . . . my breath." Racking coughs squeezed her chest. She lay on her back and gave herself to the count of ten. Then she reached her hand out, and Shula helped her to her feet. She took as deep a breath as she was able, then ran. Her feet hit the end of the roof, and she jumped, arms pinwheeling, toward the other side.

She hit the lip of the roof and bounced backward, but Baileya snatched her like a hawk grabbing a rabbit. Then Jason's hands were on her arms, and they dragged her onto the roof. Shula landed beside her a moment later.

All three of them lay on the roof, panting. Baileya let them rest for nearly a minute. "We need to move," she said. "We can rest inside Westwind."

They helped Madeline sit up, but she wasn't able to stand. The guilt over Night's Breath crippled her every time Jason looked her way. "Jason," she said. "Night's Breath—"

"Later," Jason said but not in an encouraging way. Baileya ran along the roof to make sure all was clear. Shula and Jason managed to get Madeline standing. Jason picked her up and started to move. He couldn't run, but at least they were headed in the right direction, Baileya scouting and Shula keeping a watch behind them.

Madeline tried to talk to Jason twice more, but each time he quietly rebuked her. The torches had gone out only two blocks behind them. Sweat poured down Jason's face.

Baileya came to them. "We must move faster," she whispered. "The Scim are nearly upon us." She looked Jason up and down. "Give her to me."

"I've got her," Jason said. Baileya wrapped her arms around Madeline, lifting her gently from him.

"Take my weapon," she said. Jason reached out to her waist and unlatched it from a small strap of leather. "Now we run."

Shula took the lead, and Jason came last. Westwind stood like a beacon in the distance, the walls and towers covered in torches.

A horrible croaking sound came from below. It was a laugh. A laugh Madeline recognized. "Wu Song," a voice called. "Wuuu Sooooong, do you remember me?"

"Run if you can," Baileya reminded him. "Keep moving."

"That's Break Bones," he whispered, as if she didn't understand, as if she didn't know.

"All the more . . . reason . . . to run," Madeline said.

They ran, Madeline jostling in Baileya's arms. They leapt over another small alleyway. Baileya didn't even slow. She catapulted herself across with Madeline.

Below them, a horse panicked in the street, pulling a cart of hay, running over people in the crowd. Madeline could see the Scim now, massive creatures making their way through the crowd, smashing people, hacking, cutting and crushing indiscriminately. Everyone ran. No one fought. The Scim caught anyone with a torch and stamped it out.

Jason paused at the edge of the roof, crouched low, watching the Scim.

Trying to find Break Bones, probably. One of the Scim on the ground across the street saw him. The Scim nocked an arrow to its bow, taking aim at her friend.

Without thinking she shouted, "JASON!"

Startled, he fell backward, and the arrow flew harmlessly past. He grinned at her. "Thanks."

They enjoyed a brief exchange of smiles. One of the Scim shouted, "They're on the roof!"

"Run," Baileya said. "By the time they find stairs, we could be ten buildings away."

Ugly horns sounded in the streets around them. Baileya ran, her long legs eating up the space. "They're not waiting for stairs," Jason shouted.

They scaled the walls, grey hands and granite arms hoisting them to the top, where they bared their yellow teeth and, shouting, joined the race. The Scim loped behind them with surprising speed.

"We might have reached 'hide if you must,'" Jason said, panting.

"It's too late for that," Break Bones said, climbing up from a narrow space between the buildings ahead of them. He licked his lips, then pulled a heavy stone ax from a strap on his back. More Scim followed. There were Scim ahead and behind. To each side was a sheer drop to the rioting crowds. "The girl first," Break Bones said. "Then you, Wu Song. Just as I promised."

Baileya set Madeline on her feet and held out her hands. Shula threw her half of Baileya's staff. "Jason," Baileya said, and he threw her the other half. She put the staff together and spun it. "Back to back," she said. "Fight until none remain standing."

"We skipped hiding," Jason said. "I was really looking forward to hiding."

Madeline tried to get a breath and couldn't. She grabbed Jason's sleeve, trying to keep on her feet. Then the Scim were upon them.

26
BATTLE AT WESTWIND

The knight at last his sword lays down,
His grimace gone, no more a frown,
His helm replaced with glorious crown,
A gift from the Majestic One!

FROM "THE GALLANT LIFE AND GLORIOUS DEATH
OF SIR SAMUEL GRYPHONHEART," AN ELENIL POEM

✛

Thea girl first." One of the Scim said it, his voice deep and full of violent intention.

Jason shuddered. Shula and Baileya's backs were against his, and he knew Baileya would slow the vicious Scim who advanced on them. But Madeline, doubled over and coughing, would be an easy target for Break Bones.

His stomach clenched at the thought of failure. His molars ground into each other, and his jaw ached with the sudden pressure. He hadn't left everything behind to come into this crazy place to fail. *I will protect Madeline.* He would fight Death himself if it came to that. Thoughts of

Jenny came piling in. Not the good thoughts, not the memories of how they had cared for one another, the fun times, of making jiaozi with their mom or reading books together at night. Not the memories of how she always called him didi—the Chinese word for "little brother"—and he always called her jiejie. No, he saw her upside down and covered in blood, begging him for help. Because he hadn't spoken up. He hadn't spoken the truth. His lack of courage had led the way to that moment.

That cowardice a year ago had built his courage today. The pain and suffering his silence had caused were so much more than he could have ever imagined possible. He would never take the coward's path again, especially not when the life of a friend was in danger.

Baileya's spinning blades kept the Scim at bay, and Shula stepped away from them and lit on fire. Her magic must not have left her yet. She waded into the Scim with a grim determination, and they fell away in terror. One of the Scim dropped a sword, and Jason snatched it up. He could barely lift it, but he managed one awkward swing at the Scim in front of him. They fell back. But then, with laughs like monstrous frogs croaking, they advanced again. One of them knocked the sword from his hand with ease.

Jason yelped.

Madeline leaned against him, losing consciousness. She said his name just before her eyes rolled back into her head and she fell.

He scooped his arm around her, holding her up. He couldn't pick up a sword again, not that it would help, and the Scim had him backed against the edge of the roof. Baileya saw them and spun in their direction, but there were at least four Scim between them now, and Break Bones was engaging her complete attention. Shula was at the far end of the roof, clearing a path for them, lighting the Scim like torches.

Jason wrapped his arms around Madeline's waist, holding her in front of him, whispered a quick prayer, and leaned backward. The world tilted, and they fell. His body would cushion her fall, or at least he hoped so. The looks on the faces of the Scim on the roof, peering over the edge with wide black eyes and frog-like mouths agape, was almost worth it. If it was the last thing Jason saw, he would be satisfied with that. He hadn't seen another option. He couldn't make it to the stairs, and no way would he let Break Bones murder Madeline, not if falling to their deaths could prevent it.

The impact took his breath away.

He groaned. They were still moving.

They had landed in a hay cart pulled by a stampeding horse plowing through the crowd on the street. A quick glance at the Scim showed them even more startled. If they had been cartoons, their jaws would have hit the street.

He and Madeline were alive. "I'm alive!" he shouted up to the Scim, instantly regretting it. They disappeared from the edge, then reappeared, descending the wall feet first.

The cart bucked wildly, knocking Madeline off him. He shoved her deeper in the hay, hoping it would keep her in the cart. The cart hit a hole in the street, and he flew, for a moment, off of the pile of hay and into the air. He fell into the cart, biting his tongue in the process. An arrow zipped past his head, lodging in the wooden plank beside him.

He leapt onto the driver's seat and grabbed hold of the flailing reins. "Yah, mule!" he shouted, because that's what they always shouted in movies, even though this wasn't a mule.

Or a horse.

A closer look made it clear his rampaging "horse" was actually a gigantic, furious goat.

"Yah, goat!" he yelled, and the beast came under some semblance of control. Which is to say, it stopped careening side to side on the street and ran straight ahead, scattering the crowd as Jason yelled, "Runaway goat! Make way!"

Baileya was keeping pace, running along the top of the buildings to their right. Her long legs stretched to their maximum, she vaulted over Scim, dodged weapons, and cleared the spaces between roofs. She flew from a rooftop, her legs tucked beneath her, her bladed staff held under her left arm, her hair flying out behind her. She landed in the hay beside Madeline.

She slipped beside Jason, taking the reins. "A clever escape, Wu Song."

"It was an accident," he said, and she grinned at him.

"We should be able to get to Westwind quickly with this cart," Baileya said.

Shula came falling like a white-hot meteor toward them, also landing in the hay and lighting it immediately on fire.

"Come on!" Jason yelled. He scrambled into the back and dragged Madeline clear.

Shula's flames only grew brighter. "My magic is out of control!" she shouted.

"We have to stop the cart," Jason said to Baileya.

She shook her head. "We ride as long as we can. The Scim are faster on foot than we."

She was right. The Scim were loping in their wake, in the street and along the rooftops. If they abandoned the cart, they'd be in the same situation they had been in on the roof. The cart shuddered as Baileya steered the goat around a few runaway Scim children.

Shula was shoveling flaming bales of hay out the back, sending up jets of sparks behind them. They hit a corner hard, and a wheel on the cart wobbled, letting out a tremendous shriek. "We're losing a wheel!"

Baileya whipped the reins harder, shouting at the goat. Jason wasn't sure how going faster would help, and then he saw the arched rise of a narrow bridge ahead. There was no way the cart would fit. "Hold Madeline!" Baileya cried, furiously driving the goat toward the narrow passage.

Bracing his legs as well as he could against the footboard, Jason wrapped Madeline tightly in his arms and ducked his head, waiting for the impact. Just before they hit, the right-hand wheel came off, rolling alongside them as the cart crashed to the ground, sparks rising from the cobblestone streets. Shula barely managed to grab onto the cart's rail. The terrified goat lunged for the bridge, wedging the cart between stone columns rising on either side.

His head ringing, Jason dragged Madeline over the front of the cart, weaving his way past the angry goat. Baileya motioned him forward, already beyond the animal and facing the bridge. "I will hold the Scim here. Those who refuse the bridge will be slowed by the river. Make all haste for Westwind. Do not pause, do not linger!"

"No loitering? Your advice is no loitering?"

He hoisted Madeline onto his shoulder with Baileya's help and stumbled down the street. The crowds had thinned, whether because they were farther from the square or because the goat had flattened or blocked everything headed this way, Jason didn't know. Smoke curled through the city now, along with the distant cries of terrified people. The city was no longer dark, because it was on fire.

Jason was sweating before he got out of earshot of Baileya. The whistling sound of her staff was often followed by the impact of metal on leather armor. He felt Shula before he heard her, the blazing heat of her flames moving alongside him.

"My flames won't go out," she said. "I can't help you carry her."

"We're almost there." He could, in fact, see Westwind's gate. It wasn't open, though, and he wasn't sure how they would get through it. Five blocks to go, more or less.

"I'll run a full block ahead of you," Shula said. "Make sure it's clear."

"Right," he said, gasping.

Madeline stirred. "Jason?"

"It's okay," he said. "We're almost to Westwind."

"I can . . . walk," she said.

He set her down. Walking together might make them faster. He wasn't sure. She leaned on him, and they struggled onward. Shula stood at the intersection, her head turning both ways to take in the people on the street. "Quickly," she said.

Madeline was able to nearly trot, though her breathing came in fits. Her skin was clammy and alarmingly cold. "I can carry you," he said, but Madeline shook her head, a determined look on her face.

When they reached the intersection, Shula immediately ran to the next. At the next intersection she did the same. They were three blocks away now. Jason shouted at the top of his lungs for someone to open the gate. Ruth Mbewe's tiny blindfolded face appeared at the top of the wall. "We cannot open the gate," she called. "The Scim are too close!"

Jason craned his neck to look back toward the goat cart. He couldn't see the cart anymore, or hear the battle, but there were no Scim, either. "I don't see any," he said.

"Swim the moat, and we'll throw you a rope!"

Madeline's face set in a grim, determined frown. She would try. Jason didn't see how she would do it, though. And the Scim couldn't be that close, he hadn't seen any. Shula hadn't seen any.

Then, a block ahead of Shula, on the street that crossed in front of the gate, a figure loomed out of the deep shadows of the street. His massive arms had gashes, his clothes were burned, and he was dripping with water. No doubt he had swum the river rather than fight his way over the goat cart. Break Bones.

Shula picked up the pace, deliberately running at him, her flames burning ever hotter.

"Quickly," Madeline gasped, and Jason limped alongside her, moving toward the moat.

Shula danced around Break Bones. His superior strength was nothing compared to her speed. She scalded his arms badly every time he took a swing at her, and thus far he hadn't managed to connect. Jason got Madeline to the edge of the moat. It was still a three-foot drop into the foul water around the castle. He helped Madeline to a sitting position and got ready to help her slip in, then follow.

Ruth's face appeared again above. "The knight is opening the bridge!"

The knight? Jason squeezed Madeline's hand. Why was the knight inside instead of at the festival? Why didn't he open the gates as soon as he saw Madeline and Jason on their way? Wasn't his job to fight the Scim? Why was he hiding in the castle?

They made their way toward the descending bridge. When it was nearly to the ground, Jason boosted Madeline onto it, and she hobbled inside. The Knight of the Mirror flew over the bridge on his silver stallion, Rayo.

Shula's flame went out.

Break Bones laughed. "Your magic is extinguished for the night!" He backhanded her, sending her flying into the moat.

Then the knight was upon the Scim, barely missing him with his lance. Break Bones grabbed the knight by the waist, twisted hard, and smashed him onto the stone road. The Knight of the Mirror was no fool, and he rolled to the side just before the Scim's fists pounded the pavement. "Go to the lady of Westwind at once," the knight called to Jason.

Jason, flat on his belly beside the moat, was able to reach Shula's outstretched hand. Several people ran from inside the castle and helped him pull her out of the putrid water. "What about Baileya?" he asked. The knight fought the Scim using only his sword.

"She is Kakri," Shula said. "She won't stop fighting."

"Get Madeline to the knight's solar," Jason said to Ruth. Ruth stood close to Madeline, letting the breathless girl lean on her.

Jason had to get to the wall. He needed to get to higher ground, so he could find Baileya. If he could get his hands on a bow, maybe he could help her.

When he reached the top, he was breathless and exhausted. His heart sank as he looked over the lip of the wall. It wasn't just Break Bones out there. There were hundreds of Scim, all converging on the castle like a swarm of ants. He scanned the crowd—or what he could see of it in the darkness—and saw, to his dismay, the three white-robed Skulls moving toward the castle as well.

"Send out the girl," one of the Black Skulls demanded. "The one who cannot breathe. Madeline Oliver."

A few of the castle's residents were trying to hold the drawbridge long enough to keep it open so the knight could return. Rayo was nowhere to be seen. The knight was in the thick of battle and making a slow, tortured path back. One of the Black Skulls was moving toward the drawbridge now, and nothing stood in its way.

In the guardhouse, a small room built into the stone wall, Jason found a bow. He stood as he had been taught and put his fingers on the string, an arrow nocked between them. It felt strange without the magic to guide him. He sighted along the arrow, pointing at the heart of one of the Black Skulls. He pulled back carefully, then released the string. The arrow went sideways. The string snapped his forearm, and he dropped the bow, crying out in pain. The arrow fell awkwardly into the moat, followed by the bow.

A horn blew, a brighter, higher sound than the horns of the Scim. Rondelo bounded into the fray on Evernu, his white stag. Close behind him came some of the army of the Elenil, the men and women who were loyal to the Knight of the Mirror. Rondelo, whose battle prowess had never been a gift of magic but rather of hard-earned skill, cut through the Scim. David and Kekoa came behind him. They weren't wearing their war gear, but they had their weapons of choice. They moved slower and with less fluidity than they had with magic, but still, they were making a difference in the battle.

"Hold the bridge!" Rondelo cried, and his people spread out in a semicircle, pushing the Scim away from the entrance. The fighting grew vicious along that semicircle, but the Elenil army managed to hold it. There were more Elenil warriors in the crowd than Jason had ever seen. Near Rondelo an Elenil man in a shining silver helmet repaired every break in the line, running back and forth to the places in most need. He held two swords, and when he waded into the Scim, the swords flashed with reflected firelight.

Rayo came galloping back toward the castle now, Baileya on his back. "The bridge has fallen!" she shouted. "More Scim are on their way!"

The Knight of the Mirror turned to his side, and as Baileya thundered past, he grabbed her forearm and slung himself up behind her. "Close the drawbridge!" he cried, and immediately it began to ratchet upward. Westwind's defenders continued to fight as the drawbridge inclined. The knight's horse jumped onto it, and as soon as they hit the ground inside, the knight slung himself down and joined the people in closing the bridge, lending his strength to turning the wheel.

Rondelo and Evernu and the Elenil with the silver helmet leapt off the drawbridge, remaining outside the castle. They guarded the closing gate, keeping the Scim off, pushing them back. The three Black Skulls shoved their way to the front of the conflict. The silver-helmeted Elenil spun and danced as his twin blades easily deflected two of the three Skulls. Rondelo joined him, leaping from Evernu's back to engage the third Skull, allowing the stag to hold another hole in their line.

Break Bones slunk up behind Rondelo. Jason shouted a warning, and Rondelo spun, kicking Break Bones in the chest. During this momentary distraction, the third Black Skull turned his attention to the silver-helmeted Elenil and ran a sword through his heart. He fell like a puppet with cut strings. Rondelo screamed and skidded into the trio of Skulls, fighting them with a fierce passion.

Jason ran for the gate, shouting at them to hold it. The knight heard him and paused. "The silver Elenil has fallen," Jason said, and he ran up the bridge, which was so high now he could scarcely make it to the top. He hung over the lip, swung his body twice, and just managed to jump across, landing with a bone-jarring thump.

Rondelo kept all the Scim at bay himself, with only Evernu's help. Jason scooped up the body of the silver-helmeted Elenil. He felt lighter than he should, even though he was completely limp, as if Jason had picked up a bag that should be full of bricks but was stuffed instead with pillows. "Evernu," he shouted, and the stag fell back to his side. He put the body over the stag's back and, at Rondelo's instructions, climbed on himself.

The stag leapt to the top of the bridge, skidding inside the castle walls. The Knight of the Mirror shouted for them to close the bridge, just as Rondelo vaulted through the gap. Jason slipped from the stag, pulling the Elenil man down and laying him gingerly on his back. David and Kekoa appeared beside him, helping Jason get the man's arms and legs laid out gently.

He didn't appear to be breathing. Jason carefully removed the silver helmet. The still, quiet face looked familiar.

"Aw, no," Kekoa said. "It's Vivi."

Jason knew that name, but the terror of the last hour prevented him from remembering. But David filled in the blanks when he said, "Hanali's dad."

Rondelo fell to his knees beside Vivi's body. "Ah, brave soul." Tears sprang from Rondelo's eyes. "On this night of all nights he fought, when his body cannot be mended with the magic of the Sunlit Lands. He is lost to us." He closed his eyes, and his next words came slowly but surely, like a poem being quoted: "His bowl is spilt, his thread unspun. His life is past and just begun. He treads now in a clime of sun . . . in the land of the Majestic One."

"They're climbing the walls!"

Rondelo rose smoothly to his feet. "Come, friends. Let us avenge Vivi, son of Gelintel, father of Hanali."

"No," the Knight of the Mirror said. "These three young men must come with me to my solar. Rondelo, protect Vivi's body so the Scim will not take possession of him."

Rondelo lifted Vivi in his arms and set him gently on Evernu's back. "When the wall is breached, I will take him to Hanali."

The knight put his hand on Rondelo's shoulder. "Let us pray that our people can hold the walls long enough to accomplish one more task. Come, boys. Stop staring at the walls and follow me!"

27

PARTINGS

It is no shame to travel with crows.

A KAKRI PROVERB

✦

She missed Darius. It was a ridiculous thing to think as she labored, breathing heavily, to climb the tower stairs. Nevertheless, there it was. She had met him freshman year. He was charming, kind, and smart. Rare enough in a boy at all, nearly extinct among high school freshmen. One day in English, when they were right in the middle of studying Romeo and Juliet, he had shown up at class with three roses for her.

On the note he had written, "Madeline. 'That which we call a rose by any other name would smell as sweet.' I called these 'Madeline,' and they seemed sweeter. Yours, Darius."

It wasn't the most emotionally competent way of breaking the ice, but it could have been worse. Besides, they had been freshmen. He was an emotional genius compared to some of the other kids.

And when she had gotten sick, he had been amazing. But once she knew what was going on—not just her diagnosis, but once she really understood—she'd had to break up with him. She couldn't let him spend a year of his life watching hers slip away. She knew he would stick by her until the end, and she couldn't let him do that. She regretted it now. Maybe if she had stayed with him, he'd be with her on this staircase. One thing was certain—as much as she appreciated Ruth's help climbing the stairs, and as strong as Ruth was for an eight-year-old, Darius could have scooped her up in his arms and carried her. She worried she might not make it through the night, and even after they'd broken up, she'd still secretly imagined that Darius would be there when . . . well, when she breathed her last.

"Are you able to continue?" Ruth asked, her blindfolded face turned toward Madeline's.

The clash of weapons and the cries of warriors echoed through the courtyard and up the tower. Although they ascended as quickly as Madeline was able, she was afraid the battle would overtake them before she entered the knight's quarters. "Yes," she said, and they moved forward another eight hard-won steps before she doubled over, hands on her knees, taking breaths that rasped through her like knives.

"There is a window here," Ruth said, although how she knew it with her eyes covered Madeline couldn't say. Perhaps the cool night air touched her face.

Madeline put her hand on the narrow stone window. Waves of Scim had crested the walls. Human soldiers worked to push them back. Madeline suddenly understood why the Knight of the Mirror must require those who fought at his side to do so without magic. Was it all in anticipation of this night? He would be uniquely vulnerable during this time. In fact . . . his magical blessing that nothing could be taken from his hand would be broken tonight, wouldn't it? That meant the Scim artifacts he was meant to protect would be at risk. Not to mention her and Jason.

The sound of shattering glass came from further up the tower.

Before they could investigate, a bird, green and black with a plume of bright blue on its head, landed on the window.

"Do you bring a message for the Knight of the Mirror?" Ruth asked, her words tumbling out with intense concern.

"The gates are fallen," the bird said. "Malgwin, harbinger of chaos and suffering, swims the waters of the Sunlit Lands. The Scim have taken the Court of Far Seeing—"

"That we can see ourselves," Ruth snapped. "What more?"

"They enter the Palace of a Thousand Years, intent on reclaiming the Heart of the Scim. The palace guards hold them floor by floor. The archon is wounded and has retreated to his chambers with the stone. Tirius commands the knight come lest—"

"He could not even if he wished it. The knight is trapped here in his own castle."

"Then we are lost," the bird replied. "The Court of Far Seeing is burning. Three magistrates are dead, killed in the square by the Scim. More are wounded, and hours yet remain until daylight."

"Vivi, too, has left us," Ruth said. "I have heard the mourning cry of the Elenil from the courtyard."

"Woe! Woe! Woe to the Sunlit Lands!" the bird cried. "Is the Sword of Years safe? Or have the villains retaken their instruments of destruction?"

"For now they are safe," Ruth said. "Though the Scim beat upon our very door."

"This is one bright kindling of hope."

"Is there no other news, then?"

"None good. The Black Skulls roam our streets. The Scim are fierce and the Elenil all unprepared. It is said the Maegrom have joined their side and allowed the Scim entrance through their own clever tunnels. Even now the—awk! Awk awk awk!" The bird's head bobbled, as if choking on something in its long neck. It flapped its wings and flew away, high over Westwind, headed toward the center of the city.

"What . . . what happened?"

Ruth, her face set in a grim frown, said, "The magic has faded now even for the messenger birds. It will not be long until the last of the Elenil magic fails for the night."

They made their way farther up the stairs. One of the stairway mirrors was shattered, and the broken glass crunched beneath their feet. "Is . . . someone . . ." A series of coughs battered Madeline's chest.

Ruth lowered Madeline to the stone stairs, careful to avoid the broken mirror. "Perhaps there is help above. I will go. Patience."

Help above? The only person above was Fernanda, trapped in her mirrors. Maybe Ruth was getting one of the magical artifacts. But if the magic was failing, what help would they be? Even the magic mirrors were breaking. A terrible thought crept into her mind. What if someone else was in the tower? One of the Scim or the Black Skulls? That seemed impossible, but what if they had used some sort of magic and arrived before them? Madeline had allowed an eight-year-old to go alone up the stairs.

Madeline struggled to her feet and rested her hand against the wall. Her heart beat frantically, and she felt light headed. She waited for the black waves at the edges of her vision to recede. Then she made her way, step by painful step, upward.

A yelp of surprise came from above, and Ruth pushed herself under Madeline's arm. "I told you I would bring help. You should have waited."

She *had* brought help too. Rushing down the stairs, holding the hem of her dress so she could move more easily, came Fernanda Isabela Flores de Castilla, the lady of Westwind. She draped Madeline's other arm around her neck, and together the three of them made their way steadily toward the top.

"How—?"

"On this night the cursed enchantment is broken," Fernanda said. "Tonight alone in the year I walk among you not as a ghost but as a woman."

A sob caught in Madeline's throat. She was exhausted, she couldn't breathe, and she needed to keep climbing. This poor woman, though, had been trapped in the mirrors for the entire year, and now, tonight, she was using her few moments of precious freedom to help Madeline. It was too much to bear.

"Come, come," Fernanda said. "It is not so bad. Being trapped in a mirror saves me looking in them."

They had reached the knight's solar.

"On the bed there," Fernanda said, and together she and Ruth lowered Madeline onto the rumpled bed in the main chamber. The table with the Scim artifacts sat in full view, unprotected.

"Need . . . to hide . . . the artifacts," Madeline said.

Fernanda stroked her sweating forehead. "Do not worry, child, my beloved will be here soon. He has a plan, I know, to keep them safe."

Jason burst into the room, followed by Delightful Glitter Lady trotting along in her golden retriever size. "Madeline!"

Jason's friends David and Kekoa came in behind him. Kekoa carried a strange weapon with teeth. Then Shula came behind them, her face covered in dirt and gore, her hair loose and wild. She carried a canvas package, which she immediately unfolded in the center of the floor. It was full of weapons. Then Baileya entered, panting.

"The knight bars the tower door," she said. "He will be here in a moment. For now he asks that each of you arm yourselves, for the battle to leave here will be fierce."

Shula and Jason were at Madeline's side now, talking over each other, both concerned for her and trying to figure out how they could help. Of course there was nothing to be done.

The knight appeared a moment later, his sword in hand. His eyes lingered on the magically shrunken rhinoceros, and he frowned at Jason. "Make haste," he said. "Gather quickly."

Madeline got to her feet and met them at the table. Fernanda pressed in to the knight's side, and he took her under his arm, pausing only to kiss her once and say, in barely more than a whisper, "Ah, my lady, at last I hold you for a moment. Forgive me that I must make haste in giving instructions."

She kissed his cheek and said, "My brave knight, do as you must."

The Knight of the Mirror looked around the table. "We are nine," he said. "Before you lie five magical artifacts, weapons of the Scim. Should they retrieve these weapons, tonight's attack will be only the first course in a veritable banquet of destruction."

"Maybe we could skip to dessert," Jason said. The knight ignored him.

"My magical boon returns at first light, but even now the Scim are within the walls of Westwind. I fear what may come. I must ask a brave favor of you all."

"We'll do whatever you ask," Shula said.

"Within reason," Jason said.

The knight nodded. "Your honesty does you both credit. I fear my request is neither reasonable nor easily accomplished. I desire to fling these five artifacts to the other peoples of the Sunlit Lands so the Scim will not easily recover them."

Baileya said, "I can take them to the Kakri, Sir Knight, with little difficulty."

"I hoped you would say so." He picked up the silver mask. "This is the Mask of Passing. Entrust it, please, to your tribe. I would have Jason join you in your journey."

"Whoa," Jason said. "I should go with Madeline. I came here to protect her, not your drama mask."

Baileya folded her arms. "The desert is harsh, Sir Knight. I fear Wu Song may not be easily accepted among my people. If something were to happen to me before we reached the Kakri, he would surely be lost."

"Better the mask be lost than returned to the Scim." Then, to Jason, the knight said, "I do not have the people to send more than two together, and it is more important that each artifact have a warrior to help transport it than that you be near your friend. Your pledge to the Elenil binds you to take this order."

"Except I didn't make a pledge to the Elenil, I made a pledge to Madeline," Jason said. "I'm not leaving her."

"The knight's right," Madeline said. "I will need . . . protection . . . and someone to help . . . me move. At least until . . . morning."

"Besides," Shula said. "How would you protect her? Not with bow and arrow."

Jason blushed. "You saw that, huh?"

Baileya put her hand on Jason's arm. "I heard tell of it from the knight. It is no shame. You acquitted yourself bravely. To attempt the bow is better than to have run. Better a failure than a coward."

"Thanks, I guess?" Jason said, still blushing.

The knight handed a folded robe to Kekoa. "Ruth will accompany you to the Zhanin. She knows the way. Sail west, and wait for the song of welcome. If they do not welcome you, or seem hostile, wear the Robe of Ascension for one day . . . only long enough to explain yourself and our situation. Remind their holy ones of my service to them many years ago."

Kekoa took the robe. "Okay, kid," he said. "Let's go."

"Godspeed," said the knight. "Do not fight unless you must."

"We should go as well," Baileya said.

"I want to know where everyone is going in case something goes wrong. Something always goes wrong," Jason said.

The knight nodded. "Quickly, then. David, to you I give this key, called the Disenthraller. It can open any lock: gate or door, chest or drawer. Take it to the Aluvorean people."

David nodded once, quickly, and put the key in his pocket. "Anyone I should take with me?"

"You will move faster alone, I think," the knight said. "Leave the city by the western gate if you can, and head to the southwest. You will see the great trees rise up like mountains. Follow them to the heart of the wood and say these words: 'Beneath the shadows of the great trees I beg your mercy. Take me to your heart that I might grow.' If the people reject you, speak to the trees."

"Beneath the shadows of the great trees I beg your mercy. Take me to your heart that I might grow." David looked to the knight for confirmation. They exchanged nods. "Good luck to all of you," David said. He scooped up an extra knife from the canvas covering on the floor and trotted down the stairs.

"I will bar the door behind him," Fernanda said.

"O wise woman," the knight called after her. "Shula and Madeline, you must take this stone, the Memory Stone, to the Maegrom."

Madeline held up her hand. "A bird told us . . . the Maegrom . . . have allied with . . . the Scim."

The knight deflated. "That is grave news. I fear, then, that I must take the Memory Stone and try to hold it until dawn. May I be successful! I must ask you two, then, to take the Sword of Years to the Pastisians. They live in the far northeast, beyond the mountains, near the crystal horizon."

Jason's tiny rhino whined, and Jason said, "Wait, aren't those the necromancers? I heard about them."

"Indeed," the knight said. "It is a dark time that we have come to this."

Fernanda burst into the room. "The door is barred, but the Scim are outside the tower. In moments they will knock upon the door."

The knight placed the rusted sword in Madeline's hands and the scabbard in Shula's. "This sword must not be returned to the scabbard, or it will come out new and thirsty for blood. Once awakened it cannot be put to sleep save through bloodshed. It must not fall to the Scim. Guard it with your lives!" He pulled the canvas from the floor, dropping the other weapons with a great clattering of metal. He wrapped the sword and tied it with rope. "Upon the roof a great bird awaits. You are too weak to run, Madeline, but not, I hope, too weak to fly. Head northeast until you think the very world will end, and you will see the lights of their city by night or the smoke of their magics by day. They have great contempt for the magic of the Elenil and the Scim. Tell them they may destroy this sword if they wish and if they are able!"

"Will the bird's magic last so long?" Shula asked.

A crashing sound came from below. The knight thrust a short sword at Jason. "It is a risk, Shula, but one we must take. Fly low if you can. My lady Fernanda, take Shula and Madeline above. Baileya, Jason, with me to guard their retreat."

"I thought you wanted us to leave," Jason said, taking the sword gingerly.

"I fear only Baileya can help me hold the door now," the knight said. "We must hope we can then provide an exit for the two of you."

Jason hugged Madeline. "Once we deliver the mask, I'll find you."

"Hurry, boy!" the knight cried, running down the stairs. Baileya followed. Jason winked at Madeline and shot after them, Delightful Glitter Lady at his heels.

"This way," Fernanda said urgently, leading them to a corner of the room where a wooden ladder lay, a ladder that Madeline hadn't noticed before. With Shula's help Fernanda propped it in the corner. She climbed the rungs and pushed open a sort of hatch. The roof was sloped, but built onto the side was a wide wooden platform. An enormous bird perched there, a saddle on its back.

Shula climbed on first. Madeline passed her the sword, then mounted behind her, encircling her waist with her arms. Her breathing came shallow and fast. "Farewell," Shula said.

"Go with God," Fernanda replied. "Come home once your duty is done!" Then she whispered to the bird, "To Pastisia!"

The bird let out an ear-shattering call, crouched down, and shoved itself into the sky. Its wings spread wide, and it circled once, twice, around the tower, gaining height with each pass. Far below, the Scim fought their bloody battle with the Elenil. Fires blazed throughout the city. The bird turned northeast, gliding over the city walls. A Scim far below loosed an arrow at them, but it fell away long before reaching them.

The darkness was so deep, they couldn't see the ground once they left the firelit city. Despite the knight's warning, Shula kept the bird flying high, saying she was worried about trees or other obstructions in the dark. The stars burned above, but there was no moon. A dark ribbon glittered with starlight below, a river wending its way through the land. They flew with astonishing speed, the air cold and piercing. It seemed to help Madeline's breathing a little, though she shivered almost without ceasing. It was because of her shivering that she didn't feel the bird shaking at first.

"Oh no," Shula said.

"What . . . is it?"

"Hold on," Shula said. Then again, yelling, "Hold on!"

Madeline wrapped her arms tighter around Shula.

The bird was shrinking. It was still large, large enough to hold them both, but not large enough to stay airborne. It was struggling, flapping with all its might, but they were falling, falling toward the unseen ground below. The Sword of Years tumbled from Madeline's grip. She reached for it, gasping, and then she was falling, faster than the bird and Shula. She closed her eyes and braced herself.

She hit the water, hard, before she had a chance to take even half a breath.

28
THE FALL

Thou shalt flee to the east, and walk dunes alone
in sunshine and shadow, eater of carrion.
Thy sister shall be the crow, thy brother the hyena.
FROM "THE ORDERING OF THE WORLD," AN ELENIL STORY

✦

The door shuddered in its frame, but the heavy bar held. Splinters flew, and a thick stone blade split a hole. The knight stood three steps above the door, sword at the ready. Baileya stood two steps above him, her double-bladed staff as wide as the stairway. Jason stood six steps up from Baileya. The knight had taken Jason's short sword and given him a mace. It was, essentially, a weighted club with spikes on it.

"Always keep the upper ground," the knight said. "If I fall, do as Baileya says. The narrow stairs work to our advantage. Any creature that passes me and this warrior maid must be fierce indeed, but hopefully wounded."

Jason cleared his throat. "Then I whack it in the head with the pointy club."

"The mace," the knight said. "Indeed. Well said, young warrior."

There came another shuddering crash from the door and guttural shouts from the Scim on the other side. The knight clasped Baileya's forearm, and she his. "It has been an honor to fight alongside you, daughter of the desert."

"If we live," she said, "this shall be a story of great value among my people. The honor is mine, Sir Knight."

"Likewise," Jason said. "Honor to die with everyone, et cetera."

Baileya grinned at him, and her pale-silver eyes twinkled like starlight. "Even in the face of death you raise the spirits of your companions."

He managed not to blush this time, but her words warmed him right to the tips of his fingers. He shrugged, trying to look nonchalant, something he found challenging when holding a mace. "It might be my only contribution to this fight."

"Make ready," the knight said, as another fall of the ax tore a hole in the door. Great grey fingers reached through, trying to rip the boards apart, but the knight sliced at them. Howling erupted from the other side of the door.

For a bare second a black eye peered through the hole in the door, disappearing before the knight's sword could rise to meet it. "Beware, Scim, lest thou lose thine eyes at my door."

Jason laughed. "Nice one, King James."

"It is the ancient language of kings and knights," Baileya said.

"Behold! I doth know that so much already," Jason said, swinging his mace, which hit the stone wall and jarred his arms. "Ouch."

Delightful Glitter Lady leaned against him and let loose a high-pitched whine.

There was a momentary silence on the other side. A Scim shouted, "They have a unicorn upon the stairs!"

Jason patted Dee on the back. *That's right, you nutty people of the Sunlit Lands. Be afraid of my rhino. Call it a unicorn if you like.*

The door shattered inward. The first Scim to cross the threshold fell to the knight's sword. Three more Scim rushed upon him. He sidestepped the stroke of an ax, kicked a second Scim, and drove his elbow into the jaw of a third. Baileya darted forward and stabbed a Scim over the knight's shoulder.

Then, chaos.

The knight stacked the bodies of the wounded Scim before him to impede their comrades, but the Scim snagged feet and arms and dragged them away so that a fresh wave of attackers could advance. For a time, Baileya switched places with the knight so he could rest. The fighting seemed to go on for hours, and the smell of sweat and blood and the sound of metal on metal rang endlessly in Jason's ears. When Baileya and the knight switched places again, the Scim retreated and moved away from the doorway.

"What's happening?" Jason asked.

"They will try a new approach," Baileya said. "Perhaps they will scale the tower?"

The knight shook his head and said softly, "They do not know our numbers. Perhaps we have guards above with hot pitch or bow and arrow."

"Sir Knight," came a booming voice.

"I am here," the knight called.

"In time we will take this tower. Is this not true?"

"Aye," the knight said, "unless ye be a battalion of knaves and cowards."

"Thinkest thou that we are such?"

"I said not so, sir."

"Sir Knight, may I approach in peace that we may exchange a few words before the fight recommences?"

The knight whispered something to Baileya, then called, "Aye, but with empty hands, sir."

A Scim came into view, palms up. He looked up the stairs to see the knight, Baileya, and Jason standing there, each holding a weapon, and the rhinoceros lounging at Jason's side. The Scim laughed and leaned against the doorjamb, crossing his arms. "Wu Song. Truly, you are a thorn of great length and sharpness inserted deeply into my side."

Jason waved. "Hey, Break Bones. Good to see you."

"Why dost thou seek parley?" the knight asked.

"Oh, good Sir Knight, I thought it might be pleasant to converse before thy death."

The knight set his sword against the wall, point on the stairs. He massaged his sword arm with the other. "Speak then, sir. Night is burning away, and when the sun returneth so doth the magic of the Elenil."

Break Bones laughed, his great grey boulder of a head nodding in delight. "Ah, such a pleasure, Sir Knight, to speak with thee. Thou art as fierce in words as in battle. Yes, soon the magic of the Elenil shall return." His grin disappeared, and his wide hands clenched at his side. "Not so the army of the Scim. Thou and the Kakri child have killed or wounded a full two score."

"Speak and be done," Baileya said. "I grow weary of your stalling."

Break Bones stood straight. "Ah, the child has a tongue, and sharp enough. Surrender the artifacts of the Scim to us, and we shall take you captive until first light, then release you—you and all in the tower, save Wu Song and his friend Madeline. For I have sworn to kill her and then him."

"No deal," Jason said. The knight and Baileya said nothing, staring at the Scim. "Right, guys? No deal, right?"

The knight spoke. "Break Bones. Didst thou pause our battle to insult us? I am a knight and a man of honor. Thou must live according to thy vows, and I according to mine. The artifacts of the Scim are under my protection, and I cannot give them willingly into thy hands."

"I intended no insult. My offer was meant as a kindness. We will fight ye for the hours it takes to wound or tire ye, and then take what ye will not give. In a moment we shall return." He paused, then said, "Wu Song. You have always spoken truth to me, so I must do the same."

"Is it that you like my shirt?" Jason asked. "A lot of people have said that."

"No, child. It is said among the Scim that you have murdered Night's Breath. Is this so?"

Jason considered this. When the magic had snuffed out, Jason hadn't. Which meant Night's Breath had died. Died so he could live. Madeline had made that choice, not him, but it was true. Night's Breath had died because of Jason. He took a deep breath and started to answer. Stopped. Tried again. He couldn't bring himself to say the simple answer—yes. Instead he said, "Technically, I was unconscious. So . . . not really. It wasn't my decision."

Break Bones seemed to deflate a little. "Ah. I had hoped it to be but a rumor. He was used to heal your wounds and died of them? Is that the shape of it?"

"I didn't choose it," Jason said, "if that makes a difference. It wasn't me, exactly. I'm horrified by it."

"But you are the one who benefited," Break Bones said. "You did not kill him, but you inherited his life."

"It wasn't me," Jason repeated. "It's a horrible thing, but I'm not a murderer, if that's what you're saying."

"No, it was not you," Break Bones said. "It was your allies. Now a great prince of my people lies dead, and his life throbs in your veins. His life was taken in payment for yours, and you stand upon those stairs and say it is not your fault."

"It's *not* my fault!"

"Yet he is dead, and you still breathe."

"I can't change that," Jason said. He stopped, uncertain of the rules of the Sunlit Lands. He asked Baileya, "Wait, I can't change that, can I?"

She shook her head. "Death comes but once."

"Yeah, okay," Jason said. "I can't bring Night's Breath back to life. So you can't hold me responsible for his death."

"Tell that to his orphaned children," Break Bones said. "Who will care for them now? Their father is dead, and you will use his life for some other purpose than to care for them. You will not serve his people or walk his mother to meet the Peasant King. Are these not your choices? You did not murder him, perhaps, but his blood is on your hands."

"That's not fair," Jason said.

"So says his wife. So say his children and his mother and his neighbors. Yet here you stand. Alive."

"Why are we talking about this? Did you just want me to feel bad before you killed me?"

The Scim frowned, his eyes sad. "No, Wu Song. I told you this so you would understand: every Scim in this city has made a blood oath to return Night's Breath's life to his people."

"Um," Jason said. "Just to be clear . . . Are you saying that every Scim in the city has taken an oath to kill me?"

"Indeed, and to bear your body back to Night's Breath's widow."

Jason's knees felt weak. "Well. Thanks for letting me know."

Break Bones bowed. "Sir Knight. Lady. Wu Song. In a moment our battle will recommence, at your signal. Fare ye well."

The Scim disappeared.

"Are ye ready?" the knight asked, still using his archaic speech.

Baileya shook her staff. Jason just shook. He couldn't say anything. He had known theoretically the Scim were willing to kill him, but that was a bit different than all of them taking a vow to kill him. Overwhelmed by the whole thing, he shouted, "You know, I'm actually a pretty nice guy if you take the time to get to know me!"

Break Bones's voice came echoing to them as he addressed his soldiers. "Kill whomever you must to take the tower. What belongs to the Scim we return to our people. Whoever lays hands upon the Sword of Years and returns it to our people, be it Scim or Elenil, human or Kakri, I shall be in their debt for every day of my life. Are ye ready, my brethren? Are ye prepared, sistren?"

A roar came from the army of the Scim.

The knight brandished his sword and shouted, "Come then, Scim! Do your worst."

They did. Four Scim rushed in, two in front and two in back. While the knight fought the front two, the two in the back sliced at him. He made quick work of them, but as he knocked the fourth down the stairs, it revealed a fifth Scim kneeling at the bottom of the tower, a crossbow in his hands trained directly at the knight.

The knight turned fast enough to spare his heart, but the bolt sank into his sword shoulder. With a cry, Baileya leapt over him, darted out of the stairway, and killed the Scim. She snatched the crossbow and two bolts that had fallen to the ground before scrambling back to the relative safety of the stairway.

"Well done," the knight said, pale and bleeding on the stairs.

"Whatever Scim next ascends the stairs receives a bolt for their trouble," Baileya shouted.

"Help me ascend," the knight said to Jason.

They retreated ten steps up, so that they bent around the corner and could no longer see the entrance. Baileya removed the bolt from the knight's shoulder with a swift and practiced hand. She loaded the crossbow and waited a few steps below them.

The blood flowed rhythmically from the wound. With the knight's coaching, Jason ripped some cloth from the knight's tunic and pressed it against the wound. He hadn't seen so much blood since what had happened with his sister.

"Press harder," the knight said. "Good. Now tie it. Yes, like that. Well done, Wu Song."

Baileya loosed a bolt at the first Scim to show his head, and all fell quiet again.

"Next they will overwhelm us with numbers," the knight said. "No doubt they grow restless at the thought of dawn's approach."

The next wave of Scim came in a vicious, angry mob. Baileya dropped one with a bolt, and the knight stood behind her, trying as best as he was able to keep them from passing him on the stairs. Jason reached for his mace only to realize with some horror that he had left it farther down the stairwell, leaning against the wall. He hadn't really needed it so far and had forgotten to bring it in the excitement of the knight's wound.

One Scim made it past the knight, and Jason kicked it in the teeth as hard as he was able. Baileya didn't notice, but he made a note to tell her later that her "use your feet" advice had worked.

That's when he noticed Delightful Glitter Lady twitching. Or shaking—it was hard to say. "What's wrong, girl? Are you okay?" She seemed to be having some sort of attack. She crooned to him, distressed, then ran down the stairs. "Come back, Dee! It's not safe!"

Then he understood.

The magic had worn off. The magic that made her small.

She grew to a monstrous, full-size rhino just as she squeezed between the legs of a Scim. The newly gigantic rhino smashed the Scim into the ceiling and kept growing. She filled the whole stairway. The stones started to give at her sides. No one would be getting past her. She snorted and cried, pawing at the stairs, eager to burst through the wooden doorframe and fight.

"Quickly," the knight said. "Take me up."

Together Jason and Baileya managed to get him up the stairs. Dee was snorting and shuffling below, the stairway starting to give way. The Scim were shouting and yelling from the other side. It sounded like the sudden appearance of a unicorn had frightened them so badly they were terrified to approach her. Who knew if there were more on the other side?

They passed the shattered mirror, then the garderobe, and came at last into the knight's solar. Fernanda had stacked everything heavy in the room close to the door, ready to form a barricade. The knight looked out the open windows of the tower. "Too many hours still until sunrise," he said to himself. He took Fernanda's hands, pulling them away from studying the dressings on his wound. "My lady, I must ask you a hard favor." He placed the Memory Stone in her hand.

"No!" she said. "It is too cruel. I have hours of freedom still."

The knight took the Mask of Passing from Baileya. "It is cruel, lady. And yet . . . only you can enter the mirrors. Come daylight the stone and mask will reappear in the world, and none will be able to take them from my hand. It will be some small victory tonight."

"What?" Jason stared at him, completely mystified. "Why didn't you send all of the artifacts into the mirror in the first place, then? And I thought magic didn't work right now?"

"I do not know for certain what daylight will bring," the knight said. "Perhaps the Scim will rule Far Seeing. In which case, the farther away the artifacts, the better." He paused. "And the magic that lets her enter the mirrors is not of the Elenil . . . unlike the magic that has trapped her there."

Jason picked up the Mask of Passing. "We can still get out of here," he said.

"The bird is gone," the knight said. "It won't return. There is no rope long enough, no weapon powerful enough, to remove us from this tower now."

Jason listened, his finger on his chin. "True. But you know what I always say? Poop has to go somewhere."

Baileya understood first. "No," she said. "It is too long of a drop."

"Into water," he said.

Baileya shivered. "I would not call it water."

"They will hear the splash," the knight said.

"They will be waiting for you at the lip of the moat," Fernanda said.

A chorus of shouts came from below, as well as the trumpeting of an enraged rhinoceros. Sounded like she was winning.

"I don't think they'll hear us," Jason said. Celebratory battle cries, followed by surprised shrieks of terror, drifted up the stairs. "I don't think we have much time."

Fernanda picked up the stone. She kissed the knight. "Until next year, my beloved." She walked to a mirror. She looked over her shoulder once, then stepped into the mirror, the knight running up behind her and pressing his hands flat against the glass. She put her hands on the glass too.

"Quickly," the knight said to Jason. "Head for the garderobe."

"What will you do?"

"I? I will make the Scim believe there are a hundred of us fighting them."

In the garderobe, Jason moved the stool and sat with his legs in the hole. It was a long fall to the moat. "Hurry," Baileya said. "So the knight can retreat to his solar and block the doorway." Jason had to wiggle a bit to get himself moving through, and he didn't want to think what he might be touching or about to touch in the sewage of the moat. Then he wasn't thinking anything at all but how fast and far he was falling, and he hoped he survived so he could avoid being murdered by all the Scim.

The water closed over his head, surprisingly warm. He made the dire mistake of opening his eyes, but in that darkness and the cloudy moat water, he couldn't see much. He surfaced and headed for the side of the moat.

Baileya splashed down near him. They pulled themselves from the water, and they both crouched low. Scim were everywhere . . . fighting, shouting, pulling the city apart.

Baileya checked the mask. She still had it. "Come, Wu Song. Stick to the shadows, and we may yet escape."

"I forgot my weapon," Jason said lamely.

Baileya squeezed his shoulder. "You also made our escape from Westwind possible. Fear not. We will avoid the fighting if we can."

They darted into an alley. Baileya said, "If something happens to me, Wu Song, you must keep this mask out of the hands of the Scim. Go to my people, the Kakri. If they do not kill you, then you will be safe."

If they don't kill me, I'll be safe, Jason thought. What a laugh. That nicely summed up his entire time in the Sunlit Lands so far. *If they don't kill you, you will be safe.*

He ducked low and followed Baileya across a shadowed street, his sneakers squeaking with water. They ran for the eastern gates of Far Seeing.

29

CAPTURED

Thou Scim I banish to outer darkness,
a land as black as thy heart.

FROM "THE ORDERING OF THE WORLD," AN ELENIL STORY

✛

Madeline woke lying on her belly. She couldn't move. Leather straps held her tight against a saddle of some kind. The wind was in her face, and she wondered if she had imagined falling. Had Shula tied her onto the saddle to keep her safe as they flew to Pastisia? "Shula?" she asked, but her voice swept away, drowned out by the wind.

A harsh, guttural voice answered. "I didn't kill her. I left her stranded beside the river."

She tried to lift her head and couldn't. Her breath came in such limited doses. She tried to remember what had happened. She had fallen from their bird, fallen through darkness. The bird must have been making its way down already. She had fallen into water—the voice had mentioned a river. She couldn't breathe. She had a vague memory of someone taking hold of her . . . She thought hard. Her neck? Yes, her neck ached still where she had been grabbed. They had taken hold of her neck and pulled her from the river. Someone with gloves and big hands.

She forced her eyes open and managed to lift her head. She was strapped to a giant bird. Its rider's white robes snapped and flowed around him like a flag. The black antelope skull gleamed in the starlight. He turned his head slightly, and the horns of his mask looked sharp even in this darkness. "It will be dawn soon. You will breathe easier then."

No.

"How did you . . ." But she couldn't get enough breath for the question. She coughed.

"I saw you leave from the knight's castle. I followed. I couldn't see you in the darkness, but my owl saw you easily enough. When you fell from your bird, I fished you out of the river."

"What do . . . you want?"

The Black Skull patted a canvas-wrapped parcel strapped beside him. The Sword of Years. "You are needed in the Wasted Lands. I don't know which of the other artifacts may have been recovered."

Madeline's heart sank. If they'd captured her when she had escaped the city, what were the chances the others had made it out at all? No doubt the Scim had already collected all their artifacts and were returning to their homeland now. The knight was right to worry that the Court of Far Seeing might fall.

She couldn't move her upper arms, but her forearms could still pivot. She studied the saddle, trying to see if there was something she could reach. The Black Skull was too far away. The Sword of Years couldn't be reached, either. There was a small saddle pouch near her left arm. She stretched for it. With the tips of her fingers she managed to get it open. The Black Skull didn't look back at her, didn't seem to notice.

Inside, she found a knife. It was smaller than a butcher knife but big enough to do some damage. Sharp, with a wooden handle. She tested it on the leather band around her arms. It was an awkward angle for her arms, but the band fell away easily once she got her blade on it. There was another band over her back and shoulders and one over her thighs, a fourth on her lower legs. Apparently the Black Skull believed in strapping in before flight.

She couldn't reach the Skull, not yet. Then another thought came to her. She could see the edge of the bird's saddle. What if it had a strap?

She had seen the Black Skulls in battle and knew they shrugged off even mortal wounds. A simple gash from a knife would do nothing more than annoy him. If she could cut the saddle loose, though . . . At least it would slow their progress toward the Scim homeland and give her a chance to escape. The band holding the saddle to the owl was thick. It didn't immediately give way when she found it with her knife. Her breathing came in uneven gasps, slowing her progress. She was sweating profusely and trying to keep an eye on her captor.

She was halfway through the strap when he saw her.

"What are you doing? We'll fall." The grotesque voice of the thing sounded almost panicked. The owl descended immediately, headed for the desert floor. The sun was almost here. Madeline could see the ground. She cut faster. She was still held tight by multiple straps. The one over her thighs and the one on her shoulder she was able to cut with relative ease, but she couldn't reach where it crossed her ankles, not without sitting up or moving, something she was afraid to do while the owl was still so far above the ground.

When the owl touched down, Madeline sliced the last remaining fraction of the saddle band, then cut the strap holding her ankles. She slid off, out of control, landing on her back in the sand. The Black Skull jumped from the bird, landing on his feet and facing her.

"Give me the sword!" Madeline shouted, lungs aching, the knife held toward the Black Skull. Her hand shook with adrenaline.

He stood before her in his white robes, his black gloves held up in supplication, his horrible horned head facing her. "That can't hurt me."

"Come closer and . . . we'll find . . . out."

The Black Skull reached up and put his hands on his mask. "Madeline."

His voice sounded rough and deep, but something about the way he said her name was almost familiar.

The Black Skull pulled off his mask. It came away as a complete whole, more helmet than mask. He set it aside in the sand. She couldn't breathe. She struggled to keep upright in the sand, to keep the blade pointed at him, but she wasn't sure she could do it. Consciousness was shrinking down, pushed to a small pinpoint with blurred nothingness pressing in on the edges.

"Look at me," he said. "Maddie, look."

She knew that voice.

She focused, or tried to. He had stepped closer. She spat a warning at him, swinging the knife wildly. He said her name again, crouched down in front of her. Her vision cleared, and she saw him—saw the face of the man who wore the Black Skull.

"Darius?"

"Hey," he said with a gentle smile. She knew that smile. This was her boyfriend. He wasn't a hallucination or a shape-shifter. It wasn't magic. It was him—she knew it with an immediate certainty.

Her heart beat faster, her chest hurt, she took a deep breath, tried to speak, passed out.

She came back to consciousness with an enormous, gulping, chest-expanding breath of deep air. Oxygen flooded her body, making her light headed and giddy. Her left wrist felt like it had been burned, and the sensation spread like liquid flame up her arm, over her shoulder, down her back, onto the bicep of her right arm. It throbbed a few times, then lessened. She scrambled to her feet, stumbling away from Darius.

He sat on a small folding stool made of a wooden frame with a piece of canvas stretched over it. He gestured to a second one beside him. "Sunrise," he said. "Your magic just came back."

She put her hand on her chest and took two deep breaths, forcing air through her nostrils. The scent of cool water and the faint perfume of desert flowers permeated the air.

"We've had a misunderstanding," Darius said.

"You stole my sword!" she shouted.

"It's beside you. I returned it while you slept."

Slept? While she was unconscious, he meant. But there it was, still wrapped in canvas. She pulled the rope off and inspected the sword. "How did you get here? Why are you fighting for the Scim?"

He didn't move from his stool. He watched her carefully, as if she were a wild animal and he wasn't sure what she would do. "When you and Jason disappeared into that pipe, I went crazy. I had to find you. Your parents . . . Madeline, your parents went insane. They thought maybe I had done something to you. They said maybe . . . Well, they said they thought I might have helped you commit suicide."

"WHAT?"

He made calming gestures with his hands. "They were upset. You'd been missing for months, Mads."

"For months? What are you talking about?"

"Time . . . time works strangely in the Sunlit Lands. A day here might be a few months at home. Or a century here could be four weeks there."

Madeline let that sink in before she spoke. That meant . . . a human year could be a millennium in the Sunlit Lands. Or a few weeks. "That makes no sense—is time faster or slower here?"

"Neither. Both. It's magic, Maddie. It's the weirdest thing. I came here months after you. Six months after you."

"Six? Darius, I haven't even been here two months."

"Two months in the Sunlit Lands. Six back home. And get this, Mads. I arrived before you."

"What do you mean?"

"I mean, I left six months after you, and I've been in the Sunlit Lands for a year and a half looking for you."

Madeline took another deep breath, running that through her head. "Okay. It's magic, so it doesn't make complete sense. It's not like science."

He shook his head. "Different rules. Right."

"What did Jason's parents say when the police talked with them?"

Darius threw his hands up. "Weirdest thing. They said he wasn't missing. Said he was in China visiting relatives, that they had picked him up from the hospital and taken him straight to the airport."

"Did the police believe them?"

Darius shrugged. "They didn't arrest them or anything, so I guess so. His dad acted like I wasn't in the room the one time I saw him."

Wow. Jason had said his dad hated him, but that was really strange. "So . . . how did you get here?"

"You had been gone six months. I was reading fantasy novels, trying to figure out if there was some clue, some piece of reality between the lines. Every day I hung out by that pipe where you and Jason disappeared. I had gone through Lewis and L'Engle and was almost done rereading the Meselia books. I had just started *The Azure World*, and I kept coming back to those first three chapters—"

Madeline interrupted. "The part where Okuz gathers the adventurers from across space and time."

"Right. I kept wondering, what if one of these is real? Something about the story of Karu stuck with me."

Madeline smiled despite herself. Karu had always been one of Darius's favorite characters in the Meselia books. He only appeared in a few of the books, but he was a charming adventurer who always saw the positive side of things. "Karu notices an owl in the middle of the day, blinded by sunlight, and follows it into the deep woods," Madeline said.

"Right. And I remembered that hummingbird with you and Jason. That day I went back down to the pipe where you had disappeared, and I sat by the fence and read the book. It was Saturday, just about noon, and this possum came walking down the street. All the dogs in the neighborhood howled and barked. Possums aren't usually out during the day. It stopped when it saw me, then turned and walked back the way it had come. So I followed it."

"Did it take you into the pipe?"

"No. Into an empty lot behind the houses. There was this weird dome of—I don't know how to say it—a dome of darkness. About the size of a one-person tent. The possum went into it and didn't come out. I waited for about ten minutes, then I followed." He shifted in his chair and looked off to the side. She recognized that look . . . He wasn't telling her everything. "I ended up in the Wasted Lands with the Scim. I told them I was looking for you, that the Elenil had kidnapped you . . . and they agreed to help me rescue you."

"*Rescue* me?"

"From the Elenil. Right. I became a Black Skull. Using Scim magic, I can go into battle and never be harmed, so long as I keep my helmet on. I spearheaded the new campaign against those monsters."

She crossed over to him. "Darius, you don't understand. The Elenil aren't monsters . . . they *saved* me. Their magic is why I can breathe. You've been to Far Seeing. You've seen who they are. The city is beautiful . . . It's amazing."

"Yes," Darius said, his face still as a stone. "Meanwhile everything in the

Scim territories is broken, rotting, and falling apart. It's abject poverty and ruin. And while Far Seeing has sunlight all day, every day, the Wasted Lands have night. The brightness of their day is a weak twilight. Their brightness and Far Seeing's darkness are the same. Do you see?"

She grabbed his hands. She couldn't understand how he had gone so wrong, how he had been twisted so badly. "Darius, listen to me. The Scim are *evil*. They want to destroy the Elenil. I've heard them say it themselves—they want to bring a thousand years of darkness to Far Seeing, they want to break bones and murder people. You were there tonight, you saw it!" She fell back from him, sudden realization coming to her. "You were part of it. You were part of the attack on Far Seeing."

Darius stood, anger flashing across his face. "How did they get utopia, Mads? Who paid for it? The Scim, that's who. The center of their magic, what is it called? Do you know?"

"The Heart of the Scim."

"Yes. If they want sunlight, they take it . . . from the Scim. If they want to construct a building faster, that can be accomplished by magic . . . so long as a Scim building goes up slower. If they need rain for their crops, the Scim get drought. If they need to get rid of their waste, their garbage, their sewage, they just have to find a place to put it. Why not the Wasted Lands?"

"All their magic," Madeline said. "All their wealth, their power. What are you saying?"

"Stolen, Madeline. Stolen! Is that so hard to understand, so hard to believe?" He rubbed his hands over his eyes. "Maybe it is. You've been their prisoner so long, been hearing their propaganda, of course you believe it."

Madeline's own anger flared up. "I wasn't a prisoner!"

His face softened, and he reached up with his hands, as if to put them on her shoulders. "Madeline. Were you allowed to leave the city?"

"Yes, I—" She thought of the knight. Hadn't he specifically said they weren't to leave the city? "Not without a chaperone," she said.

"Chaperone? Or guard?" Madeline didn't answer, so Darius went on: "Did they want to make sure you heard their side of things? Did they have some sort of class or book you had to read or something like that? Something that told you all about how the Elenil are the chosen ones who are meant to rule the Sunlit Lands?"

She thought of the woman in the ivy. The storyteller. "Something like that," she said.

"Did they make you take an oath of loyalty? Threaten to take away the magic if you didn't obey them?"

Yes. They had done both those things, and she had scarcely noticed. She bit her lip, willing herself not to cry. She felt the world tipping. "Darius. They gave me back my breath. I'm *alive*."

Tears welled up in Darius's eyes, and he spread his arms wide. She melted into his hug. "I know," he said. "I'm so sorry. I know."

He held her for a long time.

A sudden thought occurred to her, and she pushed him away. "Are you the one who kidnapped Shula?"

"Yes," he said. "I would have done worse things if I thought it would get me to you."

"You almost *killed Jason*," she said.

"I never—" he said. "Wait. The kid in the white armor?"

The kid in the white armor. Her hands balled into fists, and she pounded on his chest. "You didn't know it was him? Is that what you're trying to say? How does that make it any better, that you thought you were killing a stranger?"

Darius stepped away from her, the hurt clear on his face. "Do you remember in—which one was it—*The Gold Firethorns*, I think. Do you remember when Lily betrayed the Eagle King?"

Yes, of course she remembered. Lily, deceived by Kotuluk, thought her friends could only survive the flames of the firethorns if she turned her back on the Eagle King. She couldn't tell them what she was doing, or the magical agreement keeping them safe would be violated. Terrible consequences came as a result, and Lily was banished from Meselia. But her friends were safe, and as she left Meselia for the last time, she said she had no regrets. "I remember," Madeline said.

"Everything I've done has been for your protection," Darius said. "Or to protect the Scim. If that means I'll be punished, so be it. But I did it all with good intentions, just like Lily."

She knew that. She knew it before he said it. It didn't make her happy about things, but she knew he had a good heart. She crossed her arms. "Okay. Explain it to me, Darius. Help me understand."

He held his hand out to her, but she didn't take it. He nodded, put his hand back at his side. "I'd like to show you something," he said at last. "You should know both sides of the story before you make a decision. I won't take the sword away from you. If you want to go back to the Elenil, I'll take you myself. You can return the sword, stay with them, do whatever you want."

She looked him in the eyes. He was telling the truth. "And you'll go with me?"

His face hardened. "I'll take you wherever you want to go." He didn't say he would go with her, though. She knew him well enough to know that he wasn't making that part of the promise.

"Okay," she said. "Show me."

He stowed the stools and the sword on the saddle. He had repaired it while she was unconscious. He mounted and she slipped on behind him. "I have to wear my helmet," he said. "So I can fly the owl."

"Okay."

He settled the helmet on his head, his horns sharp and silhouetted against the risen sun. She wrapped her arms around his body and turned her face to lay it against his back. He ordered the bird to fly, in the fearsome, guttural voice of the Black Skull. They lifted into the air and headed toward the dark night of the Wasted Lands.

30

THE STORM

The desert claims the land, and so we,
we must claim the desert.

FROM "THE DESERTED CITY," A KAKRI LAMENT

✦

Faster, Jason." It was a mantra Baileya repeated endlessly. His legs felt like bags filled with sand, which for all he knew they now were. All he could see in any direction was sand. Sand dunes ahead. Sand dunes to the left and right. Behind them, the other sand dunes they had passed and, sometimes, the sand clouds created by their Scim pursuers.

They had lost the Scim for almost nine hours in the Tolmin Pass. Baileya knew a shortcut that required confronting an eleven-foot-tall knight with glowing eyes and a scary sword made of flaming night. Apparently she had some sort of deal going with him, though, because she said she had already paid her toll, and he let them through. The monster knight wasn't so sure about Jason, but Baileya convinced him that Jason was part of the deal.

Jason didn't know if the Scim went around or through the scary toll road, but it didn't take them long to get on his and Baileya's trail again. He wondered aloud how the Scim were surviving. Baileya knew every trick. Certain plants hoarded water in the mornings. She poured it along the leaves and into their mouths. She had hollowed a gourd for a canteen and saved some water for the evening. She made a sweet mashed food out of a certain cactus. It had tubers that grew among the roots, which she smashed and mixed sparingly with water. It had the consistency of paste, but the taste had grown on him. He was still getting his daily delivery of pudding too. He shared it with Baileya, and she seemed genuinely impressed by his ability to find a new cup of "this food you call pudding" every morning.

She warned him of the various dangers of the deserts. Sandstorms, naturally. Most of the nasty desert animals you could think of from Earth. Plus something called a ghul that changed shapes to look like your friends and then ate you. And something that sounded like a hyena, sort of, except she said it was "as smart as a woman." He wasn't sure if that meant smarter than a man or not, but he knew not to ask. Either way, it was a hyena that was smarter than a hyena. He was glad to hear it didn't have opposable thumbs, but she said it would lay clever traps and had to be avoided.

The Kharobem, too, should be avoided—a strange, magical race of creatures who changed shapes ("a common power for desert folk," Baileya said) and were known for interceding in the business of the people of the Sunlit Lands. Massively powerful, with a magic more formidable than any other, they could settle a dispute between warring peoples in a few minutes. They rarely intervened, but when they did, it was the stuff of legend. The last time had been hundreds of years ago, when they had destroyed a Kakri city called Ezerbin.

"Why is their magic so powerful?" Jason asked.

"The Kakri trade in story," Baileya said. "It is the foundation of our economy. Do you understand? It is like money for us. The Kharobem are *made* of story."

Jason snorted. "Okay. Thanks for clearing that up."

"They are world shapers. They alter things in a way no other magic can. They tell the world the way it should be, and it is."

Jason's tongue felt thick. They hadn't stopped for a drink in hours. The sun squeezed the sweat out of him. "Still, that's not the same as being made of story. That's like, I don't know, word magic or something."

"Faster, Jason," Baileya said, and for a while he didn't speak at all. Keeping up with her exhausted him, and she was going slow for him. He would be embarrassed by how easily she outpaced him if not for the fact that he wasn't sure any person he knew would be able to keep up with her. She seemed to be on a casual holiday stroll while he was doing the most strenuous march of his life.

Sometimes she would stand beside him and mark out a certain land-mark. A thorny tree, maybe. She would tell him to walk to it as quickly as he could, and then, if she wasn't back, he could rest until she returned. She would disappear then, for spans of time as long as twenty minutes. He would stand beneath the thorn tree (or lie in the narrow shade of a boulder or rest at the bottom of a dune), sweat rolling from his face, his tongue thick and dry, waiting for her to return. When she did, she would say, "Quickly, Jason." They would set off again, sometimes in the same direc-tion, sometimes in another. She never explained why she made the choices she did, but he accepted them with mute appreciation.

This time she left him in the shade of a rock jutting up from the desert floor. It angled toward the horizon in a way that let him sit beneath the overhang in the relative coolness of the shade. Baileya disappeared, telling him to be silent and conserve his strength. She would return in time.

Drowsy from the heat and exhausted from walking, he fell asleep in the shade of the stone.

"—somewhere near here," a guttural voice said.

"Climb up on the rock there," another replied. Jason shook himself awake. Those were Scim voices.

"So the Kakri woman can fill me with arrows? Do it yourself."

The second Scim grunted. "The Kakri are fearsome, but the boy . . . How could he have killed Night's Breath? Did you see him with the bow upon the walls of Westwind?"

They both chortled.

Apparently everyone had seen Jason's spectacular failure. More concern-ing was that the Scim—at least two of them—stood on the opposite side of this rock. He wished he had somehow walked faster all those times Baileya had told him to do so. He had to hope these two wouldn't want a break in the shade. What should he do? Make a run for it? He didn't think he'd have much of a chance. Maybe he could bury himself in the sand if he did it slowly so it didn't make too much sound.

"This accursed sun," one of the voices said. "Oh, for the cool embrace of night."

"I can barely speak, my throat is so parched."

"Could we sit in the shade of this stone, even for a few moments?"

"But if one of the war chiefs finds out—"

"I will not speak of it."

"Nor I. But how far behind is the rest of the war party?"

There was a pause. No doubt they were looking back, trying to judge the distance. Jason began to carefully pile sand in his lap. He didn't think he would get himself buried in time, but he had to try something.

The Scim came around the stone, still speaking to one another, and stopped, still as statues, when they saw Jason sitting in the shade. He sat up straight, doing his best to look like he had known they were coming and had been waiting for them. "Hello," he said.

The great shambling soldiers looked at one another, uncertain what to do. One had his hand on the handle of his ax, the other stood with his mouth wide open.

Jason almost laughed. "When someone says hello, it's polite to say hello back."

"Ehhhhhhh," said one of the Scim. "Hello?"

Jason smiled broadly. "That's better. Now. If you don't mind being a little crowded, all three of us should be able to fit in the shade of this rock."

"We have captured him," one of the Scim said. Jason decided he would call him Fluffy, because his thick black hair was in a braid that had come loose, giving him a fluffy halo.

"Not true," Jason said.

The second Scim (Jaws, Jason decided, because of how far his jaw had fallen open upon finding Jason sitting serenely under the rock) said, "It is true. You have no weapon. We are heavily armed. We will be joined by our army in a few minutes' time."

"Then we might as well sit in the shade and wait," Jason said.

Fluffy gave him a sour frown. "We will not sit with the murderer of Night's Breath."

Jaws said, nearly in the same moment, "It is a trap."

"A trap?" Jason laughed. "How could an invitation to sit in the shade be a trap?"

"If we could see how it worked," Jaws said, "it would not be a trap, would it?"

Jason acknowledged his point, while racing through a plan to get himself out of this mess. He might be able to hold these two off, but he couldn't expect the whole Scim army to stand in the sunshine for fear of a nonexistent trap.

"You are too clever for me," Jason admitted. He turned away from them, and when they could just barely see his face, he smirked.

"Wait," Fluffy cried. "I saw the look on your face!"

Jaws said, "Tell us, have we stumbled into your trap already?"

"There is no trap," Jason said truthfully.

Jaws pointed at him accusingly. "Precisely what someone would say if they had set a trap!"

Baileya descended on them from the top of the rock, twisting her body so that each of her feet connected with one of their jaws. They fell backward, and she snatched the ax from Fluffy's belt, flinging it toward Jason. "Catch!" she cried.

He barely avoided getting brained with the ax. He grabbed the handle and tried to lift it, but he could scarcely get it up to his shoulder. Baileya had her staff in two pieces, and she whirled like a desert wind, meeting Jaws's blade and keeping Fluffy at bay. Unable to do anything else constructive, Jason dug a hole and buried the ax.

Distracted by Jaws's sword, Baileya didn't see Fluffy reach for her hand, crushing it. She cried out and dropped half of her staff. She tried to wrench away from Fluffy, but he held her hand fast, making it nearly impossible for her to parry Jaws's blows. Jason scrambled to them, snatched up the fallen half of the staff, and drove the bladed end into Fluffy's knee.

Fluffy yowled and released Baileya, who brought the haft of her staff up into Jaws's face, hitting him hard enough to knock him, stunned, to the ground. She yanked the other half of her staff from Fluffy's knee and said, "Quickly, Jason!"

"Sorry about your knee, Fluffy!" Jason called as they scrambled over a dune.

"My name is not Fluffy!" the Scim warrior roared.

Baileya made him run for almost thirty minutes. Finally she let him collapse at the top of a dune, the sun burning his face. She crouched, facing the direction they had come. "They are craftier than I supposed. The larger part of their forces was closer than I knew, while they left another small group behind to kick up dust, so we would think them in the distance. That was a close moment, indeed."

"Thirsty," Jason said.

Baileya stood over him and shielded his face with the sleeve of her flowing shirt. "There is a small oasis near here. I will need to check it first for wylna." Those were the hyena things. Wylna. Jason thought he could fight off a pack of hyenas to get a drink of water. "First," Baileya said, "I need you to bind my hand. I fear it is broken."

Jason sat up immediately and gingerly took her wrist in his hand. A nasty bruise spread beneath her golden-tan skin. The fingers were swollen, the center of her hand like a balloon. With her good hand she unwrapped a long piece of cloth from around her waist. It held her loose garment close against her body. She tore a strip of it with the blade of her staff and handed it to Jason. "Bind it tight," she said.

He wound it around her hand.

"Tighter."

He yanked it, hard. He winced. Her face had gone pale. He didn't like to see her in pain, certainly didn't want to be the one causing her pain. But it had to be done.

"Still tighter," she said.

She gritted her teeth, and he pulled as hard as he could. Sweat beaded her face, and she gasped. "Good. Now we find water. Then we run."

He helped her to her feet. She stood, weak with pain for a moment. He gripped both her arms, keeping her steady. He carefully wiped the sweat from her face. Her eyes met his, and her lips parted, but before she could speak, Jason said, "I know, I know, 'Run faster, Jason.'"

She leaned on him while they walked down the dune, but by the time they climbed the next, she had transferred her staff into her wounded hand, flexing her hand and spinning the staff lightly. She sent him up one dune, the wind blowing so it obscured his footprints, and she went in another direction. The Scim were close enough, she said, that it was wise to give them a false trail. He objected, but she assured him her strength had returned. He didn't know how that was possible, but it was true that she looked better. He felt dehydrated, light headed, and exhausted, but she looked like she could run again. She slipped away to make the false trail.

After she rejoined Jason, she pointed out an oasis.

Oasis. The word made him think of a palm tree with coconuts next to a pure stream. This was a muddy puddle. An animal stood beside it, lapping water.

"Is that . . . a lion cub?"

"Perhaps." Baileya squinted her silver eyes. "Not all is what it seems in the desert."

Jason was reminded of her stories about the many creatures of the desert who could change their shapes.

The sand around the water hole quivered. "What's that?"

Baileya froze. So did the lion cub.

A dog-sized creature shook itself free of the sand, its jaws clamping onto the cub's rear leg. The cub cried out in panic, and two more of the creatures leapt out of the sand. They looked like wild dogs with thick, cracked lips and white patches in their sandy fur.

"Wylna," Baileya whispered. "We must go. Quickly, Jason."

"They're going to eat that cub," Jason said.

"Better than eating us."

"Give me your staff," Jason said.

"No," Baileya said. "We will not stop to fight three wylna with a battalion of Scim at our backs."

A faint sound came to them on the wind. "The Scim," he said. "They're nearby."

Baileya listened. The wylna had paused, their pointed ears pricked toward the Scim army. "They're following the fake trail," she said. "We must go now."

Jason had another idea.

He jumped to his feet and shouted as loud as he was able, "Hey, Break Bones, we're over here!"

He ran to the oasis. The wylna crouched down, watching him warily. He ran full speed toward the wylna with its maw latched onto the cub. He aimed a terrific kick at its head, but at the last moment the wylna let go, skittering away and growling at Jason.

The wylna triangulated Jason the moment he stopped moving. No matter how he turned, there was one he couldn't see. "I was a kickball champion in eighth grade," he said. "Get close enough, and I'm gonna send you sailing over the fences like a red rubber ball."

The lion cub slipped away, limping, the wylna distracted by this new, larger prey. Jason kicked toward his blind spot, hoping the third wylna wouldn't get a bite in. He turned in a circle, trying not to let any of them out of his sight for more than a second. "The Scim are gonna come over that hill soon," Jason said. "When they do, we're all going to want to run. But if you want to attack them, I won't complain."

The Scim were shouting some sort of battle march. They were close. The wylna listened, backing up slightly from Jason. The chanting grew louder, and the wylna trotted away, one of them watching Jason over its shoulder. "This way," Baileya hissed. She had crossed to the other side of the oasis. Jason fell to his chest and slurped up three quick gulps of water.

Baileya was already running.

The wind had whipped up. "I outsmarted those dog things!" Jason shouted.

Baileya's eyes flashed. "You are a fool."

That stung. She was one of the only people who had never called him a fool. "At least I'm consistent!" he shouted back. He had saved the lion cub, at least. That was something. The wind whipped past them, kicking up sand.

He heard his name and, looking back, could see the Scim loping behind them. They were much too close, and there were at least twenty of them. An arrow whistled past his ear.

"They are within bow shot," Baileya said. "Run twenty paces ahead, then turn to the left. Run until you find a garden of stone. Climb to the top of the stones and wait for me."

"But what if you don't—"

"Then I will be dead, and you will soon join me." She laughed at the look on his face. "But at least the lion cub lives!"

She spun back, staff in hand, and shouted a high-pitched, ululating war cry. Jason counted out the twenty steps, then turned left and ran full speed.

The sand stung his face. He lifted his hands, trying to shield his eyes. The wind howled, and in the distance he heard the wylna raise an answering howl. Cries and the sound of battle came from behind, and then he couldn't see more than a step or two ahead.

Baileya appeared beside him, took his hand, and corrected his course. The sand lifted for a moment, and he saw the Scim, not far behind. He saw the lion cub between them and the Scim. Or no, it wasn't the lion cub at all, it was a young girl, limping in front of the Scim, as if she could stop them herself. The girl glanced at Jason and smiled.

She held up her arms and shouted something, and a curtain of sand lowered over the Scim, eventually obscuring the girl as well.

In the cover provided by the howling sandstorm, Baileya pulled Jason up a series of solid stones jutting out of the sand. She found a cleft in the rock, pushed him in, and followed after. She loosened her belt—more of a sash, really—carefully unfolding it until it was almost the size of a bedsheet. She lifted it so it kept out the sand, tucking it into the clefts of the rock to form a makeshift tent. They settled side by side, panting, and listened to the static of sand on stone.

31
THE WASTED LANDS

Do not cry in the darkness, but follow the small bright star.

FROM A TRADITIONAL SCIM LULLABY

✦

They flew for a while in sunlight. Madeline loved the blue sky studded with white clouds. She even saw, off to the west, the sparkling expanse of the sea. The Ginian Sea, according to Darius, the home of the Zhanin, the shark people. As they continued southward, she saw an impossibly large forest, with trees as high as thin mountains. She asked Darius about it, but he pointed instead toward the southeast.

"The Wasted Lands," he said in his harsh Skull voice.

It rose up like an angry, dark cloud or a tidal wave. Somehow the sunlight didn't penetrate the column of darkness that towered over that place. Campfires and torches dotted the distant landscape. The owl descended in lazy, looping arcs as they fell toward the northern edge of the blackness. They landed in a strange twilight where bright daylight shone at their backs and full night stood before them.

Darius slid off the owl. He offered Madeline his gloved hand, a motion both familiar coming from Darius and foreign coming from a Black Skull. She took his hand and slipped down. "We will walk a short distance into the darkness," Darius said.

"Can you take that helmet off? I'd rather be with Darius than with a Black Skull."

The horned head tilted for a moment before Darius reached up and removed the helmet. "Of course," he said and took off his gloves, too. "You don't have to cover up now," Darius said. "Only the Elenil require no skin to show."

She pulled her gloves off. "Why did you cover up, then? For the sake of the Elenil?"

Darius grinned. "Scim magic might have protected me from wounds as a Black Skull, but I couldn't get over the idea that I would lose the magic and be standing around with bare arms and no gloves. I wanted protection."

"*Scim* magic?"

Darius nodded. "It's the same as Elenil magic, really. If I'm wounded in battle, a Scim takes the wound. A team of Scim stay back for each Black Skull, and healers work to try to save as many of them as they can. It's a new technique, and one of the few that has given us an upper hand against those monsters." He saw the look on her face, raised his hands, and said, "Against the *Elenil*."

"But why have humans be the Skulls? Why not other Scim? And how is that different than the way the Elenil are using the Scim?"

"It's different because the Scim are in control." He looked her in the eyes. "And it's humans because the Scim insisted I be the first Black Skull. Because the whole thing was my idea."

Madeline, stunned, started to ask him another question, but he shook his head. "We should start moving." He led her into the darkness. After a few minutes, he reached out and took her hand. It felt natural, but she couldn't stop herself from thinking about him being a Black Skull, kidnapping Shula, almost killing Jason. Or even just the fact that she had broken up with him. But she had broken up with him because of her breathing, a problem that had been solved by the Elenil. Or, at least, mostly solved. Despite all those things she still wanted to be with him. He was the only one who had stood by her after she got sick. That Darius and this one were somehow the same man.

The Wasted Lands smelled of garbage and sulfur. They walked along a sickly stream of foul water. Refuse stood in random piles. When Darius took them too close to one pile, a mangy rat bared its teeth and hissed.

Madeline found herself clutching Darius's arm with her free hand. Something about this place felt unsafe. She had felt this way before, in the "bad part of town," only here there was no town . . . just garbage and rats and the occasional stunted bush. Nothing healthy grew here. She shivered. After the temperate warmth of Far Seeing, the cold of the Wasted Lands took her by surprise. Darius noticed and, without asking, unfastened his cloak and spread it over her shoulders. They trudged on through the dark. When she had warmed herself a little, she took his hand again.

"We're here," Darius said gently.

He led her to a broken-down hut made of mud and discarded wood. It was shaped like a half-melted scoop of ice cream. The door stood crooked in the doorway. A window with no glass had been dug out of the space beside the door.

Drifting from the hovel was a woman's voice, singing. "Do not cry in the darkness," she sang, "but follow the small bright star." Madeline wanted to get closer, to see the woman in the hut. Her voice, so clear and bright, was the first beautiful thing in this wasted place. Madeline moved quietly to the window. The woman's silver hair was pulled back from a lined, pleasant face. Black tattoos curled around her wiry arms, and as she sang, she dipped a dirty rag in a bowl of grey water. The only light came from a candle—at least Madeline thought it was a candle—about the size of a softball. A tiny wick stood out of it, and a pungent odor came from it.

The woman dabbed water on a young girl's forehead. The girl, too, had black tattoos covering her arms, as well as her neck and face. She wore a pale-green nightshirt, soaked in sweat and stuck to her stick-thin body.

"Who are they?" Madeline whispered.

Darius leaned against her back, whispering in her ear. "Look at her nightshirt," he said. "Look carefully."

It was a thin material, maybe cotton. A V-neck. It was stained, as though someone had done their best to wash out mud or old, dried blood, or both.

The child broke into severe coughing—coughing so extreme Madeline's hand moved unconsciously to her own chest. The woman lifted the coughing girl's head and shoulders from the bed and held her. She didn't stop singing, even when the child's coughing drowned her out completely. Madeline recognized that sort of coughing. A pang of sympathy pierced her. Madeline knew what it was like to lie in bed perfectly aware there was nothing anyone could do for you.

Confusion washed over her. "Are these . . . Scim?" she asked.

"Yes," Darius said, but he didn't elaborate, didn't explain the answer to her question, which she was sure he must anticipate.

"Why aren't they . . . ?" She stopped herself from asking the question that burned in her mind. It seemed disrespectful. But the fact remained: they didn't have monstrous muscles or wide, frog-like mouths. Their hair was not in greasy knots, and they didn't have tusklike teeth. The best word she could think of to describe them was *graceful*. The mother's hair shone with a lustrous light, and although the daughter was not well, a vibrant aura radiated from her.

"Why aren't they ugly?" Darius asked, no hint of warmth in his voice.

Madeline's ears went hot. It was her question, yes, but the way he said it only reinforced how ugly the question itself was. "They don't look like any Scim I've ever seen."

"What you've seen," Darius said, "is their war skin. Before going to battle they transform themselves to intimidate, to cause fear, to make it clear they shouldn't be messed with. You've never seen a Scim before, not really. You've seen a people at war, not the people themselves."

Living in this terrible, corrupted place . . . Madeline was amazed these people could show any sign of weakness, ever. A moment of vulnerability, a minute of dropping their guard, could be the difference between life and death. She didn't know them, not at all. Yet she had signed away a year of her life to fight them . . . to destroy them. "I want to meet them," Madeline said.

"That's not a good idea," Darius said.

Madeline turned on him, whispering fiercely, "I thought your whole point was that I didn't know them. So let me learn."

Darius deflated. "At least let me put my helmet on."

Madeline crossed her arms. "Why?"

"So they know my position. So they know you're with me."

She didn't understand what that meant. "Fine."

Once the helmet settled on his head, they stood together in front of the broken wooden door. Darius rapped on it and called out in his altered voice, "Open!"

"Who is there?"

"A Black Skull and his honored guest."

The door flew open. A man stood before them, thin but strong. He glanced at the skull, following the long line of the horns with his eyes before bowing his head. "Sir," he said, "please sit and sup with us."

The Black Skull bowed his head so he could enter the low-ceilinged hovel. He sat at a short table near a makeshift hearth. A small kettle hung over the fire. The girl did not turn to look at them. She stared, her eyes half-lidded, at the dirt ceiling. The mother hurried to Madeline, guiding her to the table. She took Madeline's hand to seat her. Something startled the woman, and she gasped.

"What is it?" Madeline asked.

"N-n-nothing, miss." She poured a small portion of gruel from the pot and set it in front of Madeline. A second portion went to the Black Skull. A third to her husband.

"Sit and eat with us," Madeline said.

The woman blushed. "There are but three bowls."

Madeline said to Darius, "Do you have a bowl, or a cup, on the owl?"

The Black Skull stared at her, unmoving. The woman said not to bother themselves, and her husband's face turned red too. Darius, his voice rough, said, "This is all their food, Madeline. Do not embarrass them further."

Now Madeline blushed. She held the bowl up to the woman. "Please. I'm not hungry."

The woman's dark eyes widened as if she had never heard such a thing. Darius put his hand on hers. "Eat, Madeline."

His voice carried the unmistakable tone of someone correcting a child. She had been rude somehow. Maybe in this culture you couldn't refuse food. She lifted the bowl to her lips. She had been among the Elenil long enough that this seemed a strange intimacy, to eat with her hands uncovered. The simple gruel warmed her as she sipped from it. As she tipped the bowl away from her face she noticed that the network of tattoos had moved onto her right hand now. It seemed to be moving faster, like ivy covering a tree.

The girl coughed and called for her mother. The mother stayed near her guests, hovering beside them. "Go to your child," the Black Skull said. "We will call if we have needs."

The woman bowed her head in a curt, thankful nod and rushed to her daughter's side, scooping her up in her arms. Madeline watched, her heart breaking for the poor girl. "Can we help?" Madeline asked. "Does she need medicine?"

The Scim man looked to the Black Skull, seeming embarrassed. When the Black Skull didn't speak, he turned again to Madeline and said, "Medicine will not help her."

"What is her name?" Madeline asked.

"She is called Yenil. Her mother is Fera. I am Inrif."

"I'm Madeline."

"We know you, Madeline Oliver." Inrif looked down at his bowl. He had not taken even a sip. "You are our benefactor."

"Your benefactor?"

"Yes. We are honored to have you in our home."

What was he talking about? She looked more carefully around their hut. There were a few clean rags, like the kind the Elenil used instead of toilet paper. Some clothes were hung near a small window. There was only the one narrow bed. Inrif and Fera must sleep beside the fire, she decided.

Yenil coughed harder, hacking. Her mother cried out and bit her own knuckle. Madeline couldn't take it any longer. She swept across to the girl and propped her up. "Sometimes sitting up helps with the breathing," she said. "It lets the lungs expand."

Yenil said, "Thank . . . you . . . miss."

This close to her, Madeline could see the green nightshirt better on the small girl. In fact, it looked surprisingly like hospital scrubs. But how would they get those, here in the Sunlit Lands?

Or, she corrected herself, here in the Wasted Lands?

Unless.

No.

The scrubs were too large for Yenil.

No, no.

Madeline saw the swirling black tattoos on Yenil's left arm. She saw the way they branched up her arm and crept across her clavicle. They came out again on her right arm, nearly to her wrist. Oh no.

Madeline put her left arm alongside Yenil's. The patterns and whorls matched. Precisely. Every leaf, every branch.

Yenil's breathing grew faster, shallow and erratic. She coughed, trying to get a breath. A tendril of black tattoo crept up from her right hand, encircling her pinky. Madeline held up her own right hand. Her silver tattoo curled around her pinky too.

A rush of understanding coursed through her.

"No," she whispered.

The nightshirt . . . It was a pair of scrubs. Her scrubs. The ones she had thrown away once she made it to the Sunlit Lands. Somehow they had come here, to this family. The cough—that racking, awful cough—that was hers too. It all fell into place with a terrible, grinding finality. She could breathe. She could run and jump and sing and shout and dance, and all it cost was a year of service to the Elenil.

Or so she thought.

She knew—she knew!—that the magic of the Sunlit Lands worked by taking something from one person and giving it to another. Jason received the skills and abilities of a warrior by taking them from someone else. He took the skills of an archer from a true archer, and during that time the Elenil archer could no more fire an arrow than Jason had been able to from the top of Westwind.

Which meant her breath . . . Of course. She hadn't stopped to think about it, hadn't spent a single moment considering that maybe for her to breathe someone else would not be able to. Her heart clenched in her chest. She felt dizzy and nauseated. She had to get out of this place. The walls were too close, the fire too warm, the smoke in the air too thick. How could they keep Yenil in here? Wasn't it obvious it wasn't a good situation for her? A furious anger rose in her chest.

Tears burst from her eyes, and she ran from the hut. She didn't know where she was going, didn't look at the ground, she just ran and ran and felt the breath filling her lungs. A sob tore from her, and even that wasn't her own, it was borrowed from Yenil. Stolen from a child.

She fell on the ground, sobbing.

What would she do?

Deep, racking sobs shook her body.

"M-M-Madeline?"

A hand rested lightly on her shoulder. Madeline wiped at the tears on her face. It was Fera, the girl's mother.

"It is for the best," she said, "you being our benefactor."

Madeline stared at the pulsing silver tattoo on her arm. She wanted to rip it off. The bracelet if she could, her whole arm if she couldn't. "I'm going to destroy it," she said.

Fera gasped. "No!"

Madeline couldn't believe it. Why would Yenil's mother argue against getting her daughter back? "Your daughter can't breathe."

Fera turned her face away, as if ashamed. "The Elenil pay us. Every month. So that Yenil will continue to share her breath with you. We agreed to the terms so that we can feed her and ourselves."

"How could you do that?" Madeline said.

"They also send us the things you discard. We are . . ." Fera struggled for the right words. "Our neighbors are jealous."

Madeline snatched a rock and began to beat it against her wrist where the bracelet lay beneath her skin. Fera covered Madeline's arm with her own and cried, "No! Please, no!"

"She'll die," Madeline said.

Fera's face set into stone. "Without this we will have no food. Yenil will die anyway. Then I. Then her father."

"How can you do this?" Madeline asked. "She's your *daughter*. Don't you understand?"

"It is you who do not understand. Yenil has made her choice. It is I who lie beside her in the night and wipe the sweat from her face. I who bore her, who rubs her back as she sends her breath to the sunlit corners where you live." A fierce anger came into her eyes. "It is I who holds her while you run. While you jump or dance and Yenil's breath comes harder and harder. It is I who cradles her body and weeps while you sing with your friends."

Madeline burst into tears again. "I didn't know. I didn't know the cost."

Fera studied her. "You did not know because you did not think to ask. You did not wonder what the cost of this magic would be, to yourself or others. But such is the way of those who have never paid for much."

Fera stood and walked, her back straight, to the horrible dilapidated hovel she called home, leaving Madeline to weep in the darkness.

32

THE MEETING OF THE SPHERES

Let us turn our faces from this place,
let us seek solace in the desert.

FROM "THE DESERTED CITY," A KAKRI LAMENT

✝

When the storm passed, Baileya climbed from the cleft of the rock and disappeared for over an hour, checking the surrounding area for the Scim army. "I can find no sign of them," she said. "I do not think they will find us again."

The sunset painted the desert. Baileya led Jason down from the stones they had hidden in. "It is the night of the third and fourth spheres' meeting," she said. "It is a festival among my people. I hoped we would make it in time. Turn and look."

The rocks they had hidden among were not stones at all but the remnants of an ancient city. Broken towers and fallen walls protruded from the shifting sands. A statue of a Kakri couple stood above them. The woman's right arm encircled the man, and her left arm was raised to the sky. Or Jason assumed that's what it would be doing—it had broken long ago. A series of fountains remained, all filled with sand rather than water.

"What is this place?" Jason asked.

"It was called Ezerbin. Once it was the greatest city in the world. The Court of Far Seeing is a pale shadow of Ezerbin's glory."

"In the middle of the desert?"

"It was no desert then. Canals crossed the city. Fountains, irrigated fields. There were cisterns, too, yes, but mostly the water was plenteous."

Jason could barely imagine. The place looked like dried bones stacked in the sun. "What happened?"

"The city grew vile. The people oppressed their neighbors. In time they became horrible, filled with lies. The Kharobem came. They encircled the city and pronounced there would be no more water. The rain stopped. The river dried up. The people of the city had to leave or die. It is said a crow came to my ancestor and taught her to live in this new land, the desert. Others in the city denied this offer, for it was too much to humble themselves to a bird. They could not learn from such a lowly creature. But my ancestor believed it was no shame to walk with crows. So were born the Kakri, the ones who left the city and embraced the desert as our home."

Jason's mouth fell open. He had assumed the Kakri were some sort of nomadic tribal people, and maybe they were. But Baileya was telling him that they had once built the greatest city in the Sunlit Lands. "Whoa," Jason said. "Are they planning to rebuild it one day?"

Baileya leaned on her staff. "In the desert there is no room for a lie, Jason. You must walk either with truth or with death. The truth tells us that we cannot rebuild unless the water returns. It is not the choice of the Kakri people whether to rebuild. We must allow the Kharobem to tell us if such a time returns. In the meantime, every year at the meeting of the third and fourth spheres, my people congregate here and sing about the fall of old Ezerbin and tell stories." They rested in the shade of the fallen wall, and Baileya showed him where the Kakri would gather, near the statue.

Night settled in. The stars, strangely, did not appear like at home, the brightest first, in the darkest parts of the sky. They climbed up from the eastern horizon, bright and multicolored, a blanket of galaxies being pulled over the world. From the north came a small, warm moon, faster and brighter than Earth's, racing ahead of the stars at an angle like a surfer before a wave.

Somehow, while Jason had been watching the stars rise, the Kakri had entered quiet as breath and gathered before the statue. Half stood beneath the oncoming stars, the other half beneath the moon. Jason's breathing quickened. These silent warriors terrified him.

"Do not fear," Baileya whispered. "On this night there is no violence among the Kakri. It is a night of mourning our lost city and celebrating our marriage to the desert."

When the stars and the moon met, a song began among the moonside Kakri. "Where is the fountain which brought joy to the city, clean and clear at its heart?" There were no instruments, just voices.

The starside Kakri answered, also in song, "It has been carried away, the water spilled to the sand, the water given to the sun." The song, beautiful and strange, reached out to Jason like the tendrils of a plant opening in the morning dew. He felt himself alive, transported, and filled with a deep, melancholy sadness.

When the song ended, a woman ran among the singers, dressed as an enormous crow. She invited them into the desert. She told them they could become a part of it, that she would teach them how to thrive. She would teach them, she said, how to become people again, and not the corrupted creatures which had come to live in this city. They must leave everything behind—their houses, their possessions, their friends or family members who would not embrace the desert and the wisdom to be found there.

As the crow said these words, those near her cheered and embraced. They threw off their dull capes and coverings, revealing beautiful, brightly colored outfits beneath. They turned to their neighbors and shouted the news, inviting them to the desert, and color rippled through the crowd. Baileya threw off her own cloak and grabbed Jason's hand. "Come! Now we dance!"

Musical instruments came out (Jason's favorite was a stringed instrument Baileya said was called a bitarr), and the Kakri danced in a whirling, leaping style. Those who jumped highest and whirled fastest moved toward the center of the crowd. Jason tried to imitate them but found himself on the outer limits of the dance with the smallest children and most infirm elders.

At times a Kakri man would appear, laughing, and try to teach him how to leap higher. A drink that tasted like honey and goat's milk was passed around, and a crowd gathered to watch Jason take his first sip. When he held the bowl to his lips, Baileya pushed it higher, and he took in several gulps of the drink, which burned and left him sputtering and gasping. The people cheered, applauding and laughing, and a trio of muscled women lifted him up on their shoulders and began to jump in place, tossing him higher each time. "Spin!" they called to him, and he did his best, trying to spin as they had in their dances. When he reached the ground again, there were many hands clapping his back and arms thrown over his shoulders.

Sweating and exhausted, he sat down between two old women who rested on the edge of the deserted fountain. They wore bright clothes, but a chill had set in without the sun, and their dun-colored cloaks were over their legs.

"Hello," Jason said to them, wiping the sweat from his forehead.

"Greetings, Wu Song, slayer of tigers," the old woman to his left said.

His heart immediately started pounding again. How did this old woman know the story of Wu Song? Back home only people with Chinese family knew the story. "Forgive me, but I don't know your name."

The old lady on his other side chuckled. "She is Mother Crow. Do you not see her feathers?"

He looked more closely at her cloak. It did have black feathers sewn into it. She must have been the one in the play who invited the people into the desert. Mother Crow smiled at him, her face wrinkled and aged as the desert itself. "Would you leave behind all to learn the wisdom of the desert?"

"Uhhhh." Jason's mouth twitched. "I don't think so. I have things to do. My friend Madeline . . . I have to protect her."

"Indeed," Mother Crow said. "I suspected you would say so."

The other old lady patted his hand. "You cannot protect another person," she said. "Not in truth. Death comes for all. Your friend Madeline, too."

"But there's value in keeping people safe until that time," Jason said. "You can't save people forever, but if you can do it today, you should. People are . . ." He paused. He wasn't sure how to say the next bit. "People are the most important thing in the world. Anything else can be replaced, but people . . . Each one is unique, and when a person dies, they never come again. They're gone forever. Other people might come but not that one. So we have to protect them while we can. And if it's someone you love . . . you should protect them no matter what."

Mother Crow smiled. "You see? He has some of the desert in him. I see why she likes you."

"Who, Madeline?"

Both the old women laughed, and one pointed at Baileya, who leapt and spun near the center of the crowd, her bright-blue smock flying around her like wind. She caught his eye as she twirled, and she smiled, looked away, and kept dancing. He noticed the gold armband she wore. She had rolled her loose sleeves up so you could see it, glittering on her muscular arm.

Mother Crow said, "Wu Song. May I see the mask?"

Baffled that she knew so much, Jason pulled the mask from his sack. Mother Crow held it up, studying the mirrored surface as it flared and shone in the starlight. "The Knight of the Mirror asks that you keep it safe from the Scim."

"The Scim made it," the other old lady said.

Mother Crow nodded and said, "They could make another if they chose. No, we will not hold this mask for you, Wu Song. It has too little of the truth in it. This mask is deception. To live in the desert one must embrace who one is. This mask does the opposite. It tells the world you are who they desire you to be. It is a small death to cover your face in such a way."

"So I came all this way for nothing."

The old woman's eyes widened in surprise. "You gained a story, did you not?"

"Now," Mother Crow said. "When the sun rises you must leave this place. So long as you hold that mask, you are not welcome among our people. If one day you desire to leave all and learn from the desert, come and seek what you may find among the sands."

Jason tucked the mask away, disappointed. How did they know all these things before he told them? What was he meant to do now that their entire mission had failed? And of course he had been the one to fail, not Baileya, who was good at everything. He paused. "Is there, perchance, a Father Crow I could speak to?"

The old women cackled with laughter. "Sweet child, go along now. How can you protect your Madeline when she is so far away?"

He wasn't sure what to do. He wandered out beyond the new firelight flickering up near the elders. He stood and looked at the moon, now completely enveloped in stars. The music and joyful cries of the people faded as he considered all that had happened since coming to the Sunlit Lands.

After a while, Baileya leaned up against his shoulder, handing him a chunk of roasted meat. "Hare," she said. He hadn't realized how hungry he was until she put it in his hands, and he ate it gladly.

He told her all that the old women had said. She listened carefully. When he was finished, she said, "I will go back with you to Far Seeing."

"You're not upset?"

"It is foolish to be upset about what is. Let us instead attempt to shape what will be." She shivered, as if suddenly cold, and pulled her dun cloak over her shirt. "Why have you tied yourself to Madeline?" she asked. "Why do you seek to protect her even from Death, should she come?"

Jason and Baileya sat down on the edge of a broken piece of statuary. It looked like it had been a group of people sitting at a long table. The table was flat and smooth and broken in such a way that they could lean up against it like a chair. "I haven't told anyone this story," Jason said.

Baileya jumped up. "Then why tell it to me? Such a story is priceless. An unknown, untold tale?"

He had forgotten how stories were money here among the Kakri. Huh. That meant that she had shared something valuable with him when she told him the story of the crow inviting the Kakri people into the desert. "You deserve to know. You're my friend," Jason said. She looked skeptical. "It would help me to tell someone."

Her face softened, and she sat down again, legs crossed, facing him. She put her hands on her knees and said, "I will listen attentively."

"I had a sister once. Her name was Jenny. She was three years older than me." Jason cleared his throat. He hadn't said her name in a while. His eyes burned. "You have to understand that my parents . . . They meant well, I think, but they did things differently. They weren't like the other American parents, you know, even though my mom came to the United States when she was young. My dad thought the best way to encourage someone to work hard was to never be satisfied with their work. If we got straight As, he would barely acknowledge it. He'd say things like, 'Grades in middle school do not count.' But if you got terrible grades, they suddenly counted quite a lot."

"I do not know what this means, grades and As."

"Right. Think of it like . . . lessons. If we did well at our lessons, he didn't say anything, but if we did poorly, he had a lot to say. So Jenny and me, we were like a team. When I got my grades, I'd go to her bedroom, and we'd close the door, and she would look at them and tell me what a good job I was doing. She'd show me her grades, and I'd tell her how proud I was. We talked about everything. It was us versus my parents in everything, and we always stuck together."

"It is not a good way to live as a family."

Jason laughed cynically. "I don't think it's what my parents intended, but it's what happened. Well, after a while Jenny started dating this guy named Marcus. He was Korean."

"What does 'dating' mean?"

Jason stopped, trying to think of the right way to say it. "More than friends, I guess?"

"Like you and Madeline. More like siblings than friends." She raised an eyebrow, as if asking whether she had understood his relationship to Madeline correctly.

Jason ran his hands through his hair. "No . . . like husband and wife, but they weren't married yet."

"They were betrothed?"

Jason debated whether to explain the entire process in modern-day America, but decided it would cause more questions and misunderstandings. She didn't need to get it perfectly, anyway. "No, they weren't engaged. They wanted to be engaged, though." That seemed close enough.

"Ah," Baileya said. "He had not yet told her his story. I understand now."

He wasn't sure she did, but he couldn't spend forever on this little detail. "Right. So Jenny and Marcus, they were . . . they were spending a lot of time together. My parents didn't like him, though. They kept saying he was irresponsible. They wanted Jenny to date a Chinese boy, not a Korean one."

"What does this mean?"

Huh. What *did* that mean? "He came from another . . . like, another tribe than us."

"Like you and me," Baileya said.

Close enough. "Right. Yeah. So . . . my dad had a big fight with Jenny, and he told her she couldn't see Marcus anymore."

Baileya leaned forward. "She did not obey him."

Jason shook his head. "Jenny would say she was going to a friend's house or that she was working on her lessons. One night she didn't come home. She had told my parents she was meeting someone at the library, but as the hours went by, my dad started to suspect she was with Marcus."

"Your mother killed the boy," Baileya said, as if it were the most obvious thing in the world.

"What? No! My dad started asking me where Jenny was. She told me everything, and Dad knew that. I knew Jenny and Marcus had driven to a mountain near our house to watch the sunset. She had texted me from there."

"Texted?"

"Sent me a message. My dad got more and more angry as the night went on. He shouted and screamed. My mom tried to get me to tell her what was going on. I kept sending messages to my sister telling her to get home quickly. At last my dad grabbed me by the shirt and dragged me to my sister's room. He threw me on the floor and told me he knew she was seeing Marcus. That it didn't matter now, that it was three in the morning and he needed to know where she was. I was so tired. I hadn't slept. My whole body hurt. I told him what I knew. He called the police, and then he and my mother and I went to the mountain in my father's car." Then he had to explain about police and cars.

"The . . . police . . . they found your sister?"

"No," Jason said. "At sunrise my mom noticed skid marks on the road. There were broken trees. My dad stopped the car in the middle of the road, grabbed me by the neck, and dragged me to the edge of the cliff. Marcus's car was down there. My father was yelling, and I didn't know what to do, so I climbed down. By the time I got to the car, I was bruised and covered in mud. My clothes were torn."

"Did your father follow you?"

Jason shook his head. "Jenny was . . . The car was upside down. Broken. Marcus was dead. Jenny, though. She looked at me. She tried to speak. I couldn't get the door open. She said . . ." Jason couldn't get the words to come out. His lips trembled, and his throat closed tight. His hands shook, and tears spilled from his eyes. "She said, 'Didi, I was waiting for you.'"

Baileya did not say anything, but she reached across and took his hand in hers.

Jason explained to her about doctors and ambulances. "When the ambulance came, they said that Marcus had been dead for six hours. Jenny had been there beside him that whole time. If they had been able to get to her even an hour sooner, they could have saved her." He hung his head. "If I had only told them the truth."

"You have not lied since that day?"

"One lie. I told my parents that Jenny had said she loved them, and she was sorry she disobeyed."

"What did your father say?"

Jason stared into the distance. "He said I had killed my sister. He hasn't spoken to me since the funeral."

Baileya sat still, her hand resting in his. "You did not kill her," Baileya said.

"I—" Jason could not handle Baileya saying that. Even Jenny had blamed him. *I was waiting for you*, she had said. And he hadn't come, not in time. He had never told anyone that part of the story, he had only turned it over and over in his own mind. Jenny had wished he had told the truth, that he had let his parents know where she was. If he had told them right away, or even if he had told them sooner, Jenny would still be alive. "I can't let someone else die," Jason said. "I have to protect Madeline. If she were to . . . to pass, and I could have stopped it . . . I can't live with that."

Baileya said, "I have heard your story, and I will consider it carefully. It is a good story, Wu Song." She pulled the gold armband from her arm and placed it on Jason's. "I will keep the story safe." She stood. "Come, the sun is rising. Bring the mask and we will return to Far Seeing." She took his hand and helped him to his feet. "I understand now why you must protect

Madeline, and I, too, will protect her. Wait for me at the fallen gate of the city, and we will begin our journey soon."

Jason wiped his eyes, thankful for the easy way Baileya had taken his story, and thankful, too, that she had not condemned him but seemed more serious than ever about joining him. She made her way over to the remnants of the dancers. She spoke to them. He couldn't hear their words, but there was a great ululating cry, and the dancing began again with more fervor. He turned the gold band on his arm. It felt like a declaration of friendship. It meant a lot to him that she had put it on his arm, that she would loan it to him for a short time.

Mother Crow stood at the broken gate. She pressed a small bag of food and a skin of water into his hands. "For the Kakri people, courtship is different than among your people."

"Dating advice, huh, Mother Crow? No offense, but how long has it been since you dated someone?"

She ignored him. "If you wish to marry Baileya, here is how it is done among our people. First, the man has a story he has kept secret his whole life. It must be a story he has never told anyone, ever. He pulls the woman aside and shares the story with her. This is a valuable story, a secret story." Jason felt a small flutter of panic in his stomach. Mother Crow continued, "When the story is done, the woman must decide whether to marry or not. If she wishes to become betrothed, she tells the man his story was a good one and that she will consider it carefully. She has one year to think on his story."

"So if she says it's a good story, they're *engaged*?"

Mother Crow smiled and shook her head. "First she must give him a token of her affection."

Uh-oh. "Not like a gold armband, though, right?"

"That would be a fine token," Mother Crow said. "Then she tells her family, and there is a celebration."

There would be a way to explain the misunderstanding, he was sure. Celebrations weren't bad, anyway. Right?

"For the next twelve cycles of the moon," Mother Crow said, "the family tries to kill the suitor, and the woman must prevent it through the strength of her arms and her prowess as a warrior."

Wait, what? "Say that again? The family tries to murder the suitor?"

"For one year. The betrothal celebration lasts one day, after which the family seeks the suitor to kill him. If they fail to kill him, then there is great rejoicing, and he becomes a member of her household."

"And if they succeed?"

She shrugged. "What does it matter?"

"What if the suitor backs out of the engagement?"

Mother Crow narrowed her eyes. "The family still attempts to kill him, but he is no longer under the protection of his betrothed."

Great. He would be married or dead within a year. Possibly both.

"Mother Crow," he said.

"Yes, Wu Song?"

"Good-bye." He ran into the desert, knowing that Baileya would catch up easily.

She did. She was beaming. Her skin seemed to glow. She smiled at him and took his hand.

Soon her family would follow them into the desert, bent on killing him as part of their strange marriage ritual. The Kakri would move faster than the Scim military, and they knew these desert wastes.

Baileya squeezed his hand. "Faster, Wu Song."

Wu Song ran.

33

THE ELENIL AT WAR

One of the Peasant King's followers, a knight in his service,
said to him, "My lord, where are you going?"
The Peasant King replied, "Why, to meet Death.
Would you go with me, Sir Knight?"

FROM "THE TRIUMPH OF THE PEASANT KING," A SCIM LEGEND

✦

Madeline's tears had stopped. Darius found her staring silently at refuse in the field. He had taken his helmet off. He smoothed his white robes and sat beside her. "The Elenil will come soon," he said. "After our attack on the city, they will respond. You can help Yenil's family, Madeline."

"How? By throwing away better garbage?"

"You can make sure they aren't harmed. You're a high-value human to the Elenil. They want to make sure your deal is kept. They'll want you happy. Tell them to leave her family alone, and they will."

The darkness here was so deep. There were no stars. It was as if a thick cloud layer hovered overhead. "The Elenil don't fight their own battles, Darius. They won't sweep in here and hurt anyone. If anything they'll send some human soldiers. How many Elenil even died in your attack?"

Darius rubbed his jaw. "I haven't spoken to the war council yet, but no more than a hundred. They are long lived, though, and not used to death. Not anymore. You don't know them, Madeline. They'll come, and when they do, it will be to punish our people. We crossed a line by attacking during their holiday. They will make it clear that such a thing cannot happen again."

Something stirred within her. It was wrong for the Scim to murder the Elenil. The Scim were in poverty, yes, but why did that make killing others okay? "Darius, you make it sound like the Elenil could come in and wipe out the Scim in a single day."

"They could. They've taken the Scim's weapons . . . their most powerful ones, anyway." He turned to look at his owl, which had closed its golden eyes, resting perched on a log sticking out of a garbage pile. "Except for the Sword of Years, which I have now. The Elenil have all but enslaved these people by building an economy based on taking from the Scim to empower and enrich the Elenil. The Elenil could crush the Scim in an afternoon if they truly wanted to do so."

"Then how are they at war?" It didn't make any sense.

"They can't destroy the Scim completely. Who would be the object of their magic then? Where would their sewage magically disappear to? Madeline . . . if there is a Scim woman with a beautiful voice, she sells it to the Elenil. If you have talent, or ability, or anything the Elenil want, you can get ahead. If you're a gifted musician, or athlete, or artist. For a while at least. If you don't have those things, you can get a meal, maybe, or a roof over your head for a few weeks by giving them some small piece of your life. Healing magic, maybe. You take the flu for a week so the Elenil can be healthy. In exchange, three days of food. Follow the money, Madeline. When you see this sort of injustice in the world, you always follow the money. Who benefits? Who loses? Then you know what kind of game is being played."

It still didn't make sense. It was a terrible deal, and she didn't understand how getting a few days of food would be worth being sick for a week. "Why would the Scim agree to this?"

Darius looked embarrassed. He stared into the night for a while. When his eyes met hers, there was a calculation being made, a decision being weighed out. "Okay," he said. "Okay. You know my cousin Malik?"

"Yeah. The one who went away to college last year. Your mom mentioned him."

"He's not in college, Madeline. Listen, it goes like this. We start with a private prison somewhere."

"A private—?"

"Contracted. They make a deal with the government, so the government doesn't have to run a prison. It works like this. They make a deal for a bunch of money. The government guarantees a quota . . . a certain number of inmates a year or the company won't make money, right?"

Madeline shook her head. "What does this have to do with Malik?"

"Just wait for it, Mads. So to meet the quota, a certain number of people have to be arrested. But there's not enough. The cops are working hard, but they're not getting enough convictions. So the legislators, they make tighter laws. Then the cops can arrest more people, the judges can put more away. They make mandatory minimum sentences for small crimes so they can fill prison beds."

"That's a cynical way of looking at things."

Darius squeezed her hand. His eyes held something like compassion, but it might have been pity. "It's experience, not cynicism." He took his hand back. "So Malik, he's trying to make ends meet. His mom's in the hospital, and his girlfriend is pregnant. He can't get ahead fast enough, even being careful with his money. His friends keep saying he could make good money fast if he's willing to sell drugs. He keeps pushing them off. His mom would be furious if she ever found out. His girlfriend would be furious too, and he has a kid on the way. He can't risk that. But he knows who to talk to if he decides he needs the money."

Madeline could scarcely believe what she was hearing. "Did Malik start selling drugs?"

"No," Darius said, obviously frustrated. "No, that's what I'm telling you . . . he decided not to. Then one day he's hanging out with some of our friends, they're sitting on the sidewalk, just catching up, and a police car comes flying out of nowhere, up onto the curb. Everyone scatters, and Malik runs too."

"Why did he run if he didn't do anything wrong?"

"That's exactly what the cops say. And the thing is, one of Malik's friends, he was holding. He ditched his drugs on the sidewalk. The cops ask Malik who they belong to, and he knows, but he won't tell them. So they take him in, and they sweat him at the station and try to get him to talk. But he won't give them a name, so they write up the report and they say that the drugs were Malik's."

"Wait. Are you saying they lied?"

"They wanted to bust a dealer, and my cousin was sitting there, right where the drugs were found. You know, in the scramble maybe they thought they were his. Maybe they think that's what really happened. I don't know. But the cops are adamant. The public defender doesn't put up much of a fight, and Malik goes to jail."

"Malik's in *jail*?"

"In jail it costs ten bucks a minute to make a phone call, because some company has a monopoly on outgoing calls. Plus he's doing prison labor. Growing produce for some fancy big-name grocery chain."

"Malik was hanging out with drug dealers? Darius, why didn't he just give them a name?"

"Malik gets paid this tiny bit of money for his work. A lot less than the phone company, the private prison, and the grocery chain are making off him. Meanwhile his kid is growing up without a daddy, his girlfriend has no money and has to figure out who can take care of the baby so she can work, his mama can't afford the hospital. Some white dude on the television is talking about how Malik needs to learn to take responsibility for his actions, but meanwhile Malik has nothing and never has. He was loyal to his friends, that's his crime. Meanwhile he's got no safety net, no one to bail him out on rent one month."

"Are you sure he was telling the truth?"

Darius snorted. "Why would he lie at this point? He's already serving the time. He's never lied to me before, even when he did stupid things. What makes you think he's lying? Because a couple cops have a different story? A couple cops you don't even know?"

"Okay," Madeline said. She could see it happening. "It's a really terrible story. I'm sorry about Malik. But what does this have to do with the Scim?"

"Okay, I'm almost to that. So Malik, when he gets out, he won't have any money. He'll be worse off than he was going in, and what's going to happen? He tries to join the military, but they won't take him because of his record. He doesn't have a car, so he can't leave the neighborhood very easily. He's taking the bus to work on the other side of town. He can't afford to live there, so he's taking the bus two hours each way to work, where he gets just enough money to stay in debt. His kid gets sick, so he takes out a payday loan. His mom dies, he can't pay for the funeral, but he has to get the cash somehow. It starts all over again. He's gotta make the decision—is he gonna work inside the system and suffer or gamble on breaking the law to get ahead? His kid, he's going to inherit the same thing."

"If he just works hard—"

Darius slapped the back of his hand into his palm. "No, Mads, no. He's working harder than your dad. Fifty-hour weeks plus twenty-eight hours of travel. I'm not saying he can't get out, people do. You asked why the Scim would agree to this deal. It's the wrong question. The question is, how are the Elenil keeping the deal in place? You start following the money, and you find the politicians, the prison owners, the lobbyists and corporations, they need more bodies. They need legal slavery. So they write the laws tight. They make sure it's a law that will catch young black men, because the young ones are cheaper to take care of in jail. Then they wait for you to slip up. One mistake, and they've got you. That's how it works in the real world, and that's how it works here."

Madeline felt raw. Like Darius was accusing her of something, like she had participated in some way in what was being described. She felt like they were on two boats that had been lashed together, but he was cutting the ropes. He was headed out to sea, watching her drift away.

Darius crossed to the owl and came back with the sword. He unwrapped it and put it in Madeline's hands. The worn pommel, the chipped and rusted blade—the only way it could look more pitiful would be if the blade was broken.

"The Sword of Years," she said.

"Five hundred years ago, there was a battle," Darius said. "The Scim and the Elenil were at war. All the men—in those days only the Scim men fought—had gone out to battle, dressed in their war skins. They had left behind a small city, called Septil. The Elenil had fought the Scim warriors and been forced to a draw. The Scim offered to make a peace treaty, and the Elenil also agreed. They met to discuss the treaty, but one of the Elenil captains snuck away with his soldiers and came upon the city."

"During the peace negotiations? The Elenil were scouting out the Scim land at the same time?"

"Yes," Darius said. "Septil was filled with women and children and elderly men. They saw the war party come to the gates. The Scim people debated whether the Elenil might be there with peaceful intentions. They had received messenger birds saying the peace talks had begun. Others were skeptical. They had few weapons in the city, but there was one sword, rusted and nicked and half useless. The old men put a blood spell on it: the sword would be harmless except against those who harmed the Scim. If the sword found people who had harmed the Scim or gained from their harm, it would not be sheathed until it had spilled their blood. All of it."

Madeline turned the sword over in her hands. It didn't seem magic, it seemed like an old broken piece of junk. "What happened?"

"They let the Elenil in. The Elenil began to slaughter the people . . . They thought they would leave a parting gift for the Scim warriors, who would return home from their peace talks to find their families butchered. But a child picked up the sword, and when he pulled it from the scabbard, it became sharp, shiny, and new. It drank the blood of the Elenil, and that one child defeated the entire war party. They retreated."

Five hundred years, he had said. This sword was older than the United States. How strange. The bitterness between the Scim and the Elenil ran deep and ancient. "The Knight of the Mirror said not to sheathe the sword. He said it was dangerous."

Darius laughed bitterly. "To the Elenil. The sword still fulfills its calling. It spills the blood of those who would oppress the Scim. It is patient and will wait centuries to exact its vengeance. That is why it's called the Sword of Years."

A horn blew, clear and cold as the moon. Darius scrambled to his feet.

"What is it?" Madeline's hand closed instinctively around the sword's handle.

"The Elenil," Darius said. He threw the canvas to her. "Cover the sword."

Fera and Inrif burst from their hovel just as Darius pulled his helmet on. "Are they near?" Fera cried.

"Madeline will protect you," the Black Skull said, climbing onto his owl. "I must warn the elders." Then, to Madeline: "I leave the sword to you, Mads. Do what you think is right."

To Madeline's astonishment, the couple didn't ask how she would protect them. They wished the Black Skull a safe journey and returned inside. She followed, carrying the wrapped sword under her arm.

Yenil moaned. She had fallen asleep. Her breathing came in short, raspy breaths.

Inrif bolted the door, and Fera lifted squares of wood over the windows, barricading them in. The tiny hut felt claustrophobic now, and the smoke from the fire burned Madeline's eyes.

Inrif and Fera tried to hide their curiosity about the package, but their eyes drifted toward it over and over. Madeline placed it on the table, trying to be quiet so as not to wake Yenil. She unwrapped the sword. Fera gasped. Inrif hissed through his teeth.

"The Sword of Years," Madeline said.

Inrif hurriedly threw the canvas over the sword and wrapped it tightly. "The Sword of Ten Thousand Sorrows," he said. "The Sword of Pain. Blood-Spiller. The Strife of Generations."

Fera placed a hand on Madeline's arm. "It has many names. We are simple people, miss. We do not go on blood feuds with Elenil lords."

"Take my advice," Inrif said. "Do not use this sword, nor give it to any who would."

"Why? This is one of the artifacts of the Scim, made with Scim magic." She pushed the wrapped sword across the tiny table. "You should have it."

Inrif held up his hands, as if to ward off a blow. "Do not offer that foul thing to me again. It is a curse, miss, a curse whether you meet its point or its hilt."

Fera didn't look at the bundle. "My husband speaks truth. Some Scim would have it returned to us, others would have it destroyed. If such a thing were possible."

Madeline didn't understand. "What should I do with it, then?"

"Throw it in the sea," Fera said.

"Return it to the Elenil," Inrif said bitterly. "Let them keep the cursed thing within their own walls. May the Peasant King take pity on them when it is unsheathed!"

A bright light blasted through the planks on the windows. Beams of summer sunlight lit the room. When the light hit them, Fera and Inrif both twisted away, letting their arms and legs swell and grow. Tusks jutted from their faces, and their lean bodies grew heavily muscled. War skin, that's what they called it. They looked like monsters. They looked like Break Bones. Madeline couldn't help but recoil.

Yenil neither woke nor changed.

Fera cried out in her new, guttural voice and held Yenil to her chest. "She does not put on her war skin, husband."

Madeline crossed to them. "What does that mean?"

"It means," Inrif said, walking to the door, "that our sweet child is nearing the end of her illness. Her war skin should protect her when the light threatens, even when she is not conscious. This is dire news indeed."

"Our sweet child," Fera wailed. "Only yesterday she laughed and sang. Only yesterday she ran about the neighborhood and played with the other children."

Yesterday. Because of the Festival of the Turning. Because Madeline had not been stealing her breath. Madeline's tattoo burned.

A knock on the door nearly shook it from its frame. Inrif opened the door carefully. Outside stood the Elenil. No humans. No Maegrom. Nothing and no one but the Elenil.

They were dressed for war. Silver helmets. An army of shields. Swords like polished moonlight.

"Wait," Madeline shouted. She ran to the door. "I am of the Elenil. These people are under my protection."

The first blade went through Inrif's chest. He fell forward, his heavy war-skin body knocking the Elenil soldier back.

Madeline stared in horror. Fera slammed the door, wincing against the light outside.

The immediate thumping against the door moved Madeline to action. She snatched up the Sword of Years, uncovering it.

"No," Fera hissed. "The back wall. Dig!"

"But with the sword—"

"And if you fail, they will only kill more Scim. They will say we fought against them."

Madeline fell beside the wall and dug with her hands. The dirt was packed and hard. She used the sword to break into it, and it crumbled beneath the blade. The door shivered, and the Elenil shouted for them to open it.

Fera leaned against the door, grunting each time the Elenil smashed into it. "Take Yenil," she whispered, her voice a passionate plea.

"Come with us," Madeline said.

"The hole is not large enough," Fera said, tears falling.

"I can dig faster."

As if in answer, the door buckled. Fera shouted and smashed it back. "Go!"

Madeline scooped up Yenil. She weighed almost nothing. Yenil stirred but did not wake. Madeline wiggled out through the hole first. The Elenil were on the other side of the hut, light hovering over them, coming from tiny, floating orbs of sunlight. They didn't see her. She reached inside and took hold of Yenil's hands, dragging her through the hole.

She hoisted the child in her arms and ran.

She ran until she could no longer see the light, letting the darkness fold over her, envelop her. Yenil's breathing came harder while Madeline ran. They fell together into the dirt. Noises of battle came from the direction of the hut.

Fera screamed, and there was the sound of metal on stone. Shouts, distant in the darkness. Then silence. No more screams. No sounds of battle.

Tears burst from Madeline's eyes.

Yenil leaned against her. Still asleep and struggling for breath, she said, "Mother . . . I am cold."

Madeline wrapped her arms around her.

They were in a sickly garden. Orderly rows of malnourished plants lay crushed between them. Madeline listened to the harsh, labored breathing of the girl in her arms. She could feel the pulsing connection of their tattoos. She sobbed and held the girl tighter.

"Oh, sweet lamb, don't you cry now." An old woman sat beside her, a floral hat on her head, her grey hair like the straws of a broom. "I'm not saying it isn't sad, dear. But this isn't the time for tears, not yet."

It was the Garden Lady, the one who had met her in her mother's garden a million years ago. "They killed Fera and Inrif," Madeline said.

The old lady nodded. "They will kill that sweet girl you're holding too, should they find her." She rearranged herself and smoothed her skirt. "You have three favors yet, dear. If I can help, only ask the question."

Madeline wiped her face. "Can you get us somewhere safe? Westwind?"

"Hmm. Not all the way to Westwind, dear. There's no garden there for us to enter. But close. Close enough. Do you agree this will be your first favor, leaving you with only two more?"

Lights were coming toward them. The sunlight bounced and shone across the garbage and refuse of the Wasted Lands. Elenil soldiers, resplendent in the reflected sunlight, made their way toward Madeline's hiding spot, like living mirrors.

"Yes," she said. "Yes, quickly."

"Close your eyes," the old lady said.

She did.

Sunlight hit her face, and for one panicked moment she thought the Elenil had found her. Birds sang around her. They were in a lush, green garden in the shadow of the archon's palace. An Elenil couple stood a few yards away, surprised by the sudden appearance of the human and the Scim girl.

Madeline said nothing. Being this close to the archon filled her with panic. She lifted Yenil and trotted away from the garden toward Westwind and, she hoped, safety.

34
AN END TO HOPE

During the storm, hope.
After the storm, peace.
A KAKRI PROVERB

✤

So then a Kakri warrior hidden in the sand dune comes flying out with a sword, and he's shouting this crazy oooolalalalalalalala, and I'm like uh-oh, and I don't know what to do, so I run straight toward this big rock, and I climb on top, and then Baileya comes and fights the guy until she knocks his sword out of his hand, and then she steals his ride, which is this huge bird like an ostrich—"

"It is called a brucok," Baileya said, smirking.

"—steals his brucok, and after that no one else could catch us. She had left me sitting there by myself as *bait*," Jason said. He glared at Baileya accusingly.

"Not bait," she said. "You were the tantalizing reward in the center of my trap."

"That's bait!"

Madeline grinned. She had shared her story about her time in the Wasted Lands. It had been painful, telling them about Darius and the Scim family and explaining young Yenil, who even now slept on Madeline's bed. Shula hugged Madeline again. She had been terrified when she lost Madeline to the Black Skull, thinking Madeline had been imprisoned . . . or worse.

It was a relief to hear Jason share about his journeys with such wide-eyed wonder, though Madeline could tell he was holding back part of the story. He looked at Baileya with a strange nervousness, and she smiled back with a certainty and warmth she hadn't shown before. What had happened out there in the desert?

"Anyway," Jason said, "we don't have time to go into it all, but there were also gigantic moving statues, a death blimp—"

"It was the Pastisians in one of their machines. It was not a 'death blimp.'"

"You said they were necromancers, and that thing was like a . . . I don't know, some sort of weird dirigible. So death blimp is good enough for me. We had to hide! Baileya buried me—"

"You don't know how to conceal yourself properly."

"And then! Then she made her giant bird—"

"Brucok."

"—she made her giant brucok *sit on top of me*."

Baileya shrugged. "You would not stay still beneath the sand. I needed to cover you."

Yenil stirred, her body racked with coughing. The network of silver tattoos that covered much of Madeline's body tingled. That evidence of Yenil's burden—of what should be Madeline's burden—reminded Madeline who had put that burden on her back. The Elenil had taken away Yenil's breath and given it to Madeline and done it without Madeline understanding what the bargain entailed.

Jason asked, "What do you want to do, Mads?"

His quiet voice startled her from her thoughts. Jason, with a look both open and determined, waited for her response. She had harmed him, too. She had made a bargain for his life, knowing full well the consequences and not allowing him a choice. Night's Breath's life for his. He was the beneficiary of that death through no fault of his own. The blood guilt for that one lay on her.

She knew what had to be done. "Did the Scim recapture the Crescent Stone?"

"No," Shula said. "The Elenil magic returned just in time to repel them."

"Then we have to destroy it," Madeline said.

"That is the source of all Elenil magic," Baileya said. "To destabilize it would be catastrophic."

"For who? It's catastrophic already for the Scim."

Jason shook his head. "You won't be able to breathe, Madeline. We'll be kicked back to our world. Right?"

Shula, wiping the sweat from Yenil's brow, said grimly, "I can't go back to Syria. I'll be killed."

"I can breathe, but she can't," Madeline said desperately. "I need your help if we're going to do this. We need to make a plan to get our hands on that stone."

An awkward silence fell in the room. Maybe they couldn't see. Maybe they didn't understand that every beautiful tower in Far Seeing was a broken-down hovel in the Wasted Lands. The fine clothing they were all wearing was the result of putrid rags among the Scim. Every good thing the Scim had, the Elenil stole it and threw it carelessly onto their hoarded piles of wealth. Madeline benefited from this with every wonderful, full-chested breath of air she took into her lungs. She couldn't live with that, couldn't stand by and do nothing. Madeline said, "I'll do it by myself if I have to."

"Some wrongs cannot be easily righted," Baileya said. "But that does not mean we should not try. I fear the magic of the Elenil is woven so centrally through their life and culture that you cannot destroy it without destroying them. Yet it is true that their gain is the Scim's loss, and their wealth, the Scim's poverty. I do not know if removing it completely is wise, but I will stand with you, if you think this the best course."

Shula put her hand on Madeline's shoulder. "We should at least think through the consequences for others. It won't be only the five of us who are affected."

Jason shrugged. "I guess I can live without my morning pudding."

Baileya seemed to be the one who would know best what the costs would be, as she was the only native to the Sunlit Lands in the room—other than Yenil, who, in addition to being a child, still slept. Madeline asked Baileya what she thought.

"There will be some good," she said, and Madeline bristled at the "some." "My own people have chosen not to use Elenil magic since it began. Nonetheless, there are good things that come from it." She raised her hand for silence when Madeline objected. "You asked for my thoughts, you will receive them."

"What good—"

Baileya cut her off immediately. "The Aluvoreans are protected from the Scim by the Elenil. With their magic gone, the Scim will plunder Aluvorea. The Elenil also keep the Pastisians at bay. The necromancers could sweep the land if the Elenil are weakened. Make no mistake, the Elenil as you know them will cease to exist. Their long lives, for one, will disappear, and they will become like flowers in the desert . . . beautiful, but for a few moments only."

Madeline felt her face flush. "Do they shorten the lives of the Scim to make themselves live longer?"

"No, it was a payment far more terrible," Baileya said. "However, now is not the time to tell stories but to live them. The death of Elenil magic may collapse buildings. It will definitely destroy certain families. The Scim will cease to receive payment for their 'donations' to the Elenil magical economy. Their poverty will go from crippling to absolute. It will take time for them to recover. Many will die. The Elenil will, largely, keep the wealth that remains to them and many of the advances they made on the backs of the Scim and others. Make no mistake—if you choose to destroy the stone, there will be suffering and pain and death."

"What about justice?" Madeline snapped.

Baileya inclined her head. "Perhaps justice, in some measure."

"The city is a mess already," Jason said. "Parts of the wall are down, and people are in mourning after the attack on the city. You're talking about taking a bomb to the center of their culture, basically."

"They shouldn't have built it around stealing from the Scim," Madeline said, and no one seemed to have a response to that. They sat quietly, as if waiting for instructions from her. Which maybe they were. They were loyal friends . . . willing to follow her into this mess.

Shula spoke first, her voice low. "I've always been on the side of the Elenil. You know this." As Madeline had explained everything to her, it was like multiple puzzle pieces fell into place for Shula. She understood now why the Scim acted in certain ways. But what seemed to change everything for her was Yenil. Seeing that child, orphaned and on the run, changed something for her. It reminded her, she said, of herself. "I have no love for the Scim, but we can't just walk into the tower and fight the Elenil. We need a plan."

"Actually," Jason said, "we sort of can walk into the tower. There aren't any doors. I could ride Delightful Glitter Lady straight up the steps."

"They will sever you from your magic," Baileya said. She grinned at him. "Your riding and archery skills will not be of much use, I think."

"I was sort of hoping you would go with me," Jason said, smiling.

"I can almost pass for an Elenil," Madeline said. "With the right dress and a little luck . . ."

Jason pulled a small sack from his side and opened it, revealing a mirrored mask. "We have this, too. Someone could wear it."

"I want to go," said a small, weak voice. Yenil leaned on her elbow, coughing. "I want to help."

Madeline hesitated, then took her hand. "Of course you can go."

"She can hardly walk," Jason pointed out.

"The Elenil killed her parents. She deserves to be there." Madeline couldn't bring herself to add that once she destroyed the stone, it was she who would not be able to breathe or walk or run or speak.

"Humans are not allowed in the tower without an Elenil escort," Shula said. "But it might work if they think Madeline is Elenil and I'm either one of the human guards or, using the mask, an Elenil. We could say Yenil is a prisoner . . . or that we're looking for a healer. We need to gather weapons and clothing. It could get us partway to the stone at least."

"I will gather weapons," Baileya said.

"I can find the clothes we'll need," Shula said. "How soon will we go?"

Yenil lay back on the bed, sweating. She struggled for breath. Madeline rearranged her, trying to make her comfortable. Yenil's eyes closed. She groaned and slipped into sleep. They couldn't wait long. Yenil wouldn't last. "As soon as we're ready," she said.

Baileya stood. "Jason, will you come with me, or do you have other business?"

"I want to talk to Madeline for a few minutes. Then I'll go get Dee."

Baileya nodded once, curtly, and she and Shula left together, Baileya already asking her what sorts of weapons she preferred. Jason turned his attention to Madeline. She knew what was coming and felt her heart clench and shrink into a tiny ball. She didn't want to have this conversation.

"I have these memories now," he said quietly. "Almost like dreams. I can't always remember them clearly, but sometimes they are so vivid they feel more real than the world around me. Especially this world."

Madeline breathed softly, her heart pounding. "Jason—"

"Night's Breath, that was just his war-skin name, you know. His family called him Geren. He had children and a wife. His mother is old . . . She lives on the edge of the Wasted Lands in the shell of what once was their family mansion, which has been handed down through the generations. It's collapsing. None of the walls are complete. Weeds grow in the dining room. Rain falls in the bedrooms, and mold grows across the walls."

"Jason, I didn't know any of—"

"Just—" Jason paused and pressed his palms against his temples. "Just listen. For a minute." He waited for Madeline to sit back, silent, listening to the blood thrumming through her head. When she was quiet, he said, "Once a year, Geren—Night's Breath—took his children through the wastes to visit their grandmother. The children would run through the darkened hallways, and their laughter always made Geren think, *This must have been what it was like once, when my family was powerful.* He had a scar. Did you see that?"

Madeline shook her head. "I don't remember it."

"Once, in the waste, he came across an Elenil traveling alone. She demanded he give her his steed and some supplies. She was on her way to the Court of Far Seeing, and he was headed there as well on some business. So he offered to let her ride with him, to mount up behind him, and together they would split his rations and arrive in a few days." Jason's fists tightened, and his face flushed. As if this had all happened to him and not

Night's Breath. "She told him it would bring shame on her to arrive with him, and she would be needing what she had originally demanded. She sliced him across the chest with her sword and took all his provisions, not just the few days' worth it would take her to arrive at the court."

"That's terrible," Madeline said.

"It gets worse. When he arrived at the Court of Far Seeing, delirious with hunger, his chest wound infected, he found that she had left word with the city guard that he had attacked her in the wilderness. They arrested him and put him in a dungeon for fourteen months. He had been a farmer. When he returned home, his crops were dead. His family lived with his mother, barely surviving. That is when he joined the Scim army and took the name Night's Breath."

Madeline sighed. "Then I killed him."

Jason didn't answer. He stared at the palms of his hands. "I don't know, Mads. His last memories are lost. It's like I only got the strongest ones. The ones he revisited over and over. There's this one story he loved, about this magician called the Peasant King."

"The Peasant King?" Madeline had met him, had seen him in the wood of the tower door.

"There's a story about the Peasant King, about how when he built the Sunlit Lands, he went to the wealthy and the powerful people in the world and offered to let them come in. He told them it was paradise, and that meant everyone would be equal. They would leave their power and their wealth at the door, and in the Sunlit Lands all their needs would be provided for—they would never be hungry or sick. They would be happy. But they didn't want to leave their wealth and their power. The Peasant King got angry, and he said those people could never come in, ever. He cast a spell so only the outcasts, the losers, the broken, the homeless, and the wounded could enter. He made the doors hard to find and in the worst places in the world."

Madeline found herself leaning forward, eager to hear the end of the story. "What happened? Why isn't that the situation now?"

"Mads, that's the thing. I think someone broke the Sunlit Lands. Night's Breath, he had this deep conflict going on inside of him because he saw the war against the Elenil as a betrayal of the Peasant King's original purpose.

You don't fight for a higher position in the Sunlit Lands. It's the beggars who are kings, right? The wealthy and powerful, they're the fools. But his family didn't have food to eat. So what was he supposed to do? And Mads, I get it. I know why you did what you did. I've been thinking about it, and I know—I know I would have done the same thing for you. Because I know you, and I didn't know Night's Breath." He sighed heavily and looked at the little girl on the bed. He whispered, "I know you, and I don't know Yenil. I'd be lying if I said there isn't a part of me that thinks we should leave all the magic alone until your breathing . . . until the magic is permanent."

Madeline gasped. "You mean until my disease kills her."

Jason looked away, ashamed. "Yes. Listen, Mads, we've all been following along at school while you've gotten sicker. We've had the updates and passed along the rumors and felt awkward when you showed up in class. I know there's not a cure, you've told us that. There's not any hope, Madeline. There's not any hope, and what I want to do more than anything is to make you well. I want to save you, and I don't know how. Except I could let that little girl go, just like you did with Night's Breath—"

Madeline grabbed his arms. "No. Jason, promise me. No! I couldn't live with that."

His eyes brimmed with tears, and it hit her all at once that she had done the same thing to him. He would have to live with it. He didn't get a choice. The poor Scim soldier was dead so Jason could live, and that had been Madeline's decision. It had been her call, and she had chosen her friend to live and the stranger to die. It couldn't be changed now.

She leaned her forehead against Jason's. "When you're sick," she said, "when you're really sick . . . you just want one more normal day. I hated walking into school. Hated the looks on people's faces. Hated the way everything stopped while I coughed and hacked, like everyone else was holding their breath. I hated the way people who had been mean to me the year before asked how I was doing and tried to be nice to me. I wanted to have a day where I showed up and someone called me a name. I wanted the boys to flirt with me and the teachers to lecture me for not turning in my homework. Or to walk through a room and have no one notice me, just once."

"In my defense," Jason said, "I was still a jerk to you sometimes."

She grinned at him. "True." She sat beside him and leaned her head against his shoulder, and they watched Yenil struggling to breathe. "That disease will be mine again soon," she said.

"Maybe since we were gone, the doctors have found a new treatment," Jason said.

She patted his arm. "I've spent a long time trying to have hope, Jason. There's a certain point when you realize that hope isn't what you need anymore. You can't hope forever. Sometimes people die. Terrible things happen. Evil wins, and farmers end up in jail while the wealthy get richer. Injustice rules the world. Your lungs get more and more scarred and there's nothing to be done."

"But maybe—"

"No, Jason, listen to me. Sometimes hope isn't what you need. This disease is going to kill me. I'm going to take it back, and I will die. Maybe not today or tomorrow. But I will. Sometimes you don't need hope anymore."

Tears streaked Jason's face. He rubbed at them with the back of his hand. "If we don't need hope, Mads, what do we need?"

"Courage," she said. "I don't need hope anymore, Jason. I know what's coming. I need courage to face it."

He took her hand. "We'll face it together."

35

THE CHOICE

To change the world, change first a heart.

THE GARDEN LADY

✦

Jason rode on Delightful Glitter Lady's back through the crowded streets of Far Seeing, like a king. "Are you sure you don't want to ride up here?" Jason asked Baileya.

"I do not wish to be so conspicuous," Baileya said, but Jason had already seen several people take note of her Kakri clothing and her double-bladed staff and give her a wide berth.

"It's not every day you get to ride a rhino," Jason said absently, watching the tower. "Unicorn, I mean." They were at the bottom of the stairs, quite a way from the massive garden at the base of the palace. They were supposed to wait until Madeline, Shula, and Yenil reached the main entrance. If they entered without any trouble, Jason and Baileya would follow a little way behind. If there was a problem, they'd make some noise and see if that helped them slip inside the tower.

An Elenil guard stopped them. He glanced at Baileya, who had hidden her staff in her sleeves. "You cannot bring weapons into the courtyard unless you are Elenil."

Jason flexed his biceps. "You talking about these guns?"

The guard clearly had no idea what Jason was talking about. Baileya gave him a quizzical look too. Whatever. That was comedy gold. Fine. He went back to the original plan. "I don't have any weapons, sir." That was true. Jason wasn't carrying a single weapon.

The guard gestured to Dee. "This unicorn is a war beast."

"Ha!" Jason shouted. "THIS IS A PEACETIME UNICORN."

"I do not know what that means."

"It means she is retired from military service and is now a civilian unicorn."

The guard's hand fell onto the hilt of his sword. "You cannot go farther unless you shrink your unicorn to its smallest size. And where is your Elenil guide?"

Jason pulled the magic dial off the saddle. "I've got the embiggenator right here. The only problem is, I also have this." He held up a small, smooth stone.

The guard looked at it dispassionately. "A stone? Why is that a problem?"

"Well, you know how magic works, right? If something gets small, something else has to get big. I accidentally brought along the stone that gets big when Delightful Glitter Lady gets small."

"I see," the guard said.

"There's Madeline," Baileya said.

She wore a tightly bound Elenil sheath dress. Another Elenil woman he didn't recognize stood beside her, a small Scim body in her arms. A guard had stopped her and was saying something, but they were too far away to be heard.

A flurry of birds flew into the square, squawking and calling out as they delivered messages to their various recipients.

The guard Madeline was talking to drew his sword. Jason didn't know why, but he knew what it meant. It was time to shout the secret phrase he had taught Baileya as their signal. It was time for them to make their loud, impressive, over-the-top distraction.

He cleared his throat and shouted at the top of his lungs, "It's morphin' time!"

✦

With her hair pinned up and the Elenil dress on, Madeline barely recognized herself.

"The eyes give you away," Shula said. "We should remove the neck."

The high neck of the dress could be unpinned. Fernanda stood in the mirror across from them, watching closely. They weren't in the knight's upper room, so she couldn't speak, only make motions to them. Another side effect of her curse. She made it clear, though, that she agreed with Shula.

With the neck removed, however, the silver tattoos that had been spreading across Madeline's body were visible. They coiled up from her collarbones, working their way up her neck and toward her chin in the front, the nape of her neck in the back. "No one ever shows their tattoos, though," Madeline said.

Shula pulled Madeline's hair back, pinning it up. "Only the Elenil have access to this much magic. It's rare to show it off, especially if someone other than Elenil are around. But it would be unthinkable for a human to have so much magic, and it will distract them from your eyes."

Fernanda nodded her approval from within the mirror.

Madeline studied her reflection in a different mirror. Her skin was not pale enough to be Elenil, and her hair had too much yellow in it. Most of the Elenil had blonde hair that leaned toward silver. Her eyes were definitely a distraction, the wrong blue. But she might pass if no one studied her too closely.

Shula opened her knapsack. "Now this," she said. She held up the shining, mirrored Scim artifact known as the Mask of Passing. She held it up to her face and tied the ribbons behind her head.

Her clothing—jeans and a long-sleeved shirt—flickered, then became a light-violet Elenil dress. Her face reappeared, only not dark any longer . . . It was similar to Madeline's own skin color. Her hair was golden blonde rather than black.

"You look . . . surprisingly like me."

The woman who was not Shula nodded. "The mask causes you to see someone like yourself. That's how it works. Anything that might make you think I'm 'the other' goes away, so you know I'm the same sort of person you are."

"You look human still, though."

"To you. To the Elenil I'll look like an Elenil. To the Scim, a Scim."

"We should test it on the way," Madeline said.

"That would be wise."

They stopped at a market stall a few hundred meters from the main tower. Shula hailed an Elenil soldier and told her to send a message to the wall, asking if there was any danger. The soldier sent a bird without hesitation.

Yenil had tried to walk, but it had been too much. Madeline carried Yenil, perched on her back. Shula would take over when they reached the tower, they decided, and carry her in her arms. They planned to say, if stopped, that they were looking for a healer.

They were stopped. Of course. It wasn't Yenil who was the problem, at least not at first.

"Is that a sword, miss?"

Madeline hesitated. The Sword of Years, wrapped in cloth and rope, hung from her shoulder like a purse. "Yes," she said. She did her best imitation of Gilenyia. "We Elenil are allowed to walk armed wherever we please."

"Of course," the guard said, his eyes lingering on her neck. "The archon has requested, though, that we catalog the weapons as they come through."

Would he recognize the Sword of Years? She didn't know. If he did, they wouldn't make it into the tower, let alone to the top. They wouldn't get the Heart of the Scim.

"This girl is in distress," Shula said smoothly. "We seek a healer and do not have time for pleasantries."

The guard frowned. "To call the archon's order a mere pleasantry is a grave insult." He glanced at Yenil. "Is that a Scim girl? She looks almost like . . . a human."

"She is gravely wounded," Shula said.

"Gilenyia herself has ordered us to bring her," Madeline said, taking a chance.

The guard looked over his shoulder. "Gilenyia is at the ceremony within," he said.

"As is any Elenil of consequence," Madeline snapped.

The guard stepped backward as if she had struck him. She could see the truth of her own words in the shocked look on his face. The guard started to step aside, but just at that moment a flurry of birds circled the tower. Hundreds of them flew past in a great swarm, knocking the Mask of Passing from Shula's face. It clattered to the ground. The guard unsheathed his sword despite the storm of birds.

"What trickery is this?" he shouted. His gaze met Madeline's eyes, and his own widened. "You're no Elenil."

A small yellow bird perched on his shoulder. "Lieutenant," it said, "the Scim have breached the walls again."

"It is full daylight!" the soldier cried.

"They pour through the walls like water. Pray they do not drown us. Break Bones rides at their head upon a grey wolf, and the Black Skulls ride beside him."

"May the Majestic One protect us!"

Shula bent for the mask, but the guard stopped her. "I do not know what game you play, but none of you three may enter."

"She will die!" Madeline shouted, pointing at Yenil.

"Scim die," the guard said. "Such is their fate."

The sudden bellowing cry of a runaway rhinoceros echoed across the square. Shula hoisted Yenil onto her back. Madeline grabbed Shula's hand, and they ran past the terrified guard and into the tower.

✛

Whatever message the cloud of birds had brought, the Elenil guards had taken a sudden interest in Jason and his rampaging unicorn. He burst past fifteen or so guards without any trouble. He pulled Dee up short when a row of Elenil appeared ahead, each on one knee with a spear shaft pushed into the ground, the points ready to pierce the rhino's chest. He couldn't see Baileya . . . She had slipped away into the crowd somewhere.

"Halt!" one of the guards shouted.

"We already halted," Jason said.

"Don't come any closer," another shouted.

"We're not moving."

Madeline and Shula had made it into the tower already. That was the main point of the distraction, but it would be better if he and Baileya could get into the tower too, to help them get to the top and retrieve the Heart of the Scim.

Another flurry of birds sped through the crowd.

One of the guards shouted, "The Scim have breached the outer walls!"

A howling sound came from the west, just before a monstrous wolf loped into view, Break Bones on his back. "Wu Song," he called, pulling his wolf to a stop. "The Elenil have invaded our territories and murdered our people for the last time. We have come to destroy them and retrieve the Heart of the Scim."

"I am pretty sure we called dibs," Jason said. "Only we're gonna do the opposite. We're here to destroy the Heart of the Scim and . . . retrieve the Elenil?"

The massive Scim dismounted from his wolf. "You must not destroy the Heart. It is ours! It is not yours to do with as you please!"

As he spoke, the Black Skulls arrived.

"Hey," Jason said. "Good to see you all. Before anyone kills anyone, I just want to remind you that I go to the same high school with at least one of you, and I think school spirit should count for something."

The antelope-headed Black Skull spoke, and despite the magically modulated voice, Jason could recognize Darius's voice beneath it now that he knew who it was. "Return the Scim artifacts and no one need die."

"Hi, Darius!" Jason said. "I feel like we're basically on the same team here."

Break Bones laughed. "Unfortunately for you, Wu Song, I have made a blood oath to murder you."

"Um. There's no time limit on that, though, right? I mean, you could wait until I'm 130 years old."

An arrow blossomed in Break Bones's shoulder. Baileya appeared from behind a column. She didn't say anything clever. She wasn't one for talking needlessly in battle. She did, however, unsling a massive bag from her shoulder and throw it to Jason. It fell open, revealing a huge collection of weapons. Jason felt intimidated by the fact she could throw it. He pulled out a sword, his magic flowing into it, and shouted a battle cry. The Elenil and Scim met like competing waves, with Jason and Dee between them.

✠

"These plates fly," Madeline said, placing her feet on the floating panels that had taken her to the top of the tower the last time she had been here.

"You dare to bring a Scim here? On this, of all days?" It was Rondelo, dressed in beautifully brocaded white clothing from head to toe. Evernu, the stag, stood beside him.

"She's ill," Madeline said.

Gilenyia peeled off from the crowd of elaborately costumed Elenil. "This is a funeral," she said firmly. "A rare occurrence for us Elenil. A certain solemnity is encouraged. Not only that, but it is the funeral for Vivi, the father of Hanali. You, of all humans, should respect his loss. I will attend to the Scim girl, if only to keep you from interrupting." Despite Madeline's protests, she tried to take Yenil from Shula's back. Shula stepped away from her, refusing to let her touch Yenil. Gilenyia studied the girl more closely, tracing the lines of the tattoos. Her eyes widened, and her face snapped back toward Madeline. "What is this? How did you come to find this girl?"

"How did the Elenil come to find her?" Madeline said fiercely.

Shula spoke in a quiet, calm voice. "Go back to your funeral and leave us be. We don't want to harm you."

Gilenyia looked at them more carefully. "Why, Madeline. You're dressed like an Elenil. Shula appears to be—ah, but what's that? The Mask of Passing?" It hung from Shula's hand. "What mischief are you two up to?"

Madeline's jaw clenched. She slung the package on her shoulder to the front and unwrapped it. Rondelo and Gilenyia watched in curious silence. When the cloth fell away, Rondelo gasped. Madeline took the rusted, nicked, dull blade and slid it into the scabbard. When she pulled it out again, the blade vibrated like a tuning fork. Bright, polished, and sharp, the Sword of Years sang for the blood of those who had benefited from the death of Scim people.

Rondelo's sword flashed, and the point fell toward Shula. "Madeline, do not try anything. That blade—"

Gilenyia had backed away from Yenil. "This is a magic blade, Rondelo. It is called Thirsty, among other names. If there is a healing spell to counteract that blade, I do not know it. Even at the height of my powers, if Madeline were to cut an Elenil with this blade, I would not have the powers to reverse it."

The sword hummed in Madeline's hand, the edge of the blade pulling her toward the Elenil. She felt its rage, felt its desire to drain them, to drain all of them. "Stand on the plates," she said to Shula. Shula edged away from Rondelo and toward the hover plates.

"You will have to take the stairs," Gilenyia said. "Archon Thenody is no fool. He'll not speed your way to assassinate him."

Assassination was not the plan, but Madeline felt the sword hum with glee at the thought. Still, it made sense that the archon's magic would not help them to the top.

"Let me help you," Gilenyia whispered. "There are those of us who would see the current archon replaced with someone . . . younger."

Shula stepped behind Madeline. "Perhaps as a hostage," she said quietly.

"Good idea," Madeline said. "Rondelo, give Shula your sword or I'll run Gilenyia through. That's right. Good. Now—Gilenyia. Up the stairs."

Gilenyia tipped her head slightly. "A pleasure."

The Sword of Years pulled in Madeline's hand. She hoped she had the strength to keep it from striking.

✦

Delightful Glitter Lady frolicked among the warring Scim and Elenil with joyous abandon, and Jason shouted and tried not to fall off. The Elenil fought with the terrifying certainty that no wound given them was permanent, and the Scim with a desperate anger. Baileya struck among them like lightning, wounding Elenil and Scim alike if they came too close to Jason.

The Elenil were confused about whose side Jason and Baileya were on. A Scim came up behind her as she nocked her bow, and Jason brained him with the hilt of his sword. The Scim went down hard, and Baileya gave Jason such a warm smile he almost lost his grip and fell from the rhinoceros.

Just as they fought their way through the tower entrance, a wind kicked in. It howled through the palace compound, blasting them with sand. Jason covered his face. If they had broken into the tower a moment later, he might well have been blinded by the sand, but as it was, the walls of the tower had protected them. "Sandstorm?" Jason called. "Baileya, what is going on?"

Everyone stopped fighting.

Floating like monstrous columns through the melee were fifteen-foot-tall creatures covered in wings. They did not turn, and they each had four faces, each one directly facing one of the cardinal directions on a compass. To the east, a face like a lion. To the west, an ox, and to the north, an eagle. The southern face was that of a human being. The wings sparkled. Or, on closer examination, they didn't sparkle—they blinked. The wings were covered in jeweled eyes, and as they blinked, the patterns on the wings moved like a school of fish.

"Kharobem," Baileya said, wonder in her voice. "They come to watch some story that is about to unfold. The last time they came in such numbers . . . it was the fall of Ezerbin."

Jason let out a war whoop. "That must mean we're about to win!"

"The people of Ezerbin did not win," Baileya said. "Even now their city is a haunt for jackals."

"Oh," Jason said. "Good point."

A barefoot girl in clothing that was little more than a sack limped into the center of the battle.

The Kharobem did not move or speak or make a sound, but Jason knew with a deep certainty that the Kharobem knew the girl. That they were, in fact, here because of the girl.

She stood at Dee's feet and looked up at Jason. "There was a cactus," she said, "born in a city. It lived in a pot upon a counter. It did not grow large. It did not flower. Until it returned to the desert. There it lived a long and happy life, and the desert and the cactus and the sun and the moon and the water and the sand lived happily together for many a year."

Jason shrugged. "Okay, thanks, I guess. And now we fight some more?"

There was silence from the assembled warriors. Jason slid off Dee's back and stood in front of the limping girl.

Break Bones stalked among the warriors, moving toward the tower entrance.

Baileya stepped toward him, her double-bladed spear at the ready.

"Wait," Jason said. "I have a better idea." He snatched the pebble out of his pocket and threw it into the tower doorway. He grabbed the embiggenator and turned Dee all the way to kitten sized. She let out a plaintive squeak as the tiny pebble became a door-blocking boulder.

Baileya squeezed his arm, just below the gold armband she had given him. "I would rather a clever warrior than a strong one," she said.

Jason blushed. In the middle of a battle. How embarrassing. He leaned toward her.

"They are working to move the stone already," she said.

She was right. The stone shuddered, and he could hear the shouting of the Scim outside, Break Bones's voice piercing through.

"Let's get up those stairs," he said, running ahead of Baileya.

She called his name, and he stopped to find her pointing at the ground. Delightful Glitter Lady struggled to get over the first stair, her tiny war cry lost in the cavernous room. But she squeaked again, scrambling for the next stair.

"Aw," Jason said. "So cute! C'mere, Dee." He scooped her up and settled her into his pocket. The sword and the bag of weapons Baileya had thrown to him were all discarded on the ground now. He sorted through it, searching for a lighter sword. He found one and tried to lift it over his head with one hand. He almost fell, and the sword went clattering to the ground. He dug through again until he found—well, he wasn't sure if it was a small sword or a long knife. He lifted it above his head and shouted, "TO WAR!"

Baileya followed him up the stairs. The strange limping girl followed too, silent and watchful.

✦

The Heart of the Scim.

They stood in the glass room at the top of the tower. The stone was on its pedestal. It was the true stone, not the ship-sized stone that hung outside.

Their journey had been easy—suspiciously easy. The Elenil had fallen out of Madeline's way when they saw the Sword of Years in her hand. Gilenyia had helped, shouting that there would be no healing for any who opposed the sword. No doubt it also helped having an Elenil funeral taking place at the base of the tower. Near immortals being reminded of their mortality turned out to be cowards in battle.

Madeline put her hands on the stone and lifted, but it wouldn't move. "Why can't I pick it up?"

"Only certain of the Elenil can remove it," Gilenyia said.

"You're one of them," Shula said. It wasn't a question.

"It would be an act of treason for me to put the Crescent Stone in your hand," Gilenyia said.

The black and purple energy moved inside the stone, almost like water trapped in crystal. Madeline strengthened her grip on the Sword of Ten Thousand Sorrows. She lifted the blade. "I don't need to hold it," she said.

"You don't understand," Gilenyia said, falling in front of Madeline, blocking the stone. "Killing the archon, that makes sense. Let someone else take his place. Perhaps someone more . . . understanding of the Scim. Perhaps that would be wise. But Madeline, if you destroy that stone, you destroy the Elenil. If you destroy the Elenil, my dear—believe me, this is true—you will destroy the Scim, the Aluvoreans, the Pastisians, the Maegrom, and all the people of the Sunlit Lands. I do not claim the Elenil to be without fault, but you must understand we are the foundation of this society. All else is built on top of our work, our city, our magic." Madeline's tattoo was pulsing now, linked to Yenil in a way she hadn't felt before. She could feel the magic guzzling, pulling at Yenil, siphoning her breath away and into Madeline. The Scim girl slid from Shula's back and stared at the source of all their trouble, her hair disheveled and half covering her face.

From where they stood, in the glass room at the apex of the tower, Madeline could see the chaos at the base. Fire had broken out somehow, and the strange creatures Gilenyia called the Kharobem hovered unmoving all around the tower floor, some of them on the stairs, a few floating in the center of the tower. She could see Jason and Baileya running up the stairs, Scim close behind them. They were almost to the top.

She hesitated, and lowered the sword.

A Scim came slowly across the glass bridge toward Madeline. It was one of the servants of the archon. She remembered meeting him but not his name. He was dressed like an Elenil. Madeline understood now that he was wearing his war skin, but it had been modified to make him look powerless, like less of a threat. He could have merely taken on his other form, like Yenil's. Instead they had kept him in his fierce battle skin and humiliated him. They had cut off his tusks. Even in war he would be unimpressive now. She did not remember his name because he was not someone to be remembered or to be seen. He was a decoration in the living quarters of the archon.

"Miss," he said, and his voice was raw. "My lady Gilenyia says all will be lost, but they have taken everything from us. What more is there to lose? They have even taken our language."

"Taken your language? What do you mean?"

"Does it not seem strange that we diverse people speak the same tongue? We are all speaking the Elenil language, through means of their magic. When you break that stone, those who have known their mother tongues will speak them again. But my children and grandchildren will know only Elenil. I speak it only through magic. We will not be able to speak to one another. You are not speaking your native tongue, either. Nor are your friends. When magic ceases, our language will be all but dead, with only the elders knowing it well."

Madeline, wide eyed, turned to Shula. "You're not speaking English?"

"I don't know English," she said. "Only Arabic and French."

Madeline turned back to the Scim. "Are you saying to destroy it or not?"

The Scim bowed his head. "Perhaps once all has burned, my grandchildren will rise from the ashes."

Madeline lifted the sword over her head. "Yenil?"

The girl nodded, a fierce look on her face.

"You don't understand," Gilenyia shouted again. "The magic of that sword cannot be sated. It will destroy the Heart of the Scim completely. Madeline, please, listen to reason!" Shula grabbed Gilenyia and pulled her from in front of the stone.

The sword came whistling down, and a fierce joy radiated from it. It smashed into the stone. The Heart of the Scim shattered into a hundred thousand shards, which flew like shrapnel through the glass room.

Nothing happened.

Nothing changed.

Madeline took a deep breath. Yenil struggled for oxygen.

"It was a fake," Shula said. Above them, the giant facsimile of the Crescent Stone still hung over the tower, crackling with power.

Madeline gripped the sword tighter. She knew, somehow, where the true stone must be. The archon. He would be carrying it on his person. She had a sudden memory of the first time she had seen him without his sheet. She remembered the choker he'd worn, with what she had thought to be a miniature facsimile of the Crescent Stone. Of course he would keep it on him. Now that she knew, it seemed so obvious. She spoke to the old Scim servant on the bridge. "Take me to him."

The Scim bowed his head and shuffled across the bridge into the quarters of the archon.

✦

Being shot with an arrow hurt. Not in a stubbing-a-toe sort of way, but in a screaming, burning, let-me-faint-now sort of way. The arrow came in through Jason's shoulder, from behind, at a high angle so it only caught flesh and muscle. One moment he was running up the stairs, the next an arrowhead appeared, sticking out of his shoulder. It was the worst pain he had felt in his life: a throbbing, burning, pulsing nightmare of excruciation.

"A lucky wound," Baileya said.

"Lucky?"

"Clean through, the arrowhead on the other side, no bones damaged, no major bleeding." She glanced back down the stairs. Some Elenil guards had engaged with the ascending Scim, giving them a moment.

Baileya steadied him and, without warning, broke the head of the arrow off, then yanked the shaft out. Jason's vision swam, and he put his hand against the wall. Baileya pulled out a handful of leaves, chewed them, then pasted them over the hole in his shoulder. "Bloodsop," she said. "To stop the bleeding."

It had a strong, almost minty smell. "You should probably carry more of that if we're going to be hanging out."

Baileya grinned. "Wait here," she said.

"Where are you going?"

"To throw any archers I can find off the stairs."

She slipped down into the battle.

Jason set Dee down, and she explored a few different stairs. Jason sat, putting pressure on the wound. It had been several minutes, he thought, but the blood had already stopped, and the chewed-up leaves had hardened. There must have been some sort of painkiller in the leaves too, because although his shoulder felt hot, the pain had lessened considerably. The limping girl stood below him, watching, but she did not speak or intervene in any way.

Across the tower, Jason noticed a single Scim sneaking up the opposite stairway. "Dee," he said. "Come here." The little rhino trotted to him, and he slipped her into his pocket. Jason had seen the Elenil swinging across the center of the tower to reach the opposite side. He found a rope tied alongside the edge of the stairs. He tucked his tiny sword into his belt.

"Okay, shoulder," he said, "don't kill us."

He swung. Shooting pain fired through his whole body, and he screamed as the rope spun him onto the stairs on the other side, landing a full flight up from the Scim. It was, of course, Break Bones.

Break Bones curled his lip in disgust, shifting his grip on the massive stone ax in his hand. "Thou hast no weapon, Wu Song."

"Break Bones. Hey. How's it going?" Jason pulled his tiny sword out. He regretted its size now. He wasn't sure it could even get through Break Bones's thick skin. Dee climbed out of his pocket and scampered off to the side, and Jason lost sight of her.

"Thou art in my way, human child."

Jason shrugged. The sudden pain in his shoulder made him regret it. "I get that a lot. Here's the thing, though. I feel like if I let you pass, you're going to murder my friend."

"The Heart of the Scim is ours. She must not be allowed to destroy it."

"Why do you want it so bad?"

Break Bones spit on the floor. "Fool! They have enslaved us with it for centuries. The balance is shifting. I would take it back so that we can enslave them. Without the Heart of the Scim we cannot use the Heart of the Elenil. We will reverse the flow of the magic. A few hundred years of justice should make things even. We shall live in towers of glass, they in mud hovels. Our children and grandchildren will rule over them. Your friend Madeline would break our chains and deny us our crown."

"Just to be clear," Jason said. "You're planning to kill her. Instead of talking things out?"

"The Scim have talked to the Elenil for decades, and what has changed?"

"Obviously I can't stop you," Jason said. "I only have this tiny little sword." As if on cue, Delightful Glitter Lady leapt down the stairs toward Break Bones, letting loose a full-throated kitten-unicorn war cry. She crashed into Break Bones's foot. "And a tiny unicorn."

Break Bones chuckled, ignoring Dee completely. "Then stand aside. Run if you can. When I have finished your friend, I will come back for you. Let no one say Break Bones breaks oaths."

"But first," Jason said, "Delightful Glitter Lady: ATTACK!" Dee trumpeted and hit Break Bones's foot, smashing into it over and over again.

Break Bones caught her easily and lifted her to his face. "Wu Song," he said. "Your perseverance is to be commended. But this little beast is no threat to me."

Jason pulled out the embiggenator. "Heh. That's what you think." He turned the knob all the way to the right, and Delightful Glitter Lady went from kitten size to the size of a Labrador, to the size of a rhinoceros, to the size of a juvenile Tyrannosaurus rex. Break Bones fell backward, pinned beneath her.

Delightful Glitter Lady scurried to her feet and trumpeted so loud Jason could feel the stones vibrating through the soles of his shoes.

Break Bones stumbled away, rushing down the stairs.

"Dee," Jason said. The rhino's enormous head swiveled toward him. "Fetch!"

Dee bellowed her delight and charged down the stairs after the retreating Scim warrior.

Jason raced up the stairs, laughing, his wound momentarily forgotten.

✚

They found the archon, at last, sitting in a three-acre garden built, somehow, on a balcony of the tower. He was sitting at a small metal table, sipping tea with Hanali. Both of them were dressed in the extravagant head-to-toe white mourning clothes of the Elenil. The archon raised his eyebrows when he saw Madeline and Shula, Yenil and Gilenyia, and the old servant. Madeline looked up. The crescent-shaped crystal at the top of the tower could be seen from here, glinting in the bright sunlight, still emanating the power of the Crescent Stone.

"So," Thenody said. "You are the ones causing the ruckus below and interrupting poor Vivi's funeral. Now you interrupt me while I have tea with his grieving son. What have you to say for yourselves?"

Madeline still held the sword. It shook in her hands, eager to decapitate the archon of the Elenil. She could feel its attraction, could see the generations of bloodshed and murder and pain that had given him so much power, so much wealth. Her breathing quickened, and as it did, Yenil swayed, her breath rattling in her lungs. "You would kill this little girl so I can breathe," Madeline said.

The archon rubbed his earlobe. The network of golden tattoos that covered his visible skin shimmered. The choker with the small crescent crystal crackled with power around his neck. "I believe your friend Hanali made that particular deal. I was not aware of it until this moment, though I cannot say I am surprised, nor that I disagree with his choice. How do you find these dirty little things, Hanali? Do you scout the Wasted Lands yourself?"

"Many of them come to me, my lord," Hanali said. "Indeed, this young girl's family needed food and offered her service for . . . well, for whatever we had need."

"How clever of you," the archon said. "Did they understand the terms?"

Hanali held Madeline's eyes for a moment, then looked back to Thenody. "The Scim did. Their child did. The human girl did not."

"She's dying," Madeline said.

The archon stood and walked lazily to them, apparently unconcerned about the magical sword in her hands. He looked carefully at the Scim girl. "Not for several weeks at least," he said. "Would you agree, Hanali?"

Hanali didn't move from his seat. He sipped at his tea. "Two weeks at least, sir. Beyond that it is hard to say."

An owl the size of a hang glider flew to the edge of the garden, and a Black Skull dropped to the ground. He carried a sword, and his white robes were covered in blood. "Stay back," Madeline said. Darius hesitated, then stopped.

"I see," the archon said, looking at Darius with interest. "You're going to save the world, is that it?" He tugged on the fingers of his left glove, letting it fall to the grass at his feet. "The Scim obey your orders now? Hmm. Curious." The network of golden tattoos on his hand glowed with a bright, almost blinding intensity.

Jason came running into the garden, a large knife in his hand. He stopped when he saw Thenody. A young girl dressed in rags limped in behind him. "Oh," Jason said. "You again."

The archon's lips turned up in amusement, but his eyes were hard and cold. "Indeed." He turned to Hanali. "Who are we waiting for? The Scim rabble-rouser, yes? What was his name? Break Stones?"

"Break Bones?" Jason asked.

"Ah yes. Charming. Break Bones. We can wait for him, I think."

Shula balled up her fists. "Why are we all standing around like we're at a tea party? Let's get him." She ran at the archon, letting loose a savage war cry.

The archon gestured toward her, palm up, and she fell to the ground, frozen in midstep. She skidded across the ground and came to a halt near his feet. "But you *are* at a tea party, my dear. Children like yourself should sit quietly."

Baileya slipped in beside Jason, breathing heavily. She had her double-bladed staff in hand. Then Break Bones came loping across the garden, a sinister look in his eye.

"Hey, where's Dee?" Jason asked.

Break Bones sneered. "She could not fit through the doorway. She is not pleased I escaped."

"Oh dear," the archon said. "It has become much too crowded. The garden looks positively cluttered." He spoke to Break Bones. "I have soldiers in your village. I have but to touch a certain mark on my left wrist and they will receive the orders to kill. So be silent. Or at least polite."

Break Bones did not speak in response to this but tightened his grip on his ax. Madeline could see Shula breathing, so she knew she was okay. Yenil leaned against Madeline, breathing hard. Still . . . they had Baileya and Darius. She thought Hanali would help them. Break Bones would at least work to get the stone, even if he wanted to do something different with it. She thought that, even with his magic, together they might be able to take Thenody down.

Hanali said, "I would advise all of you to remain still. The archon is powerful, and if he sees you coming, he will easily stop you with his magic."

"True," the archon said. He seemed unconcerned that Hanali was warning them to bide their time. "The question you are all asking yourselves, however, is whether I have the Heart of the Scim. Of course, I do." He put his hand to the choker at his neck. He unfastened it and held up a small stone . . . shining black, oblong, with a great chip in one side. "It is not so dramatic as my decoy. Amazing, is it not, that all our magic flows through such a little thing? The great crystal above the palace, your bracelets, all of Elenil magic—powered by this bit of stone. But that is the way of magic, I suppose."

Hanali looked down at his feet. "Forgive me, Archon Thenody, but I have always understood none but the Elenil should know they have seen the true Heart of the Scim."

Gilenyia said, "Why have a decoy at all if you are going to tell such a large assembly the truth?"

Thenody laughed. "Not one of them will leave this balcony alive, so what does it matter?" He turned the little stone in his fingers, holding it up to the light. He glanced at Hanali. "I see the hunger in your eyes, Hanali."

Hanali said nothing, but for a brief second his eyes flickered toward Gilenyia.

"Yes, I know about her, too," the archon said. "Though I am surprised she allied with you given her understandable hatred of the Scim." He must have noticed the surprise on Madeline's face, because he laughed and said, "Do you mean to say you have not told your human pets? How wonderful. You brought them to this place with no knowledge. I underestimated you, I think, Hanali, son of no one."

"Son of Vivi," Hanali said.

"Yes, but Vivi died when you and the Maegrom let the Scim into the city, didn't he? It is quite a price to pay."

"Whoa, hey what?" Jason said. "When Hanali did what now?" Birds had begun to settle in all the trees and bushes around them. Large and small, brightly colored and drab. All silently perching. A few flew overhead, watching.

Thenody inclined his head toward the birds, as if greeting more guests. "I have invited the messenger birds to come see what will happen next. I would like everyone in the Sunlit Lands to see and hear what happens in this little garden."

"I don't understand," Madeline said quietly.

"It is simple enough, my dear. Hanali has always been . . . unorthodox. It has been ascribed to his youth. His recruiting of humans has become more and more . . . eccentric. A violent girl from Syria I can understand. Those two boys Jason fought alongside, perhaps. But then he chose you. A rich girl with power and privilege who would require a great deal of unjust magic simply to walk among us. A girl who would be horrified to know the price she paid, if she could be made to see it. The kind of girl who would be used to power and privilege enough to believe that she could change things. Who would have hope and confidence, not shrink away and accept her lot in life. Someone who would speak up."

Jason nodded. "It all makes sense. Then Hanali needed someone who really loved pudding. Someone who wasn't afraid to eat it every day. For breakfast most days, but maybe he would be willing to eat it for lunch sometimes. Or even for dinner, even though that would mean saving it all day and that the next meal would also be pudding."

Hanali smiled, his eyes never moving from the stone in Thenody's hand. "I needed Madeline," he said, in an almost dreamlike voice, as if he was remembering something. "An activist." His eyes moved to Jason. "I did not think I needed you at first. I do not know who put you in my path. I realize now I needed a truth teller. A prophet. To help her see, and to stand beside her."

"It is not the first time you have tried," the archon said.

"Some have shied away from the truth. Others have despaired rather than taking action," Hanali said. "This time . . . some unseen hand aided me in my choice of champions."

"All this so you could be archon in my place."

"Perhaps," Hanali said. "Though only to undo our centuries of injustice. I did give the Scim entry the night of the Turning. They were meant to take the tower, not raze the city. And not to kidnap Madeline or try to take the Scim artifacts, which I would have returned to them when I took power."

The archon laughed at that. "Oh, you are young, Hanali. How delightful. I suppose they were not meant to murder your father, either."

Break Bones lunged for the archon. Thenody gestured, a look of disgust on his face, and Break Bones crumpled to the ground, groaning in agony. The archon twisted curled fingers toward him, and Break Bones tried to stand but couldn't. Thenody released him, and Break Bones got to his knees, panting, but could rise no farther.

"Do not approach me without permission," Thenody said, his face returning to the placid calm of a moment before. "Is that the Sword of Years you carry, Madeline? Yes? How lovely."

"It is magic," Madeline said, tears burning her eyes. This wasn't how it was supposed to go. She couldn't get near him, couldn't strike at the stone or Thenody.

"Indeed. I know it well. It could shatter the Heart of the Scim, destroying the Elenil connection to those filthy creatures. It would undo centuries of progress and beauty. You know this, of course. Your world is no different. I am no scholar, but I understand your own injustices have brought progress."

"I don't know what you're talking about."

Jason cleared his throat. "He's saying that the White House was built using slave labor. Or that computers and cars and planes and . . . and rockets were made better, made possible because of World War II. That if it weren't for the Holocaust, we would never have made it to the moon. That America would never have had a black president unless we had slavery first."

Thenody sipped his tea with his left hand, the right still holding the Heart of the Scim on display, mocking them. "The gears of an empire grind without respect for individuals. One does not throw away progress because a few people die along the way."

Madeline struggled to get her words out. "But . . . but that's such a narrow, strange way to say it. It's not worth killing Jewish people so we could get, I don't know, so we could get iPhones. Some people got rich off of slavery, but that's not an argument for it, that's a sign of the sickness."

"Nonsense," the archon said. "This city—this beautiful city—would be impossible without sacrifice. The Scim entered into our agreements willingly. Who are you to say you know better? Who are you to end an agreement made by our two sovereign nations?"

"I am Madeline Oliver," she said. "I hold the Sword of Years, a magical weapon created by the Scim people. It has fallen to me to choose how to use it, and I will do the right thing. The prophecy said I would bring justice to the Scim, and that is what I am going to do."

"Who am I to stand in the way of prophecy?" Thenody said, turning to smile at the messenger birds. "Step forward then, girl, and I will give you a choice."

Madeline stepped toward him warily.

"Look back at the tower," he said.

Madeline did. It rose above them, shining in the sun. Despite everything, that white tower framed against the cloudless blue sky, the giant crystal crescent glowing with power, was strikingly beautiful.

"My archers are in the tower. I do not need them, of course, but they have trained their weapons upon your heart and the hearts of each person on this balcony."

"Including you?" Jason asked.

Thenody ignored him. "Hanali has wagered everything on you humans. He thinks you will make a decision to upend our entire society, to create chaos, to bring suffering to all the people of the Sunlit Lands, all for your simplistic notions of justice."

"And what do you say?" Madeline asked.

"Not that we care," Jason said.

"I say that you are selfish little things and that you will leave it all in place." He set his tea on the table. "I will let you choose. You may have three options. One, you may raise your sword and kill me, allowing Hanali to take my place."

"Tempting," Jason said.

"Two, you may destroy the Heart of the Scim, eradicating all Elenil magic. The Scim will be released of their bargains, as will you and the other humans." Thenody smiled. "I believe your own self-interest will prevent this choice."

"I do like pudding," Jason said, and Madeline saw that he had been edging closer to the archon.

"Or three, I will allow all of you to leave. Alive."

"We could kill you *and* leave alive," Jason pointed out.

"Ah yes," the archon said. "I should have explained that more clearly. If you choose to kill me or destroy the stone, my archers have been instructed to kill all of you save Hanali and Gilenyia, as I do no harm to the Elenil people."

"How many archers?" Madeline asked her friends.

"I count twenty," Shula said.

"Five more in the garden itself," Baileya said. "Twenty-five."

Thenody wasn't bluffing, then. At least, she didn't think so.

She examined her three options. Kill the archon and let Hanali be in charge . . . although Madeline was unclear if it were even certain that he would be the next archon. Or destroy the stone and free them all from the Elenil magic. She looked to Darius, trying to read what was in his eyes, but he only gave her a firm, supportive nod.

Break Bones said, "Kill him."

"No," Madeline said. She was not going to kill anyone. She had decided that, at least.

"To destroy the stone will kill thousands," Break Bones said. "It will be a catastrophic failure of magical systems across the Sunlit Lands. And it will deny us the power we deserve! It will destroy injustice but deny us justice!"

"It's the right thing to do," Madeline said.

"It is the right thing to do," Hanali said. "You are correct. But is it for you to do? Or should the Elenil and the Scim figure it out together? Is it your place to choose for us?"

She looked to Jason, but he only said, "I'll back your play, Mads."

"Me, too," Darius said.

She raised the sword. She could almost feel the archers taking aim, preparing to loose their arrows when she made her choice.

She couldn't kill the archon. She knew that for certain. Night's Breath was dead because of her. She had failed to save Inrif and Fera. That was already three deaths too many on her conscience. She couldn't add the archon's. Not even if it was just. What had the Peasant King told her? Stopping injustice with violence was like throwing gasoline on a fire.

So it had to be destroying the stone. It seemed right and good to destroy it, but at what cost? Would it really mean the death of thousands to so suddenly alter the magical landscape? Could she live with that, even though she wasn't the one who had built the unjust system? And was that any different, really, than killing Night's Breath?

Yenil was gasping for breath. She sank to her knees.

Madeline couldn't accept that. Maybe she couldn't destroy the whole system, but she couldn't participate in it anymore. She wouldn't. She wouldn't let Yenil pay the price, not if she could help it. The Garden Lady's advice rose in her mind. *To change the world, change first a heart.*

She was about to force the Elenil to change their system, but would it matter if they hadn't changed their hearts? Wouldn't they just find a way to rebuild it, to replace it? Was it possible to change both? She knew this much: she was still benefiting from this unjust system. She was forcing everyone else to change when she hadn't changed herself. It was *her* heart that needed to change, her heart that could change the world.

She dropped to her knees and put her left arm on the ground.

"What are you doing?" Thenody said.

She raised the sword high.

"That was not one of the choices," he said, reaching toward her.

"There are more choices than those," Madeline said.

She brought the blade down with all her strength, smashing it into the center of her bracelet. An intense flash of light burst from her arm, and her tattoo burned so brightly she could see it even with her eyes closed. Crippling pain shot through her body. She fell backward into the grass, her arm smoking. She felt the magic draining from her tattoos like molten lava coursing through causeways in her body.

She couldn't breathe. Her back arched, and she inhaled with all her might and only got a half a breath, a quarter of a breath. Darius was by her side, his arms beneath her, trying to cradle her, to comfort her.

The archon was laughing. "Hanali, how delightful! She surprised me after all. What strange and creative creatures they are. It won't change much in the scheme—"

Yenil leapt to her feet with a feral scream. Madeline turned to look at her, wanting to tell her it was going to be okay now, that she would be able to breathe and live a normal life, but she couldn't say a word, could only gasp for air and watch in horror as Yenil snatched up the Sword of Sorrows.

Jason lunged for her and missed. Baileya shouted but was too far away. Gilenyia did not move, and a smile twitched to life on Break Bones's face.

The archon turned from Hanali, startled to find the Scim girl directly before him, already swinging the Sword of Sorrows. The blade met flesh, and the archon's left forearm flew from his body, bright golden light seeping from it and from the stump of his arm.

He fell beside Madeline, his face white with shock.

Gilenyia stooped over the archon, shouting instructions to people Madeline couldn't see. The garden they were in wilted immediately, turning brown. Trees cracked and fell. Flowers dropped to the ground, dead. The garden must have been powered by the archon's magic. The balcony began to crumble. A screeching noise came from the tower, and the massive Crescent Stone above listed to one side, then shattered, great chunks of it smashing into the garden and taking pieces of the tower with them as they careened to the square below. There were screams and shouts.

Madeline felt Darius lift her in his arms, heard him whisper, "To the ends of the earth." A hummingbird zipped through the garden, its high-pitched chirp standing out, somehow, from all the panicked sounds around her.

Then it all went still.

It was dark. Black and silent as night. She could no longer see the garden, the people running, the tower. She lay on her back, staring up into darkness.

The Garden Lady stood over her, a gentle smile on her face. "Hello, dear. What a day. What a day."

"Can't . . . breathe . . ." Madeline said.

"No, child, I expect you can't. Do you want me to change that? Your friend Jason, he might pay the price if you asked. He's loyal, that one. And brave."

"No," Madeline said firmly.

"You have two more favors to ask," the old woman said.

Madeline thought of her parents. She was so tired. She didn't want to die here, in the Sunlit Lands. She wanted to go home, and she couldn't do anything else here, could she? She couldn't even breathe. She knew she wouldn't be well again. She was past hope. She had come to acceptance. She needed only courage. "Take me home," she said. "Please."

"That I can do. And one thing more. For a few minutes. Just a few. I will let you speak to your friends before you go. And I'll give you the breath for it."

She was standing in front of Darius. He wasn't in his Black Skull outfit, just his regular clothes. "I'm going home," she said.

He wrapped her in his arms. "I'll come with you," he said.

She leaned her head against his shoulder. "Darius. When Lily said, in the books, there must be something better, she knew it in her heart, do you remember?"

"Of course."

"You're different here, in the Sunlit Lands. Back home you always pretended everything was okay, but here . . . you're changing things. You're trying to make that better place." It was true. The passion with which he protected the Scim, the way he helped her understand what had happened . . . he had opened her eyes. Without him she wouldn't have figured it all out, would have just lived out her year serving the Elenil, completely unaware of the injustice she was participating in. She would have had her breath, but Yenil would be dead. "You have to stay and help them."

"I won't leave you, Mads. I can't."

She took a deep breath. "Darius, when I broke up with you, it was because . . . How do I say this?" She tried to think of another way to say it, to make him understand, but she couldn't. How could she tell him how hard this all was for her? How could she make him understand that her heart was breaking to leave him, but not just him . . . everyone and everything she loved in the whole world? "Having you by my side every day, it's making it harder for me to leave. Harder to say good-bye."

"I would follow you to the ends of the earth," Darius said, his voice catching. He grabbed both of her hands in his.

Her lips quivered, and tears welled up in her eyes. "I'm going past the ends of the earth," she said. "You can't walk this path with me. It's impossible."

He leaned his forehead against hers. "The only impossible thing is that I would leave you," Darius said, quoting the book again.

She almost smiled. *Impossible* had never been a word that held much meaning for him. "When you're with me . . . it's making it harder, Darius. Harder to walk these last few steps."

She could see that he understood now. The most loving thing he could do was to say good-bye, to let her go. Darius said, "These last months without you, Mads . . . I've been so lonely."

Tears fell down her cheeks. "Darius, even when we're apart, we're together, because you're in my heart. And if we're together . . . if we're together I won't be afraid." She was quoting from *The Gryphon under the Stairs*, so she knew what he would say next.

He took both of her hands in his own. "Then let's see what beautiful things await." His face hardened, and he wiped the tears from her cheeks. "I'm going to fix things, Mads. I'm going to save the Scim, fix the broken system here."

Darius was starting to disappear. She could see through his hands. She didn't want him to go, didn't want this to be the end. "If I go—if you come home, and I'm gone—know that I have always loved you."

"I love you," he said. "How can I go on without you?"

He faded away before she could answer.

Break Bones stood before her. "What trickery is this?" He grunted. "The old woman in the garden. Is this her doing?"

Madeline wiped the tears from her eyes. "She said I could say good-bye to my friends. I'm not sure why you're here."

He frowned, his wide face contorted in displeasure. "I made a vow to my people that whoever returned the Sword of Years to the Scim, I would be in their life debt. You gave the sword to the girl, Yenil. I am at your service."

Madeline grinned in spite of her sadness. "What does that mean?"

"I am at your service," he repeated through gritted teeth.

"Take care of Wu Song," she said. "Help him. Don't kill him. Be a friend to him." And the Scim faded away.

Jason appeared. "The Garden Lady said you're going home. Shula and Yenil, they're going with you."

"They are?" She was shocked but pleased. It was right for Yenil to come. She didn't have any parents now, and that was because of Madeline. She could have a home and a family. It should be Madeline's. And it was good for Shula to come too. Yenil would need another familiar face if—when—Madeline wasn't around anymore.

"I'm, uh . . ." Jason blushed. "I'm engaged. To Baileya. By accident."

Madeline laughed and hugged him. "That's amazing. She's wonderful."

"She's . . . she's terrifying, mostly." He gripped her forearms. "Madeline, I made a promise to stick with you. To protect you. It's because . . . well, it's a long story. I lost my sister, and I don't want to lose you. But I've come to realize that I can't protect you. I can't save you. That's not in my power."

She squeezed his arms. "That's true."

He looked down. "I need to let what happened to my sister go. It wasn't my fault."

She didn't know what had happened, not exactly, although there had been rumors around the school. "That's true." She put her hand on his cheek. "You need to let me go too. There are things for you to do here, in the Sunlit Lands. Right?"

He nodded. "Something keeps pulling at me. The stories here. I'm not done. I think . . . I think you did the right thing, not destroying the stone. It was too violent. It would *force* people to do the right thing. We need to teach them to *want* the right thing. I see this story, or a thread of a story. I think if I pull on it, see where it goes . . . I think I might be able to find the right words. Do you understand what I mean?"

She did, somehow. She saw a flash, a vision, of Jason standing in the middle of a city, weather beaten and worn. He was telling a story, and people were weeping all around him. "The Peasant King," she said. "Is it his story?"

He looked at her, startled. "Yes. I keep seeing it in Night's Breath's memories. I need to find the rest of the story, and . . . and I need to go and see his family. I need to tell them what happened."

She held him for a long time. "Wu Song," she said. "If I die before you come home—"

"I'll see you before you die," he said, with a strange firmness in his voice. "You know I never tell a lie."

Tears crowded into her eyes. She wanted to believe him, wanted to think they would see each other again. He looked so certain, so sure. And it was true, she had never known him to tell a lie. "I know you don't," she said, smiling as the tears rolled down both of their faces.

Then Wu Song was gone, and she struggled for another breath, and she felt the branches of the hedge slapping against her face, and Shula's strong arm holding her up, and Yenil on her other side, and they appeared in her backyard. It was nighttime. She couldn't breathe. She fell to the grass, sobbing. A light came on, and Sofía came running across the grass. Shouts came from the house.

She was home.

36

A NEW JOURNEY

After the rain, the desert blooms.

A KAKRI PROVERB

✦

Even from outside the city, Jason could see the corrupted palace and the way it listed to one side, its holes black against the white stone. In the chaos of the collapsing tower, they had managed to make it out with almost no fighting. The shattering of the tower's stone and the subsequent departure of the Kharobem had distracted most of the people in the city. Many of the citizens, upon hearing that another Scim attack was happening, had barred themselves into their homes. The Knight of the Mirror had ridden out with Jason and Baileya through the southern gate, following Hanali's orders. "It will take some time to put it all back together," the knight said. "The archon's magic is struggling."

"Where were you, anyway?" Jason asked. "During the big fight?" He was riding the giant bird, the brucok, his arms around Baileya's waist. It might have made him blush on another day, but honestly, too much energy was going into making sure he didn't fall off. Delightful Glitter Lady let loose a high-pitched squeak, her tiny head peeking from his pocket. He scratched behind her ears.

The knight didn't answer. He had met them halfway down the tower, as if summoned, and escorted them quickly through the ranks of Elenil. The messenger birds had begun to spread throughout the city by then, passing along the story of the girl who had destroyed the magic that kept her alive. A debate had ignited, the Elenil arguing over whether such a thing was noble or foolish.

It wasn't safe in the city for Jason, though, that much was clear. Passions ran too high. Some Scim kids had thrown stones at him for not destroying the Heart of the Scim. An Elenil woman had given him a bouquet for the same reason.

Break Bones had met them outside the city. Baileya had advanced on him with her weapon, but he had thrown his own down and explained that he owed a life debt to Jason now. Wanting to make sure he wasn't lying, Jason had commanded him to dance and sing a silly song. When Break Bones assured him he didn't know such a song, Jason had taught him "I'm a Little Teapot," complete with actions, and Break Bones had performed it admirably, despite his scowl.

Darius had flown ahead to tell the Scim elders that Jason and Baileya were coming. Break Bones had given Darius the Sword of Years and told him to return it to the elders. Jason didn't know what sort of welcome would be waiting in the Wasted Lands, but he knew it should be the first step. Of course Baileya's family was still trying to kill him, and he hadn't told her yet that their engagement was accidental. He wasn't sure he wanted to. He wasn't sure he wanted out of it, either.

Hanali had disappeared after the events in the garden, but before he went, he had assured Jason he would be fine. He felt certain Thenody wouldn't make a public move against him. "The politics of the Elenil are subtler than that," he had said. Gilenyia had stayed at the archon's side, working her magic, bringing him back to health as best she could. The wound from the Sword of Years, she said, would not heal easily or well. Jason couldn't help but think that reattaching the archon's severed arm would mean some Scim somewhere without a hand. He didn't understand why she would try to heal Thenody when she had been part of the plot to overthrow him. He had asked Hanali before he left. "We are a loyal people," the Elenil said. "Thenody is still the archon and thus should be cared for and obeyed." Jason didn't get it, but whatever.

"When you return," the knight said, "enter through the eastern gate. Undetected if you can. You will be safe in Westwind. Send a bird ahead so I can warn you if it is unsafe." He paused and looked toward the west. A messenger bird was flying toward them. The knight held his arm up, and it landed on his wrist.

"What word bring you?" the knight asked.

"Word from the realm of the Zhanin," the bird said. "From a young man named Kekoa and a girl called Ruth."

Jason almost fell off the brucok. "What? What did they say?"

The bird turned its green head to see Jason more clearly. "They are in danger," the bird said. "They request your help. They warn that the Zhanin mean to kill the one called Jason and the woman Madeline." Jason groaned. Of course there were more people wanting to kill him. He hoped David had made it safely to Aluvorea.

"Why? We don't even know them."

"They assassinate those who threaten the balance of magic in the world," the knight said. "They must see your recent actions as a threat."

Baileya looked west. "We will be careful. To see more Zhanin in this part of the world would be strange indeed."

Jason slapped his forehead. "Is there anyone *not* trying to kill me?"

"Not I," Baileya said, and she gave Jason a look so loaded with affection that he felt a flush that ran from his face all the way to his toes.

"Nor I," said the knight.

Break Bones didn't say anything, but he was cranky like that. Delightful Glitter Lady honked her approval.

"Four," Jason said. "Well, that's a start."

They turned the brucok southward, and the knight wished them safe journey.

When both Break Bones and the knight were out of earshot, Baileya patted Jason's hand gently where it encircled her waist. "Your sister would be proud," she said to him. "You are a man who shares his stories generously. You are honest and kind. Such men are always threatened with death."

"You honestly scare me so much," Jason said.

Baileya turned so her silver eyes were all he could see. "She would be proud," she repeated. She turned away again and kicked the bird. As it began to run, she said, "As I am proud."

Jason held her tighter and let the wind push the water from his eyes. He promised himself that he would be worthy of Baileya's pride, no matter the cost. He did not speak until night fell.

EPILOGUE

To see another is the birth of Compassion.

FROM "RENALDO THE WISE," A SCIM LEGEND

✦

At night, Yenil liked to play in the garden.

Tonight there was a full moon, and the blue light washed over the flowers. It reminded Madeline of the Wasted Lands. Not what it was, but what it could be. She sat wrapped in a blanket, in a wheelchair on the crushed-seashell path. She held the book Darius had given her, the first edition of *The Gryphon under the Stairs*, in her lap. She didn't like to be apart from it—it reminded her of him.

Shula sat beside her. Without the magic of the Sunlit Lands, they spoke to one another in French or, increasingly often, in Shula's hesitant English. It had been two months. Yenil's English came quickly, and Shula was not far behind her.

Madeline's parents had been astonished, grateful, and disbelieving when they saw her that first night. She had been gone ten months, they said, and they had begun to believe the worst. They had taken Shula and Yenil in with surprising good grace, though Madeline could see the strain on them. She wasn't able to answer their questions in a way they could grasp. She couldn't explain her absence, or her sudden reappearance, or her silver scars, the ones that precisely matched the ones on the little girl who showed up with her.

Yenil—unless someone looked very closely—appeared human when not in her war skin. Honestly, Shula—a Middle Eastern girl who didn't speak English—had been a harder sell than Yenil for her parents. "Does she have a green card?" her mother kept asking in a hushed whisper. When Madeline explained about the Sunlit Lands, a confused look would cross her parents' faces, and they would stop pushing. She heard them whispering sometimes, sharing their strange theories of where she had been. But eventually the gravity of "putting on their happy faces" took over. Her mom went back to managing appearances, and her dad went back to work, and things were, more or less, normal again. Soon they stopped asking questions, whether because they didn't want to or couldn't understand the answers, Madeline didn't know.

Yenil was amazed by the house. She kept saying she lived in an Elenil mansion now. Madeline had tried to correct her at first but had given up. She wasn't wrong, Madeline had realized.

She couldn't breathe freely anymore. But she saw now that her family, her upbringing . . . She was more like the Elenil than the Scim. Which wasn't bad. It wasn't wrong. But she was looking at her life now, her privileges and power and wealth, in a new way. She was looking for those places where she could breathe only because others were holding their breath. And she planned to take a sword to each and every place she discovered.

Yenil bounded up through the moonlight, delighted at some treasure she had found. She placed it in Madeline's hand. "What is it called?"

"A bottle cap," Madeline said.

"Bottle cap," Yenil repeated and giggled. "Bottle cap!" she shouted. "Bottle cap, bottle cap!"

She danced into the garden, laughing and shouting. "Chase, Shula, chase!"

Shula jumped up, running after her into the garden. "Here I come!"

Madeline loved to see Yenil playing. Some nights Yenil woke from nightmares. Some nights she couldn't sleep for weeping. Shula slept with her and sang to her. Madeline's own mother went in to comfort Yenil some nights, a strange motherly action Madeline couldn't remember her mom ever doing for her.

"She's a dear girl and knows the value of a good bottle cap." The Garden Lady stood beside Madeline, her broom-like hair bursting out from her floral fringed hat.

Madeline smiled and moved her fingers in a tiny wave. She didn't use the energy to speak. She heard Shula and Yenil on the other side of the flowers, singing a Scim lullaby, which Yenil often hummed to herself. She had taught it to Madeline and Shula. *Do not cry in the darkness, but follow the small bright star.*

The old woman grunted and rearranged her hat. "I owe you a favor yet, dear. I'm not the kind who leaves a favor unfulfilled. What would you like? Silver and gold? Your breath back again? Anything in my power, child. Ask and I'll give it."

Madeline shook her head. She knew the cost now. She couldn't ask for magic that came at another's expense. "Sit . . . beside me," Madeline said. "Tell me . . . about . . . the Sunlit Lands. Tell me . . . about my . . . friends. Tell me . . . a story . . . about them."

"That I can do, my dear, that I can do."

The Garden Lady tucked Madeline's blanket in around her shoulders and sat in Shula's chair. She sat there long into the night, while Yenil played in the garden, and told her everything her friends had been doing in the Sunlit Lands.

And Madeline closed her eyes and was happy.

THE END

APPENDIX

Stories, Songs, Proverbs, and
Poems of the Sunlit Lands

THE THREE GIFTS
OF THE PEASANT KING

A Scim Legend

A great while ago, when the world was full of wonders, there lived a wealthy king. He ate from golden plates upon a golden table. The floor of his throne room was polished silver, and his throne was studded with rare jewels. He often threw lavish banquets for his friends. Entire feasts' worth of food would go to the dogs, for the guests could not eat it all. He was called King Franklin, and he was deeply unhappy, for although he was rich, his subjects looked on him with disdain.

It came to pass that King Franklin began to hear tales of a strange king in a far country, a man beloved by all his subjects. This Peasant King, as he was called, had neither gold nor crown. But King Franklin decided he must see this strange man who was praised by so many tongues. So Franklin disguised himself as a servant and traveled through the deep forest, over the snowy mountains, and across the wide sea. And he brought with him three gifts for the Peasant King: a fine silk cape, a diamond the size of a man's fist, and a great disk of gold to fashion a royal table.

When at last King Franklin found the Peasant King, he was surprised to find him in a humble barn, where he sat upon a throne made of hay. Upon his brow he wore a circlet of holly, and his scepter was a piece of polished oak.

Franklin, in his disguise as a royal servant, presented the gifts he had brought to the Peasant King, explaining they were from his master, good King Franklin. Then he said, "I have traveled far to ask the secret of your great glory. But I stand before you now and see that a farmer in my master's land is wealthier than you."

The Peasant King stroked his beard and thought for some time. At last he said, "Tell me, O servant, did you see many of my subjects in your travels? Did they seem more fortunate than those in your own land?"

King Franklin replied, "No more fortunate than those of other lands, though happier in their misfortune. I saw a woman who sang as she slopped the pigs, though she had no apron to cover her dress. A scribe laughed to see his papers blown by the wind. A man whistled a tune when he saw his wagon wheel had broken."

The Peasant King laughed to hear this fine report and called for the woman, the scribe, and the wagoner. When they arrived, he greeted them each with a kiss upon the cheek. To the woman he said, "Good King Franklin has sent you this apron from across the wide sea," and he gave her the fine silk cape. Then he gave the scribe the diamond the size of a man's fist and said, "Good King Franklin has sent you this paperweight from over the snowy mountains." Lastly he rolled the golden tabletop to the wagoner and said, "Through the deep forest, good King Franklin has sent you this sturdy wagon wheel."

All three went away glad, thanking the Peasant King and praising the kindness and foresight of good King Franklin.

The Peasant King said, "The glory of a king comes from neither wealth nor finery but from the well-being of his people. Now I shall send you away with three gifts: a flask of local wine, a loaf of thick brown bread, and a letter for King Franklin which holds the secret to the great glory of the Peasant King."

Then the Peasant King sent King Franklin on his way. So King Franklin traveled across the wide sea, over the snowy mountains, and through the deep forest. When he had bathed and dressed again in his royal robes and returned to his grand throne room, King Franklin set out the wine and bread and opened the letter from the Peasant King. It contained only these words: "A true king must not pretend to be a servant, but rather become one."

So, too, this story bears three gifts: one for the storyteller, one for the hearer, and one for the heart which understands.

THE ORDERING OF THE WORLD

An Elenil Story

When the world was young and foolish, the people burned the cities. The oceans, enraged with violence, flooded villages and carried away children. The ground shook, and the sky wept blood. The people cried out day and night for help. And so it came to pass that a magician—the most powerful of his age or any other—set out to repair the world. He had many names, but the Elenil call him the Majestic One.

The Majestic One spoke, and his word was law.

"Order!" he called, and all the world stopped to listen. "Stop this foolish violence. Cease this chaos and come to me, for I shall remake the world."

But of all the people, only two came to him. The rest fought and tore at one another and screamed their defiance. The names of the two who came to him were Ele and Nala. He blessed them and said, in the ancient speech of wizards and knights:

I declare ye, Ele and Nala, lords of light
*   and guardians of the wide world.*
All shall be under your dominion: water and wood,
*   stone and fire, desert and ocean, light and darkness.*
And your descendants shall be called the Elenil.

And he placed a tower in the center of the Sunlit Lands and called it Far Seeing.

Together with Ele and Nala and their children, the Elenil, the Majestic One tamed the peoples who warred with one another. The conflict turned bitter more than once, but none could stand for long against the might of the Majestic One or his servants, the Elenil.

When the war was ended and all had pledged fealty to the Majestic One, he gathered the people, and divided them into seven groups to receive their rewards and punishments and to give each people their own lands and homes so there would be no more war forever. When he spoke, each person heard his voice in their own mind, as if he spoke to them and them alone. First he spoke to the raiders who had harassed and harried the Elenil camps:

Kakri, desert dweller, eyes touched by the moon!
Thou shalt be silenced by sand in thy throat.
Thou shalt flee to the east, and walk dunes alone
    in sunshine and shadow, eater of carrion.
Thy sister shall be the crow, thy brother the hyena.

And so the Majestic One sent away the Kakri, and they live in the desert to the east, beyond the Tolmin Pass. They build no houses and plant no crops.

To the children of Grom, the Majestic One said:

How often hast thou dug beneath the walls of my fortress?
Short of stature, surly and clever, O child of Grom.
Thy home shall be beneath the ground.
Thou shalt hoard silver and gold, jewels and precious metals.
None shall be as skilled with hammer and tong,
    and none more obstinate than the Maegrom.

So the children of Grom went away to the world beneath the world, and there they remain until this very day. The Majestic One watched them leave, and when they had gone, he turned to those who had fought him in the great southern forests, who had attacked from the trees as archers and bandits. To them he said:

In Aluvorea grow the mighty trees
  so tall they touch the sun!
In their shadow thou shalt dwell
  and breathe the breath of leaves.
Be thou quiet and harmless.

Thus the Aluvoreans left in peace to populate the woods of the world. They are a gentle race, though some say they have come to love their trees more than people, a great misfortune.

To those who had been pirates upon the sea, the Majestic One declared:

Live, thou Zhanin, among waves and currents,
  wind and weather and the deep!
Forever a wanderer, without a home,
  thou shalt be melancholy,
Changeable, strange, and lonely as the sea.

So the Zhanin were swept away like driftwood. They cannot live long when separated from the water. It is a great marvel to see one at the market of Far Seeing. But occasionally such traders do appear, with strange stories and stranger wares.

Those who had used magic in their battle against the Majestic One he called human, to remind them they were neither gods nor beings of power but only mortals.

Humans! Ye shall live upon another earth,
  a people of science and dust.
Bereft of magic, short lived and passionate,
  there shall still be beauty and wonder among you.
In great need may ye return to the Sunlit Lands,
  for ye are our cousins and neighbors.

At last all who remained before the Majestic One were the Elenil, his servants of old, and the most rebellious of the people, who would come to be called the Scim. They were evil things, their hearts filled with wickedness and foul deeds. They trembled before the Majestic One, for his face shone like glowing metal. Indeed, his face shone with a righteous anger, and they feared he would destroy them completely.

> *Thou Scim I banish to outer darkness,*
> *a land as black as thy heart.*
> *Thou shalt live by eating thy brethren's scraps.*
> *Servant of darkness and night, in blackness*
> *shalt thou dwell, and in that eternal midnight*
> *may thine outer appearance match thy corrupted nature!*

The Scim wailed and begged for mercy, but the Majestic One stood unmoved. He commanded his Elenil to remove the Scim from his presence, and they drove the creatures south and east to the Wasted Lands, where shadows cling and sunlight dares not go.

So it is that we say:

> *Zhanin on the western waters,*
> *Aluvoreans in forests dispersed.*
> *To the east, the Kakri wanders,*
> *the Scim in deep darkness accursed.*
> *Humans from magic are fleeing,*
> *Maegrom in dark earth beneath.*
> *Elenil rule from Far Seeing,*
> *in lands by our master bequeathed.*
> *The Majestic One keeps all in his sight,*
> *Elenil first in the warmth of his light.*

RENALDO THE WISE

A Scim Legend

A great while ago, when the summers of this land could still be counted by those with long memories, a man named Renaldo walked the paths of the world. Hated and despised by all he met, Renaldo returned the hatred of his neighbors with vigor.

Now in those days, the Peasant King ruled. The Peasant King sent out a decree into all the land, telling his subjects that he wished to increase the happiness of all his people, and so he would give each subject a boon of their choosing. Magic or money, fortune or fame, long life or lilies, no request either small or large would be turned away, so long as it be not evil.

Renaldo thought for eight days and seven nights of what might bring him happiness, but the only boons he imagined would give him pleasure were misfortunes for his neighbors. He knew the Peasant King would not grant him his wish if he said, "Make old Mrs. Gaither's goats give sour milk" or "Tear the thatch off Mr. Havill's hut" or even "Take away the tongue of that calamitous child down the lane."

The day came for his audience with the Peasant King, and Renaldo dressed in his finest clothes and walked to the woods, where the king sat upon a stone, a sprig of holly wrapped about his forehead. He was playing a merry tune on a simple flute. "This," said the Peasant King, "is the Flute of Joy. Blow into it and such joy shall fill your heart that you will be at peace with all people and with the world. I have made it, dear Renaldo, for you. For often I have passed by your home and seen you scowling in your chair." The Peasant King held out the lovely gift, but Renaldo would have none of it.

"Such a gift is too fine for me," said Renaldo. "Now, Highness, you said you would grant any boon so long as it is not evil. Have I heard it right? For I would not speak and have you deny me."

"I will not curse a person or animal, nor take away their free will, to please you."

"Not even to make a goat's milk sour?" Renaldo asked hopefully, for the bleating and stench of Mrs. Gaither's goats truly vexed him.

The Peasant King laughed and said, "Truly not!" and played upon his Flute of Joy. The whole wood filled with dancing and laughter. The birds sang, the rabbits danced, the foxes stopped their hunting and smiled. Renaldo only frowned.

"My wish, then," said Renaldo, "is to see the coming death of every person in the land." For he thought to himself, *To know the death of a person is to have great power over them.* Besides, it might please him to see his neighbors and enemies and be able to say to himself, *But six months more and that one shall be gone. But a few years for that one. Ha! She shall be no bother after next Thursday.*

The Peasant King stopped his playing, and the whole wood fell silent. "It is not an evil gift," said the king, "though it is requested with evil intent."

"You have given your word," Renaldo reminded him.

"Indeed," said the Peasant King. "I shall grant your wish and something more: not only the time of death shall you see but also the cause."

Elated, Renaldo bowed low to the king and walked backward from his presence. The joyful playing did not start again until Renaldo set foot upon the road, which was a great relief. He hurried home to try his new skill.

He came first to Mrs. Gaither's thatched hut. The stench of her goats grew ever greater. Just last week he had convinced her to move her flock to the east side of her property, for on the west side their stench lived always in his nostrils. She complained that the east side was craggy and dangerous, but every day he wheedled and complained until she at last relented.

The old woman came out of her hut, and the moment he saw her, Renaldo knew her death. In two years' time she would take her goats out in the rain and slip upon the craggy rocks of her eastern property and break her hip. She would die within six weeks, weakened and alone.

"Serves her right," Renaldo said to himself, "for keeping such filthy animals."

He continued on to Mr. Havill's hut and knocked upon his door. For many years he and Mr. Havill had feuded about their property line. The great stones separating their property would move in the night, sometimes because Mr. Havill moved them and sometimes because Renaldo moved them. Neither could remember the true property lines any longer. Renaldo saw his end too: just one year hence he would catch a sickness during a storm. His poorly thatched roof (which Renaldo often called an eyesore) would not keep out the rain, and he would die feverish and alone.

"Serves him right," Renaldo said to himself, "for taking such poor care of his home."

He continued on to find the loudmouthed child who shouted and screamed day and night, sometimes in joy, sometimes in anger. The boy shouted whether happy or sad and could neither keep his opinions to himself nor his voice low.

Renaldo gasped.

The boy, a child of only seven summers, would die in one week's time.

And he would die trying to save Renaldo from drowning in the pond.

Renaldo liked to swim on crisp summer mornings, and next week he would sink from a leg cramp. The boy would charge into the water to save him and would succeed, but at the cost of his own life.

No more would Renaldo hear the boy's booming voice as he chased the geese. No more his disappointed cries when his mother called him to dinner. Never again the echoing crow of the boy emulating the morning rooster. All this because the boy would try to save his melancholy neighbor, the one who barely said hello and often complained that the boy was too loud.

Renaldo's heart broke as if struck by a great hammer.

Renaldo hurried to the pond and stared at the cool, placid water, and it was there that he saw his own death—sitting in a chair upon his porch many years hence, bitter, angry, and alone.

He hurried back to the Peasant King and begged for another audience.

He fell on his knees in the great king's presence and cried, "O Majesty, take away this curse! Give me instead a new boon!"

"What boon is that?" the king asked.

"Majesty, I ask only this: let the boy live a long and happy life. He does not deserve to end his life in such a way."

The king gave him a look of great pity and said, in the archaic way of knights and kings, "Stay thou out of the water, Renaldo."

Renaldo thanked the king and hurried home, determined not to swim in the pond that week. But was this enough to change the boy's future? He saw the boy and was relieved to see him living until the age of twenty-three, when he would die in battle. There was time to work on that, but for now he hurried to Mr. Havill's house and, in a flurry of activity and without a single complaint, rethatched his roof.

Then he was off to Mrs. Gaither's house, where he told her to live a long life and move her goats back between their houses, which she did.

That night he sat upon his porch, smoking his pipe, when the Peasant King came along, playing his flute softly in the moonlight. The Peasant King sat on the porch with crossed legs and did not use a chair, for the Peasant King would not sit on a chair fashioned by the hands of a living being.

"Has your boon brought you happiness?" the Peasant King asked.

Renaldo thought on this for a time, puffing upon his pipe. "We have more in common than we have differences," Renaldo said at last. "In the face of death these grievances with my neighbors seem petty."

"A wise observation," the Peasant King said. "You and your neighbors shall all be better for it. Now, I think, this flute is yours . . . for it requires a loving heart to play it."

Renaldo accepted it gladly, and in the years to come he became known as Renaldo the Wise, for he seemed to know the greatest needs of his neighbors, and all who knew him lived long and healthy lives. Many were the nights when Renaldo sat upon his porch and played his flute, and the people of the village shed their cares and kicked up their heels.

When he was very old, the whole village came to his bedside. His final words, we are told, were these: "To see another is the birth of Compassion.

Compassion is a seed of Love. Love comes hand in hand with Joy. So, little children, love one another, that your joy may be complete."

So, too, this story brings three boons: one for the storyteller, one for the hearer, and one for the heart which understands.

AN EXCERPT FROM
"THE GALLANT LIFE AND GLORIOUS DEATH
OF SIR SAMUEL GRYPHONHEART"

An Elenil Poem

O'er silent tower no banner flies,
Shouted laments from soldiers rise.
Upon the battlefield he lies—
Sir Samuel Gryphonheart!
The dragon slain, the battle won.
Alone he stood, the rest had run.
Strong armed he fought, the deed was done,
And now he must depart.

Behold! Now gentle hands take hold
The corpse of our defender bold.
To save our lives, his own he sold—
Sir Samuel Gryphonheart!
'Twas he who fought the minotaur,
'Twas he who slayed the Bolgomor,
'Twas he who saved Vald's sycamores.
Now dead upon yon cart!

His broken blade, his bloodied shirt,
Our lord is dead and we unhurt.
We cannot e'er proclaim his worth—
Sir Samuel Gryphonheart.

O minstrels, sing a glorious ode
To the chief knight who ever strode
This earth. He made the sun shine gold—
Sir Samuel Gryphonheart.

'Tis true he's left these shadowed lands,
All toil and trouble and demands.
Walks he now on gold-flecked sands,
To range sans map or chart.
And now upon that rival shore
All woes be gone, and sob no more.
No death, no tears, no pain, no war
For Samuel Gryphonheart!

Now draws near the Majestic One
To celebrate a life well done.
Homecoming his adopted son—
Sir Samuel Gryphonheart!
His bowl is spilt, his thread unspun.
His life is past and just begun.
He treads now in a clime of sun
In the land of the Majestic One.

Majestic One, all wounds he heals,
All righteous traits in hearts anneals.
Samuel's life like a bell it peals
To greet the Majestic One.
Watch them walking arm in arm
In golden fields beyond all harm.
Their laughter rings with friendship warm—
The joy of the Majestic One!

The knight at last his sword lays down,
His grimace gone, no more a frown,
His helm replaced with glorious crown,

A gift from the Majestic One!
The squire has let his horse run free.
The Sunlit Lands now mourn and weep.
Our friend is gone, no more we'll see
Till we see the Majestic One.

He stands before a riotous throng,
Those who've left all woe and wrong,
They greet him with a welcome song,
"You'll nevermore depart!"
With cries of joy they welcome him.
The night is past, the day begins.
He smiles, then laughs—they dance, they spin!
Deep joy has filled his heart.

Our greatest knight, our dearest friend,
Our defender bold has met his end.
With him our love and thanks we send,
Sir Samuel Gryphonheart!

IN THE DESERT, THERE ARE NO PATHS.
IN THE DESERT, THE WAY IS MADE BY WALKING.

✦

IT IS NO SHAME
TO TRAVEL WITH CROWS.

✦

WHAT IS STILL MAY NOT SLEEP.
WHAT SLEEPS MAY NOT LIE STILL.

✦

IF TRUTH IS NOT YOUR COMPANION,
DEATH WALKS BESIDE YOU.

✦

THE DATEEN TREE BEARS ONLY DATEEN
FRUIT AND THAT ONLY IN ITS SEASON.

AFTER THE RAIN, THE DESERT BLOOMS.

+

THREE THINGS WE CANNOT LIVE WITHOUT:
CLEAR WATER, DEEP STORIES,
A HEART THAT IS LOVED.

+

DURING THE STORM,
HOPE.
AFTER THE STORM,
PEACE.

THE DESERTED CITY

A Kakri Lament (to be sung to the tune of "The Water Bearer's Daughter," on the night of the third and fourth spheres' meeting, with a divided choir)

MOONSIDE CHOIR: Where is the fountain which brought joy to the city, clean and clear at its heart?

STARSIDE CHOIR: It has been carried away, the water spilled to the sand, the water given to the sun.

MOONSIDE CHOIR: Where is the young man who played his bitarr beneath the lady's window when the hot wind blew from the east?

STARSIDE CHOIR: His eyes are open, unseeing, his bitarr shattered in his hands, his lady . . . But we do not know where his lady has gone!

MOONSIDE CHOIR: Has she not gone to the west, to the city of the shortsighted?

STARSIDE CHOIR: She weeps into the fountain. She lingers at her window and sobs to hear the silent streets.

MOONSIDE CHOIR: Look at the walls, so bright and fair, each stone placed by a master builder.

STARSIDE CHOIR: They are drunken stones . . . They cannot stand, they cannot support one another.

MOONSIDE CHOIR: What has become of the wide avenues, the shaded alleys beneath the golden trees?

STARSIDE CHOIR: Weeds grow upon the streets, dead thorns and fruitless stunted trees line them.

MOONSIDE CHOIR: What of the birds? The wrens and sparrows? The magpies and swallows?

STARSIDE CHOIR: There are only empty nests. Even the birds, yes the birds, have fallen.

MOONSIDE CHOIR: We must rebuild these walls.

STARSIDE CHOIR: No, Sisters, set your face toward the wasteland.

MOONSIDE CHOIR: We must repair these towers.

STARSIDE CHOIR: No, Brothers, entrust yourself to the sands.

> *There is no one path through the desert,*
> *the way is made by walking.*
> *Let us turn our faces from this place,*
> *let us seek solace in the desert.*
> *The sheep pens are empty,*
> *the gates broken, the king dead.*
> *What use the sheep pen in the desert?*
> *What need for gates in the waste?*
> *He who sleeps upon the roof dies upon the roof,*
> *she who sleeps in the house receives no burial.*
> *The desert claims the land, and so we,*
> *we must claim the desert.*

MOONSIDE CHOIR: But one day the King of Stories will return—

TOGETHER:

The Story King will tell a new tale,
   the vineyards shall bear grapes.
The orchards heavy with fruit,
   the high plain will bear the mašgurum tree.
Another turning shall come,
   the city rebuilt, the gates rehung.
The people will again be many.

O Keeper of Stories!
O your house!
O your city!
O your people!

A FRAGMENT OF
"THE TRIUMPH OF THE PEASANT KING"

A Scim Legend

. . . saw the Peasant King going against the tide of those who would evacuate the city. The Shadow had fallen, and destruction followed behind. The walls were breached, and the enemy swarmed down the tree-lined avenues.

One of the Peasant King's followers, a knight in his service, said to him, "My lord, where are you going?"

The Peasant King replied, "Why, to meet Death. Would you go with me, Sir Knight?" But the knight had promised to protect a caravan headed south, so he begged his leave. The king said, "Go in peace."

Another of his followers, a wealthy merchant, saw the Peasant King walking toward the city. Leaning down from his horse, he said, "Where are you going, my lord?"

The Peasant King replied, "Why, to meet Death. Would you go with me, sir?" But the merchant had a household to protect, and he begged his leave. The king said, "Go in peace."

Finally, in the rubble of the walls outside the city, the king's gardener saw him. She was an old woman, and her whole life she had been cared for by the Peasant King. The king's gardener spoke the secret language of all growing things. She knew the songs of the morning flowers and spoke the poems of the weeds. She spent long afternoons in conversation with the trees.

"Where are you going, my lord?" she asked.

"To meet Death," he replied, and she fell at his feet, weeping.

"Not so, my lord!" she cried. "But let me go in your place, for I am a simple gardener and you a majestic king. Let me go to my rest, and you go in peace."

The king raised her to her feet. "The knight offered me no sword, the merchant no steed. You have offered your life for mine." He kissed her upon both cheeks and again upon her forehead. He said, "Winter and summer, sunshine and darkness, planting and harvest. So long as these fill the Sunlit Lands, you will live. The story of what you have done will be told wherever my name is honored, and you shall ever walk among the people. To those who are pure of heart you may grant three boons with the magic I bestow you."

"But my lord, if you refuse the offer, 'tis but a small thing," she protested.

"It is the small things of the world which are most important," the Peasant King said. He continued on his way, but the gardener would not leave his side. She stayed with him through the Enemy's lines, past the looters, past the rioters, past the soldiers. They came at last to the great Enemy, who stood taller than a hill. He had no flesh but was only darkness in the shape of a giant. He wore a pale crown set with seven shining stars and carried an iron sword which wept blood. The Peasant King told the gardener she must now say farewell, for he must battle his foe.

"You have no sword," she said.

"Our great Enemy will give me a sword, and I shall give him my heart for a sheath."

"You have no steed," she said.

"I will ride Death's chariot ere morning," the king said.

"Your people have all deserted you," she said. "Throw down your holly crown. Toss away your oaken rod. If you are not king, you need not fight this evil."

The Peasant King laughed, and it was a clear bell in the clamor of war and darkness. "They have deserted me, but I have not deserted them."

She took his hands in hers and, weeping, bid him farewell. The Peasant King blessed her again and turned to face the great darkness. The sun shone upon his face as he stepped forward . . . [*Here the fragment ends.*]

THE PARTING

A Traditional Zhanin Song of Farewell for Honored Visitors

Your arrival—how like the sunrise!
When the cool eastern light shimmers
   upon the morning waves.

In the midday the birds sang,
   fish jumped, their scales aflame,
   water sparkled in our cupped hands!

We have paddled alongside you,
   but here our journeys part.
We are an island, you an ocean stream.

When the sun departs,
   she is most beautiful.
O western waters, shine!
Peace to you, come again,
   our blessed guest, beloved friend,
   charming one, farewell.

Until once more
   the cool eastern light shimmers
   upon the morning waves.

ACKNOWLEDGMENTS

Many thanks to the following people, all of whom helped make the Sunlit Lands a better place: Leilani Paiaina Andrus, Adam Lausche, Jermayne Chapman, Kat McAllister, Mark Charles, Sydney Wu, Leah Cypress, Mark Lane, Julie Chen, Gabrielle Chen, Koko Toyama, and Kiel Russell. Special thanks to my friends on the Codex writers' forum (quite possibly the kindest corner of the Internet).

Kristi Gravemann, thank you for your commitment to getting the word out about this book (and the books to come!). I am thankful for your creativity and hard work.

Wes Yoder, you are the source of magic in every project we pitch. Thank you for your unwavering belief in my books, for your advice, and for your friendship.

Thanks to Linda Howard, without whom this book could not exist. I asked, "What kind of book would you like?" and she said a book like this one. Here it is, Linda. Thank you!

Jesse Doogan lets me pitch thirty new projects a month and claims we will make them all. Jesse is a True Fan, and she can defeat all comers in Sunlit Lands–related trivia battles. Hufflechefs unite!

Matt Griffin (www.mattgriffin.online) provided the amazing art, and Dean Renninger turned it into the beautiful cover we all know and love. AND! Matt also drew the map, and Dean did the interior design. Thanks, Dean and Matt!

Sarah Rubio, you brought the music to the text, and asked the questions that deepened the relationships between the characters. Your influence is on every page, and I am grateful.

JR. Forasteros has been a source of encouragement, insight, and wisdom. Thank you (as always). And, of course, all of the StoryMen (Clay Morgan, Aaron Kretzmann, and Elliott Dodge), as well as Amanda and Jen!

Shasta Kramer, it's so strange not to hear your thoughts on this book. I'm thankful for all the times you checked in on me along the way while I was writing, and for celebrating with me when I finished. I look forward to talking about the book with you one day.

Thank you, Mom and Dad, for introducing me to Middle-earth and Narnia and for all your support and encouragement. And thank you, Janet and Terry, for being great in-laws!

To my dear wife, Krista, thank you for making room in our lives for me to go exploring fantasy worlds and for exploring fantastic places in the real world too.

Myca, you make me happy. I love reading with you and spending time with you.

Allie and Zoey, you were the first fans of the Sunlit Lands, and it was so fun sending you the chapters as they were written and talking through the story with you. I am thankful for your questions and your help in writing *The Crescent Stone*.

There are many more people at Tyndale House Publishers who have contributed to this book in big ways and small. I am thankful for your passion for this book and for the kindness you show to me in letting me be part of the Tyndale family.

Lastly, I am thankful for you, dear reader. Thank you for joining me, Jason, and Madeline on this adventure. I hope you'll join us for the next one.

ABOUT THE AUTHOR

MATT MIKALATOS entered Middle-earth in third grade and quickly went from there to Narnia, kindling a lifelong love of fantasy novels that are rich in adventure and explore deep questions about life and the world we live in. He believes in the hopeful vision of those two fantasy worlds in particular: the Stone Table will always be broken; the King will always return; love and friendship empower us and change the world.

For the last two decades Matt has worked in a nonprofit organization committed to creating a safer, more loving world by teaching people how to love one another, accept love themselves, and live good lives. He has lived in East Asia and served all over the world.

Matt's science fiction and fantasy short stories have been published in a variety of places, including *Nature Futures*, *Daily Science Fiction*, and the *Unidentified Funny Objects* anthologies. His nonfiction work has appeared on Time.com, on the *Today* show website, and in *Relevant* magazine, among others. He also cohosts the *StoryMen* podcast at Storymen.us.

Matt lives in the Portland, Oregon, area with his wife and three daughters. You can connect with him on Twitter (@MattMikalatos), Facebook (facebook.com/mikalatosbooks), or via his website (www.thesunlitlands.com).

THE ADVENTURE CONTINUES IN

THE HEARTWOOD CROWN

COMING SUMMER 2019

FOR MORE INFORMATION, CHECK OUT
WWW.THESUNLITLANDS.COM

TURN THE PAGE
FOR A SNEAK PEAK AT
THE FIRST CHAPTER!

CP1397

1

HUNTERS

Where fear is planted, hate will grow.

AN ALUVOREAN SAYING

✛

J ason Wu had wedged himself into what he suspected might be a closet. It had never occurred to him that people who lived in a fantasy world would need a place to store their clothes, but of course they did. This particular closet was narrow and located in a dilapidated three-story house that had once been a mansion. There were holes in the roof, mold on the walls, missing stairs on the long winding stairways. He had managed to find this closet, though, with its door still intact, so he could slip inside and pull it quietly shut, certain his pursuers would not find him here, not given the size of this house.

Delightful Glitter Lady, Jason's kitten-sized rhinoceros, scrabbled impatiently on the floor beside him. Jason scooped her up and held her against his chest, trying to keep her quiet. He could hear the thundering footsteps of his pursuers outside. Dee let out a low whine, and the footsteps paused. "Dee," Jason whispered, doing his best to make it clear she needed to be silent.

"I heard him," a voice called. By now he recognized the distinctive sound of a Scim. He could tell by the guttural voice that the Scim had put on his war skin, a defensive magic all Scim had that allowed them to have thicker skin, heavier muscles, and a terrifying appearance.

Dee whined again. Jason pulled her tighter against him.

Outside the closet, all sound ceased.

Jason held his breath.

"In here?" another voice asked.

"I think so. I heard the unicorn." The people of the Sunlit Lands thought Dee was a unicorn. They were a little sketchy on zoological categories. Unfortunately for Jason, their tracking skills were fully developed.

A third voice asked, "Have you checked the closet?"

"Hold," said another voice, one Jason knew well. It was deeper, more resonant, than the others. Jason could practically feel it vibrating the house. It was the voice of Break Bones, the Scim warrior who had sworn to murder Jason more than once. "I must be allowed to kill him. But each of you may say first what you wish to do with him when the door is opened."

"I will stab him in the liver," said the first voice, and cackles of laughter came from the others.

"I will break his arms," said another.

Jason shivered.

"I will crush him with my hammer," said the third.

Jason pushed as far back against the wall as he could, feeling with one hand for a crack, a hole, a way out. But there was nothing. He was trapped.

The door flew open, and three Scim shoved and pushed, all of them trying to get in the door at once. Dee let out a delighted squeak and struggled to get out of Jason's arms.

The Scim piled on top of him, laughing and cheering as they pinned him to the floor and tickled him mercilessly. Jason begged for them to stop, and after thirty seconds or so, Break Bones called the Scim children off. They bounced out of the closet, Delightful Glitter Lady gamboling at their feet.

"Six minutes," Break Bones said. "It is the best you have done so far."

"Is Baileya back yet?" Jason asked. Baileya was a Kakri woman, a powerful warrior from a desert tribe to the north. She also happened to be Jason's fiancée, ever since he had accidentally proposed to her nearly six weeks before. The last several weeks, since they had made this broken-down mansion their base of operations, Baileya had taken to going on long patrols of the area.

Break Bones held out a wide hand and helped Jason to his feet. "She is safe, Wu Song. No one is trying to kill her."

"She'd be safe even if people *were* trying to kill her." You shouldn't mess with Baileya.

"Everyone's trying to kill *you*, Wu Song," one of the children said.

"Not you, I hope," Jason said, wrapping an arm around the nearest kid's neck and wrestling him to the ground. Soon all three kids were grappling with him. These little monsters had been his almost constant companions since he, Baileya, and Break Bones had moved in here. Nightfall was the oldest, maybe ten or so, and he was delighted by Jason's refusal to ever tell a lie. He liked to ask Jason's opinion on awkward subjects in front of the adult Scim. Then came Eclipse, an eight-year-old girl who most often won these games of Hunter and Prey. Shadow, the youngest, was a boy of around six, with a nasty habit of biting.

"Enough," Break Bones said. Jason and the kids stopped wrestling. "What did Wu Song do wrong?" Break Bones asked the Scim children.

"He got found!" Shadow shouted.

"He hid somewhere obvious," Eclipse said.

"He made every person in the Sunlit Lands want to murder him." Nightfall grinned.

"Hey!" Jason said, but it was true. The Elenil wanted to kill him for his role in crippling their leader, the archon (not to mention the extensive damage that Jason and his friends had caused to the archon's palace, the literal pinnacle of Elenil architecture). The Scim wanted to kill him because one of their nobles had died so he could live. The Kakri were trying to kill him as part of his engagement process to Baileya. It was a long story, but her whole family had a year to try to kill him before they got married. There was even some group of people he had never met, called the Zhanin, who were upset because Jason had supposedly messed up the balance of magic or something. Still, it's not like *everyone* was trying to kill him. Those necromancers in the north didn't even know who he was. And the creepy shape-shifters in the south had invited him to come to their land anytime. And the . . . well, he couldn't remember all the different people in the Sunlit Lands, but so far as he knew, only four groups were trying to kill him.

"Eclipse is correct," Break Bones said. "In a closet or under a bed—this is the first place most people will look. If you are being hunted, such places are to be shunned." He looked at Jason with pity. "For the Scim, at least. Humans are not known for their cunning in battle or survival."

"Hey!" Jason said again.

"Shadow," Break Bones said. "You are the prey now."

Shadow leapt to his feet and looked around shiftily.

"Run," Break Bones said, and the boy sped from the room. Break Bones gathered the two remaining Scim children and Jason in the center of the room. "This time you will hunt as individuals, not in a pack. Eclipse, you will take the ground floor. Nightfall, the second. Wu Song, the third floor and above."

"Why are we doing this again?" Jason asked.

"To help you survive," Break Bones said.

Oh. Fine. But it's not like Jason would be hunting anyone. If anything, he would be the one hiding, just like he was hiding now in this old house. It had belonged, once, to the family of Night's Breath, the Scim prince who had died so Jason could be healed of a mortal wound. Jason had come here hoping to make peace with that—and with Night's Breath's family. But as soon as he had arrived, Night's Breath's wife and children had left. The Scim prince's elderly mother still lived here, but she had made it clear she remained only to guard the house . . . from him. The children who remained were Night's Breath's nephews and niece. The kids had taken to Jason immediately, but the old woman showed no interest in him. Jason had to admit it hurt his feelings in a weird way. He was here, far from his own family, and when he tried to connect to this woman, she shut him out. She would turn her head away any time he entered a room. Not that it surprised him. He was terrible at family stuff. His own parents hated him and wanted nothing to do with him, so why should a family that wasn't even human be any different?

Meanwhile, Jason and Baileya had friends in danger, but Baileya wouldn't agree to travel to help them. Their friend Kekoa had sent multiple messenger birds asking for assistance, but Baileya said, "It is too dangerous at this time. One of my brothers is seeking our trail. Twice I have led him away. He is cunning and swift, and should he find us, I do not doubt he would succeed in killing you, Wu Song." His name was Bezaed, and Baileya spoke of him with reverence. He had killed one of their sister's suitors, and that was a Kakri man. He would make short work of Jason. At this point in the conversation, Jason had almost tried to explain to her about their accidental engagement. He had told her a personal story, not realizing that how the Kakri got engaged was by sharing a personal story one had never told anyone else. They were a month and a half into their yearlong engagement now, and Jason didn't want to break up with her. But he didn't want their engagement to be based on a misunderstanding, either. Plus, it was weird to be seventeen and engaged to be married to a terrifying warrior maiden from a fantasy world. She wasn't even human—at least her golden skin and shining silver eyes argued for something not quite human.

"Wu Song," Break Bones said.

"Hmm?"

"It is time to hunt," the Scim said to him, shaking his shoulder gently. "The other children have already begun."

Jason glared at him. "The *other* children?"

Break Bones grinned, his yellow, tusklike teeth protruding from his mouth. "Prove me wrong. Be the first to find Shadow."

"I will," Jason said forcefully. He strode out of the room and immediately had no idea what to do next. Finding a little half-pint Scim in a dilapidated mess like this place would be a challenge.

Delightful Glitter Lady romped down the hallway. Jason followed her into what must have once been a ballroom. Or maybe something else, because Jason thought a ballroom would be on the ground floor, but this room was large, and there were many gigantic pieces of furniture covered with moldering cloths.

Dee sniffed twice, then sneezed, almost knocking herself over. He had been keeping her at kitten size because he didn't trust the floors in this place. He worried she could fall through a rotten board if he let her be even a tiny bit larger.

"I know you're in here, Shadow," Jason said. He could hear the uncertainty in his own voice. He shivered. Anything could be under these sheets. He yanked one off, letting it fall to the ground. It revealed a sort of low sofa with no arms. He pulled another sheet to discover a pair of chairs. He would have to uncover them all, he knew, because Shadow was exactly the kind of kid to hide under a moldy sheet if he thought it would give him even a minute's advantage in a game like this. There were at least thirty sheets. Jason sighed and got to work.

About ten sheets in, Dee made a high-pitched whine. "What is it, girl?"

She snorted and shuffled toward the back of the room. Jason smiled. She smelled Shadow. He bent down low and whispered, "Where's Shadow, girl? Do you smell him?"

Dee made a quiet, distressed honking, looking at another large sheet-covered item near the wall.

"In there?" Jason walked to the sheet. It had to be a cabinet or something like that. It was taller than Jason by several feet and nearly square in shape. He yanked on the sheet, and a cloud of moldy dust rained onto him. He sneezed, grumbling to himself, and tried to shake it off. He studied the wardrobe that had been revealed. It was made of some dark wood and looked ancient. A star had been carved into the front of it and painted silver. A slight shuffle came from inside. Shadow was exactly the kind of kid who would hide in a closet immediately after being told not to hide in closets.

Dee turned in a tiny circle, whining.

"What's the problem, girl?" Jason put his hand on the door. The kids liked to say all the terrible things they would do when they found him, delighting in making it sound as terrifyingly gory as possible. Since Jason didn't tell lies, his threats sounded lame in comparison. "When I find Shadow, I am going to gloat about how I found him so fast and say that I'm better at Hunter and Prey!"

Jason flung the door open.

Shadow was inside.

A golden arm was thrown across the little Scim's neck. A young man with flashing silver eyes and loose, flowing clothes stood behind him. A knife point pressed against Shadow's cheek. Shadow struggled, and the man constricted his arms, pinning the Scim child.

"Be very quiet, Wu Song," the man said. "I have no desire to hurt this child. But if you call for help, I will." Jason opened his mouth, but the stranger's knife point pressed in, and a bead of blood appeared on Shadow's cheek. "I will take his eye if you scream."

"That is what a real threat should sound like, Wu Song," Shadow said. He had that defiant, almost nonchalant look he got in his eyes right before he would bite one of his siblings. Showing fear was not encouraged among the Scim.

"Well," Jason said, very quietly, "I did find you pretty fast. I am better at Hunter and Prey. Obviously."

The man's eyes flicked toward the room's entrance and then back to Jason. "There is room in here for one more," he said.

"Um," Jason said. "Maybe if we were closer friends."

The man pushed on the knife again, and Shadow's eyes widened. Jason's hands clenched. He wasn't a warrior. He was terrible at Hunter and Prey. He needed to be protected, and he was useless with any weapon. But he wasn't about to let someone threaten a child and get away with it. He opened the second door of the wardrobe and stepped into it.

"Close the doors," the man said.

When the doors were closed, the stranger's silver eyes shone out with a powerful light. When the man spoke, his voice came steady and low. "My name is Bezaed. My mother is called Willow, and my grandmother Abronia. I am here, brother, to kill you before you can marry my sister Baileya."

6

L'ÂME DE LA FRANCE

Les ouvrages du même auteur figurent en fin de volume.

Max Gallo

L'ÂME DE LA FRANCE

Une histoire de la nation
des origines à nos jours

Fayard

© Librairie Arthème Fayard, 2007.
ISBN : 978-2-213-63007-6

Pour David.

« *Tous les siècles d'une nation sont les feuillets d'un même livre.*

« *Les vrais hommes de progrès sont ceux qui ont pour point de départ un respect profond du passé.* »

ERNEST RENAN, *La Réforme intellectuelle et morale.*

« *Il est deux catégories de Français qui ne comprendront jamais l'histoire de France : ceux qui refusent de vibrer au souvenir de Reims ; ceux qui lisent sans émotion le récit de la fête de la Fédération.*

« *Peu importe l'orientation présente de leurs préférences. Leur imperméabilité aux plus beaux jaillissements de l'enthousiasme collectif suffit à les condamner.* »

MARC BLOCH, *L'Étrange Défaite.*

« *Le peuple français est un composé, c'est mieux qu'une race, c'est une nation.* »

JACQUES BAINVILLE, *Histoire de France.*

SOMMAIRE

Chronologie I : vingt dates clés.

LIVRE IV
LA RÉPUBLIQUE IMPÉRIALE – 1799-1920

LIVRE V
L'ÉTRANGE DÉFAITE
ET LA FRANCE INCERTAINE – 1920-2007

L'âme de la France
et le pain des Français

C'était il y a un quart de siècle, en 1981.

Je me souviens de ceux qui clamaient d'une voix vibrante que l'élection de leur candidat à la présidence de la République – c'était aussi le mien – allait faire passer la France « de la nuit à la lumière ».

Vingt-cinq années se sont écoulées. On sait ce qu'il en fut. Mais les bonimenteurs sont remontés sur l'estrade et font à nouveau commerce d'espoir.

Ils ont chanté dans les années 30 du XXe siècle : « Il va vers le soleil levant, notre pays... » Trois ans après l'« embellie » du Front populaire, les nazis entraient dans Paris.

Ils ont, dans les années 80 du même siècle, promis qu'on allait « changer la vie ». Et le chômage a enseveli le pays dans la précarité, l'incertitude et l'angoisse.

Ils disent « Nous allons gravir la montagne. » Pour un « ordre juste contre tous les désordres injustes ».

C'est la même chanson.

Et je crains que cette ascension collective promise ne se réduise – nous avons vécu cela – au pèlerinage des courtisans gravissant derrière le Roi – la Reine – le petit rocher de leurs ambitions satisfaites, cependant que le peuple oublié continue de patauger, en bas, dans les marécages.

Pessimisme ?

Inquiétude, plutôt. Le réveil des peuples auxquels depuis des décennies tous les candidats au pouvoir présidentiel promettent sans tenir parole s'appelle révolte et même révolution. Et donc grand saccage.

Car on ne peut susciter l'espérance créatrice d'une nation qu'en lui disant la vérité de son histoire et de sa situation, et non en lui offrant des mirages trompeurs.

Or, pour la France, le xxie siècle tel qu'il commence, sera un temps des troubles. La nation est ankylosée par une crise profonde. Elle doute de son identité, et donc de son avenir.

Elle ne peut qu'être ébranlée par les contrecoups d'une situation internationale qui est un véritable avant-guerre.

Qu'on songe aux problèmes posés par la prolifération nucléaire, le Moyent-Orient, la question du pétrole, les conséquences d'une mondialisation non régulée, les migrations inéluctables et les bouleversements climatiques. Sans oublier la révolution scientifique et ses répercussions techniques, sociales et éthiques. Dès lors, le pays sera de plus en plus confronté à des tensions difficiles à apaiser.

Il faudra prendre des décisions rudes, peut-être cruelles. On ne pourra plus se contenter de diriger la France en flattant l'opinion.

Les candidates et les candidats aux élections prochaines en ont-ils conscience ? Y sont-ils préparés ? Ils le prétendent. Mais mesurent-ils tous la profondeur de la crise et des changements qui s'imposent ?

On peut légitimement en douter.

Pourtant, depuis le début de ce siècle dangereux, le sol de la nation s'est déjà fissuré, laissant apparaître les entrailles de notre société en crise.

L'extrême droite a été présente au second tour de l'élection présidentielle de 2002 alors que, depuis deux décennies, elle était reléguée au banc d'infamie.

Les partis de gouvernement n'ont rassemblé qu'à peine 36 % des voix.

Le président sortant n'a pas atteint 20 % des suffrages.

Les socialistes qui, souvent, font la mode, ont été éliminés par les électeurs pour la première fois depuis 1969, en dépit de l'attention qu'on leur prête, des louanges qu'on leur tresse, de l'autosatisfaction qu'ils affichent.

Ce tremblement de terre politique a été suivi d'une brutale coulée de lave du volcan social.

En novembre-décembre 2005, dans 274 communes, 233 bâtiments publics et 74 bâtiments privés ont été endommagés ou incendiés, et 10 000 voitures ont été brûlées.

Ce qui porte le total des véhicules détruits dans l'année 2005 à 45 000 !

Des engins incendiaires ont été lancés dans trois mosquées, deux synagogues ont été visées, une église a été partiellement incendiée.

Quatre personnes ont trouvé la mort durant cette période.

Mais tout va très bien, madame la marquise !

Quelques mois plus tard, le 23 mars 2006, sur l'esplanade des Invalides, dans le cœur symbolique de Paris, au terme d'une manifestation calme et autorisée, des jeunes gens encapuchonnés ont agressé et dépouillé ceux qui défilaient paisiblement.

Événements marginaux, accompagnant inévitablement la démocratie de la rue qui impose sa loi à la démocratie représentative, ou bien actes révélant les nouvelles ruptures de la société française ?

« J'ai vu, témoigne un photographe, des jeunes se faire lyncher avec une violence inouïe. Je n'avais jamais encore été confronté à de telles scènes à Paris, à des jeunes capables de faire preuve gratuitement d'une incroyable violence. »

En octobre-novembre 2006, des autobus ont été incendiés en Ile-de-France, dans le Nord et l'Est, à Marseille. Des policiers ont été attaqués.

Pour maîtriser et calmer de telles tensions, les mots et les sourires charmeurs ne suffiront pas.

L'élu(e) de la nation à la présidence de la République au printemps 2007 devra passer aux actes.

Or les Français ont beaucoup appris depuis trente ans.

Ils éliront « elle » ou « lui », mais ils ne se contenteront pas de postures avantageuses, d'habiletés, de générosités affichées.

Ils ont fait l'expérience et l'inventaire du style mitterrandien et des gesticulations chiraquiennes.

L'un était un président roué se complaisant dans les liaisons dangereuses, séducteur tout en arabesques et en hypocrites indignations de façade.

L'autre, un bateleur dressant son étalage sur les grands boulevards, retenant un instant les badauds par son insolente esbroufe.

Avec de tels acteurs, les Français ont beaucoup appris sur le théâtre politique, ses jeux de rôle et ses simulacres.

Seuls quelques compères et les croyants applaudissent aux promesses des nouveaux candidats.

Le vrai public partagé entre le scepticisme et l'espoir observe et attend.

Certes, une femme élue présidente peut renouveler le répertoire, mais on exigera d'elle plus que de la compassion ou de la séduction : des résultats !

Or les promesses seront d'autant plus difficiles à tenir que, pour être élus, les candidates et les candidats à la présidence de la République ou aux élections législatives auront d'abord divisé les Français, accusant leurs rivaux d'être responsables des maux qui frappent le pays.

Le coupable, ce n'est pas moi, c'est l'autre, c'est la droite – ou c'est la gauche !

Mais de grand guignol en farces, d'alternances en cohabitations, les Français savent que l'un vaut l'autre.

Et en 2005, au moment du référendum sur le traité constitutionnel européen, quand les acteurs cessent d'interpréter la pièce *Gauche-Droite*, renoncent aux mimiques de leurs oppositions pour inviter les Français à voter *oui*, ceux-ci saccagent le théâtre en scandant *non* !

Les Français ne se contentent donc plus des tours de passe-passe des prestidigitateurs. Ils n'attendent plus qu'on sorte du chapeau un lapin blanc.

Leur vie est difficile. Les conflits et la violence, le fanatisme, sont une réalité. L'horizon est obscurci par des risques majeurs.

Que faire ?

Il faudrait aux dirigeants le courage de dire et surtout d'agir. Car la « moraline » ne suffit pas.

Ils devraient savoir où conduit le « lâche soulagement », comme disait Léon Blum au lendemain de Munich, en 1938.

Fin, honnête, le leader du Front populaire voulait la paix, refusait l'« excitation du patriotisme » (septembre 1936), critiquait ceux qui croyaient la guerre inéluctable.

Esthète sensible, il détournait la tête pour ne pas voir les dangers.

C'est laid et brutal, la guerre.

Mais l'illusion s'est fracassée contre le réel.

Blum a été déporté par les nazis.

Des centaines de milliers de Français qui avaient défilé en clamant qu'ils voulaient *le pain*, *la paix*, *la liberté*, ont moisi quatre années dans les camps de prisonniers en Allemagne, victimes de dirigeants qui avaient préféré leur dire ce qu'ils voulaient entendre, que le temps était aux congés payés – mérités –, et non à la mobilisation et à la préparation à la guerre.

Elle eut lieu.

Et les parlementaires élus en 1936 dans l'« embellie » du Front populaire votèrent le 10 juillet 1940, à Vichy, la mort de la République. Seuls 80 d'entre eux s'y refusèrent.

Cette *étrange défaite*, le « plus atroce effondrement de notre histoire » (Marc Bloch), peut se reproduire.

Point n'est besoin d'une invasion étrangère.

Il suffit que, face à une crise intérieure avivée par une tension internationale, la lâcheté, le désir de rassurer, l'emportent sur le courage et la volonté.

Or la nation ne peut plus se permettre de dépendre des stratégies de carrière de dirigeants soucieux de rassembler leurs camps politiques, oubliant que la France les transcende.

« Je suis pour la France, disait de Gaulle en 1965 quand on l'accusait d'être le candidat de la droite. La France, c'est tout à la fois, c'est tous les Français. Ce n'est pas la gauche, la France ! Ce n'est pas la droite, la France ! Prétendre représenter la France au nom d'une fraction, c'est une erreur nationale impardonnable ! »

Pour ne pas la commettre, il faut vouloir que la France se prolonge en tant que nation une et indivisible, et non en un conglomérat de communautés, d'ethnies, de régions, de partis politiques.

Mais les élites de ce pays ont-elles ce désir d'unité nationale alors que, de concessions aux communautés en confessions et en repentances, elles déconstruisent l'histoire de ce pays ?

Certes, il faut en finir avec la légende qui fait de l'histoire française une suite d'actions héroïques dictées par le souci du bien de l'humanité !

Pour autant, la France n'est pas une ogresse dévorant les peuples – et d'abord le sien !

En fait, on ne peut bâtir l'avenir de la nation sans assumer *toute* son histoire.

Elle s'est élaborée touche après touche, au long des millénaires, comme ces paysages que l'homme « humanise » terroir après terroir, village après village, labour après labour, modelant l'espace en une sorte de vaste jardin organisé « à la française ».

Et c'est ainsi, d'événement en événement, de périodes sombres en moments éclatants, que s'est constituée l'*âme de la France*.

On peut l'appeler, avec Braudel, « la problématique centrale » de notre histoire. « Elle est, écrit-il, un résidu, un amalgame, des additions, des mélanges, un processus, un combat contre soi-même destiné à se perpétuer. S'il s'interrompait, tout s'écroulerait. »

C'est la question qui est posée en ce début du xxie siècle à la nation : « Voulons-nous nous perpétuer ? »

Nos élites le veulent-elles, partagent-elles encore la réflexion de Renan selon laquelle « tous les siècles d'une même nation sont les feuillets d'un même livre. Les vrais hommes de progrès sont ceux qui ont pour point de départ un respect profond du passé » ?

Mais qui s'exprime ainsi aujourd'hui ?

Le mot de *nation*, même s'il est à nouveau employé, est encore suspect. On évoque le pays, les régions, les provinces, l'Europe ou le monde. Rarement la patrie, mot tombé en désuétude.

Et quand quelqu'un ose parler de patriotisme, de patriotes, on ricane ou bien on le soupçonne d'être un extrémiste de droite.

La notion d'identité de la France fait même question, alors que Braudel en avait fait l'une de ses références.

« Une nation, écrivait-il, ne peut être qu'au prix de se chercher elle-même sans fin, de se transformer dans le sens de son évolution logique, de s'opposer à autrui sans défaillance, de s'identifier au meilleur, à l'essentiel de soi, conséquemment de se reconnaître au vu d'images de marque, de mots de passe connus des initiés (que ceux-ci soient une élite ou la masse entière du pays, ce qui n'est pas toujours le cas). Se connaître à mille tests, croyances, discours, alibis, vaste inconscient sans rivages, obscures confluences, idéologies, mythes, fantasmes... »

Ainsi s'est constituée, s'est maintenue, s'est déployée au cours de notre histoire l'âme de la France.

Mais les présidents qui se sont succédé depuis trente ans, au lieu de se soucier d'elle, ont préféré parler des Français, leurs électeurs...

Adieu la France, ont-ils tous lancé avec plus ou moins de nostalgie.

Le premier jugeait que la France, ne représentant plus que 1% de la population mondiale, devait se fondre dans la communauté européenne.

Le deuxième concédait qu'elle était encore notre patrie, mais que son avenir s'appelait l'Europe.

Le troisième l'invitait à la repentance perpétuelle.

L'alibi de nos trois présidents – et de nos élites – était que les Français se moquaient de la France, cette vieillerie !

Les citoyens, prétendait-on, se souciaient du régime de leur retraite, de leur emploi. Ils voulaient qu'on les protège, que les hommes politiques les débarrassent du carcan « centralisé » de l'État et choisissent la proximité, la région, non les grandes ambitions nationales.

On a donc remisé dans les caves et les greniers Jeanne d'Arc, la Sainte Pucelle, et le drapeau tricolore, nationaliste, Napoléon l'esclavagiste et *La Marseillaise*, la sanglante guerrière !

C'est là, aux oubliettes, que l'extrême droite a trouvé ces reliques abandonnées, elle les a brandies et on lui a laissé prétendre – cela arrangeait ceux que l'histoire de France gênait – qu'elle était le « Front national ».

Ainsi les élites ont-elles donné le sentiment qu'elles n'avaient plus la volonté de perpétuer la nation.

Qu'il s'agissait là à la fois d'une tâche archaïque, néfaste et impossible, voire compromettante et ridicule.

Mais, depuis qu'on ne se soucie plus de l'âme de la France, les problèmes quotidiens des Français se sont aggravés.

On leur a dit depuis trois décennies :

Oublions les rêves de grandeur !

Cessons d'être une patrie, devenons un ensemble de régions européennes !

Finissons-en avec l'exception française !

Effaçons notre histoire glorieuse de nos mémoires ! Elle est criminelle.

N'évoquons plus Versailles, Valmy ou Austerlitz, mais le Code noir, la rafle du Vel' d'Hiv', Diên Biên Phu et la torture !

Soyons d'une province, basque ou corse, poitevine, savoyarde, vendéenne ou antillaise, et non d'une nation !

Restons enracinés dans nos communautés et nos traditions d'origine. Soyons de là-bas, même si nous avons nos papiers d'ici !

Négligeons le français, conjuguons nos langues avec l'anglais bruxellois !

Ainsi nous vivrons mieux !

Nous aurons plus de *pain*, plus de *paix*, plus de *liberté* !

Un temps les Français l'ont cru.

Mais les mots deviennent peu à peu poussière face à l'expérience vécue.

Ils ne sont plus que des mensonges.

Le *pain* est rare et cher pour le chômeur.

L'insécurité, la violence et le fanatisme menacent la *paix* et la *liberté*.

Et, en 2005 comme en 2002, les Français ont sifflé les bonimenteurs.

Ils recommenceront demain si les promesses ne deviennent pas des actes.

Ils ont appris que leurs problèmes individuels, dans un monde cruellement conflictuel, ne peuvent être résolus que si, à rebours du discours des élites, le destin de la France, de son identité, de ses intérêts nationaux, est la préoccupation première de ceux qui les gouvernent.

Et qu'une nation ce n'est pas seulement une somme de régions souveraines, un « agrégat inconstitué de peuples désunis ».

Il n'y a, il n'y aura de *pain*, de *paix*, de *liberté* pour les Français que si on défend et perpétue l'âme de la France telle que notre histoire l'a façonnée.

LIVRE I

LES SEMEURS D'IDENTITÉ

Des origines à 1515

1

LES RACINES ET LES PREMIERS LABOURS

de la préhistoire à 400 après Jésus-Christ

1.

Au commencement de l'âme française il y a la terre.

Ce n'est qu'un coin d'espace encerclé par les glaciers qui s'amoncellent sur les bordures du territoire mais qui jamais ne recouvriront cet hexagone balayé par les tempêtes de poussière de lœss. Celle-ci se dépose, s'accumule, formant des terrasses dont le vent violent modifie les contours. Les glaciers avancent, reculent ; la faune, la flore changent, le climat s'adoucit, se tempère, puis le froid redouble.

Et cela durant des centaines de milliers d'années.

Qui peut concevoir ce que signifie l'épaisseur immense du temps ?

Les formes de ce territoire au long de ces trois millions d'années sont encore imprécises, le dessin est inachevé.

Mais sur cette surface d'étendue moyenne, les blocs granitiques – plateaux, monts, chaînes arasées par l'érosion – côtoient les plus récentes montagnes, les pics déchiquetés, les sommets que les glaciers ensevelissent encore.

Les roches d'âges différents – des centaines de milliers d'années des unes aux autres – sont voisines, séparées parfois par un étroit sillon où des fleuves s'installent.

L'Europe se rassemble, s'entremêle dans cet hexagone qui sera la France.

Ce pays est comme un résumé de ce qui, ailleurs, s'étale dans une monotonie semblant ne jamais devoir s'interrompre, alors qu'ici on passe d'un paysage, d'un relief à l'autre.

Et ce commencement de l'âme de la France dit ainsi la diversité, une marqueterie de différences, un lieu où l'on se rencontre et se mêle.

Ce n'est qu'une terre, mais c'est l'empreinte première.

Cependant, rien encore n'est définitif. Les assauts glaciaires se succèdent.

Autour de huit mille ans avant notre ère, la mer fait irruption, séparant ce qu'on nommera les îles Britanniques du continent, isolant le bassin fluvial de la Tamise de celui du Rhin, donnant ses limites à l'hexagone. Par ses origines, par la mémoire de la terre, il était donc lié à cette partie que la mer éloigne, qui devient îles. Ce sont désormais comme des frères siamois tranchés par l'encastrement, entre eux, de la mer du Nord. Et chacun vivra différent malgré leur souche commune.

Les formes et les limites sont ainsi en place.

La terre hexagonale enseigne la diversité des horizons, des sols et des roches aux premiers hommes qui surgissent, venant de l'est par la grande voie danubienne, et du sud par la voie méditerranéenne.

Que sait-on de ces hommes d'il y a plus d'un million d'années ?

Peut-on imaginer qu'en eux, au fond de leur regard, il y a de temps à autre – et, entre chacun de ces moments, peut-être faut-il compter cent mille années ? – une étincelle qui, un jour, après un nouveau déluge de temps – 800 000 ans ? – donnera une flammèche ?

Elle annonce qu'ici, sur ce sol, surgira – il y faudra une autre coulée gigantesque d'années – l'âme de la France.

Les premiers de ces hommes-là sont des prédateurs que leur nomadisme pousse d'un paysage à l'autre, que le froid et le vent font reculer, se réfugier dans des grottes, mais auxquels le réchauffement du climat donne l'audace de repartir.

Ils chassent. Ils pêchent. Ils cueillent. Ils taillent dans la pierre des armes et des outils rudimentaires. Ils tendent des pièges et, selon les époques – entre elles s'étendent des millénaires –, ils tuent l'hippopotame, le rhinocéros ou l'ours brun, le cerf, le sanglier ou le lapin, le bison ou le cheval sauvage, le taureau ou le bouquetin.

Ils façonnent des grattoirs, des perçoirs, et bientôt polissent la pierre, le bois de ces arbres qui, en fonction du climat, s'enracinent dans le nord ou le sud de l'hexagone : bouleaux, pins, noisetiers, chênes, ormes, tilleuls...

Et, le temps s'étant encore écoulé, voici qu'en frottant des bouts de bois l'un contre l'autre ils font jaillir des étincelles, maîtrisant ce feu que parfois déjà la foudre leur offrait.

Ils s'accroupissent autour du foyer, ces hommes qu'on nomme de Neandertal – du nom d'un site proche de Düsseldorf.

Ils ont la voûte crânienne surbaissée, des arcades sourcilières renflées, énormes, un front fuyant, leur face sans menton est un museau. Ils sont pourtant *Homo sapiens*. Après eux viendront les *Homo sapiens sapiens*, l'homme de Cro-Magnon – vieux de 35 000 ans, trouvé aux Eyzies-de-Tayac-Sireuil, dans la Dordogne –, dont la boîte crânienne s'est allongée.

Mais, pour passer de l'un à l'autre, de la pierre taillée (paléolithique) à la pierre polie (néolithique), il a fallu plusieurs milliers d'années, peut-être plus de cent mille.

Ils brisent la pierre à coups de burin. Ils la grattent. Ils la lustrent. Ils sont encore nomades, mais déjà, dans un climat plus tempéré, ils demeurent longuement sur les lieux qu'ils jugent favorables à leurs chasses.

Ils sont là, entre Loire et Garonne, et leurs générations se succèdent sans aucune interruption, faisant de cette région l'une des seules de France où l'occupation humaine ait été permanente.

Le peuplement est dense dans les vallées de la Dordogne et de la Vézère, dans le Périgord, la Corrèze.

Lesquels de ces hommes-là, qui se rassemblent autour des feux et soufflent sur les braises pour que les flammes bleutées dansent devant leurs yeux fixes, ont, quand la mort frappait l'un des leurs, décidé de l'enfouir dans une tombe afin qu'il vive une autre vie et que son corps abandonné ne soit pas livré aux rapaces, aux fauves ?

Dans la Corrèze, à La Chapelle-aux-Saints, ils ont préparé cette sépulture.

Est-ce le premier indice d'une âme qui, en eux, commence son travail de genèse de l'homme ? Pour qu'ainsi la terre de l'hexagone devienne un grand reposoir où, génération après génération, durant des millénaires, les corps fécondent le territoire, millions de morts qui sont comme l'humus de l'âme de la France ?

Cette tombe de La Chapelle-aux-Saints, les hommes l'ont conçue et creusée quarante mille ans avant notre ère. Et c'est le signe qu'ils s'interrogent à tâtons, entre effroi et rêve, sur ce qu'est cette vie qui un jour les abandonne, sur ces animaux, biches, bouquetins, chevaux, taureaux, qu'ils tuent et dont ils se repaissent, et parce qu'ils veulent les « saisir » ils les emprisonnent dans leur regard, les représentent sur les parois des grottes à Lascaux, à Rouffignac (Dordogne).

Un renne apparaît sur ces parois, seul témoin d'un temps glaciaire qui a disparu, puis viennent taureaux, bisons, cerfs, chevaux peints en noir, en jaune, en rouge, animaux d'un climat tempéré installé dans l'hexagone autour de ces années 17 000-15 000 avant notre ère.

Et c'est ainsi que sur cette terre hexagonale surgit la première civilisation connue de l'humanité, brille l'étincelle de l'art, ce phénomène majeur du paléolithique. Dans la profondeur abyssale du temps, l'âme germe là où l'homme jette un regard interrogateur sur lui-même et sur le monde.

Là, il creuse une tombe, et quelques millénaires plus tard, alors que les temps glaciaires s'achèvent, il prend soin de ses morts. Il dresse des pierres en de longs alignements, et ces menhirs, encore debout, rappellent que le temps le plus reculé, le plus obscur, est toujours le nôtre, que l'âme de la France d'aujourd'hui n'en finit pas de communier avec ses origines.

Ailleurs, l'homme d'après le paléolithique construit des dolmens, lourdes tables de granit, tombes individuelles ou collectives. Ces rites funéraires, ces monuments dressés aux disparus, ces manifestations de l'âme, révèlent que l'homme vivant veut que ses morts demeurent à ses côtés.

Il ne lui suffit plus de se livrer à des repas rituels où il mange le cœur et le cerveau, la moelle des os des disparus, manière de conserver leurs forces en lui. Il veut les honorer, les garder près de lui en ces lieux où désormais il s'installe en sédentaire, où il commence – quatre mille ans avant notre ère ? – à gratter le sol pour creuser un trou, tracer un sillon, enfouir une semence, devenant ainsi agriculteur et non plus seulement chasseur.

Les terroirs se dessinent entre les tombes.

Et ils composent aujourd'hui une cartographie de la préhistoire française.

Qui marque encore notre sol, notre présent.

Chaque année, durant le dernier quart du XXe siècle de notre ère, moins d'une dizaine de milliers d'années après la construction des menhirs et des dolmens, et moins de vingt mille ans après que les hommes eurent peint les fresques rupestres de la grotte de Lascaux, un président de la République gravissait la roche de Solutré, en Saône-et-Loire, accompagné d'une petite foule de courtisans et de journalistes.

Autour de ce rocher surplombant la plaine se trouvait un amoncellement de carcasses de plus de dix mille chevaux. Poussés vers le vide par les chasseurs préhistoriques qui, les poursuivant, les acculaient à la mort, ou bien victimes d'un cataclysme ? Le mystère demeure.

Mais ce « pèlerinage présidentiel », ce rituel, cette manière de tenir le fil noué avec les hommes des premiers temps, leurs lieux sacrés, de mettre ses pas dans l'humus humain de notre hexagone, montrait que l'âme de la France restait liée aux temps préhistoriques et qu'elle se reconnaissait comme leur fille lointaine. Mais peut-on employer ce mot pour dire vingt mille ans, après avoir parcouru des centaines de milliers d'années ?

2.

Ce n'était plus les temps glaciaires, et l'âme des hommes de cette terre hexagonale qui s'appellerait la France fixait ses premiers repères dans un climat tempéré.

De la grotte de Lascaux à la roche de Solutré et aux milliers de menhirs dressés à Carnac, les représentations picturales ou les tumulus funéraires collectifs et les tombes individuelles faisaient de la terre un espace sacré, d'autant plus qu'on apprenait à la labourer, à la ensemencer, et qu'ainsi sanctifiée par l'humus humain elle devenait la *Grande Mère* qui conservait les corps pour leur donner une autre vie, mais aussi la *Nourricière* qui compensait les aléas de la chasse et de la cueillette.

Et on voulait désormais s'enraciner, se tenir serrés les uns contre les autres pour cultiver, tisser, modeler ces poteries que l'on décorait en griffant le vase encore malléable avec des coquillages (le *cardium*). Et l'art naissait ainsi, sur les rives de la Méditerranée, pour remonter la vallée du Rhône vers le nord.

C'est là, non loin du fleuve, entre le massif hercynien et la montagne alpine, que l'on retrouve, à mi-chemin entre Avignon et Orange, les traces du premier village d'agriculteurs de la future France : Courthezon.

On y polit la pierre – c'est l'époque néolithique –, mais on y utilise bientôt les métaux, le cuivre – l'âge chalcolithique – puis le bronze, et, à la fin du néolithique, le fer.

En moins de cinq mille ans – Courthezon a été créé vers 4650 avant notre ère – il se produit ainsi plus de transformations dans notre hexagone qu'il ne s'en était accompli en plus de cinquante mille ans !

On incinère les morts, on enfouit leurs cendres dans des urnes que l'on regroupe en vastes champs ainsi peuplés de l'âme des défunts. On crée des tombes individuelles, on édifie des tumulus de bronze. Et la terre n'est plus seulement une étendue, mais un berceau de l'âme. On crée des paysages, on ouvre des clairières, on trace des chemins, des routes.

On construit des maisons sur des pieux au lac de Chalin, dans le Jura. Un village est identifié à Chassey, près de Chagny, en Saône-et-Loire. Entre les groupes de sédentaires, les échanges se multiplient, les routes forment un réseau qui peu à peu dessine la trame de l'hexagone.

Ces hommes qui façonnent des poteries, qui abattent les arbres pour aménager chemins et clairières, qui se préoccupent du destin de leurs morts, sont les premiers occupants de l'hexagone.

Ils ont le crâne court. Ils sont râblés. Mais, au cours du dernier millénaire d'avant notre ère, ils voient prendre pied sur la terre hexagonale d'autres hommes.

Les uns viennent de l'Est, du bassin du Danube, et peut-être de plus loin encore. Les Grecs les appellent Keltai, Celtes, ce qui signifie « les hommes supérieurs, sublimes ».

Les autres viennent du Sud. Ce sont des Grecs de Phocée, et, en 620 avant notre ère, ils créent Marseille, la première cité grecque de l'hexagone. Elle essaimera, donnant naissance à Nikaia-Nice, Antipolis-Antibes, Agathé-Agde, Theline-Arles.

Ces cités-là restent nos repères. Elles sont quelques-uns des premiers points d'appui de l'âme de la France qui, peu à peu, investit l'hexagone, cette terre qui est la première des régions d'Occident à entrer en contact direct avec les grandes civilisations du bassin oriental de la Méditerranée.

Ainsi, durant le premier millénaire avant notre ère, alors que commence l'âge du fer, l'hexagone s'ouvre aux Celtes et aux Grecs qui vont, à leur manière, féconder la terre de la future France et commencer à modeler son âme.

3.

C'est désormais le vent de l'histoire qui souffle sur l'hexagone. Le temps ne se compte plus en centaines ou en dizaines de milliers d'années, mais en siècles.

L'esprit qui errait dans les temps préhistoriques peut désormais concevoir ces durées qui lui sont plus familières.

De même, il voit entrer dans l'hexagone et dans l'histoire des peuples identifiés qui font partie de sa mémoire et de ses légendes.

Celtes – Gaulois –, Grecs, Romains et Germains peuplant nos mythologies sont autant d'éléments de notre âme contemporaine. Les noms de cités, les vestiges, les monuments, la symbolique qui en est issue, sont au cœur de notre présent.

Nous imaginons que nous sommes leurs descendants directs. On peut, dans un cortège d'aujourd'hui, voir un manifestant, vêtu en Gaulois de légende, porté sur un bouclier, incarner la « résistance » à une loi que l'opinion condamne !

Ainsi, à tout instant, le passé légendaire investit le présent, oriente le futur, garde vivante une âme qui se structure dans les derniers siècles d'avant notre ère.

Les Grecs sont installés le long de la côte méditerranéenne. Les Celtes demeurent au nord, au centre et de part et d'autre du

Rhin. Des tribus nouvelles – les Belges – arrivent et les refoulent. Puis surviennent les Germains, qui menacent les Celtes, les repoussent vers le sud, les font entrer en contact avec les Romains.

Ces peuples se côtoient et s'interpénètrent dans ce résumé d'Europe qu'est l'hexagone.

Il n'y a pas une seule « race », un seul « peuple », maîtres du territoire.

Ainsi, dès sa genèse, parce que l'hexagone est comme un *impluvium* qui recueille toutes les « averses » de peuples, l'âme de ce qui sera la France est ouverte. Les peuples venus d'ailleurs l'irriguent.

C'est leur présence sur le sol hexagonal, et non leur sang, qui détermine leur appartenance et bientôt leur identité, quelle qu'ait été celle de leurs origines.

Dès ces premiers siècles historiques, ce qui concerne l'hexagone touche le reste de l'Europe et toute la Méditerranée. Le bassin danubien et, au-delà, la Grèce et ses colonies d'Asie sont aux sources de ce peuplement hexagonal.

Et les Celtes ne se contentent pas de se répandre dans l'hexagone ; ils envahissent le nord de la péninsule Italique.

Ils ont le coq pour emblème et deviennent, pour les Romains, *Galli*, Gaulois, du nom de ce coq, *gallus*.

En 385 avant Jésus-Christ, ces Gaulois sont sous les murs de Rome et menacent le Capitole.

Quand ils se replient, battus par les Romains, ils s'installent dans la plaine du Pô, où l'un de leurs peuples, les Boii, fonde Bononia, Bologne.

Et cette région padane qu'ils marquent de manière indélébile – n'y a-t-il pas une *Ligue du Nord* dans l'Italie d'aujourd'hui, et les dialectes de l'Émilie ne recèlent-ils pas des mots « gaulois » ? – devient, pour les Romains, la *Gaule Cisalpine*, la première Gaule, antérieure à l'hexagonale, la « nôtre », qui ne surgira que peu à peu, trouvant son identité gauloise dans la perception de sa différence d'avec les Grecs, les Romains, les Germains.

Les Gaulois de cette *Gaule Transalpine* – ainsi nommée par les Romains – s'hellénisent au contact des Grecs des cités de la côte méditerranéenne. Le commerce unit ce Sud au Nord. Des amphores remplies de vin sont transportées sur le Rhône, la Saône, la Seine, le Rhin. D'autres marchandises – armes, tissus, poteries – franchissent les cols des Alpes.

Ainsi, en même temps que surgissent l'identité gauloise et l'âme de la Gaule, se constitue l'Occident.

Cette période de l'âge du fer est donc décisive.

La première séquence – la période dite de Hallstatt, du nom d'un village proche de Salzbourg –, jusqu'aux années 400 avant Jésus-Christ –, puis la seconde, la période de la Tène – du nom d'un village proche de Neuchâtel –, jusqu'aux années 150 avant Jésus-Christ, voient se mettre en mouvement cette dialectique de l'unité et de la division de l'Europe qui sera à l'œuvre tout au long de l'histoire de ce continent.

Les peuples et les régions se séparent et s'unissent. Le réseau des routes commerciales les rapproche, unifie peu à peu leurs mœurs.

À Vix, dans la Côte-d'Or, au pied du mont Lassois qui commande et verrouille la vallée de la Seine, la tombe d'une princesse, morte autour de sa trentième année vers l'an 500 avant Jésus-Christ, contient un immense cratère grec (1,65 mètre de haut, plus de 200 kilos). Les bijoux de cette jeune femme permettent de mesurer l'éclat de cette civilisation celtique – on dira bientôt gauloise – ouverte aux influences grecques, qui marque une étape de plus dans la construction de l'âme de la France.

Plus au sud, dans la Drôme, le village du Pègue révèle lui aussi l'influence grecque : un champ d'urnes, un ensemble de fortifications.

La civilisation celtique s'enracine ainsi en maints lieux de l'hexagone.

À Entremont, non loin d'Aix-en-Provence, on identifie un ensemble fortifié construit vers 450 avant Jésus-Christ.

Des villes : Bibracte, près d'Autun, sur le mont Beuvray, Gergovie, proche de Clermont, Alésia, dans la Côte-d'Or, témoignent du déploiement de cette âme « gauloise ».

Un président de la République, à la fin du xxe siècle, a même songé, un temps, à se faire inhumer sur le mont Beuvray. Il avait même acquis à cette fin une parcelle de terre, voulant par là s'insérer au plus profond de notre histoire, peut-être se l'approprier.

Vitalité toujours renouvelée de nos origines légendaires...

En tous ces lieux on découvre la créativité gauloise. Ils inventent le tonneau et le savon. Ils sont charrons, forgerons, charpentiers. Ils construisent des chars à deux ou quatre roues. Ils les placent parfois auprès de leurs chefs décédés, dans les tombes princières qu'ils bâtissent pour les honorer.

Ce sont des guerriers valeureux, aux armes puissantes : glaive court, hache. Ils sont bons cavaliers et chargent, casqués. Impitoyables, ils pendent à leur ceinture les têtes de leurs adversaires vaincus.

Les Romains se méfient de ce peuple gaulois qu'ils contrôlent en Gaule Cisalpine, mais qui reste tumultueux en Gaule Transalpine.

Ils veulent l'isoler de cette mer Méditerranée où se croisent et s'articulent les relations entre toutes les provinces de leur république : cette *Mare Nostrum* qui ne saurait être menacée par les Gaulois.

Alors ils font la conquête du littoral méditerranéen, y créent des villes, dont Narbonne. La province qu'ils y instituent, qui portera le nom de Narbonnaise, tient les Gaulois éloignés de la mer.

Ainsi s'ébauche à partir de cette province la surveillance – qui conduit à la domination – par les Romains de la Gaule Transalpine. Ils y interviennent, nouant des alliances avec tel ou tel des peuples gaulois, Éduens, Arvernes, Séquanes, Rèmes, Lingons. Ils jouent habilement des rivalités entre eux tous.

Dès l'origine, ce peuple gaulois qui s'unifie porte donc en lui, par sa diversité même, des ferments de division. L'âme de la France peut toujours se fissurer, une partie d'elle-même, être attirée par la rupture, la séparation, l'alliance avec l'étranger.

Et les Romains, adossés à la Narbonnaise, de définir ainsi trois Gaules : l'Aquitaine, la Celtique, la Belgique.

Ils creusent de cette manière, sur le territoire de la Gaule, des sillons, presque des frontières, qui ne s'effaceront plus.

Dans chacune de ces Gaules, les cités sont autant de lueurs qui continuent de briller depuis ces débuts de l'histoire.

Avaricum (Bourges), Cenabum (Orléans), Autricum (Chartres), Vesontio (Besançon), Lutetia (Paris), Adenatunum (Langres), Burdigala (Bordeaux), Segodunum (Rodez), Mediolanum (Saintes), Lemonum (Poitiers), Samarobriva (Amiens), Rotomagus (Rouen), Arras, Beauvais, Reims (créées respectivement par les peuples des Arelates, des Bellovaci, des Rèmes) : nommer ces cités, c'est parcourir toute l'histoire de France jusqu'à l'avènement du XXIᵉ siècle.

C'est découvrir, au cœur des villes d'aujourd'hui, des vestiges qui sont les racines de notre présent.

Ces cités et ces lieux constituent une sorte d'archipel dont la plupart des « îles » – ces villes – se perpétuent au milieu d'un grand remuement de peuples.

Les Parisii et les Séquanes quittent alors le bassin de la Seine sous la poussée des Belges, et gagnent les uns le Yorkshire, les autres la Franche-Comté.

Les Romains s'emploient à refouler les Germains, dont ils craignent l'alliance avec les Gaulois. Et en 102-101 avant Jésus-Christ, le consul Marius bat les Teutons à Aix-en-Provence, et les Cimbres à Verceil, en Gaule Cisalpine.

Ainsi se créent des séparations, des oppositions, qui vont perdurer.

La Gaule qui a rassemblé et amalgamé les peuples est aussi le lieu de leur émiettement, une source qui se déverse dans les régions voisines.

Elle est, comme sa géographie la détermine, un condensé d'Europe, le territoire où toute l'histoire du continent se noue.

Et sur ce grand berceau hexagonal où vagissent les âmes des futures nations rivales et proches s'étend l'ombre de l'aigle romaine.

4.

Quand les légions de Jules César avancent en Gaule, précédées de leurs aigles aux ailes déployées, l'histoire se mêle à la légende.

Et c'est en s'appuyant sur les *Commentaires* de César vainqueur qu'on peut se représenter comment se construit alors l'âme de la France.

On voit – on imagine – Vercingétorix, le jeune chef des Arvernes, peuple d'Auvergne, diriger et incarner durant dix mois la résistance à la plus grande armée du monde. Avant d'être battu à Alésia et de mourir étranglé dans une prison souterraine de Rome – le Tullianum – après le triomphe de César, le Gaulois aura réussi à rassembler autour de lui la plupart des peuples de la Gaule, une armée de cent mille hommes, et à infliger au général romain une défaite sous les murs de Gergovie.

Les lieux de ces affrontements entre les légions de César et les guerriers gaulois se sont inscrits dans la longue histoire française.

C'est ainsi qu'une âme nationale palpite au souvenir qu'à Cenabum (Orléans) débuta la première rébellion gauloise contre Rome, qu'elle subit une défaite à Avaricum (Bourges), puis l'emporta à Gergovie (près de Clermont), avant d'être terrassée à Alésia/Alise-Sainte-Reine, sur le mont Auxois.

Cette résistance, magnifiée par les historiens, les romantiques du XIXᵉ siècle, devient ainsi l'un des ressorts de l'âme de la France. Et le combattant gaulois apparaît comme l'ancêtre du citoyen républicain. Vercingétorix et ses guerriers préfigurent les soldats de l'an II, les francs-tireurs de 1870 et ceux de 1944. Ils les inspirent. Un peuple résiste à l'envahisseur. Vaincu, il jette ses armes aux pieds du conquérant dans un dernier geste de défi.

Vingt siècles plus tard, Astérix vengera Vercingétorix...

La légende est une potion magique.

Mais, ses vertus évanouies, il reste la réalité, l'histoire. Celle-ci contribue à faire comprendre comment se constituent une âme collective, une nation, dès le temps de César, dans les années 60-50 d'avant notre ère.

Au début, avant que les légions de César n'entrent en Gaule, cette terre est divisée en cent peuples souvent rivaux.

Mais entre eux existe la communauté d'une civilisation celtique avec sa langue, ses dieux, ses prêtres – les druides –, ses rites souvent cruels.

On sacrifie aux dieux – Ésus, Teutatès, Taranis, Lug – des hommes (on retrouvera les vertèbres brisées révélant des meurtres rituels).

Les druides et une « aristocratie » dominent ces peuples.

Le sanglier plus que le coq pourrait leur tenir lieu d'emblème.

Mais cette civilisation commune ne peut effacer les divisions. Les Éduens (établis entre la Loire et la Saône, autour de Bibracte), les Lingons (région de Langres), les Rèmes (région de Reims), sont les alliés de Rome.

Cette division des Gaulois est le levier dont se sert Jules César pour intervenir en Gaule, empêcher les tentatives d'unité entre les Éduens, les Séquanes (Seine), les Helvètes.

Alors que s'ébauche la préhistoire de ce qui deviendra la France, on mesure que l'incapacité à s'unir est comme une maladie génétique de ce territoire, lieu d'accueil de peuples différents, tentés de jouer chacun leur partie.

César exploite cette pathologie.

Il soutient ses alliés. Il protège les Éduens contre les Suèves (des Germains). Il refoule et massacre les Helvètes. Il écrase la révolte des Belges en 57. Il sépare ces peuples et fait du Rhin la frontière entre Gaulois et Germains, entre la Gaule et la Germanie.

César trace là une ligne de fracture décisive qui rejouera tout au long de l'histoire, estompée à certaines périodes, puis à nouveau creusée, un fossé de part et d'autre duquel les peuples devenus ennemis s'observent avant de s'entretuer.

Et tandis qu'il se contente de cantonner les Germains dans les forêts de la rive droite du Rhin, il opprime les peuples gaulois.

Les violences, les atrocités que leur infligent les légions romaines suscitent la rébellion.

Les peuples divisés se rassemblent autour de Vercingétorix. Après plus de cinq ans d'un impitoyable protectorat romain, la résistance s'enflamme et les dix mois de lutte qui suivent forgent la nation gauloise.

C'est dans la lutte et la résistance qu'un peuple se donne une âme.

La légende s'empare alors du dernier carré de combattants gaulois : ceux d'Uxellodunum (dans le Quercy), qui résistent jusqu'en 51 aux légions de César, et qui, afin que tous les peuples de Gaule sachent à quel point les Romains sont implacables, auront les mains tranchées ou les yeux crevés – leur mutilation paraissant à leurs vainqueurs plus exemplaire qu'une mise à mort, plus effrayante qu'un simple égorgement.

Mais le sang répandu, les violences subies, les martyres endurés, ne sont jamais oubliés.

Ils irriguent la longue mémoire d'un lieu, d'un territoire. Et les peuples qui, des siècles plus tard, y demeurent, redécouvrent ces origines englouties, rivières souterraines qui disparaissent durant de longs parcours, puis soudain refont surface.

Et l'âme s'y abreuve, découvrant ces dix mois de résistance, ce chef gaulois, Vercingétorix, qui devient un héros emblématique.

L'âme prend aussi conscience que c'est en Gaule que s'est joué le sort de l'histoire de l'Occident – l'histoire mondiale d'alors.

César, vainqueur de cette guerre des Gaules qu'il a voulue, provoquée, pour rentrer dans Rome en triomphateur, a transformé la République. L'Empire romain va naître comme ultime conséquence de son initiative.

Mais c'est en Gaule qu'il aura trouvé la force de franchir – en 49 – le Rubicon, cet acte qui va changer la face du monde connu.

Comment mieux dire l'importance décisive de ce coin de terre entre les mers, où l'Europe se rassemble ?

5.

Morte était la Gaule celtique, étranglée par la poigne romaine comme l'avait été Vercingétorix dans le Tullianum, à Rome, après six années de captivité au fond de cette prison en forme de fosse.

Mais les peuples renaissent quand ils disposent d'un territoire tel que la Gaule, carrefour entre le Nord et le Sud, lieu de passage et de rencontre.

Celui qui s'installe dans l'hexagone dispose de ce trésor – la situation géographique – qui peut ne pas être utilisé, mais qui, dès lors qu'on le découvre, donne à qui en dispose un atout maître.

Et sur le corps vaincu et blessé de la Gaule celtique surgit ainsi une Gaule latine, pièce maîtresse de l'Empire romain.

César le veut, lui qui a fixé les limites de ce qui constitue son point d'appui pour régner à Rome.

Et ses successeurs, dont certains naîtront dans ce pays gallo-romain – Claude, à Lyon, qui régnera sur l'Empire de 41 à 54 ; Antonin, à Nîmes, qui sera empereur de 138 à 161 –, veilleront sur ces trois Gaules, l'Aquitaine, la Celtique, la Belgique, les défendant contre les incursions barbares, germaniques, élevant un *limes* sur le Rhin.

Quand, à partir du IIIe siècle de notre ère, les Alamans et les Francs, des Germains, s'avanceront, les empereurs tenteront de les repousser, divisant la Gaule en deux circonscriptions administratives, l'une (au nord de la Loire et du cours supérieur du Rhône) ayant Trèves pour capitale, et l'autre, au sud, avec Vienne.

Pour trois siècles la Gaule romaine échappera aux invasions germaniques et restera unifiée.

C'est le latin, devenu la langue de ce nouveau pays, qui y structure l'âme des peuples.

On découvre ainsi que l'hexagone est un creuset assimilateur. La civilisation romaine envahit tout l'espace, conserve les lieux de culte des dieux gaulois pour y célébrer les siens propres.

Ceux qui refusent la collaboration et l'assimilation quittent la Gaule pour les îles Britanniques ou bien pour les forêts de Germanie.

Ceux des Gaulois qui ne sont pas réduits en esclavage, qui n'ont pas été mutilés, qui n'ont pas eu les yeux crevés, les mains tranchées par leurs vainqueurs, acceptent cette nouvelle civilisation, accueillante dès lors qu'on collabore avec elle, qu'on reconnaît ses dieux, son empereur, qu'on sert dans son armée – c'est ce que fait l'aristocratie gauloise.

Les Gaulois deviennent citoyens de Rome ; ils se mêlent aux vétérans romains qui fondent des colonies d'abord en Narbonnaise, puis, plus au nord, le long de la vallée du Rhône.

La paix romaine s'appuie sur ces villes nouvelles : Béziers, Valence, Vienne, Nîmes, Orange, Arles, Fréjus, Glanum – près de Saint-Rémy-de-Provence –, Cemelanum – près de Nice. On élève des trophées à La Turbie, à Saint-Bertrand-de-Comminges, pour célébrer la pacification, la victoire sur des résistances locales.

On écrase des révoltes – celle de Vindex en 68 –, des mutineries dans l'armée du Rhin en 70 de notre ère.

Mais plus jamais la Gaule tout entière ne s'embrase. Elle est désormais romaine.

Les repères que retient notre mémoire, qui balisent l'âme de la France, sont désormais des constructions romaines.

Les voies pavées se ramifient, l'une conduisant du sud (Arelate, Arles) au nord-est (Augusta Treveronum, Trèves), et l'autre d'est en ouest, les deux se croisant à Lugdunum (Lyon).

C'est la ville de l'empereur Claude, la capitale des Gaules. Un môle dans l'histoire nationale.

Ici les trois Gaules – Aquitaine, Celtique, Belgique – envoient chaque année les délégués de leurs soixante peuples pour débattre au sein d'une assemblée fédérale qui se réunit le 1er août. Là, au confluent du Rhône et de la Saône, on célèbre le culte de Rome et de l'empereur, on affirme l'unité de la Gaule romaine et sa fidélité à l'Empire.

Lugdunum devient l'un de ces lieux emblématiques qui renaissent à chaque période de l'histoire. Elle doit son nom au dieu gaulois Lug, voit s'élever un autel pour célébrer l'empereur, et c'est dans l'amphithéâtre de la ville que sont torturés les martyrs chrétiens – sainte Blandine –, en 177, sous le règne de l'empereur philosophe Marc Aurèle.

Et c'est Lugdunum qui deviendra ultérieurement le siège du primat des Gaules, capitale du christianisme comme elle avait été capitale de la Gaule romaine.

Mais Lugdunum n'est que le centre d'une constellation de villes, d'un maillage urbain qui sert de trame à l'histoire de la nation et d'armature à son âme.

Pas une de ces villes romaines (presque toutes nos villes d'aujourd'hui se sont élevées sur un premier noyau romain qui lui-même a souvent germé sur une cité gauloise) qui n'ait laissé une trace monumentale : vestiges de thermes ou d'amphithéâtres, d'aqueducs, de demeures – Maison carrée de Nîmes, pont du Gard, théâtres d'Arles, de Nîmes, d'Orange, arènes de Lutèce, thermes de Vaison-la-Romaine...

Toute une civilisation romaine s'épanouit et les campagnes se peuplent de *villae*, les clairières s'étendent, l'agriculture et l'arboriculture se répandent. Le vignoble progresse jusqu'au Rhin.

Qui se rappelle que tel temple de Janus, près d'Autun, a été construit sur un lieu de culte des dieux gaulois ? Et que l'oppidum de Bibracte – sur le mont Beuvray –, d'origine gauloise, est lui aussi devenu lieu de culte romain ?

Mais ce passé s'estompe, s'enfouit, même si on en retrouvera un jour la trace et s'il rejaillira.

Après Alésia et la reddition de Vercingétorix, la Gaule est devenue romaine sans réticence ni remords. Son âme se construit autour des valeurs et des mœurs romaines. La bière a cédé la place au vin.

Quand on s'insurge – à partir de la fin du III⁰ siècle –, c'est contre telle ou telle mesure jugée trop rigoureuse ou trop coûteuse (les impôts). Mais ces paysans révoltés, les bagaudes, ne visent pas à construire une autre unité politique.

Rome est l'horizon de tous.

Seuls les chrétiens refusent, malgré les tortures, le martyre – ainsi ceux qui ont pour théâtre Lugdunum –, de célébrer le culte de l'empereur et de Rome.

Mais les peuples barbares qui se pressent contre le *limes* rhénan rêvent, eux, de submerger la civilisation romaine. Et c'est le creuset gaulois qui, au début du V⁰ siècle, paraît, autant que l'Italie, le représenter.

Ils vont déferler, couvrir l'hexagone de leurs peuples, et, au contact d'une terre déjà imprégnée d'« âme », s'y transformer.

2

LA SÈVE ET LA TAILLE

des invasions barbares à 1328

6.

C'est le temps des barbares, et rien ne peut arrêter leur déferlement.

Ils franchissent le Rhin et les Alpes. Ils débarquent sur les côtes. Ils viennent du fin fond de l'Europe. D'autres barbares derrière eux les poussent en avant. C'est une grande migration de peuples qui s'enfoncent dans la Gaule, la traversent ou bien s'y installent, la défendent contre ceux qui arrivent après eux.

Cette terre hexagonale fécondée depuis des millénaires par les peuples divers qui, tous, y ont laissé leurs traces, leurs morts, donne ainsi naissance à une autre civilisation.

Avec ses cent cités, ses dix-sept provinces, ses deux diocèses, la Gaule gallo-romaine s'efface. Elle est démantelée comme ses monuments qui deviennent des carrières, dont on arrache les blocs de pierre pour bâtir demeures, murs d'enceinte, bientôt châteaux forts et églises.

Et ainsi, tout au long de cinq siècles obscurs – de l'an 400 à l'an mil –, les vestiges de Rome nourrissent et inspirent ce qui naît sur ce territoire qui n'est plus la Gaule, mais la France. Elle porte désormais le nom d'un peuple germanique, installé sur le Rhin inférieur et qui, depuis des décennies, est déjà en contact avec les Gallo-Romains.

Ces Francs sont devenus soldats. Ils commandent des légions. Peu à peu, ils cessent d'être des mercenaires pour devenir les maîtres de ces régions situées au-delà de l'Escaut et du Rhin.

D'autres peuples pénètrent à leur tour cette Gaule dont les villes, le sol fertile – ces grands champs de céréales –, le climat tempéré, les voies romaines, les *villae* campées au centre de vastes exploitations agricoles, les attirent. Tout est butin dans ce pays où il fait bon vivre.

Les tribus germaniques – Vandales, Suèves, Burgondes, Alamans, Goths, Wisigoths, Alains – se ruent année après année sur l'hexagone, y taillent leur territoire, sont refoulées par d'autres.

Les Wisigoths venus des Balkans sont installés dans le Sud-Ouest ; ils y fondent les royaumes de Toulouse et de Bordeaux, puis sont repoussés dans le nord de l'Espagne.

Les Burgondes dominent la région comprise entre Lyon et Genève.

Les Alamans prennent possession des régions situées de part et d'autre du Rhin supérieur.

Ainsi se dessinent des divisions nouvelles : un nord et un sud de l'hexagone, où une langue « romane » peu à peu se répand, et un Est – sur le Rhin inférieur – où s'enracine un parler germanique : frontières géographiques et linguistiques, sillons creusés profond et que le temps n'effacera pas.

Dans le même temps s'affirme la puissance d'assimilation de ce territoire. L'humus humain y est si épais et si riche, les paysages et le climat y sont si accueillants, qu'il suffit d'être sur ce sol pour y prendre racine, vouloir le défendre contre d'autres peuples venus de Pannonie (Hongrie) ou de plus loin encore.

Ce sont les Huns. Ils chevauchent, pillent. Contre eux s'allient, sous le commandement d'un dernier chef de l'armée romaine (Aetius), Francs, Burgondes, Wisigoths, pour résister aux hordes d'Attila. Celles-ci seront vaincues sur la Marne (entre Châlons et Troyes, sans doute) en 451, à la bataille des champs Catalauniques.

Victoire symbolique en une région qui sera, tout au long de l'histoire, une zone de confrontation.

Victoire lourde de sens : les barbares ligués pour combattre les Huns, les repousser, cessent, par ce simple fait, d'être des barbares. Ils ont choisi de se fixer sur ce sol, de s'allier pour le défendre.

Plus significatif encore : Burgondes et Wisigoths sont chrétiens, même s'ils sont hérétiques, adeptes de l'arianisme, qui récuse la divinité du Christ.

À Paris, cette ville vers laquelle se dirigeait Attila, c'est Geneviève, une aristocrate gallo-romaine, catholique, qui a rassuré la population, prédit la défaite des Huns, incarné cette civilisation nouvelle issue de l'Empire romain, voué au Christ depuis l'empereur Constantin (330).

Restent les Francs qui sont encore païens mais qui, en combattant les Huns, en créant leur royaume entre Rhin et Seine, sont pris par cette terre qui les conquiert autant qu'ils croient la posséder.

Car peu à peu, en deux siècles – des années 300 aux années 500 –, la Gaule romaine s'est, comme l'Empire, mais plus que la plupart des autres provinces, christianisée. Un tournant majeur de l'histoire s'est ainsi accompli. L'empreinte la plus profonde a été creusée dans l'âme des peuples qui vivent et vivront sur ce sol.

Vers l'an 500 – le 25 décembre 496 ? –, le chef franc Clovis reçoit le baptême à Reims. Le païen devient chrétien. Il renonce, comme le lui demande l'évêque Remi, à ses amulettes, il courbe la tête. Et, avec lui, ses guerriers, son peuple, s'agenouillent et reconnaissent la foi dans le Christ. Clovis devient ainsi le premier souverain issu d'un peuple barbare à choisir le catholicisme, à ne pas être l'un de ces chrétiens hérétiques comme sont les Wisigoths et les Burgondes.

Il y gagne l'appui de l'Église.

Or celle-ci détient la mémoire de Rome, la langue et les fastes de l'Empire. Les évêques sont issus depuis deux siècles de l'aristocratie romaine, et quand le dernier empereur, Romulus Augustule, disparaît, en 476, et que sombre ainsi l'empire d'Occident, la Gaule résiste encore dix années. L'Église et ses évêques maintiennent parmi les barbares la foi nouvelle et le souvenir de l'Empire.

Clovis et les Francs s'enracinent ainsi sur une terre où, dès 314, un concile a réuni en Arles douze évêques venus de toutes les cités de Gaule.

Où, à la fin du IVe siècle, un ancien soldat romain né en Pannonie, Martin, a créé un premier diocèse et commencé à évangéliser les paysans. Premier évêque élu par les fidèles, « barbare » et non issu de l'aristocratie gallo-romaine, il incarne une foi charitable – il a partagé son manteau avec un pauvre –, simple et populaire.

Les pèlerins accourent pour le rencontrer. Sulpice Sévère, un aristocrate et lettré gallo-romain, écrit sa biographie, dresse la liste de ses miracles. Ce livre se répand dans tout l'Occident, jusqu'en Égypte et en Grèce. La basilique de Tours, où repose Martin, devient le cœur de ce catholicisme qui gagne toute l'ancienne Gaule, laquelle fait figure de foyer chrétien de l'Europe. Des monastères sont fondés : ceux de l'île de Lérins (dans la baie de Cannes) et de Saint-Victor (à Marseille). Arles et Lyon – la ville qui connut les premiers martyrs chrétiens en 177 – sont des villes d'où la foi rayonne.

En se convertissant et en entraînant son peuple dans sa foi, Clovis s'appuie sur cette chrétienté déjà présente, et la renforce.

Lui qui a vaincu les Alamans – à Tolbiac, en 496, et sa conversion constitue peut-être une manière de remerciement à Dieu pour cette victoire – s'ouvre, à la bataille de Vouillé, près de Poitiers, la route de Bordeaux et de Toulouse. Il bat les Wisigoths hérétiques. Il annexe les pays situés entre la Loire et les Pyrénées. Il assemble ainsi – même s'il ne contrôle pas la côte méditerranéenne – un « royaume » dont les contours annoncent ceux de la France. Et il n'est pas jusqu'à la frontière de l'Est, tenue par les Alamans parlant le germanique, qui ne préfigure les limites françaises.

Mais Clovis ne fixe pas de frontières, celles-ci ayant été déjà esquissées par César.

Abandonnant Soissons, il choisit le futur centre national du pouvoir lorsqu'il fait de Paris – ville romaine d'importance moyenne, comparée à Lyon, Arles, Vienne, Trèves – sa capitale.

Déjà, en 502, il a choisi l'emplacement d'un mausolée sur l'une des collines de la rive gauche de la Seine, en face des îles.

Le palais du roi est situé dans la ville que domine ce sanctuaire.

Les choix sont donc clairs et dessinent un trait majeur de l'âme française : les liens tissés entre le roi et l'Église, entre monarchie et catholicisme.

Mais l'évêque Remi l'a rappelé au jeune catéchumène qu'était Clovis : les deux pouvoirs, celui de l'Église et celui du roi, restent séparés.

Si la France devient la « fille aînée de l'Église », le roi, pourtant baptisé et sacré, n'est pas confondu avec un homme d'Église.

Le roi prie. Les prêtres prient pour le roi. Mais celui-ci n'est pas l'égal d'un dieu.

Détentrice de l'héritage de Rome, l'Église ne confond pas pour autant pouvoir politique et pouvoir religieux. Elle refuse d'idolâtrer le roi comme l'était l'empereur.

Cependant, en juillet 511, c'est le souverain Clovis qui convoque à Orléans les évêques de son royaume.

Dans cette ville qui fut la première à se rebeller contre César et dont le nom va résonner tout au long de l'histoire nationale, Clovis définit les relations entre le roi et les évêques, les églises et les monastères.

Le roi des Francs veut que « son » Église échappe à l'influence de Rome et que « ses évêques » lui obéissent.

Ainsi s'annonce la singularité des rapports entre la France et Rome. Clovis est déjà un « gallican ».

La Gaule romaine et chrétienne a donc assimilé les barbares francs. Dans toute l'Europe occidentale, à ce titre, ce royaume franc catholique constitue une exception en ce début du VIe siècle.

Près d'un millénaire et demi plus tard – en 1965 –, de Gaulle, devenu président de la République, confiait : « Pour moi, l'histoire de France commence avec Clovis, choisi comme roi de France par la tribu des Francs qui donnèrent leur nom à la France... Mon pays est un pays chrétien, et je commence à compter l'histoire de France à partir d'un roi chrétien qui porte le nom de Franc. »

Écho lointain de la conversion d'un chef barbare qui lança sa hache à deux tranchants pour déterminer le lieu où s'élèveraient, sur la colline parisienne, son mausolée et celui de sainte Geneviève.

7.

En ce début du vi^e siècle, dans le royaume franc dont Paris est la capitale, le peuple prie.

Il s'agenouille devant les reliques de sainte Geneviève et le tombeau de Clovis.

Il communie à Tours devant le mausolée de saint Martin. Il participe à la messe dans ces églises qui s'élèvent ici et là, en des lieux où depuis toujours on célébrait le culte des dieux païens, qu'un seul Seigneur désormais remplace.

Parmi ce peuple des croyants, cette cohue de pèlerins qui donnent à leurs fils le nom de Martin, on ne sait plus distinguer ceux qui sont d'origine germanique de ceux issus de ces villes et de ces villages gallo-romains.

L'Église est un immense baptistère qui rassemble et unit, préside à la naissance de cet enfant encore vagissant et fragile : le peuple français.

Il est présenté sur les fonts baptismaux par la tradition romaine dont le catholicisme est l'héritier et dont l'Église conserve la richesse. C'est en latin qu'on prie.

Mais il a aussi un parrain germanique, homme libre portant les armes, se plaçant au service d'une aristocratie franque qui fusionne elle aussi avec l'aristocratie gallo-romaine. Et c'est la

7.

En ce début du vi^e siècle, dans le royaume franc dont Paris est la capitale, le peuple prie.

religion, la foi, le baptême, qui rendent possible et sanctifient cette union.

Il y a d'un côté la loi germanique – la loi salique – qui fixe les amendes à payer pour chaque délit commis et précise les conditions des successions, dont la femme peut-être exclue. De l'autre, il y a les commandements catholiques qui imposent eux aussi le respect de règles, de principes.

Le royaume franc fait ainsi le lien – incarne la rencontre et l'union – entre le monde germanique et l'héritage antique. Et la conversion de Clovis, l'église vouée à sainte Geneviève, le mausolée au cœur de Paris, affirment ce rôle décisif de la terre « française » entre les deux versants majeurs de la civilisation européenne telle qu'elle commence à apparaître.

Mais les reliques d'une sainte et le tombeau d'un roi, les prières d'un peuple, ne suffisent pas à maintenir l'unité du royaume franc.

À la mort de Clovis, le partage entre ses fils crée quatre royaumes avec à leur tête un *Rex Francorum*. Ils ont chacun une ville emblème pour capitale : Paris avec Childebert, Reims avec Thierry, Orléans avec Clodomir, Soissons avec Clotaire.

Une logique d'affrontement, exprimant le désir de réunir ce qui vient d'être partagé, se met inéluctablement en branle. En 561, après un demi-siècle de luttes, Clotaire aura reconstitué l'unité du royaume.

Mais, autour du royaume franc, au sud et au nord, d'autres royaumes se sont constitués : la Septimanie (la région de Montpellier) wisigothe, la Provence des Ostrogoths, le royaume burgonde.

En même temps, l'aller et retour entre fragmentation et réunification se prolonge, trace de nouvelles frontières, et surgissent de nouveaux chefs : Mérovée, Dagobert. L'Austrasie (entre Rhin, Meuse, Escaut : la Lorraine, la Champagne, l'Alsace avec Metz) côtoie la Neustrie (Paris et Soissons). Et, s'associant à l'un ou à l'autre au fil des rivalités et des guerres qui les opposent, subsistent le royaume de Bourgogne et celui d'Aquitaine.

En 632, le roi Dagobert fait à son profit l'unité des différentes royautés.

Ces conflits, ces retrouvailles, ces séparations, révèlent la tendance forte et contradictoire à l'émiettement de la terre hexagonale, qu'elle soit celtique, gauloise, romaine ou franque.

Durant ces siècles, c'est un incessant va-et-vient entre éclatement et cohésion, les forces qui séparent et celles qui soudent.

Mais, face à cet avenir à chaque fois incertain, le pouvoir royal, malgré l'appui que lui porte l'Église, s'affaiblit. L'aristocratie, les comtes, les maires du palais, s'en emparent.

Dès le VIIe siècle, la famille de Pépin de Landen, maire du palais d'Austrasie au temps de Dagobert (qui règne de 629 à 639), s'impose.

Au début du VIIIe siècle, l'un de ses descendants, Pépin de Herstal (il meurt en 714), devient le chef de fait de toute la monarchie franque.

C'en est fini des descendants de l'aïeul de Clovis, Mérovée, les Mérovingiens.

8.

Pour que le royaume franc recouvre l'unité et donc la force qu'il avait acquise en sa prime jeunesse, au temps de Clovis, à l'orée du VIᵉ siècle, il ne suffit pas qu'une dynastie succède à une autre et que les descendants de Pépin de Herstal écartent définitivement les Mérovingiens.

Il faut que chacun des nouveaux maîtres du pouvoir fasse la preuve de sa capacité à maintenir la cohésion de son royaume et à le défendre. S'il y réussit, alors il bénéficiera de l'appui de l'Église et du peuple des croyants.

On enfouira le souvenir des Mérovingiens dans le mépris et la réprobation, et l'âme du peuple se convaincra qu'il y a pour ce royaume – peut-être parce que les hommes et les femmes qui l'habitent, qui en labourent et en sèment le sol, sont chrétiens – une attention particulière de la Providence qui l'arrache aux abîmes pour le faire renaître.

C'est ce sentiment que les croyants éprouvent et que l'Église et ses évêques confortent quand Charles Martel – fils bâtard de Pépin de Herstal – repousse, le 17 octobre 732, sur la voie romaine reliant Poitiers à Tours – la ville de saint Martin –, les Arabes et les Berbères musulmans qui, depuis près d'une décennie, avaient commencé, à partir de l'Espagne, à lancer des razzias sur les villes de Septimanie et d'Aquitaine, s'emparant et pillant Nîmes et Carcassonne, mettant le siège devant Toulouse, saccageant Autun et Sens, Lyon, Mâcon, Beaune, toute la Bourgogne, lançant des raids dans le Rouergue, l'Aveyron, menaçant Avignon.

La victoire de Charles Martel en 732 est donc loin d'être un épisode secondaire.

Le royaume franc ne sera pas conquis, islamisé par ces guerriers qui, rassemblés à Pampelune, ont répondu à l'appel à la guerre sainte lancé par le gouverneur d'Al-Andalus, nom donné à l'Espagne occupée.

Mais, pour être un coup d'arrêt, cette victoire ne met pas fin à la menace.

La poussée musulmane conduit le duc de Provence – Mauronte – à traiter avec l'adversaire afin de partager avec les Sarrasins la domination de la vallée du Rhône. Le duc de Provence ouvre aux musulmans les portes de Saint-Remy, d'Arles et surtout d'Avignon.

On mesure là cette tentation de la séparation, de la trahison, du choix de l'« étranger », fût-il un infidèle, pour échapper à la tutelle du pouvoir central.

Périsse le royaume pourvu que je règne en maître sur ma province ! Tous les moyens sont alors bons pour y parvenir.

Mais, en 734, à la tête de l'armée franque, Charles Martel vient mettre le siège sous les murs d'Avignon, bientôt conquise, et les Arabes sont passés au fil de l'épée avec leurs alliés. La ville est pillée et incendiée.

Bientôt, après quarante années de lutte, la présence musulmane, à l'exception de quelques lieux sur la côte méditerranéenne, est chassée de la terre franque.

Et Charles Martel est inhumé en 741, à Saint-Denis, parmi les rois.

Il reste dans le légendaire français comme celui qui a préservé la terre chrétienne – et « nationale ».

Il est le vrai fondateur de la dynastie carolingienne.

Après le règne de son fils Pépin le Bref (751 à 768), c'est le fils aîné de ce dernier, Charlemagne, qui va régner, de 768 à 814.

Une autre histoire alors commence.

D'abord se confirme le rôle majeur que joue cette terre franque dans la civilisation chrétienne.

Les armées de Charles Martel ont refoulé les infidèles. Charlemagne et son frère Carloman ont été sacrés à Saint-Denis par le pape Étienne II.

Le premier est empereur en 800.

Ainsi, la tradition romaine donne sa forme à la nouvelle « race » royale issue du monde germanique. Le fils de Charlemagne, Louis le Pieux, sera lui aussi sacré. La royauté est désormais de droit divin.

L'empereur est entouré de conseillers issus de l'Église : Alcuin et Éginhard.

Ce sont eux, les lettrés, qui renouent avec la tradition antique des études et assurent ainsi la perpétuation du savoir. Les évêques sont les relais du pouvoir impérial.

Le royaume franc est certes étendu vers l'est, et Aix-la-Chapelle en devient la capitale au lieu de Paris, mais c'est tout l'ancien territoire hexagonal, la Gaule gallo-romaine, qui bénéficie de cet ordre impérial et de l'action des *missi dominici*.

Une « administration » se met en place. Les hommes doivent prêter serment de fidélité à la personne de l'empereur.

Avec Charlemagne s'incarne ce lien particulier qui unira l'ouest et l'est de la civilisation franque.

Il y a un peuple français et un peuple germanique, mais, au-delà de leurs parlers, de leurs antagonismes, s'exprime cette lointaine origine commune, cette union carolingienne. Charlemagne est inhumé en 814 dans la chapelle palatine, à Aix.

Cet empire de traditions romaine et franque est fort. Il peut surmonter les défaites face aux Basques alliés des musulmans – à Roncevaux en 778 –, consolider la frontière sud en Aquitaine contre les incursions musulmanes, envoyer aussi une ambassade au calife de Bagdad, Haroun al-Rachid (802), recevoir l'ambassadeur du calife en 807, obtenir pour les Francs le droit de garder les Lieux saints.

À ce moment se noue pour des siècles le lien singulier et contradictoire qui unit le monde musulman et ce peuple franc. Il résiste, refoule l'avancée musulmane, mais, dans le même temps, il obtient du calife cette reconnaissance symbolique qu'est la concession de la garde des Lieux saints.

C'est aussi cette présence en Palestine qui vaudra à la royauté « franque » son rôle majeur dans les croisades.

Bien des aspects fondamentaux de l'âme française, du légendaire dans lequel elle puise, naissent ainsi au cours de cette période carolingienne qui peu à peu se dégrade.

Dès le VIIIe siècle, il lui faut faire face aux incursions normandes sur toutes les côtes de l'ancienne Gaule.

À la mort de Louis le Pieux, en 840, l'empire se divise. Du serment de Strasbourg et du traité de Verdun (842-843) – en langues romane et germanique – naissent trois États dont les frontières vont rejouer sans fin durant plus de onze siècles !

L'un des fils, Louis, obtient tout ce qui se trouve au-delà du Rhin et en outre, sur la rive occidentale du fleuve, Mayence, Worms et Spire. Le royaume de Lothaire – le deuxième fils – comprend le territoire situé entre Rhin et Escaut jusqu'à la Meuse, et sa frontière occidentale longe le cours de la Saône et du Rhône jusqu'à la mer. Tout le reste revient à Charles le Chauve.

Empire partagé, royaumes affaiblis.

Comment résister à ces envahisseurs normands qui remontent la Seine jusqu'à Paris, massacrent les évêques de Chartres, de Bourges, de Beauvais, de Noyon, longent les côtes jusqu'au delta du Rhône, pillent Arles, Nîmes, Valence ?

Les paysans s'arment ou fuient, échappant ainsi souvent à la condition d'esclaves, et c'est en hommes libres qu'ils s'établissement sur d'autres terres.

Pendant que ces incursions normandes atteignent le cœur des royaumes francs, leurs rois s'entre-déchirent dans l'espoir de reconstituer à leur profit l'unité impériale perdue.

Quête vaine, épuisement d'une dynastie dans des guerres fratricides, qui tente en vain de réunir ce qu'on peut commencer d'appeler la France et l'Allemagne.

C'est l'Église qui va choisir de soutenir une nouvelle dynastie.

L'Église est d'autant plus puissante que les ordres monastiques se sont développés – l'abbaye bénédictine de Cluny est fondée en 920.

L'Église réussit au Xᵉ siècle à imposer le respect d'une « trêve » puis d'une « paix de Dieu ». Elle entend rétablir l'ordre public en protégeant les églises, les clercs désarmés, les marchands et le bétail, sous peine d'excommunication par les évêques. Des « assemblées de paix » se tiennent à l'initiative et sous l'autorité de ceux-ci. Le poids de l'Église devient ainsi déterminant.

Quand l'archevêque de Reims, Adalbéron, choisit de soutenir Hugues Capet – héritier de Hugues le Grand –, duc des Francs, contre le dernier des Carolingiens, la balance penche en faveur de ce nouveau souverain.

Hugues Capet renonce à la Lotharingie, qui restera sous l'influence allemande. Il choisit de régner sur la partie occidentale de l'ancien empire de Charlemagne, cette *Francia* qui devient alors la France.

Ainsi commence, avec le règne d'Hugues Capet (987-996), la dynastie capétienne.

Elle est déjà l'héritière d'une longue histoire qui a façonné un territoire et son âme.

9.

C'est le temps des rois de France, et c'est aussi l'an mil.

Le sacre confère aux souverains capétiens le pouvoir de faire des miracles.

Rois thaumaturges, ils sont les représentants du Christ sur la terre, les vicaires de Dieu en notre monde.

Rois-prêtres, ils ont accès au surnaturel.

Le sacre a fait d'eux des « oints du Seigneur ». Ils font sacrer leur héritier, l'aîné de leurs fils. Attenter à leur pouvoir, les menacer, les agresser, est naturellement un acte sacrilège qui se paie de la vie.

Ils sont rois de droit divin, participent à la liturgie et deviennent ainsi des hommes au-dessus des autres hommes.

Ils protègent les hommes d'Église, tous les lieux de culte : les premières cathédrales qui surgissent à Orléans, Chartres, Nevers, Auxerre, ainsi que les monastères. Et ils condamnent au bûcher les hérétiques.

Ce roi qui, le jour de son sacre, guérit en touchant les écrouelles, qui accomplit des miracles, répète les gestes de Jésus.

Il lave les pieds des pauvres assemblés autour de lui durant la semaine sainte. Il distribue du pain, des légumes, un denier. Et il peut même, tel le Christ, rendre la vue à un aveugle.

Ainsi, l'âme française s'imprègne du respect qu'elle doit à ces monarques au pouvoir surnaturel.

Elle est d'autant plus marquée par ce caractère de représentant du Christ que la peur est au cœur de ce XIe siècle durant lequel se succèdent Robert II le Pieux (996-1031), Henri Ier (1031-1060) et Philippe Ier (1060-1108).

Les chroniqueurs, les prédicateurs, les devins, annoncent la fin des temps.

Car qui pourrait réfuter, en cette millième année depuis la Passion du Seigneur, la prophétie de l'Apocalypse : « Mille ans écoulés, Satan sera relâché de sa prison et s'en viendra séduire les nations des quatre coins de la terre. »

Cette certitude fait de chaque événement un signe.

L'éclipse donne au soleil la couleur du saphir. Les hommes, se regardant les uns les autres, se voient pâles comme des morts. Les choses semblent toutes baignées d'une vapeur couleur safran. Une stupeur et une épouvante jamais vues s'emparent alors du cœur des hommes.

Comment ne se tourneraient-ils pas vers ce roi de la *Francia*, comment ne s'agenouilleraient-ils pas devant lui ? Ne tient-il pas son pouvoir de Dieu, et ne représente-t-il pas le Christ ici-bas ?

Ainsi s'amorce le mouvement qui pousse vers le souverain les habitants du royaume que tenaillent la peur, la misère, la famine, l'insécurité, la terreur devant l'apocalypse.

On saisit à l'origine ce lien particulier – religieux – qui va, siècle après siècle, unir les sujets du royaume de France à l'« oint du Seigneur ».

Le roi n'a de comptes à rendre qu'à Dieu, mais sa mission est de protéger ceux qui sont rassemblés autour de lui. S'il rompt ce lien avec Dieu – et avec l'Église, qui, elle aussi, représente Dieu en ce bas monde –, alors les régicides se lèvent pour le punir d'avoir failli à sa fonction.

Mais le meurtre du roi blesse le peuple. Il faut qu'un autre souverain renoue le lien avec le « surnaturel ».

« Le roi est mort, vive le roi ! »

Et quand la monarchie est rejetée par les représentants de toute la nation (ainsi, en 1793, avec le verdict condamnant à mort Louis XVI), un vide se crée, qu'il faut combler : Empire et Restauration d'abord, puis exaltation de la République protectrice.

L'État hérite de la divinité du roi.

Mais la force du roi de France est d'abord religieuse, intimement liée à sa personne. Et si fort est son caractère surnaturel, si personnel le lien entre lui et Dieu, entre lui et le peuple, que l'excommunication – dont Robert et Philippe sont un temps frappés pour avoir rompu des liens conjugaux – ne parvient pas à effacer l'aura surhumaine que le sacre leur a attribuée.

En outre, le royaume de France est devenu, après le temps des incertitudes, un territoire aux frontières plus précises, au centre bien identifié. C'est bien au cœur de la France que le roi réside.

Quand ses chevauchées ne le conduisent pas d'un bout à l'autre du royaume – il doit se montrer à son peuple, à ses vassaux –, il demeure à Orléans, à Étampes, à Chartres, dans cette Beauce couverte de blés, à Paris. Les grands fleuves – la Loire, la Seine, la Marne, l'Oise, la Meuse – sont les nervures de ce territoire dont Paris devient la ville la plus active.

Le roi est ainsi à même de protéger les reliques de saint Martin à Tours, celles de sainte Geneviève, le tombeau de Clovis à Paris et celui de Dagobert à Saint-Denis.

Il est sacré à Reims, où, avant d'être le pape de l'an mil, l'évêque Gerbert d'Aurillac crée des écoles. Non loin se trouvent Troyes et ses foires, où les marchands venus d'Italie et du Nord se rencontrent. Là, le rabbin Rashi (Salomon Ben Isaac, 1040-1105) rédige ses commentaires sur la Bible et le Talmud, que les moines savants consultent, méditent et contestent.

La France trouve ainsi son assise. Elle est le grand royaume de l'Ouest, et c'est la Meuse qui lui sert de frontière avec l'Empire teutonique.

Les deux souverains – le roi Robert II le Pieux et l'empereur Henri – se rencontrent au bord de ce fleuve en 1023, à Ivois.

L'empereur est reçu sur la rive « française », le roi, sur la rive

« germanique ». On s'embrasse. On célèbre la messe. On échange des cadeaux.

« Ils resserrent ainsi les liens de leur fraternité, et chacun regagne ses terres. »

Les deux identités se renforcent mutuellement.

À la périphérie du royaume de France s'affirment des entités régionales : duché de Bourgogne, duché d'Aquitaine, marquisats de Toulouse, de Provence, duché de Lorraine, duché de Normandie d'où le duc Guillaume appareillera avec une flotte et 7 000 combattants pour se lancer à la conquête de l'Angleterre (1066, bataille d'Hastings).

Dès ce XIe siècle, le royaume de France apparaît donc bien comme la clé de voûte d'une civilisation européenne qui, désormais, ne connaît plus ces grandes ruées « barbares » qui l'ont transformée au fil des siècles. Les peuples se sont enracinés.

Il y a certes encore des incursions scandinaves, ou, au sud, des razzias musulmanes (Narbonne est attaquée par les Sarrasins en 1020), mais l'heure est à l'éclosion d'une société féodale qui va structurer l'âme française.

Le roi de France est le suzerain de vassaux qui disposent à leur tour d'hommes liges.

Des châteaux, le plus souvent en bois, surgissent. « Un blanc manteau d'églises neuves » couvre le royaume. Des divisions sociales nouvelles se font jour : « Les uns prient, les autres combattent, les autres travaillent », écrit en 1030 Adalbéron, évêque de Laon.

Dans le royaume où l'espace inoccupé apparaît immense, les « pauvres » – paysans, manants – sont unis par la misère et le travail, la famine et l'absence de droits.

L'égalité entre eux s'établit, la distinction ancienne qui séparait l'esclave de l'homme libre disparaît peu à peu : c'est le « peuple ».

Au-dessus, le deuxième ordre est celui des hommes de guerre, les chevaliers, dont la monture et les armes constituent les biens les plus précieux.

Ils servent le seigneur féodal, qui les adoube.

Enfin il y a le premier ordre, celui des hommes d'Église. Certains d'entre eux choisissent de vivre retirés dans les monastères (La Chartreuse est créé en 1084) et suivent des règles strictes.

La prière et l'étude sont leur quotidien. Apparaît ainsi une génération intellectuelle séparée du peuple et des hommes de guerre, mais inculquant à ces deux ordres le sens de leur vie et régnant par là sur les âmes.

Ce sont les « hommes d'Église » qui veulent établir la « paix de Dieu », empêcher que les hommes de guerre ne se combattent. Ce sont eux qui organisent les grands pèlerinages : à Rome pour prier sur le tombeau de saint Pierre, à Compostelle pour rendre grâce à saint Jacques, à Jérusalem pour retrouver les pas du Christ.

Mais, en 1009, le Saint-Sépulcre aurait été profané par les hommes du calife du Caire. Et c'est une souffrance pour la chrétienté, en ce millième anniversaire de la Passion du Seigneur. Une preuve décisive de la présence et de l'action de Satan. Pour le combattre et le vaincre, il faut que les chrétiens cessent de s'entretuer, « car c'est répandre sans aucun doute le sang du Christ ».

On peut expulser les juifs, brûler les hérétiques, mais la trêve et la paix de Dieu doivent s'imposer aux chevaliers chrétiens ainsi qu'aux pauvres enfants de Dieu. Il ne doit y avoir de guerre que sainte.

Ainsi, peu à peu, l'âme française se constitue, acquiert une identité forte.

Il faut, dans le royaume, autour du roi et de ses vassaux, que règne la paix. Que la violence soit dirigée exclusivement contre les ennemis de Dieu.

En 1095, à Clermont, le moine clunisien Eudes de Châtillon, devenu le pape Urbain II, préside un concile de paix pour toute la chrétienté.

Les hommes de guerre, les princes et les chevaliers doivent veiller à la faire respecter. Et à protéger les chrétiens qui désirent se rendre à Jérusalem, au Saint-Sépulcre profané par les infidèles.

Il faut « délivrer » Jérusalem.

Le légat du pape, Adhémar de Monteil, évêque du Puy, va diriger cette « croisade » dont le projet s'impose peu à peu. Ainsi va se déverser sur la terre du Christ le trop-plein de chevaliers et d'hommes de guerre qui commencent à troubler la paix de Dieu en terre chrétienne.

Un religieux, Pierre l'Ermite, va prêcher les pauvres, les laïques qui ne sont pas gens de guerre, pour qu'ils se joignent au comte de Flandre, au duc de Normandie, au duc de Basse-Lotharingie, Godefroi de Bouillon, qui partent avec leurs chevaliers.

La croisade est l'affaire de toute la chrétienté. Ainsi, parmi les princes, chevauche Hugues de Vermandois, frère de Philippe Ier, roi de France.

L'âme française et son royaume sont inséparables, dès le XIe siècle, des destinées de l'ensemble de la chrétienté.

10.

L'an mil et les inquiétudes du xiᵉ siècle s'éloignent. Quand ce siècle s'achève, qui se souvient encore des prophéties de l'Apocalypse ?

Durant les règnes de Louis VI (1108-1137) et de son fils Louis VII (1137-1180), le royaume de France s'épanouit.

Le xiiᵉ siècle est, pour la France, comme une adolescence vigoureuse, quand s'affermissent les traits du visage et ceux du caractère, annonçant la personnalité et l'âme de l'âge adulte.

L'essor de Paris, qui devient capitale de fait, symbolise ce développement d'un royaume dont le nombre des habitants s'accroît.

Ils défrichent. Les clairières, les cultures, s'étendent au détriment des forêts.

Ils se déplacent le long des routes des grands pèlerinages. La moitié des chevaliers du royaume partent en croisade en Terre sainte (Jérusalem a été conquise en 1099) ou en Espagne. Les marchands vont d'une foire à l'autre. Celles de Champagne (Troyes, Bar-sur-Aube) et de Brie sont fréquentées par des Italiens, des Flamands, des Catalans.

Même si ces centres d'échanges et ces voies commerciales sont situés aux marges orientales du royaume de France, celui-ci ne reste pas à l'écart, car Paris est devenue la ville unique qui attire marchands, visiteurs, « étudiants » de tout le royaume et du reste de l'Europe.

« Elle est assise au sein d'un vallon délicieux, au centre d'une couronne de côteaux qu'enrichissent à l'envi Cérès et Bacchus, écrit Gui de Bazoches. La Seine, ce fleuve superbe qui vient de l'Orient, y coule à pleins bords et entoure de ses deux bras une île qui est la tête, le cœur, la moelle de la ville entière. Deux faubourgs s'étendent à droite et à gauche, dont le moins grand ferait encore l'envie de bien des cités. Chacun de ces faubourgs communique avec l'île par deux ponts de pierre. Le Grand Pont, tourné au nord [...], est le théâtre d'une activité bouillonnante, d'innombrables bateaux l'entourent, remplis de marchandises et de richesses. Le Petit Pont appartient aux dialecticiens qui s'y promènent en discutant. Dans l'île, à côté du palais des Rois qui domine toute la ville, on voit le palais de la Philosophie où l'étude règne seule en souveraine, citadelle de lumière et d'immortalité. »

Entouré de forêts giboyeuses – pour le plaisir des rois et des chevaliers –, Paris acquiert ainsi une prépondérance absolue sur tout le royaume.

La ville de sainte Geneviève et de Clovis, voisine de l'abbaye de Saint-Denis, où l'abbé Suger fait construire une basilique imposante, verra bientôt se dresser le chœur de la cathédrale Notre-Dame (1163), puis sa nef (1180). Les « écoles » s'y multiplient.

Le maître Pierre Abélard s'installe sur la rive gauche, sur la montagne Sainte-Geneviève, donnant ainsi naissance à un « Quartier latin » qui est l'un des visages de la ville. Il est le premier « professeur », celui qui veut concilier foi et raison : « N'emploie jamais la contrainte pour amener ton prochain à la croyance qui est la tienne, dit-il. C'est par ses lumières seules que l'esprit humain doit se déterminer. En vain essaieras-tu d'obtenir violemment une adhésion mensongère ; la foi ne vient pas de la force mais de la raison. »

Un débat s'engage : contre Paris, contre la raison, pour la « Sainte Ignorance », la mystique, la prière, la contemplation.

Bernard de Clairvaux – saint Bernard, fondateur de l'abbaye de Clairvaux, âme de l'ordre cistercien qui sème dans tout le

royaume et en Europe les « filles » de l'abbaye mère, et qui
« fait » les papes –, exhorte professeurs et étudiants : « Fuyez du
milieu de Babylone, fuyez et sauvez vos âmes ! » Il faut s'enfer-
mer dans la solitude des monastères : « Vivre dans la grâce pour
le présent, et attendre avec confiance l'avenir. » « Tu trouveras
plus dans les forêts que dans les livres. Les bois et les pierres
t'apprendront plus que n'importe quel maître. »

Cette « dispute » – c'est saint Bernard qui l'emportera ;
Abélard, condamné, sera contraint de se retirer dans une dépendance de l'abbaye de Cluny – fait de Paris le centre intellectuel
non seulement du royaume de France, mais de l'ensemble de
l'Europe chrétienne. Dès ce XIIe siècle, Paris est bien cette cité
de lumière et d'immortalité qu'elle demeurera au fil du temps.

Mais, en fait, c'est tout le royaume de France qui devient le
lieu où s'élaborent les idées, les controverses, les tendances,
les formes qui vont ensuite se répandre d'un bout à l'autre de
l'Europe chrétienne.

La France est un creuset. Elle concentre, elle transmute, elle
invente, elle diffuse, elle rayonne.

Les abbayes cisterciennes essaiment à partir de Cîteaux et de
Clairvaux dans toute l'Europe.

« Regardez les arbres de la forêt, dit saint Bernard. Notre ordre
cistercien est comme le plus puissant d'entre eux. Il y a le tronc,
c'est notre abbaye de Cîteaux, et quatre branches maîtresses, les
premières filles : Morimond, La Ferté, Pontigny, Clairvaux. Chacune d'elles, dont Clairvaux la plus puissante, a donné à son tour
naissance à d'autres. L'ordre est comme un arbre qui se ramifie ;
de chaque branche surgit un nouveau rameau et toutes montent,
verticales, vers le ciel. »

C'est saint Bernard qui, au concile de Troyes, en 1129, rédige
les règles des Templiers, ces chevaliers chargés de la défense
des pèlerins en Terre sainte.

Ils sont des moines-soldats qui ne craignent ni de pécher en
tuant des ennemis, ni de se trouver en danger d'être tués eux-
mêmes. C'est pour le Christ, en effet, qu'ils donnent la mort ou

qu'ils la reçoivent ; ils ne commettent ainsi aucun crime et méritent une gloire surabondante. S'ils tuent, c'est pour le Christ ; s'ils meurent, le Christ est en eux.

C'est saint Bernard encore qui, en Aquitaine, tente d'empêcher que se développe l'hérésie cathare qui voit des chrétiens rechercher la « perfection », entrer en contact direct – sans l'intermédiaire de l'Église – avec le Christ. Ils conçoivent la vie comme une lutte implacable entre le Bien et le Mal. Eux veulent être des « Parfaits ».

Ainsi, c'est sur la terre du royaume de France que naissent aussi bien les orientations majeures de l'Église que les hérésies.

Et c'est encore saint Bernard qui prêche la croisade à Vézelay en 1146 : « « Dieu le veut, et son souverain pontife sur cette terre nous le commande : emparons-nous pour toujours du Saint-Sépulcre ! »

Le pape Eugène III a été moine cistercien, et le roi Louis VII rejoint les croisés, laissant la régence du royaume à l'abbé de Saint-Denis, Suger.

Le royaume de France est bien le lieu d'où partent, en ce XIIe siècle, les impulsions qui orientent le destin de la chrétienté.

Le royaume a été le berceau de l'art cistercien aux fortes colonnes, aux voûtes puissantes, à l'austérité de la pierre nue, et chaque abbaye en Europe se modèle sur celles de Sénanque ou du Thoronet.

Et, de même, c'est en Ile-de-France, à Sens (1140), à Chartres (1145-1155), à Senlis (1155), à Noyon (1151), à Laon (1155-1160), à Paris (1163-1180), que les cathédrales « gothiques », avec leur croisées d'ogives, leurs vitraux, leurs nefs inondées de lumière, lancent leurs flèches verticales vers le ciel.

Le XIIe siècle voit ainsi l'âme française être l'une des sources prééminentes de l'Europe.

C'est l'abbé de Cluny, Pierre le Vénérable, qui réunit autour de lui des chrétiens espagnols qui ont vécu sous la domination musulmane. En ces temps de croisade, il veut entreprendre la traduction du Coran.

« Qu'on donne, écrit-il, à l'erreur mahométane le nom honteux d'hérésie ou celui, infâme, de paganisme. Il faut agir contre elle, c'est-à-dire écrire. »

Il ajoute : « Pour que la fidélité de la traduction soit entière et qu'aucune erreur ne vienne fausser la plénitude de notre compréhension, aux traducteurs chrétiens j'en ai adjoint un, sarrasin. »

Le royaume de France est ainsi à l'avant-garde : c'est sur son sol que la raison et la connaissance sont au travail et que l'âme française se nourrit de cette ouverture aux autres, afin de comprendre ce « qui a permis à ce poison mortel d'infester plus de la moitié du globe ».

Au XIIᵉ siècle, le royaume de France est celui du mouvement, du débat intellectuel, du changement. Ce climat modifie les habitudes, les comportements.

La femme, oubliée du monde féodal du XIᵉ siècle, est redécouverte en même temps que se répand le culte de Notre Dame, de sainte Madeleine.

C'est dans le sud de la France, en Guyenne, en Gascogne, qu'on commence à la chanter, à dresser pour elle les autels de l'amour courtois qu'exaltent les troubadours.

La reine Aliénor d'Aquitaine, un temps épouse de Louis VII (de 1137 à 1152), encourage cette évolution, en même temps que son remariage avec Henri Plantagenêt – qui est à la tête d'un domaine angevin et roi d'Angleterre – représente une menace pour le royaume de France.

Sur ses flancs ouest et sud, la présence « anglaise » obscurcit l'avenir.

Mais Louis VII, tout en proclamant la « paix du roi » pour dix ans dans tout le royaume (1155), ne cède rien aux Plantagenêts.

C'est que s'est lentement affirmé un « amour de la France » comme germe du patriotisme, comme l'un des traits majeurs de l'âme du royaume.

À la fin du XIᵉ siècle, un clerc d'Avranches a composé la première chanson de geste, 4 002 vers dans une langue qui se dégage du latin à la façon dont se brise la coquille d'un œuf.

En vers de dix pieds, le clerc raconte l'histoire du neveu de Charlemagne qui commandait l'arrière-garde de l'empereur et qui tombe, le 15 août 778, dans une embuscade tendue par les Basques – alliés des Sarrasins – à Roncevaux.

Cette *Chanson de Roland* évoque le chevalier blessé qui se soucie de ne pas laisser son glaive entre des mains ennemies.

Puisse jamais ne t'avoir un homme capable de couardise
Dieu, ne permettez pas que la France ait cette honte !

Et le poète d'ajouter :

Il vaut mieux mourir
À honneur qu'à honte vivre...
....
Que jamais de France ne sorte
La gloire qui s'y est arrêtée.

Et le « comte Roland, étendu sous un pin, la face tournée vers l'Espagne, sent que la mort l'envahit : de la tête elle gagne le cœur... Il se met à se resouvenir de bien des choses, de toutes les terres qu'il a conquises, de la douce France »...

Le royaume de France n'est plus seulement le domaine personnel des Capétiens.

Il est la « douce France », qui appartient à tous ceux, chevaliers, clercs, poètes, manants, qui la peuplent et qui l'aiment.

Tous font vivre et se partagent l'âme de cette « douce France ».

11.

Le roi Philippe Auguste, qui hérite à la mort de son père Louis VII de la « douce France », et qui va régner d'un siècle à l'autre (1180-1223), quarante-trois ans, ne veut plus se nommer « roi des Francs », comme c'était encore l'usage pour les premiers Capétiens.

Il est le « roi de France ».

Et ce changement de titulature dit son ambition, la conscience qu'il a de n'être plus seulement le suzerain de grands vassaux, le maître d'un domaine royal, mais celui de tout un peuple qui commence à faire « nation ».

Le chanoine de Saint-Martin de Tours qui brosse son portrait écrit : « Beau et bien bâti, chauve, d'un visage respirant la joie de vivre, le teint rubicond, il aimait le vin et la bonne chère, et il était porté sur les femmes. Généreux envers ses amis, il convoitait les biens des adversaires et il était très expert dans l'art de l'intrigue... Il réprimait la malignité des Grands du royaume et provoquait leurs discordes, mais il ne mit jamais à mort nul qui fût en prison. Recourant au conseil des humbles, il n'éprouvait de haine pour personne, sinon un court moment, et il se montra le dompteur des superbes, le défenseur de l'Église et le nourrisseur des pauvres. »

Sur le socle construit par ses prédécesseurs, il bâtit un État. Et tout au long de son règne prolongé par celui de son fils Louis VIII (1223-1226), avec l'aide de ses baillis, de ses prévôts, de ses sénéchaux, il agglomère autour du domaine royal de nouveaux territoires. Il domine les grands vassaux de la Flandre, de la Champagne, de la Bourgogne. Au mitan du XIIIe siècle, le royaume aura atteint la Manche, l'Atlantique et la Méditerranée.

C'est la France, et le pape Innocent III reconnaît qu'aucune autre autorité temporelle en ce monde n'est supérieure à celle de son roi.

Ainsi, en ces cinquante années qui terminent le XIIe siècle et commencent le XIIIe, la France s'est-elle imposée comme la grande puissance continentale.

Elle est riche d'hommes, chevaliers, marchands, paysans. Elle a les fleuves et les routes pour le transport des marchandises qui vont et viennent du sud au nord. Le roi lève les impôts, et, quand il le juge bon, il pressure, menace, expulse, rouvre ses portes aux juifs, manieurs et prêteurs d'argent. C'est le commandeur de l'ordre du Temple, Aimard, qui gère la trésorerie du roi. Les Templiers, présents en Terre sainte et dans toute l'Europe, assurent les transferts de fonds. On tient des comptes précis. On dispose d'archives. Une administration se met ainsi en place à Paris.

C'est la plus grande ville d'Occident (50 000 habitants). Philippe Auguste la protège par une enceinte fortifiée. Deux grandes voies pavées – Saint-Martin et Saint-Denis – la parcourent sur la rive droite de la Seine. La rue Saint-Jacques, reprenant le tracé de la voie romaine, gravit sur la rive gauche la montage Sainte-Geneviève. La ville s'étend. Les vignes reculent. L'Université conquiert des privilèges (1215), un statut qui, entre le pape et le roi, lui assurent son indépendance.

Paris révèle la puissance du roi. Dans la tour du Louvre, on enferme les trésors et les prisonniers. Dans le donjon du Temple, on entasse les coffres emplis d'argent. Qui douterait que le souverain qui dispose d'une telle capitale ne soit le plus grand ? Il peut acheter des alliés, corrompre des adversaires, garder sur pied une armée de deux à trois mille hommes, noyau autour duquel s'agrègent, en cas de besoin, des mercenaires, des routiers, des soudards, des « cotteraux » qui ne sont plus des chevaliers, mais des hommes d'armes aguerris, sergents et arbalétriers montés, fantassins.

Ainsi se constitue un pouvoir d'État disposant d'une administration, avec ses hommes et ses rouages, d'une « diplomatie », d'une force militaire capable de briser les résistances que peut rencontrer le roi de France dans ses désirs de conquête.

Le pape lui-même est contraint de composer avec ce souverain.

Quand il prononce en 1198 l'interdit du royaume pour punir Philippe Auguste d'avoir voulu répudier son épouse, cette sanction, qui prive tout un peuple des sacrements, est de peu d'effet. Le pape doit négocier, lever l'interdit (1200).

La puissance capétienne peut ainsi se déployer, et le royaume de France, se dilater jusqu'aux rives des mers qui bordent l'Hexagone.

C'est une longue entreprise où les alliances, les guerres, les trêves, les mariages, s'entremêlent.

L'avancée capétienne se fait en direction de la Flandre, au nord.

Elle vise le Languedoc et le comté de Toulouse au sud, là où, malgré les prêches des Cisterciens et des Dominicains – ordre créé en 1215 –, l'hérésie cathare s'est enracinée.

À l'ouest (de la Normandie à la Guyenne, de la Seine à la Loire et à la Garonne), le roi de France se heurte au roi d'Angleterre Henri II Plantagenêt et à ses fils Richard et Jean.

À l'est, il lui faut se mesurer à l'empire germanique d'Otton IV.

C'est encore et toujours la situation géopolitique de la France qui suscite les convoitises de l'Angleterre et de l'Allemagne, parce qu'elle est un môle qui peut empêcher la domination ou de l'Anglais ou du Germain.

L'âme de la France se forge dans ces confrontations qui, pacifiques ou guerrières, naissent de la situation géographique et des intérêts contradictoires qu'elle génère. Dans ces quatre directions

– nord, ouest, est, sud –, en un demi-siècle, le roi de France l'emporte.

L'Artois, le Valois, le Vermandois, l'Amiénois, sont acquis par le mariage avec Isabelle de Hainaut, qui descend en ligne directe des Carolingiens.

Et le Capétien peut ainsi se présenter en héritier de l'empereur Charlemagne.

À l'ouest, il faut briser la puissance anglo-angevine et aquitaine, lutter contre Richard Cœur de Lion et Jean sans Terre. La mort de Richard en 1199 facilite la tâche. Mais la guerre – avec des intervalles de paix – dure près de vingt ans. Combats difficiles, impitoyables. Ce ne sont plus seulement des chevaliers qui s'affrontent dans une guerre « réglée », mais des « routiers », des « soudards », des « cottereaux », des mercenaires qui égorgent les prisonniers. Les forts construits par les Anglo-Aquitains sont conquis (ainsi, en 1204, Château-Gaillard, censé protéger Rouen).

Jean sans Terre et ses troupes sont mis en fuite à La Roche-aux-Moines, le 2 juillet 1214.

La Normandie, l'Anjou et la Touraine passent aux mains du roi de France.

Année et mois de victoire ! Au nord, vingt-cinq jours plus tard, le dimanche 27 juillet 1214, à Bouvines, les troupes de Philippe Auguste écrasent celles d'une coalition regroupant l'empereur Otton IV, Jean sans Terre et de grands féodaux.

Ce dimanche de Bouvines est le jour de l'irruption éclatante de la nation. Les chroniqueurs exaltent les « fils de France » « à la bouillante valeur » qui « n'hésitent jamais à braver toute sorte de dangers ».

En face d'eux, il y a « ces fils d'Angleterre que les plaisirs de la débauche et les dons de Bacchus attachent avec plus de charmes que les présents de Mars ». Il y a surtout les « Teutons ».

D'un côté, des combattants « issus de parents français » (« Vous, enfants de la Gaule, vous combattez toujours à cheval ! »), de l'autre, les Germains sont des fantassins redoutables mais sans noblesse de cœur !

L'âme française se trempe à Bouvines en s'opposant, en construisant un mythe, en célébrant une victoire qui n'est plus seulement celle du roi, mais celle de tout un peuple : « Dans tout le royaume, on n'entend partout qu'un applaudissement ; toute condition, toute fortune, toute profession, tout sexe, tout âge chantent les mêmes rythmes d'allégresse... Les innombrables danses des gens du peuple, les chants suaves des clercs, les sanctuaires parés au-dedans comme au-dehors, les rues, les maisons, les routes, dans tous les villages et dans toutes les villes, tendues de courtines et d'étoles de soie, tapissées de fleurs, d'herbe et de feuillage vert... Ceci se passa sur la route jusqu'à ce qu'on fût arrivé à Paris. Les bourgeois parisiens et par-dessus tout la multitude des étudiants, le clergé et le peuple allaient au-devant du roi, chantant des hymnes et des cantiques... Durant toute la nuit, les cierges ne cessent de briller dans les mains de tout le monde, chassant les ténèbres, de telle sorte que la nuit, se trouvant subitement transformée en jour et resplendissant de tant d'éclats et de lumières, dit aux étoiles et à la lune : Je ne vous dois rien ! Tant le seul amour du roi portait les peuples à se livrer aux transports de leur joie dans tous les villages... »

L'âme de la France naît de cette représentation d'un peuple uni autour de son souverain, de cette fusion de tous et de cette ville capitale, Paris, qui l'exprime.

Ce mouvement magnifié – rêvé pour une bonne part – renforce le pouvoir royal.

Le roi soutient les seigneurs et les moines cisterciens qui ont conduit la croisade contre les terres et les villes opulentes du Languedoc, ces populations converties à l'hérésie cathare.

Simon de Montfort et l'abbé de Cîteaux, Amalric, organisent la conquête, massacrent et pillent (sac de Béziers en 1209).

Le roi d'Aragon, venu au secours de Raymond VI de Toulouse, son vassal, est battu à Muret (1213). Louis, le fils de

Philippe Auguste, cueille ces territoires et massacre à son tour (Marmande, 1218).

Roi en 1223, il apportera au royaume de France le Poitou et la Saintonge, La Rochelle et Avignon.

Le royaume de France atteint désormais la Méditerranée.

Le Nord a conquis les peuples du Sud.

En 1244, l'hérésie cathare brûle avec Montségur.

L'âme de la France se nourrit aussi de la cruelle violence de l'État.

Le peuple de France – et d'abord celui du Sud – ne l'oubliera pas.

12.

L'enfant de douze ans qui, en 1226, devient le roi Louis IX, sait que son royaume de France est, avec ses 13 millions d'habitants, le plus peuplé, le plus puissant, le plus riche, le plus influent de la chrétienté.

Il a vu son grand-père Philippe Auguste et son père Louis VIII gouverner, repousser et vaincre les Anglais et les Impériaux.

Il est entouré de leurs conseillers, de leurs évêques, de leurs chapelains, et sa mère Blanche de Castille exerce la régence avec autorité.

L'État, avec ses agents, sa monnaie, ses prévôts – le plus important est celui de Paris, qui siège au Châtelet –, a déjà sa vie propre, même quand le roi est un enfant ou bien quand, plus tard, en 1249, Louis IX partira en croisade, sera fait prisonnier et restera hors de France pendant près de cinq années.

Louis dira à ses proches, conseillers, laïques et clercs : « Gardez-vous de croire que le salut de l'Église et de l'État réside en ma personne. Vous êtes vous-mêmes l'État et l'Église ! »

Humilité d'un souverain qui veut être l'incarnation du roi chrétien idéal et qui, promulguant une Grande Ordonnance (1254), déclare :

« Du devoir de la royale puissance nous voulons moult de cœur la paix et le repos de nos sujets... et avons grande indignation encontre ceux qui injures leur font et qui ont envie de leur paix et leur tranquillité. »

Au fur et à mesure que son règne se déroule – il durera quarante-quatre ans, de 1226 à 1270, faisant de ce XIIIᵉ siècle le siècle de Saint Louis, puisque Louis IX est canonisé en 1297 par le pape Boniface VIII –, sa grande et maigre silhouette semble s'affiner encore dans une austérité mystique, comme s'il voulait mieux exprimer l'essence de la monarchie française, chrétienne en son principe fondateur.

« Le Roi, dit Joinville, son conseiller et biographe, se maintint si dévotement que jamais plus il ne porta ni vair ni petit-gris, ni écarlate, ni étriers ou éperons dorés. Ses vêtements étaient de camelin ou de drap bleu-noir. Les fourrures de ses couvertures et de ses robes étaient de peaux de daims ou de pattes de lièvres. Il était si sobre qu'il ne choisissait jamais sa nourriture. »

Ainsi, dans l'âme française, le souverain, déjà placé au-dessus des hommes par le sacre, devient-il aussi l'homme qui doit – audelà de la politique qu'il mène – incarner la piété, le souci de la justice et de la paix pour ses sujets.

Il n'est pas seulement respecté, vénéré ou craint. Il est aimé pour ses vertus. Il est « saint » avant même d'être canonisé.

Et quand, en 1228, le jeune roi de quatorze ans, pour éviter d'être enlevé par des grands qui veulent ainsi prendre barre sur lui, se réfugie, rentrant d'Orléans, derrière l'enceinte fortifiée de Montlhéry, les milices communales de Paris et d'Ile-de-France, les chevaliers du domaine royal, le délivrent, et le peuple en cortège lui souhaite longue vie en le reconduisant dans sa capitale, Paris.

La vie exemplaire de Louis IX, l'amour de son peuple, le rayonnement de Paris, la puissance de l'État, tout concourt alors à faire du royaume de France et de son roi les acteurs majeurs de la chrétienté.

C'est dans cette source rayonnante du XIIIᵉ siècle que s'épanouit l'âme de la France en sa singularité.

Il y a en effet une exception française qui s'affirme au XIIIᵉ siècle.

La vigueur et l'attrait de l'université parisienne – qui compte 5 000 étudiants, et Thomas d'Aquin est l'un d'eux –, de celles de Montpellier, de Toulouse, d'Orléans, d'Angers, font de la France le centre intellectuel de la chrétienté. Chaque « nation » d'Europe fonde son collège sur la montagne Sainte-Geneviève. En 1257, le chapelain de Louis IX, Robert de Sorbon, crée un collège destiné aux clercs séculiers, boursiers. Ces étudiants veulent voir confirmer leur autonomie universitaire. Ils cessent de suivre leurs cours (1299) et obtiennent qu'un droit de grève leur soit reconnu. Le pape garantit ces droits.

Dans le royaume de France, joyau de la chrétienté, le nombre de cardinaux passe de deux à huit. Mesure de l'influence de la France, le pape Urbain IV, élu en 1261, est un Champenois, et en 1265 c'est un Provençal, conseiller de Louis IX, qui devient pape sous le nom de Clément IV.

Cependant, le souverain de France – le roi aux fleurs de lis, emblème peut-être lié au culte marial – ne s'interdit pas de résister aux pressions de la papauté.

Une fusion intime s'opère néanmoins entre l'Église et la monarchie française.

L'abbaye du Mont-Saint-Michel, le monastère de Royaumont, l'abbaye de Maubuisson et la Sainte-Chapelle – qui contient les reliques de la Passion, un morceau de la vraie croix et la couronne du Christ – témoignent de la volonté du roi – il suscite les initiatives, finance les travaux – d'élever des chefs-d'œuvre à la gloire du Christ.

Les dernières flèches des cathédrales se dressent, et le sourire de Reims, et le Bon Dieu d'Amiens, expriment dans la pierre la foi de toute une société que magnifie la piété du roi.

Celui-ci part pour la Terre sainte. Son long emprisonnement en Orient (de 1249 à 1254) exalte sa foi. Après sa libération, lors de son débarquement à Hyères, il s'entretient avec un moine cordelier qui lui dit : « Or prenne garde le roi, puisqu'il va en France, à faire si bien justice à son peuple qu'il en conserve l'amour de Dieu et que Dieu ne lui ôte pas, pour la vie, le royaume de France. »

On saisit le lien – au XIIIe siècle, c'est une spécificité française – entre la foi exigeante et les mesures que le monarque met en œuvre. Il se veut *Rex Pacificus*, signant des traités avec le roi d'Aragon Jean Ier ou le roi d'Angleterre Henri III. Il n'utilise pas la puissance du royaume pour imposer par la guerre ses solutions.

De même, ses Grandes Ordonnances veillent à ce que les pouvoirs s'exercent avec équité. Le chêne de Vincennes, au pied duquel le roi rend la justice, en est le symbole.

Il vise à une politique « vertueuse ».

Il dit dans l'ordonnance de 1254 : « Que tous nos baillis, vicomtes, prévôts, maires et tous autres, en quelque affaire que ce soit, fassent serment qu'ils feront droit à chacun sans exception de personne, aussi bien aux pauvres qu'aux riches et à l'étranger qu'à l'homme du pays ; et ils garderont les us et coutumes qui sont bons et éprouvés, [sinon] qu'ils en soient punis en leurs biens et en leurs personnes si le méfait le requiert. »

Oui, exception française, au XIIIe siècle, que cette moralisation de l'action politique !

Cette volonté est fondée sur la foi, sur le refus du péché et sur la crainte du blasphème qui habitent Louis IX.

« Vous devez savoir qu'il n'y a pas de lèpre aussi laide que d'être en péché mortel, dit-il. Je vous prie de préférer que toutes les infortunes arrivent à votre corps, lèpre ou toute autre maladie, plutôt que le péché mortel advienne à votre âme. »

Mais alors, il faut poursuivre ceux qui sont en état de péché.

D'abord les hérétiques (massacre des cathares à Montségur), et le royaume de France sera terre d'Inquisition.

On enterre vivant. On brûle (en mai 1239, dix-huit hérétiques sont voués aux flammes au Mont-Aimé, en Champagne). En 1242, dans un grand autodafé, on brûle vingt charretées de livres talmudiques.

Il faut que « tous les juifs vivent du labeur de leurs mains ou des autres besognes qui ne comportent pas d'usure ». En 1269, on exige qu'ils portent sur leurs vêtements un signe permettant de les reconnaître. On les dénonce parce qu'ils « font circuler sous le nom de Talmud des livres emplis de blasphèmes et d'injures contre le Christ, la Vierge, les chrétiens et Dieu même ».

Certes, Lombards, Cahorsins, chrétiens qui se livrent à l'usure, sont condamnés eux-mêmes au bannissement. Mais l'antijudaïsme chrétien de Louis IX est un fait. Et il pénètre l'âme française avec d'autant plus de virulence que le roi et son royaume sont l'expression la plus achevée – et les modèles – de la chrétienté.

Louis IX est déjà le Roi Très-Chrétien quand, en 1270, il embarque une seconde fois à Aigues-Mortes – port qu'il a fait construire – pour la Terre sainte.

Il s'arrêtera à Tunis et y mourra le 25 août 1270 après avoir vu s'éteindre son fils cadet. Et c'est son aîné, Philippe III le Hardi, qui lui succédera.

Cette mort en croisé fait de lui une figure sacrée de la chrétienté, l'image pieuse de ce royaume qui a vu aussi l'épanouissement de l'art gothique, la gloire de l'université de Paris, le prestige de la langue française illustrée par un Jean de Meung – deuxième partie du *Roman de la Rose* – et les œuvres de Rutebeuf – *Renart le Bestourné*.

Quelques années avant de se croiser (en 1267), Louis IX avait voulu procéder à la réorganisation de la basilique de Saint-Denis afin qu'on pût lire dans l'agencement des tombeaux l'histoire de la dynastie du royaume de France.

Ce nouvel ordonnancement, cette réécriture de l'histoire, plaçant dans la partie sud de la nef les Mérovingiens et les Carolingiens, au nord les Capétiens, et, entre ces deux rangées, Philippe Auguste et Louis VIII, qui appartenaient aux deux lignées – ils descendaient à la fois, affirmaient les généalogistes, de Charlemagne et d'Hugues Capet –, étaient une manière d'incarner la glorieuse continuité de la royauté française.

Ces gisants conduisent à Louis IX, dont la sainteté exprime l'essence de ce royaume.

L'âme de la France en reçoit la grâce.

Louis est saint.

« Mais, dit son chroniqueur Joinville, on n'en fit pas assez quand on ne le mit pas au nombre des martyrs pour les grandes peines qu'il souffrit au pèlerinage de la Croix, et aussi parce qu'il suivit Notre Seigneur dans le haut fait de la Croix. Car si Dieu mourut sur la Croix, il fit de même, car il était croisé quand il mourut à Tunis. »

Le roi de France n'est pas seulement saint, mais martyr.

Comment certains n'imagineraient-ils pas, après un tel apogée, que la France est promise à un destin exceptionnel, qu'elle est une nation sainte ?

« J'ai d'instinct l'impression que la Providence l'a créée pour des succès achevés ou des malheurs exemplaires », écrira de Gaulle.

13.

Saint Louis, le roi martyr, le Roi Christ, aura régné quarante-quatre années. À eux tous, ses cinq successeurs – les derniers Capétiens en ligne directe – n'auront, de 1270 à 1328, gouverné le royaume de France que durant cinquante-huit ans.

Mais c'est comme si peu importaient désormais la durée de chaque règne, et même la personnalité de chacun des souverains. Il y a pourtant bien des différences entre le fils de Saint Louis, Philippe III le Hardi – qui règne quinze ans : 1270-1285 –, son petit-fils Philippe IV le Bel (1285-1314 : vingt-neuf ans de règne), et les fils de ce dernier, Louis X le Hutin (1314-1316), Philippe V le Long (1316-1322) et Charles IV le Bel (1322-1328), auquel succédera Philippe de Valois.

Ce que Saint Louis a légué, c'est l'idée que la royauté française est au-dessus de tout.

« Dans toute la chrétienté, le roi de France n'a jamais d'égal », dit un chroniqueur italien.

La couronne royale transcende toutes les circonstances, toutes les personnalités. La canonisation de Louis IX a exalté le sacre qui déjà plaçait le souverain au-dessus des simples mortels.

Les rois de France sont de la lignée d'un saint.

« Grand déshonneur à ceux de son lignage qui voudront mal faire, dit Joinville, car on les montrera du doigt et on dira que le Saint Roi dont ils sont issus eût répugné à faire une telle méchanceté. »

En fait, le grand manteau bleu à fleurs de lis d'or de Saint Louis les protège.

Ils font de son corps, qu'ils fractionnent, des reliques.

En présence de Philippe le Bel, les ossements de Saint Louis sont placés en 1298 dans une châsse d'or derrière l'autel de l'abbaye de Saint-Denis. En 1306, Philippe le Bel obtiendra que la tête du Saint Roi soit transférée à la Sainte-Chapelle. Mais on laissera le menton, la mâchoire et les dents aux moines de Saint-Denis.

Puis on fragmentera le squelette pour offrir des reliques à tel ou tel souverain, à tel ou tel homme d'Église.

Une phalange du doigt de Saint Louis sera ainsi envoyée à un roi de Norvège...

Le roi de France bénéficie de l'immunité que lui confère son ascendance sainte. Mais il tire aussi son pouvoir de lui-même :

« Que veut le roi si veut la loi », disent les conseillers, les légistes qui forment autour de lui un groupe de plus en plus nombreux.

Ils sont membres des Chambres – la plus importante est la Chambre des comptes (1320) –, des Conseils.

Ils sont rassemblés dans le palais de l'île de la Cité, que Philippe le Bel agrandit et fortifie d'épais et hauts remparts.

Il fait édifier une immense salle à deux nefs enrichies par les statues des rois de France et qui est destinée aux avocats et à leurs clients.

Les services de juridiction criminelle sont installés dans les grosses tours. L'ensemble du « personnel » royal, de leurs familles et de leur domesticité représente près de 5 000 personnes, l'équivalent de la population d'une ville du royaume.

Personne – ni grands féodaux, ni étudiants ou professeurs, ni marchands ou moine prêcheurs – ne peut échapper à l'attraction de Paris, qui est la plus grande ville de la chrétienté avec – peut-être ? – 61 098 feux ou foyers fiscaux, soit plus de 200 000 personnes.

L'État centralisé, organisé, apprend à compter.

En 1328, une enquête sur l'état des feux les évalue pour tout le royaume à 2 469 987 répartis entre 23 671 paroisses, soit plus de 13 millions d'habitants.

Ainsi s'affirme l'un des traits constitutifs de l'histoire nationale : le pouvoir est centralisé à Paris.

Il enserre tout le territoire dans une « administration » dirigée de la capitale, du palais royal, où sont concentrés tous les rouages.

Le centre est le roi.

« Le roi est empereur en son royaume. » « Le roi ne tient son royaume que de son épée et de lui. » « Le roi ne tient de personne, sauf de Dieu et de lui. » Telle est la thèse des « conseillers », qui sont souvent des « gradués en droit » issus des universités de Toulouse, de Montpellier, d'Orléans et naturellement de celle de Paris.

Ces légistes sont avocats ou procureurs de la Couronne. Quelques-uns d'entre eux accéderont au Conseil du roi ou à la Chambre des comptes.

Ils annoncent une « haute administration ».

Les légistes les plus proches du roi (pour Philippe le Bel, Pierre Flotte, Guillaume de Nogaret, Enguerrand de Marigny) concentrent sur eux les accusations, les haines et le mépris dont on ne peut pas même concevoir d'accabler le roi.

> *Trahi êtes chacun le pense*
> *Par vos chevaliers de cuisine...*

écrit-on au souverain.

Et les barons, les féodaux qui subissent l'autorité royale s'indignent de la place tenue par ces

> *Petites gens parvenus*
> *Qui sont à la cour maîtres devenus*
> *Qui cousent, règnent et taillent*
> *Toutes les bonnes coutumes défaillent*
> *Justice désormais*
> *À la cour on ne nous rend jamais*

Serfs vilains avocassiers
Sont devenus empereurs.

Ces légistes, « boucs émissaires » jalousés, paient de leur vie leur pouvoir qu'une succession royale remet en cause.

En 1278, le chambellan de Saint Louis, Pierre de la Brice, est accusé et pendu au gibet de Montfaucon comme un détrousseur ou un crocheteur. Enguerrand de Marigny connaîtra le même sort en 1315.

Car l'État royal qui concentre, centralise le pouvoir, et dont le souverain n'a pas la même exigeante vertu, la même humilité que Saint Louis, peut se montrer une machine impitoyable.

Les cinq derniers rois capétiens ont d'abord poursuivi la politique d'élargissement de leur royaume.

Agenais, Poitou, Languedoc, Guyenne, Bourgogne – et la ville de Lyon – entrent dans le domaine royal.

Mais le Comtat Venaissin, avec Avignon, est « donné » au pape en vertu d'une promesse de Saint Louis.

Et au nord-est, en Flandre, le roi de France et ses chevaliers aux « éperons dorés » sont battus à Courtrai en 1302 par les fantassins des milices des villes drapières. La Flandre industrieuse, « bourgeoise » et « marchande », résiste ainsi à l'attraction capétienne.

La France trouve là une résistance qui ne cédera pas au cours du temps. C'est un autre « monde ».

Et pourtant la « machine royale » est puissante.

Elle fait reculer le pape Boniface VIII qui voulait que tous les chrétiens, y compris le roi de France, relèvent de sa justice (1296).

En convoquant à Notre-Dame en 1302 une assemblée de plus de mille délégués – clercs et laïques –, Philippe le Bel en appelle à la fidélité monarchique qui commence à prendre les couleurs du sentiment national. Et il ne craint pas d'envoyer Guillaume de Nogaret, son légiste, tenter de s'emparer, à Agnani, de Boniface VIII, qui mourra des suites de cet « attentat » (1303).

Pour défendre ou accroître leur pouvoir, faire respecter leur souveraineté, briser les résistances, obtenir les moyens qui leur sont nécessaires, l'État, le roi, ses légistes, sont prêts à toutes les violences.

On voit s'affirmer-là une raison d'État qui marque l'âme de la France et la structure.

Capable de faire plier la papauté, elle n'hésite pas à réprimer les émeutes, les insurrections populaires (à Provins, en 1280, lorsqu'on veut prolonger la durée du travail d'une heure sans augmentation), voire à manipuler la monnaie (1295) ou à créer de nouveaux impôts (la maltôte en 1290).

On confisque les biens des juifs (1306). Pour les condamner au bûcher et les spolier, on profite des rumeurs qui les accusent d'empoisonner les puits et de se liguer avec les lépreux, à l'instigation des musulmans, aux fins d'assassiner des chrétiens.

L'État étend son empire, se ramifie. Il a besoin de ressources. Il diminue la teneur en métal fin des monnaies, lève de nouveaux impôts. Et si on dresse en 1328 un état des feux, preuve de l'efficacité administrative de l'État, c'est d'abord pour des raisons fiscales.

L'argent et le pouvoir vont de concert.

De même, quand, à partir de 1307, Philippe le Bel s'attaque à l'ordre du Temple, c'est à la fois parce que cette organisation internationale échappe à son pouvoir, et peut même s'imposer à lui, et parce qu'elle est une puissance financière.

L'ordre est supprimé en 1312.

Par la torture et au cours d'un procès, il faut obtenir les aveux des maîtres de l'ordre. Mais Jacques de Molay et Geoffroy de Charnay, devant la foule rassemblée face à Notre-Dame, proclament leur innocence et la sainteté de l'ordre. Ils seront cependant livrés aux flammes le 18 mars 1314.

Procès politique organisé par un État pour qui la justice n'est qu'un instrument parmi d'autres servant à contrôler la « totalité » des activités du royaume.

La famille royale elle-même n'est pas préservée de cette violence. D'autant que – une punition, une malédiction, murmurent certains – aucun des trois fils de Philippe le Bel n'a d'héritier mâle.

Il faut donc se montrer impitoyable avec tous ceux qui, par leur comportement, peuvent mettre en cause la légitimité de la lignée royale.

Les accusées – donc les coupables – vont être les belles-filles de Philippe le Bel : elles ont commis le péché d'adultère ou en ont été témoins. Elles sont enfermées à Château-Gaillard. Leurs amants – deux jeunes chevaliers – sont châtrés et torturés à mort (1314).

Exemplarité archaïque du châtiment, violence de cet État qui mêle modernité et barbarie, religiosité et cynisme.

Le roi vénère les reliques de Saint Louis et n'a de comptes à rendre qu'à Dieu.

Vicaire du Christ, il est à l'abri de toute critique.

Son « absolutisme » croît parce que l'État qui se construit est plus efficace, donc plus redoutable.

Au moment où, en 1328, un Valois succède aux Capétiens, l'âme de la France, la tradition nationale, conjuguent dès ces XIIIe et XIVe siècles la cruauté et la sainteté, tendances contradictoires et complémentaires.

3

LE ROYAUME DÉVASTÉ ET RENAISSANT

1328-1515

14.

Le ciel s'obscurcit vite au-dessus du royaume de France lorsque meurt en 1314 Philippe IV le Bel.

Pourtant, la France est l'État le plus peuplé, le plus riche, le plus puissant de la chrétienté.

Aucune autorité temporelle, pas plus un autre roi que l'empereur germanique, ne peut imposer sa loi au roi de France, souverain de la fille aînée de l'Église.

Le pape lui-même n'y parvient pas.

Un Capétien est maître comme Dieu en son royaume.

Et il n'est pas une seule ville qui puisse rivaliser avec sa capitale.

Paris est la ville des étudiants et des clercs, des bourgeois, des marchands, des maîtres de métier et des théologiens.

Tous ceux qui pensent et écrivent en Europe – donc tous ceux qui prient – rêvent de séjourner quelques années à l'ombre de Notre-Dame et sur les pentes de la montagne Sainte-Geneviève, dans ce Quartier latin où l'on étudie et ripaille.

Et cependant l'orage approche, dont on entend les grondements. Aucun des trois fils de Philippe IV le Bel n'a eu de descendant mâle. Seule la fille du roi, Isabelle, a donné naissance à un fils ; mais il a été couronné roi d'Angleterre.

Cet Édouard III possède les terres immenses de Guyenne. Il est le descendant lointain de Henri Plantagenêt, l'Angevin, duc de Normandie, qui, en 1154, avait épousé Aliénor d'Aquitaine, devenant ainsi le grand vassal du roi de France, et roi d'Angleterre pouvant prétendre à la couronne à Paris.

Mais les légistes français argumentent. Ils sont déjà imprégnés de ce sentiment national qu'on a vu sourdre au XIIIᵉ siècle. Les barons, les princes, ne veulent pas, eux non plus, être soumis à l'Anglais.

Certes, dans les vignobles, sur les quais du port de Bordeaux, là où l'on charge dans les navires les barriques à destination de l'Angleterre, on soutient la prétention d'Édouard à être aussi roi de France, puisqu'il est le fils de la fille de Philippe IV le Bel.

Les légistes contestent la valeur de cette ascendance : « Mais, écrivent-ils, si le fils d'Isabelle avait quelque droit à alléguer, il tenait ce droit de sa mère ; or, à cause de son sexe, sa mère n'avait aucun droit. Il en allait donc de même du fils. »

Le moine chroniqueur ajoute : « Les Français n'admettaient pas sans émotion l'idée d'être assujettis à l'Angleterre. »

On va donc sacrer à Reims, le 29 mai 1328, le comte de Valois, fils d'un des frères de Philippe IV le Bel. Et à sa mort, en 1350, lui succédera son fils, Jean le Bon.

La chaîne dynastique des Valois va se dérouler durant deux siècles et demi.

Mais qui peut croire qu'Édouard III acceptera, lui, roi d'Angleterre, d'être le vassal du roi de France alors qu'il se sent par le sang plus proche de Philippe le Bel que ce Valois sacré à Reims, célébré dans sa Cour, la plus brillante de la chrétienté ?

Qui peut croire qu'il ne trouvera pas d'alliés parmi ces barons et ces princes, français, certes, mais demeurés des féodaux que le poids d'une administration royale commence à irriter ? Ils se veulent vassaux, mais non sujets.

L'un d'eux, Charles de Navarre – Charles le Mauvais –, fils d'une petite-fille de Philippe le Bel, descend directement du roi capétien. Il faudra bien compter avec lui, qui possède Normandie, Picardie, Flandre, Champagne, Lorraine !

Et puisque s'exacerbent au sommet du royaume de telles rivalités, comment ces bourgeois de Paris, ces riches marchands que le fisc royal s'évertue à pressurer, ne joueraient-ils pas leur partie, se servant de l'un ou l'autre prétendant et des querelles entre rois pour acquérir puissance et influence ?

Ainsi s'annonce le temps des conflits, d'une guerre qui peut durer cent ans.

Il suffit de quelques années pour que le beau, le grand, le saint royaume de France soit dévasté.

Nul ne saurait l'envisager quand, après le sacre de Reims, Philippe VI de Valois préside, après avoir touché les écrouelles, les réjouissances. On y dévore 82 bœufs, 85 veaux, 289 moutons, 78 porcs, 13 chevaux ; on y met en perce des centaines de tonneaux de vin.

Trois mois plus tard, en août 1328, Philippe VI rétablit l'ordre dans les Flandres, terre de l'un de ses vassaux, et au mont Cassel, guidés par le roi, les chevaliers français, à coups d'estoc et de taille, massacrent les milices piétonnes des villes flamandes toujours rétives.

Point de quartier pour ces gens du commun, ces ouvriers tisserands !

Les barons et jusqu'à Édouard III sont enchantés de ce souverain de France, chevalier courageux, fidèle à l'ordre aristocratique.

En fait, cette victoire sur les « ongles bleus » flamands, cette tuerie de gueux qui, un temps, semble recréer l'unité de la chevalerie contre les marchands, les artisans, les ouvriers, les villes, ne peut effacer les contradictions.

Les rivalités entre grands, entre monarques, sont trop fortes, et, derrière elles, se profile le conflit entre deux nations qui s'affirment : la France et l'Angleterre.

Il suffit d'une dizaine d'années (1337-1347) pour que la guerre devienne la gangrène de ce XIVᵉ siècle. Elle le sera pour « cent ans ».

Philippe VI a voulu s'emparer de la Guyenne. Édouard évoque avec mépris un « soi-disant roi de France ». La flotte anglaise détruit la française, censée transporter les troupes pour l'invasion de l'Angleterre (bataille de L'Écluse, 24 juin 1340). À Crécy (26 août 1346), les archers anglais déciment la chevalerie française. Et le 4 août 1347, les bourgeois de Calais livrent les clés de leur ville à l'Anglais, qui s'en empare pour deux siècles.

Ainsi, un conflit aux origines dynastiques et féodales se transforme en guerre entre nations, chacune d'elles gardant la cicatrice de ces premiers affrontements qu'a suscités une naissance commune.

Le Français est le cousin de l'Anglais, et l'un et l'autre sont les plus anciens ennemis.

L'Anglais affirme sa supériorité militaire. Il détruit la flotte d'invasion – naissance d'une tradition ! Il tue méthodiquement les chevaliers français qui combattent comme autrefois et que le « soldat » anglais perce de ses flèches ou égorge au coutelas.

Face à l'Anglais, l'âme française éprouve un sentiment d'admiration et d'impuissance. Les Anglais l'emportent toujours. Après la mort de Philippe VI, en 1350, c'est son fils Jean le Bon qui, avec ses chevaliers, est battu à Poitiers en 1356, fait prisonnier, gardé à Londres, délivré contre forte rançon. Par le traité de Brétigny-Calais en 1360, il sera contraint d'abandonner à l'Anglais plus du tiers de son royaume avant d'aller mourir à Londres, où – noble chevalier – il est allé remplacer l'un de ses fils prisonnier, qui s'était enfui.

En dépit de la prise de possession par Philippe VI du Dauphiné (1343), de Montpellier (1349), puis de l'affirmation de la suzeraineté royale sur la Bourgogne, ce milieu du XIVe est, pour le royaume de France, un abîme où il s'enfonce.

Pour la toute jeune nation, c'est l'un de ces « malheurs exemplaires » qui blessent son âme et vont se répéter tout au long de son histoire.

Car le sol du royaume de France n'est pas seulement jonché des corps des chevaliers percés de flèches ou égorgés par les archers et les « routiers » anglais à Crécy puis à Poitiers. Les dix ans – 1346-1356 – qui séparent les deux défaites françaises voient s'amonceler les cadavres.

La peste noire a commencé de faucher en 1347-1348. Qu'elle soit bubonique ou pulmonaire, elle tue souvent un habitant sur deux, et la totalité de ceux de certains villages sont enfouis dans des fosses communes ou entassés sur des bûchers.

Au début du XIVᵉ siècle, la population du royaume était devenue si abondante que la disette – parfois la famine –, après des décennies de récoltes suffisantes, étaient réapparue.

La peste noire vide les campagnes sans faire disparaître la famine. Et les survivants tuent ceux qu'ils jugent responsables de l'épidémie.

On dit que les juifs empoisonnent les puits et les sources. On les traque et on les brûle. Ceux qui le peuvent se réfugient à Avignon, où le pape Clément VI les protège, excommuniant ceux qui les persécutent. Mais des milliers périssent, comme si l'épidémie de peste noire réveillait une autre maladie endémique, l'antijudaïsme, comme si celui-ci était caché au plus profond d'un repli de l'âme de la France et se tenait prêt à l'infester si les circonstances s'y prêtaient, s'il fallait désigner un bouc émissaire responsable des malheurs du temps.

Dans le désarroi et la terreur provoqués par la peste noire, des milliers de chrétiens se flagellent, « batteurs » fouettant leurs corps jusqu'au sang, zébrant leurs torses et leurs cuisses en hurlant, longues processions ensanglantées parcourant des campagnes appauvries.

D'autres paysans – ces « jacques » – affamés se rebellent. Quand la jacquerie devient menaçante, on la taille en pièces – ce que fait Charles le Mauvais en 1358, massacrant plus de vingt mille jacques après avoir, par traîtrise, capturé puis décapité le chef (Guillaume Carle, en Beauvaisis) que ces paysans se sont donné.

Sur fond de peste noire – et donc de « grande peur », comme on dira en 1789 –, de disette, de jacqueries – donc de violences – se met en place une « mécanique » sociale et politique qui caractérisera souvent l'histoire nationale.

Le pouvoir royal est affaibli : le Dauphin Charles, fils de Jean le Bon, réunit les états généraux (1357).

On voit surgir des « réformateurs » parmi lesquels s'imposent le prévôt des marchands de Paris, Étienne Marcel, l'évêque de Laon, Robert le Coq, du parti de Charles de Navarre.

Cet engrenage – querelles dynastiques, jacqueries, états généraux, volonté de réforme, rôle des « bourgeois » de Paris – « invente » un assemblage qui se recomposera à maintes reprises au cours de l'histoire de France.

À Paris, une foule en armes massacre les « mauvais conseillers » du roi (22 février 1358).

Étienne Marcel pénètre dans les appartements du Dauphin et ordonne la mise à mort des « maréchaux » de Champagne et de Normandie, qui incarnent la chevalerie incapable de remporter des victoires militaires contre les Anglais et opposée aux réformes.

Le Dauphin Charles assiste au massacre de ses proches, qu'il est contraint d'approuver. Étienne Marcel le prend alors sous sa protection, le coiffant d'un chaperon rouge et bleu, couleurs de la bourgeoisie parisienne !

On pense ici à Louis XVI qui, le 20 juin 1792, face aux sans-culottes qui ont envahi le palais des Tuileries, est contraint de « boire à la santé de la nation » et de coiffer le bonnet rouge. C'est comme si les émeutiers rejouaient, quatre siècles plus tard, la scène de février 1358 !

Les peuples ont une longue et fidèle mémoire. Les souvenirs jaillissent, ressuscitent des gestes inscrits dans l'inconscient collectif comme si, au cours des temps, s'était élaboré une génétique de la nation.

Ces mécanismes politiques et psychologiques vont s'inscrire dans l'âme de la France, où s'affirme le sentiment national.

Les partisans d'Étienne Marcel se retournent contre lui – en juillet 1358 – quand le prévôt des marchands, devenu l'allié de Charles le Mauvais, sera rendu responsable de l'entrée dans Paris de troupes anglaises.

Il est assassiné à la porte Saint-Antoine après que Jean Maillart, qui a été l'un de ses soutiens, a refusé de lui remettre la clé de la porte, et a fait au contraire appel au Dauphin, qui va pouvoir rentrer dans Paris.

On mesure ici combien la question « nationale » est intriquée avec les questions de politique « intérieure ».

Charles le Mauvais, rival du Dauphin, et Étienne Marcel, le réformateur, ont recours aux Anglais. Car ceux-ci sont certes des étrangers, mais aussi issus de la même origine « française ». Dès lors, rechercher leur appui, est-ce prendre le parti de l'étranger ? On peut d'autant plus se poser la question que le système féodal – vassalité – enserre encore le royaume.

Cependant, choisir l'Anglais pour allié, c'est déjà être, aux yeux de Français de plus en plus nombreux, du « parti de la trahison ».

Et c'est cette coalition des féodaux avec l'étranger, de Charles le Mauvais avec les Anglais, qui est défaite à Cocherel, le 16 mai 1364, par le capitaine breton Bertrand Du Guesclin.

Le Dauphin Charles, dont le père Jean le Bon vient de mourir prisonnier à Londres, peut sortir de Paris et se rendre à Reims pour s'y faire sacrer avec son épouse Jeanne de Bourbon, le 19 mai 1364.

L'abîme ne s'est pas refermé sur le royaume de France et ses souverains.

15.

En 1364, après l'avènement et le sacre de Charles V, le peuple espère que les souffrances, la disette, la peste noire, mais aussi ces compagnies de routiers, de soudards, de pillards, d'Anglais qui, entre deux batailles, écument le pays, vont s'éloigner.

Charles V n'est-il pas de « sainte lignée » ? Ne dit-il pas qu'il veut placer sa couronne sous la protection du « bienheureux Louis, fleur, honneur, bannière et miroir, non seulement de notre race royale, mais de tous les Français » ?

Il déclare que le roi « doit seigneurier au commun profit du peuple ». Il incarne la figure du souverain français tel qu'on le rêve, soucieux du sort de son peuple. Et donc ne le pressurant pas fiscalement, supprimant même certaines impositions – ce qui attire à lui les seigneurs gascons auxquels l'Anglais réclame des taxes. Un roi qui s'entoure d'hommes sages, légistes, professeurs, théologiens, lecteurs d'Aristote et de saint Thomas d'Aquin – Nicolas Oresme et Philippe de Mézières –, qui accumule dans une tour du Louvre plus de mille manuscrits, autant qu'en possède le pape. Et ses propagandistes écrivent, et on recopie leur *Traité du Sacre*, le *Songe du Vergier*, dans lesquels ils exaltent les caractères du monarque, mystique et divin, de la royauté française, tout en affirmant son indépendance vis-à-vis de la papauté.

Ce souverain-là ne veut conduire qu'une guerre victorieuse. Assez de Crécy et de Poitiers ! Ses chefs de guerre, Bertrand Du Guesclin et Olivier de Clisson, sont de prudents hommes d'armes, non des chevaliers téméraires et écervelés, cibles des archers anglais. Du Guesclin et Clisson conseillent de ne combattre les Anglais que s'ils sont en mauvaise posture : c'est ainsi seulement qu'on doit « prendre un ennemi ».

Et prudemment, de manière retorse, Charles V se réapproprie le Poitou, la Saintonge et l'Angoumois.

En 1380, à sa mort, l'Anglais ne possède plus qu'une bande de terre entre Bordeaux et Bayonne, et les villes de Calais, Brest et Cherbourg.

Le royaume reprend son souffle après des temps où la peste, la disette et la guerre l'étouffaient.

On peut semer et moissonner. On peut vendre son grain en échange d'une monnaie – un franc d'or – que de trop rapides changements de teneur en métal précieux ne dévaluent pas d'une saison à l'autre. Et à Paris on peut s'imaginer que l'ordre et la sécurité vont régner.

Charles V entreprend de renforcer les défenses de la ville. Une nouvelle enceinte est construite, englobant les nouveaux quartiers.

Il protège ainsi sa résidence de l'hôtel Saint-Paul, immense bâtiment qui possède sept jardins, une ménagerie, une volière, un aquarium. Il poursuit la construction du donjon de Vincennes et commence à ériger, à la porte Saint-Antoine, une Bastille qui comportera huit donjons reliés par un mur de vingt-quatre mètres de hauteur.

Aucune ville chrétienne ne recèle une telle forteresse. Mais Paris n'est-elle pas la plus grande ville de la chrétienté ?

Ainsi, tout au long du règne de Charles V (1364-1380), se dessine et se précise dans l'âme française le modèle du « bon souverain », lettré (on dira de Charles V qu'il est « le Sage »), entouré de conseillers dévoués – savants eux-mêmes –, prudent mais courageux défenseur du royaume, soucieux du bien commun, et, comme l'écrit sa biographe Christine de Pisan, fille d'un médecin conseiller du roi, « désireux de garder et maintenir, et donner exemple à ses successeurs à venir que par solennel ordre doit se tenir et mener le très digne degré de la haute couronne de France ».

Roi administrateur veillant à la bonne gestion du royaume, il promulgue de Grandes Ordonnances afin d'organiser sa succession – son fils Charles n'a que douze ans en 1380 – en créant un conseil de régence, mais est tout aussi préoccupé de veiller au sort de la forêt française, cette richesse du royaume dont une ordonnance, à compter de 1376, fixe les règles d'exploitation.

Ce souverain-là sait écouter son peuple.

Quand des émeutes urbaines – à Montpellier, notamment – et des jacqueries – celles des *tuchins* qui se mettent sur la touche (1379) – soulèvent le peuple contre le fisc, il réprime mais diminue les impôts. Et, peu avant sa mort, il annonce la suppression des impôts directs, les fouages (calculés par « feux »).

C'est le roi juste et sage, celui que recherchent tout au long de leur histoire les Français, et qui, parce qu'il y a eu Saint Louis et Charles V – puis d'autres, plus tard, de cette « sainte lignée » –, ne surgit ni d'un rêve ni d'une utopie. C'est celui qu'on attend dans les temps sombres, et qu'on regrette après sa mort.

« Au temps du trépassement du feu roi Charles V, l'an 1380, les choses en ce royaume étaient en bonne disposition et avaient fait plusieurs notables conquêtes. Paix et justice régnaient. N'y avait fait obstacle, sinon l'ancienne haine des Anglais... »

Il n'y a pas que l'Anglais.

Le chroniqueur Jean Juvénal des Ursins oublie que l'étranger, dans un royaume comme la France, ne peut rien s'il ne bénéficie de la complicité, de l'alliance d'une partie des grands.

Or l'œuvre de rétablissement accomplie par Charles V est minée par les privilèges, les apanages qu'il a accordés à ses trois frères : Jean de Berry, Louis d'Anjou et Philippe de Bourgogne. Ce sont eux qui vont composer le conseil de régence, puisque, à la mort de Charles V, son fils Charles VI n'a que douze ans.

Et lorsque Charles VI trépasse à son tour, en 1422, le royaume de France est plongé au plus profond des abîmes de son histoire.

Charles VI a déshérité son fils, l'a banni, l'accusant d'« horribles crimes et délits ». Il a marié sa fille Catherine au roi d'Angleterre, Henri V de Lancastre, qu'il a légitimé comme « son vrai fils et héritier ». Et le traité de Troyes conclu en 1420 a stipulé que la couronne de France est échue à Henri V et pour toujours à ses héritiers.

Il n'y a donc plus qu'une double monarchie : le roi d'Angleterre est roi de France.

Aussi, quand en 1422 Charles VI et Henri V décèdent et que le fils de l'Anglais ne peut régner, puisqu'il n'a que dix mois, c'est le duc de Bedford qui devient régent d'une France occupée par les Anglais ; quant au fils de Charles VI, qui l'a déshérité, il peut bien prendre le titre de Charles VII il est celui que, par dérision, on surnomme « le roi de Bourges » !

C'est le duc de Bedford qui a présidé à Saint-Denis aux obsèques de Charles VI, et le héraut s'est écrié : « Vive le roi Henri de France et d'Angleterre ! »

Était-ce le royaume de France que l'on portait en terre ?

« Chacun vit mourir là rien que plus qu'il aimât », écrit un témoin.

Ainsi, en l'espace de quarante-deux années, le royaume est-il retombé au fond d'un abîme bien plus profond que celui d'où Charles V le Sage avait réussi à l'arracher.

En 1422, dans ce pays occupé, le seul espoir gît dans cette blessure intime de chaque Français qui souffre de la présence anglaise, de la perte de souveraineté du royaume, gouverné au nom de Henri VI par le duc de Bedford.

Or cela fait quatre décennies que le peuple subit le malheur.

Peste, disette, famine, violences des Grandes Compagnies, pillage par les Anglais, châtiment à la moindre rébellion.

Les oncles de Charles VI, maîtres du conseil de régence, massacrent les jacques, ou les bourgeois quand ils protestent contre la levée d'impôts trop lourds, ou bien quand ils ont la disgrâce de figurer dans le camp de l'un des princes et que celui des autres est vainqueur.

Car les oncles du roi sont divisés.

Le plus puissant est Philippe de Bourgogne, opposé à ses deux frères, Louis d'Anjou et Jean de Berry.

Et l'Anglais, entre ces rivaux, peut jouer l'un ou l'autre. Il est d'autant plus fort que le royaume est appauvri, que sa population n'a jamais été aussi réduite – à peine une douzaine de millions d'habitants.

Marchands, artisans, jacques, manouvriers, bourgeois de Rouen, de Paris ou d'Orléans ont le sentiment que les oncles du roi dilapident les biens du royaume et remplissent les coffres avec des impôts de plus en plus lourds.

Dans les villes et les campagnes, on s'insurge. On massacre les percepteurs, on pourchasse les juifs (ils seront expulsés du royaume en 1394), on ouvre les portes des prisons.

À Paris, les émeutiers s'emparent, à l'Hôtel de Ville, des deux mille maillets de plomb que le prévôt avait fait entreposer là pour servir en cas d'attaque des Anglais.

Ces mouvements populaires échappent aux riches bourgeois qui voudraient les utiliser pour faire pression sur les oncles du roi.

Ceux-ci répriment. Les têtes roulent, les corps se balancent aux gibets. Mais le calme ne revient dans le royaume qu'au moment où le roi, en 1388, met fin au gouvernement des princes, et, avec l'aide des « sages » conseillers de son père Charles V, règne effectivement.

Court moment d'apaisement. C'est le temps des fêtes. Charles VI a vingt-deux ans, son épouse Isabeau en a dix-neuf, son frère Louis d'Orléans, dix-huit. Danses, jeux, déguisements. Louis d'Orléans guide le roi son frère et la reine Isabeau dans les labyrinthes du plaisir. La tragédie n'est jamais bien loin. Des travestis vêtus en sauvages, la peau enduite de poix et couverte de poils, meurent brûlés vifs à un bal donné à l'hôtel Saint-Paul.

Ce bal des Ardents est le symbole de cette période : Paris brille des milliers de feux d'une fête qui attire artistes et artisans. Louis d'Orléans « ne gouverne aucunement à son plaisir et fait jeunesses étranges ».

Le pouvoir entre les mains des oncles du roi était divisé ; il est maintenant débauché sans que cessent les rivalités. Et le peuple continue de souffrir.

Seule la présence du roi légitime empêche la désagrégation du royaume.

Mais, le 5 août 1392, dans la forêt du Mans, il suffit de la rencontre d'un mendiant, mauvais présage, et du choc bruyant d'une lance sur un casque pour que Charles VI bascule dans la démence.

Ce roi fou, Charles VI, qui dans ses périodes de lucidité sombre dans la dépression ou est influencé – manœuvré – par son entourage, va « régner » ainsi entre démence et prostration trente ans durant.

Le royaume de France s'enfonce dans l'abîme parce que son roi a sombré dans la folie et que les grands s'entre-déchirent, peu soucieux du sort du royaume.

Ce pays commence à découvrir un trait majeur de son histoire : qu'il pourrit toujours par la tête. C'est le cas avec la guerre civile entre le frère du roi, Louis d'Orléans, et son fils, Charles d'Orléans, marié à la fille du comte d'Armagnac, d'une part, et, de l'autre, Philippe de Bourgogne et son fils Jean sans Peur.

Ces deux factions – Armagnacs et Bourguignons – sont les deux fauteurs de guerre civile. Assassinats et massacres, utilisation des éléments les plus violents du peuple, sont de règle.

Jean sans Peur, le Bourguignon, fait assassiner en 1407 Louis d'Orléans, frère du roi, l'Armagnac. Dès lors, les Bourguignons traquent dans Paris tous les Armagnacs.

« On n'avait pas plus de pitié à tuer ces gens-là que des chiens : c'est un Armagnac. »

Les Bourguignons contrôlent le roi fou, s'appuient sur de « méchantes gens, tripiers, bouchers et écorcheurs, pelletiers, couturiers et autres pauvres gens de très bas état faisant de très inhumaines, détestables et très déshonnêtes besognes ».

L'un d'eux est Simon Caboche (1413), qui, avec les siens – les cabochiens –, fait régner la terreur dans Paris. Le monarque est terré dans sa folie. On impose une « ordonnance cabochienne », mais l'anarchie qui s'installe, les meurtres qui se multiplient, isolent les Bourguignons et poussent les marchands, la bourgeoisie parisienne, à changer de camp. Jean sans Peur quitte Paris, qui devient Armagnac avec Charles d'Orléans.

Que fait le camp perdant dans une guerre civile ? Il devient le parti de l'étranger. Le prince bourguignon s'allie alors avec l'Anglais.

Une pratique française se confirme : la division au sommet de l'État provoque la crise du royaume et la guerre civile dont l'étranger tire profit.

Le nouveau roi d'Angleterre, Henri V, est un souverain remarquable, grand chef de guerre, fin politique et homme pieux. Il entend se réapproprier l'héritage des Plantagenêts.

Son armée débarque en Normandie, gagne les pays de la Somme.

Les chevaliers français sont entassés sur le plateau d'Azincourt. Le sol est boueux, ce 25 octobre 1415. L'armure pèse au moins vingt kilos. Si l'on tombe à terre, on ne peut se relever. Alors on charge les archers anglais sans attendre qu'arrive la piétaille des gens d'armes. Les chevaux se heurtent, renversent leurs cavaliers, qu'il ne reste plus aux Anglais qu'à égorger, car Henri V a ordonné qu'on ne fasse prisonniers que les grands et qu'on tue tous les autres.

Ils seront trois mille chevaliers, barons, baillis, grands officiers de l'administration du royaume à être ainsi massacrés.

Charles d'Orléans, prisonnier, est transféré en Angleterre, où, de prison en prison, il passera vingt-cinq années à se morfondre et à rimer :

> *En regardant vers le pays de France*
> *Un jour advint à Douvres sur la mer*
> *Qu'il me souvint du doux plaisir*
> *Qu'en ce pays je trouvais*
> *Et mon cœur commença à soupirer*
> *Mais à mon cœur amer*
> *Voir la France faisait grand bien.*

Cette nostalgie charnelle du royaume perdu, cette souffrance et cette humiliation, il n'est pas besoin d'être prisonnier en Angleterre pour les ressentir.

On souffre de la guerre civile : les Bourguignons massacrent encore les Armagnacs à Paris en 1418 ; Jean sans Peur le Bourguignon est assassiné à Montereau le 10 avril 1419 – est ainsi vengé Louis d'Orléans, qu'il avait fait tuer le 23 novembre 1407.

On souffre de l'avancée des troupes anglaises, armée d'occupation qui prend possession sans ménagements du royaume de son roi, imposant à Rouen un siège impitoyable, remontant la Seine : « Les Anglais font autant de mal que les Sarrasins. » Mais on en veut aussi au Dauphin Charles, devenu lieutenant général du royaume en 1417.

On désire la paix.

On approuve donc le traité de Troyes (20 mai 1420). Henri V de Lancastre épouse la fille de Charles VI et devient, de fait, fils et héritier du roi de France.

Charles le Dauphin n'est plus qu'un banni.

Le 1er décembre 1420, Henri V, Charles VI, le pauvre roi fou, son épouse Isabeau et Philippe le Bon, le nouveau prince bourguignon, entrent dans Paris.

« Jamais princes ne furent reçus à plus grande joie qu'ils furent. »

La capitale du royaume de France est aux mains des Anglais, mais la foule assoiffée de paix applaudit.

Après la mort de Henri V et celle de Charles VI, en 1422, le duc de Bedford est régent du royaume au nom de Henri VI de Lancastre.

Malheureux Charles VII, roi de Bourges !

Un pouvoir divisé, une guerre civile, un parti de l'étranger, un peuple exsangue et désorienté, la souffrance d'une âme française humiliée, bafouée, niée : tel est l'abîme où a chuté le royaume de France.

Quelle providence ou quelles circonstances, quels héros pourront-ils lui permettre de resurgir au grand jour de l'unité et de la souveraineté nationales ?

16.

Où s'est réfugiée l'âme de la France, puisque le territoire du royaume est partagé et que celui qui se proclame roi de France, ce pauvre Charles VII, n'a pas même été sacré à Reims, qu'il tient sa Cour à Bourges et qu'Orléans est assiégée par l'Anglais ?

Car le roi anglais, Henri VI de Lancastre, est roi de France, lui aussi, fort de la légitimité que lui confère le traité de Troyes. Et à Paris, qu'il contrôle, les bourgeois, les maîtres de l'Université, les marchands, les évêques, « collaborent » avec le régent anglais, le duc de Bedford.

D'autant plus que l'Anglais a pour allié Philippe le Bon, le Bourguignon, le plus fastueux des princes de la chrétienté, qui possède trois capitales : Lille, Bruges et surtout Dijon. Riche, il l'est par les vignobles de Beaune – on construira dans cette ville, en 1443, un magnifique hôpital –, par les voies commerciales qu'il contrôle, par les Flandres ou cliquètent les métiers mécaniques à tisser.

Il attire peintres, artistes, sculpteurs.

Le duc de Bretagne, à l'autre extrémité du territoire, est lui aussi l'allié de l'Anglais.

Ainsi, cette « France anglaise » dispose de presque tout le pays au nord et à l'est de la Loire, et il faut encore y ajouter la Guyenne.

Telle est ainsi brisée l'ancienne unité française liée à la « sainte lignée » des rois de France.

Et lorsque les chevaliers du roi de Bourges tentent une fois encore de bousculer les archers anglais, ceux-ci, comme à Crécy, Poitiers, Azincourt, les massacrent de leurs flèches et de leurs coutelas, le 17 août 1424, à Verneuil-sur-Avre.

Charles VII doute aussi de lui, de ses droits. Hésitant, il songe parfois à se retirer en Dauphiné, à renoncer à la reconquête du royaume, qui lui paraît si difficile qu'elle en devient improbable.

Cependant, les provinces qu'il contrôle sont riches – les pays de Loire, notamment –, elles ont été peu touchées par les ravages de la guerre. Il a autour de lui non seulement les membres du vieux parti Armagnac, mais ceux qui sont restés fidèles à la dynastie capétienne.

Sans doute certains membres de sa Cour sont-ils tentés par des rapprochements avec les Bourguignons, et lui-même, miné par l'incertitude, n'est-il pas capable de prendre la tête de la résistance à l'Anglais, de se faire le héraut du royaume de France.

Élites collaborant avec l'occupant, pouvoir royal impuissant, armée défaite : l'âme de la France réside encore et résiste dans son peuple humilié et exploité par l'Anglais.

« Toujours le régent Bedford enrichissait son pays de quelque chose, et quand il en revenait il n'en rapportait rien qu'une nouvelle taille », écrit un témoin.

En Normandie, où l'Anglais, de Rouen à Caen, s'est fortement implanté, on se rebelle contre les impôts nouveaux. Et l'occupant réprime, sévit, pend, décapite.

Un patriotisme populaire naît de cette résistance. Il s'exprime partout, l'Anglais agissant partout selon son intérêt.

On murmure même à l'université de Paris, quand les professeurs y apprennent que Bedford veut créer une université à Caen afin d'y former des « administrateurs » au service des Anglais.

On mesure l'âpreté et la rapacité anglaises. Dans les années qui suivent le traité de Troyes, un témoin écrit : « Les Anglais ont détruit et gâté tout le royaume, et tant de dommages y ont fait au temps passé et de présent que si tout le pays d'Angleterre était rendu et mis à deniers, on n'en pourrait pas recouvrer la centième partie des dommages qu'ils ont faits audit royaume de France. »

L'âme de la France se forge ainsi dans la défaite et l'occupation étrangère. Un « parti français » s'affirme au sein du peuple.

Jeanne la Pucelle, fille de « labours aisés » et fille du peuple – analphabète, donc –, est l'une de ces Françaises qui, au nom de Dieu, protecteur du royaume de France, répondent à l'appel de ces voix – celle du Seigneur, celles du peuple – qui les incitent à se lever pour sauver le royaume.

Jeanne, qui est née entre la Champagne et le Barrois, est l'incarnation de ce mouvement surgi des profondeurs nationales.

Mais il y avait aussi Péronne, de Bretagne, et Catherine, de La Rochelle. Et combien de femmes et d'hommes agenouillés prient pour que soit sauvé le royaume et sacré le roi français ? La foi chrétienne enflamme le sentiment national. Jeanne est portée par cette croyance qui l'« oblige » à agir, lui insuffle la force de conviction bousculant les hésitations.

Le représentant du Dauphin, Robert de Baudricourt, capitaine de Vaucouleurs, bien que sa terre relève du duc de Bourgogne, va l'aider, lui permettre de rejoindre Chinon. Elle y reconnaîtra le Dauphin et s'imposera aux chefs de guerre après avoir été reconnue pucelle.

C'est une vierge qu'on attendait, puisqu'une débauchée, la reine Isabeau, avait corrompu le roi Charles VI et perdu le royaume.

Jeanne convainc les théologiens chargés de l'interroger : « Au nom de Dieu, les gens d'armes batailleront et Dieu donnera la victoire. »

De Blois elle prévient le roi d'Angleterre : « Je suis venue ici de par Dieu le Roi du Ciel pour vous bouter hors de France. »

En trois mois, Jeanne va changer la donne de cette guerre de cent ans en révélant la force du patriotisme populaire.

De la Bourgogne à la Normandie, de la Bretagne à l'Aquitaine, et à Paris même, on va rapidement savoir qu'une pucelle, menant au combat Dunois le Bâtard, demi-frère de Charles d'Orléans, La Hire, le duc Jean d'Alençon, et ses capitaines de compagnie, a, le 8 mai, fait lever le siège d'Orléans, et, le 18 juin, remporté la victoire de Patay.

Le Dauphin peut enfin, l'étreinte anglaise desserrée, se rendre à Reims et s'y faire sacrer le 7 juillet 1429.

Il est désormais le roi de France légitime.

« Gentil roi, dit la Pucelle, ores est exécuté le plaisir de Dieu qui voulait que levasse le siège d'Orléans et que vous emmenasse en cette cité de Reims recevoir votre Saint Sacre, en montrant que vous êtes vrai Roi de France et celui auquel le royaume de France doit appartenir. »

Victoire miraculeuse, née du peuple patriote et de la foi en Dieu.

Victoire décisive et pourtant gaspillée.

Charles VII et sa Cour n'agissent pas, veulent d'abord se réconcilier avec le duc de Bourgogne. Le roi laisse Jeanne, sans appui, tenter de prendre Paris (elle y est blessée), La Charité-sur-Loire. Elle entre dans Compiègne qu'assiège une armée bourguignonne. Mais elle ne connaît pas la fortune des armes comme à Orléans. Elle est faite prisonnière le 24 mai 1430 et vendue pour 10 000 écus aux Anglais.

Elle est jugée hérétique et schismatique à Rouen suivant une procédure inquisitoriale. Les clercs sont français (l'évêque de Beauvais, Pierre Cauchon) ; les soldats, anglais. Condamnée, elle est brûlée vive le 30 mai 1431, place du Marché, à Rouen : « Elle fut arse cestui jour. »

Rien n'avait été tenté par Charles VII pour arracher celle que les Anglais et les juges ecclésiastiques à leur service tenaient pour une sorcière, et qui avait tiré le royaume de France de l'abîme.

Mais Jeanne la Pucelle n'allait pas être oubliée, devenant dans l'âme de la France, le symbole du patriotisme, et, pour les chrétiens, la preuve que la Providence veille sur le royaume.

Son procès en réhabilitation aura lieu en 1456. Mais la Pucelle continue de chevaucher tout au long de l'histoire nationale : patriote revendiquée par la IIIe République, béatifiée en 1900, elle est canonisée en 1920 par Benoît XV. Et le 8 mai fut proclamé fête nationale.

« Lance au poing et dans son étui de fer aussi claire que le soleil d'avril à sept heures,
« Voici Jeanne sur son grand cheval rouge qui se met en marche contre les usurpateurs [...]
« Et maintenant écoutez, Messieurs les hommes d'État, et vous tous, Messieurs les diplomates, et vous tous, Messieurs les militaires...
« Jeanne d'Arc est là pour vous dire qu'il y a toujours quelque chose de mieux à faire que de ne rien faire...
« Cette Pucelle et cette patronne et cette conductrice au plus profond de la France arrachée par l'aspiration du Saint-Esprit... »

On peut refuser cette vision mystique de « sainte Jeanne » et de la France qu'exprime Paul Claudel, mais, après son « passage » – « Cette flamme déracinée du bûcher ! elle monte ! » –, tout change. Comme si le patriotisme populaire et la foi qu'il exprime obligeaient les « élites » à constituer ce « parti français » qui fait de l'Anglais l'ennemi dans tout le royaume, et Charles VII, sacré à Reims, le seul roi de France.

Une paix est conclue entre Bourguignons et Armagnacs (Arras, 1435). Charles VII entre le 12 novembre 1437 dans un Paris ruiné où errent les loups, mais c'est sa capitale. Elle est à l'image d'un royaume dévasté, parcouru par les Grandes Compagnies. Les campagnes sont vides d'habitants ; de rares paysans affamés y sont guettés par les « écorcheurs », les routiers en maraude, ou frappés par les retours de la peste noire (ainsi en 1438).
De tout le royaume monte vers le roi le désir de le voir agir.
« Il faut que vous vous éveilliez, car nous n'en pouvons plus », lui lance Jean Juvénal des Ursins.
Charles VII acquiert de la détermination. Il se montre combatif et volontaire. Il affiche ses maîtresses – Agnès Sorel –, et le Dauphin Louis supporte mal cette autorité nouvelle. Le futur

Louis XI s'éloignera de ce père devenu, pour les vingt dernières années de son règne, un vrai roi de France.

Charles VII réforme. Par les ordonnances de mai 1445, à partir de ces routiers, de ces écorcheurs, de ces soldats désœuvrés entre deux batailles, il crée une armée soldée par le Trésor royal et donc permanente. Ces « Compagnies de l'Ordonnance du Roi » sont logées en forteresse ou chez l'habitant, et complétées par des « francs archers » à raison d'un par cinquante feux. Le franc archer, dispensé d'impôts, doit s'entraîner au tir à l'arc ou à l'arbalète.

Le roi tire enfin la leçon des défaites de la chevalerie française en créant cette « infanterie à l'anglaise ».

Pontoise (1441), Le Mans (1448), Rouen, Caen, Cherbourg (1449) sont reconquises. Et, avec ces villes, le prestige royal.

L'entrée de Charles VII à Rouen est solennelle. Ce 10 novembre 1449, il est accueilli par l'archevêque Raoul Roussel, par les évêques qui furent les acteurs du procès de Jeanne d'Arc et par les témoins de son supplice.

Mais, après avoir été les alliés intimes des Anglais, les dignitaires s'inclinent désormais devant Charles VII, qui avance sous un dais, précédé par un cheval portant le sceau aux trois lis.

La fonction royale est séparée du corps du roi.

La victoire de Castillon, en Guyenne – le 17 juillet 1453 –, clôt la guerre de Cent Ans.

Trois cents bouches à feu ont écrasé la chevalerie et l'infanterie anglaises dans cette Aquitaine liée à l'Angleterre depuis trois siècles.

Tant de batailles perdues sont ainsi vengées.

Le pouvoir a toujours besoin de gloire. Dans l'histoire nationale, depuis les origines, ce sont les glaives et les armées qui l'ont apportée.

Le chevalier, le soldat – et le clerc – sont en France, plus que les marchands, faiseurs de prestige. L'argent, le commerce, plient devant le pouvoir. Et Charles VII fait emprisonner Jacques

Cœur (1451), grand argentier et grand marchand. L'argent n'est jamais une fin, pour un roi de France, au contraire de la gloire.

Ce n'est qu'un indispensable moyen.

Quand, le 22 juillet 1461, Charles VII s'éteint, le royaume de France a recouvré une part de sa puissance, de sa gloire et de sa richesse.

Est-ce par une attention de la Providence ?

Celui qui n'avait jamais été qu'un « gentil Dauphin », Charles VII, est devenu, grâce à Jeanne la Pucelle, grâce à tous les Français, attachés à leur nation, et aux conseillers qui l'ont à sa Cour assisté, Charles VII le Bien servi.

17.

« Je suis France », dit Louis XI.

Il vient enfin, à trente-huit ans, de succéder à son père, Charles le Bien servi.

Voilà près de vingt ans qu'il attend, plein d'impatience et même de rage. Il a quitté le royaume de France pour se réfugier chez le Bourguignon, Philippe le Bon. Il a conspiré contre son père, organisé complots et même prises d'armes.

Enfin Charles VII est mort.

Le 13 août 1461, Louis entre dans la cathédrale de Reims : cérémonie fastueuse dont les détails et la magnificence ont été voulus par le duc de Bourgogne ; c'est d'ailleurs lui qui a posé la couronne sur la tête de Louis XI.

C'est à ses côtés qu'il entrera dans Paris, le 31 août.

« Je suis France », dit alors Louis.

Manière d'affirmer qu'il sera souverainement roi de France, donc prêt à secouer toutes les tutelles qu'on voudrait lui imposer. Et d'abord celle de l'héritage de Charles VII. Il renvoie les conseillers de son père : vingt-cinq baillis et sénéchaux. Et il suffit de quelques semaines pour que l'on comprenne que ce souverain au visage de fouine, d'une piété superstitieuse, remuant entre ses doigts des médailles saintes comme s'il s'agissait d'amulettes, est un monarque déterminé et autoritaire.

Il se méfie des grands, donc en tout premier lieu du duc de Bourgogne, le plus puissant. Il préfère s'entourer d'hommes simples mais dévoués corps et âme – Tristan L'Hermite, Olivier Le Daim, l'évêque Balue, bientôt disgracié et emprisonné sans procès –, le chroniqueur Commynes, corrompu, et Francesco Sforza, venu de l'Italie de Machiavel et des Médicis.

Ainsi, pour la première fois dans l'histoire nationale, un souverain esquisse un pouvoir « absolutiste » en s'appuyant non plus sur ses vassaux, les grands, mais sur des hommes liés à lui par un lien de « service », serviteurs du roi et donc de l'État.

Gouvernement impitoyable : le roi réprime avec sauvagerie – pendaisons, mutilations, bannissements – la « tircotterie » d'Angers et la « mutemaque » de Reims, des émeutes anti-fiscales.

Car ce pouvoir qui se ramifie a besoin d'argent. Il multiplie par quatre la taille. Il resserre les rouages de l'État, contrôle les villes, le clergé. Il renforce l'armée des compagnies d'ordonnances. Il favorise les cités marchandes. Il crée une quatrième foire à Lyon, ce qui fait de cette ville un centre d'attraction pour les banquiers et marchands italiens. De nombreuses routes sont pavées et les « chevaucheurs » du roi, qui transportent les plis officiels, trouvent aux relais des montures fraîches.

Et à sa manière autoritaire, en renforçant l'État, le roi exprime les souhaits du peuple, de ce « parti français » né dans la guerre contre le « parti de l'étranger », et qui, même s'il en craint la violence, approuve un souverain affirmant : « Je suis France. »

Avec Louis XI surgit ainsi un nouveau type de souverain français, de pouvoir national, peu respectueux des « règles » et de la morale – les conseillers de Louis XI sont des hommes de police, et même, à l'occasion, des bourreaux –, comme si le service du royaume autorisait – au nom de Dieu aussi, car le roi est pieux, il invoque saint Michel – l'emploi de toutes les habiletés et de toutes les violences.

Parce que la ville d'Arras a résisté en 1479, tous les habitants en sont chassés, remplacés par d'autres, et la ville, débaptisée, devient un temps « Franchise ».

Mais ce pouvoir est national. Louis XI se rend en pèlerinage à l'abbaye du Mont-Saint-Michel, il crée l'ordre de Saint-Michel parce que, dix ans durant – 1424-1434 –, la place a résisté au siège des Anglais, parce que Jeanne d'Arc a invoqué saint Michel qui allait l'aider à terrasser l'Anglais comme il avait terrassé le dragon.

Et les premières imprimeries qui se créent à Paris à partir de 1470 – il y en aura neuf, contre quarante en Italie – diffusent à des centaines d'exemplaires, peut-être même à un ou deux milliers, ces invocations à saint Michel et ces apologies du roi de France. Les grands qui ont montré contre les Anglais leur impuissance, leur désir de collaborer avec l'occupant et de constituer un parti de l'étranger, et les chevaliers qui ont donné la preuve de leur incapacité à vaincre les archers anglais voient ainsi leur pouvoir réduit au bénéfice de celui du roi et de l'État.

Au contraire, comme jamais, les marchands, les bourgeois, les manouvriers, considèrent que le pouvoir royal est le garant de leur prospérité :

> *Et quand Anglais furent dehors*
> *Chacun se met en ses efforts*
> *De bâtir et de marchander*
> *Et en biens superabonder.*

Ce « parti français », ce peuple « patriote », n'est évidemment pas conscient de la politique que conduit Louis XI, mais, lorsqu'il est averti de ce qui se trame, il soutient l'« universelle aragne » qui tisse sa toile pour réduire les ducs et les princes à l'impuissance et les dépouiller de leurs possessions au profit du royaume.

Tel est l'axe de cette politique française de Louis XI, qui parfois trébuche sur les propres pièges qu'elle tend à ses adversaires.

Les grands ont jaugé la menace. Ils mènent dès 1465 une guerre ouverte contre Louis XI. Le duc de Bourgogne, Philippe le Bon et son fils Charles le Téméraire, le duc de Bretagne, ont formé ce qu'ils appellent la ligne du Bien Public et ont enrôlé dans leurs rangs le propre frère du roi.

Après la bataille incertaine de Montlhéry (16 juillet 1465), les ligueurs menacent Paris. Louis XI négocie (traité de Conflans, 1465), mais sa détermination ne faiblit pas. Il incite les Flandres à se soulever contre Charles le Téméraire, et prend le risque de se rendre à Péronne, défier le duc de Bourgogne et négocier avec lui en dépit de l'insurrection des Liégeois, que, l'accord une fois intervenu, on réprimera (1468).

Ce souverain bavard, retors et superstitieux, auteur de plus de sept volumes de lettres, a une vision claire des dangers qui menacent le royaume. Il doit briser le duché de Bourgogne, empêcher que Charles le Téméraire ne conquière l'Alsace et la Lorraine, réunissant ainsi territorialement la Flandre et la Bourgogne. Et il doit plus encore empêcher que se renoue l'alliance anglo-bourguignonne.

Or Édouard IV débarque en 1475 une armée de 25 000 hommes à Calais. Pour le faire renoncer, il faut lui verser 75 000 écus plus 50 000 écus de rente annuelle.

Le peuple approuve cette politique. Les villes ont résisté aux Bourguignons (ainsi Jeanne Hachette à Beauvais). Il se félicite de l'accord intervenu entre Louis XI et Édouard IV d'Angleterre (à Picquigny, 1475) :

> *J'ai vu le Roi d'Angleterre*
> *Amener son grand ost*
> *pour la Française terre*
> *Conquérir bref et tost*
> *Le Roi voyant l'affaire*
> *Si bon vin leur donna*
> *Que l'autre sans rien faire*
> *Content s'en retourna.*

Ce roi réussit. Charles le Téméraire, qui a repris la guerre, meurt devant Nancy (1477), et en jouant des successions, en mêlant habile diplomatie et menaces, Louis XI agrandit le royaume de France du Roussillon, de la plus grande partie de la Bourgogne (duché), de la Picardie, de l'Anjou, du Maine et de la Provence.

Avec Marseille, le royaume s'ouvre ainsi sur la Méditerranée et recouvre les limites de la Gaule romaine.

Certes, il a fallu accepter que Marie de Bourgogne – fille de Charles le Téméraire – épouse l'empereur Maximilien d'Autriche. Les Habsbourg sont aux portes du royaume de France. Mais Louis XI a obtenu que la fille de Marie de Bourgogne épouse le Dauphin Charles, et elle apporte dans sa dot la Franche-Comté, l'Auxerrois, le Mâconnais et l'Artois.

Au sud, Isabelle de Castille a épousé Ferdinand d'Aragon, et ces Rois Catholiques vont reconquérir toute l'Espagne, en chasser les musulmans.

Ces modifications portent en germe une nouvelle géopolitique de l'Europe occidentale. Le royaume de France ne peut qu'y être directement impliqué.

Le 30 août 1483, quand meurt Louis XI à Plessis-lès-Tours, le royaume de France n'est plus l'État exsangue de la première moitié du xv\ siècle.

L'âme du pays a été trempée par la guerre. Elle se sait et surtout se veut française.

Au lent processus d'agrandissement et d'unification du royaume, Louis XI, en vingt-deux ans de règne, a apporté une contribution majeure.

Dans le fonctionnement du pouvoir, il a tout subordonné au succès de la politique qui sert la gloire et les intérêts du royaume tels que le roi les conçoit.

Ceux qui ne partagent pas cette vision doivent être brisés. Le royaume de France ne doit compter que des sujets soumis au pouvoir royal.

L'âme de la France se souviendra de l'« universelle aragne ».

18.

La mort a saisi Louis XI et c'est un enfant de treize ans qui est sacré roi de France. Point de conseil de régence pour Charles VIII : le défunt roi a choisi deux tuteurs, sa fille Anne et son époux, Pierre de Beaujeu, un Bourbon dont il sait qu'ils continueront sa politique avec ténacité et prudence. « Anne, disait-il, est la femme la moins folle du monde. »

Et, précisément, elle doit faire face avec Pierre de Beaujeu à la « Guerre folle » que mènent contre ces deux tuteurs les princes qui veulent dominer le roi, retrouver leur influence. Parmi eux, il y a le cousin du souverain, Louis d'Orléans, fils du poète Charles d'Orléans, retenu si longtemps prisonnier en Angleterre. Vaincu par les troupes royales, Louis d'Orléans passera trois années en prison (1488-1491) avant de devenir, à la mort de Charles VIII (1498), Louis XII, roi de France.

Et, revêtant les habits du souverain, il combat à son tour les princes. Il peuple son Conseil de roturiers, comme l'avaient fait Louis XI et Charles VIII. Il écoute les avis de cet « humaniste » – un des hérauts de la révolution culturelle qui, portée par l'imprimerie, bouleverse des valeurs réputées immuables – nommé Guillaume Budé (1467-1540), dont Charles VIII avait fait son secrétaire.

Fini le temps des chroniqueurs à la Commynes. Charles VIII les a renvoyés.

Avec le roturier progresse l'esprit profane.

La Sorbonne admet les *studia humanitatis* – études profanes. Un Robert Gaguin publie pour Charles VIII les *Commentaires* de César, et une *Histoire française* qui se donne Tite-Live pour modèle.

Les imprimeries se multiplient à Paris et à Lyon. En 1514, Louis XII dispensera les livres de taxe à l'exportation. Les librairies disposent en réserve de plusieurs dizaines de milliers de volumes à eux tous.

On imprime, on réimprime François Villon, sa *Ballade des dames du temps jadis* :

> *Où est la très sage Héloïse*
> *Pour qui châtré fut et puis moine*
> *Pierre Abélard à Saint-Denis [...]*
> *Et Jeanne la bonne Lorraine*
> *Qu'Anglais brûlèrent à Rouen [...]*
> *Mais où sont les neiges d'antan ?*

La nation naît de cette langue qui s'affine, se crée en forgeant des mots neufs, en exprimant une sensibilité nouvelle et en donnant à des milliers de lecteurs la conscience forte d'appartenir à une communauté nationale. Le chant profane, les livres, la poésie, tous ces textes qui commencent à circuler constituent une mémoire collective, une légende et une mythologie partagées.

La France commence à vivre en chaque Français grâce au pouvoir des mots :

> *Frères humains qui après nous vivez*
> *N'ayez les cœurs contre nous endurcis [...]*
> *Mais priez Dieu que tous nous veuillent absoudre !*

Heureusement, entre le moment où Villon écrit cette *Ballade des pendus* – vers 1461 – et la fin du siècle (Charles VIII : 1483-1498 ; Louis XII : 1498-1515), la mort recule.

Les grappes de pendus au gibet de Montfaucon sont moins serrées.

La peste noire et la disette frappent encore au début du règne de Charles VIII, mais le pays se repeuple ; les étrangers sont admis sans avoir à payer le droit d'aubaine pour obtenir la « naturalité ».

Castillans et Italiens arrivent nombreux dans les villes, dont la population augmente (Paris : 250 000 ; Lyon, Nantes, Rouen, Toulouse : entre 25 000 et 50 000).

Les défrichements reprennent, les villages abandonnés retrouvent vie.

À Lyon, à Troyes, à Paris, du tissage à la fabrication de papier pour l'imprimerie, les ateliers se multiplient, en même temps que des modes nouvelles, venues d'Italie, répandent le goût du luxe, des tissus en soie, de la joaillerie.

En deux décennies, la France a retrouvé sa richesse. Elle est la plus vaste des nations – 450 000 kilomètres carrés –, la plus peuplée – 20 millions d'habitants –, celle dont l'organisation étatique, la plus élaborée, permet de recouvrer les impôts avec le plus d'efficacité.

Ainsi s'inscrit dans la mémoire nationale l'expérience à la fois du malheur exemplaire et du redressement miraculeux qui remet la France à sa place : au premier rang.

Le passage de la dévastation provoquée par la guerre – civile et étrangère – à ce renouveau, cet éloignement des temps de malheur, sont des éléments déterminants dans l'élaboration de l'âme de la France.

Hier, c'était la peur qui étreignait les campagnes menacées par les routiers des Grandes Compagnies.

À la fin du XVe siècle, Claude de Seyssel publie *Louange au Roi Louis XII,* et il décrit une France paisible, gouvernée par un « Père » :

« Tous, dit-il, labourent et travaillent, ainsi avec les gens croissent les biens, les revenus et les richesses. »

La croyance s'enracine qu'il existe un miracle français, que la Providence veille sur le royaume.

Mais, rassurés, satisfaits, les souverains et leur entourage – et, naturellement, les grands, soucieux de recouvrer leur influence – ne réalisent pas que la France ne regarde pas vers l'Atlantique, où Portugais, Espagnols et Italiens s'aventurent (1492 : Christophe Colomb aborde les terres américaines), et qu'ainsi le royaume de France ne participera pas à ce partage du monde – et de l'or ! Les souverains français préfèrent chevaucher en Italie, qui, émiettée, sans État, est cependant le grand pôle économique et financier de l'Europe avec les Flandres.

S'il ne peut être question de conquérir ces dernières, l'Italie, elle, semble facile à saisir.

C'est le mirage de la monarchie française. Pour le matérialiser, on veut avoir les mains libres.

On rend le Roussillon à Ferdinand d'Aragon, l'Artois et la Franche-Comté aux Habsbourg. Une « politique étrangère » française se dessine, où l'illusion, le souci de la gloire, l'emportent sur la raison. Et dans laquelle on sacrifie le gain sûr, réalisé, au rêve.

Charles VIII entre dans Naples en février 1495, vêtu du manteau impérial et de la couronne de Naples, de France, de Jérusalem et de Constantinople.

Car le roi de France entend aussi libérer ces deux dernières villes (Constantinople a été conquise en 1453 par les musulmans). Mais il lui faudra rebrousser chemin devant la coalition italienne qui se forme, et quitter l'Italie malgré la *furia francese* victorieuse à Fornoue (5 juillet 1495).

Mêmes difficultés pour Louis XII, qui se heurte à une Sainte Ligue animée par le pape Jules II, peu soucieux de voir le grand royaume de France dominer l'Italie.

De cette aventure italienne resteront le renforcement d'un courant d'hommes et d'idées, et l'influence dominante de la création artistique italienne dans le royaume de France.

D'un côté, les hommes d'armes (Charles VIII est entré en Italie à la tête de près de trente mille hommes) ; de l'autre, les peintres, les musiciens, les architectes, les théologiens, les philosophes, de Savonarole à Machiavel.

D'un côté le roi, de l'autre le pape.

Un lien ambigu est ainsi noué entre l'âme de la France et celle de l'Italie, qui, quelles que soient les circonstances – incompréhensions, rivalités, conflits –, ne sera jamais tranché.

C'est que les libres décisions des hommes sont orientées par des logiques enserrées dans des structures qui posent les termes d'une équation que, par leurs choix, les acteurs auront à résoudre ou à compliquer.

Le royaume de France n'a, en matière de politique extérieure, le choix qu'entre une expansion vers le nord-est (la Flandre, les Pays-Bas), l'est (au-delà du Rhin), le sud-est (l'Italie) et le sud (l'Espagne).

L'Italie est le seul territoire qui, par son morcellement et sa richesse, attire les convoitises. Et il en sera ainsi jusqu'à ce qu'il soit unifié.

À l'intérieur du royaume, le pouvoir royal est aussi confronté à des problèmes qui ne sont jamais définitivement résolus, puisqu'ils font partie de la nature même de la société française.

Que faire des grands ?

Les tuteurs de Charles VIII ont brisé leur « Guerre folle ». Et, comme Louis XI avant lui, comme Louis XII après lui, Charles VIII s'appuie sur des « roturiers », des « bourgeois » qui deviennent ses conseillers.

De même, comme Charles VII – qui avait, dans la Pragmatique sanction de Bourges, affirmé en 1438 la nécessaire obéissance du clergé français au roi de France et non au pape, sauf en matière théologique –, Charles VIII favorise l'indépendance du clergé français.

Reste le troisième ordre (après l'aristocratie et le clergé), représenté au sein des états généraux, qui reflètent l'ensemble de la nation.

Charles VIII réunit les états en 1484 et leur annonce... une réduction des impôts (de la taille).

Quant à Louis XII, il les assemble à Tours en 1506 pour leur faire rejeter le projet de mariage entre l'héritière du duché de Bretagne – sa fille Claude de France – et le petit-fils de Maximilien d'Autriche, Charles de Habsbourg... futur Charles Quint !

Quel roi de France et quels représentants des Français eussent accepté de voir le royaume pris en tenailles par les Habsbourg, écrasant l'Ile-de-France entre leurs possessions de l'Est et de l'Ouest ?

C'eût été retrouver, en pis, la situation qui avait donné naissance à la guerre de Cent Ans.

En 1514, Claude de France épouse François de Valois et apporte en dot le duché de Bretagne.

Lorsque, le 1er janvier 1515, Louis XII, « Père du Peuple », meurt sans héritier mâle, c'est son cousin, François de Valois, qui monte sur le trône sous le nom de François Ier.

Des temps nouveaux commencent, dont on pressent qu'ils sont porteurs de bouleversements majeurs dans l'ordre des valeurs – mais l'âme de la France est déjà si forte, si structurée, qu'on ne pourra la nier.

CHRONOLOGIE I

Vingt dates clés (des origines à 1515)

35 000 avant J.-C. : L'homme de Cro-Magnon, aux Eyzies-de-Tayac-Sireuil (Dordogne)

15 500 avant J.-C. : Grotte de Lascaux

620 avant J.-C. : Fondation de Marseille

500 avant J.-C. : Début des invasions celtes

58-52 avant J.-C. : Jules César en Gaule

177 : Martyrs chrétiens de Lyon

498 : Baptême de Clovis

800 : Charlemagne empereur

843 : Partage de Verdun

910 : Fondation de Cluny

987-996 : Hugues Capet

1096-1099 : Première croisade

1180-1223 : Philippe Auguste

1244 : Prise de Montségur, citadelle cathare

1285-1314 : Philippe le Bel

1348 : Épidémie de peste noire

1429 : Jeanne d'Arc délivre Orléans (8 mai), est suppliciée à Rouen le 30 mai 1431

1461-1483 : Louis XI

1495 : Entrée de Charles VIII (1483-1498) à Naples

1511 : Sainte Ligue (pape, Angleterre, Espagne, Venise, Suisse) contre la France de Louis XII (1498-1515)

LIVRE II

GUERRES CIVILES, GLOIRE DU ROI, PUISSANCE DE L'ÉTAT

1515-1715

1

LA GUERRE AU NOM DE DIEU

1515-1589

19.

Que devient le royaume de France après que Luther a affiché, en 1517, sur les portes de la chapelle du château de Wittenberg, 95 propositions pour réformer l'Église catholique, et que dans toute l'Europe, et d'abord dans l'Empire germanique, se déchaîne la guerre des religions entre huguenots et papistes, réformés et catholiques ?

Quelles blessures seront infligées à l'âme de la France dans cet affrontement des croyants qui devient vite une guerre civile et une guerre sociale ?

Comment un royaume dont le roi est le représentant de Dieu sur terre, qui accomplit en son nom des miracles, qui détient de fait un pouvoir quasi sacerdotal, pourrait-il traverser cette épreuve sans que les passions le bouleversent et le déchirent ?

Cependant, durant quarante-cinq ans, de 1515 à 1560, la tourmente qui ravage l'Allemagne – la révolte des paysans, une vraie guerre aux arrière-plans religieux, y commence en 1524 – semble épargner la France. On y poursuit les hérétiques, on y brûle les imprimeurs, on y conspire déjà, mais le royaume ne s'embrase pas.

Le vent souffle fort, la mer se creuse dès 1520, mais le royaume continue de voguer. Ce n'est qu'en 1559-1560 que la tempête se lève et que s'approche l'heure des massacres.

Les deux premiers souverains Valois, François Ier (1515-1547) et Henri II, son fils (1547-1559), ont affirmé avec force leur foi catholique et ont condamné les huguenots.

La guerre civile, la persécution généralisée, n'éclatent pas pour autant.

Mais voici que, le 30 juin 1559, au cours d'un tournoi – vestige et rituel médiévaux –, Henri II a l'œil et le crâne transpercés par un morceau de la lance de son adversaire, Gabriel de Montgomery. Longue agonie, symbole de la souffrance nationale à venir.

Son frêle fils aîné (quinze ans), François II, lui succède, mais régnera à peine un an et demi.

Va commencer alors le temps de la guerre civile. Mais l'on se souviendra des quarante-cinq premières années du XVIe siècle comme d'une époque encore paisible.

Et pourtant, entre le 25 janvier 1515, sacre du duc de Valois, devenu François Ier, et la mort tragique de Henri II en 1559, que de transformations dans la vie du royaume, qui déterminent son avenir et marquent pour des siècles l'âme de la France !

D'abord le roi.

Il est, avec François Ier, glorieux vainqueur des Suisses à Marignan (13 et 14 septembre 1515) après avoir franchi les Alpes au col de l'Arche, 3 000 sapeurs ouvrant la route à 40 000 hommes et à 300 canons.

La tradition militaire nationale s'enracine. Sur le champ de bataille, le roi se fait sacrer chevalier par Bayard. Ce geste n'est pas la vaine tentative de faire revivre un rituel anachronique, mais l'expression d'une volonté de nouer le présent au passé. François Ier et Bayard sont des chevaliers. Il n'y a pas rupture entre les époques. L'institution monarchique est éternelle. Ainsi se créent et se renforcent les mythes nationaux.

François Ier annonce les campagnes de Bonaparte en Italie – les cols d'où l'on tombe par surprise sur l'ennemi, l'emploi de l'artillerie pour arracher la victoire. Et les avantages qu'on glane : concordat avec le pape en 1516 – le roi nomme aux charges de l'Église de France et bénéficie ainsi de sa richesse, qui devient un instrument politique pour s'attacher les candidats aux fonctions ecclésiastiques.

Il signe un traité de paix perpétuelle avec les cantons suisses : coûteux, parce qu'il faut les acheter, mais le royaume dispose ainsi d'une frontière sûre et de mercenaires courageux, dévoués, aguerris.

François Ier se sent si fort qu'il brigue en 1519 la dignité impériale. Mais l'argent des banquiers augsbourgeois – les Fugger – permet à Charles d'Espagne d'acheter les électeurs et de devenir Cnarles Quint.

Toute la géopolitique française s'en trouve changée : l'ennemi n'est plus l'Anglais. En 1520, François Ier accueille Henri VIII au camp du Drap d'or, mais le Habsbourg, Charles Quint, prend le royaume de France en tenailles entre le Rhin et les Pyrénées, et revendique l'héritage bourguignon.

L'Italie n'est plus seulement la terre des richesses, des arts, des créateurs qu'il faut attirer en France (Léonard de Vinci et sa *Joconde*, le Primatice, le Rosso, Cellini), mais le champ clos de l'affrontement entre le roi de France et l'empereur Charles Quint et son fils Philippe II. Entre le Français et les Habsbourg, dix-huit ans de guerre.

À la victoire de Marignan – jamais oubliée, magnifiée – succèdent les défaites, et d'abord la plus grave, le 24 février 1525 : le « désastre » de Pavie.

François Ier est fait prisonnier : « De toutes choses ne m'est demeurée que l'honneur et la vie sauve », dit-il. Transféré à Madrid, il n'est libéré qu'en signant sous la contrainte un traité léonin et en donnant ses fils en gage contre sa libération.

Humiliation.

Nécessité de trouver contre le Habsbourg des alliances nouvelles : celles des hérétiques allemands ! Et celle, encore plus scandaleuse, de Soliman le Magnifique.

Avec la complicité française, la flotte turque viendra bombarder en Nice 1543, et, pour que les équipages et les navires de Soliman puissent hiverner, François Ier les accueillera à Toulon après avoir vidé la ville de ses habitants.

L'intérêt dynastique et le « patriotisme monarchique » sont plus forts que la foi catholique !

La France inaugure ainsi une diplomatie « nationale » et « laïque » qui ne répugne pas à chercher l'appui de l'infidèle contre l'empereur chrétien, qu'il soit Charles Quint ou Philippe II d'Espagne.

Stratégie fructueuse qui permet de compenser la puissance des Habsbourg (deux après l'abdication et la mort de Charles Quint – 1556, 1558 : l'empereur Ferdinand et le roi d'Espagne Philippe II) et de consolider la présence française en Orient.

Les « capitulations » de 1536 accordent des avantages aux vaisseaux et aux marchands français au Levant, et confirment que la France est la protectrice des Lieux saints.

Au terme des affrontements (victoire française à Cérisoles en 1544, résistance de Metz en 1554, puis défaite française à Saint-Quentin en 1557), le traité du Cateau-Cambrésis (1559) marque l'épuisement des deux adversaires.

Henri II conserve les trois évêchés (Metz, Toul et Verdun), rend ses États au duc de Savoie, et les Anglais rétrocèdent Calais.

Mais ces aléas de la guerre – et même la captivité de François Ier – n'ont en rien atteint le prestige du roi.

François Ier est le « César triomphant », l'égal de Cyrus et de Constantin.

Il est pour la première fois « Sa Majesté ».

Les états généraux ne sont plus convoqués (de 1484 à 1560). « Car tel est notre bon plaisir. » « Car ainsi nous plaît-il être fait. »

Le roi gouverne en réunissant des conseils : Conseil secret, Conseil étroit, Conseil des affaires.

La centralisation renforce l'absolutisme.

L'ordonnance de Villers-Cotterêts, le 10 août 1539, manifeste cette volonté royale de réglementer, de contrôler, de tenir d'une main ferme tout le royaume.

Pièce maîtresse dans cette unification, c'est, au bénéfice du roi et de toutes les juridictions du royaume, un acte juridique et politique majeur qui marque profondément l'âme de la France.

Il vise, en 192 articles, à créer une nation « homogène » :

« Le langage maternel français » est obligatoire dans les actes publics.

La langue est l'instrument de la politique : le français est la langue de l'État.

La justice devient une arme étatique : les juridictions ecclésiastiques ne peuvent juger que les affaires concernant l'Église.

Dans la procédure pénale, l'accusé se voit privé de moyens de défense au bénéfice de l'accusation. Le pouvoir royal a tiré la leçon des émeutes qui se sont produites à Lyon en 1529, et la nouvelle législation permettra de réprimer avec encore plus de sévérité la révolte de 1543-1548 qui dresse la Guyenne contre les hausses d'impôts. De même, parce qu'il a fallu faire face en 1539 à une grève des imprimeurs lyonnais, l'ordonnance de Villers-Cotterêts interdit les confréries de métier.

Une monarchie absolue se met en place au moment où l'humanisme de la Renaissance imprègne les élites tout en les séparant du reste du peuple.

Le pouvoir se ramifie. Il construit ou réaménage les châteaux de Chambord, Fontainebleau, Amboise, Anet, ainsi que le Louvre. Il augmente sa puissance militaire : il paie les mercenaires suisses, « solde » les compagnies, les dote d'armes nouvelles (arquebuses, bombardes, couleuvrines, pistolets). Il se veut resplendissant – la Cour autour du roi compte plusieurs milliers de courtisans –, rayonnant : Bibliothèque royale, Typographie royale, Collège des lecteurs royaux, « noble et trilingue Académie » – latin, grec, hébreu –, futur Collège de France.

Et il a dès lors de plus en plus besoin d'argent.

Il faut, pour lever l'impôt, connaître le nombre des habitants.

Les curés sont chargés de tenir des registres des naissances et des baptêmes.

En 1523 est créé un Trésor de l'épargne. On emprunte aux villes. On multiplie les créations d'« offices » qui sont vendus afin d'augmenter les recettes.

On applique avec rigueur le concordat de 1516 :

« Le Roi nomme, dit l'ambassadeur de Venise, à 10 archevêchés, 82 évêchés, 527 abbayes, à une infinité de prieurés et canonicats. Ce droit de nomination lui procure une grandissime servitude et obéissance des prélats et laïques par le désir qu'ils ont des bénéfices. Et de cette façon il satisfait ses sujets, mais encore il se concilie une foule d'étrangers. »

Les sujets paient et reçoivent, mais le pouvoir absolu exige obéissance.

« En quelque chose que le Roi commande, il est obéi aussitôt comme l'homme l'est des bêtes ! » dit Maximilien d'Autriche.

Et ceux qui ne plient pas, ou ceux qui, dans le domaine financier, essentiel pour la monarchie absolue, fraudent, sont châtiés.

Le roi ne peut pardonner les malversations, même s'il en bénéficie un temps. À la fin, il condamne et s'approprie.

Ainsi le surintendant Jacques Beaume de Semblançay est-il pendu le 9 août 1527 au gibet de Montfaucon :

> *Frères humains qui après nous vivez*
> *N'ayez les cœurs contre nous endurcis...*

Mais l'« humaniste » François Ier ne transige pas à propos de son pouvoir.

« Il n'y a qu'un roi de France, dit-il, et garderais bien qu'il n'y aurait en France un Sénat comme à Venise... »

Pas de Parlement outrepassant ses fonctions judiciaires :

« Le roi vous défend que vous ne vous entremettiez en quelque façon que ce soit du fait de l'État ni d'autre chose que de la justice. »

Ainsi, dans cette première moitié du XVIe siècle, on ne peut se contenter de regarder les tableaux inspirés de l'école italienne ou les châteaux. Il ne faut pas s'en tenir à cette Renaissance qui change le décor, les costumes et les mœurs.

On assiste en fait à l'affirmation d'une monarchie nouvelle, centralisatrice, unificatrice, autoritaire.

L'absolutisme encadre la nation, dicte ses ordonnances. En imposant la langue de l'État, le français, la monarchie entend régir l'âme de la France. Elle renforce la nation, même si sa rigidité tout comme le mécanisme de vente des offices nécessaire à son financement portent en eux, à long terme, des éléments de faiblesse.

Mais, vers 1550, c'est la force de la royauté française qui frappe.

Pour Machiavel, elle est un modèle. Nation la plus peuplée d'Europe, elle est efficacement gouvernée.

« Nul pays n'est aussi uni, aussi facile à manier que la France, écrit un ambassadeur vénitien en 1546. Voilà sa force, à mon sens : unité et obéissance. Les Français, qui se sentent peu faits pour se gouverner eux-mêmes, ont entièrement remis leur liberté et leur volonté aux mains de leur roi. Il lui suffit de dire : "Je veux telle ou telle somme, j'ordonne, je consens", et l'exécution est aussi prompte que si c'était la nation entière qui eût décidé de son propre mouvement. »

Cette relation particulière entre un peuple et son souverain est la traduction politique d'un sentiment partagé entre celui-ci et les Français : le patriotisme.

Et les poètes, les écrivains – ils forment une Pléiade incomparable, de Clément Marot à Ronsard, de Rabelais à Du Bellay, de Montaigne à Desportes –, les juristes, l'expriment, chantent la patrie :

> Plus me plaît le séjour qu'ont bâti mes aïeux
> Que des palais romains le front audacieux
> Plus que le marbre dur me plaît l'ardoise fine
> Plus mon Loire gaulois que le Tibre latin
> Plus mon petit Liré que le mont Palatin
> Et plus que l'air marin la douceur angevine,

dit Du Bellay, évoquant son village natal et rêvant de « vivre entre ses parents le reste de son âge ».

Il ajoute en 1559 :

> Laisse-moi donques là ces Latins et Grégeois
> Qui ne servent de rien au poète françois
> Et soit la seule cour ton Virgile et Homère
> Puisqu'elle est, comme on dit, des bons esprits la mère.

Les auteurs anonymes de chansons populaires riment autour des mêmes thèmes.

Ils exaltent « le noble roi François », vainqueur à Marignan, et pleurent lors de sa détention à Madrid après le désastre de Pavie.

Mais, durant toute sa captivité – un an –, la fidélité au souverain n'est jamais remise en cause.

Alors que la régente – Louise de Savoie, mère du roi – est à Lyon, les Parisiens, craignant l'invasion, créent une assemblée représentative qui s'arroge certes des pouvoirs, mais qui s'affirme décidée à combattre l'ennemi « impérial ». Et il en est ainsi dans tout le royaume.

Ce « patriotisme » est une des spécificités françaises, et les femmes en sont souvent les porte-parole, comme si elles reprenaient le glaive de Jeanne d'Arc.

D'ailleurs, autour de François Ier et de Henri II, les femmes jouent un rôle décisif.

Louise de Savoie mène les négociations pour la libération de son fils. Sa sœur Marguerite, sa maîtresse Anne, duchesse d'Étampes, sont des actrices de la vie culturelle et favorisent la diffusion de l'humanisme.

Diane de Poitiers, maîtresse de Henri II, et naturellement son épouse Catherine de Médicis, fille de Laurent de Médicis, nièce de deux papes, mère de François II, puis de Charles IX (1560-1574) et de Henri III (1574-1589), d'une reine d'Espagne et d'une reine de Navarre, ont elles aussi un grand poids politique.

Ce rôle des femmes au sommet de l'État, dans le cœur du pouvoir absolutiste, que Jeanne d'Arc avait incarné au siècle précédent, se trouve ainsi confirmé au XVIe siècle et devient l'un des traits majeurs de l'« âme de la France ».

Ce sentiment national, ce patriotisme, cet absolutisme, se renforcent mutuellement et accroissent le pouvoir du roi.

Ils vont être confrontés à la Réforme, c'est-à-dire à la possibilité, pour l'un des sujets du royaume, d'opter pour une autre religion que celle de son souverain.

Et, de surcroît, une foi souvent étrangère, hérétique (Luther a été excommunié par la diète de Worms en 1521).

Le risque d'une résurgence d'un « parti de l'étranger » est, au fur et à mesure que le siècle s'avance, de mieux en mieux perçu par ceux qui, « politiques », souhaitent préserver l'unité du royaume et donc organiser la « tolérance » pour les adeptes de la « religion prétendument réformée ».

Durant toute la première moitié du xvɪᵉ siècle – jusqu'en 1560, date de la mort de François II –, la situation oscille.

Marguerite, sœur de François Iᵉʳ, humaniste, influence le roi, favorable à ceux (Lefèvre d'Étaples, un érudit ; Briçonnet, évêque de Meaux), qui veulent, en bons lecteurs de la Bible – dont les exemplaires imprimés se répandent –, purifier l'Église.

Le 5 février 1517, François Iᵉʳ a même chargé Guillaume Budé d'inviter Érasme à venir à Paris : « Je vous avertis que si vous voulez venir, vous serez le bienvenu », lui écrit le monarque.

La création du Collège trilingue (latin, grec, hébreu) des lecteurs royaux participe de cette ouverture humaniste tolérée et même souhaitée dès lors qu'elle ne touche que le monde intellectuel et ne met pas en cause le pouvoir politique.

Mais l'excommunication de Luther, la publication en français de *L'Institution chrétienne* de Calvin, le choix de l'« hérésie » par près de la moitié de la noblesse (les Condés, les Montmorencys, les Bourbons), inquiètent les souverains.

C'est leur pouvoir absolu que leur « tolérance » remet en cause.

Et l'Église catholique, dont ils sont en fait les maîtres politiques, est un rouage trop important de leur système absolutiste pour qu'ils acceptent de la voir attaquée ou simplement concurrencée.

Pour un roi de France – même prince de la Renaissance, même humaniste comme François Iᵉʳ –, le fait que certains de ses sujets rompent avec le pape, refusent les sacrements, quittent donc l'Église catholique, la religion dont il est le « représentant » et qui le sacre, est inacceptable.

Dès lors, durant cette première moitié du xvɪᵉ siècle, la persécution des huguenots va s'accentuer, sans provoquer encore de guerre civile.

Dès 1523, des hérétiques sont brûlés à Paris, place Maubert.

Il suffit qu'une statue de la Vierge ait été mutilée pour que d'autres soient torturés, condamnés au bûcher.

En 1529, un gentilhomme, Berquin, est ainsi exécuté.

En 1534, le roi s'indigne et s'inquiète qu'on ait osé placarder sur la porte de sa chambre, à Amboise, mais aussi au Louvre, des textes hostiles à la messe.

Cette « affaire des placards » le persuade que les huguenots sont des ennemis du pouvoir royal.

La persécution s'intensifie. On torture. On brûle. L'imprimeur Étienne Dolet est ainsi exécuté (1546), et le roi laisse le parlement d'Aix exterminer dans le Luberon 3 000 hérétiques « vaudois » dont les villages sont détruits.

La machine à massacrer est en marche.

Une « Chambre ardente » est créée dès 1551 auprès du parlement de Paris, et un inquisiteur dominicain y siège. Elle rendra en trois ans plus de 500 arrêts contre l'hérésie.

Un édit d'Écouen autorise en 1559 à abattre tout huguenot révolté ou en fuite. Et le conseiller Anne Du Bourg, qui s'oppose à cet édit, est étranglé et brûlé.

Mais cette persécution n'empêche pas, en 1555, Calvin, réfugié à Genève, d'organiser les églises réformées de France. En 1560, on en compte plus de 150, représentant deux millions de fidèles. Un synode national se réunit même à Paris.

Sur son lit de mort, Henri II a beau murmurer : « Que mon peuple persiste et demeure ferme en la foi en laquelle je meurs », des protestants chantent des psaumes sur l'autre rive de la Seine, en face du Louvre.

Ce défi à l'autorité royale, à l'absolutisme, à la règle fondatrice – « religion du roi, religion du royaume » –, constitue une lourde menace.

D'autant plus politique que des conjurés huguenots cherchent à s'emparer du roi en résidence à Amboise. Cette conjuration ourdie par des gentilshommes va échouer, et les nobles « catholiques » conduits par François de Guise exécuteront plus d'une centaine de conjurés, dont certains sont pendus aux balcons du château.

Est-ce le temps des massacres qui commence ?

La mort de François II permet à sa mère Catherine de Médicis de faire promulguer deux édits qui tentent d'éviter la guerre civile.

Le premier amnistie les conjurés d'Amboise.

Le second, distinguant l'hérésie de la rébellion, entrouvre ainsi la porte à la tolérance religieuse dès lors qu'elle ne se mue pas en force politique hostile au pouvoir royal.

Est-ce possible ?

Un imprimeur est encore brûlé vif pour écrits séditieux ; des huguenots sont massacrés à Lyon.

Comment établir une frontière nette entre critique de l'Église et opposition au roi qui en est le protecteur ?

D'ailleurs, les protestants recommencent à conspirer. Ils tentent de s'emparer de Lyon (septembre 1560). Alors la répression s'abat sur eux.

Devant les états généraux réunis à Orléans peu après la mort du roi François II – le 5 décembre 1560 –, le chancelier Michel de L'Hospital lance un appel à la tolérance qui est aussi l'expression d'un désir d'unité française, de sagesse politique et de tolérance.

On ne peut, dit-il, convaincre les huguenots qu'avec les « armes de la charité, les prières, persuasions, paroles de Dieu qui sont propres à tel combat. Le couteau vaut peu contre l'esprit. Ôtons ces mots diaboliques, luthériens, huguenots, papistes : ne changeons pas le nom de chrétien ! »

Cette voix est aussi celle d'une autre spécificité française.

Elle affirme qu'entre les camps opposés, entre les violences qui s'exacerbent l'une l'autre, il existe un choix « médian » récusant l'extermination d'un camp par l'autre, parce que la première victime en serait le royaume, la nation elle-même.

20.

La France de 1560 peut-elle entendre la voix de la sagesse et de la tolérance ?

Les passions religieuses qui se déchaînent nourrissent les ambitions, les haines, les ressentiments, les convictions, les croyances que la monarchie centralisatrice, autoritaire, marchant vers l'absolutisme, a jusque-là réussi à contenir, à refouler, à étouffer.

Et toutes les vieilles blessures se rouvrent au moment où le pouvoir se trouve affaibli.

En 1560, un enfant de dix ans est devenu Charles IX, roi de France. Il est maladif, dépressif, velléitaire.

Et c'est sa mère, Catherine de Médicis, « par la grâce de Dieu, reine de France, mère du Roy », qui exerce la régence, avec l'habileté, le sens de l'intrigue, l'absence de scrupules, le cynisme d'une fille des Médicis de Florence, élèves de Machiavel.

Elle n'a qu'un seul but : ne rien céder du pouvoir royal, celui de Charles IX, c'est-à-dire le pouvoir qu'elle détient, et peut-être demain celui de son fils préféré, Henri – sans compter qu'après lui reste encore un frère cadet, François.

Quant à sa fille Marguerite, elle la mariera le moment venu à l'un des grands, duc ou prince, et pourquoi pas au roi de Navarre, Henri de Bourbon ?

Elle se méfie de tout et de tous.

De ces Guises – François, le général ; Charles, l'archevêque de Reims – qui prétendent descendre en ligne directe de Charlemagne et qui incarnent un catholicisme intransigeant. Ils sont pénétrés de l'esprit du concile qui, réuni à Trente, après 1545, ne cède rien aux « réformés », mais élabore au contraire une Contre-Réforme, qui recrée l'Inquisition sous le nom de Congrégation de la Suprême Inquisition, qui s'appuie sur la Compagnie de Jésus – l'armée noire du pape – pour diriger les consciences des hommes et des femmes d'influence, et établit les listes des livres « diaboliques » à proscrire.

De ces autres grands, les Bourbon-Condé, qui soutiennent les huguenots.

Des Bourbon-Navarre, eux aussi tentés par la religion prétendument réformée.

Catherine de Médicis s'inquiète de voir ces protestants se doter d'une organisation militaire, exprimant, sous le couvert de la foi nouvelle, les volontés d'autonomie des grands seigneurs et des villes brisées par le pouvoir royal.

Cette situation religieuse, politique, sociale – la disette reparaît, les prix des denrées montent, la misère, qui semblait contenue, se répand à nouveau avec, ici et là, des poussées de peste noire –, est d'autant plus lourde de menaces que chaque camp regarde vers l'étranger.

Les catholiques vers l'Espagne, les huguenots, vers ces « Gueux » des Pays-Bas qui combattent l'Espagnol Philippe II et affirment leur religion et leur désir d'indépendance.

L'Allemagne s'émiette.

La religion du prince est celle de son peuple.

Il en ira ainsi en Angleterre, quand Élisabeth, après le schisme de Henri VIII, choisira en 1563 de créer l'Église anglicane, antipapiste, mais hiérarchisée à l'instar de l'Église catholique.

Dans cette nouvelle configuration des forces en Europe, la France hésite encore.

Étrange moment, révélateur du caractère complexe de l'histoire nationale et de l'âme de la France.

Autour d'elle, les peuples s'alignent. Les uns entrent au temple, les autres, dans l'Église romaine ou dans l'Église anglicane.

Les peuples obéissent à leur souverain : *Cujus regio, ejus religio.*

Mais la France, fille aînée de l'Église, hésite et débat.

Le patriotisme, le sentiment familial, sont déjà si forts que, durant deux années encore (1560-1562), Catherine de Médicis et ses conseillers tentent d'éviter la guerre civile.

Ronsard, « papiste », s'adresse au souverain :

> *Sire, ce n'est pas tout que d'être Roi de France*
> *Il faut que la vertu honore votre enfance...*

Et dans cette *Institution pour l'adolescence du roi Charles IX* (1561), il convoque l'histoire devenue référence, légende :

> *Du temps victorieux vous faisant immortel*
> *Comme Charles le Grand ou bien Charles Martel...*

L'invincible, l'indomptable Charles Martel...

La régente organise à Poissy, en septembre 1561, un colloque où des représentants de la religion catholique et de la religion réformée débattent, échangent avec vigueur des arguments en faveur de leur foi.

Dialogue de la dernière chance – mais significatif de la singularité française – où les plus radicaux des intervenants – Théodore de Bèze pour les huguenots, le général des jésuites Lainez – empêchent que la tolérance l'emporte.

Cependant, un édit – de Saint-Germain, le 17 janvier 1562 – reconnaît dans certaines conditions le droit pour les pasteurs de prêcher à l'extérieur des villes, qui leur demeureront closes.

C'est un pas vers l'apaisement, vers la reconnaissance de l'autre.

Mais les passions débordent, entraînent le peuple.

Des protestants saccagent des églises. Des catholiques, des temples. Les uns et les autres prennent les armes, s'affrontent déjà.

Et premier massacre à Vassy, non prémédité.

Il a suffi, le 1er mars 1562, à François de Guise et à ses hommes d'entendre chanter des psaumes dans la ville – en contradiction avec l'édit de Saint-Germain – pour qu'ils tuent des dizaines de huguenots. On massacre des « religionnaires » dans plusieurs villes. En guise de riposte, les protestants s'emparent d'autres cités.

La porte de la cruauté et de la guerre civile vient de s'ouvrir, et elle ne se refermera – jamais totalement – que trente-six années plus tard, en 1598, avec l'édit de Nantes, pacification précaire.

Cependant, comme si dès 1562 les Français pressentaient que le pire pour le royaume était encore à venir, s'exprime alors le désarroi, la souffrance devant ce malheur qu'est la guerre entre Français.

Réfugié à Bâle, un huguenot (Castellion) écrit dans son *Traité des hérétiques* : « Supportons-nous l'un l'autre et ne condamnons incontinent la foi de personne. »

Quant à Ronsard, dans la *Continuation du Discours sur la misère de ce temps*, il décrit :

> *L'extrême malheur dont notre France est pleine*
> ....
> *Comme une pauvre femme atteinte de la mort*
> *Son sceptre qui pendait et sa robe semée*
> *De fleurs de lis était en cent lieux entamée*
> *Son poil était hideux, son œil hâve et profond*
> *Et nulle majesté ne lui haussait le front.*

Castellion, dans son *Conseil à la France désolée*, insiste sur le malheur absolu qu'est la guerre civile : « Ce ne sont pas les étrangers qui te guerroient comme bien autrefois a été fait lorsque par dehors tu étais affligée, pour le moins tu avais par dedans l'amour et accord de tes enfants quelque soulagement. Aujourd'hui, ce sont tes propres enfants qui te désolent et affligent. Tes villes et villages, voire les chemins et les champs, sont couverts de corps morts, tes rivières en rougissent et l'air en est puant et infect. Bref, en toi il n'y a ni paix ni repos, ni jour ni nuit, et on n'entend que plaintes, et hélas de toutes parts sans y pouvoir trouver lieu qui soit sûr et sans frayeur et meurtre, crainte et épouvantement. »

La France se déchire et les Français s'entretuent. L'âme de la France souffre.

Le patriotisme et la conscience nationale éplorés ne peuvent pourtant empêcher les affrontements de se succéder – quatre « guerres » de 1562 à 1574 –, ni les camps en présence de faire appel à leurs « coreligionnaires » des pays voisins.

Ainsi, en même temps que resurgissent, derrière les engagements religieux, les ambitions des grands féodaux, les colères sociales, on voit renaître le « parti de l'étranger ».

Les huguenots livrent Le Havre aux Anglais, en appellent aux reîtres et aux lansquenets allemands, cependant que les catholiques se tournent vers l'Espagne de Philippe II.

De même se profile le risque d'éclatement du royaume.

Des « républiques théocratiques », des places de sûreté « huguenotes », se constituent.

Les villes de La Rochelle, de Nantes, de Nîmes, de Bourges, de Montpellier, de Montauban, échappent à l'autorité royale, alors que Paris – et son parlement, dont la juridiction s'étend à une grande partie de la France, hors le sud du pays – est farouchement, fanatiquement catholique.

On voit ainsi s'organiser une sorte de république des Provinces-Unies du Midi dont les capitales sont Nîmes et Montauban et qui dispose d'un port, La Rochelle.

Mais l'attachement à l'unité nationale perdure.

Des édits (celui d'Amboise en 1563), qui sont autant le résultat du rapport des forces que la manifestation de l'espérance dans le retour à la paix civile, suscitent des trêves précaires.

Et le roi continue d'incarner la nation.

Profitant d'une longue suspension des combats, Catherine de Médicis tente de rassembler les adversaires autour de Charles IX.

Elle parcourt la France à ses côtés dans un long périple de vingt-sept mois (1564-1566). Les populations divisées, les villes huguenotes, l'accueillent, se retrouvent autour de lui, attestant qu'il est la clé de voûte du pays, que sa force symbolique est grande et que ses sujets veulent croire en la fin de leurs affrontements fratricides.

À dire vrai, chaque camp voudrait avoir à sa tête ce roi-emblème. Les huguenots essaient même de l'enlever, à Meaux, en 1567 ! Ils échouent.

Catherine de Médicis ne renonce pas.

Elle veut réaliser le projet de mariage entre sa fille Marguerite et Henri de Bourbon, roi de Navarre, union d'une catholique de sang royal et d'un hérétique. Ce faisant, la réconciliation est-elle possible ? L'unité du royaume va-t-elle se reconstituer ?

Charles IX a vingt ans en 1570. L'amiral de Coligny, la plus forte personnalité huguenote, est admis au Conseil du roi.

Lui aussi a le projet de reconstituer l'unité du royaume en concevant une grande politique étrangère « nationale ». La France prendrait la tête d'une large coalition protestante en s'alliant avec les « Gueux » des Pays-Bas et en menant à leurs côtés la guerre contre Philippe II, le Habsbourg, le roi de cette Espagne ennemie de la France.

On saisit ici combien, quand il s'agit de la France – de la grande puissance européenne –, sont toujours intriquées la politique intérieure et la politique extérieure.

La « géopolitique » commande cette liaison. C'est là une caractéristique permanente de l'histoire nationale.

Le mariage de Marguerite et de Henri de Navarre doit se célébrer en août 1572.

C'est un moment charnière. L'apparence est à l'unité retrouvée.

Les nobles huguenots entrent dans Paris pour participer aux fêtes nuptiales. Coligny est devenu le conseiller influent du roi.

Mais aucun camp n'a désarmé.

Catherine de Médicis a organisé le piège en même temps qu'elle œuvrait à la réconciliation. Les Guises n'ont pas renoncé. Une tentative d'assassinat de Coligny échoue. L'ordre est donné de massacrer les protestants pour noyer l'attentat contre Coligny dans un flot de sang.

C'est la Saint-Barthélemy, le dimanche 24 août 1572.

On poignarde. On noie. On égorge. On dépèce. On brûle. On pille.

Le peuple – femmes et enfants – arrache les membres des victimes, jette les nouveau-nés dans la Seine. On trouve des morceaux de chair dans toutes les rues de Paris. Crimes barbares et rituels.

Le peuple échappe à ses chefs.

Le massacre, à Paris, par la foule enivrée de passion, s'inscrit dans l'âme de la France, annonce d'autres massacres.

La Saint-Barthélemy devient un repère, une référence. En août-septembre 1792, on craindra – deux cent vingt ans plus tard, donc ! – une « Saint-Barthélemy des patriotes », et les massacres de Septembre rappelleront, par leur violence rituelle, leur barbarie, ceux d'août 1572.

Tout au long de notre histoire, dans nos « guerres de religion » – qui se nommeront alors guerres de classes –, on massacrera (1834, 1848, 1871, 1934, 1944).

Paris n'est pas une ville paisible, mais une capitale ensanglantée, l'épicentre des passions françaises.

Le massacre se propage et fait trembler toute la France.

On tue dans de nombreuses villes : à Meaux, Orléans, Bourges, Troyes, Rouen, Bordeaux, etc.

Les huguenots se vengent, une furie iconoclaste se répand. D'autres protestants quittent le pays.

Tuer ou être tué, combattre et se protéger dans les places de sûreté, se terrer, fuir : telles apparaissent à beaucoup les seules issues.

Le pouvoir royal ordonne les massacres ou ne les empêche pas. Dès lors, comment faire encore confiance à ce roi, hésitant, il est vrai, placé devant le fait accompli, mais finalement l'acceptant, le couvrant, le légitimant – qui a laissé égorger jusque dans les chambres du Louvre ?

Quant à Henri de Navarre, il n'a dû son salut qu'au fait qu'il a – comme Henri de Condé – promis d'abjurer (il le fera le 3 septembre 1572).

Ces massacres se poursuivent d'août à octobre 1572 et font entre 15 000 et 30 000 victimes.

Une procession royale, le 4 septembre, rend grâce pour la victoire de la Juste Foi. À Rome, le pape Grégoire XIII célèbre un *Te Deum*.

Le parti huguenot est décapité.

Le roi peut donc, dans une ordonnance, exiger que l'on arrête de tuer, d'attenter à la vie et aux biens de « ceux de la religion nouvelle ».

Mais comment le croire ?

Un protestant, Duplessis-Mornay, écrira : « L'État s'est crevassé et ébranlé depuis la journée de la Saint-Barthélemy, depuis que la foi du Prince envers le sujet et du sujet envers le Prince, qui est le seul ciment qui entretient les États en un, s'est si outrageusement démentie. »

Dans l'âme de la France plane désormais le soupçon que le pouvoir peut mentir, trahir, qu'il faut se méfier de lui.

Certes, cela n'efface pas le sentiment enraciné que le roi est, comme dit Duplessis-Mornay, « le seul ciment » de la nation.

Mais il faut, en face de lui, rester sur ses gardes, et donc le contrôler.

Et pourquoi ne pas élire le roi, affirmer la supériorité des états généraux sur le monarque, exiger de pouvoir le désavouer, le renvoyer et même le condamner ? Car le tyrannique ne peut devenir légitime.

Entre le roi et certains de ses sujets – les huguenots, en l'occurrence –, c'est l'ère du soupçon qui commence.

La Saint-Barthélemy fait naître de nouveaux adversaires de l'absolutisme, des ennemis des rois (les « monarchomaques », tels Théodore de Bèze et François Hotman).

Faut-il s'étonner que les protestants soient, trois siècles plus tard – les nations ont une longue mémoire –, parmi les plus ardents défenseurs du libéralisme politique, et qu'ils jouent un rôle majeur dans le mouvement et le gouvernement républicains ?

Ainsi, la Saint-Barthélemy, si elle a arrêté la progression de la religion prétendument réformée, a aggravé les tensions. Les blessures sont profondes.

Les « malcontents » sont nombreux même chez les catholiques, que les massacres ont effrayés.

Quand Charles IX meurt à Vincennes, le 30 mai 1574, à vingt-quatre ans, Catherine de Médicis exerce la régence, puisque son avant-dernier fils, Henri, a été élu roi de Pologne.

Henri III va succéder à Charles IX à la tête d'un royaume divisé vers lequel, quittant Cracovie, il se dirige à petite allure.

Ce roi qui traverse l'Europe, qu'on fête à Vienne et qui s'attarde à Venise parce qu'il aime les plaisirs, a vingt-trois ans. C'est un Valois, fils de la Renaissance, beau, séducteur, brillant et lettré.

Il raffole du luxe, des parfums, des tissus.

Il est sensible aux charmes des jeunes femmes, et, assure-t-on, des jeunes gens qui l'entourent, ces *mignons* qu'il dote et qui forment une Cour joyeuse.

Pourtant, il n'ignore rien de la cruauté des temps.

Catholique, il peut – mais joue-t-il ? – manifester une piété exaltée, baroque.

Il n'a pas hésité à participer au massacre de la Saint-Barthélemy. La Contre-Réforme lui convient, même si, dans sa vie privée, rien ne le freine.

Il est le roi, c'est-à-dire qu'il n'a de comptes à rendre qu'à lui-même et à Dieu.

Il a le sens de ses devoirs politiques. Il doit gouverner ce royaume déchiré où le sang n'en finit pas de couler. Et où, il le sait, son pouvoir royal et sa personne sont mis en cause.

Il veut renforcer l'État. Et il est lui aussi pénétré de l'idée que l'autorité du roi est la condition de l'unité et de la paix.

Il est ainsi un continuateur de Louis XI et de François Ier, cherchant à accroître l'efficacité du gouvernement, transformant le Conseil du roi en un Conseil d'État qui se divise en Conseil des parties et en Conseil des finances.

Il gouverne avec l'aide de ces « gens de robe », nobliaux aux origines modestes mais que l'ambition et la volonté de s'enrichir transforment en grands serviteurs de l'État.

Ainsi – c'est là un trait français, une tendance longue et puissante de notre histoire –, le désir du renforcement de l'État ne disparaît pas, alors que les obstacles qu'il rencontre se multiplient, que les « monarchomaques » se nourrissent des haines religieuses pour justifier leur théorie d'un pouvoir royal contrôlé, limité.

Les ennemis du roi recrutent certes parmi les huguenots, soucieux de défendre leur « sûreté », mais aussi parmi les grands seigneurs, héritiers et nostalgiques des pouvoirs féodaux.

Les Guises sont des catholiques intransigeants – ultras et même fanatiques –, comme le roi, mais ils contestent son pouvoir. Les Bourbons sont huguenots, mais sont aussi des « féodaux », tel Condé, et l'un d'eux, Henri, est même roi de Navarre.

Celui-ci, qui peut croire à la sincérité de son abjuration, obtenue alors qu'on pressait la pointe d'une épée sur sa gorge durant la Saint-Barthélemy ?

Henri III doit aussi compter avec ce tiers parti des « malcontents », des « politiques », qui trouve en François de Valois, frère cadet du roi, un soutien considérable.

Ces oppositions suscitent contre le monarque et ses « mignons » – le duc de Joyeuse, le duc d'Épernon – des libelles, des pamphlets, une floraison de rumeurs et de reproches visant les mœurs dissolues, la prodigalité, les fêtes fastueuses du souverain.

Le pouvoir royal est devenu une cible.

On le vise de toutes parts pour des raisons différentes : religieuses, féodales, morales, vindicatives ou même sociales – la disette serre souvent le peuple à la gorge et l'épidémie relaie la faim.

Situation d'autant plus difficile pour le roi qu'il a besoin d'argent, qu'il demande aux états généraux de lui voter des subsides alors même qu'on le critique et le conteste.

Il suffit d'un événement – l'évasion de Paris, en 1575, de François, frère du roi, et de Henri de Navarre, tous deux retenus prisonniers – pour que la tension se mue en nouvelle guerre.

Relaps, hérétique à nouveau, Henri, roi de Navarre, va devenir le chef et le protecteur des Églises réformées de France.

Ainsi s'aggrave une crise politique et nationale complexe où se conjuguent des déterminants divers et contradictoires. Ce sera là un des traits permanents de notre histoire : le pouvoir central est toujours contraint de tenir compte de forces qui souvent s'équilibrent, s'opposent entre elles. L'unité nationale, qui est pourtant un désir permanent, demeure précaire. L'autorité de l'État – dont la puissance pourtant se renforce d'autant plus que les tendances à l'éclatement sont puissantes – ne cesse d'être remise en cause.

Quand le pouvoir ne peut être le fédérateur de toutes les forces, il doit s'allier à certaines d'entre elles, au risque de voir toutes les autres se liguer contre lui.

Henri III choisit ainsi en 1576 – après des batailles perdues – de négocier avec les huguenots et de leur concéder des avantages considérables (édit de Beaulieu, 7 mai 1576).

Quatre ans seulement après le massacre de la Saint-Barthélemy, le culte de la nouvelle religion peut être célébré partout sauf à Paris.

Les huguenots non seulement peuvent conserver huit places de sûreté, mais ils seront représentés à égalité avec les catholiques dans les parlements.

Et, décision lourde de symbole, les victimes de la Saint-Barthélemy sont réhabilitées.

On mesure, à cet édit, combien les préoccupations politiques l'emportent, chez le roi, sur les engagements religieux. C'est son pouvoir et l'unité du royaume autour de sa personne qui comptent au premier chef.

Mais, par l'étendue des concessions consenties aux huguenots, il affaiblit sa position face aux catholiques.

Des ligues se constituent, fédérées par Henri de Guise. Et lorsque les états généraux se réunissent à Blois (1576), une majorité de parlementaires obligent Henri III à renoncer à l'édit de Beaulieu et lui refusent les subsides qu'il réclame.

Pis : la tentation est grande, chez nombre d'entre eux, de contester son pouvoir, même si la majorité craint l'éclatement du royaume.

En France, la conscience nationale est déjà persuadée qu'il n'est pire malheur que la rupture de l'unité du royaume.

C'est ce qu'exprime, dans ses *Six livres de la République*, Jean Bodin, quand il développe l'idée de la nécessité d'un pouvoir fort, au-dessus des factions, assurant l'unité nationale, et, en politique extérieure, l'indépendance.

Le pouvoir central – royal – était alors seul capable d'assurer ces deux conditions de la paix civile. Et la tolérance entre religions antagonistes sera possible à condition précisément que le pouvoir soit fort.

L'idée d'un pouvoir arbitre – et, à terme, laïque – commence ainsi à sourdre.

Et, contradictoirement, les partisans d'un pouvoir limité sont aussi les adversaires de la tolérance.

Voilà encore une spécificité française qui s'esquisse.

La logique de l'affrontement est encore la plus forte. Même si, durant quelques années, la guerre cède la place à des trêves, à des paix provisoires, à des édits de conciliation qui permettent, en 1578-1579, à Catherine de Médicis de visiter, en compagnie de Henri de Navarre, les provinces huguenotes dans l'espoir d'en obtenir des subsides – l'argent, ressort indispensable du pouvoir –, la situation est par trop dégradée pour qu'une paix véritable soit possible.

Disettes, tremblements de terre, inondations, épidémies et poussées de peste noire ravagent le royaume : on dénombrerait 50 000 victimes de l'épidémie rien qu'à Paris ! Et, dans les territoires qu'ils contrôlent, les Guises et Henri de Navarre se préparent à une nouvelle guerre.

Quand on apprend que le frère du roi, François, est mort, le 10 juin 1584, et que, Henri III n'ayant point de fils, c'est Henri de Navarre, chef des Églises réformées, qui est le seul héritier légitime de la couronne, les hostilités paraissent inéluctables. Les catholiques ne peuvent accepter d'avoir pour souverain un hérétique et un relaps.

C'est un nouvel abîme qui s'ouvre, où le royaume risque fort de basculer et d'être enseveli.

Une fois de plus s'opère la conjonction entre situation intérieure et politique extérieure.

Les Guises concluent un accord avec l'Espagne. C'est un grand projet politique contraire à celui qu'avait tenté de mettre sur pied Coligny en 1572. Il s'agit, avec l'appui de Philippe II (qui verse des subsides), d'extirper l'hérésie, de s'allier avec le Habsbourg pour faire la guerre aux « Gueux » des Pays-Bas et y assurer ainsi la domination de l'Espagne.

Naturellement, ce « parti de l'étranger » espère s'emparer en France du pouvoir royal.

Les Guises prétendent descendre de Charlemagne : ne valent-ils pas mieux qu'un roi de Navarre hérétique ? Ils peuvent compter sur la Sainte Ligue, qui a pris le contrôle de Paris.

On voit se développer en effet dans la capitale (à partir de 1576, et surtout de 1585) un vrai parti politique qui associe un catholicisme intransigeant à des aspirations et à des structures démocratiques.

Les « militants » – plusieurs milliers – sont encadrés par des « moines » ligueurs ; ils élisent des responsables de quartier. Un conseil des Seize les représente.

Cette conjonction d'une idéologie radicale et de la volonté populaire d'exercer directement le pouvoir annonce elle aussi une des lignes de force de l'histoire nationale.

La « propagande » condamne le « tyran » et ses mœurs. Elle appelle au tyrannicide.

Il n'a servi de rien à Henri III de se rallier aux positions des catholiques intransigeants (au traité de Nemours, en 1585), de ne laisser aux huguenots que le choix entre l'abjuration et l'exil, et d'interdire partout le culte protestant. On le soupçonne : n'est-il pas celui qui a, neuf ans auparavant, accordé aux mêmes hérétiques, par l'édit de Beaulieu, la possibilité pour leurs pasteurs de prêcher partout en France sauf à Paris ?

Or c'est Paris qui est le foyer le plus vif de l'intransigeance catholique. Là règne la Sainte Ligue, véritable mouvement populaire qui échappe en partie au contrôle des Guises, même si le peuple de la cité les suit.

Avantage considérable dans l'affrontement entre catholiques et huguenots, car chaque camp comprend que celui qui tient Paris peut l'emporter dans le reste du royaume. Condition nécessaire, en tout cas, même si elle n'est pas suffisante.

C'est également une donnée majeure de l'histoire nationale, et elle surgit avec force, en cette fin de XVIe siècle, pour ne plus jamais s'effacer.

Mais Paris est d'autant plus difficile à maîtriser par le pouvoir que, peu à peu, la population parisienne, consciente de la symbolique de la ville (qu'on se souvienne de Clovis et de sainte Geneviève, de Philippe Auguste et d'Étienne Marcel), est toujours prête à manifester son indépendance. Elle est nombreuse, et le pouvoir s'en méfie. Le roi n'aime plus résider à Paris : Henri III lui préfère Blois.

Quand il envoie des troupes dans la capitale, même s'il affiche désormais un catholicisme aussi radical que celui de la Ligue, la ville se couvre de barricades (12 mai 1588).

Le peuple de Paris, ligueur, craint une Saint-Barthélemy des catholiques, et vient d'inventer ainsi son mode spécifique de protestation. Celui-ci se transmettra d'un siècle à l'autre, comme si les barricades devenaient un symbole et le mode d'expression de Paris, donc aussi de la France.

Quel choix politique peut faire Henri III ?

Les Guises ont ouvert la porte à l'Espagnol. Ils visent non seulement à affaiblir le pouvoir royal, mais à s'emparer du trône. Ce serait la fin de l'unité du royaume, de sa souveraineté – Philippe II subventionne les ligueurs et leur envoie des troupes –, de son indépendance. Le roi se rebelle. Le pouvoir monarchique, le sens de l'État, sont plus forts que l'appartenance religieuse.

Le 25 décembre 1588, Henri III organise à Blois l'assassinat des Guises – « À présent, je suis roi ! » s'écriera-t-il – et confirme que Henri de Navarre, l'hérétique, sera son héritier.

Pour les ligueurs, le souverain n'est plus qu'un « tyran Sardanapale » contre qui le tyrannicide est légitime.

Le 1er août 1589, le moine Jacques Clément éventrera d'un coup de poignard Henri III, qui, dans son agonie, confirmera son choix dynastique.

Henri de Navarre deviendra donc Henri IV, mais le monarque mourant lui demande de se convertir.

La France n'en a pas fini avec la guerre. Henri IV va devoir conquérir et son royaume et Paris.

Et le poète Agrippa d'Aubigné, qui, enfant de huit ans en 1560, fut témoin, à Amboise, des premiers massacres de huguenots, qui a combattu, a été blessé dans les rangs protestants, qui est devenu en 1573 l'écuyer de Henri de Navarre et est en 1589 encore à ses côtés, décrit l'état du royaume avec la compassion et la révolte désespérée d'un « patriote » :

> *Je veux peindre la France une mère affligée*
> *Qui est, entre ses bras, de deux enfants chargée.*
> *Le plus fort, orgueilleux, empoigne les deux bouts*
> *Des tétins nourriciers ; puis, à force de coups*
> *D'ongles, de poings, de pieds, il brise le partage*
> *Dont Nature donnait à son besson l'usage.*
> ....
> *Elle dit : « Vous avez, félons, ensanglanté*
> *Le sein qui vous nourrit et qui vous a portés,*
> *Or vivez de venin, sanglante géniture,*
> *Je n'ai plus que du sang pour votre nourriture !*

Cette souffrance française devant la tragédie nationale fait la force de ceux qui veulent rétablir l'unité, la souveraineté et la paix dans le royaume.

Le « parti de l'étranger » et de la division devrait, pour l'emporter, guérir l'âme blessée de la France, or il exacerbe sa douleur.

2

LA MESSE DU ROI ET DES CARDINAUX

1589-1661

22.

Comment Henri IV, hérétique et relaps, qu'un souverain a choisi pour lui succéder après avoir été frappé par le poignard d'un moine fanatique, peut-il rassembler autour de lui son royaume déchiré par les haines religieuses ?

À peine un sixième de la France l'a reconnu.

La capitale est entre les mains de la Sainte Union des ligueurs, soumise aux Guises. Les Parisiens suivent les processions des prêtres, des moines, qui, brandissant crucifix et portraits de la Vierge, exaltent le tyrannicide et la vraie foi. Le pape les soutient. L'Espagne de Philippe II finance les Guises, envoie ses soldats pour renforcer les rangs des ligueurs, et rêve de voir monter sur le trône de France Isabelle, l'infante, la petite-fille de Henri II, et de soumettre ainsi la France aux Habsbourg.

Et c'est cependant Henri IV qui va l'emporter.

Il lui faut d'abord conquérir son royaume comme s'il s'agissait d'une terre étrangère, et, pour cela, faire appel à l'aide des soldats d'Élisabeth Ire, ces anglicans, adversaires des papistes.

Il a besoin d'argent.

Il se dirige donc vers la Normandie, la grasse province qui verse le plus d'impôts et dont les ports nombreux peuvent accueillir les navires anglais.

Le 21 septembre 1589, il remporte la victoire à Arques – près de Dieppe – contre les troupes de Guise, du duc de Mayenne, et il est à nouveau vainqueur des ligueurs et des Espagnols à Ivry (le 14 mars 1590).

Il a lancé : « Ralliez-vous à mon panache blanc ! »

Cela vaut certes pour une bataille, mais le royaume ne se soulève pas en sa faveur, même si les provinces et les parlements de Rennes et de Bordeaux se rallient à lui.

Cela ne représente encore jamais que la moitié du royaume. Et s'il réussit à s'emparer de Chartres, il a échoué devant Rouen, et n'a pu longtemps faire le siège de Paris.

La France est divisée. Les moines casqués, les ligueurs, les milices, tiennent la capitale. Et ce roi qui aspire à gouverner la France commence par faire mourir de faim les Parisiens en les enfermant dans un blocus impitoyable : on fabrique du pain en broyant les os des squelettes arrachés au cimetière des Innocents ! On dénombrera près de cinquante mille victimes de la disette, de la maladie et des combats.

Ce sont les troupes espagnoles d'Alexandre Farnèse qui viennent desserrer le siège et prennent garnison dans Paris.

Telle est la France : quand elle n'est pas unie, elle s'entre-dévore, elle en appelle à l'étranger.

Les passions s'y exacerbent, mais, en même temps, dans chacun des camps, des « politiques », des « réalistes », commencent à penser qu'il faut trouver des solutions de compromis.

Et ces « raisonnables » se séparent peu à peu d'avec les plus « zélés » de leurs compagnons. La France apparaît aux « politiques » si divisée que, sous peine de la voir éclater, disparaître, il leur faut trouver des solutions qui ne satisfont pas les « zélés », mais expriment l'équilibre des forces.

Les passions françaises conduisent ainsi paradoxalement à l'« arrangement » qui permet la reconstitution de l'unité nationale. Mais cette « sagesse » ne l'emporte qu'après que l'on a éprouvé l'impossibilité et souffert des cruautés des solutions extrêmes.

C'est à Paris que tout se joue et que se confirme le rôle décisif, *central*, de la capitale, et qu'ainsi s'accuse un trait majeur de l'histoire française.

Là s'esquisse parmi les ligueurs des revendications politiques extrêmes. Les « catholiques zélés » veulent un roi contrôlé par les états généraux. Le conseil des Seize de la Ligue et un comité secret des Dix dressent des listes de proscription de personnalités à « épurer ».

On perquisitionne. On menace.

Le « papier rouge » énumère les noms de ceux qui doivent être « pendus, dagués, chassés ». Les lettres P, D, C, indiquent le châtiment prévu.

Et trois magistrats, dont le président Brisson, soupçonnés d'être des « politiques », c'est-à-dire des « modérés » indulgents envers l'hérésie, donc des traîtres, sont pendus et leurs cadavres exposés en place de Grève.

Un climat de terreur s'installe ainsi dans Paris.

Les « zélés » développent dans un même mouvement une conviction religieuse radicale – contre les huguenots – et une idéologie égalitaire.

Ils contestent la transmission héréditaire des titres nobiliaires.

Ils s'en prennent à ceux qui, en pleine disette – due au blocus de Paris par les armées de Henri IV –, ont leurs plats « pleins de grasse soupe ».

Ces revendications inquiètent les gentilshommes, le duc de Mayenne et les bourgeois aisés.

Des divisions se font jour parmi les ligueurs. Le roi, redécouvre-t-on, est le garant de l'ordre, et les « zélés » répandent au contraire des ferments de désordre, voire de révolution.

On aspire à la paix, à l'unité du royaume autour du souverain. Et le patriotisme vient s'ajouter à ces motivations sociales. On se veut « vrai Français ». On rejette et on craint la présence et la politique des Espagnols.

On craint l'éclatement du pays. On s'inquiète de ces villes « qui veulent un conseil à part, comme si chacune d'elles eût voulu se former sur le modèle et le plan d'une république ». La

France ne risque-t-elle pas de devenir « une Italie, et les villes changées en Sienne, Lucques et Florence, ne ressentant plus rien de leur ancien gouvernement et du bel ordre de l'illustre monarchie » ?

Ainsi le « bloc » catholique se fissure-t-il.

La passion religieuse et les revendications républicaines et égalitaires qu'elle charrie, la « terreur » qu'elle commence à répandre, rencontrent les réticences, l'opposition des « politiques », des « nobles », des « bourgeois », des patriotes attachés au modèle monarchique français.

Et le duc de Mayenne, les Guises, les chefs traditionnels de la Ligue, préfèrent en définitive choisir l'ordre.

Les plus zélés des ligueurs sont arrêtés.

Les responsables des exécutions du président Brisson et des deux autres magistrats sont pendus.

En décembre 1589, le duc de Mayenne vide de ses pouvoirs le conseil des Seize et les concentre dans ses mains.

Le « dérapage » de la Sainte Union vers des solutions extrêmes est arrêté.

En France, les poussées « révolutionnaires » sont rapidement enrayées par l'attachement à l'unité du royaume – à celle de la nation – et à l'ordre social.

Le « moment » de l'extrémisme laisse des cicatrices, développe des conséquences politiques, mais, à la fin, c'est le compromis qui s'impose.

La violence est présente dans l'histoire nationale, mais cette tempête est de brève durée et un équilibre national finit par se reconstituer, recimentant la nation et restaurant la cohésion du corps social.

L'intelligence de Henri IV est de l'avoir compris.

Il mesure qu'il ne peut conquérir son royaume par le seul usage de la force.

Il n'a pas pu entrer dans Paris. Les ligueurs ne sont pas vaincus. Il doit, s'il veut régner et être reconnu comme souverain, incarner l'unité du royaume, faire une concession majeure, abjurer sa foi huguenote afin d'exprimer, par ce choix, qu'il s'inscrit dans la tradition nationale, et donc sacrifier sur l'autel de l'unité sa foi protestante.

Le 25 juillet 1593, en la basilique de Saint-Denis, il abjure, entend la messe et communie.

Le 27 février 1594, il est sacré à Chartres, puisque Reims est encore aux mains des ligueurs.

À Pâques, il touchera les écrouelles. Il entrera dans Paris le 22 mars 1594, entendra un *Te Deum* à Notre-Dame avant de faire son entrée solennelle dans la capitale le 15 septembre.

Les politiques, les patriotes, tous ceux qui sont soucieux d'ordre social et qui veulent « recoudre » le tissu national, sont satisfaits.

Les villes se rallient à Henri IV.

Les garnisons espagnoles quittent le pays.

Les états généraux, qui voulaient contrôler le roi, sont discrédités.

Les Jésuites, accusés de prôner le tyrannicide, sont expulsés en 1594, et le pape, dans une cérémonie d'expiation à Rome, reconnaît l'abjuration de Henri IV et son retour au sein de la Sainte Église catholique.

Les Français, écrivent les partisans du roi dans des textes de propagande, ont refusé d'avaler le « catholicon d'Espagne », cette drogue étrangère qu'on voulait leur faire boire.

« Notre roi est maintenant catholique, il va à la messe, il faut le reconnaître et il ne faut plus que l'on nous trompe. »

Mais la souveraineté de Henri IV ne sera définitivement établie qu'après qu'il aura brisé les résistances armées des Guises en Bretagne (le duc de Mercœur) et en Bourgogne (le duc de Mayenne).

En fait, ces victoires militaires ne sont que de façade. Henri IV achète les ralliements. Le Trésor royal déboursera à cette fin 32 millions de livres.

L'unité du royaume se paie cher. C'est dire que si la raison l'emporte, si les « politiques » ont triomphé, en fait les divisions demeurent. On choisit l'équilibre, non l'adhésion enthousiaste.

Et il faut encore, pour empêcher les cicatrices de se rouvrir, en finir avec l'action de l'étranger.

Henri IV déclare la guerre à l'Espagne en sorte que l'unité nationale s'affirme aussi dans le combat contre les Habsbourg. Il est victorieux des Espagnols à Fontaine-Française, sur les bords de la Saône.

Mais les Espagnols assiègent Amiens, et la paix ne sera conclue que le 2 mai 1598, à Vervins.

Henri IV a pu signer à Nantes un traité avec les huguenots (30 avril 1598).

Moment important dans la construction de l'âme de la France. En refusant d'envoyer des renforts alors que les Espagnols assiégeaient Amiens, les huguenots ont montré leur détermination, leur amertume, leurs réticences face à ce roi qui a abjuré leur foi, même si de nombreux pasteurs ont fait le même choix que lui. L'édit de Nantes – ville ligueuse ! – leur accorde la liberté de conscience, l'égalité des droits, la liberté de culte, et des articles secrets leur assurent d'une part le versement par le roi de 45 000 écus par an – les pasteurs en exercice seront payés –, d'autre part le contrôle de 150 villes qui seront des « refuges de sûreté » possédant une garnison dont le souverain sera le gouverneur et dont il paiera l'entretien.

Les huguenots constituent ainsi un État dans l'État.

C'est dire que l'édit de Nantes n'est qu'un traité de compromis, de paix civile. Il marque cependant la difficile naissance, à l'avenir incertain, d'une exception française : l'acceptation de la coexistence, en un seul royaume, de deux religions ; et donc, en germe, la séparation de la religion et de l'État.

Quelles que soient les arrière-pensées des uns et des autres, les soupçons, les regrets des catholiques devant l'hérésie qui, loin d'être « extirpée », est ainsi reconnue, et les amertumes inquiètes des protestants face à ce monarque qui les a reniés, un sillon commence à être tracé.

Il n'est pas encore profond.

On pense toujours qu'un royaume n'est réellement uni que si tous les sujets du roi partagent avec lui la même foi, qui ne saurait être que catholique.

Mais l'amorce de ce sillon existe, et une graine fragile y a été semée.

23.

À peine douze années séparent la signature de l'édit de Nantes, le 30 avril 1598, et ce 14 mai 1610, quand, à Paris, dans l'étroite rue de la Ferronnerie, vers six heures de l'après-midi, François Ravaillac – « la barbe rousse et les cheveux tant soit peu dorés » – profite d'un arrêt du carrosse royal pour tuer de deux coups de poignard Henri IV, que les poètes de la Cour avaient comparé à Mars, à Hercule, à Charlemagne, et qu'ils avaient surnommé Henri le Grand.

Même si Ravaillac n'a été le bras armé d'aucune conspiration, cet acte criminel révèle le rapport complexe que les Français entretiennent désormais avec leur roi.

Depuis le début des guerres de Religion, des moines, des prédicateurs – curés ou pasteurs –, ont légitimé le tyrannicide. Il faut châtier l'hérétique ou le huguenot qui a abjuré, et Henri III a succombé aux poignards. La personne du roi est certes « sacrée ». Y attenter est donc « sacrilège ». Mais, en même temps, elle peut être « sacrifiée » afin d'expier ses fautes. Et le régicide est célébré comme un martyr : le moine Jacques Clément, assassin de Henri III, a été sanctifié par les moines ligueurs.

Il y a ainsi un double mouvement contradictoire autour de la personne du roi.

Celui-ci renforce ses pouvoirs, et jamais souverain n'a été plus encensé que ne l'est Henri IV, mais l'idée s'est peu à peu répandue qu'on pouvait le punir de mort – ce qui est fait. Ou le désigner, le renvoyer, cela qui a été réclamé par les états généraux, même si cette éventualité n'est jamais devenue réalité. Cependant, l'hypothèse demeure dans les grimoires et les mémoires.

Et personne ne l'oublie.

Ainsi, lorsque Henri IV s'emploie à affirmer et élargir son autorité, les parlements résistent et il doit faire plier chacun d'eux afin qu'il enregistre l'édit de Nantes.

C'est dire que les parlementaires – comme la majorité de la population – n'admettent pas que des sujets du roi pratiquent une religion différente de celle de leur souverain, et que cette communauté ait obtenu des garanties – juridiques et même militaires – particulières à ce sujet.

Ces réticences révèlent que les guerres de Religion marquent le début d'une ère du soupçon entre le monarque et son peuple.

Certes, Henri IV s'impose avec habileté et détermination.

Il dit aux parlementaires : « Je couperai la racine à toute faction et à toute prédication séditieuses. »

Il sait bien que les universités et les assemblées du clergé condamnent l'édit de Nantes. Lorsqu'elles invoquent la papauté, il les admoneste :

« Être bien avec le pape ? J'y suis mieux que vous ; je vous ferai tous déclarer hérétiques pour ne me pas obéir ! »

Et, habilement, il accepte le retour des Jésuites dans le royaume, et choisit pour confesseur le père Coton, membre de la Compagnie.

Cette concession ne le conduit pas pour autant à admettre l'application des décrets du concile de Trente. La France « gallicane » ne s'ouvrira que difficilement à la Contre-Réforme, et s'affirme ainsi une particularité française : le royaume est catholique, mais proclame son indépendance à l'égard de la théologie – et de la politique – vaticanes.

Henri IV répète qu'« un roi n'est responsable qu'à Dieu et à sa conscience ».

Il faut que les décisions et les actes du monarque confirment cette souveraineté qui ne se reconnaît que des limites divines et personnelles.

Dès lors, la glorification de la personne du souverain et de sa politique est essentielle.

Les poètes officiels – François de Malherbe –, les sculpteurs, les architectes, les peintres, s'emploient à exprimer, à illustrer, à construire la « représentation » du roi :

> *La rigueur de ses lois, après tant de licence,*
> *Redonnera le cœur à la faible innocence,*

écrit Malherbe dans sa *Prière pour le Roi Henri le Grand.*

> *La terreur de son nom rendra nos villes fortes,*
>
> ....
>
> *Et le peuple qui tremble aux frayeurs de la guerre,*
> *Si ce n'est pour danser n'orra plus de tambours.*
>
> ....
>
> *Tu nous rendras alors nos douces destinées :*
> *Nous ne reverrons plus ces fâcheuses années*
> *Qui pour les plus heureux n'ont produit que des pleurs :*
> *Toute sorte de biens comblera nos familles,*
> *La moisson de nos champs lassera les faucilles*
> *Et les fruits passeront la promesse des fleurs.*

Cette mise en scène des actions du roi – la « poule au pot » ! – constitue, par son ampleur, une novation, et souligne cette exaltation du pouvoir royal qui caractérisera la monarchie française. Celle-ci est « sacrée ». Elle œuvre pour le bien du royaume.

Manière de contenir le « soupçon » qui la menace, et de justifier la répression qui frappe ceux qui se rebellent : les grands et leurs clientèles.

Le maréchal de Biron, qui a conspiré avec le duc de Savoie, sera décapité en 1602.

Les duels sont interdits, la haute aristocratie est surveillée, et certains de ses membres sont emprisonnés ou contraints à la fuite (Condé et sa jeune femme, poursuivie par les assiduités du monarque, se réfugieront dans les Pays-Bas espagnols).

Le gouvernement est resserré, quelques dynasties ministérielles – les Pomponne, les Jeannin, les Villeroy – s'affirment, tandis qu'une politique cohérente, centralisée, interventionniste dans l'économie et la finance, se met en place. Des hommes comme Sully et Barthélemy de Laffemas élaborent un « modèle français ».

Un Olivier de Serres publie le *Théâtre d'agriculture et ménage des champs*. De grands travaux – routes, drainage des marais poitevins, canal de Briare, construction d'arsenaux et de galères – sont lancés.

Les châteaux – Chambord, Fontainebleau, Saint-Germain –, l'aménagement de Paris – le Louvre, le Pont-Neuf, les places Royale et Dauphine – matérialisent cette politique.

Paris, un temps délaissée par les Valois, qui lui avaient préféré les bords de Loire, redevient le centre d'un royaume repris en main : une capitale, « miracle du monde ».

Ce « modèle français » est soutenu par une démographie vigoureuse. En l'espace de ces quelques années, le royaume de France redevient le plus puissant, le plus peuplé, le plus riche des royaumes de la chrétienté.

C'est une « seconde Renaissance » qui se déploie malgré la hausse des prix, la ruine de nombreux petits propriétaires paysans étranglés par le renchérissement des fermages, le poids de l'usure.

Sully et Barthélemy de Laffemas réussissent à stabiliser le cours de la monnaie, à reconstituer un trésor royal, et l'activité économique dans les manufactures (tapisseries, soieries, métallurgie, constructions navales) anime un « mercantilisme » : il faut « exporter » et non importer.

Mais – c'est un autre trait de l'âme de la France – l'État centralisé joue là le rôle majeur. C'est lui qui crée, incite, oriente, contrôle.

C'est autour de lui que tout s'organise. Dès lors, la question de ses finances est capitale.

Il faut trouver de l'argent.

On a abaissé la taille, mais on augmente la gabelle. Et la

misère paysanne perdure. Le besoin d'argent comme l'attrait qu'exerce le pouvoir expliquent la création de l'« impôt » de la paulette (du nom du financier Paulet), qui va orienter l'évolution de la société française et peser sur l'avenir de la monarchie.

Il s'agit de faire payer chaque année une taxe aux titulaires d'offices, qui leur assurera l'hérédité des charges qu'ils ont acquises.

La *vénalité* des offices – moyen de faire rentrer de l'argent dans les caisses – est ainsi associée à l'*hérédité* de ces offices. Est ainsi créée une bourgeoisie d'officiers, une noblesse de robe liée au pouvoir monarchique et donc le soutenant, mais devenant une « caste » proliférante, un véritable « quart état » constitué d'officiers héréditaires.

Ils renforcent l'absolutisme et le pouvoir de la monarchie. Ils en dépendent. Ils en sont donc solidaires, mais, d'une certaine manière, ils l'emprisonnent. Ils ossifient le pouvoir et la société. Et, au lieu d'investir dans les activités économiques, dans la production ou le commerce, ils gèrent leur bien prestigieux : leur charge héréditaire.

Le pouvoir royal mesure à la fois l'intérêt de cette « noblesse de robe » qui l'alimente, et la difficulté qu'il éprouve à se servir d'elle.

L'État multiplie alors les « commissaires », les « intendants », qui sont ses agents zélés et obéissants.

Ainsi se dessine au début du XVIIᵉ siècle le pouvoir français : un centre lié à cette noblesse de robe et agissant par l'intermédiaire d'agents à son service, exécutants efficaces et dévoués.

Cette armature, si elle maintient le pays rassemblé autour du pouvoir central, si elle fait du royaume de France, dès les années 1600, le plus structuré des États d'Europe, si elle favorise le rôle de l'État, risque de faire perdre à la société sa souplesse, sa capacité d'initiative.

Elle peut conduire de ce fait, en cas de conflit, à une remise en cause du pouvoir central, à qui chacun est lié et dont tout dépend.

On le mesure au printemps de 1610 quand Henri IV décide d'entrer en guerre contre l'Espagne, manière d'affaiblir l'empereur du Saint Empire romain germanique, qui, par le jeu de la succession ouverte en deux duchés – Clèves et Juliers –, peut se retrouver sur les bords du Rhin. Or le Habsbourg allié de l'Espagne est l'ennemi.

Henri a rassemblé une armée de 100 000 hommes. Il est d'autant plus impatient d'intervenir aux Pays-Bas espagnols que Condé et son épouse s'y sont réfugiés. Et que Henri IV, le « Vert-Galant », entend bien conquérir la jeune femme.

Mais ce n'est là qu'un aspect anecdotique, significatif du rôle des femmes et des passions qu'elles suscitent dans le fonctionnement de la monarchie française. Elle ne doit pas masquer le grand projet de politique extérieure du roi : s'allier aux princes luthériens, aux Hollandais calvinistes, pour mieux s'opposer aux Espagnols catholiques.

Henri IV a veillé à faire couronner, le 13 mai 1610, la reine Marie de Médicis, qui assurera ainsi, tandis qu'il sera en campagne, la présidence du conseil de régence.

Mais cette entreprise ambitieuse, qui vise à faire de la France l'arbitre de l'Europe en réduisant l'influence des Espagnols et des Habsbourg d'Empire, a des conséquences dans le royaume même : elle ravive les soupçons envers ce roi qui fut huguenot, relaps avant d'abjurer.

Tout ceux qui ont condamné l'édit de Nantes s'inquiètent de voir ce souverain faire peut-être le jeu des hérétiques.

Et François Ravaillac, posant le pied sur l'un des rayons de la roue du carrosse royal, rue de la Ferronnerie, poignarde le souverain, le 14 mai vers six heures de l'après-midi.

Ravaillac sera soumis à la question. Les jambes brisées, le corps tailladé, il sera écartelé en place de Grève et le peuple brûlera ses restes.

Le cœur de Henri IV, enchâssé dans un reliquaire, est déposé au collège jésuite de La Flèche, son corps embaumé repose à Saint-Denis.

Le roi est mort, vive le roi !

C'est Louis XIII, un enfant de neuf ans.

Marie de Médicis assurera la régence du royaume.

24.

Qui tue le roi blesse le royaume.

Et ce d'autant plus qu'au souverain assassiné succède un enfant, symbole de la faiblesse, incapable de tenir les rênes.

Or la nation française est couturée de cicatrices mal refermées, d'ambitions refoulées, de haines, d'amertumes et de regrets.

Il y a les grands – le prince de Condé, le duc de Longueville, les ducs de Guise et de Bouillon – et, derrière eux, leurs clientèles, toute cette noblesse d'épée que Henri IV a humiliée, vaincue, et qui rêve à nouveau, comme aux pires moments des guerres civiles, de se partager le royaume, de dominer le sommet de l'État.

La scène centrale n'est occupée que par une régente, la reine Marie de Médicis, entourée de ce couple que l'on présente comme des aigrefins, des pilleurs de trésors : Concino Concini et sa « sorcière » de compagne, Leonora Galigaï.

Les libelles contre eux se multiplient. Les grands s'impatientent, rejoints par la noblesse de robe, parlementaires, officiers propriétaires de leurs charges qu'ils peuvent désormais léguer.

Marie de Médicis, croyant renforcer son pouvoir, s'est présentée devant le parlement de Paris pour se faire confirmer par l'assemblée qu'elle était bien la régente « des affaires du royaume pendant le bas âge dudit seigneur son fils ».

Elle semble ainsi avouer sa faiblesse, ce besoin de reconnaissance, alors que Henri IV avait veillé à ce qu'elle fût *sacrée* régente.

Or, quand en France la clé de voûte du pouvoir s'affaiblit, ne peut tenir toute sa place, c'est l'édifice entier qui se fissure.

Les factions animées par les grands se reconstituent. Les protestants, autour du duc de Rohan, créent des assemblées permanentes afin d'être prêts à réagir à toute remise en cause de l'édit de Nantes. Ils renforcent leur organisation militaire et politique. Ils craignent qu'un changement d'orientation du pouvoir ne s'opère à leur détriment.

C'est que les signes ne manquent pas, montrant une nouvelle fois qu'en France la politique intérieure et les choix de politique étrangère sont toujours intimement liés.

Par sa situation géopolitique, la France est l'épicentre de l'Europe, et s'il se met à trembler – si le roi ou l'État sont contestés –, c'est tout le système des relations internationales européennes qui se recompose.

Henri IV avait déclaré la guerre à l'Espagne en s'appuyant sur les puissances protestantes, contestant ainsi la suprématie des Habsbourg d'Allemagne et d'Espagne.

Le nouveau pouvoir signe la paix avec l'Espagne, à la grande satisfaction du « parti dévot », mais en suscitant l'inquiétude des « politiques », de ces « bons Français » qui placent les considérations religieuses au second plan, cherchant d'abord à conforter la puissance du royaume face aux Habsbourg.

Dès 1612, Marie de Médicis, dévote, prépare des « mariages espagnols » : Louis XIII épousera l'infante Anne d'Autriche, et Élisabeth, sœur de Louis XIII, se mariera avec le futur Philippe IV d'Espagne.

C'est bien une réorientation majeure de la politique étrangère du royaume qui se précise. Elle place la France dans une situation de dépendance à l'égard de l'Espagne ou des Habsbourg d'Allemagne au moment même où commence le grand affrontement de la guerre de Trente Ans (1618-1648), dans laquelle la France laisse les Impériaux envahir le Palatinat ou briser la révolte tchèque, ou encore Philippe IV d'Espagne faire la guerre aux Provinces-Unies.

La politique du parti dévot l'emporte. Elle est aux antipodes des choix d'un François Ier s'alliant avec Soliman le Magnifique pour s'opposer à Charles Quint, ou encore de ceux de Henri IV s'appuyant sur les princes luthériens et les Provinces-Unies.

Ce choix d'un traité d'alliance avec l'Espagne (1612), qui conduit à la conclusion des « mariages espagnols », ne s'explique pas seulement par des raisons religieuses.

Les décrets du concile de Trente sont désormais appliqués en France. Un renouveau religieux se manifeste avec la création d'ordres mendiants, de collèges jésuites, et l'émergence de fortes personnalités comme saint François de Sales, saint Vincent de Paul, Bérulle.

En fait, le royaume est trop divisé, trop déchiré en factions rivales pour appliquer un projet de politique extérieure qui consisterait – comme l'avait esquissé Henri IV – à faire de la France l'arbitre de l'Europe en assurant ainsi la prépondérance française et en supplantant par là les Habsbourg, qu'ils soient d'Allemagne ou d'Espagne.

Il faudrait, pour y parvenir, rassembler le royaume. Or les grands conduisent des guerres civiles contre la régente et le roi mineur (1614-1616 ; 1616-1617). Les protestants du Béarn prennent à leur tour les armes.

Les états généraux réunis à Paris en octobre 1614 montrent l'impossibilité de formuler des propositions – fiscales, par exemple – rassemblant les trois ordres (clergé, noblesse, tiers état).

On voit la vieille noblesse s'opposer à la nouvelle, définie par ses fonctions.

Incapable de rassembler, le pouvoir est cependant servi par ces divisions qui réduisent les états généraux à une impuissance comparable à la sienne.

Les « officiers » proclament orgueilleusement qu'ils sont, de par leurs fonctions, liés au monarque : « Nous représentons Votre

Majesté en nos charges, dit le prévôt des marchands de Paris, Miron. Qui nous outrage, viole Votre autorité, voire commet en certains cas le crime de lèse-majesté. »

En France, la carence ou le trouble au sommet de l'État provoquent inéluctablement l'éclatement de la nation en groupes rivaux.

Dans ces conditions, le pouvoir n'échappe pas à la critique. Chaque clan formule ses « remontrances ».

Le parlement de Paris présente les siennes en mai 1615, et élabore un véritable programme, demandant le retour à la politique extérieure de Henri IV, critiquant les conseillers de la reine, ces « étrangers » prévaricateurs.

Quelques semaines plus tard, Condé publie un manifeste exigeant que la Cour suive les cahiers des états généraux. C'est dire que le « soupçon » à l'égard de la monarchie est devenu acte d'accusation.

Les mesures prises par Concini pour tenter de faire face à ces oppositions – il fait entrer au Conseil Armand Jean Du Plessis, futur cardinal de Richelieu, chargé des Affaires étrangères –, l'emprisonnement de Condé à la Bastille, puis l'envoi de troupes en Champagne et dans le Nivernais pour réduire une rébellion du duc de Nevers, si elles recréent un semblant d'ordre, ne peuvent rétablir l'unité et l'autorité du pouvoir.

Car dans la monarchie française, qui est déjà absolutiste, c'est le roi qui les incarne. Il est le cœur du royaume et de la construction politique. S'il est absent ou empêché, le royaume entre en crise.

L'âme de la France ne peut vivre sans un « centre », une clé de voûte.

Ainsi le coup d'État organisé par Charles d'Albert de Luynes avec l'assentiment du roi est-il un premier pas nécessaire vers le retour à l'ordre.

Le 24 avril 1617, Concini est assassiné. Son corps, déterré par la foule, est dépecé, brûlé, ses cendres répandues, et Leonora Galigaï exécutée à son tour comme sorcière. Marie de Médicis chassée, Louis XIII, âgé de seize ans, confie le pouvoir réel à Luynes.

Mais le roi doit s'imposer par les armes : contre Marie de Médicis – la guerre de la mère et du fils –, contre les grands en Guyenne et en Normandie, contre les protestants en Béarn.

Luynes tout comme le dévot Louis XIII continuent la « politique » qui privilégie les mobiles religieux et ne se dresse donc pas contre le Habsbourg.

Les Espagnols prennent pied dans la Valteline, et la France se retrouve ainsi menacée d'encerclement, les armées espagnoles étant désormais toutes proches de celles de l'empereur de Vienne.

La mort de Luynes, en 1621, permet le raccommodement du roi et de sa mère.

Or celle-ci a eu pour conseiller le cardinal de Richelieu, longtemps partisan de l'alliance avec l'Espagne, mais qui, devant les initiatives de Madrid et de Vienne, a pris conscience de l'effacement et de la subordination qu'elles impliquent pour la France.

Avec son entrée au Conseil, le 29 avril 1624, les conditions d'un changement de politique, si le roi l'entérine, sont réunies.

Quinze années viennent d'être perdues, le royaume étant paralysé par des luttes vaines.

Elles ont cependant confirmé que la France, à tout moment de son histoire, peut s'enfoncer dans le marécage de ses divisions, connaître l'impuissance, les haines fratricides, les violences, les assassinats, les exécutions les plus barbares, puis recouvrer l'unité un temps perdue et donc sa force.

25.

La France était entravée.

Or il faut moins de vingt ans à Richelieu et à Louis XIII pour en faire l'un des acteurs majeurs de la politique européenne, et donc aussi pour remodeler le gouvernement, la société et l'âme du royaume.

En 1624, lorsque Richelieu est appelé au Conseil du roi, la France hésitait à choisir une politique.

Le 4 décembre 1642, quand meurt le Cardinal, suivi le 14 mai 1643 par le roi, le royaume est engagé sur une trajectoire qui détermine son avenir.

En fait, tout s'est joué en quelques semaines, même s'il a fallu plusieurs années pour déployer les conséquences du diagnostic que, dès le mois de novembre 1624 – il est entré au Conseil le 29 avril –, formule Richelieu :

« Les affaires d'Allemagne sont dans un tel état, écrit-il à Louis XIII, que si le roi les abandonne, la Maison d'Autriche se rendra maîtresse de toute l'Allemagne, et ainsi assiégera la France de tous côtés. »

Le souverain partage cette analyse.

Il a renouvelé en juin 1624, malgré les « dévots », son alliance avec les Provinces-Unies protestantes. Or elles sont en guerre avec l'Espagne catholique.

Mais Louis XIII n'a pas encore tranché définitivement. Il demeure fidèle au rapprochement avec l'Espagne, dont le roi est son beau-père. Louis reste un dévot.

Le Cardinal, lui, a choisi. L'ambassadeur de Venise note : « En toutes choses, Richelieu se fait connaître plus homme d'État que d'Église. »

C'est là une orientation décisive.

Elle place la politique au cœur de toutes les décisions. Elle est laïque dans son essence. Elle ne vise pas des objectifs « religieux », mais est portée par l'« idée que la place du royaume de France parmi les nations » doit être la première.

Encore, pour y parvenir, faut-il tout subordonner à cette ambition nationale et dynastique.

Cela suppose une direction ferme et unifiée de l'État. Une société soumise où les corps intermédiaires (parlements, états provinciaux) ne jouent qu'un rôle mineur, où l'on ne tolère aucune indépendance des grands, ces princes toujours tentés de se partager le royaume ; et où l'on ne peut non plus accepter que les huguenots constituent un « État dans l'État » avec des places fortes, des villes de sûreté, une organisation politico-militaire.

Quant au peuple de va-nu-pieds, de manants et de croquants, il faut réprimer sans pitié toutes ses protestations, ses rébellions, d'autant plus nombreuses que les impôts sont multipliés par trois entre 1635 et 1638, et que la disette menace toujours les pauvres.

Or la grande politique étrangère exige d'immenses ressources. Il faut armer 150 000 hommes, les doter d'une artillerie, les « solder », construire des navires, payer les Suédois ou les Hollandais, ces alliés qui mènent seuls la guerre contre l'Espagne, puisque Louis XIII ne l'a pas déclarée et que la France conduit donc contre les Habsbourg une « guerre couverte », « douce » mais fort coûteuse.

Il faut par conséquent abandonner « toute pensée de repos, d'épargne et de règlement du dedans du royaume », diagnostique Richelieu.

C'est bien le choix d'une politique étrangère destinée à assurer la grandeur du royaume qui détermine le programme de Richelieu.

Ceux qui s'opposent à lui invoquent les souffrances, les sacrifices qui vont être demandés au peuple si la guerre s'engage.

Ils sont hostiles à l'idée d'une politique antiespagnole, donc anticatholique.

Ils refusent, en fait, le caractère absolutiste de la monarchie.

Ils soutiennent les complots que les grands ourdissent contre Richelieu, envisageant de le faire assassiner. On voit se liguer des dévots, comme le garde des Sceaux Marillac, des grands, comme le comte de Chalais.

On conspire avec l'accord du frère du roi, Gaston d'Orléans, de la reine mère Marie de Médicis, ou même de la reine Anne d'Autriche, fille du roi d'Espagne.

On conteste l'interdiction des duels.

De leur côté, les protestants – les ducs de Rohan et de Soubise – entendent défendre leurs places fortes, donc le port de La Rochelle, qui peut leur permettre de recevoir l'aide anglaise.

Le programme que Richelieu élabore est d'une force et d'une limpidité implacables.

Il faut, dit-il, « ruiner le parti huguenot », « rabaisser l'orgueil des grands », « réduire tous les sujets à leurs devoirs, et relever le nom du roi dans les nations étrangères au point qu'il doit être ».

Les têtes des grands – pour un duel, un complot, une trahison – roulent : Marillac, le duc de Montmorency-Bouteville, Cinq-Mars, le comte de Chalais, sont décapités.

Les huguenots de La Rochelle sont assiégés : ils capituleront en 1628, la population de la ville étant alors passée de 25 000 à 6 000 habitants.

La détermination de Richelieu est impitoyable.

Il brise les résistances des protestants dans les Cévennes. Et même si, par l'édit de grâce d'Alès (1629), il leur accorde la liberté de conscience et de religion, ils perdent toutes les garanties « militaires et politiques » que Henri IV leur avait accordées.

Ils sont dans la poigne du roi, sans autre défense que son bon vouloir.

« Les sources de l'hérésie et de la rébellion sont maintenant éteintes », constate Richelieu.

L'essentiel n'est cependant pas dans la victoire de l'Église contre les adeptes de la religion prétendument réformée, mais bien dans ce que l'on peut faire de ce royaume qu'on maîtrise désormais.

Or le but est clair : la grandeur du royaume, la gloire du roi, qui ne sauraient s'obtenir que par la domination sur les autres nations.

Or il faut que la France soit la première des nations. Richelieu ne veut pas d'une Europe impériale, mais de nations alliées, subordonnées à la nation française.

Ce choix de la « grandeur nationale » passe par l'intervention dans les affaires européennes.

Richelieu est ainsi le premier des hommes d'État français à formuler clairement l'ambition qui va devenir l'un des traits distinctifs de l'âme de la France.

« Maintenant que La Rochelle est prise, écrit le Cardinal à Louis XIII, si le roi veut se rendre le plus puissant du monde, il faut avoir un dessein perpétuel d'arrêter le cours des progrès d'Espagne, et au lieu que cette nation a pour but d'augmenter sa domination et étendre ses limites, la France ne doit penser qu'à se fortifier en elle-même et s'ouvrir des portes pour entrer dans tous les États de ses voisins et les garantir des oppressions d'Espagne. »

Richelieu oppose ainsi une Europe des nations, dont la France serait la protectrice, à une Europe « impériale ».

Pour mettre en œuvre cette politique, encore faut-il que le roi la soutienne. Or Louis XIII est soumis à la pression de son entourage : Anne d'Autriche, l'épouse espagnole, Marie de Médicis, la mère dévote, et tous ceux du « parti dévot » que révulse l'idée de faire la guerre à l'Espagne ou qui prévoient le coût d'hostilités prolongées et les souffrances qu'elles provoqueront.

Le 16 novembre 1630, Marie de Médicis croit avoir obtenu d'un Louis XIII malade le renvoi de Richelieu, mais le roi va finalement conforter le Cardinal, chasser le garde des Sceaux, Marillac, et la reine mère, Marie de Médicis. Le tournant décisif est pris.

La guerre « ouverte » ne sera néanmoins déclarée à l'Espagne qu'en 1635.

C'est qu'il faut de l'argent pour la conduire. Les impôts sont augmentés, affermés à des « financiers », des « traitants », des « partisans » qui avancent à l'État les sommes qu'ils empruntent aux grandes familles de la noblesse d'épée et de robe, auxquelles est versé un intérêt. Quelles que soient leurs positions politiques, elles sont ainsi tenues par la dépendance financière qui les lie au roi.

Si l'on ajoute que Richelieu a dû renoncer à mettre fin à la vénalité des offices, à l'impôt de la paulette qui les rend héréditaires, on mesure combien la monarchie absolutiste est en même temps comme un Gulliver pris dans la toile d'araignée de ses besoins d'argent. Elle est dans la main des prêteurs, eux-mêmes attachés à cette monarchie qui les prive du pouvoir politique mais qu'ils financent et qui leur paie des « rentes », qui crée des offices de plus en plus nombreux pour les leur faire acheter puis transmettre.

Ainsi se ramifie la structure d'une société où le propriétaire d'un office préfère le prestige de sa fonction, de son titre, de la rente, aux aventures du commerce et aux risques de l'investissement dans les grandes compagnies.

Ankylose française au moment où Hollandais et Anglais courent les mers du monde.

Cependant, le royaume est riche, il demeure le plus puissant et le plus peuplé d'Europe. Il met sur pied six armées. Et même si, en 1636, Corbie est assiégée, les cavaliers espagnols parvenant à Pontoise, la nation ne cède pas. Le patriotisme conduit plus de trente mille volontaires à se rassembler pour défendre Paris. Au bout de sept années, cette guerre commencée en 1635 permet aux troupes royales de conquérir Arras, Bapaume, le Roussillon, Perpignan.

La Gazette (créée en 1631 par Théophraste Renaudot), l'Académie française, conçue par Richelieu dès 1635, exaltent ces victoires. Car c'est le rôle des écrivains, des « gazettes », de chanter la gloire du souverain et la grandeur du royaume.

Le régime absolutiste est un tout : la littérature – *Le Cid* est joué en 1636, année de Corbie – et la peinture doivent concourir à la célébration de la France et de son monarque.

L'Académie française est l'illustration de cette volonté politique de rassembler les sujets autour du pouvoir royal et de conforter le patriotisme.

On ignore les libertins (au sens d'incroyants), et le baroque cède peu à peu la place au classicisme.

Certes, il ne se passe pas d'année, entre 1624 et 1643, sans qu'il y ait une jacquerie, une émeute paysanne, une révolte dans les villes, ainsi à Dijon, Aix-en-Provence, Lyon, Rouen.

Que ce soit en Quercy, en Saintonge, en Angoumois, en Poitou – en 1636, année de Corbie –, que les rebelles se nomment « croquants » en Périgord ou « va-nu-pieds » en Normandie, il s'agit toujours de protester contre les hausses d'impôts, l'augmentation des taxes, et, souvent, des « privilégiés » soutiennent ces mouvements parce que eux-mêmes perdent peu à peu de leur pouvoir au bénéfice des « intendants de police, de justice et de finance ».

Mais on ne s'attarde pas sur la misère des humbles ni sur les malheurs de la guerre.

Ce ne sont pas les gravures de Callot montrant les grappes de pendus aux arbres, sur les champs de bataille, qu'on retient, mais les écrits d'académiciens français « célébrant les victoires des armées du roi ».

On s'inquiète pourtant, à la mort de Louis XIII, le 14 mai 1643. Son fils, né en 1638, n'est âgé que de quatre ans et huit mois.

Le temps des troubles va-t-il revenir ?

Depuis le 5 décembre 1642, sur la recommandation de Richelieu, Louis XIII a fait du cardinal Jules Mazarin son principal ministre et le parrain de son fils, le futur Louis XIV.

26.

Quand le pouvoir s'affaiblit, il redevient une proie que tous cherchent à dépecer.

Dans la monarchie française déjà absolutiste au milieu du XVIIe siècle, c'est la force du roi qui fait la force de l'État.

Or voici que l'histoire semble se répéter, offrir l'occasion d'une revanche aux grands, aux parlementaires, à tous ceux qui avaient dû ployer l'échine devant Louis XIII régnant de concert avec Richelieu.

Le Cardinal avait cherché et réussi à « rabaisser l'orgueil des grands ». Ils le revendiquent et se redressent.

Le roi n'est-il pas qu'un enfant ?

Et pourquoi respecter cette Anne d'Autriche, espagnole, reine mère comme l'avait été Marie de Médicis, l'Italienne gouvernant avec Concini, déjà un Italien comme l'est ce principal ministre légué par Richelieu à Louis XIII et à Anne d'Autriche, ce cardinal tonsuré mais non ordonné prêtre, Giulio Mazarini ?

Le pouvoir semble d'autant plus chancelant qu'Anne d'Autriche, pour obtenir la plénitude de la régence, fait casser par le parlement de Paris, dans un lit de justice, le testament de Louis XIII en même temps qu'elle confirme Mazarin dans ses fonctions.

Il suffit de quelques mois pour qu'une « Cabale des Importants », animée par le duc de Beaufort (petit-fils de Henri IV et de Gabrielle d'Estrées), envisage d'assassiner Mazarin.

Louis XIII n'avait-il pas laissé tuer Concini et supplicier Leonora Galigaï ? La « Cabale des Importants » est démasquée, Beaufort, emprisonné, mais le ton est donné.

Mazarin sera la cible, puisque, entre une reine mère étrangère et un Louis XIV encore enfant, il est le seul capable, et pour plusieurs années, de diriger l'État et de faire face.

Pour l'abattre, puisqu'on n'a pu l'assassiner, on va le larder de toutes les calomnies, de toutes les accusations.

Plus de quatre mille pamphlets – des *mazarinades* – seront publiés contre lui.

Il est, dit-on, le suborneur d'Anne d'Autriche. Il est porteur du « mal de Naples » – la syphilis –, et adepte du « vice italien », l'homosexualité.

Il pille à son profit les caisses du royaume – ce qui est vrai. Sa fortune est si grande qu'il achète des œuvres d'art par centaines – elles rempliront le musée du Louvre.

Par une politique matrimoniale minutieusement calculée, il place ses trois neveux et ses six nièces, les filles de sa sœur Mancini. Et, avec cela, habile, séducteur, grand manœuvrier, continuant la politique de Richelieu avec une égale obstination dissimulée sous des manières douces.

Mazarin illustre ainsi cette particularité française : admettre que des « étrangers » puissent servir le pouvoir au plus haut niveau de l'État.

Ces hommes qui parfois – comme Mazarin – parlent maladroitement le français deviennent des « patriotes » attachés aux intérêts du roi, soucieux de contribuer à la grandeur de la nation.

Remarquable capacité du pays – de l'État monarchique et plus tard républicain – de s'ouvrir. Car il ne s'agit pas là de la conséquence d'une pratique « féodale » pour laquelle les nationalités ne seraient pas encore définies, mais bel et bien d'un trait spécifique de la nation française.

D'ailleurs, ce n'est pas d'abord l'« étranger » qu'on attaque, mais le principal ministre, celui qui incarne la politique absolutiste, la guerre qui se poursuit contre l'Espagne catholique. Car si les protestants ont été réduits au silence par Richelieu, le parti dévot est toujours aussi puissant, toujours aussi hostile à la politique étrangère qui dresse la France contre les Habsbourg de Madrid et de Vienne.

Les parlementaires sont les plus déterminés. Ils ne sont pas sensibles à la victoire de Condé à Rocroi (le 19 mai 1643), puis aux succès du même Grand Condé et de Turenne sur la Moselle et le Rhin (Fribourg, Nördlingen), ou dans le Nord (prises de Furnes et de Dunkerque).

Ils sont dressés contre la monarchie absolutiste, contre les impôts, les taxes que le pouvoir veut prélever, la guerre dévorant l'argent.

Un des traits majeurs de l'histoire nationale réside en effet dans cette question financière.

Les caisses de l'État, qui mène une grande politique, sont toujours vides. Il épuise les recettes fiscales des années à venir. Endetté, il pressure les plus pauvres.

Mal endémique, révoltes dans toutes les provinces, misère accablante à laquelle s'ajoutent les malheurs de la guerre et les poussées de la peste.

Les grands et les parlementaires conduisent leurs « frondes » contre le pouvoir, mais ce sont les humbles qui pâtissent des récoltes saccagées, des pillages perpétrés par la soldatesque.

En Champagne, « toutes les églises et les plus saints mystères sont profanés, les ornements pillés, les fonts baptismaux rompus, les prêtres ou tués ou maltraités ou mis en fuite, toutes les maisons démolies, toute la moisson emportée, les terres sans labour et sans semence, la famine et la mortalité presque universelles, les corps sans sépulture et exposés la plupart à servir de curée aux loups. Les pauvres qui restent de ce débris sont presque tous malades, cachés dans des cabanes découvertes ou dans des trous que l'on ne saurait presque aborder, couchés la plupart à plate terre ou sur la paille pourrie, sans linge ni habits que de méchants lambeaux. Leurs visages sont noirs et défigurés, ressemblant plutôt à des fantômes qu'à des hommes. »

Ce n'est pas cette situation cruelle qui pousse les parlementaires, en 1644, en 1648, en 1650, ou les grands, de 1650 à 1653, et les assemblées du clergé et de la noblesse, en 1650 et 1651, à conduire contre le pouvoir royal qu'incarne Mazarin la Fronde parlementaire ou la Fronde des princes.

Il s'agit, pour ces « élites » qui détiennent la richesse, les offices, le prestige, d'arracher à la monarchie absolutiste la réalité du pouvoir et de sauvegarder, de reprendre ou de multiplier leurs privilèges.

Cette opposition entre le pouvoir royal et les privilégiés est profonde et renaissante.

Mais la position des grands et des parlementaires est difficile à tenir, car d'autres forces entrent dans le jeu : pauvres des villes, artisans, ouvriers, apprentis, domestiques, appartenant à des couches sociales qui n'ont pas de biens à défendre ou à arrondir, mais qui veulent obtenir de quoi survivre.

Et les parlementaires comme les grands craignent par-dessus tout ces « sans-culottes », et à la fin les liens d'intérêt et la solidarité qui unissent les privilégiés au roi, en dépit de leurs divergences, l'emportent.

Ce jeu complexe des forces politiques et sociales structure notre histoire nationale.

On l'a déjà vu à l'œuvre plusieurs fois. Qu'on se souvienne d'Étienne Marcel (1358), ou des guerres de Religion, notamment à Paris.

Il ne peut que se reproduire.

Les besoins financiers d'un l'État absolutiste s'accroissant, il multiplie les créations d'offices, renforce les « corps intermédiaires » qu'il dépouille de tout pouvoir, mais dont il dépend. Dans le même temps, il s'endette, augmente les impôts, ce qui unit un temps contre lui toutes les couches de la société. La réunion des états généraux devient alors une revendication commune. Les derniers se sont tenus en 1614. On les réclamera à nouveau en 1651, mais ils ne se réuniront que quelque cent quarante ans plus tard, à la fin du XVIIIe siècle. Ce sera en 1789.

Ce qui est chaque fois en question, c'est la nature même du pouvoir, et donc le visage de la nation.

Ainsi, quand, le 13 mai 1648, le parlement de Paris invite les autres cours souveraines à se réunir à lui, les propositions élaborées visent à en finir avec l'absolutisme, à placer la monarchie sous la tutelle des parlementaires, c'est-à-dire à garantir aux membres des cours le pouvoir – et les privilèges – dont le souverain entend conserver ou s'arroger le monopole.

C'est déjà là une « réaction » nobiliaire et parlementaire. Les parlementaires veulent révoquer les intendants et les commissaires que les cours souveraines n'auront pas légitimés.

Le roi ne saurait de même, sans leur autorisation, créer des taxes et des impôts nouveaux.

Les sujets du royaume ne pourraient être détenus plus de vingt-quatre heures sans être déférés devant leurs juges.

En outre, le pouvoir ne pourrait plus fixer les conditions de la transmission des offices ou de leur création.

Les prérogatives de l'État absolutiste seraient transférées à ces parlementaires, propriétaires de leurs charges, privilégiés par excellence.

Or ces corps intermédiaires, qui détiendraient le pouvoir réel, ne sont évidemment pas représentatifs de la société. Les croquants du Rouergue, les rebelles de Bordeaux, les miséreux de Champagne, victimes des mauvaises récoltes ou de la soldatesque, ne sont pas concernés par ces revendications.

Cependant, quand Mazarin, qui se croit renforcé par la victoire de Condé à Lens, le 20 août 1648, ordonne l'arrestation, le 26, de parlementaires – dont le populaire conseiller Broussel –, la population parisienne dresse plus de 1 500 barricades (28 août). Et le pouvoir recule, libérant les parlementaires incarcérés et fuyant Paris pour Saint-Germain dans la nuit du 5 au 6 janvier 1649.

La capitale échappe une fois de plus au pouvoir royal, mais laisse, face aux parlementaires et aux grands qui les ont rejoints, ce « peuple » que les « élites » sociales craignent tant.

Et d'autant plus que l'exemple anglais – avec Cromwell et la décapitation de Charles Ier, marié à une sœur de Louis XIII,

Henriette, réfugiée en France – montre le danger qu'il y a à laisser se déchaîner contre le pouvoir royal la colère populaire. Les parlementaires signent donc avec le roi la paix de Rueil – 11 mars 1649 –, et, en août, la Cour peut rentrer à Paris.

La partie n'est pas terminée pour autant.

La Fronde des grands (Condé, Gondi de Retz) se déchaîne à son tour de 1650 à 1653. Les assemblées du clergé et de la noblesse réclament la convocation des états généraux.

Les parlementaires rentrant en scène, la tête de Mazarin est mise à prix (150 000 livres), car il est un « perturbateur du repos public ». La haine contre lui est attisée par les milliers de mazarinades : « Adieu, cause de nos ruines ! Adieu, l'abbé à vingt chapitres ! Adieu, seigneur à mille titres ! Allez sans jamais revenir ! » Et on lui promet le sort de Concini, puisqu'il est présenté comme le responsable de tous les maux du royaume, et d'abord de la création des nouvelles taxes contre lesquelles les Parisiens se sont révoltés en dressant leurs barricades.

Mais cette révolte populaire affaiblit les frondes plus qu'elle ne les renforce, car elle fait craindre des désordres sociaux, des revendications extrêmes mettant en cause les biens des « élites » mutinées.

Celles-ci s'étaient déployées parce que le pouvoir royal était affaibli.

Or il a remporté des succès.

Le traité de Westphalie a mis fin le 24 octobre 1648 à la guerre avec les Impériaux. Le royaume y gagne l'Alsace, moins Strasbourg.

Surtout, le 7 septembre 1651, Louis XIV est proclamé majeur, et ce simple fait relégitime le pouvoir. Le roi en est la clé de voûte. Par sa seule accession à la majorité, qui marque la fin de la régence, il rassemble autour de sa personne.

La France est attachée à la symbolique du pouvoir royal. Une procession manifeste cette adhésion populaire.

Mais les princes et les parlementaires les plus déterminés persistent encore dans leur opposition. C'est l'ultime partie.

Condé rejoint la Guyenne, se range aux côtés des révoltés qui se sont emparés de Bordeaux. Puis il regagne Paris, et ses partisans s'opposent, porte Saint-Antoine (juillet 1652), aux troupes royales qui veulent entrer dans la capitale.

Un pouvoir insurrectionnel est créé, des centaines d'exécutions ont lieu, la terreur s'installe. Par une manœuvre habile, le roi fait mine d'exiler Mazarin.

Ce dernier épisode – une sorte de simulacre – montre cependant la vigueur et l'enracinement des contradictions entre la monarchie absolue et les corps intermédiaires associés aux princes.

La victoire de Louis XIV, qui peut enfin rentrer à Paris en octobre 1652, puis le retour de Mazarin, acclamé par la population de la capitale le 30 janvier 1653, ne doivent pas dissimuler le fait que les problèmes demeurent.

Les « élites » françaises sont divisées. Les uns se rangent derrière la monarchie absolutiste et sont favorables au renforcement de l'État. Les autres rêvent d'un gouvernement de l'aristocratie et des parlementaires, d'une monarchie bridée par les corps intermédiaires.

Le désir de paix des populations appauvries et le patriotisme ont pesé de façon déterminante sur la fin de ces frondes.

Condé, par un véritable acte de trahison, s'est mis au service des Espagnols. Mais il est battu par les troupes de Turenne (en 1658, aux Dunes).

L'opposition parlementaire est matée.

Les dévots, engagés dans une guerre théologique contre les jansénistes (Pascal publie les *Provinciales* en 1657), ne protestent guère contre la conclusion d'un traité entre Mazarin et... Cromwell (1654) ! Et toute la nation est satisfaite de la fin de la guerre avec l'Espagne, conclue par le traité des Pyrénées le 7 novembre 1659.

Le royaume s'agrandit de l'Artois, de la Cerdagne et du Roussillon. Condé est pardonné. Surtout, le mariage de l'infante Marie-Thérèse d'Espagne et de Louis XIV est annoncé. L'infante doit remettre une dot de 500 000 écus d'or en échange du renoncement des époux au trône d'Espagne.

Ce « mariage espagnol », le traité des Pyrénées signé après celui de Westphalie, renversent la situation de la France en Europe.

Malgré les Habsbourg et contre eux, elle a établi sa prépondérance.

Les deux traités ont d'ailleurs été rédigés en français, non en latin.

Le 26 août 1660, Louis XIV et Marie-Thérèse font leur entrée solennelle dans Paris au milieu des acclamations.

Le 9 mars 1661, Mazarin meurt.

Cet Italien honni, calomnié, a poursuivi l'œuvre de Richelieu. Il n'a certes jamais oublié son clan familial. Stratège habile, il a fait de Louis XIV le légataire universel de son immense fortune, sachant que le roi va refuser la succession de son parrain. Et c'est Colbert, le financier de Mazarin, qui la règle.

Mais le jeune monarque et l'État sont les bénéficiaires de l'héritage politique que Mazarin a accumulé pour le service de la France.

Louis XIV peut régner.

3

LE GRAND SOLEIL FRANÇAIS

1661-1715

27

« La face du théâtre change », dit Louis XIV à ses ministres et secrétaires d'État, le 10 mars 1661, lendemain de la mort de Mazarin.

Ce roi de vingt-trois ans, qui s'adresse aux membres de son Conseil, debout, le chapeau sur la tête, est impatient de régner.

Il ajoute :

« Je vous défends de rien signer, pas une sauvegarde, pas un passeport sans mon ordre, de me rendre compte chaque jour à moi-même et de ne favoriser personne. »

Ce roi veut tout voir, tout contrôler, tout décider.

« C'est par le travail que l'on règne, ajoute-t-il. C'est pour cela que l'on règne. »

Chaque jour, et durant les cinquante-quatre années de son gouvernement personnel, jusqu'à la veille de sa mort – le 1er septembre 1715 –, il accomplit avec ponctualité et gravité son « métier de roi ».

Dans chacune de ses paroles, de ses écrits, de ses décisions, de ses postures, il est l'incarnation de l'absolutisme.

Ce qui était en germe dès les origines de la monarchie française, que les hésitations des monarques, la vigueur des résistances des grands, des féodaux, des parlements, des cours souveraines, avaient empêché de l'emporter, atteint avec Louis XIV sa pleine maturité.

Dans tous les aspects de la vie nationale, cet absolutisme s'impose. Richelieu et Mazarin ont renversé les derniers obstacles au terme de guerres et de frondes qui ont marqué l'enfance et l'adolescence de Louis XIV.

Sa volonté d'exercer un pouvoir absolu est aussi le fruit d'une expérience douloureuse. Il prend sa revanche. Il se défie de tous. Il a connu les conspirations de ses plus proches parents. Il a affronté la Fronde des princes et celle des parlementaires. Il a subi la trahison de Condé. Il a dû fuir Paris. Et il ne peut pas aimer cette capitale dont la population, depuis des siècles, soutient les adversaires du roi et dresse des barricades.

La détermination de Louis XIV et la longueur de son règne font de cet absolutisme l'une des données majeures de l'histoire nationale. Pour le meilleur et pour le pire, il est au cœur de l'âme de la France.

Et ce d'autant plus que Louis XIV ne cherche en rien à dissimuler le principe absolutiste de son règne, mais qu'au contraire il l'affiche avec force, il le revendique comme l'essence même du pouvoir monarchique.

Le roi n'est-il pas choisi et jugé seulement par Dieu ? Voilà qui fonde l'absolutisme.

« Celui qui a donné des rois aux hommes, écrit Louis XIV, a voulu qu'on les respectât comme ses lieutenants, se réservant à lui seul le droit d'examiner leur conduite. Sa volonté est que quiconque est né sujet obéisse sans discernement. »

Nul ne peut contester, juger, refuser d'appliquer une décision du souverain.

Aucune autorité n'existe en dehors de la sienne. Aucune assemblée – même celle du clergé, et même le pouvoir pontifical –, aucune cour, aucun parlement, et naturellement pas les états généraux ne peuvent se dresser contre le roi, ou simplement l'interroger.

« Il est Dieu, dit une cousine de Louis XIV. Il faut attendre sa volonté avec soumission et tout espérer de sa justice et de sa bonté, sans impatience, afin d'en avoir plus de mérite. »

Plus aucun corps intermédiaire, plus aucune fonction n'existent hors de la volonté royale.

Les maires des villes, les gouverneurs des provinces, les évêques, sont désignés par le monarque, ou, si leurs nominations échappent à son autorité, ils perdent tout pouvoir. Un lieutenant général de police – celui de Paris, La Reynie – restera en poste de 1667 à 1697. Un intendant de police, de justice et de finance, et les subdélégués au service de celui-ci, sont les agents d'exécution des volontés royales.

L'armée – jusqu'alors aux mains des nobles, propriétaires des grades – devient un rouage essentiel de la monarchie absolutiste. Elle est l'instrument de sa politique étrangère, mais aussi de la répression contre ceux qui se rebellent. Elle est puissante : 67 000 hommes en 1677, 400 000 en 1703. La flotte passe de 18 navires en 1661 à 276 en 1683 !

Des officiers roturiers sont nommés au mérite, leurs grades échappant ainsi à la vénalité des offices.

L'armée est aux ordres exclusifs du roi. Et l'hôtel des Invalides accueille ceux des soldats qui ont été blessés à son service.

Tout est dans les mains du souverain.

Ainsi les Conseils du roi qui se réunissent quotidiennement. Ainsi le Conseil étroit (en présence du monarque), les intendants des provinces, mais aussi les académies créées par Colbert – surintendant des finances et des bâtiments – autour de l'Académie française (Académies des inscriptions et belles-lettres, des sciences, de musique, d'architecture).

L'image de ce pouvoir personnel est Versailles, où la Cour symbolise par sa soumission, son étiquette réglée comme celle d'une cérémonie religieuse, que le roi est au-dessus de tous et que chacun lui doit une obéissance servile.

Hors de son autorité – et de son regard –, personne n'existe.

L'âme de la France est modelée par cette servitude exigée qui devient vite volontaire. Le « fonctionnement » du gouvernement de la France, de toute la société, est déterminé par une « volonté » unique, celle du monarque, qui élève ou brise au gré de son « bon vouloir », de son intérêt dynastique ou de la vision qu'il a de l'intérêt du royaume.

Nicolas Fouquet était surintendant des finances. Le souverain le soupçonne d'avoir une ambition autonome, de parvenir peut-être à regrouper autour de lui des opposants à l'absolutisme, ou simplement d'affaiblir par sa propre lumière le rayonnement solaire du pouvoir royal. Aussi est-il arrêté, emprisonné à vie, sans aucune possibilité de recours (septembre 1661). La lettre de cachet condamne sans explication. L'État absolutiste est un État « totalitaire ». Aucun domaine ne lui échappe : Colbert crée des manufactures, de grandes compagnies de commerce qui devraient concurrencer les hollandaises et les anglaises. Le roi a son historiographe : Racine ; son peintre : Le Brun ; son archi-tecte : Le Vau ; son musicien : Lully. Molière joue ses pièces devant le souverain ; il est son protégé.

L'âme de la France apprend à servir et à louer, à attendre l'impulsion ou l'ordre de l'État pour créer.

Elle vit de l'État et sous la protection de l'État (un tarif protec-teur est institué à nos frontières par Colbert en 1667) ; c'est par le service de l'État qu'on s'élève dans la hiérarchie sociale.

Chacun dépend du roi, est son courtisan et son serviteur, mais, par-delà la personne du monarque, c'est le royaume que l'on sert.

Le roi s'identifie à la France. Et le peuple ne sépare pas le corps symbolique du roi du corps de la nation.

Mais chaque serviteur du roi, lieutenant général de police, intendant ou officier, veut être à son tour un souverain absolu, si bien que la société française devient ainsi une société de castes d'autant plus rigides qu'elles sont constituées de propriétaires de leurs charges. Colbert, qui doit faire face au gouffre financier que creuse la politique de grandeur, multiplie les ventes d'offices, ce qui, à moyen terme, ne peut que saper l'absolutisme.

Le roi risque en effet de ne plus être maître que d'une appa-rence de pouvoir absolu, celui-ci se réduisant à un rituel et à une étiquette, à une Cour.

Car, les grilles du parc franchies, les propriétaires de charges se sont emparés du pouvoir, puisqu'ils lui fournissent l'argent dont il a besoin.

L'endettement de l'État absolutiste, le déséquilibre endémique des comptes – les recettes n'étant jamais suffisantes, il faut créer de nouveaux impôts, vendre de nouveaux offices –, deviennent ainsi, dès 1670, une maladie pernicieuse qui ronge le royaume.

Mais, au début du règne personnel de Louis XIV, les effets de cette pathologie française – aucun régime n'y échappera – ne sont pas encore trop inquiétants.

L'ambassadeur vénitien souligne en 1661 que « la France est un pays riche de terroirs fertiles, composé de provinces réunies en un corps unique où les communications sont facilitées par les nombreuses rivières... Le royaume n'a pas cessé de s'agrandir depuis deux cents ans... Ses principales richesses, la France ne les tire pas des Indes, mais de son propre sol... La force du royaume vient aussi de son armée, car il est plein de soldats qui par leur instinct naturel sont braves et courageux... Je parlerai maintenant du roi Louis XIV..., prince de complexion vigoureuse, de haute taille, d'aspect majestueux... On ne le voit jamais s'emporter ou se laisser dominer par la passion... Il se consacre effectivement et assidûment aux affaires du gouvernement... »

Cette richesse du royaume semble d'abord inépuisable.

Le roi y puise pour ses « bâtiments » – Versailles, où il s'installe en 1682, Marly –, ses fêtes, ses « jeux », ses « dons » aux courtisans, puisque tout homme est à vendre et que le monarque sait les acheter par des gratifications symboliques – être à la Cour, servir le souverain, assister à son lever, à son coucher – et ses distributions d'argent.

Tout courtisan devient un domestique qui attend son pourboire !

Telle est la logique du pouvoir absolu – qui sera celle de tout pouvoir français : il veut qu'on le serve. Il distingue parmi ses serviteurs, il nomme, promeut, favorise, rétribue, renvoie, bannit.

Car le pouvoir se méfie de ceux qui, par indépendance d'esprit, force de caractère ou orgueil de caste, pourraient ne pas se soumettre à cette domestication généralisée.

Ainsi, la haute noblesse est écartée des responsabilités politiques, à la fois parce que Louis XIV a vécu la Fronde des princes, mais aussi parce qu'il se méfie de l'orgueil de caste des grands.

Les trois ministres composant le Conseil étroit qui gouverne l'État sous la direction personnelle et quotidienne du roi sont de « pleine et parfaite roture », selon Saint-Simon.

C'est le cas de Jean-Baptiste Colbert – et plus tard de son fils et de ses parents – aux Finances, de Michel Le Tellier – puis de son fils Louvois – à la Guerre, de Hugues de Lionne aux Affaires étrangères.

L'amertume pincée des grands se mue en désir de paraître aux côtés du roi à Versailles, à Marly (« Sire, Marly ! »), de partager sa vie quotidienne – les jeux, les dîners, les chasses, les fêtes, les représentations théâtrales, les ballets –, de se repaître de rumeurs, de ragots, de connaître les favorites – mademoiselle de La Vallière, madame de Montespan –, de pousser leurs filles ou leurs épouses dans les bras du roi.

Ce paraître est onéreux. On s'y ruine. On dépend du roi, qui peut rembourser les dettes qu'on a contractées.

Mais il vous faut être près de lui, afin qu'il vous voie.

Des rivalités haineuses déchirent les courtisans. Des intrigues se nouent, certaines criminelles. L'affaire des poisons compromet madame de Montespan ; le roi clôt l'enquête, mais trente-six personnes sont condamnées, exécutées, parmi les complices ou clients de l'avorteuse, sorcière, empoisonneuse, vendeuse de « filtres », organisatrice de messes noires : la Voisin.

Ainsi dépendante du roi, la haute noblesse n'a plus les moyens de se dresser contre le souverain. On ne prend plus les armes. On ose à peine prendre la plume.

La servilité, qui masque sa lâcheté sous le nom de « service de l'État », alors qu'elle n'est que soumission pour la recherche d'une charge, d'une distinction, d'une rétribution, s'inscrit elle aussi dans l'âme de la France.

Et Louis XIV fait preuve d'une lucidité cynique et machiavélienne lorsqu'il écrit :

« Je crus qu'il n'était pas dans mon intérêt de chercher des hommes d'une qualité plus éminente – pour me servir –, parce que ayant besoin sur toutes choses d'établir ma propre réputation, il était important que le public connût par le rang de ceux dont je me servais que je n'étais pas en dessein de partager avec eux mon autorité, et qu'eux-mêmes, sachant ce qu'ils étaient, ne conçussent pas de plus hautes espérances que celles que je leur voudrais donner. »

Il ajoute, dévoilant sa méthode de gouvernement solidaire excluant la désignation d'un ministre principal : « Il était nécessaire de partager ma confiance et l'exécution de mes ordres sans la donner entière à personne. »

Ce changement dans l'administration du royaume (conseillers d'État, maître des requêtes, intendants, subdélégués et officiers appliquent le plus souvent avec rudesse les ordres du roi), s'il en renforce la cohésion, ne fait pas pour autant disparaître la misère des plus humbles.

Au contraire. C'est en cascade que les besoins financiers de l'État vont écraser de taxes et d'impôts les « jacques ».

Ceux-ci se rebellent dès 1661-1662 dans tout le nord du royaume, puis en Sologne, en Bretagne. Les troupes répriment avec une cruelle efficacité ces « émotions paysannes » que la disette ou la famine provoquent.

On pend les « meneurs ». On condamne aux galères : les navires construits sur l'ordre de Colbert ont besoin de bras. On sévit sans hésitation, sans remords ni regrets. Se rebeller contre le souverain est sacrilège. Le pouvoir absolu l'affirme avec netteté :

« Quelque mauvais que puisse être un prince, écrit Louis XIV, la révolte de ses sujets est toujours infiniment criminelle. »

Le roi peut donc gouverner selon son « bon plaisir », qui est aussi, par nature, le choix propre à assurer sa gloire et celle du royaume.

Dans le pouvoir absolu, il n'y a pas séparation entre les désirs du monarque et les besoins de la nation.

Tout gouvernement de la France sera plus ou moins consciemment l'héritier de cette conviction et de cette pratique absolutiste dont Louis XIV a imprégné l'âme de la France.

Le roi en fait le ressort de sa politique religieuse et de sa politique étrangère.

Il s'agit là des deux domaines où il est confronté à d'autres pouvoirs éminents : ceux du pape et des autres souverains.

Il veut affirmer face au pape son autonomie, alors qu'il est le Roi Très-Chrétien de la fille aînée de l'Église, et montrer aux autres monarques qu'il leur est supérieur.

En 1682, dans la Déclaration des quatre articles, Louis XIV s'arroge notamment le droit de nomination des évêques, exaltant ainsi le « gallicanisme » traditionnel de l'Église de France.

Il affirme : « Les rois et les souverains ne peuvent être soumis par ordre de Dieu à aucun pouvoir ecclésiastique dans les choses temporelles, ni déposés directement ou indirectement par l'autorité des chefs de l'Église, ou leurs sujets dispensés de foi et d'obéissance et déliés de leur serment de fidélité. »

Dans cette compétition de pouvoir entre le roi et le pape, Louis précise que les conciles sont supérieurs au souverain pontife et qu'il ne saurait donc être question d'infaillibilité pontificale.

Le pouvoir absolu se veut seul de son espèce.

Le roi de France est supérieur à tous les autres.

L'âme de la France se grisera de ces certitudes.

Le roi peut à sa guise, selon son bon plaisir, mettre fin à la « paix établie » avec ses voisins.

« Tout était calme en tous lieux, reconnaît-il. Vraisemblablement pour autant que je le voudrais moi-même. »

Mais le veut-il ?

« Mon âge et le plaisir d'être à la tête de mes armées m'auraient fait souhaiter un peu plus d'affaires au-dehors », admet-il encore.

C'est qu'il s'agit de sa gloire.

Et à Londres comme à Rome, pour des questions de préséance, ou après un incident diplomatique, il réagit en affirmant sa prééminence et en obtenant réparation.

« Je ne sais si depuis le commencement de la monarchie il s'est jamais passé rien de plus glorieux pour elle, écrit Louis XIV. C'est une espèce d'hommage de roi à roi, de couronne à couronne, qui ne laisse plus douter à nos ennemis mêmes que la nôtre ne soit la première de la chrétienté. »

En 1664, six mille soldats français iront combattre aux côtés des Impériaux et seront victorieux des Turcs au Saint-Gothard.

C'est manière d'affirmer que le roi de France peut agir dans toute l'Europe selon sa volonté, et qu'il ne craint ni les Habsbourg de Vienne ni ceux d'Espagne.

À la mort du roi d'Espagne, Louis XIV réclame les biens de Marie-Thérèse, son épouse, dont la dot n'a pas été versée par Madrid. C'est la guerre de Dévolution (1667-1668). La France obtient Lille, Tournai et Douai au traité d'Aix-la-Chapelle.

De 1672 à 1679, il mène la guerre contre la Hollande, la plus grande puissance marchande d'Europe et donc du monde. Les peintres, les écrivains, les musiciens, Racine, l'historiographe du roi, célèbrent le « passage du Rhin » à Tolhuis, le 16 juin 1672.

Mais la guerre est longue, coûteuse, incertaine malgré les victoires de Condé et de Turenne. Louis XIV et la Cour sont présents sur le front. La guerre est pour eux un grand jeu glorieux qui enfle l'endettement de l'État. Mais la gloire n'a pas de prix, et le royaume s'agrandit de la Franche-Comté au traité de Nimègue, en 1679.

La prépondérance française – déjà inscrite dans les traités de Westphalie (1648) et des Pyrénées (1659) – en sort renforcée.

Qui pourrait dès lors s'opposer à la politique de « réunion » de villes au royaume de France – Strasbourg en 1681 –, qui ne sont que des annexions masquées par des arguties juridiques, voire des coups de force que l'armée et le royaume le plus puissant d'Europe imposent ?

Ceux qui ne se plient pas doivent méditer le sort de Gênes, bombardée par la flotte française qui l'écrase sous dix mille bombes incendiaires (19 mai 1684) pour la punir d'avoir fourni des galères à l'Espagne.

À Ratisbonne (15 août 1684), une trêve est conclue entre l'empereur, l'Espagne et Louis XIV : le roi de France est l'arbitre de l'Europe. Non seulement il paraît capable d'imposer sa loi à tous les autres royaumes, mais il est un « modèle ».

La langue française est devenue la langue diplomatique. Versailles et sa Cour sont imités dans toute l'Europe.

Cette prééminence fait naître parmi les élites, puis parmi le peuple français, un sentiment de supériorité, d'impunité, même, qui va caractériser l'âme de la France.

En 1683, quand meurent l'épouse de Louis XIV, Marie-Thérèse, et Colbert, qui a été le bon ouvrier de l'absolutisme, Louis XIV est dans la plénitude de sa force. Il n'a que quarante-cinq ans.

Il est le Roi-Soleil.

28

La mort, en 1683, a donc commencé à rôder dans les galeries du château de Versailles inachevé où le roi et sa Cour se sont installés.

Le soleil brille encore, mais il est froid comme dans un précoce automne qui annonce un hiver rigoureux.

L'absolutisme a sa logique. Il veut tout dominer : les grands, les humbles, les États étrangers. Comment accepterait-il qu'une minorité conserve ses croyances, continue de se rassembler autour de pasteurs formés en Angleterre, dans les Provinces-Unies, ces puissances ennemies du royaume, et à Genève ?

« Je crus au début, dit Louis XIV, que le meilleur moyen pour réduire peu à peu les huguenots de mon royaume était de ne les point presser du tout par quelques rigueurs nouvelles, de faire observer ce qu'ils avaient obtenu sous les règnes précédents, mais aussi de ne leur accorder rien de plus et d'en renfermer même l'exécution dans les plus étroites bornes que la justice et la bienséance le pouvaient permettre. »

Les intendants, dans les provinces, serrent le lacet, appliquent les édits qui restreignent ou interdisent le culte protestant. Les huguenots ne peuvent exercer certains métiers et n'ont pas l'accès à la maîtrise.

Une Caisse de conversion est créée pour les inciter à quitter la religion prétendument réformée et à rejoindre celle du roi, censée être celle de tous les sujets du royaume.

L'émigration est contrôlée.

Un édit royal – du 14 juillet 1682 – interdit aux sujets de quitter la France pour s'installer à l'étranger sans en avoir obtenu l'autorisation.

Parce qu'il est le plus centralisé, le plus administré d'Europe, le royaume de France esquisse avant tous les autres certaines des formes totalitaires de l'État.

On est condamné pour son être ou sa foi avec une rigueur qui devient peu à peu implacable, les rouages de l'État gagnant en efficacité et les édits royaux étant appliqués dans toutes les provinces.

Le seul fait d'être bohémien est ainsi un délit.

Les agents du roi doivent « faire arrêter tous ceux qui s'appellent bohémiens ou égyptiens, leurs femmes, enfants et autres de leur suite, faire attacher les hommes à la chaîne des forçats pour être conduits dans nos galères et y servir à perpétuité ; et à l'égard de leurs femmes et filles, ordonnons de les faire raser la première fois qu'elles auront été trouvées menant la vie de bohémienne, et de faire conduire, dans les hôpitaux les plus prochains des lieux, les enfants qui ne seront pas en état de servir dans nos galères, pour y être nourris et élevés comme les autres enfants qui y sont enfermés ».

Une ordonnance de 1684 décide que tous les déserteurs des troupes ne seront plus exécutés, « mais condamnés à avoir le nez et les oreilles coupés, à être marqués de deux fleurs de lis aux joues, et à être rasés et enchaînés pour être envoyés aux galères ».

L'âme de la France s'accoutume à cette violence étatique, à cette discrimination des individus en fonction non seulement de la faute commise, mais de leur qualité, de leur origine, de leur confession.

Cette mise à l'Index de certaines catégories de sujets, puis cette sélection en fonction de la « race », de la « foi », et la traque des « exclus », doivent se conclure par une peine dont l'exécution sert le royaume : la flotte royale a besoin de bras pour la chiourme de ses galères !

C'est aussi parce que le contrôle par l'État absolutiste veut s'étendre à tous les domaines, régenter les différentes activités du royaume, qu'est édictée en 1685 l'ordonnance coloniale, ou Code noir, « touchant la police des îles de l'Amérique ».

Il s'agit de définir les droits et devoirs des propriétaires d'esclaves dans les colonies françaises des Antilles : la Martinique, la Guadeloupe, Saint-Domingue.

La traite négrière transporte dans des conditions inhumaines des milliers d'Africains vers ces îles où les plantations de canne à sucre se sont étendues et où leur production donne naissance à un commerce fructueux, « triangulaire », entre l'Afrique, les îles et les ports de l'Atlantique (Bordeaux, Nantes).

Le Code noir reconnaît la légitimité de la traite, il fait des Africains des « biens meubles ».

L'État absolutiste devient ainsi le garant et le régent de l'esclavage, en même temps qu'il veille à rendre le baptême des esclaves obligatoire, leur interdisant toute autre religion, définissant juridiquement tout ce qui concerne l'État et la qualité d'esclave.

L'État absolutiste légifère, surveille, fait entrer l'esclavage dans les rouages juridiques – modernes – du royaume. La vie quotidienne des esclaves est réglementée. Quant à la justification de l'esclavage, elle est double : d'une part, elle exprime « le besoin indispensable qu'on a d'eux pour les cultures des sucres, des tabacs, des indigos » ; d'autre part, on leur apporte le salut « à raison de l'instruction chrétienne qu'on leur donne ».

Car l'État absolutiste a désormais explicitement comme l'un de ses buts majeurs de contraindre tous les sujets du royaume – et les esclaves eux-mêmes – à pratiquer la religion du roi.

Les huguenots ne sont plus seulement dépossédés de leurs droits, cantonnés, surveillés, ils sont désormais « forcés ».

La conversion des enfants de sept ans est autorisée.

Les intendants peuvent imposer une « garnison de gens de guerre » aux religionnaires réticents.

Ces « dragonnades », qui entraînent humiliations, déprédations et saccages, vols, violences, viols, morts, sont mises en œuvre avec zèle par les intendants. Dans le Poitou, Marillac aurait ainsi obtenu plus de 30 000 conversions. Convertir devient une manière, pour les agents du roi, de faire leur cour. Car Louis XIV, remarié secrètement à madame de Maintenon, pieuse et habile ambitieuse qui l'entoure de ses attentions, est désormais résolu à extirper l'hérésie.

La Cour est devenue dévote. Madame de Maintenon et le confesseur jésuite du monarque l'en félicitent.

« La conversion du roi est admirable, écrit madame de Maintenon, et les dames qui en paraissaient les plus éloignées ne partent plus de l'église... Les simples dimanches sont comme autrefois les jours de Pâques. »

Chaque jour, le roi se réjouit des listes de conversions qu'on lui envoie, qui ne relatent pas les scènes cruelles que provoquent les dragonnades ni les résistances qui déjà s'organisent dans les Cévennes.

Car le système absolutiste, en même temps qu'il accroît le contrôle et la domination de l'État sur tout le royaume, rend opaque la réalité.

Le souverain ne tolère plus qu'on échappe à l'État. « Il est de plus en plus jaloux et amoureux de gloire et d'autorité » (Saint-Simon), mais il ne connaît pas la situation réelle du royaume alors qu'ici et là, devant l'augmentation des taxes et des impôts, la misère s'aggrave, la disette reparaît et les communautés protestantes sont occupées par les dragons.

En fait, le roi ne veut pas voir.

Il veut à n'importe quel prix en finir avec « les obstinés religionnaires », ces « mauvais Français ».

Il décide donc, le 18 octobre 1685, par l'édit de Fontainebleau, la révocation de l'édit de Nantes, qui entraîne aussitôt l'exil de près de deux cent mille huguenots en Angleterre, dans les Provinces-Unies et au Brandebourg. Ils apportent à ces États leur savoir, leur esprit d'initiative, leur énergie, mais aussi leur haine envers celui qu'ils vont décrire comme le « souverain turc des chrétiens », et contre lequel ils vont contribuer à dresser toute l'Europe, inquiète de cette prépondérance française qui ne se reconnaît pour limites que celles qu'elle se donne elle-même.

Mais la révocation de l'édit de Nantes est approuvée dans le royaume de France. L'unité de la foi apparaît comme l'état naturel et indispensable de la monarchie.

Et Louis XIV, en conflit avec la papauté, jaloux de la victoire remportée par l'empereur Léopold et ses armées chrétiennes sur les 200 000 Turcs qui assiégeaient Vienne – bataille du Kalhenberg, le 12 septembre 1683 –, veut, avec la révocation, confirmer qu'il est bien le Roi Très-Chrétien.

Cette mesure absolutiste marque très profondément l'âme de la France.

L'unité religieuse autour du pouvoir royal – central – y est confirmée, renforcée. La puissance étatique doit l'imposer aux sujets réticents.

L'État est violence. Contre lui, on en vient à se dresser, à prendre les armes : ce que feront les huguenots dans les Cévennes. Et les paysans se rebellent contre les « percepteurs » d'impôts. C'est dire que l'âme de la France est aussi marquée par ces résistances.

Plus l'État est unifié, mieux il impose sa loi en tous domaines, plus il risque de susciter des oppositions, d'autant plus violentes qu'aucun espace de tolérance ne leur est ménagé.

Le royaume doit affronter non seulement ces risques d'insurrection intérieure – de guerre civile –, mais aussi ceux de guerre contre l'Europe coalisée, dressée contre Louis XIV, « souverain turc des chrétiens ».

Dans une dialectique équivalant à celle qui régit la vie intérieure du royaume – contrôle de plus en plus étendu de l'État, et résistances –, l'Europe est subjuguée par le royaume de France, fascinée par la majesté de Louis XIV, par sa puissance, sa Cour, Versailles, et en même temps décidée à se coaliser contre lui dans une guerre prolongée, si nécessaire.

Le maître d'œuvre de cette coalition est Guillaume d'Orange.

Au terme d'une révolution (1688), il a chassé d'Angleterre le roi Jacques II Stuart, catholique, qui se réfugie en France. Il a reconnu les droits du Parlement anglais et s'est fait proclamer par lui roi d'Angleterre.

Deux « modèles » s'opposent ainsi en Europe : le français, continental, absolutiste, catholique, et l'anglais – lié aux Provinces-Unies –, antipapiste, s'appuyant sur une Déclaration des droits, instaurant une « monarchie » contrôlée.

La guerre entre les deux « modèles » paraît inéluctable.

L'empereur des princes allemands, l'Angleterre et les Provinces-Unies, mais aussi l'Espagne catholique, se rassemblent dans la ligue d'Augsbourg dès 1686.

Quant à Louis XIV, renforcé par le succès de sa révocation de l'édit de Nantes, sûr de sa puissance, il a une ambition plus grande encore : il est le « Nouveau Constantin » dont les courtisans chantent les mérites, que madame de Sévigné, La Fontaine et La Bruyère louent pour son action pieuse.

Il n'est que Vauban pour mesurer les conséquences négatives du départ de tant de talents huguenots à l'étranger alors même que le royaume est de plus en plus endetté, qu'au lieu d'investir leur fortune dans les activités manufacturières ou marchandes les riches préfèrent l'achat de terres, le prêt à intérêt, l'acquisition d'offices, les garanties offertes par un État absolutiste plutôt que les risques économiques.

Car les huguenots exilés étaient précisément ouverts sur l'économie moderne telle qu'elle se pratiquait aux Provinces-Unies et déjà en Angleterre.

Sur ce plan-là aussi, le « modèle français » s'oppose au « modèle anglo-hollandais ».

Louis XIV a une vision de la puissance et de la gloire qui s'accorde à ce goût de la terre, de la rente et de l'héritage qui caractérise les élites françaises.

Il revendique ainsi – au nom de sa belle-sœur, la princesse Palatine – le Palatinat.

Ses troupes entrent en Dauphiné pour y combattre les vaudois hérétiques.

Louis tente d'aider Jacques II à reconquérir son trône, mais le débarquement de troupes dans l'Irlande catholique se solde par un échec.

Reste donc la guerre continentale contre la ligue d'Augsbourg, conduite depuis 1686 mais déclarée le 15 avril 1689. Et marquée par l'impitoyable violence des troupes françaises, qui mettent le Palatinat à sac en 1688-1689 :

« Je vois le roi assez disposé à faire raser entièrement la ville et la citadelle de Mannheim, écrit Louvois, et, en ce cas, d'en faire détruire entièrement les habitations. »

On brûle « les villes que l'on ne peut forcer », on fait mettre « le feu dans les villages et leurs dépendances ».

La France apparaît ainsi au reste du continent comme une puissance menaçante et oppressive, persécutrice de ses propres sujets protestants, et les huguenots exilés – Pierre Bayle, Jurieu – décrivent les horreurs des dragonnades, la menace que Louis XIV fait peser sur l'Europe entière.

Ces années 1683-1689 sont bien le tournant du règne de Louis XIV. L'absolutisme s'y déploie et y dévoile sa violence.

Devenu dévot, en quête de toujours plus de gloire et d'autorité, le monarque commence aussi à être harcelé par la maladie – on procède à « la grande opération » d'une fistule le 18 novembre 1686. « Le roi a souffert aujourd'hui sept heures durant comme s'il avait été sur la roue », confie madame de Maintenon.

Louis XIV fait face à la douleur comme à l'Europe coalisée.

Mais on ne danse plus le ballet à Versailles.

29.

C'est la guerre. Elle écrase le dernier quart de siècle du règne de Louis XIV et marque de son empreinte profonde et cruelle l'âme de la France.

Le roi a voulu imposer aux États d'Europe la prépondérance française. Mais, malgré les victoires militaires – Fleurus en 1690, Steinkerke en 1692, Neerwinden en 1693 –, la suprématie navale de l'Angleterre (bataille de la Hougue, 1692) et la résistance des États obligent Louis XIV, aux traités de Turin et de Ryswick (1696, 1697), à renoncer à toutes ses conquêtes. Il ne conserve que Strasbourg. La leçon est nette : une nation ne peut dominer par la force le reste de l'Europe.

Et pourtant la guerre reprend dès 1701.

Le petit-fils de Louis XIV, le duc d'Anjou, devient Philippe V, roi d'Espagne, sans renoncer pour autant à la couronne de France.

Les Français gouvernent à Madrid.

Une compagnie française se voit attribuer l'*asiento*, le privilège du transport des esclaves vers l'Amérique ; Philippe V et Louis XIV sont actionnaires de cette compagnie négrière.

Ce n'est plus seulement à un empire occidental que s'opposent l'Angleterre, la Hollande, les princes allemands. Au-delà de la question de la succession d'Espagne, la guerre a pour enjeu la domination économique, le grand commerce.

Aux traités d'Utrecht et de Rastadt (1713, 1714), Philippe V doit renoncer à la couronne de France.

L'Angleterre, puissance maritime, commence son ascension. Elle conserve Gibraltar. Elle a brisé l'empire continental qui risquait de se constituer entre Madrid et Paris ; elle s'apprête à contrôler les mers.

Deuxième leçon pour le royaume de France : les États – et d'abord l'Angleterre et les Provinces-Unies – n'acceptent pas le risque de voir un nouvel empire à l'image de celui de Charles Quint se reconstituer en Europe, cette fois au bénéfice de la France.

Ces deux leçons infligées à la France, Louis XIV, qui meurt le 1er septembre 1715, les a-t-il comprises, et ses successeurs les ont-ils retenues, ou, au contraire, voudront-ils poursuivre cette ambition d'une prépondérance française sur le continent ?

Pour le royaume de France – et pour le Grand Roi –, ces années de guerre ont été un long hiver au terme duquel les gains ont été nuls, les souffrances, immenses, les morts, nombreuses, les transformations de la monarchie, profondes.

Si l'on ajoute que les rapports avec les États européens ennemis ont été dominés par ces guerres, on mesure que ces vingt-cinq années ont été décisives pour le royaume et pour l'image que la France a donnée d'elle-même aux peuples d'Europe.

Elle est la nation militaire : plusieurs centaines de milliers d'hommes – de 200 à 400 000 – engagés dans ces guerres.

Elle est la nation guerrière : les défaites, nombreuses, n'ont pas découragé le royaume, les victoires – Denain en 1702 – ayant permis le redressement de la situation.

Elle est la nation brutale (le sac du Palatinat), impérieuse, aux ambitions démesurées, le royaume dont il faut se méfier parce qu'il est puissant, riche et peuplé.

L'âme de la France a enregistré en elle-même ces éléments contradictoires qui ont été à l'œuvre durant ce quart de siècle français (1689-1715).

Et d'abord le coût de la guerre.

Le problème financier est bien la maladie endémique du royaume. L'endettement, l'emprunt, la manipulation des monnaies, l'augmentation des impôts, sont les caractéristiques permanentes des finances de la France.

Pour tenter de colmater le déficit, on multiplie les créations d'offices : vendeurs de bestiaux ou emballeurs, experts jurés, procureurs du roi, contrôleurs aux empilements de bois, visiteurs de beurre frais, visiteurs de beurre salé, etc.

L'argent rentre, mais la société française se fragmente en milliers d'officiers héréditaires.

Les fonctions de maire et de syndic sont mises en vente. Un édit de 1695 décide de l'anoblissement, moyennant finance, de 500 personnes distinguées du royaume.

On crée des « billets de monnaie », et le contrôleur général des finances, Chamillart, écrit à Louis XIV, faisant le bilan de cette introduction du « papier-monnaie » : « Toutes les ressources étant épuisées (en 1701), je proposai à Votre Majesté l'introduction de billets de monnaie non pas comme un grand soulagement, mais comme un mal nécessaire. Je pris la liberté de dire à Votre Majesté qu'il deviendrait irrémédiable, si la guerre obligeait d'en faire un si grand nombre, que le papier prît le dessus de l'argent. Ce que j'avais prévu est arrivé, le désordre qu'ils ont produit est extrême. »

Sur une idée de Vauban, on crée un impôt de capitation qui devrait être payé par tous (1694), puis ce sera l'impôt du dixième (1710).

Ces mesures – qui ne résolvent en rien la crise financière – permettent de payer la guerre, mais appauvrissent le pays, et, conjuguées à des hivers rigoureux, à des printemps pluvieux, aggravent en 1693-1694, puis en 1709 – le grand hiver –, la crise des subsistances, la disette, la famine.

Ainsi s'installe dans l'âme française le sentiment que l'État est un prédateur, que l'inégalité s'accroît, qu'elle s'inscrit définitivement dans ces « statuts » d'officiers qui ont le droit de transmettre leurs charges.

Les « réformateurs » comme Vauban (dans son ouvrage *Projet d'une dîme royale*) ou Boisguilbert (dans *Le Détail de la France, ou Traité de la cause de la diminution de ses biens et des moyens d'y remédier*) ont le sentiment qu'ils ne sont pas entendus quand l'un propose un impôt levé sur tous les revenus sans aucune exception, et quand l'autre, condamnant la « rente », l'usure, les ventes d'offices, affirme que « la richesse d'un royaume consiste en son terroir et en son commerce ».

En fait, le cancer du déséquilibre des finances s'installe et commence à ronger l'État, la confiance qu'on lui porte, à désagréger la société et à rendre quasi impossibles les réformes.

Pour trouver des ressources, l'État crée des cohortes d'officiers en leur vendant des parcelles de son autorité, en leur concédant des privilèges qui ne pourront être annulés sans épreuve de force.

Or le privilège est le cœur même du principe social sur lequel s'est bâtie la monarchie, société d'ordres.

Et voici que la noblesse elle-même est mise en vente !

D'un côté, on domestique les grands et les nobles ; de l'autre, on multiplie leur nombre, on vend les privilèges afférents à cet ordre, qui en font un obstacle à la réforme !

Certes, il y a la gloire du monarque, que la guerre accroît. Et son historiographe, Racine, s'enthousiasme quand, en 1692, il assiste à une revue de 120 000 hommes, « ce plus grand spectacle qu'on ait vu depuis plusieurs siècles... Je ne me souviens point que les Romains en aient vu un tel ».

Boileau n'est pas en reste, qui exalte la présence du roi au siège de Namur (1692) et la capitulation de la ville, que César lui-même n'avait pas obtenue.

Louis XIV est bel et bien le Roi-Soleil :

> *À cet astre redoutable*
> *Toujours un sort favorable*
> *S'attache dans les combats*
> *Et toujours avec la Gloire*
> *Mars amenant la Victoire*
> *Vole et le suit à grands pas.*

Par cette propagande, célébration de la gloire militaire du monarque, le pouvoir absolutiste cherche à se consolider, à justifier la guerre.

Dans le même temps, les exigences nées du conflit le conduisent à accroître le contrôle des activités. La guerre impose une concentration des pouvoirs. Elle entraîne non seulement un perfectionnement technique de l'armée – fusil, baïonnette, artillerie –, mais aussi une rationalisation de toute la vie civile.

Colbert crée ainsi des administrations nouvelles, des bureaux des hypothèques. Un Conseil du commerce est mis en place. Dans chaque ville – comme cela s'est fait à Paris dès 1667 – son nommés des lieutenants de police.

Car la guerre entraîne un renforcement de la surveillance. Le courrier, et d'abord celui des courtisans, est surveillé, lu.

« C'est une misère, la façon dont on agit avec les lettres », écrit la princesse Palatine, belle-sœur du roi et grande épistolière.

De même, la répression exercée contre tous ceux qui tentent de se dresser contre l'autorité royale ou de lui échapper est implacable.

C'est l'armée du maréchal de Villars qui fait la guerre aux camisards des Cévennes, ces huguenots que commande Jean Cavalier.

Des gentilshommes traquent les jeunes paysans qui cherchent à éviter l'enrôlement dans la milice royale.

L'armée a besoin d'hommes, et ce service militaire obligatoire avec tirage au sort permettra de lever, entre 1705 et 1713, 455 000 hommes !

« La jeunesse épouvantée allait se cacher dans les réduits les plus écartés et parmi les plus grandes forêts », note un témoin, « ou bien ils cherchaient à se marier afin d'échapper à la Milice, mais certains vautours, à qui l'on donnait le nom odieux de vendeurs de chair humaine, les enlevaient jusque dans le sein de leurs familles pour les traîner au champ de Mars, servir à émousser les épées anglaises et germaniques ».

Cette « militarisation » de la société, qui est une des conséquences de l'absolutisme et un produit de la guerre, suscite la méfiance envers l'État, et la situation dramatique du royaume, à partir des années 1690, fait naître de nombreuses critiques qui mettent en cause – c'est un signe de la profondeur de la crise – la personnalité même du souverain.

Fénelon, archevêque de Cambrai, ose écrire à Louis XIV, roi désormais dévot :

« Vous n'aimez pas Dieu, vous ne le craignez même que d'une crainte d'esclave, votre religion ne consiste qu'en superstition et en pratique superficielle. »

Ce propos violent complète une *Lettre anonyme à Louis XIV* qui est une critique radicale de l'absolutisme et de la politique suivie.

« On n'a plus parlé de l'État et de ses règles, on n'a plus parlé que du Roi et de ses plaisirs », souligne Fénelon.

L'une des manifestations de cette évolution absolutiste est la guerre.

« On a causé depuis plus de vingt ans des guerres sanglantes..., la guerre de Hollande (1672-1678) a été la source de toutes les autres. Elle n'a eu pour fondement qu'un motif de gloire et de vengeance, ce qui ne peut jamais rendre une guerre juste. »

Et la conséquence en est que « la France entière n'est plus qu'un grand hôpital désolé et sans provisions. Les magistrats sont avilis et épuisés. La noblesse, dont tout le bien est en décret, ne vit que de lettres d'État... Le peuple même qui vous a tant aimé commence à perdre l'amitié, la confiance et même le res-pect. Vos victoires et vos conquêtes ne le réjouissent plus, il est plein d'aigreur et de désespoir. La sédition s'allume un peu de toutes parts... Voilà, Sire, l'état où vous êtes. Vous vivez comme ayant un bandeau fatal sur les yeux. »

On est loin des louanges de Racine et de Boileau !

En 1709, la misère empoigne tout le royaume. Nicolas Desma-rets, contrôleur général, note la « mauvaise disposition des esprits et des peuples ».

Il souligne que des mouvements de révolte ont lieu ici et là dans les provinces où la hausse du prix du blé – consécutive à de mauvaises récoltes – provoque la disette, la famine ; et où les fermiers généraux ne réussissent plus à lever l'impôt et n'ont plus aucun crédit : ne parvenant plus à emprunter, ils ne prêtent plus et n'avancent plus le montant des impôts.

La dégradation de la situation (levée forcée de soldats, misère, etc.) conduit à cette montée des critiques.

On mesure ainsi qu'en dépit des renforcements continus de l'absolutisme, du développement de la coercition, de la réglementation, de la centralisation, du culte du roi, l'âme de la France est encore capable de se rebiffer.

Sous la chape de l'absolutisme, le pays – du peuple aux aristocrates – conteste ce mode de gouvernement, et les oppositions se raniment aussitôt. On n'accepte et subit l'absolutisme que parce que l'État exerce avec violence son autorité, mais cela ne vaut que si sa politique est favorable aux intérêts de la nation et à la prospérité de son peuple.

Que les résultats soient mauvais, que l'inégalité s'aggrave, et l'esprit de critique et de sédition reparaît. Contre l'absolutisme, on dresse le souvenir des états généraux, du gouvernement des princes, de l'aristocratie, des cours souveraines.

Le roi se retrouve ainsi isolé. Et il n'a pour toute ressource que de faire appel au « patriotisme » de la nation afin qu'elle se rassemble autour de lui, non plus dans un mouvement imposé par la répression, les édits, mais dans un mouvement d'adhésion nationale.

C'est ainsi que, le 12 juin 1709, dans l'abîme qu'est cet hiver de glace et de misère, de défaites et de doutes, Louis XIV adresse un Appel à ses évêques et à ses gouverneurs afin qu'ils le diffusent dans toutes les paroisses du royaume.

Louis XIV se dépouille de son autorité de souverain absolu.

Il ne dit plus : « Tel est mon bon plaisir. » En s'adressant à ses sujets, en leur expliquant les raisons de ses choix politiques, il les élève à la dignité d'interlocuteurs habilités à comprendre, à approuver, et donc aussi à discuter et à contester.

Louis XIV explique pourquoi il n'a pas pu conclure la paix : « Quoique ma tendresse pour mes peuples ne soit pas moins vive que celle que j'ai pour mes propres enfants, quoique je partage tous les maux que la guerre fait souffrir à des sujets aussi fidèles, et que j'aie fait voir à toute l'Europe que je désirais sincèrement de les faire jouir de la paix, je suis persuadé qu'ils s'opposeraient eux-mêmes à la recevoir à des conditions également contraires à la justice et à l'honneur du nom français. »

L'intérêt dynastique devient là, simplement, le visage de l'intérêt national, la gloire et l'honneur du roi ne sont que l'expression de la « justice et de l'honneur du nom français ».

Face à l'échec de la politique de Louis XIV, cet appel royal, au cœur de la détresse qui frappe le royaume, exprime la force et la réalité de la conscience nationale. Mais cet appel confirme dans l'âme française que le roi n'est un souverain pleinement légitime que par la politique qu'il mène, et qu'en dernier ressort c'est le peuple qui l'adoube, qui lui accorde le second sacre déterminant la valeur du premier.

La contestation de l'absolutisme, l'importance du peuple, la permanence des « ordres » traditionnels du royaume, refont ainsi irruption au bout de près d'un demi-siècle – depuis 1661 – de monarchie absolutiste.

L'appel de Louis XIV au patriotisme est entendu.

La foule attend devant les imprimeries le texte du roi.

On l'approuve de ne pas avoir accepté de contribuer par les armes, comme le demandaient les puissances en guerre, à chasser son propre petit-fils, Philippe V, du trône d'Espagne.

Le maréchal de Villars lit l'appel aux troupes, qui l'acclament. Et le 11 septembre 1709, à Malplaquet, au terme d'une bataille sanglante, incertaine, s'il n'est pas victorieux de Marlborough et du prince Eugène de Savoie, il arrête l'avance ennemie.

Puis, le 24 juillet 1712, à Denain, il bat le prince Eugène.

Les alliés doivent alors se convaincre qu'ils ne pourront pas écraser la France et qu'il vaut mieux traiter, d'autant plus que l'Angleterre et les Provinces-Unies ne veulent pas que l'Empire germanique profite de la défaite française.

Dès lors que Philippe V renonce à la couronne de France, la paix est possible.

Les traités d'Utrecht et de Rastaadt la rétabliront en 1713 et 1714.

Mais le royaume et la dynastie sont affaiblis.

« Sire, vous le savez, écrit dans une lettre anonyme Saint-Simon, votre royaume n'a plus de ressources... Jetez, Sire, les yeux sur les trois états qui forment le corps de votre nation... Le clergé est tombé dans une abjection de pédanterie et de crasse qui l'a tout à fait enfoncé dans un profond oubli... La noblesse n'est pas plus heureuse... Ce n'est plus qu'une bête morte, qu'un mari insipide, qu'une foule séparée, dissipée, imbécile, impuissante, incapable de tout et qui n'est plus propre qu'à souffrir sans résistance... Le tiers état, infiniment élevé dans quelques particuliers qui ont fait leur fortune par le ministère ou par d'autres voies, est tombé en général dans le même néant que les deux premiers corps. »

Certes, la description de Saint-Simon est en fait un plaidoyer en faveur d'un gouvernement aristocratique.

« Que Votre Majesté règne enfin par elle-même », dit-il, contestant l'action des ministres, de l'épouse, madame de Maintenon, ou du confesseur jésuite, et rêvant à des princes entourant le roi.

Mais, au-delà de cette limite, c'est la succession de Louis XIV elle-même qui semble menacée.

La mort a frappé comme à grands coups de hache.

En 1711, le Grand Dauphin, fils de Louis XIV, est mort.

Puis, en 1712, le duc et la duchesse de Bourgogne (le petit-fils de Louis XIV et son épouse).

En 1712 encore, le duc de Bretagne, arrière-petit-fils aîné de Louis XIV, et, en 1714, Charles, duc de Berry, petit-fils du roi et frère de Philippe V d'Espagne – autre petit-fils de Louis XIV –, mais qui a renoncé à la couronne de France.

Ne survit donc qu'un arrière-petit-fils, le duc d'Anjou, d'à peine cinq ans et demi en 1715.

Le régent serait le neveu de Louis XIV, Philippe d'Orléans, fils du frère du roi et de la princesse Palatine.

Mais la défiance de Louis XIV est grande envers lui, qu'à la Cour on a même soupçonné d'avoir fait empoisonner les membres de la famille royale afin d'accéder au trône.

Louis XIV a d'ailleurs créé un conseil de régence afin de contrôler Philippe d'Orléans, qui en assurera cependant la présidence.

Le 1er septembre 1715 à 8 h 15, Louis XIV meurt au château de Versailles à l'âge de soixante-dix-sept ans.

Il était monté sur le trône soixante-douze ans auparavant et avait régné personnellement cinquante-quatre ans.

À sa mort, c'est à nouveau un enfant – Louis XV – qui accède au trône.

L'absolutisme survivra-t-il à la régence de Philippe d'Orléans, prince libertin ?

CHRONOLOGIE II

Vingt dates clés (1515-1715)

1515 : Victoire de Marignan, remportée par François Ier (1515-1547) sur les Suisses alliés du duc de Milan

1519 : Début de la construction du château de Chambord

1522 : Début de la première guerre contre Charles Quint

1539 : Ordonnance de Villers-Cotterêts – tous les actes officiels doivent être rédigés en français

1562 : Première guerre de Religion

1572 : Massacre de la Saint-Barthélemy (24 août)

1593 : Abjuration de Henri IV à Saint-Denis

1598 : Édit de Nantes

1624 : Richelieu, Premier ministre de Louis XIII (1610-1643)

1643 : Mort de Louis XIII et de Richelieu ; Régence d'Anne d'Autriche

1648 : Traité de Westphalie

1649 : Fuite du roi Louis XIV, onze ans, de Mazarin et d'Anne d'Autriche, de Paris à Saint-Germain

1661 : Mort de Mazarin, gouvernement personnel de Louis XIV

1682 : Le roi s'installe à Versailles

1684 : Mariage secret de Louis XIV et de madame de Maintenon

1685 : Révocation de l'édit de Nantes

1685 : Code noir sur l'esclavage

1701 -1714 : Guerre de Succession d'Espagne

1709 : L'année terrible – défaite, froid, famine

1715 : Mort de Louis XIV

LIVRE III

L'ÉCLAT DES LUMIÈRES – L'IMPOSSIBLE RÉFORME ET LA RÉVOLUTION ARMÉE

1715-1799

1

LOUIS XV

Le vent se lève
1715-1774

30

1715 : on entre dans un nouveau siècle.

C'est le temps des salons parisiens et non plus celui de la chapelle et des confessionnaux de Versailles.

On loue en Louis XIV « cette fermeté d'âme, cette égalité extérieure, cette espérance contre toute espérance, par courage, par sagesse et non par aveuglement », mais, après avoir ainsi salué le monarque défunt, édenté et dévot, Saint-Simon, l'ami et porte-parole du Régent Philippe d'Orléans, le pousse à rompre et à oublier le vieux roi qui s'était prolongé en ce xviiie siècle et qu'on ne supportait plus.

On veut participer aux fêtes du Régent, pétillantes et libertines.

On veut tomber le masque. On rejette les bigoteries et les jésuites.

Les élites françaises – princes du sang, haute noblesse – désirent à la fois retrouver leur pouvoir et leur influence, contenus par l'absolutisme de Louis XIV, et se mêler aux beaux esprits, aux jeux de l'amour et de la pensée.

En 1715, Marivaux a déjà vingt-sept ans, Montesquieu, vingt-six, Voltaire, vingt et un.

Philippe d'Orléans, homme de tous les talents, brillant et beau, libertin mais conscient de ses devoirs, incarne cette dizaine d'années de régence. Il meurt en 1723, l'année de la majorité de

Louis XV, et le duc de Bourbon lui succède jusqu'en 1726
– cette année-là, le roi, assisté du cardinal Fleury, gouverne.

La décennie de la Régence est, après le long hiver du Grand
Roi, une période de retournement et de créativité qui marque
l'âme et la mémoire de la France.

Louis XIV a tenté de prolonger son règne au-delà de sa propre
mort. Le conseil de régence doit tenir en tutelle ce neveu,
Philippe d'Orléans, dont il s'est toujours méfié : trop beau, trop
talentueux, donc trop ambitieux, trop dangereux pour un
monarque absolutiste.

Avant de mourir, Louis XIV a fait de ses deux bâtards légitimés – les fils de madame de Montespan –, le duc du Maine et
le comte de Toulouse, des princes du sang ayant le droit de succéder à leur père. Pis : le duc du Maine a été désigné par
Louis XIV pour prendre en main l'éducation de Louis XV.

Le Régent veut le pouvoir. Il fait casser le testament de
Louis XIV par le parlement de Paris, auquel il rend en échange
son droit de remontrance ; il fait de même pour toutes les cours
souveraines.

Ainsi les parlementaires, écartés du jeu par la monarchie absolutiste, retrouvent-ils leur pouvoir de contrôle, de contestation,
d'opposition.

Défaite posthume de Louis XIV et de la volonté absolutiste
qui, depuis la dernière convocation des états généraux, en 1614
– il y a alors un siècle –, l'avait emporté. Le Parlement et les
cours souveraines se présentent à nouveau comme le « corps »
de la nation.

Imposture, puisque les parlementaires sont propriétaires de
leurs charges héréditaires, qu'ils représentent un groupe social
puissant qui peut certes s'attribuer le rôle de « défenseur » du
peuple, mais qui est partie prenante dans la caste des privilégiés.
Cependant, en réintroduisant les parlements dans le jeu politique
comme acteurs influents, le Régent veut aussi faire contrepoids
aux princes, à la haute noblesse, à laquelle – dans sa lutte contre
les bâtards de Louis XIV – il a sacrifié le gouvernement ministériel, celui de « la vile bourgeoisie », instrument de l'absolutisme
royal.

Durant trois années (1715-1718), huit Conseils – de conscience, des finances, de justice, etc. – peuplés par la haute noblesse gouvernent en lieu et place des descendants des familles ministérielles, les Colbert, les Louvois, les Pontchartrain, etc.

Cette « polysynodie » est une réaction aristocratique à la pratique de Louis XIV. Elle tente de mettre sur pied un autre mode de gouvernement, mais l'incompétence, la futilité de cette haute noblesse, ses rivalités, tout comme le désir du Régent de gouverner lui-même, mettent fin à cette expérience qui avait aussi un but tactique : permettre à Philippe d'Orléans de s'imposer en rassemblant autour de lui les princes contre les bâtards de Louis XIV et contre les parlementaires, auxquels on a rendu leurs pouvoirs.

Cet exercice d'équilibre, qui se termine par la création de secrétariats à la Guerre, aux Affaires étrangères (pour le cardinal Dubois), donc par un retour du gouvernement ministériel, n'en a pas moins fissuré l'absolutisme.

On mesure même, à cette occasion, combien les élites françaises sont divisées, le pouvoir, fragmenté, les ambitions de chaque « clan », contradictoires.

Les risques d'éclatement du groupe social des élites ne sont pas encore perçus. Et cependant, en 1721, paraissent les *Lettres persanes* de Montesquieu. En 1720, Marivaux, sur le modèle anglais du *Spectator*, lance un périodique, *Le Spectateur français*.

Ainsi, une « opinion » souvent critique – prenant modèle sur ce qui se passe à Amsterdam, à Londres – commence d'apparaître. Elle est influente dans les salons. Elle attire telle ou telle personnalité de la haute noblesse, du Parlement.

En face d'elle, le pouvoir est hésitant.

Voltaire a déjà connu la Bastille en 1717. Mais, à sa sortie, ses premières œuvres lui ont valu la notoriété. Ses pièces sont jouées en 1725 lors du mariage du roi avec Marie Leszczynska, fille du roi de Pologne détrôné. Une épigramme contre le Régent le renvoie à la Bastille. En 1726, il s'exilera en Angleterre au terme d'une querelle avec le chevalier de Rohan qui l'a fait bâtonner, refusant de se battre en duel avec un homme qui

« n'a même pas de nom ». Et Voltaire a répondu, comme s'il pressentait l'avenir : « Mon nom je le commence, vous finissez le vôtre ! »

Épisode symbolique illustrant comment, sous l'apparence d'un système politique et social qui est l'ordre naturel et sacré du monde, des ferments de division prolifèrent.

Et si les « idées nouvelles » – les « Lumières », dira-t-on bientôt – sont acceptées, c'est que le royaume continue d'être rongé par la « maladie » financière, l'endettement, la recherche haletante de revenus, l'anticipation des recettes pour faire face aux dépenses courantes, à l'impossibilité de prélever de nouveaux impôts.

Naturellement, le regain de pouvoir des parlements et de la haute noblesse réduit encore les marges de manœuvre de la monarchie.

Comment faire payer les privilégiés qui sont le socle du système social et le symbole même de la société d'ordres ?

Ce dilemme, la Régence essaie de le contourner, à défaut de le résoudre.

La fondation en 1716 par l'Écossais John Law d'une Banque générale est le point de départ de cette tentative.

Il s'agit de créer des billets circulant rapidement, en nombre suffisant pour impulser la croissance économique, favoriser le grand commerce maritime et, sinon remplacer, en tout cas entamer le monopole des « espèces sonnantes et trébuchantes », or ou argent, dont la frappe est limitée.

Ce modèle de banque – devenue Banque royale – est emprunté à la Hollande et à l'Angleterre, qui ont créé leurs propres banques respectivement dès 1609 et 1694.

C'est aussi sur les modèles anglais et hollandais que Law fonde en 1717 la Compagnie d'Occident, devenue Compagnie française des Indes.

Ces premières initiatives sont un succès.

Elles permettent, par le jeu de la valeur des billets, des taux d'intérêt, de réduire les endettements – ce qui ruine certains prêteurs. Elles facilitent les investissements, donnent une impulsion aux manufactures et à l'artisanat de luxe favorisés par le grand commerce.

Mais cette économie et cette finance nouvelles se heurtent à la réalité du modèle français.

Law propose une circulation rapide de la monnaie et la prépondérance du commerce dans un royaume où la fortune est foncière, liée à la rente, aux revenus que l'on tire de son statut, de son office, au rôle que l'on joue dans le prêt d'argent à l'État.

Or, en 1719, Law se fait attribuer la Ferme générale – la levée des impôts –, puis, en 1720, il devient contrôleur général des finances.

Cette rencontre entre fonctions liées à l'État et nouvelle économie et nouvelle finance suscite des inquiétudes parmi les princes, prêteurs habituels. Ils retirent leur or de la Banque, la valeur du papier s'effondre, la Bourse de la rue Quincampoix ferme.

Le système novateur a fait faillite. Il s'est brisé contre la structure traditionnelle de la finance dans le royaume. Et aussi sur la rapacité des grands, qui se sont enrichis dans cette spéculation sur le « papier-monnaie », entraînant, par leur volonté de sauver leurs gains en or, le naufrage de la Banque.

Les conséquences de la « banqueroute » de Law vont s'inscrire dans la longue durée de la mémoire nationale.

La défiance à l'égard de l'État, des « élites » qui se sont enrichies, des affaires d'argent, en est renforcée.

Elle se double d'un rejet du « papier-monnaie », d'un attachement aux pièces d'or ou d'argent – la livre-tournoi, dont le cours est stabilisé en 1726 et le restera pour près de deux siècles.

La conviction s'enracine dans l'âme des Français que les « rentes » d'État ou les fermages, l'achat de terres ou d'immeubles, sont les seuls moyens de protéger sa fortune.

Ainsi, le « modèle » marchand et l'aventure coloniale tels que les pratiquent les Hollandais et les Anglais n'entraîneront jamais la totalité des élites françaises dans un projet commun.

Certes, l'économie, grâce à la circulation des billets de John Law, a été fouettée, le commerce du sucre, la traite négrière, se sont développés, de même que les villes portuaires : Bordeaux,

Nantes, Lorient, et aussi, pour le commerce avec le Levant, Marseille. Mais le « système » – rente, usure, propriété foncière, achat d'« offices » – n'est pas modifié en profondeur.

Quant à la crise financière, elle n'est pas réglée.

La tentative du duc de Bourbon, principal ministre après la mort du duc d'Orléans en 1723, de créer un impôt du cinquantième – sur les revenus de tous les propriétaires – est rapidement abandonnée.

La monarchie se révèle capable de formuler le diagnostic de sa maladie financière, mais est impuissante à appliquer les thérapies qu'elle élabore.

Le mal et les remèdes sont identifiés, connus ; mais le régime est incapable d'entreprendre l'opération qui permettrait d'extirper la tumeur.

D'autant que le pouvoir des parlementaires rend encore plus difficile l'action du roi.

Cependant, une partie des élites – dans le gouvernement (ainsi le cardinal Dubois, chargé des Affaires étrangères jusqu'à sa mort en 1723) mais aussi dans les mondes juridique et littéraire – regarde les modèles anglais et hollandais avec attention, persuadée qu'il y a là une voie nouvelle pour l'organisation sociale et politique, économique et financière.

C'est une des raisons qui expliquent le « retournement » de la politique extérieure du royaume.

On s'allie avec l'Angleterre et la Hollande, puis avec le Habsbourg de Vienne (1717-1718), et l'on renonce ainsi au rôle d'arbitre ou à une posture impériale en Europe, au bénéfice d'une pacification des rapports avec la puissance britannique, différente mais alors en plein essor.

Et on n'hésite pas, en 1719, à faire la guerre à l'Espagne où continue de régner le petit-fils de Louis XIV, Philippe V, pour lui imposer de se joindre à l'accord passé avec Londres !

L'Angleterre est la référence et en même temps la vraie rivale.

Ruiné par la banqueroute de Law, Marivaux imite les Anglais quand il veut créer un périodique.

Et Voltaire, sortant de la Bastille, s'exile outre-Manche en 1726.

Louis XV, qui, cette année-là, décide de gouverner avec son précepteur, le cardinal de Fleury, n'a encore que seize ans.

Va-t-il, peut-il saisir l'avantage que lui donne la perspective d'un long règne ?

31.

Le temps n'a pas manqué à Louis XV.

Lorsque le cardinal de Fleury, son ancien précepteur devenu en 1726 son principal ministre, meurt en 1743 à l'âge de quatre-vingt-neuf ans, le roi n'en a que trente-trois.

Il règne sur un royaume taraudé par une crise financière permanente, mais qui connaît un vif essor économique.

Fleury a gouverné prudemment. Des guerres, certes, mais qui n'épuisent pas le pays. Les blés sont abondants. Le grand commerce, actif. Les foires, prospères. L'administration du royaume – intendants, subdélégués, gouverneurs –, efficace. On trace des routes. On enquête pour connaître la réalité des fortunes, des récoltes, des revenus, le nombre des habitants. On en dénombre une vingtaine de millions, soit la population la plus importante d'Europe.

Certes, les inégalités s'accroissent entre fermiers, coqs de village et manouvriers. Mais chacun se souvient du pire qu'ont connu ses aïeux : disette, famine, épidémies, peste, guerres civiles, soldatesque répandue comme une vermine sur les campagnes.

L'ordre règne. L'armée est réorganisée. On crée des écoles militaires. On ouvre des classes pour apprendre à lire aux fils de paysans. La misère s'éloigne un peu des masures.

On sait que le monarque est jeune, beau, séducteur, conquérant. À Paris, on connaît le nom de ses maîtresses, nombreuses,
titrées, comtesses, duchesses ou marquises : la Pompadour, la
Du Barry. Mais au royaume de France on ne juge pas un roi sur
ses fréquentations d'alcôve.

Le sacre en fait un être distingué par Dieu, homme au-dessus
des autres humains.

Les conseillers, ses ministres, ses maîtresses, ses confesseurs,
peuvent le tromper, lui faire commettre des erreurs. Mais lui est
sacré. On prie pour son salut, afin que Dieu l'éclaire dans les
choix qu'il doit faire pour ses sujets.

Quand, en 1744, il tombe malade à Metz, les églises se remplissent. Il faut sauver *Louis le Bien-Aimé*.

Mais, treize ans plus tard, quand, dans les jardins du château
de Versailles, un domestique, Robert François Damiens, frappera
le roi d'un coup de canif, l'écorchant à peine, on ne relèvera
aucune émotion dans le royaume, plutôt une indifférence méprisante. Et presque de la pitié et de l'indulgence pour ce Damiens
qu'on va rouer, cisailler aux aines et aux aisselles pour faciliter
l'écartèlement par quatre chevaux attelés à ses membres.

Au mitan du XVIIIᵉ siècle, dans les années 1740-1760, quelque
chose de décisif s'est donc produit dans le rapport du peuple et
de son roi.

Le monarque et l'institution monarchique paraissent désacralisés.

Dans la constitution et l'évolution de l'âme de la France, ce
tournant est capital.

Il s'agit en fait d'une véritable révolution intellectuelle.

Les esprits de ceux qui pensent, écrivent, publient, font jouer
leurs pièces sur les scènes des théâtres, lisent leurs œuvres dans
les salons parisiens, entretiennent une correspondance quotidienne avec Londres ou Berlin, ont échappé à la monarchie
absolue.

Ils portent un regard différent sur le monde.

La raison plus que la foi guide leur pensée. Ils décrivent, ils
analysent. Ils sont écoutés, applaudis.

Face à ce mouvement des idées, à ces *Lumières* qui se répandent, la monarchie est hésitante.

Ces esprits indépendants n'appellent pas à la révolte. Cette fronde intellectuelle ne fait pas tirer le canon sur les troupes royales. Ces « philosophes » – puisque c'est ainsi qu'on les nomme – fréquentent les salons, sont accueillis à la Cour, courtisés et protégés par les aristocrates.

Mais cette révolution dans les esprits sape les fondements de la monarchie absolue.

Marivaux, Voltaire (les *Lettres philosophiques* en 1734, *Zadig* en 1747, l'*Essai sur les mœurs et l'esprit des nations* en 1757, année de Damiens, le régicide), Rousseau, qui, lui, s'avance au nom de l'égalité et ébranle ainsi les bases sociales du système monarchique, font triompher l'esprit laïque.

Quand, en 1752, Voltaire publie *Le Siècle de Louis XIV*, il jauge le règne avec une indépendance d'esprit qui, par-delà les jugements qu'il porte sur la période, sont un acte révolutionnaire.

Et la parution en 1751 du premier tome de l'*Encyclopédie*, qui s'approprie tous les domaines pour les reconstruire hors de la « superstition », a la même signification.

Que faire avec ces philosophes ?

En 1749, Diderot a été emprisonné à Vincennes. En 1752, un arrêt du Conseil annule l'autorisation de paraître des deux premiers volumes de l'*Encyclopédie*.

Mais, outre que les philosophes bénéficient de la protection de membres influents de la Cour (madame de Pompadour), chaque mesure prise à leur encontre les renforce en attirant l'attention sur leurs discours. Un « parti philosophique » se constitue ainsi, vers les années 1750, autour de l'*Encyclopédie*, de Voltaire, de Diderot et de d'Alembert.

Il devient un acteur déterminant de l'évolution du royaume. Sa vigueur, sa créativité et sa diversité en font un des éléments constitutifs de l'âme de la France.

Pour la première fois dans l'histoire nationale, un pouvoir « intellectuel » se crée hors des institutions – la Cour, l'Église, les parlements, etc. –, transcendant les ordres, les classes – noblesse, clergé, tiers état –, et fait face à celui de la monarchie.

Avec *De l'esprit des lois*, Montesquieu lui confère en 1748 une dimension politique en mettant l'accent sur le risque de dérive despotique de la monarchie absolue.

Il souligne que la seule manière de l'empêcher est de dresser contre le pouvoir un autre pouvoir. Ce « contre-pouvoir », les corps intermédiaires en sont l'expression.

Ainsi se dessine une caractéristique majeure de l'histoire française : le parti philosophique devient un pouvoir intellectuel qui intervient dans l'arène politique.

Ces philosophes, ces écrivains transmettent l'exemple d'une monarchie contrôlée telle qu'elle existe en Angleterre. Voltaire est le propagateur de ce modèle. Rousseau s'interroge sur l'origine de l'inégalité. L'*Encyclopédie* – dont le pouvoir se voit contraint de tolérer la diffusion – examine dans un esprit laïque tous les sujets.

La diffusion de cet « esprit des Lumières » imprègne toutes les élites.

Le débat intellectuel, la polémique, deviennent un des traits significatifs de la vie parisienne, des théâtres aux salons.

On discute, on conteste. Plus rien ne va de soi.

Une idéologie nouvelle aux multiples nuances se constitue. Les divergences et les polémiques qui la caractérisent – entre Voltaire et Rousseau, il y a un fossé – n'empêchent pas qu'elle porte une critique radicale de la monarchie absolue et qu'elle exprime, avec Montesquieu, un « libéralisme » politique, une idée de l'équilibre et de la limitation des pouvoirs qui s'inscrit à contre-courant de l'évolution du régime en place.

Cette influence des « philosophes » au cœur du XVIIIe siècle donne ainsi naissance à une spécificité nationale, à une orientation singulière de l'âme de la France.

Le parti philosophique pèse d'autant plus que sa contestation de la monarchie absolue rencontre celle que, pour des raisons différentes, conduisent les parlementaires.

Ces privilégiés auxquels le Régent a rendu leur pouvoir de remontrance contestent la plupart des décisions de la monarchie.

Quel que soit le sujet – création d'un impôt du vingtième sur tous les revenus (1749) ou bien problèmes posés au clergé français par la bulle pontificale *Unigenitus* –, les parlementaires se dressent contre le pouvoir royal en affirmant qu'ils représentent les corps intermédiaires, là où se conjoignent l'autorité souveraine et la confiance des sujets. Qu'en somme rien ne peut se faire sans leur approbation.

Les « lits de justice » – ces manifestations de l'autorité royale censées imposer sa décision – sont inopérants.

Les parlementaires se mettent en grève. Le pouvoir les exile hors de Paris, à Pontoise en 1752. Mais les cours souveraines de province relaient le parlement de Paris empêché.

Contre les évêques décidés à suivre le pape et donc à reconnaître l'autorité de la bulle *Unigenitus* contre les jansénistes, les « convulsionnaires », les parlementaires se présentent comme les défenseurs des traditions gallicanes, alors que le roi choisit pour sa part de soutenir les décisions pontificales.

Une véritable opposition frontale – à propos des sacrements refusés aux mourants qui ne disposent pas d'un billet de confession signé par un prêtre favorable à la bulle *Unigenitus* – se manifeste ainsi entre les parlements et le pouvoir royal.

C'est bien l'ancienne querelle sur la question de la monarchie absolue qui se rejoue à propos du gallicanisme, celui-ci n'étant qu'un prétexte, mais dans un contexte nouveau déterminé par l'esprit des Lumières.

S'il y a désaccord profond entre les parlementaires et les philosophes, ils se retrouvent côte à côte contre la monarchie absolue.

Et Louis XV cède.

Le pouvoir monarchique est ainsi atteint alors que le pays voit non sans inquiétude les guerres succéder aux guerres.

Elles ne pèsent pas encore sur la vie du royaume – rien qui rappelle le « grand hiver » de 1709 –, mais on n'en comprend pas les mobiles. Elles sont décidées hors du Conseil, dans le « secret du roi ». Elles apparaissent plus dynastiques que nationales. Encore et toujours, il faut les financer.

La première, la guerre pour la succession de Pologne, contre l'Autriche qui réussit à imposer son candidat en empêchant le retour du beau-père de Louis XV, se solde au traité de Vienne (1738) par la promesse qu'à la mort de Stanislas Leszczynski la Lorraine, qu'on lui a attribuée en compensation, reviendra à la France.

On mesure à cette occasion, puis surtout à propos de la succession d'Autriche – à la mort de l'empereur, sa fille Marie-Thérèse lui succède, mais la France conteste qu'elle puisse être élue au trône impérial –, que la situation a profondément changé en Europe.

La Prusse est devenue un royaume puissant que Frédéric II a doté d'une remarquable armée. La France s'allie à lui dans un premier temps contre l'Angleterre, la Hollande, la Russie, qui soutiennent Marie-Thérèse d'Autriche et ses ambitions impériales.

Les Français entrent dans Prague, remportent le 11 mai 1745 la bataille de Fontenoy contre les Anglo-Hollandais. Mais, à la paix d'Aix-la-Chapelle, Louis XV renonce à ses conquêtes : « Nous ne faisons pas la guerre en marchand, mais en roi. »

Il a, en fait, « travaillé pour le roi de Prusse » alors que, durant cette guerre inutile, s'est profilé le concurrent principal : l'Angleterre.

Cette rivalité avec Londres est « atlantique », « moderne », lourde d'avenir, puisqu'elle a pour enjeu le contrôle des colonies américaines, des Antilles, des comptoirs des Indes.

Elle supposerait soit qu'on passe un accord avec l'Angleterre – une bonne entente ne prévaut-elle pas depuis vingt ans ? –, soit, si on choisit la guerre, que la France réoriente ses efforts vers la constitution d'une puissante marine et d'une économie ouverte, structurée par de grandes compagnies marchandes.

Mais la fortune française est « rentière », foncière. Et Paris poursuit son rêve de dominer le continent, d'arbitrer les conflits européens.

Dès lors, autour du roi, les « conservateurs » choisissent l'alliance avec Vienne au traité de Versailles de 1756.

C'est là un véritable renversement d'alliance.

Or cette nouvelle orientation est pleine de contradictions. Le parti philosophique admire l'Angleterre – l'adversaire –, ses institutions, ses mœurs. Il est fasciné par Frédéric II, le souverain philosophe, alors que la Prusse est l'ennemie de Vienne.

Ainsi, alors que commence en 1756 une nouvelle guerre, celle-ci franco-anglaise, le royaume de France est parcouru de courants contradictoires.

Le roi n'est plus Louis le Bien-Aimé. Et Voltaire, en brossant l'histoire du *Siècle de Louis XIV*, fait à sa manière une critique de celui de Louis XV : le Roi-Soleil, majestueux, était implacable mais glorieux. Louis XV est un souverain de cinquante-sept ans qui n'inspire plus la ferveur quasi religieuse qu'on doit à celui que Dieu a sacré.

Le geste de Robert François Damiens, le 5 janvier 1757, même s'il n'inflige qu'une blessure légère au souverain, frappe durement le principe de la monarchie absolue.

32.

Louis XV va encore régner dix-sept ans.

Le temps ne lui est donc pas compté. Mais son gouvernement personnel est déjà vieux de trente et une années. Et l'on s'est lassé de ce roi dont les pamphlets affirment qu'il ne s'intéresse qu'à la chasse et aux dames.

Certes, l'économie est prospère, le commerce, actif, les récoltes, abondantes, car l'embellie climatique se poursuit et les « physiocrates » élaborent les premiers rudiments d'une science des échanges, une réflexion sur l'économie.

En juin 1763 est même autorisée la libre circulation des grains.

Cependant, le monarque n'est ni vénéré ni respecté.

On est impitoyable avec sa maîtresse, la comtesse Du Barry, auquel le banquier de la Cour remet 300 000 livres par mois.

On serait indulgent pour la débauche de luxe qui entoure la favorite si le roi n'apparaissait pas seulement comme l'homme des plaisirs, mais comme un souverain attentif au sort de son royaume, homme au-dessus des autres hommes, incarnation de la majesté et de la gloire.

Or la guerre contre l'Angleterre et la Prusse est une succession humiliante de désastres.

Elle blesse le sentiment national.

En 1757, à Rossbach, Soubise cherche son armée franco-autrichienne défaite par les Prussiens. Et toute l'Europe salue le roi Frédéric II, constructeur d'une nation puissante, modèle d'administration, qui change la donne sur le continent.

Le parti philosophique loue le prince éclairé et conteste l'alliance française avec l'Autriche.

Le pacte de famille conclu entre Louis XV et les Bourbons de Madrid et de Naples ne peut changer l'équilibre des forces.

Les colonies tombent les unes après les autres : le Canada est perdu, Montréal capitule (1759-1760), Pondichéry connaît le même sort en 1761.

Le 10 février 1763, le traité de Paris dépouille la France de l'essentiel de ses possessions d'outre-mer.

Comment faire face à cette humiliante défaite infligée par ceux qu'on admire, Anglais, Prussiens, les « modernes », alors qu'on a pour alliée cette Autriche archaïque à laquelle Louis XV veut rester fidèle, mariant son petit-fils Louis avec l'archiduchesse Marie-Antoinette, une Habsbourg (mai 1770).

L'opinion, suivant le parti philosophique, ne peut que se détourner de ce roi et de son gouvernement qui infligent à la nation une telle banqueroute internationale.

On se moque des ministres (Choiseul), des généraux (Soubise), du monarque lui-même.

Le pouvoir royal n'est plus respecté. On l'accuse d'avoir sacrifié les intérêts de la nation. Comment, dès lors, accepterait-on que la monarchie demeure absolue alors qu'elle est si peu glorieuse ?

Chanter les louanges de Frédéric II et de la Prusse, c'est une manière de refuser d'être confondu avec un pouvoir incapable. Et c'est un ministre, le cardinal de Bernis, qui, jugeant le rôle des différents États, écrit : « Le nôtre a été extravagant et honteux. »

On mesure à quel point s'élargit la faille, si souvent présente dans notre histoire, entre le « pouvoir » et l'« opinion ». Comment se reconstitue, pour les meilleures raisons philosophiques, et parce que en effet la politique extérieure a eu des résultats désastreux, un « parti de l'étranger » d'autant plus menaçant, cette fois-ci, qu'il rassemble contre le pouvoir politique le pouvoir intellectuel.

Ce dernier devient une véritable force capable de mener des campagnes politiques au nom des principes « éclairés » qu'il défend.

Le pouvoir politique apparaît ainsi acculé, affaibli, injuste et corrompu.

Mais le roi n'est pas seul atteint. Ce sont les piliers de la monarchie qui se fissurent.

On critique le clergé. On critique les parlementaires, même si parfois on se ligue avec eux contre l'absolutisme.

Le « pouvoir » en tant que tel est ainsi remis en cause.

Voltaire prend parti pour le huguenot Calas, roué en mars 1762, accusé à tort d'avoir tué son fils afin de l'empêcher d'abjurer la foi réformée.

La campagne que mène Voltaire renvoie tous les « pouvoirs » – religieux, judiciaire, monarchique – du côté de l'injustice. La réhabilitation de Calas, en 1765, est une victoire du parti philosophique et une nouvelle perte d'autorité des institutions « monarchiques ».

Même combat pour faire acquitter un autre protestant, Sirven. Mêmes campagnes pour tenter de sauver du bourreau Lally-Tollendal, gouverneur de Pondichéry, condamné pour s'être rendu sans combattre, et le jeune chevalier de La Barre, condamné à mort pour un geste sacrilège.

Les deux hommes sont exécutés, mais l'obstination du pouvoir – le roi a refusé la grâce de La Barre – l'isole, et constitue pour lui, en fait, une défaite morale.

La légitimité sans laquelle il n'est pas de pouvoir fort et respecté passe du côté du parti philosophique, qui étend son influence (le Grand Orient de France est créé en 1773 ; le duc d'Orléans lui-même, neveu du roi, est initié à la franc-maçonnerie).

Les loges maçonniques sont des lieux de débat, des « sociétés de pensée » où se constitue une « opinion éclairée » qui reconnaît le « Grand Architecte de l'Univers » et critique les Églises au nom du déisme.

Les représentants du pouvoir politique en prennent conscience, et, en 1770, l'avocat général Séguier prononce un réquisitoire lucide, mais qui est un constat de défaite :

« Les philosophes se sont élevés, dit-il, en précepteurs du genre humain. Liberté de penser : voilà leur cri, et ce cri s'est fait entendre d'une extrémité du monde à l'autre. Leur objet était de faire prendre un autre cours aux esprits sur les institutions civiles et religieuses, et la révolution s'est pour ainsi dire opérée. »

En 1717, Voltaire était emprisonné à la Bastille. En 1770, madame Necker, épouse de financier, ouvre une souscription pour lui faire élever une statue.

Ces années sont décisives pour l'évolution de l'âme de la France. Paris est la capitale des Lumières. Le roi est vaincu sur les champs de bataille, mais les « philosophes », lus dans toute l'Europe, sont invités à Berlin et à Saint-Pétersbourg.

Ce que le pouvoir monarchique a perdu en gloire et en influence en Europe, les philosophes l'ont reconquis.

La dissociation s'accuse encore entre pouvoir politique et pouvoir intellectuel.

Mais – c'est une autre spécificité française qui apparaît là – une séparation s'opère au sein du parti philosophique, entre ceux – tel Voltaire – qui ne remettent pas en cause l'organisation sociale, et ceux – tel Rousseau – qui condamnent l'« inégalité ».

Radicale, cette pensée se répand aussi dans la société, enflamme les esprits, isole davantage encore le pouvoir monarchique, dont le mode de vie, naguère accepté comme naturel et légitime, devient une manifestation de l'injustice :

« Le goût du faste ne s'associe guère dans les mêmes âmes avec celui de l'honnête, écrit Rousseau. Non, il n'est pas possible que des esprits dégradés par une multitude de soins futiles s'élèvent jamais à rien de grand, et quand ils en auraient la force, le courage leur manquerait. »

Plus critique encore, cette dénonciation du luxe comme cause de la pauvreté : « Le luxe nourrit cent pauvres de nos villes et en fait périr cent mille dans nos campagnes... Il faut des jus dans nos cuisines ; voilà pourquoi tant de malades manquent de bouillon. Il faut des liqueurs sur nos tables ; voilà pourquoi le paysan ne boit que de l'eau. Il faut de la poudre à nos perruques ; voilà pourquoi tant de paysans n'ont pas de pain. »

Critiqué, dénoncé, accusé, méprisé, le pouvoir royal, affaibli et isolé, est contesté par les parlementaires, ces « Grandes Robes » privilégiées qui prétendent défendre les sujets du royaume alors que, propriétaires de leurs charges, ils se soucient d'abord et avant tout des intérêts de leur caste.

Le roi, dont ils sont fondamentalement solidaires, est cependant leur adversaire. Ils réclament la convocation des états généraux. Ils se mettent en « grève ». Ils décident – contre lui – l'expulsion des Jésuites en 1764. Ils contestent toute remise en cause des privilèges fiscaux. Et, pour donner plus de force à leurs prises de position, ils organisent la concertation du parlement de Paris avec ses homologues provinciaux.

Ce sont là deux conceptions de la monarchie qui s'opposent. En mars 1766, dans un lit de justice, la « séance de la flagellation », Louis XV rappelle que les cours souveraines ne forment pas un seul corps, mais qu'elles tiennent leur autorité du roi :

« C'est en ma personne seule que réside la puissance souveraine, déclare Louis XV. C'est à moi seul qu'appartient le pouvoir législatif, sans dépendance et sans partage. L'ordre public tout entier émane de moi, et les droits et les intérêts de la nation, dont on ose faire un corps séparé du monarque, sont nécessairement unis avec les miens et ne reposent qu'en mes mains. »

Il y a ainsi forte contradiction entre le roi et les parlementaires, en même temps qu'une complicité de fait.

Quand le parlement de Paris a à juger le chevalier de La Barre, en 1766, il le condamne à mort pour marquer qu'en dépit de sa décision d'expulser les Jésuites il ne protège pas l'impiété ni le parti philosophique – n'a-t-on pas trouvé chez La Barre un exemplaire du *Dictionnaire philosophique* de Voltaire ? –, mais sait se ranger à l'avis du roi, hostile à la grâce du jeune homme.

Mais les parlementaires et le souverain, complices, perdent aux yeux de l'opinion toute autorité morale.

Ces Grandes Robes « font périr dans les plus terribles supplices des enfants de seize ans ! » s'écrie Voltaire.

Diderot ajoute : « La bête féroce a trempé sa langue dans le sang humain, elle ne peut plus s'en passer, et n'ayant plus de jésuites à manger, elle va se jeter sur les philosophes ! »

Quand, en 1771, le nouveau chancelier et garde des Sceaux, Maupeou, et l'abbé Terray, contrôleur général des finances, décident, devant l'attitude des parlements, de faire un « coup de majesté », autrement dit d'arrêter les parlementaires, de restreindre la juridiction du parlement de Paris, de mettre fin à la vénalité des offices et de la justice, de nommer dans les cours souveraines des « fonctionnaires » au service du roi, Voltaire soutient ce qui constitue à ses yeux une mesure révolutionnaire, une tentative de la monarchie de réaffirmer ses pouvoirs contre le « féodalisme » des Grandes Robes.

Mais d'autres écrivains – tel Beaumarchais – défendent les parlementaires et entraînent derrière eux l'opinion, tant le rejet de la monarchie absolue est devenu grand.

La réforme vient trop tard.

La monarchie est déjà trop affaiblie pour la mettre à exécution !

La maladie du roi, en avril-mai 1774, illustre de manière tragique cette situation nouvelle de la monarchie. Le monarque est atteint de la petite vérole, son visage se couvre de croûtes ; méconnaissable, il exhale une odeur fétide.

Son confesseur a beau murmurer : « Messieurs, le roi m'ordonne de vous dire que s'il a causé du scandale à ses peuples, il leur en demande pardon », le peuple ne pardonne pas.

En 1744, alors que le souverain était tombé malade à Metz, six mille messes avaient été célébrées pour le salut de Louis le Bien-Aimé. Trente ans plus tard, on n'en compte plus que trois.

Et après la mort du roi, le 10 mai 1774, le cortège qui conduit la dépouille de Versailles à Saint-Denis n'est accompagné dans la nuit que par des gardes et quelques domestiques.

Se souvenant des passions du défunt, certains, parmi ceux qui voient passer le cortège, lancent : « Taïaut ! Taïaut ! » et : « Voilà le plaisir des dames ! Voilà le plaisir ! »

C'est un roi de vingt ans, Louis XVI, qui doit assumer le périlleux héritage.

2

L'IMPUISSANCE DU ROI

1774-1792

33.

Il va suffire de dix-neuf ans pour que Louis XVI, accueilli avec enthousiasme et espérance en mai 1774 par le peuple de Paris, gravisse, le 21 janvier 1793, les marches de l'échafaud et que sa tête tranchée soit montrée par le bourreau au peuple fasciné, rassemblé sur la place de la Révolution.

Événement majeur, fondateur d'une nouvelle période de l'histoire nationale.

L'exécution du roi est une rupture symbolique avec la monarchie, mais qui, cependant, plonge ses racines profond dans le passé.

C'est un orage dévastateur et créateur qui n'a pas surgi d'un coup dans un ciel serein.

On l'a vu s'avancer, on a craint sa venue, sans jamais imaginer sa violence destructrice.

On a voulu le tenir à distance, résoudre les problèmes qui le nourrissaient, mais sans y parvenir.

Et, de ce fait, il est apparu à certains comme une fatalité, une punition divine, voire comme le résultat d'un complot dont on s'est mis à rechercher bien en amont les prémices : l'une des causes en aurait été l'expulsion des Jésuites, en 1764, ou encore les agissements du parti philosophique et des sociétés de pensée conjoignant leurs efforts pour saper les fondements de la monarchie.

En fait, l'orage n'est puissant et sa venue inéluctable que parce que la monarchie est aboulique, qu'elle n'ose affronter les forces qui sont liées à elles et qui l'épuisent comme les sangsues vident un corps de son énergie.

C'est dès les premiers mois du règne de Louis XVI, roi si bien accepté qu'on l'appelle *Louis le Bienfaisant* et qu'on s'entiche de sa jeune épouse Marie-Antoinette, qu'on voit ce pouvoir capituler.

Les « réformateurs », le chancelier Maupeou et le contrôleur général des finances Terray, qui ont privé les parlements de leurs privilèges et de leurs exorbitantes prétentions politiques, sont renvoyés.

Dès le 12 novembre 1774, le nouveau contrôleur des finances, Turgot, rétablit les parlements dans leurs fonctions et leur rend leurs prérogatives. Dès lors, ce réformateur, avant même d'avoir agi, est affaibli.

Il veut rétablir la libre circulation des grains, sur laquelle Terray était revenu. Mais les récoltes sont mauvaises, la spéculation fait monter le prix du blé. Les émeutes se multiplient, parce que le pain est devenu rare et cher. C'est la « guerre des farines ». Et quand Turgot veut supprimer les corvées et les corporations afin de modifier le système fiscal et de libérer le travail, le Parlement proteste.

Un « front » se constitue ainsi entre les parlementaires, qui ne sont que des privilégiés, et le « peuple » misérable. La réforme n'a plus que le roi pour soutien.

Or la Cour elle-même est divisée.

Le duc d'Orléans est un « opposant » riche et ambitieux. Les frères du roi, le comte de Provence (futur Louis XVIII) et le comte d'Artois (futur Charles X), la jeune reine, sont hostiles aux réformes qui mettent en cause les privilèges fiscaux, les statuts immuables qui sont, dans le domaine du travail (les corporations), autant de formes de privilèges.

Turgot est renvoyé le 12 mai 1776 ; la corvée et les corporations, rétablies dès le mois d'août.

Ainsi, la réforme amorcée sous Louis XV est effacée, et la monarchie révèle son impuissance à l'imposer.

D'abord parce qu'il y faudrait un grand roi mû par une volonté inflexible, capable de domestiquer son entourage – à la manière d'un Louis XIV –, de rabaisser l'orgueil des grands et les pouvoirs des parlements, comme l'avait fait un Richelieu. Louis XVI est honnête, mais il ne sait pas s'arracher à ses proches, à leur influence. Et on colporte – les pamphlets en répandent la rumeur – qu'il ne réussit pas même à consommer son mariage.

Sans roi déterminé – ou soutenant contre tous un ministre de combat –, il ne peut y avoir de monarchie forte ni donc de réforme d'envergure.

Il y a aussi le fait que personne ne peut concevoir l'avenir cataclysmique qui attend les privilégiés et le royaume.

Qui peut jamais imaginer la fin d'un monde ?

Les acteurs sont aveugles.

Mais, à cette caractéristique partagée par tous les régimes, s'ajoutent, pour la France de la fin du XVIIIe siècle, des circonstances particulières.

Une crise de subsistances frappe le royaume. Le peuple souffre dans les villes et les campagnes. Il est souvent au bord de l'émeute. Il s'en prend aux « puissants », et donc à la Cour, aux privilégiés, à la reine. Ces « émotions populaires », cette exacerbation des tensions sociales, prennent une signification politique, parce que l'esprit des Lumières s'est répandu non seulement parmi les élites, mais aussi au sein du peuple.

On sait ce qui se joue au théâtre : en 1775, Beaumarchais donne *Le Barbier de Séville*, et bientôt ce sera *Le Mariage de Figaro*. On n'a pas feuilleté l'*Encyclopédie*, mais on connaît son existence. Malesherbes, que Louis XVI a appelé à son Conseil, s'en est fait le protecteur. Lorsque, en mars 1778, il séjourne à Paris – où il meurt –, Voltaire, dont on n'ignore pas qu'il a contesté avec succès les verdicts de la justice – Calas, Sirven, La Barre, Lally-Tollendal –, est célébré comme le roi des Lettres et du parti philosophique. On couronne en sa présence son buste sur la scène de la Comédie-Française.

Tel est le climat social et intellectuel qui cerne la monarchie et ses privilégiés.

Or ce pouvoir « central » est divisé : les parlementaires et les grands sont hostiles aux réformes qui amputeraient leurs privilèges. Le roi ne pourrait s'opposer à eux qu'en s'appuyant sur la volonté réformatrice du tiers état, qu'anime désormais une bourgeoisie d'affaires et de talent.

Mais celui-ci est le groupe social le plus pénétré par l'esprit des Lumières. Il se rend au théâtre. Il lit. Il participe aux assemblées des sociétés de pensée, aux tenues des loges maçonniques.

Ce tiers état – et de jeunes nobles : La Fayette, le comte de Ségur, le duc de Noailles – s'enthousiasme pour la rébellion des « Américains » (des *Insurgents*) contre l'Angleterre.

Volonté de revanche contre Londres après la guerre de Sept Ans – c'est Vergennes, chargé des Affaires étrangères, qui aura conduit avec talent la diplomatie française jusqu'à la guerre en 1778 –, mais, surtout une sympathie pour la « révolution américaine » semble portée par les Lumières.

On publie à Paris les textes de la Déclaration des droits de Philadelphie, la Constitution républicaine de la Virginie (1776) et la Déclaration d'indépendance (4 juillet 1776).

Ces textes qui affirment que « tous les hommes sont par nature libres et indépendants », que « tout pouvoir appartient au peuple et donc dérive de lui », sont lus comme autant d'incitations à contester la monarchie absolue.

On y évoque la séparation des pouvoirs, on y déclare qu'il existe des droits inaliénables, et que les gouvernements n'ont été institués que pour les faire respecter.

« Ils ne tirent leur juste pouvoir que du consentement de ceux qui sont gouvernés. »

« *Liaisons dangereuses* » (le livre de Laclos paraît en 1782) que celles qui se nouent entre une monarchie arc-boutée sur des principes immuables et les États-Unis d'Amérique, que cette même monarchie aide à vaincre et donc à instaurer un pouvoir républicain !

Même si le traité de Versailles – 3 septembre 1783 – marque la revanche française sur Londres et efface l'humiliation subie, conférant une once de gloire à Louis XVI, ce succès est lourd de conséquences.

Le retour de La Fayette à Paris, en 1782 est triomphal. Il est nommé maréchal de camp. L'esprit des Lumières, réformateur, est hissé au cœur du pouvoir.

Louis XVI a d'ailleurs choisi comme « directeur du Trésor » – il n'est pas membre du Conseil du roi – un banquier suisse, huguenot, donc hérétique, Necker, dont le salon parisien – son épouse est fille de pasteur ; sa fille Germaine est la future madame de Staël – est un lieu de rencontres entre tenants du parti philosophique et hommes de pouvoir.

Mais cette situation même affaiblit Necker aux yeux des adversaires des réformes.

Or, chargé par le roi de rétablir les finances du royaume, il ne peut que songer à réformer le système fiscal.

Afin de tourner l'opposition des parlements, il crée des assemblées territoriales où le tiers état obtient autant de sièges que ceux, additionnés, des ordres de la noblesse et du clergé. Il tente donc par là une politique qui cherche à s'appuyer sur l'opinion éclairée.

Le problème est d'autant plus grave qu'il a fallu financer la guerre d'Amérique, que les emprunts contractés ont été levés à 10 % d'intérêt et que la moitié des dépenses du royaume est affectée au service de la dette !

À la recherche du soutien de l'opinion, Necker, qui se heurte aux milieux privilégiés, publie un *Compte rendu au roi sur l'état des finances du royaume*. Il y dissimule l'ampleur du déficit, mais dévoile les dépenses de la Cour, le coût des fêtes, des cadeaux offerts par le roi ou la reine à tel ou tel membre de son entourage. Les chiffres cités – 800 000 livres de dot pour la fille d'une amie de la reine ! – représentent, pour l'opinion, des sommes inimaginables : le salaire quotidien d'un ouvrier est alors d'environ une livre...

Comment ne pas s'indigner, alors même que le pouvoir célèbre la victoire des Insurgents dont les textes constitutionnels affirment : « Tous les hommes ont été créés égaux et ont reçu de leur Créateur des droits inaliénables » ?

Le pouvoir monarchique est pris dans une contradiction difficile à résoudre.

Solidaire des privilégiés, il ne peut faire la réforme que contre eux, mais il n'ose la conduire, et, pour le peuple et le tiers état, il est l'incarnation même des privilégiés et de l'inégalité.

Lorsque, le 12 mai 1781, Necker remet sa démission au roi, constatant que le souverain ne le soutient pas, il est, pour le parti philosophique et l'opinion, la preuve vivante que le souverain ne veut pas introduire plus de justice et d'égalité dans le système fiscal, mais est le défenseur des ordres privilégiés.

On ne s'étonne donc pas que Louis interdise la représentation aux Menus Plaisirs du *Mariage de Figaro*, et qu'il nomme en novembre 1783, comme contrôleur général des finances, un ancien intendant, Charles Alexandre de Calonne.

Necker est l'homme du parti philosophique ; Calonne apparaît comme le serviteur du monarque, donc le défenseur des privilèges.

L'un est populaire, l'autre, suspect à l'opinion éclairée.

Mais l'un et l'autre, comme Louis XVI, sont confrontés en fait au même problème : comment résoudre la crise financière du royaume ?

34.

Que peut encore le roi de France en ces années 80 du XVIIIᵉ siècle ?

Rien ne paraît devoir changer dans le grand apparat du pouvoir monarchique.

Et cette permanence du décor et du rituel, cette succession des fêtes, cet isolement de la Cour, dans les jardins illuminés de Versailles, renforcent le sentiment des souverains que rien ne saurait détruire l'ordre royal, qu'on peut indéfiniment continuer la partie, même s'il faut rebattre les cartes, changer les hommes.

Mais qu'à la fin le roi, parce qu'il est le roi, finira bien par imposer son autorité.

C'est le propre d'une vieille et grande nation, d'un pouvoir plusieurs fois séculaire, que de donner l'illusion qu'ils ne peuvent s'effondrer.

La politique de Calonne entretient ce mirage.

Il multiplie les emprunts, creuse encore le gouffre du déficit, mais l'argent roule.

Il achète les châteaux de Saint-Cloud et de Rambouillet pour le roi. Il investit dans la Compagnie des Indes orientales.

Disciple des physiocrates, il pense qu'une politique « libérale », facilitant la circulation des marchandises et de l'argent, fera naître la prospérité, mettra fin à cette crise économique qui ronge le royaume, suscite rébellion et misère.

Il signe le premier traité de libre-échange avec l'Angleterre en 1786. Il entend supprimer toutes les douanes intérieures.

Mais la réalité des finances vient crever le soyeux rideau de l'illusion.

Calonne est confronté, comme Turgot, comme Necker, à l'obligation de modifier le système fiscal afin de faire payer les privilégiés, ceux qu'on commence à appeler les *aristocrates*.

Il imagine un impôt général – la subvention territoriale – et reprend l'idée de Necker d'assemblées territoriales, tournant ainsi les parlements et même les intendants.

Il va jusqu'à envisager l'aliénation du domaine royal afin de rembourser les dettes ! Et il croit habile de faire approuver ces mesures par une assemblée de notables.

Il dénonce devant elle les supercheries de Necker, qui a dissimulé l'ampleur du déficit dans son *Compte rendu au roi*.

En attaquant l'homme du parti philosophique, Calonne renforce encore l'opposition de l'opinion éclairée, et en proposant des réformes à des notables, il se condamne à leurs yeux.

La reine et son entourage obtiennent son renvoi le 9 avril 1787. Il est remplacé par le cardinal Loménie de Brienne, un de ces notables qui l'ont combattu.

Turgot, Necker, Calonne, Loménie de Brienne : le roi, changeant les hommes, croit renouveler la donne, mais c'est à chaque fois son autorité qui est entamée, son impuissance qui est dénoncée, sa soumission à la reine qui concentre sur elle les critiques.

La crise financière devient aussi une crise morale qui exige des solutions politiques. Elle cesse d'être seulement financière pour devenir une crise de régime.

Les rumeurs, les libelles, les pamphlets, font de la reine une pervertie, capable de se vendre à un cardinal de Rohan, grand aumônier de France, de le rencontrer dans les bosquets de Versailles et de se faire offrir – en échange de quoi, sinon de ses faveurs ? – un collier de 1 600 000 livres.

Les bijoutiers, grugés, portent plainte, et le parlement de Paris se saisit de l'affaire. L'assemblée générale du clergé proteste contre l'arrestation de Rohan, qui sera acquitté ; une comtesse descendante des Valois, qui a abusé de la naïveté de Rohan, sera seule condamnée mais s'enfuira en Angleterre.

La reine, innocente, est à jamais compromise. Et le roi devient, aux yeux de l'opinion, le jouet d'une épouse corrompue.

L'opinion s'indigne, s'abreuve de ragots, partage le sentiment de ce magistrat : « Un cardinal escroc, la reine impliquée dans une affaire de faux ! Que de fange sur la crosse et le sceptre ! Quel triomphe pour les idées de liberté ! »

C'est une constante de l'histoire française – peut-être aussi de l'histoire de toutes les autres nations – qu'une rupture morale entre le pouvoir et l'opinion précède toujours la rupture politique. En France, c'est le mépris de l'opinion qui donne naissance à la crise de régime.

On ne rejette un pouvoir que lorsqu'on s'est convaincu qu'il n'est plus vertueux.

Naturellement, les opposants à ce pouvoir, quand ils ne les créent pas, exploitent les conditions pour que le mépris isole le pouvoir et le mine.

Que peut encore le roi alors que son autorité morale est atteinte et que, face à l'opposition aux réformes indispensables, il n'apparaît plus légitime, qu'on cherche donc ailleurs – dans l'esprit des Lumières – d'autres sources de légitimité ?

Les sociétés de pensée et les « clubs » se multiplient.

Au club Valois, à la Société des trente, à la Société des amis des Noirs, dans les loges maçonniques, on rencontre le duc d'Orléans, Mirabeau, Sieyès, La Fayette, Condorcet, Talleyrand, des membres de la noblesse « libérale », des représentants du tiers état et du clergé.

Une « opinion publique » se crée, nourrie par les pamphlets, les « correspondances », les livres ; publiés en 1788, ceux de Sieyès – *Essai sur les privilèges, Qu'est-ce que le tiers état ?* – sont parmi les plus lus.

On voit ainsi se dessiner une confrontation entre les « patriotes »
– mot venu d'Amérique – et les aristocrates.

Or c'est dans ce contexte qu'avec Loménie de Brienne
– l'homme de la reine – Louis XVI tente une nouvelle politique
qui apparaît comme un regain d'absolutisme.

Il impose au Parlement un emprunt de 420 millions de livres.
« C'est légal parce que je le veux », répond-il au duc d'Orléans,
qui juge cet emprunt « illégal ».

Il exile les parlementaires ; deux d'entre eux sont arrêtés.

Ces « privilégiés », dans le climat de crise du régime, apparaissent comme les défenseurs de la nation.

Il n'est pas jusqu'à l'assemblée du clergé qui ne proclame, en
juin 1788, que « le peuple français n'est pas imposable à volonté.
La propriété est un droit fondamental et sacré, et cette vérité se
trouve dans nos annales... Le principe ne se perd jamais de vue
que nulle imposition ne peut se lever sans assembler les trois
états et sans que les gens de ces trois états y consentent. »

À Grenoble – *journée des Tuiles*, 7 juin 1788 –, la foule s'insurge pour défendre les parlementaires. L'armée intervient, tire.

Au château de Vizille, le 21 juillet 1788, les états du Dauphiné
se réunissent et se présentent comme porte-parole de la nation.

Dès lors, les réformes esquissées par Loménie de Brienne et
par son garde des Sceaux Lamoignon (qui veut retirer le pouvoir
judiciaire aux parlements) sont dans l'impasse. Et le mot de
Louis XVI – « C'est légal parce que je le veux » – n'est plus que
ridicule, en ce qu'il témoigne de la prétention et de l'impuissance
royales.

Outre le droit à l'état civil accordé aux protestants et la reconnaissance des quarante mille juifs de France, ne reste du passage
de Loménie de Brienne au pouvoir que la décision de convoquer
les états généraux pour le 1er mai 1789.

Mais dans quelles conditions les délégués seront-ils désignés ?

C'est Necker, que le roi appelle en août 1788, qui va définir
ces modalités.

Le retour de l'homme des Lumières apparaît comme une victoire du parti philosophique après l'échec de la solution « libérale » (Calonne) et de la tentative absolutiste (Brienne).

Mais Necker commence par reculer : il abroge les édits royaux, annule la réforme judiciaire de Lamoignon, rappelle les parlements.

Reste une décision confirmée par le roi le 27 décembre 1788, qui double le nombre des députés du tiers état aux états généraux.

Face à l'ordre du clergé et à celui de la noblesse, le tiers état rassemblera donc autant de députés qu'eux.

La manœuvre se veut habile. Elle satisfait les « patriotes », mais inquiète les ordres privilégiés. Elle ne paraît pas décisive, car si le vote par ordre est maintenu, le tiers état restera toujours minoritaire. En revanche, si le vote par tête s'impose, la règle « un délégué, une voix » ouvrira le jeu, car des curés élus dans les baillages pourront rallier le tiers état, et des nobles « éclairés », patriotes, pourront faire de même.

La majorité pourra alors changer de camp.

Une bataille politique capitale va donc s'engager autour de la question du vote par ordre ou par tête.

Que peut encore le roi de France ?

L'heure n'est plus aux hésitations et à l'habileté, mais au choix.

Or, à la fin de l'année 1788, Louis XVI a seulement redistribué les cartes sans fixer de règle du jeu.

35

Voici l'année 1789 qui commence.

D'aucuns voient la France naître avec elle, comme si, avant, il n'y avait eu qu'un Ancien Régime et non une nation millénaire changeant de route, certes, en 1789, mais restant elle-même.

Comme le dira plus tard, analysant les circonstances et les causes de l'« étrange défaite » de 1940, l'historien Marc Bloch : « Il est deux catégories de Français qui ne comprendront jamais l'histoire de France : ceux qui refusent de vibrer au souvenir du sacre de Reims, ceux qui lisent sans émotion le récit de la fête de la Fédération (1790). Peu importe l'orientation de leurs préférences, leur imperméabilité aux jaillissements de l'enthousiasme collectif suffit à les condamner. »

La France, donc, avant et après 1789.

Témoin des événements de cette année qui se conjuguera avec le mot *révolution*, Chateaubriand écrit :

« Les moments de crise produisent un redoublement de vie chez les hommes. Dans une société qui se dissout et se recompose, la lutte des deux génies, le choc du passé et de l'avenir, le mélange des mœurs anciennes et des mœurs nouvelles, forment une combinaison transitoire qui ne laisse pas un moment d'ennui, les passions et les caractères en liberté se montrent avec une énergie qu'ils n'ont point dans la cité bien réglée. L'infraction des lois, l'affranchissement des devoirs, des usages et des bienséances, les périls même ajoutent à l'intérêt de ce désordre. Le genre humain en vacances se promène dans la rue, débarrassé de ses pédagogues, rentré pour un moment dans l'état de nature, et ne recommençant à sentir la nécessité du frein social que lorsqu'il porte le joug des nouveaux tyrans enfantés par la licence. »

Au cours des premiers mois de 1789, c'est l'effervescence.

« Dans tous les coins de Paris il y avait des réunions littéraires, des sociétés politiques et des spectacles, les renommées futures étaient dans la foule sans être connues », écrit encore Chateaubriand.

Jamais, à aucun moment de son histoire, la France n'a connu – ni ne connaîtra – une telle multitude de débats dans des assemblées électorales, des réunions tenues dans les plus petits villages, avec la participation du plus grand nombre. Il suffit, pour avoir le droit de suffrage, d'avoir vingt-cinq ans et d'être inscrit sur le rôle des contributions.

Chacun s'exprime, participe à l'élaboration des Cahiers de doléances, ou bien approuve et recopie ceux que font circuler les sociétés de pensée, le parti des patriotes.

Des journaux se créent chaque jour, des libelles et des pamphlets sont imprimés (plus de cent par mois en 1788, davantage en 1789). On peut y lire : « Point d'ordres privilégiés, plus de parlement, la Nation et le Roi ! » Le paysan revendique la propriété de la terre, l'égalité, la juste répartition des impôts, la fin de la misère.

Ce débat qui s'étend à toutes les classes de la société, cette liberté de parler, de tout dire, de tout revendiquer, cette exigence d'égalité, cette fraternité, le recours à l'élection pour désigner les délégués aux états généraux qui vont « représenter » leurs électeurs, marquent en quelques mois, de façon définitive, l'âme de la France.

C'est comme si la tradition du débat, confinée dans les parlements, les cours souveraines, les assemblées de notables, les états généraux eux-mêmes, s'était étendue à tout le territoire national, au peuple entier.

La réforme démocratique, le droit universel au suffrage, la prise de parole, l'égalité entre tous les intervenants, se dessinent en ce printemps 1789.

Moment capital dans l'histoire nationale : « L'esprit de la révolution qui agitait les bourgeois des villes, écrira Tocqueville, se précipita aussitôt par mille canaux dans cette population agricole ainsi remuée à la fois dans toutes ses parties et ouverte à toutes les impressions du dehors, et pénétra jusqu'au fond... Mais tout ce qui était théorie générale et abstraite dans l'esprit des classes moyennes prit ici des formes arrêtées et précises. Là, on se préoccupa surtout de ses droits ; ici, de ses besoins. »

Car la misère et la faim sont là, aggravées par la crise des subsistances, la hausse du prix du pain.

Le salaire d'un ouvrier (quinze sous par jour) lui permet seulement d'acheter du pain pour sa famille.

Dès lors, en même temps que surgit une démocratie, la violence sociale ensanglante ce printemps et cet été.

Les paysans attaquent les châteaux. Ils arrêtent, pillent des convois de grain.

À Paris, les 27 et 28 avril 1789, dans le faubourg Saint-Antoine, des milliers d'ouvriers des manufactures, toute une foule, assiègent les fabriques de papier peint appartenant à un riche membre du tiers état, Réveillon. On brûle son effigie en place de Grève. On pille sa maison. L'armée intervient. On dénombre au moins 300 morts et des milliers de blessés.

Ainsi s'affirme une caractéristique française : la conjonction entre le débat politique, la pratique – naissante – de la démocratie électorale, et les question sociales posées par et dans l'émeute, à Paris mais aussi dans les campagnes.

À côté du tiers état – aucun paysan, aucun artisan parmi les délégués, mais 300 avocats ou juristes, des hommes d'affaires, etc. – existe un quart état, celui des « infortunés ».

Les liens ou les ruptures entre ces deux réalités sociales, leur alliance ou leur guerre, vont donner un visage nouveau à l'histoire nationale.

Il se dessine dès ce printemps 1789.

L'existence à l'arrière-plan de ce quart état – le peuple des pauvres, manouvriers et brassiers, paysans ne disposant que d'un petit lopin, ouvriers, artisans, infortunés des villes – amplifie la force du tiers état.

« Qu'est-ce que le tiers état ? interroge Sieyès. Tout. Qu'a-t-il été jusqu'à présent dans l'ordre politique ? Rien. Que demande-t-il ? À y devenir quelque chose. »

Ce « quelque chose », imprécis et modeste au mois de janvier 1789, devient en quelques semaines – de la réunion des états généraux, le 5 mai, à Versailles, au 23 juin, quand les députés du tiers refusent de quitter la salle du Jeu de paume où ils se sont rassemblés dès le 20 juin, le roi ayant fait fermer les portes de la salle des séances – le « tout ».

Le tiers état se donne le 17 juin le nom d'Assemblée nationale et fait le serment de ne se séparer qu'après avoir donné une Constitution au royaume.

Le roi invite le 27 juin le clergé et la noblesse à se réunir au tiers état. Il y aura donc vote par tête, et non plus par ordre.

La réunion des députés devient « Assemblée nationale constituante ».

Une révolution politique vient de se produire, renversant l'absolutisme royal, affirmant la primauté de la nation, incarnée par ses représentants et régie par une Constitution.

Parce que l'opinion – le quart état – emplit de sa rumeur et de sa violence encore contenue la salle du théâtre politique, et parce que les acteurs sur la scène l'entendent « remuer », on est passé des suppliques et des souhaits à l'exigence politique.

Cette conquête du pouvoir constituant par la « représentation nationale » s'opère contre l'exécutif royal, qui a tenté chaque jour d'enrayer ce processus.

On ferme la salle du jeu de Paume, et le 23 juin encore le roi menace de dissoudre les états généraux : « Si vous m'abandonniez dans une si belle entreprise, dit-il, seul je ferais le bonheur de mes peuples... Je vous ordonne de vous séparer tout de suite et de vous rendre demain matin chacun dans les salles affectées à votre ordre pour y reprendre vos délibérations. »

« La nation rassemblée ne peut recevoir d'ordres », réplique l'astronome Bailly, doyen du tiers état, et Mirabeau ajoute : « Nous ne quitterons nos places que par la force des baïonnettes ! »

La violence est brandie.

C'est contre l'exécutif que le constituant s'affirme.

Il y aura toujours, depuis ce temps, un rapport fait de tensions, de soupçons, entre l'exécutif et l'assemblée.

Cette caractéristique nationale se fait jour en ce mois de juin 1789.

Le pouvoir a paru céder. En fait, il prépare sa contre-attaque. La « radicalité » est déjà devenue une donnée essentielle de la vie politique française.

Des troupes royales sont ramenées des frontières à Paris. Il y aura trente mille hommes, armés de canons de siège, autour de la capitale.

Le 11 juillet, le roi renvoie Necker : la contre-attaque est ouvertement déclenchée.

Il suffira de cinq jours pour que Louis XVI rappelle Necker, avouant sa défaite, perdant encore un peu plus d'autorité et de légitimité.

C'est que, durant ces cinq journées, l'opinion – le quart état – s'est embrasée.

Les précédents historiques rappelés par les journaux frappent l'opinion : on craint une « Saint-Barthélemy des patriotes ».

On affronte les mercenaires du régiment de cavalerie Royal-Allemand.

On pousse les gardes-françaises à la désobéissance et à la désertion avec leurs armes.

Le pouvoir perd son glaive. Puis son symbole.

Le 14 juillet, la Bastille est prise après de réels combats – 98 morts, 73 blessés –, et la violence devient terreur dès ces jours de juillet : les têtes de Launay, gouverneur de la Bastille, de Foulon de Doué, du nouveau ministre Breteuil, de Bertier de Sauvigny, intendant de Paris, sont promenées au bout des piques.

Le quart état, qui a donné l'assaut à la Bastille, exerce à sa manière sa justice terroriste.

Le 16 juillet, le roi rappelle donc Necker. Le 17, il se rend à l'hôtel de ville, où Bailly a été élu maire de Paris, et La Fayette, désigné pour commander la milice constituée afin de défendre la capitale.

Le monarque arbore la cocarde bleu et rouge.

On lui dicte ce qu'il doit faire : « Vous venez promettre à vos sujets que les auteurs de ces conseils désastreux [le renvoi de Necker] ne vous entoureront plus, que la vertu [Necker] trop longtemps exilée reste votre appui. »

Le fracas de la foudre, la violence, la terreur, le heurt sanglant avec le pouvoir : tous les traits de la vie politique française sont dessinés.

Chateaubriand ne s'y trompe pas quand il mesure la significa-tion de la prise de la Bastille : « La colère brutale faisait des ruines, et sous cette colère était cachée l'intelligence qui jetait parmi ces ruines les fondements du nouvel édifice. »

Mais les « déguenillés » agitent devant ses yeux les têtes « échevelées et défigurées » portées au bout d'une pique.

« Ces têtes, et d'autres que je rencontrai bientôt après, chan-gèrent mes dispositions politiques, écrit Chateaubriand. J'eus horreur des festins de cannibales, et l'idée de quitter la France pour quelque pays lointain germa dans mon esprit. »

L'émigration commence dès ce printemps de 1789.

Il y aura bientôt, comme si souvent dans notre histoire natio-nale, un « parti de l'étranger » pour se vouloir, se rêver et se proclamer parti de la « vraie France ».

36.

Le bruit que font les tours de la Bastille en s'effondrant sous la pioche des démolisseurs, ces ouvriers à demi nus que la foule acclame, pas un Français qui ne l'entende.

La surprise, l'angoisse, l'enthousiasme et la colère se mêlent, créant en quelques jours une « émotion nationale » qui prolonge les débats auxquels ont donné lieu, au printemps, les élections des délégués aux états généraux. Jamais l'existence d'une nation centralisée, déjà fortement unifiée, ne s'était manifestée avec une telle force, une telle rapidité.

C'est bien une spécificité française qui est à l'œuvre : entre la capitale – l'épicentre – et les périphéries, entre les villes et les campagnes, un échange s'établit, les événements se renforçant les uns les autres.

C'est l'état du royaume, secoué par les jacqueries, et les questions fiscales qui ont conduit à la réunion des états généraux ; ce sont les événements parisiens qui attisent maintenant les foyers provinciaux.

Il y a bien, en cet été 1789, une nation qui se reconnaît comme « une » en réagissant avec la même exaltation aux nouvelles et aux rumeurs que répandent journaux, pamphlets et voyageurs. Et que rapportent les députés du tiers quand ils retournent auprès de leurs mandants, ou que, comme presque chaque jour, dans leurs lettres détaillées, ils leur font le récit de ce qui se passe à l'Assemblée nationale constituante, dans les rues de Paris ou autour de cette Bastille où l'on a dressé des tentes pour des cafés provisoires, où l'on se presse comme à la foire Saint-Germain et à Longchamp, où l'on rencontre « les orateurs les plus fameux, les gens de lettres les plus connus, les peintres les plus célèbres, les acteurs et les actrices les plus renommés, les danseuses les plus en vogue, les étrangers les plus illustres, les seigneurs de la Cour et les ambassadeurs de l'Europe : la vieille France était venue là pour finir, la nouvelle pour commencer » (Chateaubriand).

Mais, devant ce champ de ruines, cette forteresse abattue, ce qui l'emporte dans tout le royaume, c'est une « grande peur ». On craint les brigands, on redoute les troupes étrangères appelées par le roi pour mettre fin à cette « jacquerie » nationale.

Les rumeurs se répandent. Les paysans se souviennent des grappes de pendus aux arbres après chacune de leurs jacqueries. Ils s'arment. Ils pillent les convois de grain. Ils tuent. Ils attaquent les châteaux. Ils incendient. Ils réclament la fin des privilèges. Ils veulent la terre. Ils exigent l'égalité.

Comment arrêter cette marée du quart état, des « déguenillés », des « infortunés », paysans pauvres, manouvriers et sansculottes des villes ?

Tous réclament la « fin d'un monde », un renversement de l'ordre, afin de voir naître une autre organisation sociale dont ils savent seulement qu'elle doit mettre fin aux privilèges.

L'Assemblée nationale constituante les entend, veut les apaiser : elle abolit les privilèges dans la nuit du 4 août, et vote la Déclaration des droits de l'homme et du citoyen, le 26 août de cette même année 1789.

On proclame que « les hommes naissent libres et égaux en droit », que « les distinctions sociales ne peuvent être fondées que sur l'utilité commune ».

Pensées et principes radicaux. La France fait l'expérience nationale unique de la naissance, à partir d'une rébellion nationale, d'une révolution. De l'avènement d'un nouveau monde.

La violence a imposé la défaite politique et militaire du pouvoir en place.

Mais, dans le même temps, le peuple va découvrir que les principes d'égalité s'arrêtent à la porte des propriétés.

On abolit le régime féodal, mais seulement pour ce qui concerne les droits personnels. Ceux qui sont liés à la terre doivent être rachetés.

On décrète que les « hommes sont égaux », mais seuls voteront les citoyens « actifs », seuls seront élus ceux qui disposent de plus encore de biens.

Démocratie limitée, égalité bornée : la devise de ce monde nouveau est « Liberté, égalité, propriété ».

L'expérience de la nation, au terme de cet été 1789, est donc complexe. Le peuple a fait l'apprentissage de la démocratie politique ; il sait qu'il pèse, que les luttes qu'il mène peuvent être fructueuses, mais, en même temps, ses victoires sont bornées.

Il a des droits, mais il a faim.

Il voit, il éprouve l'existence d'une fracture entre lui, le déguenillé, le quart état, et le tiers état des citoyens actifs qui, payant l'impôt, sont les vrais acteurs du jeu politique institutionnel – vote, élections, décisions.

Et comme la faim perdure, qu'on craint la répression organisée par le roi et la reine, toujours en leur château, arborant au cours d'un banquet la cocarde noire avec des officiers du régiment de Flandre, on marche sur Versailles, les 5 et 6 octobre. Il y a là des milliers de femmes. On force les grilles. On pénètre dans les appartements de la reine. On tue les gardes du corps, on brandit leurs têtes. On ramène à Paris « le boulanger, la boulangère et le petit mitron ».

Victoire de la violence, révolution qui s'amplifie au lieu de s'atténuer.

On veut masquer cette réalité. Le maire de Paris parle d'un « peuple humain, respectueux et fidèle, qui vient de conquérir son roi ».

Et Louis XVI se déclare « fort touché et fort content », affirmant qu'il est venu à Paris « de son plein gré ».

« Indignes faussetés de la violence et de la peur qui déshonoraient alors tous les partis et tous les hommes. Louis XVI n'était pas faux, il était faible ; la faiblesse n'est pas la fausseté, mais elle en tient lieu et elle en remplit les fonctions » (Chateaubriand).

En fait, on soupçonne – ou on accuse – le roi, et surtout la reine et le parti des aristocrates, de préparer avec la complicité de l'étranger – Marie-Antoinette n'est-elle pas « l'Autrichienne » ? – cette « Saint-Barthélemy des patriotes » qui leur permettrait de rétablir leur pouvoir absolu.

On souhaiterait qu'il n'en soit pas ainsi, et l'opinion oscille entre l'espérance d'une « fraternité », d'une « union » autour du roi, et la crainte d'une trahison. Dans les clubs – les Jacobins, les Feuillants –, dans les « sections » électorales, chez les « sansculottes », on surveille avec plus ou moins de suspicion le parti de la Cour.

Il y a donc un double mouvement :

Il conduit d'une part à l'organisation de la fête de la Fédération, le 14 juillet 1790, où 100 000 personnes rassemblées sur le Champ-de-Mars prêtent serment à la Constitution. Des pancartes répètent aux citoyens : « La Nation, c'est vous ; la Loi, c'est vous ; le Roi en est le gardien ». C'est la mise en place d'une monarchie constitutionnelle où le roi de France n'est plus que le « roi des Français », où ce qui le sacre n'est plus l'onction de Reims, mais le choix du peuple de par la Constitution. Et Louis XVI paraît accepter ce régime qui met fin à la monarchie absolue : « Moi, roi de France, dit-il, je jure à la Nation d'employer tout le pouvoir qui m'est délégué par la loi constitutionnelle de l'État à maintenir la Constitution et à faire exécuter les lois. »

Mais, d'autre part, on soupçonne le roi et le parti des aristocrates de ne pas accepter la nationalisation des biens du clergé – décidée le 17 avril 1790 pour garantir la monnaie des assignats créée en décembre 1789 –, puis la Constitution civile du clergé, qui fait de celui-ci un « corps de l'État » et exige des fonctionnaires qu'ils prêtent serment d'accepter cette mesure « gallicane » que le pape, pour sa part, condamne (13 avril 1791).

Ainsi les choix politiques deviennent-ils aussi, de par cette Constitution civile du clergé, des choix religieux.

Et la « politique » renvoie dès lors aux passions des guerres de religion.

Il ne s'agit plus seulement de monarchie constitutionnelle ou de monarchie absolue, mais de fidélité au pape ou de rejet de son autorité.

On est prêtre jureur ou prêtre réfractaire.

Et, le 17 avril 1791, la foule empêche Louis XVI de se rendre au château de Saint-Cloud où il doit entendre une messe célébrée par un prêtre réfractaire.

Parce que le sacre du roi de France en fait le représentant de Dieu sur la terre du royaume, entrer en conflit avec lui, c'est commettre un acte sacrilège, attester qu'on veut créer une « Église » constitutionnelle.

La cohérence existant sous la monarchie absolue entre religion et royauté, l'Assemblée constituante semble vouloir la maintenir, mais entre un monarque constitutionnel et une Église soumise à l'État, et non plus au pape.

« L'Église est dans l'État, l'État n'est pas dans l'Église », dira un député du tiers.

Mais si le roi, en bon catholique, refuse la Constitution civile du clergé, cela signifie aussi qu'il rejette l'idée de monarchie constitutionnelle à laquelle il a semblé se rallier.

Quand il tente de fuir avec la famille royale, le 20 juin 1791, il manifeste, comme il l'écrit, qu'il ne peut accepter les nouveaux pouvoirs, ceux des députés, des clubs, des citoyens. Il se dit fidèle au gouvernement monarchique « sous lequel la nation a prospéré pendant mille quatre cents ans ».

Arrêté à Varennes, reconduit à Paris, il aura fini de perdre, aux yeux de la foule silencieuse qui assiste à son retour dans la capitale, tel un prisonnier, toute légitimité. Les soupçons se sont mués en accusation.

Et certains, le 17 juillet 1791, au Champ-de-Mars où Louis XVI avait juré fidélité à la Loi, déposent une pétition réclamant sa déchéance et la proclamation de la république.

L'engrenage révolutionnaire a franchi une nouvelle étape.

Mais l'Assemblée, le tiers état, tous ceux qui veulent enrayer cette fuite en avant, cette radicalité qui peut remettre en cause toute l'organisation sociale (les propriétés), échafaudent la fiction d'un enlèvement du roi, et la garde nationale commandée par La Fayette ouvre le feu sur les pétitionnaires.

Le souverain sera maintenu au prix d'un mensonge et d'une cinquantaine de morts.

Journée décisive, lourde de conséquences non seulement pour le mouvement de la Révolution, mais pour l'histoire nationale.

Un fossé sanglant vient de se creuser entre « modérés », partisans de la monarchie constitutionnelle, et « radicaux », entre ceux qui recherchent un compromis politique – donc un accord avec le roi – et ceux qui jugent que le monarque est un traître.

Louis XVI innocenté – mais nul n'est dupe de cette fable de l'enlèvement – va prêter serment à la Constitution le 14 septembre 1791.

Et l'Assemblée nationale constituante cède la place le 30 septembre 1791 à l'Assemblée législative.

Après la fuite manquée du roi, l'émigration de la noblesse s'est accélérée. L'armée est en crise et le soupçon de trahison pèse sur toute la Cour.

Avec une lucidité aiguë, Barnave – avocat libéral, élu du Dauphiné, partisan d'une monarchie constitutionnelle, un des acteurs de la réunion de Vizille en 1788 – écrit :

« Ce que je crains, c'est le prolongement indéfini de notre fièvre révolutionnaire. Allons-nous terminer la révolution, allons-nous la recommencer ? Si la révolution fait un pas de plus, elle ne peut le faire sans danger ; c'est que, dans la ligne de la liberté, le premier acte qui pourrait suivre serait l'anéantissement de la royauté ; c'est que, dans la ligne de l'égalité, le premier acte qui pourrait suivre serait l'attentat à la propriété... »

Mais comment stabiliser une situation dès lors que l'une des pièces principales de l'échiquier politique – le roi, la Cour, le parti aristocratique – cherche à reprendre le royaume en main comme si rien ne s'était passé depuis le printemps 1789 ?

37

C'est une France nouvelle que représentent les 745 députés de l'Assemblée législative qui se réunissent à Paris pour la première fois le 1er octobre 1791.

Robespierre avait fait voter par l'Assemblée constituante une proposition décrétant, avant de se séparer, l'inéligibilité de ses membres.

Ce sont donc des hommes nouveaux, surgis des assemblées locales, qui ont été élus.

Avocats, médecins, militaires, ils sont le visage de cette France qui, depuis près de trois ans, est labourée par les événements révolutionnaires, les affrontements sociaux, les bouleversements institutionnels et cette nouvelle guerre de religion qui oppose prêtres jureurs et prêtres réfractaires.

Ainsi naissent à partir des débats électoraux et des « émotions » populaires – Grande Peur, jacqueries, émeutes, cortèges, violences urbaines – les pratiques politiques de la France contemporaine.

Depuis 1788, dans le creuset de la Révolution, ces comportements et ces sensibilités politiques vont s'inscrire dans l'âme de la France.

Comme l'écrit Chateaubriand, témoin privilégié, l'Assemblée constituante avait déjà été, « malgré ce qui peut lui être reproché, la plus illustre congrégation populaire qui ait jamais paru chez les nations, tant par la grandeur de ses transactions que par l'immensité de leurs résultats ».

L'Assemblée législative est tout aussi importante : elle précise les contours d'une exception française.

Aucun peuple n'a fait à un tel degré, dans toute son épaisseur sociale, une telle expérimentation politique.

La France devient la nation politique par excellence.

Il y a à l'Assemblée et dans le pays une « droite » et une « gauche ».

Des ébauches de partis politiques reclassent les députés, rassemblent leurs partisans dans des débats passionnés.

Une opinion politique se constitue, se déchire, excommunie telle ou telle de ses tendances.

Le club des Feuillants (Barnave, La Fayette) est partisan de la monarchie constitutionnelle. Il veut arrêter la révolution au point où elle est parvenue.

Les clubs des Jacobins (Robespierre) et des Cordeliers (Danton, Desmoulins) veulent démasquer les trahisons de la monarchie.

La presse – Marat et son *Ami du peuple*, l'abbé Royou et son *Ami du roi* –, les libelles, expriment ces combats d'idées, galvanisent les « aristocrates » ou les « patriotes ».

La foule fait irruption dans la salle du Manège, où siège l'Assemblée. Elle envahit les tribunes, distingue parmi les députés ces élus de Bordeaux, ces Girondins – Brissot, Vergniaud, Roland... – au grand talent oratoire.

Ceux-là clament que l'Europe doit suivre l'exemple français.

Ainsi se forge, dans ces premiers mois de la Législative, l'idée que la nation française a une mission particulière, qu'elle est exemplaire. Il lui faut devancer par une guerre patriotique celle que s'apprêtent à lui faire – lui font déjà – les émigrés rassemblés dans une armée des princes qui se constitue à Coblence autour des frères du roi, les comtes de Provence et d'Artois.

Le girondin Isnard déclare : « Le peuple français poussera un grand cri, et tous les autres peuples répondront à sa voix. »

Certains – tel Robespierre – récusent cette prétention, se méfient de ce patriotisme révolutionnaire qui devient belliciste, qui s'imagine que les peuples vont accueillir avec enthousiasme les « missionnaires armés ». Mais l'idée de guerre s'impose et paraît une solution aux problèmes auxquels est confronté le pays.

Surtout, elle canalisera la passion révolutionnaire.

Elle permettra par les prises de guerre – le butin – de faire face à la crise financière et économique qu'aggrave la mauvaise récolte de 1791.

Dans les campagnes, dans les villes, le pain, la viande et le sucre manquent ou sont hors de prix. Dans le débat politique, des voix de plus en plus nombreuses, venues du quart état, mais qui trouvent écho dans *L'Ami du peuple* et dans les clubs, réclament la taxation des denrées.

La faim, la cherté de la vie poussent à l'émeute, aux violences.

On dénonce les « accapareurs ». On impose par la force les prix de vente.

Une aile radicale s'exprime, s'organise, agit, élargissant encore la palette des courants politiques, enfournant dans la machine révolutionnaire de nouveaux combustibles.

Flambent cependant déjà, dans de nombreuses régions, les oppositions entre prêtres jureurs et réfractaires.

Les paysans de l'Ouest s'opposent à ce que de nouveaux prêtres viennent dire la messe en lieu et place de leurs curés.

Ici et là, en Bretagne, en Provence, dans la vallée du Rhône, des « aristocrates » s'organisent militairement, parfois en liaison avec les émigrés.

Le 9 novembre 1791, l'Assemblée législative vote un décret exigeant de tout émigré qu'il rentre en France avant le 1er janvier 1792 sous peine d'être coupable de conspiration.

Le 21 novembre, un autre décret exige des prêtres qu'ils prêtent serment à la Constitution.

À chacun de ces décrets, le roi oppose, conformément aux pouvoirs que lui accorde la Constitution, son droit de veto.

Une épreuve de force s'ébauche entre le pouvoir exécutif et le pouvoir législatif appuyé sur le mouvement des clubs et sur cette opinion publique soupçonneuse envers un monarque qui a déjà tenté de prendre la fuite et que les Jacobins, les Cordeliers, les Girondins et naturellement Marat suspectent d'être complice des émigrés – ses frères ! –, du nouvel empereur germanique, François II, et du roi de Prusse Frédéric-Guillaume.

Au plus grand nombre, la guerre paraît le moyen de dénouer ces contradictions.

Le roi sera contraint de se démasquer, de choisir son camp. Et elle obligera les monarchistes, les ennemis de l'intérieur, à prendre soit le parti de la France, soit celui de l'étranger.

Cette fuite en avant, rares sont ceux qui mesurent qu'elle ne peut que favoriser une dictature militaire et la radicalisation de la situation.

Le « parti de la Cour » la souhaite.

Le roi nomme donc un ministre girondin favorable à la guerre.

Le 20 avril 1792, un ultimatum est lancé à l'empereur et aux princes allemands pour qu'ils dispersent les émigrés massés sur leurs territoires.

La Cour imagine que l'armée française, affaiblie par les luttes politiques et l'émigration de nombre de ses officiers, va s'effondrer, et qu'avec le concours des Prussiens et des Autrichiens l'ordre sera rétabli dans le royaume, et le peuple, enfin châtié.

Ainsi la France s'engage-t-elle dans la politique du pire.

3

LA LOI DES ARMES

1792-1799

38.

La guerre commence le 20 avril 1792.

Premières défaites sur les frontières nord et est, le long des routes traditionnelles des invasions.

Le peuple se souvient. Il s'inquiète pour le sort de cette ville-verrou, Verdun, qui commande le chemin de Paris et dont le nom, depuis le temps de Charlemagne, est inscrit dans la mémoire nationale.

La guerre ravive les souvenirs de tous les combats pour la défense de la patrie.

Quand, le 25 avril 1792, à Strasbourg, Rouget de L'Isle entonne pour la première fois son *Chant de guerre pour l'armée du Rhin*, il emprunte ces mots : *Aux armes, citoyens !* aussi bien aux affiches de la Société des amis de la Constitution, qui invitent à s'enrôler, à « vaincre ou à mourir », qu'aux appels à résister à l'armée espagnole lancés en 1636 et qui souhaitaient qu'un « sang impur abreuve nos sillons ».

Quant à la musique de son *Chant de guerre*, elle s'inspire d'un thème de Mozart, le franc-maçon, le musicien des Lumières, mort en 1791.

Dans un pays centralisé où existe depuis des siècles un sentiment patriotique, la guerre, dès les premiers combats de 1792, associe nation et révolution, défense de la patrie et défense des droits nouveaux.

Le citoyen est patriote.

L'ennemi de la révolution est un traître à la nation.

À ceux qui crient « Vive le roi ! » on répond « Vive la nation ! ».

La loi des armes simplifie, radicalise, exclut, condamne.

Point de place pour les modérés – les Feuillants – adeptes du compromis, par sagesse, par intérêt, pour protéger les propriétés, maintenir la monarchie constitutionnelle, garante de la paix civile et de l'ordre social.

En choisissant la politique du pire – la guerre –, le parti de la Cour a cru pouvoir éteindre le brasier révolutionnaire. C'est l'incendie général qu'il déchaîne contre lui.

En souhaitant la guerre, les Girondins, qui espéraient ainsi gouverner la révolution, ont ouvert la porte aux hommes les plus décidés, aux « sans-culottes » les plus radicaux.

Le temps n'est plus ni à Louis XVI, ni à Barnave ou La Fayette, ni même à Brissot, mais à Danton, Desmoulins et bientôt Robespierre.

La loi des armes, les idées extrêmes, imposent dès lors leur empreinte profonde dans l'âme de la France.

Que le roi – en mai puis en juin – oppose son veto à un décret instituant la déportation des prêtres réfractaires, puis à un autre créant un camp de 20 000 fédérés à Paris, et aussitôt on demande sa suspension.

On envahit le 20 juin les Tuileries, on contraint Louis XVI à se coiffer d'un bonnet phrygien, on l'humilie.

Il ne cède pas.

La presse royaliste invite les amis du roi à rejoindre Paris pour défendre le souverain.

L'amalgame est fait entre les aristocrates, le monarque, et ces Autrichiens et Prussiens qui avancent vers la capitale. On crie : « Périssent les tyrans ! Un seul maître, la Loi ! » Et on proclame « la patrie en danger » (le 11 juillet). L' amalgame se fait entre citoyens et patriotes.

Toute la France entend rouler le tambour, battre le tocsin ; 200 000 volontaires s'enrôlent dans les armées de la nation.

Les fédérés marseillais marchent vers Paris en entonnant le *Chant de guerre pour l'armée du Rhin*, devenu *La Marseillaise*.

Les camps sont face à face. Entre eux, ce ne peut plus être que la guerre, la victoire de l'un et l'écrasement de l'autre.

La loi des armes est sans appel.

Elle s'exprime dans le manifeste, connu à Paris le 28 juillet, du général prussien Brunswick.

Il a été écrit par le marquis de Limon, un émigré.

Il menace Paris d'une « exécution militaire et d'une subversion totale, et les révoltés au supplice si les Parisiens ne se soumettent pas immédiatement et sans condition à leur roi ».

« Les vengeances approchent », écrivent les journaux royalistes.

C'est la guerre dans Paris.

Le 10 août 1792, l'assaut est donné aux Tuileries.

Les défenseurs du roi sont des aristocrates et des mercenaires suisses ; les gardes-françaises ont rejoint les assaillants, les sans-culottes et les fédérés marseillais. Vrais combats : plus de mille morts, dont six cents défenseurs massacrés.

Une Commune insurrectionnelle est créée.

Désormais, il existe encore une Assemblée législative – auprès de laquelle le roi s'est réfugié –, mais cette démocratie représentative a en face d'elle, détenant la force des sans-culottes en armes, la Commune, démocratie directe, vrai pouvoir qui fait emprisonner le monarque et sa famille au Temple, obtient sa suspension et la création d'un tribunal extraordinaire.

Commence le temps des suspects, des visites domiciliaires.

Sous la pression de la guerre, l'engrenage de la violence et de la terreur tourne de plus en plus vite, parce que les troupes austro-prussiennes avancent, qu'elles occupent Verdun le 2 septembre, et que la peur des représailles, de la vengeance annoncée par le manifeste de Brunswick, suscite la haine.

On massacre, dans les premiers jours de septembre, les suspects emprisonnés à Paris – plus de 1 300 victimes –, et cette « Saint-Barthélemy » révolutionnaire s'étend à tout le royaume.

On tue sans jugement, on profane les corps – ainsi celui de la princesse de Lamballe.

La révolution engendre une nouvelle passion « religieuse », terroriste ; deux cent vingt ans après la Saint-Barthélemy, les rues de Paris sont à nouveau rouges de sang.

La patrie en danger, les volontaires, l'assaut des Tuileries, le 10 août, *La Marseillaise*, la Commune, les massacres de Septembre : autant de références qui se gravent dans la mémoire nationale, dans l'âme de la France.

L'élan des volontaires, le sang de la guerre et des massacres, déchirent et cimentent à la fois la nation.

Parti des aristocrates contre parti des patriotes.

Ennemis de la révolution face aux révolutionnaires.

Drapeau blanc et fleur de lys contre drapeau tricolore.

Blanc contre bleu.

Mais aussi « bleu » différent du « rouge », car l'exigence d'égalité s'est imposée en même temps que la guerre.

Mourir pour la patrie ? Soit. Mais qu'elle devienne alors aussi la patrie du quart état !

Ces divisions, ces revendications, sont autant de nervures qui se superposent ou s'opposent dans l'âme de la France.

Mais la guerre favorise aussi l'amalgame des patriotes contre l'étranger et ses alliés, les émigrés.

Les paysans mènent une guerre de partisans contre les troupes austro-prussiennes qui avancent vers Valmy, une fois Verdun conquise.

Les troupes françaises composées de jeunes enrôlés, encadrées par des généraux (Dumouriez, Kellermann) et des officiers de l'armée du roi, avec, parmi eux, des aristocrates, comme le duc de Chartres – futur Louis-Philippe –, font reculer les troupes de Brunswick au cri de « Vive la Nation ! »

Mais ce « Vive la Nation ! » a valeur universelle.

« De ce lieu, de ce jour date une nouvelle époque de l'histoire du monde », dira un témoin de l'affrontement de Valmy.

Il se nomme Goethe.

39.

La victoire de l'armée de la nation signe la défaite de la monarchie et la condamnation du roi.

La nouvelle Assemblée, la Convention, abolit à l'unanimité la royauté dès le lendemain de Valmy, le 21 septembre 1792.

Elle proclame la « République une et indivisible ».

Ainsi s'ouvre une séquence majeure de l'histoire nationale, après plus d'un millénaire de monarchie.

Mais cette rupture institutionnelle naît dans le fracas des armes.

La République est combattante. Elle n'a pas surgi du lent travail consensuel de partis qui s'opposent en se respectant. Elle n'est pas enfantée par des débats parlementaires dans le cadre d'une assemblée.

La Convention entérine et traduit le rapport des forces sur le champ de bataille.

Les soldats criaient : « Vive la Nation ! » Cela devient : « Vive la République ! »

Après Valmy, il y aura Jemappes – le 6 novembre 1792 –, l'invasion, l'occupation, l'annexion de la Belgique.

La République est conquérante.

Elle se veut libératrice. Elle annexe les royaumes, les villes, les principautés, pour le bien des peuples. Elle est le germe d'une « Grande Nation ».

Elle apporte « secours et fraternité à tous les peuples qui veulent recouvrer la liberté ». Et la Convention « charge le pouvoir exécutif de donner aux généraux les ordres nécessaires pour porter secours et défendre les citoyens qui auraient été vexés et pourraient l'être pour la cause de la liberté ».

Voici venu le temps des « missionnaires armés » et celui des coalitions antifrançaises qui vont – de 1793 à 1815 – rassembler, au gré des circonstances, l'Angleterre – qui ne saurait tolérer un Anvers français –, l'Autriche, la Hollande, la Prusse, l'Espagne, la Russie, Naples, la Sardaigne...

La République vit sous la menace. L'armée est son glaive et son bouclier.

Mais la guerre n'est pas qu'aux frontières.

Parce qu'il faut une levée en masse pour constituer une armée immense – 400 000 volontaires, 700 000 soldats –, il faut des réquisitions, des fournitures – vivres, armes, uniformes, etc. –, et l'assignat s'effondre. Tandis que les « munitionnaires » font fortune, les paysans se rebiffent contre cet impôt du sang.

Il faut tenir, sévir. La terreur est l'envers de la guerre. Soixante départements – sur quatre-vingt-trois – seront bientôt en insurrection.

La République une et indivisible crée, en même temps qu'elle unifie, le sillon qui divise la nation.

L'âme de la France est ainsi couturée par ces cicatrices sanglantes qui défigurent le pays, en ces années cruciales 1793-1794, et le marquent aussi profondément que des siècles de monarchie.

Il y a la division entre républicains au sein de la Convention.

Les Jacobins « montagnards » – ils siègent en haut de l'Assemblée – sont centralisateurs comme l'étaient – car, sous la rupture, les continuités s'affirment – Richelieu et Louis XIV.

En face, les Girondins sont fédéralistes, veulent réduire « Paris à un quatre-vingt-troisième d'influence ».

Mais la guerre exige – techniquement, mentalement – que la nation se plie à la discipline unique qui s'impose à toute armée. Et les défaites (Neerwinden en mars 1793), les trahisons (Dumouriez passe à l'ennemi), les insurrections (en Vendée, à Lyon, en Provence, où les royalistes livrent Toulon aux Anglais), condamnent en juin 1793 les Girondins – arrêtés, jugés, décapités.

Dès les origines, la République a ainsi deux visages : le jacobin s'oppose au girondin.

Cette division perdurera, rejouant la scène sans fin sous des noms différents, avec plus ou moins de violence : Parisiens contre provinciaux « décentralisateurs », républicains autoritaires contre républicains démocrates.

En fait, cette fracture entre républicains est d'autant plus nette qu'elle se superpose à d'autres divisions, et qu'ainsi, malgré l'affirmation réitérée de *République une et indivisible*, la France, pays toujours menacé de tensions et de déchirements, reste aussi émiettée qu'elle l'a souvent été.

D'un côté, on retrouve ceux qui veulent ouvrir le procès du roi afin de le condamner, de l'exécuter. De l'autre se regroupent les modérés, les attentistes qui craignent une division radicale entre la France ancienne et la nouvelle.

Mais la guerre est là. Les royalistes sont à Toulon, à Lyon, à Nantes, aux côtés des armées ennemies.

Le procès du monarque est un des aspects de la guerre. La Convention l'ouvre dès novembre 1792. « L'élimination du roi est une mesure de salut public, une providence nationale », dit Robespierre.

« Tout roi est un rebelle et un usurpateur, ajoute Saint-Just. Louis est un étranger parmi nous. On ne peut régner innocemment, la folie en est trop évidente. »

La mort est votée par 361 voix contre 360. Louis Capet sera exécuté le 21 janvier 1793, et sa tête montrée, sanglante, au peuple rassemblé.

Cette mort de Louis XVI laisse un vide béant au cœur de l'histoire nationale.

Plus d'un millénaire d'acceptation, de respect, de vénération, d'obéissance à l'égard de ce roi sacré, thaumaturge, représentant de Dieu sur terre, unissant la France à l'Église et au divin, se trouve ainsi tranché net.

La France, nation mystique et politique, en est profondément divisée et blessée.

Et alors que les rébellions armées – en Vendée notamment – se prolongent, s'amplifient, que l'élan patriotique est nécessaire pour repousser l'ennemi aux frontières, il ne faut pas que soit entendue la voix de Louis XVI qui, sur l'échafaud, crie, dans les roulements des tambours : « Français, je meurs innocent, je pardonne à mes ennemis, je souhaite que ma mort soit utile au peuple ! Je remets mon âme à Dieu. »

On a besoin d'une autre « religion », d'une autre mystique pour soutenir la République.

D'abord, il faut qu'on en finisse avec le christianisme, lié à la monarchie.

Voltaire a été admis au Panthéon dès le 11 juillet 1791, et on a célébré « l'homme qui combattit les athées et le fanatique, qui inspira la tolérance, qui réclama les droits de l'homme contre la servitude de la féodalité ».

La Convention a réhabilité le chevalier de La Barre. Elle abolit l'esclavage le 4 février 1794. Elle va tenter, avec un nouveau calendrier – le décadi remplaçant le dimanche, thermidor, juillet, brumaire, novembre, etc. –, de parachever la déchristianisation.

Elle organise le culte de la Raison, adopte le « déisme voltairien », célèbre l'Être suprême.

Elle veut transformer la République en mystique.

Mais elle dresse ainsi contre cette parodie de religion aussi bien les catholiques que les sceptiques, les croyants que les cyniques.

Dans l'âme de la France, ces divisions aux origines de la République, cette fracture entre plusieurs France, ce mysticisme républicain, cette idée d'une mission universelle de libération des peuples assumée par la nation, sont autant de sources de frictions, de ferments de guerre civile.

La France de 1793-1794 est une fois encore le pays de la Saint-Barthélemy, des guerres de Religion.

Si la nation n'éclate pas, c'est d'abord que le pays défend son sol contre l'étranger. Que le patriotisme – « Mourir pour la patrie est le sort le plus beau, le plus digne d'envie », chante-t-on – soulève et rassemble la majorité de la nation.

Celle-ci est en armes. Elle résiste.

L'amalgame entre soldats volontaires, conscrits de la levée en masse, anciens des régiments du roi promus officiers de la République, bientôt jeunes généraux, se réalise.

Le patriotisme et l'héroïsme, la jeunesse de ce pays, le plus peuplé d'Europe et à l'armée la plus nombreuse, cimentent la nation.

L'âme de la France, monarchiste aussi bien que républicaine, est martiale.

Cela ne suffirait pas à empêcher la désagrégation.

Si la République en armes dessine l'ébauche d'un pouvoir totalitaire, c'est moins par la mise en œuvre d'une idéologie qui en contiendrait le germe que par les nécessités « techniques » de la guerre aux frontières, et surtout à l'intérieur.

Si la France est divisée, c'est qu'il existe des « traîtres ». On ouvre les « armoires de fer » de la monarchie ; on y trouve les noms des « stipendiés » de la Cour, et, parmi eux, Mirabeau et Barnave. Dumouriez, le vainqueur de Valmy, est passé à l'ennemi. La Fayette l'a déjà fait, comme des milliers d'officiers, d'émigrés.

Il faut un Tribunal révolutionnaire, une loi des suspects, un Comité de sûreté générale, un Comité de salut public. D'abord à Paris, puis dans les départements, près de 200 000 sans-culottes sont réunis et organisés en parti révolutionnaire, le parti jacobin, qui s'appuie sur des représentants en mission.

Le parti est l'œil de la surveillance. Il dénonce. Il châtie.

Car, au bout de cette suspicion, la Terreur est à l'ordre du jour.

On dénombre 500 000 suspects. On guillotine. Peut-être y a-t-il plus de 100 000 victimes.

On confisque, avec les lois de ventôse (février 1794), les biens des suspects.

On veut s'attacher, avec les lois sur le maximum des prix, les citoyens les plus pauvres. On leur promet l'« égalité sainte » en votant la Constitution de l'an I (24 juin 1793), laquelle ne sera pas appliquée puisque, face à la guerre, le gouvernement est dit « révolutionnaire jusqu'à la paix ».

La répression – à Lyon on tire au canon sur les « royalistes », à Nantes on les noie, en Vendée on les fusille, partout on les décapite – n'épargne personne, puisque tout le monde, dès lors qu'il s'oppose à la politique du Comité de salut public où Robespierre a fait son entrée en juillet 1793, est suspect.

On guillotine les « enragés » qui réclamaient pour le quart état une « révolution sociale », un nouveau maximum des prix, et non pas l'application d'un maximum pour les salaires.

Marat a été assassiné le 13 juillet 1793 par Charlotte Corday, sinon il aurait été de la charrette qui, au printemps 1794, conduit les enragés à l'échafaud.

Puis ce sera le tour des « indulgents » – Danton, Desmoulins –, accusés de vouloir mettre fin à la Terreur, à la guerre, donc à la révolution, et soupçonnés de vouloir abandonner la mystique républicaine.

Procès bâclé pour étouffer la grande voix de Danton en ce printemps 1794.

Certes, les armées de la République terroriste sont victorieuses en ce même printemps (Fleurus, le 26 juin), mais le pouvoir est isolé.

Les enragés sont toujours en quête de pain bon marché, et crient devant le blocage de leurs salaires : « Foutu maximum ! »

La République n'est plus pour eux qu'un régime parmi d'autres.

La nation est épuisée, et chacun se sent suspect.

Pourquoi cette surveillance, ces exécutions, si la victoire est acquise ?

Robespierre et ses partisans se retrouvent seuls parmi les cadavres des enragés et des indulgents, cibles toutes désignées pour tous ceux qui, après avoir mis en œuvre une implacable terreur (Barras, Fouché), craignent qu'elle ne se retourne contre eux.

Le 9 thermidor an II (27 juillet 1794), Robespierre est renversé. Cent sept de ses partisans sont décapités. Jamais on n'a autant exécuté en un jour.

Ce paroxysme terroriste et républicain, cette politique mystique et patriotique, ces luttes inexpiables entre factions, se gravent dans l'âme de la France.

Au moment où le pays invente la démocratie moderne – élections aux états généraux, débats, Constitution –, il en génère aussi les pathologies : le parti « unique », la loi des suspects, le Tribunal révolutionnaire, la Terreur.

La guerre contamine ainsi tout l'ordre politique.

Saint-Just, l'une des victimes du 9 thermidor, a dit : « La Révolution est glacée. »

La République l'est tout autant.

40.

Cinq années seulement, mais un fleuve d'événements et de sang, séparent cet été 1794 de l'an 1789, quand la prise et la destruction de la Bastille allaient faire entrer la France dans ce territoire inconnu nommé Révolution.

Les hommes qui siègent à la Convention, après la chute des robespierristes, savent qu'ils sont tous des survivants de cette imprévisible et interminable odyssée.

Pendant la Terreur, comme le dira Sieyès, ils ont « vécu » en s'enfonçant dans le « marais », évitant de choisir entre Girondins et Jacobins, pour échapper à la loi des suspects, au Tribunal révolutionnaire, à la colère des enragés.

Mais, à la Convention, ils ont approuvé les mesures de salut public, pas seulement parce qu'ils craignaient, en s'y opposant, de faire figure de suspects et de monter dans la charrette pour l'échafaud, mais parce qu'ils ne voulaient pas du retour à l'Ancien Régime. Ils en auraient été les premières victimes, trop révolutionnaires pour ces émigrés qui se pressaient aux frontières avec les armées étrangères.

Maintenant que la « crête » de la Montagne a été arasée, ils veulent endiguer le fleuve, le canaliser afin qu'il s'apaise, que la République profite aux républicains, c'est-à-dire à eux.

Car, après ces temps tumultueux, ces jours de terreur, les survivants aspirent à jouir de leur victoire. Ils sont la République.

Ceux qui, comme les frères du défunt roi, le comte de Provence (successeur en titre de Louis XVI après la mort à la prison du Temple, le 8 juin 1795, du Dauphin Louis XVII), le comte d'Artois, imaginent qu'ils vont pouvoir restaurer l'Ancien Régime (catholicisme religion d'État, ordres reconstitués, parlements rétablis, déclare le futur Louis XVIII dans sa proclamation de Vérone, le 24 juin 1795), ne comprennent pas que les conventionnels entendent créer « leur » République.

Ils ne veulent ni de l'Ancien Régime ni même d'une monarchie constitutionnelle que les plus lucides parmi les royalistes envisagent encore.

Ce « marais », ces habiles, ces prudents, ces chanceux, ces réalistes, ces survivants qui détiennent enfin le pouvoir, veulent le garder pour eux. Certains se sont enrichis. Ils expriment le désir de cette couche sociale qui a acheté les biens confisqués aux émigrés, aux suspects, à l'Église. Ces hommes sont patriotes par conviction autant que par intérêt. Ils ne veulent être spoliés ni par les aristocrates réclamant leurs biens, ni par les sans-culottes exigeant qu'on les partage.

Avec cette Convention thermidorienne, la France expérimente une forme politique nouvelle : le gouvernement républicain du centre, une sorte de « troisième force » hostile avec autant de détermination aux royalistes qu'aux jacobins sans-culottes.

Et se servant de l'une ou l'autre de ces factions pour écraser la plus menaçante des deux et renforcer ainsi le centre.

Certes, pour briser ces extrêmes, il faut disposer d'une force armée.

Précisément, les soldats de la nation sont victorieux aux frontières. Après la Belgique, la Hollande est conquise. On imagine des « républiques sœurs », un agrandissement de la France jusqu'aux frontières « naturelles » (le Rhin). Et la première coalition se disloque : la Prusse, la Hollande et l'Espagne s'en retirent.

Reste l'intraitable Angleterre, toujours menaçante, ravivant la guerre en débarquant dans **la** presqu'île de Quiberon 4 000 émigrés (26 juin 1795) afin de ranimer dans tout l'Ouest l'insurrection vendéenne avec laquelle Paris avait réussi à négocier une trêve.

En quelques semaines, le général Hoche va écraser ces émigrés : on les fusillera par centaines, et leurs chefs, Stofflet, Charette, seront exécutés quelques mois plus tard.

Ces conventionnels qui veulent gouverner « au centre » ne sont pas des hommes à scrupules.

En cinq années, ils ont appris qu'il faut savoir annihiler l'adversaire, détruire la faction rivale. La Révolution a fait de tous les hommes politiques français des cyniques qui se déterminent en fonction du rapport des forces.

Ces thermidoriens n'ont pas hésité à se servir de la « jeunesse dorée », de ces « muscadins » royalistes, pour fermer le club des Jacobins (12 novembre 1794), briser les sans-culottes, cette « queue de Robespierre » qui réclamait du pain pour les plus pauvres.

Car on a faim, dans le quart état. L'assignat n'est plus qu'à 8 % de sa valeur nominale. Les prix des denrées (viande, pommes de terre) ont augmenté de 400 à 900 %.

Des mères se suicident avec leurs enfants en se jetant dans la Seine.

D'un côté, ces républicains thermidoriens jouissent de leurs biens, mais, à la porte des cafés où ils se gobergent, des républicains sans-culottes crient famine.

Le peuple fait l'expérience que la République peut le laisser mourir de faim, que les changements institutionnels n'effacent pas la misère.

Alors on se rassemble, on se souvient des « journées révolutionnaires ». Les femmes et les sans-culottes envahissent la Convention le 12 germinal (1er avril 1795) et le 1er prairial (20 mai 1795). On lance aux conventionnels : « Que le sang coule, celui des riches, des monopoleurs et des spéculateurs ! Du temps de Robespierre, la guillotine fonctionnait, mais on mangeait à sa faim ! »

Le pouvoir laisse l'insurrection se déployer, certains députés montagnards se rallier à elle, puis l'armée et les sections modérées de l'ouest de Paris encerclent le faubourg Saint-Antoine. Après quelques jours de résistance, cette « Commune » de sans-culottes est écrasée par les armes.

On exécute. On condamne à mort. Six députés montagnards se suicident.

Les républicains du centre prouvent qu'ils savent eux aussi se montrer impitoyables.

Ainsi s'inscrit dans l'âme de la France l'idée que l'ordre, le respect des biens et des propriétés, l'emploi de la force contre ceux qui veulent les violer, peuvent aussi faire partie d'une politique républicaine.

Un jour, dans les années 1870, Thiers dira : « La République sera conservatrice ou ne sera pas. » Et les troupes versaillaises materont le Paris de la Commune.

La période révolutionnaire a aussi « inventé » cette politique-là.

Elle laisse faire les bandes royalistes qui, à Lyon, à Marseille, en Provence, traquent les Jacobins, les massacrent dans les prisons – à Aix, à Tarascon, à Marseille, etc., on dénombrera près d'un millier de victimes de cette « terreur blanche ».

Mais, dès lors que ces mêmes royalistes représentent à nouveau une menace pour le pouvoir, les thermidoriens sont prêts à tout pour défendre *leur* République, qui est aussi *la* République.

Ils l'ont montré dans la presqu'île de Quiberon en fusillant les émigrés débarqués par les navires anglais et faits prisonniers.

Pour défendre le nouveau régime, ils dressent aussi une forteresse constitutionnelle, la Constitution de l'an III (août 1795), qui comporte deux Conseils élus par les 20 000 Français les plus riches : celui des Anciens et celui des Cinq-Cents, ainsi que cinq Directeurs, renouvelables les uns et les autres par tiers chaque année ou tous les trois ans. Le peuple « approuve » par un million de voix pour, 50 000 contre et... cinq millions d'abstentions.

Mais peu importe : la procédure est « démocratique », elle est bien formellement républicaine. Et les royalistes, qui espéraient subvertir la République en pénétrant légalement ses institutions par la voie électorale, sont bernés.

Par 200 000 voix contre 100 000, les conventionnels ont en effet fait adopter un décret dit des *deux tiers* qui précise que les deux tiers des membres des nouveaux Conseils législatifs devront être choisis parmi les... conventionnels ! Les royalistes et le peuple découvrent qu'on peut concevoir des institutions formellement républicaines qui permettent de contrôler les élections par un jeu politique truqué.

Nouvelle leçon de politique « moderne » donnée par la Révolution, la grande école du cynisme politique.

Il ne reste plus aux royalistes qu'à tenter eux aussi une « insurrection », une « journée révolutionnaire ».

Le 13 vendémiaire (5 octobre 1795), ils rassemblent vingt mille manifestants en armes qui se dirigent vers la Convention.

Barras – ancien terroriste, bien décidé à jouir des biens et du pouvoir dans ce régime qui désormais est le sien –, chargé du commandement des troupes de Paris, va s'adjoindre des généraux connus pour leurs sentiments jacobins. L'un d'eux, suspect de « robespierrisme », a même été arrêté en thermidor. Depuis lors, il traîne son sabre inutile dans Paris.

Il va disperser au canon les royalistes, qui laissent trois cents morts sur les marches de l'église Saint-Roch et dans les rues avoisinantes.

La République est donc « sauvée ». La Convention peut se séparer, le 26 octobre 1795, pour laisser place au Directoire.

Mais ce « centre » républicain n'a survécu, ne l'a emporté que parce que l'armée lui a obéi.

La guerre aux frontières a fait de l'armée la garante de l'ordre intérieur, et donc de la République.

Elle est entrée sur la scène politique et y a joué aussitôt un rôle déterminant.

Peut-elle accepter de retourner dans l'ombre ?

Le « général Vendémiaire » se nomme Napoléon Bonaparte.

41.

Ce général Bonaparte qui noie dans le sang, à coups de canons, une tentative d'insurrection royaliste, la France ne pourra plus l'oublier.

Ainsi, le 13 vendémiaire (5 octobre 1795) commence à se creuser un nouveau sillon dans l'histoire nationale. L'âme de la France va s'en trouver marquée en profondeur. Une tradition, celle de l'homme providentiel, de l'homme du recours, hissé au-dessus des factions – ou des partis – qui s'opposent, se dessine de plus en plus nettement durant ces quatre années qui vont se terminer par le coup d'État des 18 et 19 brumaire an VIII (9 et 10 novembre 1799), quand Bonaparte mettra fin au Directoire et s'emparera de la réalité du pouvoir.

La Révolution qui avait mis en place un régime d'assemblée, qui s'était définie, avec la République, comme la structure la plus opposée à la monarchie absolue, donne donc naissance au pouvoir personnel d'un général, lecteur et admirateur de César.

Les thermidoriens, qui avaient affirmé qu'ils ne voulaient ni « de la dictature de César ni de la royauté de Tarquin », ont fait appel pour les défendre à un homme qui se rêve empereur après avoir conquis la gloire sur les champs de bataille, à l'image de César.

Dans l'âme de la France, son aventure devient une référence.

Pour certains, il est l'antimodèle, l'ogre « infamant », le général putschiste. Pour d'autres, il est le chef exemplaire, charismatique, qui balaie les politiciens corrompus, lâches, incapables, petits hommes sans gloire que la vue d'un manipule suffit à disperser comme des oiseaux apeurés.

Mais, quel que soit le jugement qu'on porte sur le personnage, il est l'un des môles qui marquent les débuts de la période contemporaine de notre histoire.

Un courant politique se forme autour de lui : espérance ou menace, c'est le *bonapartisme*. Face à l'impuissance des politiciens, l'homme du recours, par un coup d'État que légitime la situation de la nation et restaure l'ordre et l'autorité. Il unifie le peuple. Il défend les intérêts de toute la patrie contre ceux qui, révolutionnaires ou monarchistes, n'agissent qu'en fonction de leur idéologie ou de leur clientèle.

Il incarne le centre opposé aux extrêmes.

Sa force lui vient de ce qu'il a le soutien du peuple et des armées.

Si ce général de coup d'État, ce dictateur – ou bien ce héros météorique – s'est imposé jusqu'à occuper pareille place dans l'âme de la France, c'est que la situation de la nation favorise son entreprise et permet à son ambition de se réaliser.

En ces dernières années du XVIIIe siècle, après la tourmente révolutionnaire, la société française a soif de paix intérieure et de stabilité.

Les notables, les nantis, les paysans, qui ont profité les uns de la vente des biens nationaux, les autres, de la suppression des droits seigneuriaux, aspirent au calme.

La guerre ne les affecte qu'indirectement (conscription, impôts). Elle se déroule loin de la France : en Italie, contre l'Autriche, et Bonaparte, qui s'est vu confier le commandement de l'armée d'Italie en guise de récompense pour les services rendus en vendémiaire, s'y couvre de gloire à Arcole, à Rivoli. Il signe le traité de Campoformio. Il envoie son butin – argent et œuvres d'art – au Directoire.

À la manière de César, il écrit sa propre légende, transforme chacune de ses actions en triomphe, conquiert l'opinion.

Il met ainsi en œuvre une stratégie qui combine la gloire militaire (il montre du génie dans cette campagne d'Italie de 1796 à 1797) et la sociabilité politique (il est l'homme de Barras, proche de Sieyès, de Fouché, de Talleyrand) qui le fait apparaître comme le général au service des Directeurs, mais il est aussi le chef indépendant qui porte les espoirs de l'opinion.

Avec son épée, il peut trancher le nœud gordien des intrigues politiciennes.

Son aventure égyptienne – mai 1798 – et son retour « miraculeux », en octobre 1799, font de lui un héros de légende.

Mais il ne peut jouer ce rôle que parce que le Directoire ne parvient pas à stabiliser la situation.

Le pouvoir des Directeurs, qui, comme celui des thermidoriens, entend se situer au centre, est menacé : d'un côté, les héritiers des Jacobins et des enragés parlant au nom du peuple des « infortunés » rêvent d'une société égalitaire ; de l'autre, par le simple jeu électoral, les institutions risquent d'être pénétrées par les « Jacobins blancs », ces royalistes qui veulent en finir avec la République, même s'ils divergent sur le type de monarchie à rétablir (absolue ou constitutionnelle).

Gauche, droite, centre : figures désormais classiques de la politique française.

En mai 1796, le Directoire déjoue la « conspiration des Égaux » fomentée par Babeuf, qui vise à établir un communisme de répartition supprimant la propriété privée.

Babeuf se poignardera au cours de son procès, et une trentaine de ses compagnons seront fusillés en 1797.

Mais leur souvenir, transmis par quelques survivants – Buonarroti –, fera germer au XIXe siècle les idées « babouvistes », créant un socle pour le communisme et le socialisme français dont on mesure ainsi l'enracinement profond dans l'histoire nationale.

Le 18 fructidor (avril 1797), le Directoire doit faire face à une poussée électorale royaliste ; les Directeurs font alors appel au général Bonaparte, qui leur délègue le général Augereau.

Terreur froide : arrestations, épurations, déportations.

La preuve est faite à nouveau que le centre ne peut imposer sa politique républicaine – défendant les transferts de propriété qui ont eu lieu pendant la Révolution, affirmant le caractère laïque de l'État dans une perspective voltairienne – que s'il dispose du soutien de l'armée.

Ce soutien est d'autant plus nécessaire qu'en 1798 (le 21 floréal), le Directoire doit faire face à une poussée électorale de la « gauche », cette fois, et que seul un coup de force – un vrai coup d'État – permet d'exclure les députés élus de cette tendance.

Malgré cela, l'influence des néojacobins s'accroît en juin 1799. On parle à nouveau de « bonheur du peuple ». On exige des mesures en sa faveur : « Élaguez ces fortunes immenses qui font le scandale des mœurs, établissez l'impôt progressif sur les fortunes, réduisez les impôts indirects, faites des économies en renvoyant les fonctionnaires inutiles, en diminuant l'indemnité des députés et les pensions des Directeurs ! »

Des revendications « modernes » se font ainsi jour dans le langage politique. Elles traverseront les décennies.

En même temps, on veut en finir avec le « système de bascule », l'instabilité qui fait soutenir la gauche contre la droite, et vice versa.

Derrière les néojacobins se profile le parti des généraux. Ils sont victorieux. Ils ont créé des républiques sœurs : la Batave, la Cisalpine, la Romaine, l'Helvétique, la Parthénopéenne (napolitaine). Ils ont accumulé des « trésors de guerre ». Les soldats leur sont dévoués, puisque ce sont les généraux qui les paient.

Ce néojacobinisme « armé » annoncerait-il le retour à un robespierrisme rebouilli ?

Sieyès s'en inquiète. Il dénonce la « sanglante tyrannie » des Jacobins de l'an II et leur « pouvoir monstrueux », dont il faut empêcher la renaissance.

Les « républicains du centre » – Sieyès, Fouché, Talleyrand – se tournent vers Bonaparte rentré d'Égypte.

Il est l'homme providentiel. Il se présente comme sans ambition personnelle, prêt seulement à mettre sa popularité au service du parti de l'ordre.

Son frère Lucien a été élu président du Conseil des Cinq-Cents, mais lui, « le plus civil des généraux », évoque moins ses exploits militaires que les découvertes que les savants qui l'ont accompagné en Égypte ont réalisées au pays des pharaons.

À Saint-Cloud, où se sont réunis les conseillers, après un moment difficile, Murat, à la tête d'une compagnie de grenadiers, disperse les élus en criant à ses soldats : « Foutez-moi tout ce monde-là dehors ! »

C'est la technique d'un coup d'État moderne, mêlant le coup de force parlementaire à l'action armée, l'apparence légale à la violence, que Bonaparte et ses complices ont appliquée.

Bonaparte peut se présenter comme l'homme du centre, au-dessus des partis, incarnant l'union des Français contre les « anarchistes » et les « royalistes ».

« Tous les partis sont venus à moi, m'ont confié leurs desseins, dévoilé leurs secrets, et m'ont demandé mon appui : j'ai refusé d'être l'homme d'un parti », dit-il.

En fait, il veut rassembler tous les notables et, autour d'eux, le peuple, en ne revenant pas sur les conquêtes majeures de la Révolution dans l'ordre social : abolition des droits seigneuriaux, liberté de la propriété, vente des biens nationaux.

Le ciment de cette union, c'est le patriotisme.

Il dit : « Ni bonnet rouge [révolutionnaire] ni talon rouge [aristocratique] : je suis national ! »

La Révolution, la République, sont l'assomption de la nation.

CHRONOLOGIE III

Vingt dates clés (1715-1799)

1715-1723 : Régence de Philippe d'Orléans. Louis XV a cinq ans

1757 : Attentat de Damiens contre Louis XV (1715-1774)

1771 : Réformes de Maupeou : abolition de la vénalité des offices, gratuité de la justice, etc.

1774 : Louis XVI (1774-1792) rétablit les parlements dans leurs privilèges

1784-1785 : Affaire du « collier de la reine » qui discrédite la monarchie

1788 : À Vizille, les états du Dauphiné réclament la convocation des états généraux

5 mai 1789 : Ouverture des états généraux à Versailles

14 juillet 1790 : Fête de la Fédération au Champ-de-Mars

20-21 juin 1791 : Fuite du roi à Varennes

20 avril 1792 : Déclaration de guerre à l'Autriche et à la Prusse

20 septembre 1792 : Victoire de Valmy et, le 21 septembre, abolition de la royauté, puis proclamation de la République une et indivisible (25 septembre)

21 janvier 1793 : Exécution de Louis XVI

Mars 1793 : Soulèvement de la Vendée contre la Convention

Septembre 1793 : Loi des suspects et loi sur le maximum des prix et salaires

8 juin 1794 : Fête de l'Être suprême

27 juillet 1794 : (9 thermidor an II) Chute de Robespierre

5 octobre 1795 : (13 vendémiaire) Bonaparte écrase un soulèvement royaliste

1796 : Bonaparte général de l'armée d'Italie

Mai 1798 – août 1799 : Bonaparte conduit l'expédition d'Égypte

9-10 novembre 1799 : (18 et 19 brumaire) Coup d'État de Bonaparte, fin du Directoire, Bonaparte premier consul

LIVRE IV

LA RÉPUBLIQUE IMPÉRIALE

1799-1920

1

LA COURSE DU MÉTÉORE

1799-1815

42

Il suffit à Napoléon Bonaparte de moins de cinq années – 1799-1804 – pour, comme il le dit, « jeter sur le sol de la France quelques masses de granit ».

Ces menhirs et ces dolmens institutionnels, du Code civil à l'Université et à la Banque de France, y demeurent souvent encore, et même quand ils ont été érodés, remodelés, parfois enfouis, les empreintes qu'ils ont laissées dans l'âme de la France sont si nettes qu'on peut dire que Napoléon Bonaparte, premier consul ou empereur, a dessiné la géographie administrative et mentale de la nation.

Certes, il a souvent utilisé les « blocs » déjà mis en place par la Révolution – les départements – et, avant elle, par des souverains qui voulaient bâtir une monarchie centralisée, absolue.

Symboliquement, dès le 19 février 1800, Bonaparte s'est d'ailleurs installé aux Tuileries.

Il y a trois consuls dans la nouvelle Constitution, mais Bonaparte est le premier ; les deux autres ne sont que les « deux bras d'un fauteuil dans lequel Bonaparte s'est assis ».

Il suffira de ces cinq années pour que le général de Brumaire devienne d'abord consul pour dix ans, puis à vie, enfin empereur, sacré par le pape Pie VII à Notre-Dame.

Mais à chaque étape de cette marche vers l'Empire – la souveraineté absolue – le peuple a été consulté par plébiscite. Et, quelles que soient les limites et les manipulations de ces scrutins, ils ont ancré dans le pays profond l'idée que le vote doit donner naissance au pouvoir, et que le suffrage populaire lui confère sa légitimité.

Le premier plébiscite – en février 1800 – rassemble 3 millions de oui et 1 562 non ; le consulat à vie est approuvé le 2 août 1802 par 3 568 885 voix contre 8 374 ; le 2 août 1804, le plébiscite en faveur de l'Empire recueille 3 572 329 voix contre 2 568 !

Sans doute, au moment du sacre, Napoléon s'est-il agenouillé devant le pape, mais le plébiscite a précédé cette « sacralisation » traditionnelle, suivie par le geste de Napoléon se couronnant lui-même et couronnant Joséphine de Beauharnais, puis prêtant serment devant les citoyens.

« Ce n'est qu'en compromettant successivement toutes les autorités que j'assurerai la mienne, c'est-à-dire celle de la Révolution que nous voulons consolider », explique-t-il.

Comme le dira une citoyenne interrogée après le sacre : « Autrefois nous avions le roi des aristocrates ; aujourd'hui nous avons le roi du peuple. »

C'est bien, dans des « habits anciens » – ceux de la monarchie, voire des empires romain ou carolingien –, un nouveau régime qui surgit et qui entend élever sur le double socle – monarchique et révolutionnaire – une nouvelle dynastie, une noblesse d'Empire rassemblée dans un ordre (celui de la Légion d'honneur), hiérarchisée (les maréchaux d'Empire), héréditaire, mais ouverte par le principe réaffirmé de l'égalité.

Les émigrés sont amnistiés (en 1802), ils peuvent s'insérer dans les rouages du pouvoir, mais la rupture avec la monarchie d'Ancien Régime est franche et tranchée.

En septembre 1800, à Louis XVIII qui l'invite à rétablir la monarchie légitime, Bonaparte répond : « Vous ne devez pas souhaiter votre retour en France. Il vous faudrait marcher sur 100 000 cadavres. »

Et au mois de mars 1804, le duc d'Enghien, soupçonné de préparer le retour de la monarchie en prenant la tête d'un complot monarchiste (Cadoudal, les généraux Pichegru et Moreau), est enlevé dans le pays de Bade et fusillé dans les fossés de Vincennes (21 mars).

Cadoudal le Vendéen est guillotiné en place de Grève par le fils du bourreau Sanson qui avait décapité Louis XVI.

Même quand il entre dans la grande nef de Notre-Dame pour s'y faire sacrer empereur, Napoléon est l'héritier des Jacobins. Les membres de l'ordre de la Légion d'honneur, lorsqu'ils prêtent serment, s'engagent à conserver les territoires français – donc les conquêtes de la Révolution – dans leur intégrité, à défendre la propriété libérée des contraintes féodales, à reconnaître comme définitif le transfert de propriété résultant de la vente des biens nationaux et à affirmer le principe d'égalité.

Dès le lendemain du coup d'État de Brumaire, Bonaparte avait dit : « La Révolution est fixée aux principes qui l'ont commencée : elle est finie. »

« Je suis la Révolution », a même ajouté Bonaparte en commentant et assumant l'exécution du duc d'Enghien.

Mais c'est un régime original qui façonne l'âme de la France.

La consultation des citoyens par le moyen de votes successifs tamise une minorité de notables désignant les représentants des Français au Tribunat – qui discute mais ne vote pas – au Corps législatif – qui vote mais ne discute pas.

Par le jeu des plébiscites, Napoléon est formellement l'empereur des Français, alors que l'autorité vient en fait d'en haut, et non du peuple.

Mais les « apparences » démocratiques sont capitales.

L'âme de la France va s'en imprégner.

Elle y voit conforté le principe d'égalité, ressort de l'histoire nationale. Un libéral comme Benjamin Constant peut bien dire que le Consulat, puis l'Empire sont des « régimes de servitude et de silence », rappeler le rôle de la police, les nombreuses violations des droits de l'homme, la censure généralisée, le peuple mesure la différence avec l'Ancien Régime.

Le vent de l'égalité continue de souffler : chaque soldat a un bâton de maréchal dans sa giberne. Illusion, certes, mais le mirage dure, enivre l'âme de la France.

En même temps, la société s'imprègne des valeurs militaires que Napoléon Bonaparte incarne : ordre, autorité, héroïsme, gloire, nation.

Et ce régime est accepté, plébiscité.

C'est une dictature, mais le despote est éclairé. Il est homme des Lumières.

Son frère Lucien est Grand Maître du Grand Orient de France, qui regroupe alors toutes les loges maçonniques.

Quand la paix religieuse est rétablie – le concordat date du 16 juillet 1802 –, le catholicisme n'est pas décrété religion d'État, mais seulement religion de la majorité des Français. Nombreux, parmi les officiers, les voltairiens de son entourage, sont ceux qui bougonnent, mais ce compromis leur convient. Juifs et protestants trouveront d'ailleurs leur place aux côtés des catholiques sous la férule d'un empereur qui se serait fait « mahométan chez les mahométans ».

Cette pacification religieuse, qui place les Églises dans la dépendance de l'État, n'est qu'un des aspects de ce régime d'autorité et d'ordre qu'en l'espace de cinq années Napoléon Bonaparte met en place.

Banque de France, Code civil, préfets et sous-préfets, lycées, école de Saint-Cyr, réorganisation de l'Institut en quatre classes, chambres de commerce, divisions administratives, dotation à la Comédie-Française, pension de retraite des fonctionnaires, préfecture de police à Paris, organisation hiérarchisée de l'Université, Légion d'honneur : la France moderne, fille de la monarchie et de la Révolution, sort de terre.

À cela s'ajoute la gloire militaire, après que Napoléon Bonaparte a défait les Autrichiens en Italie, à Marengo (14 juin 1800).

Bataille et victoire exemplaires, puisque le mérite en revient à

Desaix – qui y trouve la mort – et à Kellermann, mais dont la presse aux ordres attribue tout le mérite à Napoléon Bonaparte.

Ainsi se confirme le rôle moderne de la propagande dans le fonctionnement d'un régime qui accentue la personnalisation – les grands tableaux historiques, les images d'Épinal, figurent et diffusent sa geste héroïque – et construit ainsi la légende napoléonienne.

Elle masque les répressions et les reniements : ainsi du plus symbolique et du plus inacceptable d'entre eux, le rétablissement, le 20 mai 1802, de l'esclavage aboli par la Convention, la déportation et la mort de Toussaint-Louverture, les massacres de Noirs à Saint-Domingue.

Ou bien la surveillance policière qui, par le biais du « livret ouvrier », contrôle la population laborieuse des villes, la plus rebelle parce que ne bénéficiant pas, comme la paysannerie, du transfert de propriété, de l'abandon des droits seigneuriaux réalisés pendant la Révolution.

Le régime s'appuie ainsi sur la gloire du premier consul, la paix qu'il apporte – elle est signée avec l'Angleterre à Amiens en 1802, mais ne durera qu'un an –, le silence qu'il impose.

Il assure la protection des propriétés et la stabilité monétaire avec la création du franc germinal et la concession à la Banque de France du privilège de l'émission.

Les notables, les propriétaires et les rentiers sont satisfaits. Les formes de la politique propres à la France contemporaine se dessinent ici.

Le fonctionnement démocratique – le vote – est corseté et manipulé par le pouvoir incarné par une personnalité héroïque au-dessus des factions, des partis et des intérêts. C'est un régime de notables, de « fonctionnaires » d'autorité (militaires, préfets), auquel la paysannerie sert de base populaire. Mais Napoléon Bonaparte en est la clé de voûte.

C'est dire que cette construction politique dépend étroitement de la « gloire » du « héros », donc d'une défaite militaire ou de la disparition de la personne du consul.

Ainsi, la rumeur de la défaite et de la mort de Napoléon à Marengo ébranle tout le régime en 1800.

La création de l'Empire est une tentative pour le pérenniser.

Un député du Tribunat – Curée – déclare ainsi le 30 avril 1804 : « Il ne nous est plus permis de marcher lentement, le temps se hâte. Le siècle de Bonaparte est à sa quatrième année ; la Nation veut qu'un chef aussi illustre veille sur sa destinée. »

Napoléon Bonaparte est sacré empereur des Français le 2 décembre 1804.

Mais la course d'un météore ne peut que s'accélérer.

43

En cinq nouvelles années, de 1804 à 1809, Napoléon plonge l'âme de la France dans l'ivresse de la légende. Et durant deux siècles la nation titubera au souvenir de ce rêve de grandeur qui a le visage des grognards d'Austerlitz, d'Iéna, d'Auerstaedt, d'Eylau et de Friedland.

Napoléon entre et couche dans les palais de Vienne, de Berlin, de Varsovie, de Madrid, de Moscou. Il est le roi des rois.

À Milan, il s'est fait couronner roi d'Italie. Son frère Joseph est roi de Naples avant d'être roi d'Espagne. Son frère Louis est roi de Hollande. Sa sœur Elisa est princesse de Lucques. Les maréchaux d'Empire deviennent à leur tour rois selon le bon plaisir de l'Empereur.

Ses soldats sont à Lisbonne et sur les bords du Niémen. Ils occupent Naples et Rome.

Cette légende napoléonienne n'imprègne pas seulement la France, elle bouleverse l'Europe, dont elle modifie l'équilibre et change l'âme.

La Grande Armée apporte dans ses fontes le Code civil, mais aussi les semences de la révolte contre cette France impériale qui annexe et qui s'institue, de la Russie au Portugal, maîtresse du destin des peuples.

Or ceux-ci, de Madrid à Berlin, du Tyrol à Naples, affirment leur identité.

Fichte écrit ses premiers *Discours à la nation allemande* (1807) et Goya peint les insurgés qui, *el dos y el tres de Mayo* – les 2 et 3 mai 1808 –, attaquent les troupes françaises à Madrid, puis dans toute l'Espagne et sont réprimés.

De 1804 à 1809 s'esquisse l'Europe du XIXᵉ siècle et de la plus grande partie du XXᵉ, dans laquelle les nations, nouant et dénouant leurs alliances, s'affrontent dans des guerres dont ces cinq années napoléoniennes auront été les ferments.

L'âme même de la France est profondément modelée par cette période où se fixent son destin, celui de l'Empire napoléonien et le regard que ce pays porte sur lui-même et sur l'Europe.

Car on n'est pas impunément la nation dont les soldats ont vu se lever le soleil d'Austerlitz le 2 décembre 1805.

D'abord, cette nation s'imprègne des valeurs d'autorité.

Le régime n'est pas seulement cet Empire plébiscitaire où l'égalité et les bouleversements produits par la Révolution sont admis, « codifiés ».

Il est aussi une dictature militaire, avec son catéchisme impérial, son université impériale, ses lycées qui marchent au tambour (1 700 bacheliers en 1813), sa noblesse d'Empire (1808).

La France voit ainsi se poursuivre la tradition d'une monarchie absolue, centralisée.

Le contrôle de tous les rouages de la nation est même plus pointilleux, plus efficace, plus « bureaucratique » qu'il n'était au temps des monarques légitimes, quand le pays restait souvent « un agrégat inconstitué de peuples désunis ».

Napoléon, empereur « jacobin », régente toutes les institutions. Il a ses préfets, ses évêques, ses gendarmes, sa Légion d'honneur, son Code civil et sa Cour des comptes (1808) pour tenir toute la nation serrée.

Il promeut aux « dignités impériales ». Il dote les siens. Car l'Empire des Français entend bien devenir celui d'une dynastie.

Dès 1807, on s'inquiète, dans l'entourage de Napoléon, de sa descendance. On songe au divorce de l'Empereur d'avec Joséphine de Beauharnais, incapable de donner naissance à un fils.

Napoléon a marié son frère Louis, roi de Hollande, à Hortense de Beauharnais, fille de Joséphine, et en 1808 naîtra de cette union Louis-Napoléon, futur Napoléon III, qui régnera jusqu'en 1870.

À cette réalité dynastique, on mesure le prolongement, durant tout le XIXe siècle français, de ce qui s'est joué au cours de ces années légendaires.

Napoléon renforce – aggrave – les traits de la monarchie, qu'il associe à l'héritage révolutionnaire. Et toutes les intrigues de la Cour, les pathologies politiques liées au pouvoir d'un seul, s'en trouvent soulignées.

Car Napoléon a la vigueur brutale d'un fondateur de dynastie. C'est un homme d'armes. Il a conquis son pouvoir par l'intrigue et le glaive, non par la naissance.

Il est vu et se voit comme un « homme providentiel », une sorte de substitut laïque – même s'il a été sacré par le pape – au monarque de droit divin.

Dans son entourage, il y a d'ailleurs des régicides.

Ainsi ce Fouché, homme de toutes les polices, auquel Napoléon reproche de susciter rumeurs et intrigues. Ou bien ce Talleyrand qui a célébré comme évêque d'Autun la fête de la Fédération (14 juillet 1790) et que, publiquement, l'Empereur rudoie :

« Vous êtes un voleur, un lâche, un homme sans foi ! Vous avez toute votre vie trompé, trahi tout le monde. Je vous ai comblé de biens et il n'y a rien dont vous ne soyez capable contre moi. Vous mériteriez que je vous brisasse comme du verre, j'en ai le pouvoir, mais je vous méprise trop pour en prendre la peine. Oh, tenez, vous êtes de la merde dans un bas de soie » (janvier 1809).

Après la longue durée monarchique et la période sanglante de la Révolution, ces années napoléoniennes achèvent d'éclairer la nation sur la nature du pouvoir politique.

Elle en mesure l'importance et en même temps s'en méfie. Elle s'en tient à distance tout en rêvant à l'homme placé par le destin au-dessus des autres et qui, un temps, est capable de l'incarner, elle.

Elle rejette et méprise ceux qui grouillent et grenouillent autour de lui. Elle n'est pas dupe du pouvoir, qu'il se présente comme monarchique ou révolutionnaire.

Mais elle continue d'espérer en l'homme providentiel capable de résoudre ses contradictions, de la porter un temps au-dessus d'elle-même, dans l'éclat de sa gloire.

Napoléon conforte ce penchant national.

Il l'encourage par une propagande systématique.

Les *Bulletins* de la Grande Armée (le premier date d'octobre 1805) rapportent ses exploits, reconstituent les batailles pour en faire autant de chapitres de la légende.

Le 30 décembre 1805, le Tribunat lui décerne le titre de Napoléon le Grand. On fête le 15 août la Saint-Napoléon. On célèbre ses victoires par des *Te Deum* et des salves de canons. On édifie des arcs de triomphe à sa gloire.

Car la réalité quotidienne de ces années, c'est la guerre dans toute l'Europe.

Les coalitions anti françaises se succèdent, rassemblant, selon les séquences, l'Autriche, la Russie ou la Prusse autour de la clé de voûte qu'est l'Angleterre.

Ainsi se dessine une géopolitique européenne qui perdurera et dont Napoléon est à la fois l'héritier et le concepteur.

L'âme de la France en épouse les contours.

Il y a l'Angleterre, qu'on ne peut conquérir (le 21 octobre 1805, Trafalgar a vu le naufrage de la flotte franco-espagnole). Elle est l'organisatrice de la résistance à cet effort d'unification du continent européen qu'est aussi la conquête impériale. Que Londres rallie la totalité des puissances européennes ou seulement quelques-unes, son dessein reste inchangé : réduire les ambitions françaises, empêcher la création du Grand Empire, s'appuyer sur l'Autriche, la Prusse, la Russie.

À rebours, Napoléon s'efforce de détacher l'une ou l'autre de ces puissances de la coalition anglaise.

Il annexe. Il se fait roi d'Italie. Il couronne ses frères. Il est le protecteur de la Confédération du Rhin. Il songe déjà à un mariage avec une héritière des Habsbourg pour renouer avec la tradition monarchique de l'alliance avec Vienne.

Le 21 novembre 1806, à Berlin, il décrète que les îles Britanniques sont en état de blocus. Et ce *Blocus continental* – interdiction à l'Angleterre de vendre ou d'importer, saisie de ses navires et des bâtiments qui commercent avec elle – contient le principe d'une guerre infinie, puisque, pour être efficace, la mesure doit s'appliquer à toute l'Europe, au besoin par la force.

Réciproquement, l'Angleterre ne peut accepter l'existence de cet Empire continental qui menace sa suprématie commerciale et diplomatique.

De même, les puissances monarchiques européennes – de plus en plus soutenues par une opinion qui découvre la nation, le patriotisme – ne peuvent admettre cet empereur qui chevauche la Révolution et diffuse un Code civil, un esprit des Lumières sapant l'autorité des souverains.

La guerre est donc là, permanente, grande consommatrice d'hommes et de capitaux, modelant l'âme de la France, valorisant l'héroïsme, le « militaire » plutôt que le « marchand », « brutalisant » la France et l'Europe.

C'est un engrenage où il faut non point de « l'humeur et des petites passions, mais des vues froides et conformes à sa position ».

Dès lors, l'inspiration « révolutionnaire » de l'Empire napoléonien cède la place aux exigences géopolitiques. L'idée s'impose que l'on pourrait contrôler l'Europe continentale en la serrant entre les deux mâchoires d'une alliance franco-russe.

Après Eylau et Friedland (1807), Napoléon rencontre le tsar Alexandre au milieu du Niémen et signe avec lui le traité de Tilsit (1807).

Ainsi naît une « tradition » diplomatique liant Paris à Saint-Pétersbourg, fruit de l'illusion plus que de la réalité.

Mais il faut aussitôt courir à l'autre bout de l'Europe parce que le Portugal est une brèche dans le Blocus continental, qu'il convient de refermer.

Les troupes françaises s'enfoncent en Espagne, dont Lucien Bonaparte devient roi, mais le peuple espagnol se soulève.

La France n'est plus la libératrice qui porte l'esprit des Lumières, mais fait figure d'Antéchrist.

« De qui procède Napoléon ? interroge un catéchisme espagnol. De l'Enfer et du péché ! »

Ainsi se retourne l'image de la France, nation tantôt admirée, tantôt haïe.

Ce sont ses soldats, parfois des anciens de Valmy, devenus fusilleurs, que Goya peint dans *Les Horreurs de la guerre*.

44.

Cinq années encore – 1809-1814 –, et la course du météore Napoléon s'arrête.

Les « alliés » – Russes, Autrichiens, Prussiens – entrent dans Paris. Le 31 mars, une foule parisienne – des royalistes – acclame le tsar Alexandre : « Vive Alexandre ! Vivent les Alliés ! » On embrasse ses bottes.

Quelques jours plus tard, le 20 avril, après avoir abdiqué, Napoléon s'adresse à sa Garde.

Les mots sonnent comme une tirade d'Edmond Rostand, ils s'inscrivent dans la mémoire collective, reproduits par des millions d'images d'Épinal montrant les grognards en larmes écoutant leur chef.

Le météore s'est immobilisé, mais la légende s'amplifie, envahit l'âme de la France, répète les mots de l'Empereur :

« Soldats de ma vieille Garde, je vous fais mes adieux. Depuis vingt ans, je vous ai trouvé constamment sur le chemin de l'honneur et de la gloire.

« Avec des hommes tels que vous, notre cause n'était pas perdue, mais la guerre était interminable : c'eût été la guerre civile, et la France n'en serait devenue que plus malheureuse. J'ai donc sacrifié tous nos intérêts à ceux de notre patrie.

« Je pars. Vous, mes amis, continuez à servir la France. Je voudrais vous presser tous sur mon cœur ; que j'embrasse au moins votre drapeau !

« Adieu encore une fois, mes chers compagnons ! Que ce dernier baiser passe dans vos cœurs ! »

Napoléon échappe ici à l'histoire pour entrer dans le mythe. Mais c'est l'histoire qui, au jour le jour de ces cinq dernières années, l'a vaincu.

Pourtant, la légende est si puissante, si consolante, que l'âme de la nation aura de la peine à reconnaître que, contre la France, ce sont les peuples d'Europe qui se sont dressés.

En Espagne, la guérilla ne cesse pas.

Pour obtenir la reddition de Saragosse, « il a fallu conquérir la ville maison par maison, en se battant contre les hommes, les femmes et les enfants » (février 1809).

En Autriche, un jeune patriote, Friederich Staps, tente à Schönbrunn d'assassiner l'Empereur, qui s'étonne : « Il voulait m'assassiner pour délivrer l'Autriche de la présence des Français » (octobre 1809).

Les victoires des armées impériales (Eckmühl, Essling, Wagram) ne peuvent contenir ce mouvement patriotique qui embrase l'Europe contre la France impériale.

Sous la conduite d'Andreas Hofer, les Tyroliens se soulèvent. Hofer est fusillé. La résistance persiste, encouragée par l'Angleterre, l'Autriche, la Prusse, la Russie.

Les annexions françaises – la Hollande est rattachée à l'Empire, tout comme la Catalogne, Brême, Lübeck, Hambourg, le duché d'Oldenburg, les États de l'Église – ne renforcent pas l'Empire, mais, au contraire, créent de nouvelles oppositions.

La Russie, dont Napoléon espérait faire un partenaire, rejoint les coalisés.

L'Europe des nations refuse l'Empire napoléonien, qui reste, aux yeux des souverains, une excroissance de la Révolution.

Napoléon n'était qu'un Robespierre à cheval !

Là gît la contradiction majeure de la politique impériale. Elle explique pour une part la place de la légende napoléonienne dans l'âme de la France. On oublie les peuples dressés contre la nation révolutionnaire pour ne retenir que la guerre que lui font les rois.

De fait, Napoléon a tenté de mettre fin à la guerre en concluant le traité de Tilsit avec le tsar, ou par son mariage avec Marie-Louise d'Autriche (1810). Cette union entre l'ancien général – arrêté en 1794 pour robespierrisme – et la descendante des Habsbourg est un acte symbolique de Napoléon pour devenir un « souverain comme les autres », peut-on dire, dans la lignée d'un Louis XVI époux de Marie-Antoinette d'Autriche !

Comme il le déclarera à Metternich, Napoléon espère ainsi « marier » les « idées de mon siècle et les préjugés des Goths », l'empereur des Français issu de la Révolution et la fille de l'empereur d'Autriche.

Ce « mariage » échouera.

La légende réduit à une déception amoureuse ce qui est l'échec d'un compromis politique.

L'Europe monarchique – soutenue par ses peuples dressés contre les armées françaises – se refuse à reconnaître la dynastie napoléonienne. Elle veut briser en Napoléon la Révolution française. L'Autriche elle-même entrera dans la coalition antifrançaise en 1813.

Quant à l'Angleterre, elle poursuit son objectif particulier : empêcher la constitution de l'Empire continental, l'unité de l'Europe sous direction française.

Napoléon est ainsi contraint à la guerre, puisque ce que l'Angleterre et l'Europe monarchique recherchent, c'est non pas un compromis, mais sa capitulation, laquelle serait, plus que la défaite de sa dynastie, celle de la Révolution.

Mais la guerre incessante sape les bases de sa popularité et mine la situation de la nation. Crise financière et crise industrielle affaiblissent le pays en 1811. Il suffit d'une mauvaise récolte, en 1812, pour que le prix du blé augmente, pour que dans de nombreux départements on revive une « crise des subsistances », avec ses conséquences : attaque de convois de grains, émeutes.

Et ce ne sont pas les distributions quotidiennes et gratuites de soupe qui les font cesser, mais une répression sévère qui se solde par de nombreuses exécutions.

Cependant, la guerre ne peut être arrêtée.

Elle s'étend au contraire à la Russie, qui ne respecte pas le Blocus continental et exige l'évacuation de l'Allemagne par les troupes françaises.

Cette campagne de Russie, qui s'ouvre le 24 juin 1812, porte à incandescence toutes les contradictions de la politique napoléonienne.

L'Empereur se heurte à une résistance nationale exaltée par le tsar :

« Peuple russe, plus d'une fois tu as brisé les dents des lions et des tigres qui s'élançaient sur toi, écrit le souverain russe dans une adresse à ses sujets.

« Unissez-vous, la croix dans le cœur et le fer dans la main... Le but, c'est la destruction du tyran qui veut détruire toute la terre.

« Que partout où il portera ses pas dans l'empire, il vous trouve aguerris à ses fourberies, dédaignant ses mensonges et foulant aux pieds son or ! »

Napoléon entre dans Moscou, mais n'a pas osé proclamer l'abolition du servage qui eût pu, peut-être, lui rallier les paysans. Il fait désormais partie de la « famille des rois », et se refuse à provoquer « l'anarchie ».

Mais ses difficultés, son éloignement, sa retraite – il franchit la Bérézina le 29 novembre 1812 –, fragilisent son régime au point qu'un complot, celui du général Malet, se développe à Paris. On tente de s'emparer du pouvoir en prétextant la mort de l'Empereur.

Dans l'entourage même de Napoléon, les généraux faits rois – Bernadotte et Murat en Suède et à Naples – et une bonne partie de la noblesse impériale ne songent plus qu'à trahir ou à s'éloigner de l'Empereur afin de parvenir à un compromis avec les « alliés ».

Au Corps législatif, le 29 décembre 1813, un rapport voté par 223 voix contre 51 décrit une France épuisée et condamne implicitement la politique impériale.

« Une guerre barbare et sans but engloutit périodiquement une jeunesse arrachée à l'éducation, à l'agriculture, au commerce et aux arts... Il est temps que l'on cesse de reprocher à la France de vouloir porter dans le monde entier les torches révolutionnaires. »

C'est un appel à la restauration de l'ordre monarchique.

Face à cet abandon des notables, et avant de choisir d'abdiquer, Napoléon tente, par une brillante campagne de France, d'arrêter l'avance des troupes des coalisés qui, pour la première fois depuis 1792, pénètrent sur le sol national.

Napoléon retrouve alors les tactiques et les mots du général de 1793, de l'empereur qui a été « choisi par quatre millions de Français pour monter sur le trône ».

Et la légende napoléonienne se grossit de ce retour au patriotisme de l'époque révolutionnaire.

« J'appelle les Français au secours des Français ! » s'écrie Napoléon.

« La patrie est en danger, il faut reprendre ses bottes et sa résolution de 93 ! »

Les victoires de Champaubert, de Montmirail, de Château-Thierry, scandent ce retour. Des paysans, sur les arrières des coalisés, mènent une guerre d'embuscades contre les troupes occupantes.

Mais, abandonné par ses généraux, trahi, Napoléon sera contraint de capituler et de faire à Fontainebleau ses adieux à la Garde impériale avant de gagner l'île d'Elbe, dont les coalisés lui ont offert la royauté.

Première Restauration.

Les frères de Louis XVI, Louis XVIII et le comte d'Artois, rentrent à Paris.

La France est « ramenée » aux frontières de 1792.

Une charte est octroyée.

La Révolution a-t-elle eu lieu ? Le drapeau blanc à fleurs de lys remplace le drapeau tricolore.

Des milliers de soldats et d'officiers, les grognards qui ont construit la légende napoléonienne, sont placés en demi-solde.

La maison militaire du roi est rétablie.

Les nobles rentrent de l'émigration. Certains sont réintégrés dans l'armée ; ils ont acquis leurs grades dans les armées des coalisés.

On célèbre le sacrifice de Cadoudal, et une cérémonie expiatoire est organisée à la mémoire de Louis XVI et de Marie-Antoinette.

Ici et là, des actes de vengeance sont perpétrés. Et le ministre de la Guerre nomme généraux des contre-révolutionnaires qui ont participé aux guerres de Vendée.

Il semble à la nation qu'une France, celle des princes, des émigrés, de ceux qui ont fait la guerre aux côtés de l'étranger, veuille imposer sa loi et ses valeurs à la France non plus de 1794 – celle de la Terreur –, ni à celle de 1804 – celle du sacre de Napoléon –, mais à celle de 1789.

Les ci-devant ont en effet recouvré leur arrogance, et souvent leurs châteaux.

Ce n'est donc pas une nation réconciliée que désirent Louis XVIII et les royalistes, mais cette France d'Ancien Régime que les Français avaient rejetée.

Dans l'âme de la nation, dès ces années 1814-1815, la monarchie apparaît ainsi liée à l'étranger.

Elle est rentrée dans les fourgons des armées ennemies.

Dans ce climat, Napoléon incarne, au contraire, l'amour de la patrie.

Le 1er mars 1815, il débarque à Golfe-Juan.

Il adresse une proclamation à l'armée :

« La victoire marchera au pas de charge ; l'Aigle avec les couleurs nationales volera de clocher en clocher jusqu'aux tours de Notre-Dame : alors vous pourrez montrer avec honneur vos cicatrices – vous serez les libérateurs de la France ! »

Le souffle de la légende balaie à nouveau le pays.

Napoléon est l'homme des trois couleurs de la Révolution et de *La Marseillaise*, du patriotisme et de la gloire. Et même, ô paradoxe, de la République !

45.

En cent jours, du 1er mars au 22 juin 1815, du débarquement de Golfe-Juan à l'abdication, la légende s'empare de tous les actes de Napoléon et achève de transformer son parcours historique en mythe qui, irriguant l'âme de la France, oriente par là l'histoire de la nation.

Homme providentiel, Napoléon est grandi par la défaite, la déportation à Sainte-Hélène.

Il devient le persécuté, le héros crucifié, et ces Cent-Jours, la défaite sacrificielle de Waterloo, font de lui, par une forme de « sacre », ainsi que l'écrira Victor Hugo, l'« homme-peuple comme Jésus est l'homme-Dieu ».

Lucidement, méticuleusement, lorsque, à Sainte-Hélène, il dicte à Las Casas ses Mémoires, ce *Mémorial de Sainte-Hélène* qui deviendra le livre de chevet de centaines de milliers de Français – mais aussi d'Européens –, Napoléon s'applique à faire coïncider l'histoire avec le mythe, avec les désirs des nouvelles générations, et à transformer son destin en épopée de la liberté.

Hugo, Stendhal, Vigny, Edmond Rostand, une foule d'écrivains ont contribué à façonner cette légende, et, par là même, à créer dans l'imaginaire français – dans l'âme de la France – une nostalgie qui est attente de l'homme du destin.

Tel Napoléon Bonaparte, celui-ci sera l'incarnation de la nation, il lui procurera grandeur et gloire, confirmera qu'elle occupe avec lui une place singulière dans l'histoire des nations.

Il sera aussi un homme du sacrifice, gravissant le Golgotha, aimé, célébré, entrant au Panthéon de la nation après avoir été trahi par les judas qui l'auront vendu pour quelques deniers.

La légende napoléonienne sous-tend à son tour et renforce cette lecture « christique » de l'histoire nationale.

La France se veut une nation singulière, et il lui faut des héros qui expriment l'exception qu'elle représente.

Elle les attend, les sacre, s'en détourne, puis elle prie en célébrant leur culte.

« Fille aînée de l'Église », cette nation a gardé le souvenir des baptêmes et des sacres royaux, des rois thaumaturges.

La Révolution laïque n'a changé que les apparences de cette posture.

Robespierre lui-même ne conduisit-il pas un grand cortège célébrant l'Être suprême dont il apparaissait comme le représentant sur terre ? Et sa chute, sa mort, ne furent-elles pas autant de signes de cette « passion » révolutionnaire qui l'habitait ?

Et lorsque l'on célèbre, dans une cérémonie expiatoire, la mort de Louis XVI et de Marie-Antoinette, c'est, sur l'autre versant du Golgotha, le même sacrifice, le même destin qu'on magnifie.

Plus prosaïquement, et avec habileté, durant les Cent-Jours, Napoléon joue du rejet par l'opinion de la restauration monarchique.

Il se présente comme l'homme de 1789 et même de 1793.

Dès le 12 mars, par les décrets de Lyon (ville d'où le comte d'Artois vient de s'enfuir), il réaffirme que l'ancienne noblesse est « abolie », que les chambres sont dissoutes, que les électeurs sont convoqués pour en élire de nouvelles, et que le drapeau tricolore est à nouveau celui de leur nation.

Tout au long de cette marche vers Paris, les troupes se rallient – autant de faits qui deviendront des images d'Épinal, des épisodes de légende –, les paysans l'acclament. Il a choisi de passer par les Alpes et non par la vallée du Rhône, « royaliste ». On plante des « arbres de la liberté », comme en 1789. Il répond qu'il compte « lanterner » les prêtres et les nobles qui veulent rétablir la dîme et les droits féodaux, et il affirme même : « Nous recommençons la Révolution ! »

À son arrivée à Paris, le 20 mars, le « quart état » manifeste dans les faubourgs du Temple, de Saint-Denis, de Saint-Antoine, en chantant *La Marseillaise* et en brandissant des drapeaux tricolores.

Le Paris des journées révolutionnaires qui, depuis 1794, n'a connu que des défaites et des répressions sort de sa torpeur.

Et les vieux jacobins régicides appellent à soutenir ce nouveau Napoléon qui promulgue l'« Acte additionnel aux Constitutions de l'Empire », texte libéral qui élargit les pouvoirs des élus.

1 536 000 oui contre 4 802 non approuveront ces nouvelles dispositions.

Ce n'est pourtant là qu'une face de la réalité.

Napoléon n'est pas un jacobin, mais un homme d'ordre, qu'il ne veut pas rompre avec les « notables » qui l'accueillent aux Tuileries pendant que l'on manifeste dans les faubourgs.

« Il faut bien se servir des jacobins pour combattre les dangers les plus pressants, dit Napoléon. Mais soyez tranquilles : je suis là pour les arrêter. »

Le cynisme de l'homme d'action dévoile, dans cette déclaration, l'une des caractéristiques essentielles de l'histoire politique française telle que la Révolution en a redessiné les contours.

La France est une nation « politique ».

Depuis la préparation des élections aux états généraux et par le biais des cahiers de doléances, le peuple est descendu dans l'arène non pas seulement pour protester ou défendre telle ou telle revendication particulière, mais pour intervenir et même s'emparer des problèmes politiques généraux de la nation.

Il y a donc désormais une « opinion populaire », celle qui a provoqué les journées révolutionnaires.

Les « sections » de sans-culottes et les clubs l'orientent.

Elle a pesé sur le sort de la Révolution. Elle est responsable de ses « dérapages » – les massacres de Septembre, la Terreur, l'ébauche de dictature jacobine –, qui, selon certains historiens, sont venus rompre le raisonnable ordonnancement de la monarchie constitutionnelle.

Napoléon Bonaparte a tenté de gouverner au centre de l'échiquier – « ni bonnets rouges ni talons rouges, je suis national » –, mais les « extrémistes » continuent de peser.

Ces néojacobins peuvent servir de contrepoids aux royalistes.

Pour les rallier, il lui faut emprunter leur langage, faire mine de « recommencer la Révolution ».

Et alors que Louis XVIII vient à peine de s'enfuir de Paris pour gagner Gand avec la Cour, Napoléon nomme le régicide Carnot, ancien membre du Comité de salut public, ministre de l'Intérieur.

Manière de rallier à soi les jacobins, de montrer aux royalistes qu'on n'est prêt à aucun compromis avec eux, mais façon aussi de persuader les notables qu'on ne cédera pas aux « anarchistes ».

Cette posture ultime renforce l'image « révolutionnaire » et « républicaine » de l'Empereur.

Ce jeu de bascule – s'appuyer sur le quart état, les sentiments révolutionnaires d'une partie du peuple, pour combattre les royalistes tout en rassurant les notables, puis, une fois le pouvoir consolidé, se dégager du soutien jacobin – devient une figure classique de la vie politique française.

Napoléon Bonaparte en fut l'un des premiers et grands metteurs en œuvre.

Mais, au printemps de 1815, alors que toute l'Europe monarchiste se rassemble pour en finir avec cet « empereur jacobin », la manœuvre ne peut réussir.

Certes, un frémissement patriotique parcourt le pays. On s'enrôle pour aller combattre aux frontières. On entonne *Le Chant du départ* et *La Marseillaise*. Et Napoléon ne manquera pas d'hommes pour affronter la septième coalition.

Certes, les fédérés des faubourgs parisiens réclament des armes. Mais Napoléon ne leur en donne pas.

Il veut l'appui des notables, de ce Benjamin Constant qui a rédigé l'« Acte additionnel aux Constitutions de l'Empire » et

qui est précisément un adversaire résolu de la Révolution et de...
l'Empire !

Quant aux royalistes, ils se soulèvent en Vendée. Et les électeurs – ce sont des notables – élisent pour la Chambre des représentants des « libéraux » qui aspirent à l'ordre et à la paix.

Or Napoléon ne peut leur apporter que la guerre – puisque les
coalisés ont refusé d'entendre ses appels à la paix –, et les
notables savent d'expérience que la guerre est un engrenage d'où
peut surgir une nouvelle fois le désordre, la terreur, et, au mieux,
un renforcement des pouvoirs de ce Napoléon dont l'Europe ne
veut plus.

Ainsi, avant même que ne s'engage la bataille de Waterloo,
Napoléon a-t-il perdu la guerre politique.

La défaite militaire ne peut que se traduire par une abdication.

Sans doute, après l'annonce de la défaite de Waterloo – un
18 juin –, la foule continue-t-elle à défiler dans Paris, réclamant
des armes et criant « Vive l'Empereur ! ». Et Carnot de proposer
l'instauration d'une dictature de salut public confiée à Napoléon
Bonaparte.

Mais la Chambre des représentants et la Chambre des pairs ne
laissent à Napoléon que le choix entre la déchéance – qu'elles
voteraient – et l'abdication.

Il faudrait faire contre elles un « 18 Brumaire » du peuple.
Mais Napoléon – l'ancien lieutenant qui, en 1789, avait réprimé
des émeutes paysannes sans états d'âme – déclare qu'il ne veut
pas être « le roi de la Jacquerie ».

Ce ne sont pas ces mots-là que retiendra la légende, mais le
retour, le 8 juillet 1815, après la défaite des armées françaises,
de Louis XVIII, la trahison de Talleyrand et de Fouché, nommés
par le roi l'un à la tête du ministère, l'autre à celle de la police.

La nation retient la Terreur blanche qui se déchaîne contre
les bonapartistes et les jacobins, les exécutions de généraux qui
ont rejoint Napoléon à son retour de l'île d'Elbe, l'élection d'une
Chambre « introuvable » composée d'ultraroyalistes, et la
conclusion, le 26 septembre, au nom de la sainte Trinité, d'une
Sainte-Alliance des souverains d'Autriche, de Prusse et de
Russie pour étouffer tout mouvement révolutionnaire en Europe.

La France, qui subit cette réaction, est fascinée par la déportation de Napoléon – il arrive à Sainte-Hélène le 16 octobre 1815.

Elle pleurera sa mort le 5 mai 1821.

Elle lira avec passion le *Mémorial de Sainte-Hélène* et, en 1840, elle célébrera le retour de ses cendres.

En 1848, elle élira comme président de la République Louis Napoléon Bonaparte, auteur d'un essai sur *L'Extinction du paupérisme*, et bientôt du coup d'État du 2 décembre 1851.

Brève – quinze ans –, la séquence napoléonienne s'inscrit ainsi de manière contradictoire dans la longue durée de l'âme et de la politique françaises.

2

L'ÉCHO DE LA RÉVOLUTION

1815-1848

46.

Quel régime pour la France ?

Cette nation qui, en 1792, a déchiré le pacte millénaire qui en faisait une monarchie de droit divin réussira-t-elle, maintenant que l'« Usurpateur » n'est plus que le prisonnier d'une île des antipodes où tous les souverains d'Europe sont décidés à le laisser mourir, à renouer le fil de son histoire après un quart de siècle – 1789-1814 – de révolutions, de terreurs et de guerres ?

Ou bien le pouvoir n'apparaîtra-t-il légitime qu'à une partie seulement de la nation, et la France continuera-t-elle d'osciller d'un régime à l'autre, incapable de trouver la stabilité institutionnelle et la paix civile ?

C'est l'enjeu des trente-trois années qui vont de 1815 à 1848, longue hésitation comprise entre le bloc révolutionnaire et impérial et la domination politique de Louis Napoléon Bonaparte qui va durer vingt-deux ans, de 1848 à 1870.

C'est comme si, de 1815 à 1848, des répliques – en 1830, en 1848 – du grand tremblement de terre révolutionnaire venaient périodiquement saper les régimes successifs, qu'il s'agisse de la restauration monarchique – drapeau blanc et Terreur blanche, fleur de lys et règne des frères de Louis XVI, Louis XVIII et Charles X, renversée en juillet 1830 – ou bien de la monarchie bourgeoise – drapeau tricolore et roi citoyen, Louis-Philippe d'Orléans, fils de régicide, combattant de Jemmapes, balayé lui aussi par une révolution, en février 1848, donnant naissance à une fugace deuxième République qui choisit pour président un Louis Napoléon Bonaparte élu au suffrage universel !

Parmi les élites de cette France de la Restauration, puis de la monarchie orléaniste dite de Juillet, il existe des « doctrinaires » libéraux.

Après les « dérapages » révolutionnaires et la dictature impériale, ils voudraient voir naître une France pacifique et sage gouvernée par une monarchie constitutionnelle, retrouvant ainsi les projets des années 1790-1791.

Ces hommes – Benjamin Constant, François Guizot... – sont actifs, influents ; ils seront même au pouvoir aux côtés de Louis-Philippe d'Orléans.

Comme Constant, ils affirment : « Le but des modernes est la sécurité dans les jouissances privées, et ils nomment liberté les garanties accordées par les institutions à ces jouissances... Par liberté, j'entends le triomphe de l'individualité tant sur l'autorité qui voudrait gouverner par le despotisme que sur les masses qui réclament le droit d'asservir la minorité à la majorité » (1819).

Guizot inspire les lois de 1819 sur la presse, qui précisent dans leur préambule que « la liberté de presse, c'est la liberté des opinions et la publication des opinions. Une opinion quelle qu'elle soit ne devient pas criminelle en devenant publique. »

Les journaux peuvent désormais paraître sans autorisation préalable. Les jurys d'assises sont seuls juges des délits de presse.

Après les années de censure et de propagande napoléoniennes, ainsi surgissent, en pleine Restauration, des journaux d'opinion qui vont peser sur la vie politique. Et la bataille pour la liberté de la presse devient dès lors un élément majeur du débat public. Un tournant est pris à l'initiative des libéraux :

« La liberté de la presse, c'est l'expansion et l'impulsion de la vapeur dans l'ordre intellectuel, écrit Guizot, force terrible mais vivifiante qui porte et répand en un clin d'œil les faits et les idées sur toute la face de la terre. J'ai toujours souhaité la presse libre ; je la crois, à tout prendre, plus utile que nuisible à la moralité publique. »

Ce mouvement que les pouvoirs vont tenter d'entraver est cependant irrésistible, parce que l'aspiration à la liberté, après la discipline militaire d'un Empire engagé en permanence dans la guerre, est générale.

C'est ainsi que le romantisme, qui marquait par de nombreux aspects une rupture avec l'esprit des Lumières et le triomphe de la Raison, et donc un retour à la tradition, à la sensibilité, rencontre le « libéralisme ».

L'évolution de Victor Hugo, poète monarchiste en 1820 – il célèbre le sacre de Charles X en 1825 –, le porte à écrire dans la préface de *Cromwell*, en 1827 :

« La liberté dans l'art, la liberté dans la société, voilà le double but auquel doivent tendre d'un même pas tous les esprits conséquents et logiques. Nous voilà sortis de la vieille formule sociale. Comment ne sortirions-nous pas de la vieille formule poétique ? »

Phénomène générationnel : en 1827, les deux tiers de la génération nouvelle sont nés après 1789, et la majorité du corps électoral (100 000 notables) avait moins de vingt ans lors de la prise de la Bastille.

Cependant, ces « libéraux », ces « modernes », qui ont un projet politique clair, des convictions arrêtées, ne parviennent pas, malgré leur proximité du pouvoir et l'influence qu'ils exercent, à l'emporter.

Un Bonaparte va sortir vainqueur de l'épisode 1815-1848.

Un empire va succéder à une monarchie qui s'était voulue « constitutionnelle » et à une république « conciliatrice ».

Des « journées révolutionnaires se sont succédé, renversant des régimes en juillet 1830 et en février 1848, ou provoquant des heurts sanglants en 1831, 1832 et juin 1848.

Cet échec des « libéraux », cet écho de la révolution répercuté tout au long du XIXe siècle, marquent profondément l'âme du pays et orientent son histoire.

De 1815 à 1848, la France n'a pas pris le tournant libéral, mais est restée une nation partagée en camps qui s'excluent l'un l'autre de la légitimité.

On le voit bien de 1815 à 1830. Les doctrinaires libéraux, les partisans de la prise en compte des conséquences politiques, sociales, économiques et psychologiques de la Révolution, sont constamment débordés par les ultraroyalistes sans obtenir pour autant l'appui des révolutionnaires « jacobins » ou des bonapartistes.

Une fois encore, la France élitiste, celle des « notables » du centre, est écrasée par les « extrêmes » qui les excommunient tout en se combattant, selon la règle : « Qui n'est pas avec moi totalement est contre moi ! »

Le réaliste Louis XVIII et les libéraux ont d'abord accepté, en 1814-1815, que la Terreur blanche massacre, que des bandes royalistes – les Verdet – se comportent en brigands, qu'on proscrive et qu'on assassine les généraux Brune et Ramel, qu'on fusille le maréchal Ney et le général de La Bédoyère.

Il faut peser les conséquences de cette politique terroriste de revanche et de vengeance royaliste, appliquée alors que le pays est encore occupé – jusqu'en 1818 – par des troupes étrangères.

Elle achève de « déchirer » le lien entre le peuple et les Bourbons.

Ils apparaissent comme la « réaction », la « contre-révolution », le « parti de l'étranger ». Certes, le monde paysan (75 % de la population) reste silencieux, mais, dans les villes et d'abord à Paris – 700 000 habitants –, la rupture est consommée entre une grande partie de la jeunesse des « écoles » et le camp « légitimiste ».

Durant la Restauration, ce dernier joue son avenir.

Plus profondément encore, le retour en force du clergé catholique et d'associations secrètes liées à l'Église qui contrôlent l'esprit public – Chevaliers de la foi, Congrégation – dresse contre le « parti prêtre » une partie de l'opinion.

L'Université, placée sous l'autorité du grand maître, monseigneur de Frayssinous, bientôt ministre des Cultes, est mise au pas.

Les Julien Sorel grandissent dans ce climat politique d'ordre moral, de surveillance et de régression.

L'âme de la France, déjà pénétrée par les idées des Lumières, se rebiffe contre cette « conversion » forcée que pratiquent « missions » et directeurs de conscience.

L'anticléricalisme français qu'on verra s'épanouir dans la seconde moitié du siècle trouve une de ses sources dans ces quinze années de restauration et de réaction.

Cette politique ultra ne peut changer qu'à la marge (dans la période 1816-1820) sous l'influence du ministre Decazes, qui a la confiance de Louis XVIII.

Les ultraroyalistes la condamnent, pratiquent la politique du pire : « Il vaut mieux des élections jacobines que des élections ministérielles », disent-ils.

Ils favorisent ainsi l'élection du conventionnel Grégoire, ancien évêque constitutionnel, partisan de la Constitution civile du clergé.

Or « jacobins » et bonapartistes se sont organisés en sociétés secrètes (sur le modèle de la Charbonnerie, ou dans la société « Aide-toi, le Ciel t'aidera »). Ils complotent.

Le 13 février 1820, le bonapartiste Louvel assassine le duc de Berry, fils du comte d'Artois, seul héritier mâle des Bourbons.

La France se trouve ainsi emportée dans un cycle politique où s'affrontent tenants de la réaction, ultraroyalistes et révolutionnaires. À peine entr'ouverte, la voie étroite de la monarchie constitutionnelle se referme.

Quand il déclare, parlant de Decazes : « Les pieds lui ont glissé dans le sang », Chateaubriand exprime l'état d'esprit ultra, mettant en accusation les « modérés », les royalistes tentés par le libéralisme.

« Ceux qui ont assassiné monseigneur le duc de Berry, poursuit-il, sont ceux qui, depuis quatre ans, établissent dans la monarchie des lois démocratiques, ceux qui ont banni la religion de ses lois, ceux qui ont cru devoir rappeler les meurtriers de Louis XVI, ceux qui ont laissé prêcher dans les journaux la souveraineté du peuple et l'insurrection. »

La mort de Louis XVIII en 1824, le sacre de Charles X à Reims en 1825, creusent encore le fossé entre les « deux France ».

La répression des menées jacobines et bonapartistes (exécution en 1827 des quatre sergents de La Rochelle qui ont comploté contre la monarchie), les nouvelles lois électorales – un double vote est accordé aux plus riches des électeurs –, révoltent la partie de l'opinion qui reste attachée au passé révolutionnaire et napoléonien.

Elle ne peut accepter le gouvernement du duc de Polignac, constitué en août 1829, au sein duquel se retrouvent le maréchal Bourmont et La Bourdonnais.

Une nostalgie patriotique l'habite. Elle a été émue par la mort de Napoléon à Sainte-Hélène, le 5 mai 1821.

Elle lit le *Mémorial de Sainte-Hélène*, publié en 1823, qui connaît d'emblée un immense succès. À gauche, l'historien Edgar Quinet peut écrire :

« Lorsque, en 1821, éclata aux quatre vents la formidable nouvelle de la mort de Napoléon, il fit de nouveau irruption dans mon esprit... Il revint hanter mon intelligence, non plus comme mon empereur et mon maître absolu, mais comme un spectre que la mort a entièrement changé... Nous revendiquions sa gloire comme l'ornement de la liberté. »

Et Chateaubriand de noter lucidement :

« Vivant, Napoléon a manqué le monde ; mort il le conquiert. »

Dans ce climat, le ministère Polignac-Bourmont-La Bourdonnais apparaît comme une provocation ultraroyaliste.

Il manifeste la fusion qui s'opère dans les esprits entre les Bourbons, l'étranger et donc la trahison, et, réciproquement, entre leurs adversaires et le patriotisme. Dès lors, le pouvoir royal n'est plus légitime, et rejouent toutes les passions de la période révolutionnaire.

Le Journal des débats écrit ainsi : « Le lien d'amour qui unissait le peuple au monarque est brisé. »

Quelques jours plus tard, Émile de Girardin ajoute : Polignac est « l'homme de Coblence et de la contre-révolution ». Bourmont est le déserteur de Waterloo et La Bourdonnais, le chef de la « faction de 1815, avec ses amnisties meurtrières, ses lois de proscription et sa clientèle de massacreurs méridionaux »... « Pressez, tordez ce ministère – Coblence, Waterloo, 1815 –, il ne dégoutte qu'humiliation, malheurs et chagrins ! »

Bertin l'aîné, propriétaire du *Journal des débats*, sera condamné à six mois de prison pour la publication de ces articles.

La réaction se déploie : la pièce de Victor Hugo, *Marion Delorme*, est interdite, et une commission examine les cours donnés par Guizot et Victor Cousin.

L'affrontement avec le pouvoir est proche.

Le 3 janvier 1830, Thiers, Mignet et Armand Carrel fondent le journal *Le National*.

On mesure alors combien le patriotisme est le ressort de l'opposition.

C'est la question nationale qui met l'âme française en révolte.

Mais la confrontation est en fait limitée à Paris.

La France paysanne reste calme, presque indifférente à ces déchaînements politiques qui, s'ils vont prendre la forme de journées révolutionnaires – les 27, 28 et 29 juillet 1830 –, et, à ce titre, s'inscrivent dans la « mythologie révolutionnaire », marquent davantage un glissement de pouvoir qu'une profonde rupture.

Les acteurs de ces journées de juillet ne sont en effet qu'une minorité, une nouvelle génération romantique (la « bataille » d'*Hernani* est de 1830, et c'est cette année-là que Stendhal écrit *Le Rouge et le Noir*). Les inspirateurs politiques sont des « libéraux » (Thiers, La Fayette, Guizot) qui vont réussir à imposer leur candidat au trône : Louis-Philippe d'Orléans.

Ils réalisent ainsi avec le fils ce que d'autres « modérés » (déjà La Fayette) avaient tenté, en 1790-1791, avec le père, Philippe Égalité.

Ils veulent instaurer une monarchie constitutionnelle qui arborera les trois couleurs. Le monarque sera un roi citoyen.

Le peuple, utilisé et dupé, doit se contenter de cette mutation politique qui ne change rien à sa condition.

Après ces « trois glorieuses » journées de juillet 1830, Stendhal écrira :

« La banque est à la tête de l'État, la bourgeoisie a remplacé le faubourg Saint-Germain, et la banque est la noblesse de la classe bourgeoise. »

Et le banquier Laffitte de conclure : « Le rideau est tombé, la farce est jouée. »

Mais, dans la mémoire de la nation – dans l'âme de la France –, ces journées de 1830 sont l'un des maillons qui confortent et enrichissent la légende de la France révolutionnaire dont Paris, qui s'est couvert de six mille barricades, est le cœur.

Une source qui n'est pas tarie peut jaillir à nouveau avec d'autant plus de force qu'elle a été détournée, contenue.

47.

Dans ce deuxième tiers du XIXe siècle, l'histoire de France semble bégayer.

Paris a pris les armes en juillet 1830 pour chasser Charles X et les légitimistes, mais en février 1848 les émeutiers parisiens contraignent les orléanistes et Louis-Philippe, vainqueurs en 1830, à l'exil.

Par leur éclat symbolique – Paris se couvre de barricades, Paris s'insurge, Paris compte ses morts et les charge sur les tombereaux, allumant partout dans la capitale l'incendie de la révolte –, ces journées révolutionnaires qui voient surgir puis disparaître la monarchie bourgeoise de Louis-Philippe marquent l'importance, pour le destin français, de ces dix-huit années.

Car ce qui s'est scellé, entre 1830 et 1848, c'est le sort final de la monarchie.

Les journées de 1830 ont signé l'échec du retour à l'Ancien Régime, tenté avec plus ou moins de rigueur par Louis XVIII et Charles X.

Mais la France ne veut ni d'une charte octroyée, ni d'un roi sacré à Reims, ni d'un drapeau à fleurs de lys cachant sous ses plis le tricolore de Valmy et d'Austerlitz.

Les monarchistes partisans d'une royauté constitutionnelle l'ont compris. Ce sont eux qui provoquent, puis confisquent, les journées révolutionnaires de juillet 1830.

Ces idéologues – des historiens (Guizot, Thiers, Mignet) et des banquiers (Laffitte, Perier) – veulent renouer avec la « bonne Révolution », celle des années 1790-1791, quand les modérés espéraient stabiliser la situation et instaurer avec Louis XVI une monarchie constitutionnelle.

Leur grand homme, le garant militaire de leur tentative, leur glorieux porte-drapeau, c'était La Fayette, et c'est encore lui qui, en juillet 1830, présente à la foule le « roi patriote », Louis-Philippe.

Cette monarchie-là se drape dans le bleu-blanc-rouge.

Si elle parvient à s'enraciner, alors le sillon commencé avec la fête de la Fédération en 1790, puis interrompu par la Terreur et détourné au profit de Bonaparte, pourra enfin être continué.

Thiers, Guizot, qui gouverneront si souvent de 1830 à 1848, rêvent de ce pouvoir à l'anglaise, avec des Chambres élues au suffrage censitaire, un roi qui règne mais ne gouverne pas.

Malheureusement pour eux, Louis-Philippe veut régner et ne joue pas le jeu du Parlement.

Certes, le « roi citoyen » rompt avec l'idée d'un retour à l'Ancien Régime. Cela suffit d'ailleurs à dresser contre lui tous les monarchistes légitimistes.

Mais, naturellement, les républicains et les révolutionnaires qui découvrent que leur héroïsme de juillet 1830 n'a servi qu'à installer sur le trône un monarque, à la place d'un autre, le haïssent.

On essaiera – des régicides issus de toutes les oppositions – à six reprises de le tuer. Et on visera aussi son fils, le duc d'Aumale.

On ignorera les réussites d'une monarchie qui conclut une entente cordiale avec l'Angleterre et ne se lance dans aucune aventure guerrière.

Elle achève de conquérir l'Algérie et de la pacifier.

Elle jette les bases d'un empire colonial.

Elle unifie le pays en créant soixante mille kilomètres de chemins vicinaux, 4 000 kilomètres de voies ferrées, qui contribuent à renforcer la centralisation de la nation.

Paris est la tête où tout se décide, où tout se joue.

Les campagnes restent soumises à leurs nobles légitimistes, méprisants envers ce roi boutiquier, inquiets de voir Guizot exiger des communes qu'elles créent une école primaire, et de certains départements, qu'ils bâtissent une école normale d'instituteurs.

Cet enseignement n'est encore ni obligatoire, ni gratuit, ni laïque, mais il ouvre le chemin à l'Instruction publique.

Cependant, la monarchie constitutionnelle reste une construction fragile, et son renversement en février 1848 clôt, dans l'histoire nationale, le chapitre de la royauté.

On ne confiera jamais plus le pouvoir à un souverain issu de l'une ou l'autre des branches de la dynastie, qu'il arbore les fleurs de lys ou les trois couleurs.

Ce que le peuple de France rejette depuis 1789, ce n'est point tant le gouvernement d'un seul homme – Napoléon fut le plus autoritaire, le plus dictatorial des souverains – que l'accession au trône par filiation héréditaire.

Même le fils de Napoléon ne peut accéder au trône. Le roi de Rome n'est que le sujet d'une pièce mélodramatique qui sera écrite beaucoup plus tard.

Ce ne sont plus ni les liens de sang ni le sacre qui légitiment le pouvoir, mais l'élection.

En 1848, quand Louis-Philippe part en exil, alors que Paris ignore que le roi a abdiqué en faveur de son petit-fils, le comte de Paris, une nouvelle période de l'histoire de France commence.

Les nostalgies monarchiques – légitimistes ou orléanistes – pourront bien perdurer, susciter d'innombrables manœuvres politiques, elles ne donneront plus naissance qu'à des chimères et à des regrets.

Des quatre modèles politiques qui ont composé la combinatoire institutionnelle de la France à partir de 1789 – monarchie d'Ancien Régime, monarchie constitutionnelle, empire, république –, il ne restera plus, après l'échec de la monarchie constitutionnelle, que les deux derniers.

C'est dire l'importance du sort de cette monarchie louis-philipparde pour l'orientation de toute l'histoire nationale à partir des années 1830-1848. En fait, se mettent alors en place de nouvelles forces sociales et politiques, des manières de penser – des idéologies – qui coloreront l'âme de la France durant le dernier tiers du XIXe siècle et tout le XXe.

De nouveaux mots apparaissent : socialisme, socialistes, communisme, prolétaires.

Surtout, s'opère la fusion entre ces « prolétaires », ces ouvriers, et le mouvement républicain. On se souvient de la conspiration des Égaux de Babeuf, du Comité de salut public.

Pour les notables, les propriétaires, ce sont là des « monstruosités » dont il convient d'éviter à tout prix le retour.

Pour d'autres – les républicains révolutionnaires –, c'est un exemple, une voie à prolonger. Au bout, il y a la république sociale fondée sur l'égalité.

L'un de ces idéologues – Laponneraye – écrira en 1832 : « Il s'agit d'une république où l'on ne connaîtra point la distinction de bourgeoisie et de peuple, de privilèges et de prolétaires, où la liberté et l'égalité seront la propriété de tous et non le monopole exclusif d'une caste. »

Dans les campagnes, chez les idéologues libéraux, on craint ces « partageux ». Et ce d'autant plus qu'on a pu mesurer en 1830 la force révolutionnaire de Paris.

Un notable libéral, Rémusat, avouera : « Nous ne connaissions point la population de Paris, nous ne savions pas ce qu'elle pouvait faire. »

On s'inquiète de la prolifération des sociétés secrètes, de la liaison entre « républicains déterminés » et prolétaires.

En 1831, les canuts lyonnais se révoltent. Les « coalitions » (grèves) se multiplient.

La condition ouvrière est en effet accablante : « Le salaire n'est que le prolongement de l'esclavage », résume Chateaubriand. La misère, le chômage, la faim, l'absence de protection sociale, le travail des enfants et la mortalité infantile sont décrits par toutes les enquêtes. Un christianisme social – Lamennais, Lacordaire – se penche sur cette situation insoutenable.

Ces foules « misérables », entrant en contact avec les républicains, modifient la donne politique. Cette rencontre entre le social et la République est encore une exception française.

Après la révolte des canuts, on peut lire sous la plume de Michel Chevalier : « Les événements de Lyon ont changé le sens du mot politique ; ils l'ont élargi. Les intérêts du travail sont décidément entrés dans le cercle politique et vont s'y étendre de plus en plus. »

Cette présence ouvrière et sa jonction avec les républicains terrorisent les notables, les modérés, les propriétaires – et, à leur suite, la paysannerie.

« La sédition de Lyon, écrit Saint-Marc de Girardin dans *Le Journal des débats*, a révélé un grave secret, celui de la lutte intestine qui a lieu dans la société entre la classe qui possède et celle qui ne possède pas. Notre société commerciale et industrielle a sa plaie, comme toutes les autres sociétés : cette plaie, ce sont ses ouvriers. Les barbares qui menacent la société sont dans les faubourgs de nos villes manufacturières ; c'est là qu'est le danger de la société moderne. Il ne s'agit ici ni de république, ni de monarchie, il s'agit du salut de la société. »

Et Girardin de lancer un appel à l'union :

« Républicains, monarchistes de la classe moyenne, quelle que soit la diversité d'opinion sur la meilleure forme de gouvernement, il n'y a qu'une voie portant sur le maintien de la société ! »

Mais ce discours d'ordre, d'intérêt, de raison, prônant l'unité de tous ceux dont les intérêts sociaux convergent, même si leurs préférences politiques divergent, se heurte à la passion républicaine, à la nostalgie révolutionnaire ravivée par la misère, la répression, l'autoritarisme d'un pouvoir qui ne réussit pas ou ne tient pas à s'ouvrir, à concéder des avantages aux classes les plus démunies, mais qui, au contraire, avec Guizot en 1836, s'insurge contre les revendications des « prolétaires » :

« Nous sommes frappés de cette soif effrénée de bien-être matériel et de jouissances égoïstes qui se manifeste surtout dans les classes peu éclairées. »

Ce sont en fait, selon les mots de Victor Hugo, les « misérables » qui « meurent sous les voûtes de pierre » des caves des villes ouvrières.

Et Guizot, pour contenir cette révolte qui couve, de suggérer : « Croyez-vous que les idées religieuses ne sont pas un des moyens, le moyen le plus efficace, pour lutter contre ce mal ? »

Cette attitude répressive et aveugle du pouvoir, que les « scandales » et la corruption délégitiment un peu plus, favorise l'amalgame entre républicains, mouvement, revendications sociales et même anticléricalisme. C'est là un trait majeur de notre histoire.

Et puisque les revendications partielles ne sont pas entendues, que le souvenir de la Révolution revient hanter les mémoires, le « mouvement » remet en cause toute structure de la société, comme le perçoit bien Tocqueville, qui note en janvier 1848 :

« Il se répand peu à peu, dans le sein des opinions des classes ouvrières, des idées qui ne visent pas seulement à renverser telles lois, tel ministère, tel gouvernement, mais la société même, à l'ébranler des bases sur lesquelles elle repose aujourd'hui. »

Et d'ajouter :

« Le sentiment de l'instabilité, ce sentiment précurseur des révolutions, existe à un degré très redoutable dans ce pays. »

Si la situation est à ce point menaçante en janvier 1848, c'est que, tout au long de ces dix-huit années, le mouvement républicain, social et révolutionnaire s'est renforcé.

D'abord, les émeutes parisiennes – mais la révolte des canuts de 1831 a déjà fissuré à elle seule la société – naissent du sentiment que les protagonistes des journées de juillet 1830 ont été bernés, spoliés de leur victoire.

Cette manipulation politique réussie par Thiers, La Fayette et Louis-Philippe conforte l'opinion « avancée » dans l'idée que les « élites » trompent le peuple et se jouent de lui. Qu'à l'hypocrisie de la politique il faut opposer la brutale « franchise » de l'insurrection armée.

En 1831, 1832, 1834, puis en 1839, des groupes d'insurgés dressent des barricades à l'occasion de l'enterrement d'un général républicain (Lamarque, juin 1832) ou pour tenter de s'emparer de l'Hôtel de Ville de Paris en 1839 (Blanqui et Barbès).

Paris est le creuset où, émeute après émeute, se perpétue et se forge la légende révolutionnaire.

C'est le temps de la « grandeur de l'idéologie » (Fourier, Proudhon, Pierre Leroux), de l'alliance des révolutionnaires avec certains écrivains (Sue, Hugo, Sand, Lamartine).

Les opinions sont radicales : « La propriété c'est le vol », décrète Proudhon. Mais le mouvement insurrectionnel et politique reste faible. La répression conduite par Thiers ou Guizot est implacable : un « massacre » est perpétré rue Transnonain, le 14 avril 1834, par Bugeaud, qui plus tard sera gouverneur de l'Algérie (1840).

On voit ainsi s'entrelacer en des nœuds complexes mais serrés les traditions révolutionnaires, le recours à la violence, le rôle de Paris, la liaison entre républicains et ouvriers (surtout parisiens). Et, malgré le recours à la force armée, la monarchie constitutionnelle paraît de plus en plus incapable de contrôler une situation qui inquiète les possédants.

Depuis 1836, un Bonaparte s'est campé dans le paysage politique. Ce Louis Napoléon, neveu de l'Empereur, a tenté un coup de force à Strasbourg (1836), un autre à Boulogne (1840). Emprisonné, il s'évade du fort de Ham en 1846.

On voit ainsi réapparaître l'un des quatre modèles institutionnels de la France du XIXe siècle. Louis Napoléon Bonaparte propose en effet une « synthèse » :

« L'esprit napoléonien peut seul concilier la liberté populaire avec l'ordre et l'autorité », dit-il.

Il publie *De l'Extinction du paupérisme* (1844) :

« La gangrène du paupérisme périrait avec l'accès de la classe ouvrière à la prospérité », y affirme-t-il.

S'esquisse là, adossé à la légende napoléonienne, un « national-populisme » autoritaire, incarné mais recherchant le sacre du peuple et non d'abord la légitimité par la filiation dynastique, même si elle tient lieu de point d'appui essentiel.

La situation du pays est incertaine.

« Il se dit que la division des biens jusqu'à présent dans le monde est injuste..., que la propriété repose sur des bases qui ne sont pas des bases équitables, note Tocqueville. Et ne pensez-vous pas que quand de telles opinions descendent profondément dans les masses, elles amènent tôt ou tard les révolutions les plus redoutables ? »

Or, pour y faire face, le national-populisme autoritaire n'est-il pas mieux armé que la monarchie constitutionnelle ?

On se souvient de Bonaparte brandissant le glaive de la force et de la loi contre tous les fauteurs de désordre, garantissant les fortunes à la fois contre les partisans de l'Ancien Régime et les jacobins.

Ainsi resurgit de la mémoire française cette solution « bonapartiste », puisque la monarchie constitutionnelle est un système « bloqué », freiné sur la voie parlementaire par l'autoritarisme du monarque – ce qui déçoit ses partisans modérés – et incapable de se doter d'un soutien populaire.

Il n'y a plus alors que deux issues : la république ou le bonapartisme.

La crise que provoque le doublement du prix du pain à la suite des mauvaises récoltes de 1846 est donc essentiellement politique : face à la montée des oppositions, le pouvoir refuse d'ouvrir le « système », de faire passer le nombre des électeurs de 240 000 à 450 000.

Il se coupe ainsi de ceux (Thiers) qui souhaitent élargir la base de la monarchie constitutionnelle pour la préserver, cependant que ses adversaires républicains et révolutionnaires, de leur côté, se renforcent. Presse « communiste », troubles dans les villes ouvrières, émeutes de la misère : les signes de tension se multiplient.

Des anciens ministres sont accusés de concussion. Un modéré – Duvergier de Hauranne – peut écrire :

« Tous ces scandales, tous ces désordres, ne sont pas des accidents, c'est la conséquence nécessaire, inévitable, de la politique perverse qui nous régit, de cette politique qui, trop faible pour asservir la France, s'efforce de la corrompre. »

Dès le mois de janvier 1847, une « campagne de banquets » mobilise l'opinion modérée sur le thème des « réformes ». L'un de ces banquets, prévu à Paris le 14 février 1848, est interdit. Un manifeste réformiste est lancé.

Il ne s'agit pas de renverser Louis-Philippe, mais de le contraindre à renvoyer Guizot, à élargir le corps électoral, à donner vigueur et perspective à la monarchie constitutionnelle.

Mais Paris, quand il voit les corps des manifestants tués au cours d'une fusillade avec la troupe, s'enflamme.

La ville est celle des minorités révolutionnaires. Ce sont elles qui agissent, débordant les réformistes.

L'Hôtel de Ville est envahi. Lamartine et les manifestants proclament la république le 24 février.

Ce qui avait été manqué en juillet 1830 réussit en février 1848. Par un bel effet d'éloquence, Lamartine parvient à faire écarter le drapeau rouge que les manifestants voulaient d'abord imposer à « leur » république. Elle restera « tricolore ». Mais on mesure, à l'ambiguïté et à la complexité de ces événements, que rien n'est tranché.

La révolution de Février n'est qu'une émeute de plus qui a réussi. Ce succès est dû au fait que la France rurale est restée passive, que les forces de l'ordre ont été hésitantes, et que l'assise sociale et politique du pouvoir s'est divisée.

Dans le même temps, cette « révolution » entre dans le légendaire national. La république et la révolution sont associées dans la reconstruction de l'événement. Dans cette « imagerie », il a suffi au peuple de se révolter, de dresser des barricades dans Paris, pour l'emporter sur le pouvoir.

48.

Quel peut être le destin de cette république officiellement proclamée le 26 février 1848 et née d'une révolution ambiguë ?

Elle est la deuxième, et elle fait resurgir tous les souvenirs de la Grande Révolution et de la Iʳᵉ République, celle de 1792. Mais son sort sera scellé avant la fin de l'année, puisque le 10 décembre 1848 Louis-Napoléon Bonaparte en sera élu président par 5 434 000 voix.

Les autres candidats, – Cavaignac, Ledru-Rollin, Raspail et Lamartine – rassemblent respectivement 1 448 000, 371 000, 37 000, et, pour le dernier, Lamartine, le héros de Février, celui qui a réussi à maintenir le drapeau tricolore... 8 000 voix !

C'est une période charnière que ces dix mois de l'année 1848.

Ils dessinent une fresque politique qui sera souvent copiée dans l'histoire nationale, parce qu'elle met en jeu des forces et des idées qui resteront à l'œuvre durant le reste du XIXᵉ et tout le XXᵉ siècle.

Au cours de ces dix mois, les illusions de Février sont déchirées.

Deux mesures capitales permettent ce retour à la réalité.

D'abord, sous la pression populaire, et parce qu'il faut bien satisfaire ces ouvriers, ces partisans de la république sociale qui, armés, manifestent, le gouvernement crée pour les chômeurs des ateliers nationaux.

Les chômeurs y percevront un salaire.

L'État prend ainsi en charge l'assistance sociale, en même temps que des lois fixent la durée quotidienne maximale du travail à dix heures à Paris, à onze heures en province, puis à douze heures sur l'ensemble du territoire national.

Il faut payer ces « ouvriers » qu'on n'emploie guère et qui deviennent une masse de manœuvre réceptive aux idées « socialistes » ou bonapartistes.

C'est en même temps un abcès de fixation. Il suffira de le vider pour que soit brisée l'avant-garde, écho de ce « printemps des peuples » qui fait souffler le vent de la révolution sur l'Europe entière.

La seconde mesure, décisive, est l'instauration, le 5 mars 1848, du suffrage universel (masculin).

Le droit de vote est accordé à tous les Français dès lors qu'ils ont atteint vingt et un ans.

Innovation capitale qui va devenir le patrimoine de toute la nation.

Mesure anticipatrice, comparée aux régimes électoraux en vigueur dans les autres nations européennes.

Au lieu de 250 000, la France compte désormais dix millions d'électeurs, dont les trois quarts sont des paysans et plus de 30%, des illettrés.

Les « révolutionnaires », les « républicains avancés », qui se proclament l'« avant-garde », comprennent que le suffrage universel va se retourner contre eux.

Ils connaissent le conservatisme des campagnes, le poids des notables sur les paysans, le rôle qu'y joue l'Église.

Ils manifestent donc à Paris pour tenter de faire reculer la date des élections.

Paradoxe : le peuple est craint par ceux qui prétendent défendre ses intérêts.

Le suffrage universel devient l'arme des « conservateurs » contre les « progressistes » !

Les élections sont fixées au 25 avril 1848, malgré les manifestations des « révolutionnaires ». Et les « modérés » peuvent brandir devant les électeurs rassemblés le « spectre rouge », la menace des « partageux », celle de la dictature et du retour de la Terreur, comme en 1793-1794.

L'Assemblée constituante élue ne compte qu'une centaine de « socialistes » sur près de neuf cents sièges. La République a accouché d'une Assemblée conservatrice et orléaniste. Le pouvoir exécutif se donne pour chef le général Cavaignac, et des scrutins complémentaires permettent la désignation de Thiers, de Proudhon et de... Louis Napoléon Bonaparte.

Cette Assemblée régulièrement élue au suffrage universel représentant, contre les minorités révolutionnaires, le « pays réel », peut, maintenant qu'elle détient le pouvoir légal, supprimer les ateliers nationaux – pourquoi verser un franc par jour à des chômeurs ? –, viviers de la contestation, symboles d'une république sociale dont la France ne veut pas.

L'annonce de la fermeture des ateliers – les ouvriers n'ont le choix qu'entre le licenciement, le départ vers la Sologne pour assécher les marais et l'engagement dans l'armée – provoque l'émeute.

Ces journées de juin 1848 – du 22 au 26 – sont une véritable guerre sociale, opposant l'est de Paris, qui se couvre de barricades, et le Paris de l'Ouest, d'où partent les troupes de ligne.

Celles-ci vont perdre un millier d'hommes, contre 5 000 à 15 000 chez les insurgés, fusillés le plus souvent. Quinze mille prisonniers seront déférés à des conseils de guerre, déportés en Algérie (5 000), les autres étant emprisonnés au terme de ces « saturnales de la réaction » (Lamennais).

« Les atrocités commises par les vainqueurs me font frémir », écrit Renan.

En même temps, les libertés – accordées en février – sont rognées : « Silence aux pauvres ! » lance encore Lamennais.

Pourtant, en août, on vote – toujours au suffrage universel – pour élire les conseils généraux, d'arrondissement et municipaux.

Le peuple s'exprime, apprend à choisir, à peser par le scrutin sur les décisions.

Ambiguïté de cette République qui massacre ceux qui veulent aller au-delà des limites fixées par les notables, mais qui apprend au peuple les règles de la démocratie !

Ainsi se façonne l'âme française.

Les « prolétaires », les révolutionnaires, mesurent que la république aussi peut être conservatrice et durement répressive. Leur méfiance envers le suffrage universel s'accroît. Ils découvrent le *Manifeste du parti communiste*, publié par Marx et Engels à Londres le 24 février 1848.

Ils vont se persuader que les « avant-gardes » doivent choisir pour le peuple, y compris même contre les résultats du suffrage universel.

Et ce d'autant plus que, aux élections du 10 décembre 1848, Louis Napoléon Bonaparte écrase tous les autres candidats, à commencer par le général « républicain » Cavaignac, qui a conduit la répression de juin.

En un tiers de siècle, de 1815 à 1848, les Français ont donc vu se succéder à la tête de la nation une monarchie légitimiste, une monarchie constitutionnelle, une république dont le président est un Bonaparte, neveu de l'empereur Napoléon Ier !

Les Français ont voulu ces changements ou les ont laissé faire. Ils ont usé de la violence ou du bulletin de vote pour les susciter.

Mais ceux qui ont pris part aux journées révolutionnaires n'ont représenté que des minorités.

Rien de comparable au mouvement qui avait embrasé le pays en 1789 et l'avait soulevé en 1792.

Peu à peu, acquérant une expérience politique qu'aucun autre peuple au monde ne possède à un tel degré, et qui fait de la France la nation politique par excellence, la majorité des Français aspire en fait à la paix civile.

Dans ses profondeurs, le peuple a découvert que le vote peut être un moyen pacifique de changer les choses, lentement et sans violences.

Ainsi, cette nation révolutionnaire qui périodiquement dresse dans Paris des barricades est aussi désireuse d'ordre.

Elle continue d'osciller, comme si après la gigantesque poussée révolutionnaire de 1789 elle n'avait pas encore recouvré son équilibre. Les journées d'émeutes – les révolutions – se répètent, les régimes se succèdent, mais, dans le même temps, elle ne souhaite plus retomber dans les violences généralisées.

À Paris, grand théâtre national, elle met en scène la révolution comme pour se souvenir de ce qu'elle a vécu.

Puis elle interrompt le spectacle et sort du théâtre aussi vite qu'elle y est entrée.

Elle veut, au fond, vivre tranquillement, jouir de ses biens, de son beau pays.

C'est cette réalité contradictoire qui caractérise, au mitan du XIXᵉ siècle, l'âme de la France.

3

RENOUVEAU ET EXTINCTION DU BONAPARTISME

1849-1870

49.

À partir de décembre 1848, la République est donc présidée par un Bonaparte que le peuple a élu au suffrage universel.

Peut-on imaginer que cet homme-là, symbole vivant de la postérité napoléonienne, incarnation de la tradition bonapartiste, se contentera d'un mandat de président de la République de quatre années, non renouvelable ?

Cependant, son entreprise – conserver le pouvoir au-delà de 1852, fût-ce par le recours au coup d'État, et peut-être proclamer l'Empire – paraît aléatoire et difficile.

Les élites politiques conservatrices sont désireuses de garder, par le moyen des Assemblées, la réalité du pouvoir. Elles sont favorables à un régime – monarchie ou république – constitutionnel dans lequel le président ou le monarque n'aura qu'une fonction de représentation.

Elles se défient d'un Bonaparte, élu d'occasion, qu'elles espèrent manœuvrer à leur guise.

Elles craignent davantage encore les « rouges », les partageux, ce peuple auquel on a dû accorder le droit de vote.

Elles aspirent à l'ordre.

Leur parti s'appellera d'ailleurs le parti de l'Ordre.

Mais Louis Napoléon Bonaparte trouve aussi sur sa route ces « démocrates socialistes – « démocsoc » – qui se réclament de la Montagne et de 1793, qui aspirent à une république sociale et constitueront le parti des Montagnards, hostile à la fois au prince-président et au parti de l'Ordre.

C'est donc un jeu politique à trois qui va commencer dès le lendemain de l'élection de Louis Napoléon Bonaparte à la présidence de la République.

Partie difficile, car il existe un quatrième joueur, le plus souvent sur la réserve, mais toujours sollicité par les trois partis – le bonapartiste, le parti de l'Ordre et les Montagnards : il s'agit du peuple.

Et puisqu'il y a suffrage universel, la bataille politique s'étend des villes aux campagnes, là où se concentre la majeure partie de la population.

Celui qui tient et convainc le monde paysan, celui-là peut imposer ses choix.

Le suffrage universel est ainsi un facteur d'unification politique de la nation, et, en même temps, il divise le monde paysan en partisans de l'un ou l'autre des trois « partis ».

Les paysans apporteront-ils toujours leurs voix à un descendant de Napoléon (ils viennent de le faire en décembre 1848), ou aux représentants des notables, ou encore seront-ils gagnés par les idées socialisantes des « démocrates socialistes », et suivront-ils les Montagnards ?

Les quatre années qui vont de décembre 1848 à décembre 1852, date de la proclamation du second Empire, sont décisives pour la vie politique nationale. C'est là, autour de la République, du suffrage universel, du conflit entre bonapartisme, parti de l'Ordre et Montagnards, que se précisent les lignes de fracture politiques de la société française.

L'âme de la France contemporaine y acquiert de nouveaux réflexes.

Les thèmes de l'homme providentiel – au-dessus des partis – et du coup d'État (celui que va perpétrer Louis Napoléon Bonaparte) s'enracinent dans les profondeurs nationales.

Naturellement, la référence au passé pèse sur les choix. Marx qualifie ainsi le coup d'État du 2 décembre 1851 de « 18 Brumaire de Louis Napoléon Bonaparte ».

Mais cette « répétition », cinquante-deux ans après la prise du pouvoir par Napoléon Bonaparte, peut-elle être autre chose qu'une farce, comme si l'histoire se parodiait, comme si Napoléon le Petit pouvait être comparé à Napoléon le Grand, et le républicain socialisant Ledru-Rollin, à Robespierre ?

Marx conclut à la « farce ».

Dans l'histoire nationale, les événements de ces quatre années n'en sont pas moins d'une importance majeure : ils suscitent des comportements politiques, des réactions « instinctives » qui détermineront les choix du pays.

Ainsi, alors que le pouvoir personnel de Louis Napoléon est installé à l'Élysée, que quelques observateurs lucides craignent « une folie impériale » que « le peuple verrait tranquillement », les élections législatives du 13 mai 1849 marquent la constitution et l'opposition à l'échelle de la nation – et non plus seulement dans les villes – du parti de l'Ordre et du parti montagnard.

Deux blocs – on dira plus tard une droite et une gauche – se sont affrontés. Les résultats sont nets : le parti de l'Ordre – religion, famille, propriété, ordre – remporte 500 sièges à l'Assemblée législative, contre 200 aux Montagnards de Ledru-Rollin, et moins d'une centaine à un « centre ».

« La majorité – sur 750 sièges – est aux mains des ennemis de la République », note Tocqueville.

Mais le parti de l'Ordre n'est pas pour autant rassuré par cette victoire.

Les milieux ruraux ont été – fût-ce marginalement – pénétrés par les idées des Montagnards.

Dans le nord du Massif central – de la Vienne à la Nièvre et à la Saône –, dans les départements alpins (de l'Isère au Var) et dans l'Aquitaine (Lot-et-Garonne, Dordogne), les démocrates sociaux sont présents.

Les villes moyennes sont touchées.

Le parti de l'Ordre mesure qu'à partir de Paris – et des villes ouvrières – les idées socialistes se sont répandues par le biais du suffrage universel dans tout le territoire national.

Elles sont minoritaires, mais le germe en est semé.

Au sein du parti montagnard, on commence à croire que le socialisme peut vaincre pacifiquement grâce au suffrage universel. Des associations et des sociétés secrètes se constituent pour diffuser les idées « montagnardes » et organiser les « militants ».

Dès lors, il reste au parti de l'Ordre, majoritaire à l'Assemblée, à faire adopter un ensemble de lois qui interdiront la propagande socialiste (lois Falloux livrant l'enseignement à l'Église, lois restreignant la liberté de la presse).

L'élection de l'écrivain socialiste Eugène Sue (28 avril 1850) contre un conservateur conduit le parti de l'Ordre à voter, le 31 mai 1850, l'abrogation de fait du suffrage universel, les plus pauvres, par une série de dispositions, se voyant retirer le droit de vote.

Mais puisque la voie électorale est ainsi fermée, resurgissent dans la « Nouvelle Montagne » les idées de prise du pouvoir par les armes.

La fascination et la mystique de la révolution, de la « journée » révolutionnaire, des barricades, trouvent alors une nouvelle vigueur.

Cela ne concerne évidemment que des « minorités ». Mais le peuple constate qu'on le prive de ce droit de vote qu'il avait commencé à s'approprier.

Le parti de l'Ordre croit avoir remporté la mise contre les Montagnards. Fort de cette victoire, il s'oppose à toute révision constitutionnelle qui aurait permis à Louis Napoléon, en 1852, de se présenter pour un nouveau mandat.

Les Montagnards ont voté en l'occurrence avec le parti de l'Ordre. Mais ils mêleront leurs voix à celles du parti bonapartiste pour s'opposer à la constitution d'une force militaire destinée à protéger l'Assemblée d'un coup d'État.

En fait, ces manœuvres politiciennes laissent Louis Napoléon Bonaparte maître du jeu.

Le 13 novembre 1851, il peut proposer à l'Assemblée l'abrogation de la loi du 31 mai 1850 qui a aboli le suffrage universel.

L'Assemblée conservatrice repousse cette proposition, et le prince-président apparaît ainsi comme l'homme qui, contre les notables, mais aussi contre les rouges partageux, entend redonner la parole au peuple.

Il retrouve de cette manière l'une des sources du bonapartisme, qui veut tisser un lien direct avec la nation en se dégageant de l'emprise des partis.

Il dispose dans l'armée – épurée par ses soins – du soutien que lui apporte le « souvenir napoléonien ».

Et parce qu'il est au cœur de l'institution – à l'Élysée –, il va pouvoir préparer son coup d'État, exécuté le 2 décembre 1851, jour anniversaire d'Austerlitz.

Des députés, dont Thiers, sont arrêtés.

Ceux qui résistent et tentent de soulever le peuple parisien sont dispersés par la troupe, qui tire.

Le député Baudin est tué sur une barricade pour avoir montré au peuple comment on meurt pour 25 francs par jour, cette indemnité parlementaire que le peuple, spectateur, conteste.

Sur les boulevards, dans Paris, afin d'empêcher par la terreur l'extension de la résistance, les troupes de ligne ouvrent le feu sur la foule des badauds (trois à quatre cents morts).

La résistance est vive dans les départements pénétrés par les idées républicaines, ceux qui ont voté « rouge » en 1849. La répression est sévère : 84 députés expulsés, 32 départements en état de siège, 27 000 « rouges » déférés devant des commissions mixtes (tribunaux d'exception : un général, un préfet, un procureur), dix mille déportés en Algérie et en Guyane, des milliers d'internés et d'exilés.

Mais le suffrage universel est rétabli, et, le 20 décembre, 7 500 000 voix approuvent le coup d'État, contre 650 000 opposants. On compte un million et demi d'abstentions.

Un an plus tard, un nouveau plébiscite – 7 800 000 oui – permet à Louis Napoléon, devenu Napoléon III, de rétablir l'Empire. Celui-ci est proclamé le 1er décembre 1852, cinquante-huit ans après le sacre du 2 décembre 1804.

C'est le renouveau du bonapartisme, mais aussi le début de son extinction.

Car la résistance au coup d'État et la rigueur de la répression marquent une rupture irréductible entre une partie du peuple et la figure de Bonaparte.

Certes, l'immense succès des plébiscites de 1851 et 1852 montre bien que le mythe demeure, que l'homme providentiel, la figure d'un empereur tirant sa légitimité du peuple consulté dans le cadre du suffrage universel, continuent de fonctionner.

Mais les républicains ont une assise populaire.

La grande voix de Victor Hugo, l'exilé, va commencer de se faire entendre.

Le 2 décembre 1851 sera qualifié de « crime ».

Louis Napoléon est un « parjure » que Marx désigne sous le nom de Crapulinsky.

Louis Napoléon a beau répéter : « J'appartiens à la Révolution » et décréter la mise en vente de tous les biens immobiliers des Orléans, on sait aussi que les préfets ont reçu l'ordre, dès le 6 janvier 1852, d'effacer partout la devise « Liberté, Égalité, Fraternité ».

Et le ralliement de la plupart des conservateurs du parti de l'Ordre à l'Empire confirme que ce régime n'est pas au-dessus des « partis » : il est « réactionnaire ».

On le sait, même si on le soutient ou si on l'accepte par souci de paix civile.

Mais les républicains refuseront ce « détournement » du suffrage universel. Et, fruit de cette expérience, ils garderont une défiance radicale à l'endroit du plébiscite, de la consultation directe du peuple mise au service d'un destin personnel.

L'âme de la France contemporaine vient d'être profondément marquée. La République avait massacré les insurgés de juin 1848, ce qui avait conduit le « peuple » à choisir pour président Louis Napoléon Bonaparte.

Après le coup d'État du 2 décembre 1851, il y a désormais, minoritaire mais résolu, un antibonapartisme populaire.

Ce Napoléon III, c'est Badinguet, Napoléon le Petit !

La colère et le mépris qu'il suscite renforcent le désir de République et le souvenir de la Révolution.

50.

Au lendemain de la création du second Empire, les Français ne croient pas à la longévité de ce régime né d'un coup d'État sanglant et que deux plébiscites ont légitimé.

L'âme de la France est une âme sceptique.

Depuis le 21 septembre 1792, les citoyens de cette nation « politique » ont vu se succéder la Ire République, le Directoire, le Consulat, l'Empire, une monarchie légitimiste, une monarchie orléaniste et constitutionnelle, la IIe République et enfin le second Empire. Déclarations, Chartes, Actes additionnels, Constitutions ont tour à tour régenté la vie publique.

On a débattu, en 1789, dans les villages des cahiers de doléances, on a voté pour celui-ci ou pour celui-là, on a disposé du droit de vote, puis on l'a perdu, et on en a de nouveau bénéficié.

Le Français, si éprouvé par les changements politiques, est devenu prudent, attentiste.

Puisque la monarchie millénaire de droit divin s'est effondrée et que Louis XVI a été décapité, lui qui avait été sacré à Reims, qui peut croire qu'en ce bas monde un régime politique soit promis à la longue durée ?

Le sacre par le pape de Napoléon Ier n'a pas empêché l'Empereur d'être vaincu et de mourir en exil à Sainte-Hélène.

Et Charles X n'a pas durablement bénéficié de la protection divine, bien qu'il eût été lui aussi sacré à Reims.

Comment imaginer dès lors que ce Louis Napoléon Bonaparte, même devenu Napoléon III, puisse régner plus longtemps que son oncle Napoléon Ier ?

Nul ne peut le concevoir.

On observe. On ne commente pas : trop d'argousins, trop de mouchards, trop de gendarmes. Trop de risques à prendre parti pour un régime dont on comprend bien qu'il est fragile, comme tous les régimes, et que viendra son tour de chanceler, de se briser.

Telle est alors l'âme de la France, qui, en soixante années, a subi tant de pouvoirs, entendu tant de discours, qu'elle baisse la tête et fait mine de se désintéresser des affaires publiques que gèrent ces messieurs les intelligents, les notables.

Or ceux-ci, précisément, ne croient guère à la longévité du second Empire.

Guizot, qui exprime la pensée des milieux de la bourgeoisie libérale, déclare : « Les soldats et les paysans ne suffisent pas pour gouverner. Il y faut le concours des classes supérieures, qui sont naturellement gouvernantes. »

Tocqueville est tout aussi réservé sur l'avenir du régime quand il écrit en 1852 :

« Quant à moi qui ai toujours craint que toute cette longue révolution française ne finît par aboutir à un compromis entre l'égalité et le despotisme, je ne puis croire que le moment soit encore venu où nous devrions voir se réaliser définitivement ces prévisions, et, en somme, ceci a plutôt l'air d'une aventure qui se continue que d'un gouvernement qui se fonde. »

Il n'empêche : l'« aventurier » Louis Napoléon, entouré d'habiles et intelligents complices – dont Morny, son demi-frère –, va régner de 1852 à 1870, soit sept ans de plus que Napoléon Ier, sacré en 1804 et définitivement vaincu en 1815 !

Cette longue durée du second Empire et les transformations qui la caractérisent vont servir de socle à la fin du XIXe siècle et aux premières décennies du XXe.

Le second Empire dit « autoritaire » est ainsi, durant quinze années – de 1852 à 1867 –, le moule dans lequel l'âme de la France prend sa forme contemporaine.

L'État centralisé – répressif, policier même – organise et régente la vie départementale, sélectionne les candidats aux élections.

Ces « candidatures » officielles bénéficient de tout l'appareil de l'État.

Le préfet devient pour de bon la clé de voûte de la vie locale sous tous ses aspects. Il fait régner l'« ordre » politique et moral. Il est le lien entre le pouvoir central – impérial – et toutes les strates de la bourgeoisie : celle qui vit de ses rentes, de la perception de ses fermages ; celle qui est, d'une certaine façon, l'héritière des « robins » : avocats, médecins et apothicaires, notaires, parfois tentée par un rôle politique, mais prudente et surveillée.

L'Empire n'aime pas les esprits forts, les libres penseurs.

D'ailleurs, aux côtés du préfet, l'évêque est, avec le général commandant la place militaire, le personnage principal. Il a la haute main sur l'enseignement, entièrement livré à l'Église. Les ordres religieux – au premier rang desquels les Jésuites – ont été à nouveau autorisés.

L'Empire est clérical.

La police et les confesseurs veillent aux bonnes mœurs.

Le réalisme de certains peintres (Manet, Courbet) est suspect. *Madame Bovary*, *Les Fleurs du mal*, sont condamnées par les tribunaux.

Les journaux sont soumis à l'autorisation préalable.

Un « homme de lettres » qui est perçu comme un opposant, un rebelle – ainsi Jules Vallès –, est réduit à la misère, voire à la faim. Il n'écrit pas dans les journaux, il ne peut enseigner – l'Église est là pour le lui interdire –, il remâche sa révolte. Il se souvient des espoirs nés en février 1848 et noyés dans le sang des journées de juin. Il rêve à de nouvelles journées révolutionnaires qui lui permettraient de prendre sa revanche.

On voit ainsi s'opposer deux France complémentaires mais antagonistes.

Une France « officielle », adossée aux pouvoirs de l'État, qui cherche dans l'Église, l'armée, la police, la censure, les moyens de contenir l'autre France.

Celle-ci est minoritaire, souterraine, juvénile, conduite parfois par le sentiment qu'elle ne peut rien contre la citadelle du régime à une sorte de rage désespérée.

L'hypocrisie du pouvoir, qui masque sa corruption et sa débauche sous le vernis des discours moralisateurs, révolte les « vieux » républicains révolutionnaires – ils avaient, pour les plus jeunes, une vingtaine d'années en 1848. Ils sont rejoints par des éléments des nouvelles générations, « nouvelles couches » elles aussi républicaines.

Mais, jusqu'aux années 1860, le pouvoir semble enfermé dans son autoritarisme. C'est Thiers qui, en 1864, parle au Corps législatif des « libertés nécessaires ».

Il reste aux opposants à s'enivrer, à vivre dans la « bohème », à clamer leur athéisme, leur anticléricalisme, leur haine des autorités.

Mais ils sont le pot de terre heurtant le pot de fer.

Car la France se transforme, et son développement sert le second Empire.

C'est sous Napoléon III que le réseau ferré devient cette toile d'araignée de 6 000 kilomètres qui couvre l'Hexagone.

C'est durant cette période que la métallurgie – et le Comité des forges, où les grandes fortunes se retrouvent – augmente ses capacités. Houillères et sidérurgie dressent pour plus d'un siècle leurs chevalets, leurs terrils et leurs hauts-fourneaux dans le Nord, au Creusot, en Lorraine.

C'est le second Empire qui dessine le nouveau paysage industriel français, qui trace les nouvelles voies de circulation, en même temps qu'ici et là des progrès sont accomplis dans l'agriculture.

Les traités de libre-échange contraignent les industriels français à se moderniser.

Et c'est une fois encore l'État qui donne les impulsions nécessaires, qui soutient le développement du système bancaire.

Vallès écrira : « Le Panthéon est descendu jusqu'à la Bourse. »

Car l'argent irrigue la haute société et ses laudateurs (journalistes, écrivains), ses alliés (banquiers, industriels), ses protecteurs (les militaires, les juges), ses parasites (les corrompus).

Le visage de Paris se transforme : Haussmann perce les vieux quartiers, crée de grands boulevards qui rendront difficile à l'avenir la construction de barricades.

Et chaque immeuble construit sur les ruines d'une vieille demeure enrichit un peu plus ceux qui, avertis parce que proches du pouvoir, anticipent les développements urbains.

Le modèle français se trouve ainsi conforté.

Le pouvoir personnalisé est entouré de ses courtisans et de ses privilégiés.

Centralisé, autoritaire, il préside aux bouleversements économiques et sociaux qu'il encadre. Et la richesse nationale s'accroît.

On fait confiance à cet État qui maintient l'ordre : les emprunts lancés sont couverts quarante fois !

Structure étatique et fortunes privées, pouvoir et épargne, se soutiennent mutuellement.

Quant aux pauvres, aux salariés, aux « misérables », aux « ouvriers » – Napoléon III se souvient d'avoir écrit et voulu *L'Extinction du paupérisme* –, ces humbles obtiennent quelques miettes au grand banquet de la fête impériale.

C'est la particularité d'un pouvoir personnel issu d'un coup d'État, mais aussi du suffrage universel, de n'être pas totalement dépendant des intérêts de telle ou telle couche sociale.

Napoléon III va accorder en 1864, dans un cadre très strict, le droit de grève.

Dès 1862, il a permis à une délégation ouvrière de se rendre à Londres à l'Exposition universelle, d'adhérer à l'Association internationale des travailleurs à l'origine de laquelle se trouvent Marx et Engels.

Ces ouvriers peuvent faire entendre leurs voix dans le « Manifeste des 60 » sans connaître la prison de Sainte-Pélagie (1864).

Ainsi s'esquisse, toujours en liaison avec l'État – et dans le cadre de sa stratégie politique –, une nouvelle séquence de

l'histoire nationale : elle voit apparaître sur la scène sociale des
« ouvriers » d'industrie qui manifestent au cours de violentes
grèves et créent à Paris, en 1865, une section de l'Internationale
ouvrière.

Pourtant, ces manifestations, ces novations, n'affaiblissent
pas le régime. L'État les encadre, il conserve l'appui des bour-
geoisies et la neutralité bienveillante des paysans, qui constituent
encore la majorité de la population française.

Mais Napoléon le Petit aspire à chausser les bottes de Napoléon le Grand. Sa politique étrangère active, après une période
de succès, connaîtra des difficultés qui saperont son régime.

La tradition bonapartiste, qui a été l'un des leviers de la
conquête du pouvoir, devient ainsi la cause de sa perte.

Dans l'âme française, la quête d'un grand rôle international
pour la nation aveugle le pouvoir.

Il croit avoir barre sur le monde comme il a barre sur son
pays.

Là est l'illusion mortelle.

Certes, Napoléon III jette les bases d'un empire colonial français au Sénégal, à Saigon. La Kabylie est « pacifiée » ; Napoléon III pense à promouvoir un « royaume arabe » en Algérie, et
non pas une domination classiquement coloniale : anticipation
hardie !

Il intervient en Italie en s'alliant au Piémont contre l'Autriche,
et les victoires de Magenta et de Solferino (4 et 24 juin 1859)
permettront à la France, en retour, d'acquérir, après plébiscite,
Nice et la Savoie (1860).

Pourtant, la guerre contre la Russie (1855) en Crimée, pour
défendre l'Empire ottoman contre les visées russes, était déjà une
entreprise discutable.

Elle avait cependant pour contrepartie l'alliance avec l'Angleterre, dont Napoléon III, tirant les leçons de l'échec du premier
Empire, voulait faire le pivot de sa politique étrangère, prolon-
geant ainsi l'Entente cordiale mise en œuvre par Louis-Philippe.

Cette alliance Paris-Londres demeurera d'ailleurs, durant toute la fin du XIXe siècle et tout le XXe siècle – et malgré quelques anicroches –, l'axe majeur de la politique extérieure française.

Mais l'expédition au Mexique « au profit d'un prince étranger (Maximilien d'Autriche) et d'un créancier suisse », dira Jules Favre, républicain modéré, alors que la situation en Europe est mouvante et périlleuse pour les intérêts français, constitue un échec cuisant (1863-1866).

Plus graves encore sont les hésitations devant les entreprises de Bismarck, qui, le 3 juillet 1866, écrase l'Autriche à Sadowa, la Prusse faisant désormais figure de grande puissance allemande.

Toutes les contradictions de la politique étrangère de Napoléon III apparaissent alors au grand jour.

Il a été l'adversaire de l'Autriche, servant ainsi le Risorgimento italien. Mais les troupes françaises ont soutenu le pape contre les ambitions italiennes. Et Napoléon III a perdu de ce fait le bénéfice de ses interventions en Italie. À Mentana, en 1867, des troupes françaises se sont opposées à celles de Garibaldi : il fallait bien satisfaire, en défendant le Saint-Siège contre les patriotes italiens, les catholiques français, socle du pouvoir impérial.

Et c'est seul que Napoléon III doit affronter Bismarck, qui, en 1867, rejette toutes les revendications de compensation émises par Paris (rive gauche du Rhin, Belgique, Luxembourg...). Ni l'Angleterre, ni la Russie, ni l'Italie, ni bien sûr l'Autriche, ne soutiennent la France contre la Prusse.

Comme toujours en France, politique extérieure et politique intérieure sont intimement mêlées.

Le premier Empire avait succombé à la défaite militaire et à l'occupation.

Napoléon III peut se souvenir de Waterloo.

51.

Voilà quinze ans que le second Empire a été proclamé.

C'est le temps qu'il faut pour que de nouvelles générations apparaissent et que les conséquences des transformations politiques, économiques et sociales produisent leurs effets.

En 1869, des grèves meurtrières – de dix à quinze morts à chaque fois –, réprimées par la troupe, éclatent à Anzin, à Aubin, au Creusot. Des troubles se produisent à Paris. Des « républicains irréconciliables » s'appuient sur ce mécontentement qui sourd et sur les échecs humiliants subis en politique extérieure – Mexico a été évacué par les troupes françaises en février 1867 – pour rappeler les origines du régime impérial.

On célèbre les victimes du coup d'État du 2 décembre.

On veut dresser une statue au député Baudin.

On manifeste en foule, armes dissimulées sous les redingotes, en janvier 1870, quand le cousin germain de l'empereur, Pierre Bonaparte, tue le journaliste Victor Noir.

Des hommes nouveaux – Gambetta – font le procès du régime, s'expriment au nom des « nouvelles couches », formulent à Belleville un programme républicain : séparation de l'Église et de l'État, libertés publiques, instruction laïque et obligatoire. Les candidats républicains au Corps législatif sont élus à Paris. À ces élections du mois de mai 1869, un million de voix seulement séparent les opposants résolus des candidats de la majorité.

Mais ces derniers sont des partisans de l'ordre plutôt que des « bonapartistes ».

À leur tête, le « vieux » Thiers, qui rassemble autour de lui les « modérés », les anciens soutiens de la monarchie constitutionnelle, ceux que le coup d'État du 2 décembre 1851 a privés du pouvoir.

Ils se sont ralliés à Louis Napoléon Bonaparte. Ils ont participé à la « fête impériale », mais Napoléon III ne leur semble plus capable d'affronter les périls intérieurs et extérieurs. Lorsqu'il était l'efficace défenseur de l'ordre, brandissant le glaive et faisant de son nom le bouclier de la stabilité sociale, on l'acceptait, on l'encensait. Mais le « protecteur » semble devenu impotent.

Thiers l'avertit au printemps de 1867 : « Il n'y a plus une seule faute à commettre. »

Le préfet de police de Paris, Piétri, déclare : « L'empereur a contre lui les classes dirigeantes. »

C'est ce moment où le gouffre se crée sous un régime, et la France, vieille nation intuitive et expérimentée, attend la crise, continuant de vivre comme si de rien n'était, mais pressentant la tempête comme une paysanne qui en flaire les signes avant-coureurs.

Cependant, le décor impérial est toujours en place.

En 1867, Paris est illuminé pour l'Exposition universelle que visitent les souverains étrangers. Victor Hugo a même écrit la préface du livre officiel présentant l'Exposition et le nouveau Paris de Haussmann. N'est-ce pas la preuve que l'Empire autoritaire devient libéral ?

Napoléon III desserre tous les liens : ceux qui étranglaient la presse, qui limitaient le droit de réunion ou les pouvoirs des Assemblées.

L'Empire semble recommencer. Des républicains modérés s'y rallient. L'un d'eux, Émile Ollivier, devient chef du gouvernement.

Au plébiscite du 8 mai 1870, 7 358 000 voix contre 1 572 000 et 2 000 000 d'abstentions approuvent les mesures libérales décidées par l'empereur.

Une fois encore, le suffrage universel – contre les élites – ratifie ses choix.

Napoléon III paraît demeurer l'homme providentiel capable d'entraîner le pays et de le faire entrer dans la « modernité ». C'est un Français, Lesseps qui, en présence de l'impératrice, inaugure en 1869 le canal de Suez, son œuvre.

« L'Empire est plus puissant que jamais », constatent les républicains accablés.

« Nous ferons à l'empereur une vieillesse heureuse », déclare Émile Ollivier en commentant les résultats du plébiscite : après plus de quinze ans de règne, Napoléon III a « retrouvé son chiffre ».

Pourtant, en quelques mois, le régime va s'effondrer. Le piège est ouvert par Bismarck.

Candidature d'un Hohenzollern au trône d'Espagne. Indignation de Paris ! Retrait de la candidature, mais dépêche d'Ems (où le roi prussien Guillaume Ier est en villégiature), humiliante.

Embrasement à Paris. L'entourage de Napoléon III, l'impératrice, les militaires : « La guerre sera une promenade de Paris à Berlin ! » Les journalistes à gages, les courtisans poussent à la guerre afin de laver l'affront et de recouvrer, par la victoire sur la Prusse, l'autorité que l'on a perdue par les réformes libérales.

Illustration et confirmation d'une caractéristique française : un monarque – ici l'empereur – n'accepte pas de n'être qu'un souverain constitutionnel dépendant des élus.

Le pouvoir exécutif refuse d'être entravé ou contrôlé ou orienté par les députés.

La politique étrangère étant le terrain sur lequel il est le seul maître, il va donc y jouer « librement », en souverain absolu, sa partie.

Encore faut-il qu'il soit victorieux.

Le 19 juillet 1870, Émile Ollivier salue la déclaration de guerre à la Prusse d'un « cœur léger ».

La France est pourtant seule face à Berlin, qui dispose d'une armée deux fois plus nombreuse et d'une artillerie – Krupp ! – supérieure.

Ni l'Autriche ni l'Italie ne s'allient à Paris. Et en six semaines de guerre l'état-major français montre son incapacité.

On perd l'Alsace et la Lorraine. On se replie sur Metz, où le maréchal Bazaine – le vaincu du Mexique – s'enferme.

À Sedan, le 2 septembre, Napoléon III – à la tête de ses troupes depuis le 23 juillet – se constitue prisonnier avec près de cent mille hommes.

Que reste-t-il d'un empereur qui a « remis son épée » ?

L'humiliation, cependant que la nation est entraînée dans la débâcle.

La France connaît là un de ces effondrements qui, tout au long des siècles, ont marqué son âme.

Le pays est envahi. L'armée, vaincue. Le pouvoir, anéanti. C'est l'extinction du bonapartisme.

Les républicains, les révolutionnaires qui, en juillet, avaient tenté – c'est le cas de Jules Vallès – de s'opposer au délire guerrier, et que la foule enthousiaste avait failli lyncher, envahissent le Corps législatif.

Ils déclarent l'empereur déchu.

Le 4 septembre 1870, ils proclament la république.

Au coup d'État originel répond ainsi le coup de force républicain et parisien.

Le 2 décembre 1851 a pour écho le 4 septembre 1870.

Au second Empire succède, par et dans la débâcle, la IIIe République.

Mais l'émeute républicaine, révolutionnaire et patriote – on veut organiser la défense nationale contre les Prussiens – n'a pas changé le pays, celui qui, en mai, a apporté 7 358 000 voix à l'empereur, ou plutôt au pouvoir en place, garant pour l'écrasante majorité de l'ordre et de la paix civile.

Rien n'a changé non plus dans les hiérarchies sociales, les rouages du pouvoir.

Les préfets sont en place.

Les généraux vaincus par les Prussiens gardent le contrôle de cette armée qui a été l'armature du pouvoir impérial.

Or tous les notables – le parti de l'Ordre – craignent que la débâcle ne soit l'occasion, pour les « rouges », de s'emparer du pouvoir. L'armée, à leurs yeux, est le recours contre les « révolutionnaires ».

L'un de ces « modérés » – républicain – déclare dès le 3 septembre : « Il est nécessaire que tous les partis s'effacent devant le nom d'un militaire qui prendra la défense de la nation. »

Ce sera le général Trochu.

« Participe passé du verbe trop choir », écrira Victor Hugo.

4

LES VÉRITÉS DE MARIANNE

1870-1906

52.

En neuf mois, entre septembre 1870 et mai 1871, l'âme de la France est si profondément blessée que, durant près d'un siècle, les pensées, les attitudes et les choix de la nation seront influencés, voire souvent dictés, par ce qu'elle a souffert après la chute du second Empire.

C'est là le legs du régime impérial.

Il ne se mesure pas en kilomètres de voies ferrées, en tonnes d'acier, en traités de libre-échange, en longueurs de boulevards tracés à Paris.

L'héritage de Napoléon III, cette honte qu'il a inoculée à la nation, s'appelle la débâcle, la défaite, la reddition du maréchal Bazaine, l'occupation du pays, l'entrée des troupes prussiennes dans Paris, la proclamation de l'Empire allemand dans la galerie des Glaces, à Versailles, le 18 janvier 1871.

Le roi de Prusse devient, par le génie politique de son chancelier de fer, Bismarck, l'empereur Guillaume. Et c'est comme si la botte d'un uhlan écrasait la gorge des patriotes français.

Ils songeront à la revanche, à leurs deux « enfants », l'Alsace et la Lorraine, livrées aux Prussiens en dépit des protestations des députés de ces deux provinces.

Et cette peste, cette guerre perdue, cette suspicion entre les peuples français et allemand, l'un voulant effacer la honte de la défaite et recouvrer Strasbourg, l'autre soucieux d'empêcher ce réveil français, la haine mêlée de fascination qui les unit, ne pouvaient que créer les conditions psychologiques d'une nouvelle guerre. Puis, elle-même, en générer une autre !

Bel héritage que celui de Napoléon III !

Et, comme si cela ne suffisait pas, la guerre contre les Prussiens nourrit la guerre civile.

Le parti de l'Ordre, même s'il fait mine, après Sedan et le siège de Paris, de vouloir poursuivre la guerre, songe d'abord à conclure au plus vite l'armistice puis la paix avec Bismarck.

Les Thiers, les Jules Favre, les Jules Ferry, les notables du parti de l'Ordre et, derrière eux, l'immense majorité des Français craignent que de la prolongation de la guerre ne jaillisse la révolution parisienne.

Alors, même si Gambetta réussit à quitter Paris en ballon, à rejoindre Tours et à constituer sur la Loire une armée de 600 000 hommes, même si des généraux comme Chanzy et Bourbaki, des officiers valeureux comme Denfert-Rochereau ou Rossel, se battent vaillamment et remportent quelques victoires, la guerre est perdue.

Jules Favre rencontre Bismarck dès le 15 septembre 1870. Les républicains, les révolutionnaires, les patriotes, rêvent encore de mener la lutte jusqu'au bout, de « chasser l'envahisseur » ; ils en appellent aux souvenirs des armées révolutionnaires. Victor Hugo, septuagénaire, veut s'engager, exalte les combats des « partisans et francs-tireurs ». Mais ces irréductibles sont minoritaires.

Toutes les consultations électorales pour approuver les mesures gouvernementales – le 3 novembre 1870, à Paris, 550 000 voix pour, 68 000 contre, puis dans toute la France, le 8 février 1871, donnent une majorité écrasante en faveur de la paix à n'importe quel prix : cinq milliards de francs-or pour les Prussiens et, par surcroît, l'Alsace et la moitié de la Lorraine.

L'Assemblée qui se réunit à Bordeaux en février 1871 est l'expression de ce désir d'ordre et de paix, mais aussi de cette haine contre les révolutionnaires parisiens, cette minorité qui crée une Commune de Paris, un Comité de salut public, qui, le 18 mars 1871, quand on veut lui reprendre les canons qu'elle a payés, se rebelle – et les soldats rejoignent les insurgés, et l'on fusille deux généraux dont l'un avait participé à la répression des journées de juin 1848 !

Car, de manière inextricable, le passé se noue au présent, et ce nœud emprisonne l'avenir.

Les « communards » de 1871 sont les jeunes gens de 1848, vaincus, censurés, marginalisés durant tout l'Empire.

C'est long, vingt ans à subir un régime arrogant, soutenu par des majorités plébiscitaires, vainqueur jusqu'au bout, avant, « divine surprise », de s'effondrer tout à coup comme une statue de plâtre.

Ce sont ces jeunes gens devenus des hommes de quarante ou cinquante ans qui manifestent, imposent la proclamation de la république, puis s'arment dans Paris parce que la Révolution c'est Valmy, et qu'ils veulent donc défendre Paris contre les Prussiens.

Pour ces hommes-là, sonne l'heure de leur grande bataille, l'épreuve décisive, la chance à saisir.

À l'enthousiasme se mêle chez eux l'angoisse, car ils sont divisés. Ils savent qu'ils ne sont qu'une minorité, que le pays ne les suit pas, que les quartiers ouest de Paris se sont vidés de leurs habitants, que les Prussiens ont libéré des prisonniers afin qu'ils rallient l'armée hier impériale, aujourd'hui « républicaine », mais ce sont toujours les mêmes officiers qui commandent – bonapartistes ou monarchistes, soldats de l'ordre qui, vaincus par les Prussiens, veulent écraser ces révolutionnaires, ces républicains.

Entre la République et la reddition aux Prussiens, le maréchal Bazaine, à Metz, choisit de déposer les armes.

Ainsi se creuse le fossé entre les révolutionnaires, les républicains patriotes et l'armée. Et, réciproquement, l'armée ne se sent pas républicaine : quand elle entrera dans Paris, le 21 mai 1871, elle fusillera ces insurgés, ces communards.

Trente mille morts. Des milliers de déportés en Guyane ou en Nouvelle-Calédonie. Pour cette fraction minoritaire du peuple, déjà soupçonneuse envers la République fusilleuse de juin 1848, la conviction s'affirme qu'il n'y a rien à attendre de ce régime-là, pas plus que d'un autre.

L'idée s'enracine que les régimes politiques, quelle que soit leur dénomination, monarchie, empire, république, ne sont que des « dictatures ».

Alors, pourquoi ne pas imposer la dictature du prolétariat pour remplacer la dictature militaire, celle des aristocrates ou des notables ?

On mesure ce qui germe dans cette « guerre civile » du printemps 1871 – la qualification est de Karl Marx, qui publie *La Guerre civile en France* –, et comment la violence des combats dans Paris – exécution d'otages par les communards qui incendient les Tuileries, l'Hôtel de Ville, répression sauvage par les troupes, tout cela sous l'œil des Prussiens – crée des divisions politiques profondes, des cicatrices qui marqueront longtemps l'âme de la France.

L'on s'accusera mutuellement de barbarie, de faire le jeu du Prussien, et toutes les oppositions anciennes – monarchistes contre républicains, patriotes contre « parti de l'étranger » – sont confirmées par cette impitoyable « guerre civile » qui voit Paris perdre au terme des combats, en mai, 80 000 de ses habitants.

Cet événement devient une référence pour confirmer les accusations réciproques. Il est un mythe que l'on exalte, comme un modèle à suivre, avec ses rituels – ainsi le défilé au mur des Fédérés, chaque 28 mai.

Il est la preuve de l'horreur et de la barbarie dont sont capables et coupables ces « rouges » qui ont tenté d'incendier Paris.

La Commune s'inscrit dans la longue série des « guerres civiles » françaises – guerres de Religion, Révolution avec ses massacres de Septembre, la Vendée, la guillotine, les terreurs jacobine ou blanche, les journées révolutionnaires et les révolutions de 1830 et de 1848 qui en sont l'écho, les journées de juin – dont le souvenir réverbéré rend difficile toute politique apaisée.

Avec de telles références mythiques, le jeu démocratique aura du mal à être considéré comme possible, comme le but à atteindre.

Les oppositions sont d'autant plus marquées que le parti de l'Ordre s'inscrit lui aussi dans une histoire longue.

Thiers, qui est désigné par les élections du 8 février 1871 « chef du pouvoir exécutif du Gouvernement provisoire de la République », a été l'un des ministres de Louis-Philippe. En février 1848, il a conseillé que l'on évacue Paris, abandonnant la capitale à l'émeute pour la reconquérir systématiquement et en finir avec les révolutionnaires. Puis il a été le mentor de Louis Napoléon, qu'il a cru pouvoir mener à sa guise et qu'il a fait élire président de la République en 1848.

En 1871, face à la Commune, Thiers applique son plan de 1848 avec une détermination cynique. L'Assemblée s'installe à Versailles pour bien marquer ses intentions : Paris doit être soumis à un pouvoir qui, symboliquement, siège là où le peuple parisien avait imposé sa loi à Louis XVI et à Marie-Antoinette dès octobre 1789.

En 1871, c'est la revanche de Versailles : versaillais contre communards, province contre Paris, l'armée fidèle contre les émeutiers, parti de l'Ordre contre révolutionnaires.

Et le pays dans sa majorité soutient l'entreprise de Thiers.

Il faut extirper les rouges de l'histoire nationale en les fusillant, en les déportant.

Au terme de la Semaine sanglante, le 28 mai 1871, le mouvement révolutionnaire est brisé pour une vingtaine d'années.

La France des épargnants fait confiance à Thiers.

Les emprunts lancés pour verser aux Prussiens les cinq milliards de francs-or prévus par le traité de paix signé à Francfort le 10 mai 1871 sont largement couverts.

La France est riche.

Les troupes prussiennes évacueront le pays à compter du 15 mars 1873. Thiers est le « libérateur du territoire ».

La France est calme.

Elle est prête à accepter une monarchie constitutionnelle. Mais alors que la majorité de l'Assemblée est monarchiste, les deux branches de la dynastie – la branche aînée, légitimiste, avec le comte de Chambord ; la branche cadette, orléaniste, avec le comte de Paris – ne peuvent s'entendre.

Le pays « entre ainsi dans la République à reculons ».

Thiers est élu président de la République le 31 août 1871. Mais les institutions ne sont pas fixées. Et lorsque, constatant la division des monarchistes, Thiers se rallie à la République en précisant : « La République sera conservatrice ou ne sera pas », la majorité monarchiste l'écarte, le 24 mai 1873, préférant élire comme nouveau président de la République le maréchal de Mac-Mahon, l'un des chefs de l'armée impériale, l'un des vaincus de la guerre de 1870, l'un des responsables de la débâcle !

Mais le mérite de Mac-Mahon est de n'être pas républicain. L'Assemblée peut donc, puisque le comte de Chambord refuse de renoncer au drapeau blanc, ce symbole de l'Ancien Régime, voter la loi qui fixe à sept ans la durée du mandat du président de la République, en espérant que ce délai sera suffisant pour que les prétendants monarchistes se réconcilient, acceptent les principes d'une monarchie constitutionnelle et le drapeau tricolore qui en est l'expression.

L'entente ne se fera pas, et, le 29 janvier 1875, l'amendement du député Wallon est voté à une voix de majorité, introduisant donc le mot « république » dans les lois constitutionnelles.

C'est ainsi, au terme d'un compromis entre républicains modérés – Jules Grévy, Jules Ferry – et monarchistes constitutionnels, que la République s'installe presque subrepticement.

Avec son Sénat, contrepoids conservateur à la Chambre des députés, son président qui ne peut rien sans l'accord du président du Conseil des ministres responsable devant les Chambres, la République est parlementaire.

Mais ces lois constitutionnelles peuvent aussi bien servir de socle à une monarchie constitutionnelle qu'à une république conservatrice.

L'âme de la France blessée, gorgée de mythes du passé, a vécu durant les deux premiers tiers du XIXᵉ siècle des alternances chaotiques entre les régimes, les brisant l'un après l'autre par le biais des révolutions ou à l'occasion d'une défaite devant les armées étrangères.

Révolution et débâcle, guerre civile et pouvoir dictatorial, se sont ainsi succédé.

Mais les passions politiques ont de moins en moins concerné la majorité du pays.

La nation a appris à user du suffrage universel. À chaque fois, elle a voté pour l'ordre – fût-il impérial –, pour la paix, pour le respect des propriétés.

Les journées révolutionnaires ont certes occupé le devant de la scène. Elles ont constitué l'imaginaire national. Elles font partie du rituel français. Elles sont célébrées par une minorité qui veut croire que le pays la suit. Pourtant, dans sa profondeur et sa majorité, le peuple choisit la modération, même s'il écoute avec intérêt et peut même applaudir, un temps, les discours extrêmes, les utopies qui se nourrissent de la sève nationale.

Même si, rituellement, chaque année, les cortèges couronnés de drapeaux rouges célèbrent, au mur des Fédérés du cimetière du Père-Lachaise, la mémoire des insurgés du printemps 1871, les institutions de la IIIᵉ République, nées de la débâcle et du massacre des communards, expriment le choix de la modération.

53.

En 1875, rien n'est encore définitivement acquis pour la République.

Elle n'est qu'un mot dans les lois constitutionnelles.

Ce mot peut en devenir la clé de voûte ou bien être remplacé par cette monarchie constitutionnelle qui est le régime de prédilection de la majorité des députés et du président de la République, Mac-Mahon.

Ils attendent l'union des héritiers de la monarchie. Ils s'emploient à faire régner dans le pays l'« ordre moral », à leurs yeux condition indispensable de l'ordre public et de la préservation des traditions, si nécessaire à une restauration monarchique.

C'est encore un moment important pour l'âme de la France. On la voue au Sacré-Cœur. On construit, pour expier les crimes de la Commune, la basilique du Sacré-Cœur, sur la butte Montmartre. On fait repentance. On multiplie les processions, les messes d'expiation. Et l'on ravive ainsi, en réaction, l'esprit des Lumières.

L'ancienne et profonde fracture qui, au cours des décennies, avait séparé les Français en défenseurs de l'Église et en libertins, esprits forts, laïques et déistes, redevient une césure majeure.

« Le cléricalisme, voilà l'ennemi ! » s'écrit Gambetta.

C'est un combat passionnel qui s'engage et qui sert de ligne de front entre monarchistes et républicains.

D'un côté les cléricaux, de l'autre, les anticléricaux.

La France croit se donner ainsi une vraie division qui est en même temps un leurre. Car elle dissimule l'entente profonde qui existe entre les « modérés » que sont les monarchistes constitutionnels et les notables républicains.

Tout les rapproche : la même crainte du désordre, le même refus de remettre en cause la propriété et l'organisation sociale, le même souci d'éradiquer les révolutionnaires, les socialistes, et de se garder de ces « républicains avancés » à la Gambetta qui veulent obtenir l'amnistie pour les communards condamnés ou en exil.

Lorsque Jules Ferry déclare : « Mon but est d'organiser l'humanité sans Dieu et sans roi » (« Mais non sans patron... », commentera Jaurès), il marque ce qui l'oppose aux cléricaux. Mais lorsqu'il dit, évoquant la répression versaillaise de la Commune : « Je les ai vues, les représailles du soldat vengeur, du paysan châtiant en bon ordre. Libéral, juriste, républicain, j'ai vu ces choses et je me suis incliné comme si j'apercevais l'épée de l'Archange », il est en « communion » avec le parti de l'Ordre.

Rien, sur ce point-là comme sur les orientations économiques et sociales, ne l'en sépare.

Et il en va de même de Jules Grévy, de Jules Favre ou de Jules Simon, qui déclare : « Je suis profondément républicain et profondément conservateur. »

Il faut donc, pour souligner l'opposition qui sépare républicains et monarchistes, choisir ce terrain du rapport entre l'État et l'Église.

Ce qui unira les républicains, de Jules Simon à Gambetta, et même aux communards, c'est l'anticléricalisme.

Cette posture – cette idéologie – a l'avantage de laisser dans l'ombre des divergences qui opposent les républicains « avancés », devenant peu à peu socialistes, et les républicains conservateurs.

L'alliance entre tous les républicains sur la base de l'anticléricalisme est d'autant plus aisée que la répression versaillaise a décapité pour une longue durée le mouvement ouvrier et le mouvement social.

Les « notables », monarchistes ou républicains, peuvent se défier sans craindre qu'un troisième joueur ne vienne troubler leur partie en parlant salaires, durée du travail, organisation sociale, égalité...

C'est ainsi que, assurés du maintien de l'ordre, les modérés peuvent glisser peu à peu vers une République dont ils savent qu'hormis le thème de l'anticléricalisme elle sera conservatrice dans ses institutions et dans sa politique économique et sociale.

Surtout, ces adeptes d'un régime « constitutionnel » qui veulent à tout prix le maintien de l'ordre peuvent désormais – c'est une grande novation dans l'histoire de la nation – régler leurs différends politiques sur le terrain parlementaire.

Alors que, depuis un siècle, c'est l'émeute, la révolution, le coup d'État, la journée révolutionnaire, les « semaines sanglantes », la violence, la terreur, la répression, qui départagent les adversaires politiques, c'est maintenant dans l'enceinte des Chambres (celle des députés et le Sénat) et par le recours au suffrage universel que s'évalue le rapport des forces.

Il a donc fallu près d'un siècle (1789-1880) pour que le parlementarisme l'emporte enfin en France.

Et c'est une dernière crise – frôlant les limites de la légalité institutionnelle – qui permet la victoire parlementaire de la République.

Mac-Mahon a, en effet, imposé à une Chambre « républicaine » le duc de Broglie comme président du Conseil.

Ce 16 mai 1877 marque un tournant politique. De Broglie va être contraint de démissionner en novembre. Les 363 députés qui se sont opposés à lui seront réélus après que la Chambre aura été dissoute par Mac-Mahon.

« Il faudra se soumettre ou se démettre », a lancé Gambetta, stigmatisant « ce gouvernement des prêtres, ce ministère des curés ».

Le 30 janvier 1879, quand le Sénat connaîtra à son tour une majorité républicaine, Mac-Mahon démissionnera et sera remplacé par Jules Grévy, républicain modéré.

Le pays, « saigné » par un siècle d'affrontements sanglants, a résolu cette crise dans un cadre où les violences ne sont plus que verbales.

En quelques mois, la IIIe République s'installe.

Jules Ferry, ministre de l'Instruction publique, crée un enseignement laïque, veille à la formation des instituteurs dans ces « séminaires républicains » que sont les écoles normales départementales. Il s'attaque aux congrégations, notamment aux Jésuites.

La République, c'est l'anticléricalisme.

Elle prend des décisions symboliques : les deux Chambres quittent Versailles pour siéger à Paris. Le 14 juillet devient fête nationale à compter de 1880, et *La Marseillaise* sera l'hymne de la nation.

Le 11 juillet 1880, Gambetta incite les députés à voter une loi d'amnistie pour les communards condamnés ou exilés.

« Il faut que vous fermiez le livre de ces dix années, dit-il. Il n'y a qu'une France, et qu'une République ! »

Mais le retour des communards signe aussi le retour de la contestation sociale. Donc celui de visions différentes de la France et de la République.

Sur la scène politique où monarchistes et bonapartistes viennent de quitter les premiers rôles, d'autres acteurs vont faire leur entrée.

54.

En un quart de siècle – 1880-1906 –, un modèle républicain français se constitue.

Des lois fondamentales sont votées, des forces politiques prennent forme, partis et syndicats structurent la vie sociale.

Profondes, les crises sont gérées pacifiquement, même si elles dressent encore les Français les uns contre les autres. La violence est certes présente, mais contenue.

Ainsi se fixent des traits majeurs de l'âme de la France qui se conserveront jusqu'aux années 40 du XXe siècle, au moment où l'« étrange défaite » de 1940, cette autre débâcle, entraînera la chute de la IIIe République et renverra aux pires souvenirs de 1870.

Mais, jusque-là, le bâti qui a été construit entre 1880 et 1906 tient.

D'ailleurs, les hommes politiques qui ont surgi dans les années 1890 occupent encore, pour les plus illustres d'entre eux – Poincaré (1860-1934), Barthou (1862-1934), Briand (1862-1932) –, des fonctions éminentes dans les années 30 du XXe siècle. Philippe Pétain (1856-1951) est un officier déjà quadragénaire en 1900. À cette date, Léon Blum (1872-1950) est un intellectuel d'une trentaine d'années engagé dans les combats de l'affaire Dreyfus. Le journal *L'Humanité* de Jaurès (1859-1914) est créé en 1904.

Pétain couvrira de son nom et de sa gloire de maréchal la capitulation de 1940, et on le qualifiera de nouveau Bazaine.

En 1936, Léon Blum sera le président du Conseil du Front populaire, et *L'Humanité*, le quotidien emblématique des communistes.

C'est dire que la IIIe République a su traverser le traumatisme de la Première Guerre mondiale (1914-1918), et, dans l'apparente continuité des institutions et des hommes, « digérer » les bouleversements des premières décennies du xxe siècle.

La Russie, l'Italie, l'Allemagne et l'Espagne sont submergées par le communisme, le fascisme, le nazisme, le franquisme. La France républicaine, elle, résiste aux révolutions et aux contre-révolutions.

Comme si elle était sortie définitivement, pour les avoir vécus jusqu'aux années 1870, de ces temps de guerre civile, et qu'elle avait construit au tournant du siècle, entre 1880 et 1906, un modèle adapté enfin à la nation.

On le constate en examinant les lois proposées par les républicains modérés. Elles sont à leur image – prudentes –, mais elles définissent les libertés républicaines, qui concernent aussi bien le droit de réunion, d'association, de création de syndicats, de publication, que l'élection des maires, mais aussi le droit au divorce.

Ces lois votées entre 1881 et 1884 expriment à la fois la résolution et l'opportunisme de leurs initiateurs. Elles créent un « État de droit ».

Elles sont l'affirmation d'une démocratie parlementaire qui suit une voie moyenne, « modérée ».

De ce fait, Gambetta est écarté après un court et grand ministère d'une dizaine de semaines (novembre 1881-janvier 1882). L'homme est considéré comme trop « avancé », à l'écoute des couches populaires. Son échec comme président du Conseil, alors qu'il est le « leader » le plus prestigieux des républicains, qu'il a animé les campagnes contre le second Empire, puis Mac-Mahon, est révélateur d'un trait du fonctionnement politique de cette IIIe République.

Puisque le président de la République, quelle que soit son influence, se tient en retrait dans une fonction de représentation et d'arbitrage, l'exécutif est dans la dépendance des majorités parlementaires. Celles-ci varient au gré des circonstances et des ambitions individuelles qui, déplaçant quelques dizaines de voix, font ainsi « tomber » les gouvernements.

Cette faiblesse de l'exécutif, cette instabilité ministérielle, seront, dès les origines, une tare du régime républicain, qui le caractérisera jusqu'à sa fin, en 1940. Si un gouvernement veut « durer », il doit « composer ».

Un Jules Ferry le dira clairement : « Le gouvernement est résolu à observer une méthode politique et parlementaire qui consiste à ne pas aborder toutes les questions à la fois, à limiter le champ des réformes..., à écarter les questions irritantes. »

Cependant, Ferry est l'un des initiateurs majeurs de ce « modèle républicain ».

Ses lois scolaires (1882-1886) introduisent la laïcité aux côtés de l'obligation et de la gratuité de l'instruction publique.

Elles créent un enseignement féminin.

Jules Ferry est ainsi celui qui, avec lucidité et conviction, veut arracher les citoyens à l'emprise cléricale identifiée à la cause monarchiste.

Cette « laïcité » déborde le domaine scolaire en devenant, à partir de 1901, le grand thème républicain.

Des lois sur les associations visent les congrégations enseignantes, puis imposent l'inventaire des biens de l'Église.

On débouche ainsi sur la loi capitale de séparation des Églises et de l'État en 1905. Ses deux premiers articles précisent que la République garantit la liberté de conscience et qu'elle « ne reconnaît, ne salarie ni ne subventionne aucun culte ».

Cette « séparation » crée une « exception française ». Elle définit la République.

Elle a été voulue par des forces politiques nouvelles – radicaux, socialistes (son rapporteur est Aristide Briand) –, des courants de pensée – franc-maçonnerie du Grand Orient de France, farouchement anticlérical et vigoureusement athée depuis 1877 ; protestantisme.

Hostile à tout « ralliement » des catholiques à la République, l'attitude de la papauté a conféré à cette législation laïque le caractère d'une politique de « défense républicaine ».

La laïcité, disent Jean Jaurès et Émile Combes (1835-1921, ancien séminariste), est une manière de « républicaniser la République ». « Le parti républicain a le sentiment du danger. Il a perçu […] que la congrégation s'était accordée avec le militarisme. Il exige qu'il soit agi contre elle. »

Car la République, en ces années 1880-1906, se sent en effet menacée.

Dans ses profondeurs, le pays reste rural et modéré. Le nouveau régime ne s'y enracine que lentement.

L'élection des maires, le rôle des instituteurs (les « hussards noirs de la République »), l'action des notables laïques « libres penseurs », opposés au curé, à l'aristocrate, au grand propriétaire, au milieu clérical, favorisent le développement de l'esprit républicain.

L'école laïque gratuite et obligatoire enseigne un « catéchisme républicain » qui redessine les contours de l'histoire officielle.

Il est relayé par les symboles et rituels républicains : *La Marseillaise*, le 14 Juillet, Marianne...

Mais le fonctionnement politique du régime – l'instabilité ministérielle, la corruption, les scandales (celui du canal de Panama, dans lequel des députés sont compromis : la « plus grande flibusterie du siècle ») – crée des foyers de troubles.

Nostalgie du militaire providentiel : le général Boulanger, « brave général », « général revanche », un temps ministre de la Guerre (1887), soutenu par la Ligue des patriotes de Paul Déroulède, est tenté de prendre le pouvoir. Ce n'est qu'un rêve vite brisé.

Un courant anarchiste se dresse contre la « société bourgeoise », contre l'État, veut mener une « guerre sans pitié » contre cette société injuste. Une vague d'attentats – la « propagande par le fait », à savoir des actes de délinquance comme la « reprise individuelle » – culmine avec l'assassinat, en 1894, du président de la République Sadi Carnot par l'anarchiste Caserio.

La guillotine fonctionne.

La police, qui manipule parfois ces anarchistes de manière à déconsidérer toute protestation sociale, contrôle en fait cette poussée qui ne met pas le régime en péril.

Derrière l'autosatisfaction des « notables » républicains et les « frous-frous » de la « Belle Époque », ces troubles n'en révèlent pas moins l'existence d'une question sociale, de plus en plus présente.

Des syndicats se créent par branches professionnelles. La CGT, née en 1895, les regroupe.

En 1906, au congrès d'Amiens, elle adopte une charte « anarcho-syndicaliste ». La charte d'Amiens préconise la grève générale, affirme la volonté d'en finir un jour avec le patronat et le salariat. Dans le même temps, cette confédération veut rester « indépendante des partis et des sectes qui, en dehors et à côté, peuvent poursuivre en toute liberté la transformation sociale ».

Cette radicalité syndicale et ce souci d'autonomie sont d'abord le reflet de la violence de la répression qui frappe les ouvriers grévistes à Anzin (1884), à Fourmies (1899-1901), à Courrières (1906) après un accident minier qui a fait 1 100 morts. Clemenceau (1841-1929), ministre de l'Intérieur, « premier flic de France », fait donner la troupe qui ouvre le feu, et qui, le 1er mai 1906, met en état de siège la capitale, où toute manifestation est interdite.

Face aux socialistes et aux revendications ouvrières, un bloc républicain s'est constitué ; il regroupe les radicaux-socialistes (Clemenceau), les modérés (Poincaré, Barthou). Il s'oppose aux socialistes (leur premier congrès a lieu en 1879). Ceux-ci s'unifieront dans la Section française de l'Internationale ouvrière (SFIO) en 1905.

Il y a là, en fait, deux conceptions de la République qui s'opposent. Cet affrontement est symbolisé par le débat qui met face à face, à la Chambre des députés, en avril 1906, le radical Clemenceau et le socialiste Jaurès.

Jaurès dénonce l'inégalité, dépose une proposition de loi sur la transformation de la propriété individuelle en propriété collective.

Clemenceau voit dans le socialisme une rêverie prophétique et choisit « contre vous, Jaurès, la justice et le libre développement de l'individu. Voilà le programme que j'oppose à votre collectivisme ! »

En fait, pour importants qu'ils soient et pour majeurs que soient les enjeux qu'ils sous-tendent, ces débats ne mobilisent pas les grandes masses du pays. Elles s'expriment néanmoins dans le cadre du suffrage universel.

Le nombre des électeurs qui votent pour le Parti socialiste augmente ainsi lentement.

Mais ce parti, comme les syndicats ou comme le Parti radical, ne compte que peu d'adhérents. Le citoyen est individualiste et sceptique. Il accepte le système politique en place. Ceux qui le contestent autrement que dans les urnes ne sont qu'une minorité.

La République « intègre » : en 1899, Millerand devient le premier socialiste à accéder à un ministère, et Jaurès soutient ce gouvernement Waldeck-Rousseau « de défense républicaine », bien que le ministre de la Guerre y soit le général de Galliffet, l'un des « fusilleurs » des communards.

Maurice Barrès (1862-1923), écrivain et député nationaliste, avait écrit à propos du ministère Jules Ferry : « Il donne à ses amis, à son parti, une série d'expédients pour qu'ils demeurent en apparence fidèles à leurs engagements et paraissent s'en acquitter, cependant qu'ils se rangent du côté des forces organisées et deviennent des conservateurs. »

Tel sera le chemin suivi par Alexandre Millerand ou Aristide Briand, tous deux socialistes, puis ministres « républicains » et cessant, du coup, d'agir en socialistes.

Produit d'une longue histoire « révolutionnaire », la IIIᵉ République a construit entre 1880 et 1906 un système représentatif imparfait, contesté, mais capable de résister, dès lors qu'il sent sa politique républicaine modérée menacée soit par l'Église (et ce sont les lois laïques), soit par l'anarchisme et le socialisme (et c'est la répression), soit par le « militarisme », et ce seront les combats contre le général Boulanger ou pour la défense de l'innocent capitaine Alfred Dreyfus.

Par l'ampleur qu'elle prend de 1894 à 1906 – de la condamnation du capitaine pour espionnage à sa réhabilitation complète et à sa réintégration dans l'armée –, l'affaire Dreyfus est significative des divisions de l'âme de la France en cette fin de siècle.

Car la culpabilité de Dreyfus est dans un premier temps acceptée : seuls quelques proches la contestent.

Cela reflète d'abord la confiance que l'on porte à l'autorité militaire, liée à la volonté de revanche. Personne ne doute que l'Allemagne ne soit l'ennemi, capable de toutes les vilenies.

Ensuite, la vigueur de l'antisémitisme donne un crédit supplémentaire à la culpabilité de Dreyfus, Alsacien d'origine juive.

Cet antisémitisme ne touche pas seulement les milieux conservateurs qui condamnent le « peuple déicide » dans la tradition de l'antisémitisme chrétien. Il existe aussi un antisémitisme « populaire », républicain, socialiste, anticapitaliste. On répète les thèses de Toussenel exposées dans son livre *Les Juifs, rois de l'époque, histoire de la féodalité financière*. Juif, usurier et trafiquant sont « pour lui synonymes ».

Le livre d'Édouard Drumont (1844-1917), *La France juive*, rencontre un large écho, tout comme son journal, *La Libre Parole*, lancé en 1892. La presse catholique – *La Croix, Le Pèlerin* – reprend quotidiennement ces thèmes.

On mesure la difficulté qu'il y a à obtenir une révision du procès d'Alfred Dreyfus.

On se heurte à l'antisémitisme.

On est accusé d'affaiblir l'armée, donc, d'une certaine manière, de prendre parti pour l'Allemagne.

Dans ces conditions, le rôle d'un Clemenceau, d'un Péguy (1873-1914), d'un Jaurès, des intellectuels – le terme apparaît à l'époque –, de la Ligue des droits de l'homme qu'ils constituent, est déterminant.

C'est dans *L'Aurore* de Clemenceau que, le 14 janvier 1898, Zola, au faîte de sa gloire, publie son « J'accuse » : « Je n'ai qu'une seule passion, celle de la lumière... La vérité est en marche, rien ne l'arrêtera ! »

Le pays se divise en dreyfusards et antidreyfusards.

Les corps constitués, les monarchistes, les catholiques, les ligues – des patriotes, de la patrie française –, la France antirépublicaine, sont hostiles à la révision.

Les républicains avancés, les « professeurs », les socialistes – après avoir longtemps hésité : Dreyfus n'est-il pas un « bourgeois » ? – en sont partisans.

Cette bataille qui prend l'opinion à témoin, qui pousse les « intellectuels », les écrivains, à s'engager – Barrès contre Zola –, ces valeurs de vérité et de justice désormais considérées comme plus importantes que la « raison d'État », font de l'affaire Dreyfus un événement exemplaire témoignant qu'il y a bien une « exception française ».

La justice ne doit pas s'incliner devant l'armée.

Les valeurs de vérité et le respect des droits de l'homme sont supérieurs aux intérêts de l'État dès lors que celui-ci viole les principes.

Il est capital pour l'âme de la France qu'à la fin d'un combat de plus de dix ans les dreyfusards l'emportent.

Les « valeurs » s'inscrivent ainsi victorieusement au cœur du patriotisme républicain qui s'oppose à un nationalisme arc-bouté sur une vision sincère mais étroite des intérêts de l'État.

En ce sens, l'affaire Dreyfus prolonge la tradition qui avait vu Voltaire prendre parti pour Calas et le chevalier de La Barre contre les autorités cléricales et royales.

L'esprit républicain qui l'a emporté au terme de l'affaire Dreyfus va s'affirmer tout au long du XXᵉ siècle avec le rôle combiné des intellectuels et de la Ligue des droits de l'homme (40 000 adhérents en 1906).

Mais ce sont davantage des personnalités extérieures à la société politique qui se sont engagées. Pour un Jaurès, que de silences prudents !

Quant au pays provincial et rural, aux notables locaux, ils ont été bien moins concernés par l'« Affaire » que les milieux parisiens. Les élections de 1898 changent peu la composition de l'Assemblée : Jaurès, dreyfusard, soutien de Zola, est battu.

Le souci de ne point affaiblir l'armée, dans la perspective d'une future confrontation avec l'Allemagne, en proclamant qu'elle a failli, intervient sans doute dans la réticence d'une large partie de l'opinion.

Ce qui tendrait à montrer qu'au fond les Français, qu'ils soient dreyfusards ou antidreyfusards, républicains ou ennemis de la « Gueuse », sont d'abord des patriotes, les uns privilégiant les valeurs des droits de l'homme identifiées à la République, les autres, la tradition étatique, certes, mais patriotique elle aussi.

À l'heure où, par l'alliance franco-russe (1893) et par le maintien, malgré des différends coloniaux, de bons rapports avec le Royaume-Uni, les gouvernements successifs préparent la « revanche », il est vital que la IIIe République soit capable de susciter, malgré les fractures de l'opinion, une « union patriotique ».

5

L'UNION SACRÉE

1907-1920

55.

De 1907 à 1914, la France marche vers l'abîme de la guerre en titubant.

D'un côté, elle semble décidée à l'affrontement avec l'Allemagne de Guillaume II afin de prendre sa revanche et de récupérer l'Alsace et la Lorraine tout en effaçant le souvenir humiliant de Sedan et de la débâcle de 1870.

Dans les milieux littéraires parisiens, après la réhabilitation de Dreyfus en juillet 1906, et comme pour affirmer que l'on continue à avoir confiance dans l'armée, on constate un renouveau du nationalisme et du militarisme.

Barrès, Maurras (1868-1952), mais aussi Péguy, l'ancien dreyfusard, chantent les vertus de la guerre : « C'est dans la guerre que tout se refait ; la guerre n'est pas une bête cruelle et haïssable, c'est du sport vrai, tout simplement », va-t-on répétant.

On vante la « race française », catholique, on se dit prêt au sacrifice, on institue la célébration nationale de Jeanne d'Arc.

On manifeste. On conspue les pacifistes, les socialistes, ce « Herr Jaurès qui ne vaut pas les douze balles du peloton d'exécution, une corde à fourrage suffira »...

En janvier 1913, une coalition rassemblant des élus traditiona-listes (monarchistes), des républicains modérés, des radicaux-socialistes, élit Raymond Poincaré, le Lorrain, incarnation de l'esprit de revanche, président de la République.

Les diplomates et les militaires, qui échappent de fait au contrôle parlementaire, trouvent ainsi au sommet de l'État un appui déterminé. Ils font de la France la clé de voûte de la Triple-Entente entre Royaume-Uni, France et Russie.

Elle n'a pas été ébranlée par la défaite de la Russie face au Japon, en 1905, ni par la révolution qui a suivi. Elle souscrit des emprunts russes à hauteur de plusieurs milliards de francs-or. Elle appuie le tsar, qui tente de moderniser son pays sur les plans économique et politique.

Elle ne tient aucun compte de l'agitation « bolchevique » qui se déclare hostile à la guerre contre l'Allemagne et qui, à cette « guerre entre impérialismes », oppose le « défaitisme révolu-tionnaire ».

Dans cette préparation à la guerre, le haut état-major français obtient le vote d'une loi portant le service militaire à trois ans (avril 1913) pour faire face à une armée allemande plus nom-breuse, la France ne comptant que quarante millions d'habitants et l'Allemagne, soixante.

Mais ces signes, ces décisions, les initiatives françaises prises au Maroc pour y instaurer un protectorat auquel l'Allemagne est hostile, et qui manifestent une volonté d'affrontement, le choix délibéré du risque de guerre, sont contredits par d'autres atti-tudes.

C'est comme si, à tous les niveaux de la vie nationale, le pays était divisé.

D'abord, les conflits sociaux se durcissent : la troupe inter-vient à Draveil en 1908 et tire sur les cheminots grévistes.

En 1909, les électriciens plongent Paris dans l'obscurité.

Ministre de l'Intérieur, puis président du Conseil, Clemen-ceau réagit durement face à ce syndicalisme révolutionnaire qui paralyse les chemins de fer cependant que les inscrits maritimes bloquent les ports.

Opposés à la troupe dans ces conflits sociaux, les ouvriers développent un antimilitarisme radical, cependant qu'en 1907 les viticulteurs ruinés par le phylloxéra réussissent à gagner à leur cause des soldats du 17e régiment d'infanterie, qui se mutinent : « Vous auriez, en tirant sur nous, assassiné la République. »

Ces incidents semblent miner la cohésion nationale indispensable à une entrée en guerre.

Les socialistes sont gagnés par ce climat. Ils prônent dans leurs congrès la « grève générale » pour s'opposer à la guerre.

« Prolétaires de tous les pays, unissez vous ! » scande-t-on.

Cette poussée verbalement révolutionnaire fait contrepoids, en même temps qu'elle le renforce, au courant nationaliste et belliciste.

De là ces appels au meurtre lancés contre Jaurès, le pacifiste, membre de l'Internationale socialiste, qui déclare à Bâle en juin 1912 : « Pour empêcher la guerre, il faudra toute l'action concordante du prolétariat mondial. »

Il rêve de préparer une grève générale « préventive » pour dissuader les gouvernements de se lancer dans un nouveau conflit.

Jaurès sous-estime ainsi la logique mécanique des blocs – à la Triple-Entente s'oppose la Triple-Alliance (Allemagne, Autriche-Hongrie, Italie). Il ne mesure pas l'engrenage des mesures militaires, les décisions d'un état-major entraînant la réplique d'un autre, et, une fois les mobilisations commencées, comment freiner un mouvement lancé, doté d'une puissante force d'inertie ?

En outre, Jaurès ne perçoit pas que des groupes marginaux – ainsi les nationalistes serbes –, des États « archaïques » – dans les Balkans, mais la Russie est aussi l'un d'eux –, peuvent, par leurs initiatives échappant à tout contrôle, déclencher des incidents qui entraîneront dans un conflit régional les grands blocs alliés, lesquels, par leur intervention, généraliseront le conflit.

En fait, en ces années cruciales durant lesquelles se jouent le sort de la paix et le destin de la France, le système politique de la IIIe République révèle ses limites. Car il ne s'agit plus seulement de constituer un gouvernement, de voter des lois, de trouver une issue à telle ou telle affaire intérieure – affaire Dreyfus ou scandale de Panama –, mais bien de prendre des décisions qui engagent la France sur le plan international.

Ici, le rôle du président de la République, celui du ministère des Affaires étrangères et du ministère de la Guerre, échappent en partie au contrôle parlementaire.

De plus, la grande presse – *Le Matin, Le Petit Parisien* – pèse sur l'opinion et influe donc sur le choix des députés, qui ne respectent pas les accords passés entre leurs partis.

On perçoit aussi un fossé entre les manœuvres et rivalités politiciennes des leaders parlementaires – Clemenceau est le rival de Poincaré, celui-ci, l'adversaire de Joseph Caillaux (1863-1944) et de Jaurès – et la gravité des problèmes qui se posent aux gouvernements alors que s'avivent les tensions internationales.

C'est le cas entre le Royaume-Uni et l'Allemagne à propos de la question de leurs flottes de guerre respectives ; entre la France et l'Allemagne sur la question du Maroc ; entre l'Autriche-Hongrie, liée à l'Allemagne dans le cadre de la Triple-Alliance, et la Serbie, soutenue par la Russie, orthodoxe comme elle, une Russie qui est l'alliée de la France dans le cadre de la Triple-Entente.

Une République dont l'exécutif est ainsi soumis aux combinaisons parlementaires peut-elle conduire une grande politique extérieure alors que le chef de son gouvernement est menacé à tout instant de perdre sa majorité ?

Cette interrogation se pose dès les années 1907-1914, qui comportent deux séquences électorales : en 1910 et en 1914.

Au vrai, le problème est structurel : il demeurera, puisqu'il est le produit du système constitutionnel qui a été choisi.

Ce système a une autre conséquence : il facilite l'émergence des médiocres et écarte les personnalités brillantes et vigoureuses.

On l'a vu dès l'origine de la République – en 1882 – avec Gambetta.

Cela se reproduit, à partir de 1910, avec Joseph Caillaux, le leader radical qui, en 1911, a résolu par la négociation une crise avec l'Allemagne à propos du Maroc. Il a accepté des concessions pour éviter ou faire reculer la guerre, ce qui le désigne comme un complice du Kaiser. Caillaux est aussi partisan de la création d'un impôt sur le revenu, refusé par tous les modérés. Il est donc l'homme à ostraciser.

D'autant plus qu'il associe le Parti radical au Parti socialiste de Jaurès en vue des élections de mai 1914. Au cœur de leur programme commun : l'abolition de la loi portant le service militaire à trois ans.

Or c'est cette coalition présentée comme hostile à la défense nationale qui l'emporte, faisant élire 300 députés radicaux et socialistes contre 260 élus du centre et de la droite conservatrice.

Est-ce le socle d'une autre politique étrangère ?

En fait, la France continue de tituber. Les députés radicaux élus ne voteront pas l'abolition de la loi des trois ans, soumis qu'ils sont à la pression de l'« opinion » telle que la reflètent les grands journaux parisiens, eux-mêmes sensibles à la fois aux fonds russes qui les abreuvent et au renouveau nationaliste d'une partie des élites intellectuelles.

Et le président de la République, que le vote de mai 1914 vient de désavouer, n'en continue pas moins de prôner la même politique étrangère. Il agit dans l'ombre pour dissocier les députés radicaux de Caillaux et de Jaurès.

De toute façon, il est bien tard pour changer d'orientation.

Le 28 juin 1914, l'archiduc François-Ferdinand est assassiné à Sarajevo par des nationalistes serbes. La mécanique des alliances commence à jouer.

Les ultimatums et les mobilisations se succèdent.

Le 31 juillet 1914, Jaurès est assassiné.

Le 1er août, la France mobilise.

Le 3, l'Allemagne lui déclare la guerre.

La décision a échappé aux parlementaires, à la masse du pays engagée dans les moissons, avertie seulement par le tocsin et les affiches de mobilisation.

Elle répond sans hésiter à l'appel de rejoindre ses régiments.

Mais des différences apparaissent entre l'enthousiasme guerrier qui soulève, à Paris et dans quelques grandes villes, les partisans de la guerre en des manifestations bruyantes – « À Berlin ! » y crie-t-on – et l'acceptation angoissée des nécessités de la mobilisation par la majorité des Français. Les slogans proférés dans la capitale ne reflètent pas l'état d'âme du reste de la France.

On est partout patriote. On part donc faire la guerre. Mais on n'est pas belliciste.

C'est plutôt la tristesse et l'angoisse qui empoignent la masse des Français.

Ceux qui, pacifistes intransigeants, partisans de la grève générale, s'opposent à la guerre sont une minorité isolée. Le gouvernement n'a pas à sévir contre les révolutionnaires, les syndicalistes, ceux qui hier se déclaraient contre la guerre. Les socialistes s'y rallient.

« Ils ont assassiné Jaurès, nous n'assassinerons pas la France », titre même un journal antimilitariste.

Jules Guesde (1845-1922), le « marxiste » du Parti socialiste, qui accusait Jaurès de modérantisme, devient ministre.

C'est donc l'« union sacrée » de tous les Français.

La République rassemble la nation, condition nécessaire de la victoire.

56.

La Grande Guerre qui commence en 1914 est l'ordalie de la France, et donc de la IIIe République qui la gouverne.

L'épreuve, qu'on prédisait courte, de quelques semaines, va durer cinquante-deux mois.

Le 11 novembre 1918, quand, le jour de l'armistice, on dressera un monument aux victimes, on dénombrera 1 400 000 tués ou disparus (10 % de la population active), 3 millions de blessés, dont 750 000 invalides et 125 000 mutilés.

Sur dix hommes âgés de 25 à 45 ans, on compte deux tués ou disparus, un invalide, trois handicapés.

Si l'on recense les victimes par profession, on relève que la moitié des instituteurs mobilisés – les « hussards noirs de la République », officiers de réserve, ont encadré leurs anciens élèves – ont été tués.

Polytechniciens, normaliens, écrivains – d'Alain-Fournier à Péguy – et surtout paysans et membres des professions libérales ont payé leur tribut à la défense de la patrie.

Durant toute la guerre, une large partie du territoire – le Nord et l'Est –, la plus peuplée, la plus industrielle, a été occupée.

En septembre 1914, la pointe de l'offensive allemande est parvenue à quelques dizaines de kilomètres de Paris, et en août 1918 la dernière attaque ennemie s'est rapprochée à la même distance de la capitale.

Des offensives de quelques jours, lançant les « poilus » en Champagne, au Chemin des Dames (en 1915, en 1917), ont coûté plusieurs centaines de milliers d'hommes.

29 000 meurent chaque mois en 1915 ; 21 000 encore en 1918.

La France a été « saignée », et c'est son meilleur sang – le plus vif, parce que le plus jeune – qui a coulé durant ces cinquante-deux mois.

Qui ne mesure la profondeur de la plaie dans l'âme de la France !

Le corps et l'âme de la nation sont mutilés pour tout le siècle.

Chaque Français a un combattant, ou un tué, ou un gazé, ou un invalide dans sa parentèle.

Chacun, dans les générations suivantes, a croisé, côtoyé un mutilé, une « gueule cassée ».

Chacun, jusqu'aux années 40, a vu défiler des cortèges d'anciens combattants.

Puis d'autres, par suite d'autres guerres, les ont remplacés, et à la fin du XXᵉ siècle il n'y avait plus qu'une dizaine de survivants du grand massacre, de celle qui restait la « grande » guerre et dont on avait espéré qu'elle serait la « der des der ».

Sonder la profondeur de la plaie – toutes ces femmes en noir qui n'ont pas enfanté, qui se sont fanées sous leurs voiles de deuil –, prendre en compte les traumatismes des « pupilles de la nation » et ceux de ces survivants qui pensaient à leurs camarades morts près d'eux, c'est réaliser que la Première Guerre mondiale a été pour plusieurs décennies – au moins jusqu'à la fin des années 40 du XXᵉ siècle – le grand déterminant de l'âme de la France.

À prendre ainsi conscience de l'étendue de la blessure, de la durée de cette épreuve de cinquante-deux mois, on devine que c'est au plus profond de l'« être français » que le peuple des mobilisés et celui de l'arrière ont dû aller puiser pour « tenir ». Et d'autant plus qu'année après année la conduite des opérations militaires n'a pas permis de repousser l'ennemi hors du territoire national.

Dès l'été 1914, sous le commandement de Joffre, le front français est percé. Des unités – en pantalons rouges ! – sont décimées et se débandent.

On fusille sans jugement ceux qu'on accuse d'être des fuyards.

Mais ce ne sera pas l'effondrement. Le pouvoir politique tient. Il quitte Paris pour Bordeaux – sinistre souvenir de 1871 ! –, mais demande aux militaires de défendre Paris.

Et c'est la bataille de la Marne, le front qui se stabilise, les soldats qui s'enterrent dans les tranchées.

La République ne s'est pas effondrée. Il n'y aura pas de débâcle comme en 1870. Nul ne manifeste contre le régime et les soldats résistent.

Ces « poilus » sont des paysans. La terre leur appartient. Un patriotisme viscéral, instinctif, les colle à ces mottes de glaise.

Mais, poussés par les politiques, les chefs croient à l'offensive.

Offensive en Champagne en 1915. Échec : 350 000 morts.

En 1916, on s'accroche à Verdun.

En 1917 – la révolution russe de février a changé la donne –, le général Nivelle, qui vient de remplacer Joffre, lance l'offensive du Chemin des Dames.

Échec. Hécatombe. Mutineries.

Pétain, économe des hommes, partisans de la défensive, le remplace. Il veut attendre « les Américains et les tanks ».

Quand les Allemands lancent leurs dernières offensives, en 1918, Foch, généralissime de toutes les armées alliées, dispose d'une supériorité écrasante. Craignant que sa propre armée ne s'effondre – comme s'est dissoute l'armée russe après la révolution d'octobre 1917 –, l'état-major allemand fait pression sur Berlin pour qu'on sollicite un armistice. Ainsi, le sol allemand n'aura pas été envahi.

C'est donc, le 11 novembre 1918, la victoire de la France.

La nation a été le théâtre majeur de la guerre.

Elle a sacrifié le plus grand nombre de ses fils – seuls les Serbes, proportionnellement à leur population, ont subi davantage de pertes.

Le peuple français sous les armes et l'arrière ont tenu parce que l'« intégration » à la nation issue d'une histoire séculaire a été réalisée.

Ce patriotisme aux profondes racines a été revivifié par les lois républicaines, par le suffrage universel, par le « catéchisme national » enseigné par les « hussards noirs de la République ».

Chaque soldat est un citoyen.

Cet attachement à la terre de la patrie – le poilu est souvent un paysan propriétaire de sa ferme – explique sa résistance. Il se bat. Il s'accroche au sol non parce qu'il craint le peloton d'exécution pour désertion ou refus d'obéissance, mais parce qu'il défend sa propre parcelle du sol de la nation.

Et s'il se mutine en 1917, s'il fait la « grève des combats », c'est parce qu'on ne respecte pas en lui le citoyen, que l'on est « injuste » dans la répartition des permissions ou dans la montée en première ligne, qu'on « gaspille » les vies pour « grignoter » quelques mètres, tenter des percées qui ne peuvent aboutir.

Certes, la lassitude, la contestation, la fascination pour la révolution russe, l'antimilitarisme – si présent en 1914 –, progressent en même temps que la guerre se prolonge et que les offensives inutiles se multiplient.

Le poilu se sent solidaire de ses camarades qui « craquent », qui se rebellent et qu'un conseil de guerre expéditif condamne à mort.

Mais le patriotisme l'emporte sur l'esprit de révolte.

Le sol de la patrie occupé appartient aux citoyens. Il leur faut le défendre, le libérer.

Ce sont des citoyens-soldats qui ont remporté la victoire. En première ligne, ils avaient le sentiment de vivre avec les officiers de troupe dans une « société » républicaine où chacun, à sa place, risquait sa vie.

Ils n'avaient pas le même rapport avec les officiers supérieurs, perçus comme des « aristocrates ». Et les généraux qu'ils ont appréciés sont ceux qui, comme Pétain, les respectaient, rendaient hommage à leur courage, ne les considéraient pas comme de la chair à canon.

À la tête du pays, l'union sacrée à laquelle participaient les socialistes confirmait ce sentiment d'une cohésion de tous les Français.

Sans doute les socialistes quittent-ils le gouvernement en novembre 1917, reflétant par là la lassitude qui affecte tout le pays. Mais la personnalité de Clemenceau, président du Conseil, prolonge l'union sacrée. Il a un passé de républicain dreyfusard, même si, dans les milieux ouvriers, on se souvient du « premier flic de France », adversaire déterminé du socialisme. Il incarne un patriotisme intransigeant.

Sa volonté de « faire la guerre » et de conduire le pays à la victoire, la chasse qu'il fait à tous ceux qui expriment le désir d'en finir au plus vite par une paix de compromis donnent le sentiment que le pays est conduit fermement, que la République a enfin un chef à la hauteur des circonstances.

Certes, en poursuivant Joseph Caillaux, qui a été partisan d'une autre politique, pour intelligence avec l'ennemi, il règle de vieux comptes, en habile politicien. Mais, avec Clemenceau, avec Foch et Pétain, la République, qui reçoit en outre le soutien de centaines de milliers de soldats américains, doit et peut vaincre.

Après le 11 novembre 1918, Clemenceau sera surnommé le « Père la Victoire ».

La République et la France auront surmonté l'épreuve.

On sait à quel prix.

57

La France a vaincu et survécu.

Mais l'ivresse qui a accompagné l'annonce de l'armistice n'a duré que quelques jours.

L'émotion et la joie se sont prolongées en Alsace et en Lorraine quand Pétain, Foch, Clemenceau et Poincaré ont rendu visite, en décembre 1918, aux provinces et aux villes libérées.

L'humiliation de 1870 était effacée, la revanche, accomplie.

Mais cette fierté n'empêche pas la France de découvrir quelle a, comme trop de ses fils, la « gueule cassée ».

On s'est battu quatre ans sur son sol. Forêts hachées par les obus, sols dévastés, villages détruits, mines de fer ou de charbon inondées, usines saccagées : il va falloir réparer.

L'amertume, la rancœur, parfois la rage, se mêlent, dans l'âme de la France, à l'orgueil d'avoir été vainqueur et au soulagement d'avoir survécu.

Les anciens combattants, qui se rassemblent, veulent rester « unis comme au front ». Ils ont des « droits », parce qu'ils ont payé l'« impôt du sang ». Ils exigent que le gouvernement se montre intransigeant, qu'il obtienne le versement immédiat des « réparations ». « Le Boche doit payer ! »

Et le gouvernement répond : « L'Allemagne paiera. »

Mais, déjà, l'historien Jacques Bainville écrit : « Soixante millions d'Allemands ne se résigneront pas à payer pendant trente ou cinquante ans un tribut régulier de plusieurs milliards à quarante millions de Français. Soixante millions d'Allemands n'accepteront pas comme définitif le recul de leur frontière de l'Est, la coupure des deux Prusse, soixante millions d'Allemands se riront du petit État tchécoslovaque... »

Ces lignes sont publiées dans *L'Action française* en mai 1919, au moment où les conditions du traité de paix sont transmises aux délégués allemands.

Les exigences sont dures, non négociables. Ce traité sera perçu comme un « diktat ».

Il prévoit la démilitarisation partielle de l'Allemagne. Le bassin houiller de la Sarre devient propriété de la France. Les Alliés occupent la rive gauche du Rhin ainsi que Mayence, Coblence et Cologne. Une zone démilitarisée de 50 kilomètres de large est instaurée sur la rive droite du Rhin.

L'Allemagne est jugée responsable de la guerre. Elle doit payer des réparations, livrer une partie de sa flotte, des machines, du matériel ferroviaire. Sur la frontière orientale, la Tchécoslovaquie est créée, la Pologne renaît, la Roumanie existe. Autant d'alliés potentiels pour la France.

Mais chaque clause du traité contient en germe une cause d'affrontement entre l'Allemagne et la France.

D'autant que celle-ci est seule : le président des États-Unis, Wilson, qui a réussi à imposer la création d'une Société des Nations, est désavoué à son retour aux États-Unis. Ceux-ci ne ratifieront pas les conclusions de la conférence de la paix (novembre 1919).

Le Royaume-Uni ne veut pas que l'Allemagne soit accablée, contrainte de payer. L'Italie a le sentiment que sa « victoire est mutilée ».

La France est seule. Orgueilleuse et amère, elle célèbre sa revanche.

Le traité de Versailles est signé dans la galerie des Glaces du château de Versailles, le 28 juin 1919, là même où a été proclamé l'Empire allemand, le 18 janvier 1871.

L'honneur et la gloire sont rendus à la patrie.

La fierté des anciens combattants est aussi méritée que sourcilleuse.

Mais on sent l'angoisse et une sorte de désespoir poindre et imprégner l'âme de la France.

Chaque village dresse son monument aux morts, et le deuil – le sacrifice des fils – se trouve ainsi inscrit au cœur de la vie municipale, dans les profondeurs de la nation.

C'est autour de ce monument aux morts qu'on se rassemble, que les anciens combattants se retrouvent « unis comme au front ».

Aux élections législatives du 16 novembre 1919, le Bloc national, constitué par les partis conservateurs et par les républicains modérés, remporte une victoire éclatante et constitue une « Chambre bleu horizon ». De nombreux anciens combattants y ont été élus.

C'est une défaite pour le Parti socialiste, dont le nombre d'adhérents a augmenté rapidement après l'armistice, qui regarde avec passion et enthousiasme les bolcheviks consolider leur pouvoir, qui s'insurge contre l'envoi de militaires français en Pologne, de navires de guerre en mer Noire, d'armes aux troupes blanches qui combattent les rouges.

Mais le verdict des urnes est sans appel : le suffrage universel renvoie l'image d'une France modérée, patriote, qui refuse l'idée de révolution. Même s'il existe des révolutionnaires dans les rangs de la CGT et au sein du Parti socialiste, qui souhaitent la sortie de l'Internationale socialiste et l'adhésion à la IIIe Internationale communiste.

Les oppositions sont vives entre la majorité Bloc national et la minorité séduite par le discours révolutionnaire.

Un signe ne trompe pas : en avril 1919, un jury d'assises a acquitté Raoul Villain, l'assassin de Jaurès.

Une manifestation de protestation rassemblant la « gauche » a eu lieu à Paris – la première depuis 1914. Elle montre la vigueur de cette composante de l'opinion, mais illustre aussi son caractère minoritaire.

En fait, après l'effort sacrificiel de la guerre, le pays se divise.

Chacun puise dans l'histoire nationale les raisons de son engagement.

Les socialistes tentés par le léninisme font un parallèle entre jacobinisme et bolchevisme. La révolution de 1789 – et surtout de 1793 –, la Commune de 1871, leur paraissent préfigurer la révolution prolétarienne et le communisme. La Russie est une Commune de Paris qui a réussi.

On affirme sa solidarité avec les soviets. Des marins de l'escadre française envoyée en mer Noire pour aider les blancs se mutinent.

On conteste la politique d'union sacrée qui a été suivie par les socialistes en 1914. On se convainc que c'était Lénine qui, en prônant le défaitisme révolutionnaire, avait raison.

Au mois de décembre 1920, à Tours, la majorité du Parti socialiste – contre l'avis de Léon Blum – accepte les conditions posées par Lénine pour l'adhésion à l'Internationale communiste.

À côté de la SFIO va désormais exister un Parti communiste, Section française de l'Internationale communiste (SFIC). *L'Humanité* de Jaurès devient son journal.

C'est donc sur la tradition française qu'est greffée la souche bolchevique.

En soi, cette volonté d'imitation d'une expérience étrangère, la soumission acceptée à Moscou, sont la preuve que, alors qu'elle est la première puissance du continent après la défaite de l'Allemagne, la France est devenue moins « créatrice » d'histoire, plutôt l'« écho » d'une histoire inventée ailleurs.

Le pays se replie sur sa victoire et sur ses deuils.

Quand le débat s'engage pour savoir quelles dispositions militaires prendre pour se protéger d'une future volonté de revanche et de la contestation allemande du traité de Versailles, le maréchal Pétain propose un système de forteresses qui empêchera toute invasion.

C'est la prise de conscience d'un affaiblissement, malgré la victoire du pays.

On peut lire dans *La Nouvelle Revue française*, en novembre 1919, sous la plume de l'écrivain Henri Ghéon :

« L'être de la France est en suspens. Si le triomphe de nos armes l'a sauvée de la destruction et du servage, il la laisse si anémiée, et de son plus précieux sang, et de son capital-travail, et de son capital-richesse, que sa position, son assiette, est matériellement moins bonne, moins sûre, moins solide, malgré la récupération de deux provinces et l'occupation provisoire du Rhin, qu'en juillet 1914. »

Et Ghéon d'ajouter :

« Il nous paraît que la France n'aura vaincu, qu'elle ne sera, ne vivra qu'en proportion de nos efforts nouveaux pour faire durer sa victoire. »

Mais, après la tension de la guerre, les sacrifices consentis, l'âme de la France a-t-elle encore les ressources pour faire face aux problèmes que la guerre – et la victoire – lui posent : déclin démographique, reconstruction, accord entre les forces sociales et politiques pour adapter le pays, affronter les périls, crise financière d'une nation endettée, appauvrie ?

Or c'est la division qui s'installe.

Les ouvriers, les cheminots et les fonctionnaires se lancent dans la grève, manifestent pour la journée de huit heures (deux morts le 1er mai 1919).

En utilisant la réquisition et la mobilisation du matériel et des cheminots, le gouvernement brise la grève dans les chemins de fer au printemps de 1920.

Échec syndical et politique : des milliers de cheminots (18 000, soit 5 % de l'effectif) sont révoqués.

La justice envisage même la dissolution de la CGT.

Fort de la majorité qu'il détient, le Bloc national, républicain conservateur, inquiet de la vague révolutionnaire qui, à partir de la Russie, semble déferler sur l'Europe, est décidé à briser le mouvement social, donc à creuser un peu plus le fossé entre la majorité de la population et une minorité plus revendicative et contestatrice que révolutionnaire.

L'union sacrée est bien morte.

Pourtant, au-delà des divisions politiques, la république parlementaire continue d'écarter ceux qui, par leur personnalité, leur popularité, tentent de résister aux jeux des combinaisons politiciennes.

En janvier 1920, les parlementaires ont écarté la candidature à la présidence de la République de Georges Clemenceau, homme politique à l'esprit indépendant. À sa place, ils élisent Paul Deschanel.

Quand la folie aura contraint ce dernier à démissionner, en septembre 1920, ils choisiront Alexandre Millerand, ancien socialiste, devenu homme d'ordre et chef du Bloc national.

Mais dès que le même Millerand s'efforcera de donner quelque pouvoir à sa fonction, il rencontrera des oppositions.

Ainsi, deux ans seulement après l'armistice, la France apparaît à la fois épuisée, saignée par la guerre et divisée, cherchant des modèles dans les révolutions et les contre-révolutions qui fleurissent en Europe.

D'aucuns regardent vers Moscou et adhèrent au bolchevisme.

D'autres se tournent vers Rome, où l'on entend résonner le mot « fascisme », inventé en mars 1919 par Benito Mussolini.

Quant au pays profond, il se souvient de ceux qui sont tombés, il fleurit les tombes et les monuments aux morts.

CHRONOLOGIE IV

Vingt dates clés (1799-1920)

1804 : 21 mars, promulgation du Code civil ; 2 décembre, couronnement de Napoléon empereur

1805 : 2 décembre, Austerlitz

1812 : Campagne et retraite de Russie

1815 : 1er mars, retour de l'île d'Elbe, et, le 18 juin, Waterloo

5 mai 1821 : Mort de Napoléon à Sainte-Hélène

1824 : Mort de Louis XVIII. Accession au trône de son frère Charles X

27, 28, 29 juillet 1830 : les Trois Glorieuses – Louis-Philippe d'Orléans, roi des Français

1831 : Révolte des canuts lyonnais

25 février 1848 : Proclamation de la République

Juin 1848 : Répression contre les ouvriers des ateliers nationaux

10 décembre 1848 : Louis-Napoléon Bonaparte élu président de la République

2 décembre 1851 : Coup d'État. L'Empire sera proclamé le 1er décembre 1852

4 septembre 1870 : Déchéance de l'Empire. IIIe République

21-28 mai 1871 : Semaine sanglante. Fin de la Commune

1875 : Vote de l'amendement Wallon. Le mot « république » dans les textes constitutionnels

1er mai 1891 : Grèves et incidents à Fourmies

30 janvier 1898 : « J'accuse ! », de Zola, en défense d'Alfred Dreyfus

9 décembre 1905 : Loi de séparation de l'Église et de l'État

3 août 1914-11 novembre 1918 : Déclaration de guerre de l'Allemagne à la France – armistice de Rethondes

28 juin 1919 : Signature du traité de Versailles.

LIVRE V

L'ÉTRANGE DÉFAITE
ET LA FRANCE INCERTAINE

1920-2007

1

LA CRISE NATIONALE

1920-1938

58.

En une quinzaine d'années – des années 20 aux années 30 du
XXe siècle –, la France, passe d'un après-guerre à un avant-guerre,
même si elle refuse d'imaginer que ce qu'elle vit à partir de
1933 annonce un nouveau conflit contre les mêmes ennemis allemands qu'elle croyait avoir vaincus.

Mais il existe, en fait, plusieurs France, comme si, après la
« brutalisation » exercée par la guerre, l'âme de la nation avait
non seulement été traumatisée, mais avait éclaté.

Il y a les Français qui pleurent dans les cimetières et se recueil-
lent devant les monuments aux morts.

Il y a les anciens combattants qui se regroupent à partir des
années 30 dans une ligue patriotique antiparlementaire rassemblant ceux qui ont combattu en première ligne : les Croix-de-
Feu. Ils seront près de cent cinquante mille.

Il y a ceux que la « boucherie » guerrière a révoltés, qui ne
veulent plus revoir « ça ». Ils sont pacifistes. D'autres se pensent
révolutionnaires parce que, selon Jaurès « le capitalisme porte en
lui la guerre comme la nuée porte l'orage ». Ceux-là sont devenus communistes.

Il y a ceux qui croient à l'entente possible entre les États.

Ils font confiance à la Société des Nations pour régler les différends internationaux. Ils pleurent en écoutant Aristide Briand, pèlerin de la paix, plusieurs fois président du Conseil et ministre des Affaires étrangères durant sept années –, lorsqu'il salue l'adhésion de l'Allemagne à la Société des Nations (1926), signe le pacte Briand-Kellog mettant la guerre hors la loi (1928) ou appelle à la constitution d'une Union européenne (1929) et déclare : « Arrière, les fusils, les mitrailleuses, les canons ! Place à la conciliation, à l'arbitrage, à la paix ! »

Il y a ceux qui, après la « marche sur Rome », la prise du pouvoir par Mussolini (octobre 1922), veulent imiter le fascisme italien et sont parfois financés par lui.

Ils créent un Faisceau des combattants et des producteurs (Georges Valois, 1925), des mouvements qui se dotent d'un uniforme – les Jeunesses patriotes, les Francistes –, comme si ces jeunes hommes qui ont vécu la discipline militaire et porté le bleu horizon ne pouvaient y renoncer et voulaient pour la France un « régime fort », ce que Mussolini a qualifié, dans les années 30, d'État « totalitaire », inventant ce mot.

Et puis il y a les hommes politiques qui continuent à renverser les gouvernements au Parlement – la moyenne de durée d'un président du Conseil est de six mois !

Ils sont radicaux-socialistes, le parti clé de voûte de la IIIᵉ République, dont les chefs – Édouard Herriot (1872-1957), Édouard Daladier (1884-1970) – peuvent s'associer aussi bien avec les socialistes qu'avec les républicains modérés, comme Poincaré – président de la République jusqu'en 1920, puis plusieurs fois président du Conseil.

Il y a ceux qui veulent oublier et la guerre et l'avenir.

Ils dansent et boivent (la consommation d'alcool a été multipliée par quatre entre 1920 et 1930). Ils se laissent emporter par les rythmes nouveaux des « années folles » (autour de 1925).

Car la France n'est pas seulement une « gueule cassée », elle a aussi « le diable au corps ».

L'auteur de ce roman, publié en 1923, Raymond Radiguet, écrit : « Je flambais, je me hâtais comme les gens qui doivent mourir jeunes et qui mettent les bouchées doubles. »

Et Léon Blum, le socialiste qui, en décembre 1920, au congrès de Tours, avait dit à ses camarades qui, majoritaires, allaient fonder le Parti communiste : « Pendant que vous irez courir l'aventure, il faut que quelqu'un reste pour garder la *vieille maison* », se souvient de ces années-là : « Il y eut quelque chose d'effréné, écrit-il, une fièvre de dépenses, de jouissance et d'entreprise, une intolérance de toute règle, un besoin de mouvement allant jusqu'à l'aberration, un besoin de liberté allant jusqu'à la dépravation. »

En fait, ceux qui s'abandonnent ainsi tentent de fuir la réalité française qui les angoisse.

Ils expriment avec frénésie leur joie d'avoir échappé à la mort, aux mutilations que leurs camarades, leurs frères, leurs pères, ont subies et dont ils portent les marques sur leurs visages, dans leurs corps amputés.

Ils rêvent à l'avant-guerre de 14, devenu la « Belle Époque », oubliant les violences, les injustices, les impuissances, les aveuglements qui avaient caractérisé les années 1900.

L'âme de la France se replie ainsi sur les illusions d'un passé idéalisé, d'un avenir pacifique, et, pour certains, d'une force capable d'imposer aux autres les solutions françaises.

C'est cette combinaison entre refus de voir, angoisse, désir de jouir, souvenir des morts et des malheurs de la guerre, croyance en l'invincibilité française, qui caractérise alors l'âme de la France.

On veut croire en 1923 que Poincaré, en faisant occuper militairement la Ruhr, en s'emparant de ce gage, réussira à obtenir que l'Allemagne paie les réparations que le traité de Versailles a fixées.

On veut croire qu'en construisant une ligne fortifiée (la ligne Maginot, du nom du ministre de la Guerre), comme le souhaite Pétain, on se protégera de l'invasion.

On imagine qu'en s'alliant avec les nouveaux États de l'Europe orientale (Pologne, Tchécoslovaquie, Yougoslavie), on contraindra l'Allemagne « cernée » à une politique pacifique.

Mais on sait aussi que la France s'est affaiblie. Moins de naissances. Aristide Briand confie : « Je fais la politique étrangère de notre natalité. »

On sait que le franc s'est effondré, que l'inflation ronge la richesse nationale, que les prix ont été multipliés par sept entre 1914 et 1928. Les rentiers et les salariés sont les victimes de cette érosion. Et le rétablissement de la stabilité monétaire entre 1926 et 1929 – le « franc Poincaré » – n'est qu'un répit.

On ne respecte pas les politiciens qui occupent à tour de rôle, comme au manège, les postes ministériels, et dont on sent bien qu'ils sont incapables d'affronter la réalité.

Les radicaux-socialistes sont de toutes les combinaisons. Le Cartel des gauches issu des élections de 1924 ne dure que deux années, et Herriot, le leader radical qui dit s'être heurté au « mur de l'argent », se retrouve dans le même gouvernement que Poincaré...

Les communistes, pour leur part, ont transformé leur parti en machine totalitaire, et leur leader, Maurice Thorez (1900-1964), suivant les directives de Moscou, mène une politique « classe contre classe » dont les premières cibles sont les socialistes. Le parti de Léon Blum est qualifié de « social-fasciste », de « social-flic » !

En fait, la France est divisée entre de grandes masses électorales stables. En 1924, en 1932, en 1936, ce sont quelques centaines de milliers d'électeurs – moins de 5 % du corps électoral – qui se déplacent pour donner une majorité de gauche.

La dépendance accrue de l'exécutif à l'égard des combinaisons parlementaires, la « mobilité » des radicaux qui parlent à gauche mais s'associent souvent avec la droite ou freinent les volontés de réforme, conscients du « conservatisme » de leurs électeurs, empêchent toute politique à longue portée.

Un républicain modéré comme André Tardieu (1876-1945), ancien collaborateur de Clemenceau, qui sera à l'origine de la création des assurances sociales (1928) et des allocations familiales (1932), jauge l'impuissance du système politique : il évoque la « révolution à refaire », mais quittera la vie politique devant l'impossibilité de réformer ce système.

Mais voici que la crise économique de 1929 bouleverse en quelques mois la situation mondiale.

Les hommes politiques français, eux, continuent à s'aveugler.

On célèbre l'empire colonial français lors de l'Exposition coloniale de 1931. On parle d'une France de 100 millions d'habitants au moment même où des troubles nationalistes secouent l'Indochine, où, après la guerre du Rif (1921-1923), la situation au Maroc reste périlleuse, où le nationalisme se manifeste en Algérie et en Tunisie.

Mais c'est surtout la politique de Briand qui vole en éclats.

L'Allemagne, frappée par la crise, ne paie plus les réparations.

Hitler devient chancelier le 30 janvier 1933 et le Reich quitte la Société des Nations, décide de réarmer et de remilitariser la rive gauche du Rhin.

Hitler tente même, en 1934, de s'emparer de l'Autriche (l'Anschluss).

Un front antiallemand se constitue, qui rassemble la France, le Royaume-Uni et l'Italie... fasciste.

Pour quelle politique ?

Quelle confiance peut-on avoir en Mussolini pour défendre les principes de la Société des Nations ?

Le ministre des Affaires étrangères, Barthou, retrouve la tradition de l'alliance franco-russe d'avant 1914. Mais la Russie, c'est l'URSS communiste, et le pacte franco-soviétique suscite l'opposition des adversaires du communisme. Barthou sera assassiné à Marseille en 1934 en même temps que le roi de Yougoslavie. La politique internationale avive ainsi les divisions de la vie politique française.

Contre l'Allemagne, soit ! Mais avec qui ? Mussolini ou Staline ?

Et pourquoi pas l'apaisement avec l'Allemagne nazie ? N'est-ce pas plus favorable aux intérêts français, à « nos valeurs » traditionnelles, que l'entente avec la Russie soviétique ?

Les passions idéologiques déchirent l'âme de la France. Des scandales – Stavisky – secouent le monde politique et font se lever une double vague d'antiparlementarisme : celui des ligues – Croix-de-Feu, Jeunesse patriotes, francistes – et celui des communistes.

Lorsque le gouvernement Daladier déplace le préfet de police de Paris – Chiappe –, soupçonné de complicité avec les ligues, celles-ci manifestent, le 6 février 1934.

Journée d'émeute : une dizaine de morts, des centaines de blessés place de la Concorde.

Paris n'avait pas connu une telle violence depuis plusieurs décennies.

Les Croix-de-Feu ne se sont pas lancés à fond dans la bataille. La prudence et la retenue de leur chef, le colonel de La Rocque, ont empêché qu'on jette « les députés à la Seine ».

Le 12 février, les syndicats, les socialistes et les communistes – unis de fait dans la rue – manifestent au cri de « Le fascisme ne passera pas ! ».

On peut craindre que ces affrontements ne conduisent à une situation de guerre de religion ou de guerre civile comme la France en a si souvent connu.

Perspective d'autant plus grave et « classique » que les camps qui s'affrontent affichent aussi des positions radicalement différentes en politique extérieure.

Dès ce mois de février 1934, alors que Hitler passe en revue les troupes allemandes, que Mussolini déclare qu'il faut que l'Italie obtienne en Afrique (en Éthiopie) des récompenses pour sa politique européenne, qu'en Asie le Japon a attaqué la Chine, la République semble être incapable de susciter une nouvelle « union sacrée ».

Où est le parti de la France ? Chacun se réclame de la nation mais regarde vers l'étranger.

Le pouvoir républicain a d'ailleurs cédé devant l'émeute du 6 février.

Daladier a démissionné.

Il est remplacé par Gaston Doumergue (soixante et onze ans) qui a été naguère président de la République. Ce radical-socialiste modéré est entouré de Tardieu et Herriot.

Le ministre de la Guerre est un maréchal populaire parmi les anciens combattants, Philippe Pétain (soixante-dix-huit ans).

Comment ces septuagénaires pourraient-ils unir et galvaniser l'âme de la France blessée, angoissée, repliée sur elle-même ?

De l'autre côté du Rhin, la jeunesse acclame le chancelier Hitler.

Il n'a que quarante-cinq ans.

59.

À partir de 1934, il n'y aura plus de répit pour la France. Durant quelques semaines, au printemps et au début de l'été 1936, l'opinion populaire aura beau se laisser griser par les accordéons des bals du 14 Juillet dans les cours des usines occupées par les ouvriers en grève, ce ne sera qu'une brève illusion.

L'espoir, le rêve, la jouissance des avantages obtenus du gouvernement du Front populaire – congés payés ; quarante heures de travail par semaine, etc. –, seront vite ternis, effacés même, par le déclenchement de la guerre d'Espagne, le 17 juillet 1936, et l'aggravation de la situation internationale.

La France est entrée dans l'avant-guerre.

Mais le pays refuse d'en prendre conscience.

Qui peut accepter, vingt ans seulement après la fin de la Première Guerre mondiale, si présente dans les corps et les mémoires, qu'une nouvelle boucherie recommence à abattre des hommes dont certains sont les survivants de 14-18 ?

Dès lors, on ne veut mourir ni pour les Sudètes, ces 3 millions d'Allemands de Tchécoslovaquie séduits par le Reich de Hitler, ni pour Dantzig, cette « ville libre » séparée du Reich par un « corridor » polonais.

Certes, la France a signé des traités avec la Tchécoslovaquie et la Pologne !

Mais quoi, le respect de la parole donnée vaut-il une guerre ?

Il faut la paix à tout prix, à n'importe lequel !

Et quand, à Munich, le 29 septembre 1938, Daladier et l'Anglais Chamberlain abandonnent sur la question des Sudètes, et donc, à terme, livrent la Tchécoslovaquie à Hitler, c'est dans toute la France un « lâche soulagement », selon le mot de Léon Blum.

Embellie illusoire du Front populaire !

Apparente sagesse de Léon Blum de ne pas intervenir en Espagne pour soutenir un *Frente popular* menacé par le *pronunciamiento* du général Franco !

Lâche soulagement au moment de Munich.

Ce sont là les signes de la crise nationale qui rend la France aboulique, passant de l'exaltation à l'abattement, de brefs élans au repliement.

Aussi les volontaires français qui s'enrôlent dans les Brigades internationales pour aller combattre auprès des républicains espagnols – Malraux est le plus illustre d'entre eux – sont-ils peu nombreux (moins de 10 000).

Même si le « peuple » ouvrier est solidaire de ses camarades espagnols, il aspire d'abord à « profiter » des congés payés et des auberges de jeunesse !

Attitude significative : elle révèle qu'on imagine que la France peut rester comme un îlot préservé alors que monte la marée guerrière.

Et, avec la non-intervention en Espagne, la ligne Maginot, l'accord de Munich, les élites renforcent cette croyance, cette illusion.

Comment, dans ces conditions, préparer la France à ce qui vient : la guerre contre l'Allemagne nazie ?

En fait, durant ces quatre années (de 1934 à 1938), c'est comme si le pays et ses élites avaient été incapables – ou avaient refusé – de voir la réalité, de trancher le nœud gordien de cette crise nationale qui mêlait chaque jour de façon plus étroite politiques intérieure et extérieure.

Au temps du Front populaire, le 14 Juillet, on défile avec un bonnet phrygien, et l'entente des communistes, des socialistes et des radicaux se fait ainsi dans l'évocation et la continuité de la tradition révolutionnaire.

L'hebdomadaire qui exprime cette sensibilité du Front populaire s'intitule *Marianne*.

On célèbre aussi – en mai 1936 – le souvenir de la Commune de Paris en se rendant en cortège au mur des Fédérés en hommage aux communards fusillés au cimetière du Père-Lachaise.

Nouvelle référence révolutionnaire alors que les mesures du Front populaire sont importantes – congés payés, scolarité obligatoire et gratuite jusqu'à quatorze ans –, mais ne « révolutionnent » pas la société française.

Au reste, les radicaux de Daladier, interprètes des classes moyennes, sont des modérés qui n'accepteront jamais une dérive révolutionnaire du Front populaire. D'autant moins que le basculement électoral qui a permis la victoire du Front, aux élections d'avril-mai 1936, ne porte que sur... 150 000 voix !

Les « discours » et « références » révolutionnaires ne sont donc qu'illusion, simulacre.

Mais ils sont suffisants pour provoquer l'inquiétude et même une « grande peur » parmi l'opinion modérée, dans les couches moyennes, chez les paysans.

Parce que, derrière le Front populaire, on craint les communistes ; ils ont désormais 76 députés – plus que les radicaux –, et il y a 149 députés socialistes. Ils ont refusé de participer au gouvernement radical et socialiste de Léon Blum, tout en le « soutenant ». Pourquoi, si ce n'est pour « organiser » les masses (les adhérents du Parti communiste sont passés de 40 000 en 1933 à plus de 300 000 en 1937) ?

Les propos révolutionnaires, joints à ces réalités, aggravent les tensions.

Lorsqu'on entend chanter les militants du Front populaire, portant le bonnet phrygien, « *Allons au-devant de la vie. Allons au-devant du bonheur. Il va vers le soleil levant, notre pays* », l'opinion modérée ne craint pas seulement un retour à la terreur de 1793. Ce chant est soviétique.

On a donc peur des « bolcheviks » au moment précis où les grands procès de Moscou dévoilent la terreur stalinienne.

Donc, indissociablement, à chaque instant de la vie politique, la situation intérieure renvoie à des choix de politique extérieure.

La peur, la haine entre Français, s'exacerbent. Salengro, ministre de l'Intérieur de Blum, est calomnié et se suicide. Georges Bernanos écrira : « L'ouvrier syndiqué a pris la place du Boche ». La nation, sur tous les sujets, est divisée.

Ainsi, en 1935, les élites intellectuelles s'indignent dans leur majorité que la France, à la Société des Nations, vote des sanctions contre l'Italie fasciste qui a entrepris la conquête de l'Éthiopie, État membre de la SDN.

Dans les rues du Quartier latin, à Paris, les étudiants de droite manifestent contre le professeur Jèze, défenseur du Négus.

Les académiciens évoquent la mission civilisatrice de l'Italie fasciste face à l'un des pays les plus arriérés du monde : cette « Italie fasciste, une nation où se sont affirmées, relevées, organisées, fortifiées depuis quinze ans quelques-unes des vertus essentielles de la haute humanité ». Et c'est pour protéger l'Éthiopie qu'on risque de déchaîner « la guerre universelle, de coaliser toutes les anarchies, tous les désordres » !

D'un côté, les partisans du Front populaire crient : « Le fascisme ne passera pas ! » ; sur l'autre rive de l'opinion, on affirme que le fascisme exprime les « vertus » de la civilisation européenne.

Quand la guerre d'Espagne se déchaîne, cette fracture ne fait que s'élargir, même si des intellectuels catholiques tels Mauriac, Bernanos et Maritain tentent d'empêcher l'identification entre christianisme et fascisme ou franquisme.

Ces oppositions donnent la mesure de la profondeur de la crise nationale française.

Le gouvernement du Front populaire – avec les peurs et les haines qu'il suscite, dont l'antisémitisme est l'un des ressorts –

avive ces tensions, même s'il refuse d'intervenir officiellement en Espagne. Les radicaux s'y seraient opposés. De même, les Anglais sont partisans de cette politique de non-intervention qui est un laisser-faire hypocrite, puisque Italiens et Allemands aident Franco.

Si « le Juif » Léon Blum a dissous les « ligues », elles se reconstituent sous d'autres formes : les Croix-de-Feu deviennent le Parti social français (PSF). Son « chef », le colonel de La Rocque, rassemble plus de deux millions d'adhérents qui défilent au pas cadencé !

Un autre mouvement, le Parti populaire français (PPF), créé par un ancien dirigeant communiste, Doriot, réunit plus de 200 000 adhérents autour de thèmes fascistes.

À ces partis légaux s'ajoutent des organisations « secrètes », comme le Comité social d'action révolutionnaire – la « Cagoule » –, financé par l'Italie fasciste, qui se livre à des attentats provocateurs et, à la demande de Mussolini, perpètre l'assassinat d'exilés politiques italiens comme celui des frères Rosselli.

Tous ces éléments semblent préfigurer une « guerre civile », même si la masse de la population reste dans l'expectative, d'abord soucieuse de paix intérieure et extérieure.

C'est cette tendance de l'opinion que les élites politiques suivent et flattent au lieu de l'éclairer sur les dangers d'une politique d'apaisement.

Dans ces conditions, aucune politique étrangère rigoureuse et énergique, à la hauteur des dangers qui menacent le pays, n'est conduite.

D'ailleurs, le système politique marqué par l'instabilité et l'électoralisme l'interdit.

Les radicaux demeurent le pivot sensible de toutes les combinaisons gouvernementales.

Le 21 juin 1937, ceux du Sénat font tomber Léon Blum, qui, sans illusions, demandait les pleins pouvoirs en matière financière.

C'en est fini du Front populaire, et, en novembre 1938, un

gouvernement Daladier reviendra même sur les quarante heures. La grève générale lancée par la CGT sera un échec.

Ceux qui avaient cru à l'embellie, à l'élan révolutionnaire, sont dégrisés. Le mirage s'est dissipé. L'amertume succède à l'espérance.

On avait voulu croire aux promesses et aux réalisations du Front populaire.

On retrouve le scepticisme et on s'enferme dans la morosité et la déception.

La politique extérieure, elle, provoque le désarroi.

Quand, le 7 mars 1936, Hitler, en violation de tous les engagements pris par l'Allemagne, a réoccupé militairement la Rhénanie, le président du Conseil, le radical Albert Sarraut, a déclaré :

« Nous ne sommes pas disposés à laisser placer Strasbourg sous le feu des canons allemands ! »

Une réponse militaire française aurait pu alors facilement briser la faible armée allemande et le nazisme.

Mais, après ses rodomontades, le gouvernement français recule. Il ne veut pas se couper de l'Angleterre. Et, à la veille des élections législatives, il pense que le pays n'est pas prêt à une mobilisation que le haut état-major juge nécessaire si l'on veut contrer l'Allemagne.

Capitulation de fait, lâche soulagement...

Mussolini a compris où se situent la force et la détermination : en janvier 1937, il crée un « axe » italo-allemand, abandonnant à leur sort la France et l'Angleterre.

Même impuissance quand Hitler, en mars 1938, réalise l'Anschluss et entre, triomphant, dans Vienne.

Même renoncement à Munich, le 29 septembre 1938, et même lâche soulagement.

On veut croire que c'est « la paix pour une génération ». À son retour de Munich, on acclame Daladier, « le sauveur de la paix ».

Mais c'est tout le système d'alliances français qui se trouve détruit.

La Tchécoslovaquie est condamnée.

Pourquoi se battrait-on pour la Pologne, maintenant menacée par l'Allemagne qui veut recouvrer Dantzig ?

Et que peut penser l'URSS de cet accord de Munich qui, comme l'écrit un journal allemand, « élimine la Russie soviétique du concept de grande puissance » ?

Car la volonté d'écarter l'URSS de l'Europe et de pousser Hitler vers l'est est évidente à la lecture de l'accord de Munich.

En décembre 1938, le ministre des Affaires étrangères du Reich, Ribbentrop, vient signer à Paris une déclaration franco-allemande.

Ce n'est pas une alliance, mais c'est plus qu'un traité de non-agression.

Pour ne pas heurter les nazis, on a conseillé aux ministres juifs du gouvernement français de ne pas se rendre à la réception donnée à l'ambassade d'Allemagne.

Voilà jusqu'où sont prêtes à s'abaisser les élites politiques françaises !

Et c'est le gouvernement républicain d'un pays souverain, qu'aucune occupation ne contraint, qui prend cette décision !

Elle condamne un système politique et les hommes qui le dirigent.

Comment pourraient-ils demain, dans l'orage qui s'annonce, prendre les mesures radicales et courageuses qu'impose la guerre ?

En fait, écrit Marc Bloch, « une grande partie des classes dirigeantes, celles qui nous fournissaient nos chefs d'industrie, nos principaux administrateurs, la plupart de nos officiers de réserve, défendaient un pays qu'ils jugeaient d'avance incapable de résister ».

Marc Bloch ajoute : « La bourgeoisie s'écartait sans le vouloir de la France tout court. En accablant le régime, elle arrivait, par un mouvement trop naturel, à condamner la nation qui se l'était donné. »

2

L'ÉTRANGE DÉFAITE

1939-1944

60.

Pour l'âme de la France, 1939 est la première des années noires.

Le lâche soulagement qui avait saisi le pays à l'annonce de la signature des accords de Munich, la joie indécente qu'avaient manifestée les cinq cent mille Français massés de l'aéroport du Bourget à l'Arc de triomphe pour accueillir le président du Conseil Édouard Daladier, ne sont plus que souvenirs.

La guerre est là, fermant l'horizon.

Des dizaines de milliers de réfugiés espagnols franchissent la frontière française pour fuir les troupes franquistes qui, le 26 janvier 1939, viennent d'entrer dans Barcelone.

On ouvre des camps pour accueillir ces réfugiés qui incarnent la débâcle d'une République qui s'était donné un gouvernement de *Frente popular*.

Quelques semaines plus tard, le 15 mars, les troupes allemandes entrent dans Prague : violation cynique par Hitler des accords de Munich, et mort de la Tchécoslovaquie.

Quelques semaines encore, et Mussolini signe avec le Führer un *pacte d'acier*. Les deux dictateurs se sont associés pour conclure avec le Japon un pacte *anti-Komintern*, se constituant en adversaires de l'Internationale communiste dirigée par Moscou.

La France doit-elle dès lors conclure une alliance avec l'URSS contre l'Allemagne nazie ?

La question qui avait taraudé les élites politiques françaises revient en force. Elle provoque les mêmes clivages.

La droite rejette toujours l'idée d'un pacte franco-soviétique. Elle affirme qu'on doit poursuivre la politique d'apaisement, voire de rapprochement avec ces forces rénovatrices mais aussi conservatrices que sont le fascisme, le nazisme, le franquisme.

Bientôt – le 2 mars 1939 –, le maréchal Philippe Pétain sera nommé ambassadeur de France en Espagne auprès de Franco.

Mais, dans le même temps, quelques voix fortes s'élèvent à droite pour affirmer que parmi les périls qui menacent la France, « s'il y a le communisme, il y a d'abord l'Allemagne » (Henri de Kérillis).

L'industriel français Wendel est encore plus clair : « Il y a actuellement un danger bolchevique intérieur et un danger allemand extérieur, dit-il. Pour moi, le second est plus grand que le premier, et je désapprouve nettement ceux qui règlent leur attitude sur la conception inverse. »

En ces premiers mois de 1939, l'âme de la France est ainsi hésitante et toujours aussi divisée.

Mais on sent, de la classe politique au peuple, comme un frémissement de patriotisme, une volonté de réaction contre les dictateurs pour qui les traités ne sont que « chiffons de papier ».

On est révolté par les revendications des fascistes, qui, à Rome, prétendent que Nice, la Corse, la Tunisie et la Savoie doivent revenir à l'Italie.

À Bastia, à Nice, à Marseille, à Tunis, on manifeste contre ces prétentions qui donnent la mesure de l'arrogance du fascisme et de l'affaiblissement de la France.

Daladier, l'homme de Munich, prend la pose héroïque et patriotique : « La France, sûre de sa force, est en mesure de faire face à toutes les attaques, à tous les périls », déclare-t-il le 3 janvier 1939.

On se rassure.

Un million de Parisiens acclament le défilé des troupes françaises et anglaises, le 14 juillet 1939. Douze escadrilles de bombardement survolent Paris, Lyon et Marseille.

On se persuade – les observateurs du monde entier en sont convaincus – que l'armée, l'aviation et la marine françaises constituent encore la force militaire la plus puissante du monde.

Et il y a la ligne Maginot qui interdit toute invasion !

Car aucun Français ne veut la guerre, et l'on espère que la force française suffira à dissuader Hitler de la commencer. Les Allemands doivent se rappeler que la France les a vaincus en 1918.

Ainsi, chaque Français continue de penser que le conflit peut être évité.

Au gouvernement, Paul Reynaud, libéral, indépendant, qui joue aux côtés de Daladier un rôle de plus en plus important, prend des mesures « patriotiques ».

Les crédits militaires, que le Front populaire avait déjà très largement augmentés, le sont à nouveau.

L'ambassadeur allemand Otto Abetz, qui anime ouvertement un réseau proallemand dans les milieux intellectuels et artistiques, est expulsé (29 juillet 1939).

À Londres comme à Paris, des déclarations nombreuses réaffirment que les deux nations démocratiques n'accepteront pas que Hitler, sous prétexte de reprendre Dantzig, entre en Pologne.

« Nous répondrons à la force par la force ! »

Et à la question posée dans un sondage : « Pensez-vous que si l'Allemagne tente de s'emparer de Dantzig, nous devions l'en empêcher, au besoin par la force », 76 % des Français consultés répondent oui, contre 17 % de non.

Ce n'est ni l'union sacrée ni l'enthousiasme patriotique, plutôt une sorte de résignation devant les nécessités. Une acceptation qui pourrait devenir de plus en plus résolue si les élites se rassemblaient pour exprimer l'obligation nationale d'affronter le nazisme et le fascisme, de se battre et de vaincre parce qu'il n'y a pas d'autre issue.

Mais on entend toujours, parmi les élites, le refus de « mourir pour Dantzig ». Et c'est un ancien socialiste, Marcel Déat, qui le répète.

Le pacifisme reste puissant, toujours aussi aveugle à la menace nazie.

Il est influent dans les syndicats de l'enseignement proches des socialistes et au sein même de la SFIO.

Naturellement, le refus de la guerre antinazie est par ailleurs le ressort des milieux attirés par le nazisme, le fascisme ou le franquisme. L'écrivain Robert Brasillach, l'hebdomadaire *Je suis partout*, représentent ce courant.

À l'opposé, les communistes apparaissent comme les plus résolus à l'affrontement avec le « fascisme ».

Thorez, leur leader, propose un « Front des Français ».

Le PCF se félicite que des négociations se soient ouvertes, à Moscou, entre Français et Soviétiques. Ces derniers réclament le libre passage de leurs troupes à travers la Pologne pour s'avancer au contact des Allemands. Les Polonais s'y refusent. Ils savent depuis des siècles ce qu'il faut penser de l'« amitié » russe.

Seuls quelques observateurs avertis, comme Boris Souvarine, ancien communiste devenu farouchement antistalinien, n'écartent pas l'éventualité d'un accord germano-soviétique, sorte de figure inversée des accords de Munich, par lequel les deux partenaires, oubliant leurs oppositions idéologiques radicales, associeraient leurs intérêts géopolitiques : les mains libres pour Hitler à l'Est, assorties d'un nouveau partage de la Pologne entre Russes et Allemands, et, à l'Ouest, guerre ouverte contre la France et l'Angleterre.

Ni Berlin ni Moscou n'excluent la guerre entre eux, mais chacun pense que le temps gagné permettra de renforcer sa propre position.

L'aveuglement français face à cette éventualité d'un accord germano-russe participe aussi de la crise nationale.

Les idéologies paralysent la réflexion et repoussent la notion d'intérêt national loin derrière les préoccupations partisanes.

La nation, sa défense et ses intérêts ne sont ni le mobile des choix politiques ni le cœur de l'analyse politique.

C'est là un fait majeur.

Ainsi, pour les communistes, il faut d'abord défendre la politique soviétique, dont ils sont l'un des outils.

Ils en épousent tous les méandres, et, de cette manière, estiment sauvegarder les intérêts de la classe ouvrière française, autrement dit de la France elle-même.

L'idéologie communiste empêche la « compréhension » de ce que sont les intérêts de la nation, qui ne sauraient se réduire à ceux d'une classe, fût-elle ouvrière, encore moins à ceux d'une autre nation, se prétendrait-elle communiste.

Pour les pacifistes, le patriotisme n'est qu'un mot destiné à masquer le nationalisme qui est à l'origine de la guerre. Les nations ne sont que des archaïsmes, des structures d'oppression. Ce ne sont pas leurs intérêts qu'il faut défendre, mais ceux de l'humanité...

Ces pacifistes – qui influencent les socialistes – ne pensent plus en termes de nation.

Les radicaux-socialistes et les socialistes sont des politiciens enfermés dans les jeux du parlementarisme, incapables le plus souvent de prendre une décision et de l'imposer, fluctuant donc entre le désir de paix à tout prix – le « lâche soulagement » – et les rodomontades patriotiques – celles d'un Daladier – intervenant trop tard et qui ne sont pas suivies d'actes d'autorité.

Les modérés, les conservateurs, se souviennent de la « Grande Peur » qu'ils ont éprouvée à nouveau au moment du Front populaire.

Ils craignent les désordres. La guerre antifasciste pourrait permettre aux communistes de prendre le pouvoir, créant une sorte de Commune victorieuse grâce à la guerre.

Ils sont sensibles aux arguments des minorités favorables à une entente avec le fascisme, le franquisme et même le nazisme.

Le succès en Europe de ces régimes d'ordre les fascine. Ils estiment que le moment est peut-être venu, pour les « modérés », de prendre leur revanche sur les partisans d'une République « sociale » qui, à leurs yeux, ont dominé depuis 1880 et sûrement depuis 1924.

Ce courant est influencé par Charles Maurras, qui identifie les intérêts de la nation à ceux des partisans de la « royauté ».

Ainsi, aucune des forces politiques ne place au cœur de son projet et de son action la défense bec et ongles de la nation.

Chacune d'elles est dominée par une idéologie ou par la défense de la « clientèle » qui assure électoralement sa survie.

De ce fait, les « instruments » d'une grande politique extérieure – la diplomatie et l'armée – ne sont ni orientées ni dirigées par la main ferme du pouvoir politique.

Seules quelques personnalités indépendantes d'esprit accordent priorité aux intérêts de la nation et sont capables de prendre des décisions au vu des nécessités nationales sans se soumettre à des présupposés idéologiques.

Mais ces individualités sont peu nombreuses et ne peuvent imposer leurs vues et leurs décisions aux forces politiques ou aux grands corps.

Un Paul Reynaud, par exemple, a soutenu les idées novatrices du colonel de Gaulle – création de divisions blindées – sans réussir à imposer assez tôt leur constitution.

De Gaulle (1890-1970) est évidemment l'un de ces patriotes lucides qui n'ont pas encore le pouvoir de décision ni même celui de l'influence.

Dès 1937, il peut écrire : « Notre haut commandement en est encore aux conceptions de 1919, voire de 1914. Il croit à l'inviolabilité de la ligne Maginot, d'ailleurs incomplète (elle ne couvre pas le massif des Ardennes, réputé infranchissable). [...] Seule la mobilité d'une puissante armée blindée pourrait nous préserver d'une cruelle épreuve. Notre territoire sera sans doute une fois de plus envahi ; quelques jours peuvent suffire pour atteindre Paris. »

De Gaulle anticipe aussi les évolutions de la situation internationale lorsqu'il identifie la menace nazie et le risque d'un accord germano-russe que n'empêchera pas le heurt des idéologies, car, estime-t-il, la géopolitique commande à l'idéologie.

Ils ne sont qu'une poignée, ceux qui ont envisagé cette hypothèse, relevé les signes avant-coureurs du double jeu de Staline.

Le maître de l'URSS négocie avec les Français et les Anglais, d'une part, et, de l'autre, avec les Allemands.

Il écarte le ministre des Affaires étrangères juif, Litvinov, et le remplace par Molotov dès le mois de mai 1939.

Des réfugiés antinazis sont livrés par les Russes aux Allemands.

Le 23 août 1939, la nouvelle de la signature d'un pacte de non-agression germano-soviétique plonge les milieux politiques dans la stupeur, le désarroi, la colère.

Malgré de nombreuses défections, les communistes français vont justifier la position soviétique. Se plaçant ainsi en dehors de la communauté nationale, ils vont subir la répression policière.

Car le pacte signifie évidemment le déclenchement de la guerre.

Le 1er septembre 1939, les troupes allemandes entrent en Pologne – Russes et Allemands se sont « partagé » le pays. L'Angleterre d'abord, puis la France, le 3 septembre, déclarent la guerre à l'Allemagne.

On n'avait pas voulu se battre pour les Sudètes.

On va mourir pour Dantzig.

L'opinion française perd tous ses repères. Les communistes sont désormais hostiles à la « guerre impérialiste » !

La guerre s'impose comme une fatalité.

On la subit sans enthousiasme.

Le frémissement patriotique qui avait saisi l'âme de la France pendant les six premiers mois de 1939 est retombé.

Restent le devoir, l'acceptation morose, l'obligation de faire cette guerre dont on ne comprend pas les enjeux parce qu'à aucun moment les élites politiques n'ont évoqué clairement les intérêts français ni n'ont agi avec détermination.

Les élites ont oublié la France, prétendant ainsi suivre les Français qui, au contraire, attendaient qu'on leur parle de la nation et des raisons qu'il y avait, vingt ans après la fin d'une guerre, de se battre à nouveau et de mourir pour elle.

61.

En onze mois, de septembre 1939 à juillet 1940, la France, entrée dans la guerre résignée, mais qui s'imaginait puissante, a été terrassée, humiliée, mutilée, occupée après avoir succombé à une « étrange défaite », la plus grave de son histoire.

Car ce n'est pas seulement la crise nationale qui couvait depuis les années 30 qui est responsable de cet effondrement.

Si des millions de Français se sont jetés sur les routes de l'exode, si Paris n'a pas été défendu, si deux millions de soldats se sont rendus à l'ennemi, si la IIIᵉ République s'est immolée dans un théâtre de Vichy, et si seulement 80 parlementaires ont refusé de confier les pleins pouvoirs à Pétain, alors que 589 d'entre eux votaient pour le nouveau chef de l'État, c'est que la gangrène rongeait la nation depuis bien avant les années 30.

C'était comme si, en 1940, la débâcle rouvrait les plaies de 1815, de 1870, qu'on avait crues cicatrisées et qui étaient encore purulentes.

Pis : c'était comme si, à l'origine et à l'occasion de l'« étrange défaite », toutes les maladies, les noirceurs de l'âme de la France s'étaient emparées du corps de la nation, comme s'il fallait faire payer au peuple français aussi bien l'édit de Nantes, la tolérance envers les hérétiques, que la décapitation de

Louis XVI et de Marie-Antoinette, la loi de séparation de l'Église et de l'État, la réhabilitation de Dreyfus et le Front populaire !

Le désastre de 1940 fut un temps de revanche et de repentance, le châtiment enfin infligé à un peuple trop rétif.

Il fallait le faire rentrer dans le rang, lui extirper de la mémoire Henri IV et Voltaire, les communards et Blum, et même ce dernier venu, ce grand rebelle, de Gaulle, ce colonel promu général de brigade à titre temporaire en juin 1940 et qui, depuis Londres, clamait que « la flamme de la Résistance française ne doit pas s'éteindre et ne s'éteindra pas ».

Il osait dénoncer le nouvel État français, refuser une « France livrée, une France pillée, une France asservie ».

Le 3 août 1940, on le condamnait à mort par contumace pour trahison et désertion à l'étranger en temps de guerre.

Et Philippe Pétain, beau vieillard patelin de quatre-vingt-quatre ans, derrière lequel se cachaient les ligueurs de 1934, les politiciens ambitieux vaincus en 1936, dont Pierre Laval, tous les tenants de la politique d'apaisement, invitait au retour à la terre, parce que la « terre ne ment pas ».

Il morigénait le peuple, l'invitait à un « redressement intellectuel et moral », à une « révolution nationale » – comme en avaient connu l'Italie, l'Allemagne, l'Espagne. Mais celle-ci serait une contre-révolution française : il fallait oublier la devise républicaine, « Liberté, Égalité, Fraternité », et la remplacer par le nouveau triptyque de l'État français : Travail, Famille, Patrie.

L'ordre moral, celui des années 1870, s'avance avec ce maréchal qui avait dix-sept ans au temps du maréchal de Mac-Mahon et du duc de Broglie.

« Depuis la victoire [de 1918], dit Pétain, l'esprit de jouissance l'a emporté sur l'esprit de sacrifice. On a revendiqué plus qu'on n'a servi. On a voulu épargner l'effort. On rencontre aujourd'hui le malheur. »

Le malheur s'est avancé à petits pas sournois.

« Drôle de guerre » entre septembre et mai 1940.

On ne tente rien, ou presque – une offensive en direction de la Sarre, vite interrompue – pour secourir les Polonais broyés dès le début du mois d'octobre.

Et Hitler, le 6 de ce mois, lance un appel à la paix qui trouble et rassure.

Peut-être n'est-ce là qu'un simulacre de guerre ?

Les Allemands ont obtenu ce qu'ils voulaient ; pourquoi pas une paix honorable ?

Ce qu'il reste de communistes prêche pour elle, contre la guerre conduite par la France impérialiste. Ils ne dénoncent plus l'Allemagne. On les emprisonne, ces martyrs de la paix, et leur secrétaire général, Thorez, a déserté et gagné Moscou !

D'une certaine manière, et bien qu'ils ne soient qu'une minorité, leur propagande renoue avec le vieux fonds pacifiste, antimilitariste, qui travaille une partie du peuple français.

On s'arrange donc de cette « drôle de guerre » sans grande bataille offensive, ponctuée seulement d'« activités de patrouille ». Les élites cherchent tant bien que mal à sortir d'un conflit qu'elles n'ont pas voulu.

Quand les Soviétiques agressent – en novembre – la Finlande, on s'enflamme pour l'héroïsme de ce petit pays dont la résistance est aussi soutenue par... l'Allemagne. On rêve à un renversement d'alliance, à attaquer l'URSS par le sud, à prendre Bakou.

L'idée d'une paix avec Hitler fait son chemin et prolonge la politique d'apaisement de 1938.

Comment, dans ces conditions, le peuple et les troupes seraient-ils préparés à une « vraie » guerre ?

Qui lit, parmi les 80 personnalités auxquelles il l'adresse, le *mémorandum* du général de Gaulle intitulé *L'Avènement de la force mécanique*, dans lequel il écrit : « Cette guerre est perdue, il faut donc en préparer une autre avec la machine » ?

On se réveille en plein cauchemar le 10 mai 1940.

La pointe de l'offensive allemande est dans les Ardennes,

réputées infranchissables, et Pétain avait approuvé qu'on ne prolongeât pas la ligne Maginot dans ce massif forestier : la Meuse et lui ne constituaient-ils pas des obstacles naturels bien suffisants ?

Symboliquement, c'est autour de Sedan, comme en 1870, que se joue le sort de la guerre.

Les troupes françaises entrées en Belgique sont tournées.

Il suffit d'une bataille de cinq jours pour que le front soit rompu. À Dunkerque, trois cent mille hommes sont encerclés et évacués par la flotte britannique qui sauve d'abord ses propres soldats.

En six semaines, l'armée française n'existe plus.

Le 14 juin, les Allemands entrent dans Paris.

L'exode de millions de Français – mitraillés – encombre toutes les routes.

Un pays s'effondre.

Le 16 juin, Paul Reynaud, qui a succédé en mars comme président du Conseil à Daladier – et qui a nommé de Gaulle, le 5 juin, sous-secrétaire d'État à la Guerre –, démissionne, remplacé par Philippe Pétain. Le général Weygand, généralissime, a accrédité la rumeur selon laquelle une Commune communiste aurait pris le pouvoir à Paris. La révolution menace. Il faut donc arrêter la guerre.

Le 17 juin, sans avoir négocié aucune condition de reddition et d'armistice, Pétain, s'adresse au pays :

« C'est le cœur serré que je vous dis aujourd'hui qu'il faut cesser le combat. Je me suis adressé cette nuit à l'adversaire pour lui demander s'il est prêt à rechercher avec nous, entre soldats, après la lutte, dans l'honneur, les moyens de mettre un terme aux hostilités. »

Des centaines de milliers de soldats se battaient encore.

Cent trente mille étaient déjà tombés dans cette guerre où les actes d'héroïsme se sont multipliés dès lors que les officiers menaient leurs troupes à la bataille.

Mais le discours de Pétain paralyse les combattants. Pourquoi mourir puisque l'homme de Verdun appelle à déposer les armes alors que l'armistice n'est même pas signé ?

De Gaulle, qui a déjà jugé que la prise du pouvoir par Pétain « est le *pronunciamiento* de la panique », s'insurge contre cette trahison.

La France dispose d'un empire colonial, lance-t-il. La France a perdu une bataille, mais n'a pas perdu la guerre.

Le 18 juin, il parle de Londres : « Le dernier mot est-il dit ? L'espérance doit-elle disparaître ? La défaite est-elle définitive ? Non ! La France n'est pas seule... Cette guerre est une guerre mondiale... Quoi qu'il arrive, la flamme de la Résistance française ne doit pas s'éteindre et ne s'éteindra pas. »

Voix isolée, qui n'est pas entendue dans un pays vaincu, envahi, livré.

Certes ici et là on refuse la reddition. On veut gagner l'Angleterre. On accomplit les premiers gestes de résistance – ce mot que de Gaulle vient de « réinventer ».

À Chartres, le préfet Jean Moulin tente de se suicider pour ne pas signer un texte infamant pour les troupes coloniales.

Mais la France, dans sa masse, est accablée, anéantie.

À Bordeaux, où le gouvernement s'est replié, on arrête Georges Mandel, l'ancien collaborateur de Clemenceau, républicain intransigeant, patriote déterminé.

On le relâchera, mais le temps de la revanche des anti-républicains commence.

C'est le triomphe, par la défaite et l'invasion, d'une partie des élites, celles qui, dans la République, s'étaient senties émigrées, ou bien dont les ambitions n'avaient pu être satisfaites.

Quant au peuple, il pleure déjà ses soldats morts – et les prisonniers.

Il est à la fois désemparé et soulagé.

Comment ne pas avoir confiance en Pétain, le vainqueur de Verdun ?

À Vichy, le 10 juillet 1940, le Maréchal devient chef de l'État.

Il annonce une Révolution nationale.

Dans quelques mois, on fera chanter dans les écoles, en lieu et place de *La Marseillaise* bannie :

Maréchal, nous voilà
Devant toi le sauveur de la France
Nous saurons, nous tes gars
Redonner l'espérance
La patrie renaîtra
Maréchal, Maréchal, nous voilà !

62.

1940 : pour la France, c'est le malheur de la défaite et de l'occupation, le règne des restrictions et des vilenies, des lâchetés, même si brûlent quelques brandons d'héroïsme que rien ne semble pouvoir éteindre.

Mais ce sont bien les temps du *malheur*.

Pétain répète le mot comme un vieux maître bougon qui sait la vérité et veut en persuader le peuple.

Il fustige : le malheur est le fruit de l'indiscipline et de l'esprit de jouissance, mâchonne-t-il. Et tout cela, qui remonte à la Révolution française, doit être déraciné.

Plus de *Marseillaise*, donc, mais *Maréchal nous voilà*.

Plus de 14 Juillet, mais célébration de Jeanne d'Arc et institution de la fête des Mères.

Plus de bonnet phrygien, mais la francisque, devenue emblème du régime. Il ne faut plus laisser les illusions, les perversions, corrompre les jeunes qu'on rassemble dans les « Chantiers de jeunesse ».

Quant aux anciens de 14-18, dont Pétain est le glorieux symbole, ils doivent se réunir dans la Légion française des combattants. On les voit, la francisque à la boutonnière, acclamer Pétain à chacun de ses voyages officiels.

Il est le « Chef aimé ». Il suit la messe aux côtés des évêques. Il se promène dans les jardins de l'hôtel du Parc, à Vichy, devenu capitale de l'État français.

On le vénère. On le croit quand il dit, de sa voix chevrotante, pour consoler et rassurer :

« Je fais à la France le don de ma personne pour atténuer son malheur. »

Mais l'armistice a attaché la France à la roue d'une vraie capitulation. Et l'occupant, « correct » et « souriant » aux premiers mois d'occupation, pille, démembre, tente d'avilir le pays.

La nation est partagée en deux par une ligne de démarcation : zone occupée, zone libre.

Il y aura même un ambassadeur de France – du gouvernement de Vichy – à Paris !

L'Alsace et la Lorraine sont allemandes, gouvernées par un *Gauleiter*. Les jeunes gens vont être enrôlés dans la Wehrmacht.

Le Nord et le Pas-de-Calais sont rattachés au commandement allemand de Bruxelles, et une zone interdite s'étend de la Manche à la frontière suisse.

L'Allemand puise dans les caisses : chaque jour, la France lui paie une indemnité suffisante pour nourrir dix millions d'hommes. Il achète avec cet argent les récoltes, les usines, les tableaux.

Les Français qui avaient espéré le retour rapide à l'avant-guerre, le rapatriement des prisonniers, le départ des occupants, s'enfoncent dans l'amertume et le désespoir. Le rationnement, la misère, le froid et l'humiliation ne prédisposent pas à l'héroïsme.

En zone occupée, la présence allemande – armée, police, Gestapo – rappelle à chaque pas la défaite.

En zone libre, on s'illusionne, on arbore le drapeau tricolore le jour de la fête de Jeanne d'Arc. Une « armée de l'armistice » cache ses armes, préparant la revanche, et à Vichy même les officiers du Service de renseignements arrêtent des espions allemands.

La défaite et l'occupation, ce sont aussi ces ambiguïtés, ce double jeu, ces excuses à la lâcheté, aux malversations, au « marché noir », à toute cette érosion des valeurs morales et républicaines.

Le malheur corrompt le pays.

Et la silhouette chenue d'un Pétain en uniforme couvre toutes les compromissions, les délations, les vilenies.

On livre à la Gestapo les antinazis qui s'étaient réfugiés en France.

On promulgue, à partir d'octobre 1940, des lois antisémites, sans même que les Allemands l'aient demandé. Et la persécution commence à ronger la société française, avec son cortège de dénonciations, d'égoïsmes, de lâchetés.

Les 16 et 17 juillet 1942, grande rafle des Juifs à Paris : la tache infamante, sur l'uniforme de l'État français, a la forme d'une étoile jaune.

80 000 de ceux qui ont été raflés, avec le concours de la police française, disparaîtront, déportés, dans les camps d'extermination.

L'ogre nazi est insatiable. Il exige, pour faire fonctionner ses usines de guerre, un Service du travail obligatoire (STO) en Allemagne qui s'applique à tous les jeunes Français.

L'âme de la France est souillée par cette complicité et cette collaboration avec l'occupant, fruits de la lâcheté, de l'ambition – le vainqueur détient le pouvoir, il favorise, il paie, il ferme les yeux sur les malversations –, mais aussi d'un accord idéologique.

Car toutes ces motivations se mêlent.

On est un jeune homme qui, en 1935, manifeste contre les sanctions de la SDN frappant l'Italie fasciste qui a agressé l'Éthiopie.

On a des sympathies pour la Cagoule. On a baigné dans la tradition antisémite illustrée par les œuvres de Drumont, qui ont imprégné les droites françaises.

On aurait été antidreyfusard si l'on avait vécu pendant l'Affaire.

On est aussi patriote, défenseur de cette France-là, « antirévolutionnaire », antisémite.

On fait son devoir en 1939. On est prisonnier, on s'évade comme un bon patriote. On retrouve ses amis cagoulards à Vichy. On y exerce des fonctions officielles. On ne prête pas attention aux lois antisémites. C'est le prolongement naturel de la Révolution nationale.

On est décoré de la francisque par Pétain. Et on a pour ami le secrétaire général de la police, Bousquet, qui organise les rafles antisémites de Paris et fera déporter la petite-fille d'Alfred Dreyfus.

On est resté un beau jeune homme aux mains pures, et quand, en 1943, le vent aura tourné, poussant l'Allemagne vers la défaite, on s'engagera contre elle dans la Résistance.

On pourrait s'appeler François Mitterrand, futur président socialiste de la République.

Jamais d'ailleurs on n'a été pronazi ni même pro-allemand. On a été partisan d'une certaine France, celle du maréchal Pétain, de la Révolution nationale, qui voit bientôt naître un Service d'ordre légionnaire, noyau de la future Milice, force de police, de répression et de maintien de l'ordre aux uniformes noirs, imitation malingre de la milice fasciste, des SA et des SS nazis.

On n'a pas été choqué quand, le 24 octobre 1940, à Montoire, Pétain a serré la main de Hitler et déclaré : « J'entre aujourd'hui dans la voie de la collaboration. »

On écoute d'autant plus cette voix qui prêche pour une « Europe nouvelle » continentale – Drieu la Rochelle le faisait dès les années 30 – que les événements ont ravivé le vieux fonds d'anglophobie d'une partie des élites françaises.

Il y a eu l'évacuation du réduit de Dunkerque, où les Anglais ont d'abord embarqué les leurs.

Il y a eu surtout, le 3 juillet 1940, l'attaque de la flotte française en rade de Mers el-Kébir par une escadre anglaise : 1 300 marins français tués, l'indignation de toute la France contre cette agression vécue comme une trahison, alors qu'elle n'était pour les Anglais qu'une mesure de précaution contre un pays qui, contrairement à ses engagements, venait de signer un armistice séparé. Et qu'allait devenir cette flotte ? Un butin pour les Allemands ?

Mais le ressentiment français est grand. Et les cadres de la marine (l'amiral Darlan) sont farouchement antianglais.

Le ressentiment vichyste est alimenté chaque jour par la présence à Londres du général de Gaulle, la reconnaissance par Churchill de la représentativité de cette « France libre » qui s'adresse par la radio au peuple français – « Ici Londres, des Français parlent aux Français » –, l'incitant à la résistance.

Il y a en effet des Français qui résistent et qui veulent exprimer et incarner les vertus propres à l'âme de la France.

Car le patriotisme d'une vieille nation survit au naufrage de la défaite. Il est si profondément ancré dans le cœur des citoyens qu'il est présent jusque chez ceux qui « collaborent » ou s'enrôlent dans la Milice ou dans la légion des volontaires français pour défendre – sous l'uniforme allemand – l'Europe contre le bolchevisme.

C'est un patriotisme « dévoyé », criminel, mais même chez un Joseph Darnand – chef de la Milice, héros des guerres de 14-18 et de 39-40 –, il est perceptible.

Et on peut en créditer, sans que cela leur tienne lieu de justification ou d'excuse, bien des serviteurs de l'État français qui côtoient cependant à Vichy des aigrefins, des cyniques, des ambitieux sordides, des politiciens aigris et ratés, voire des fanatiques, journalistes, écrivains, que la passion antisémite obsède.

Mais la pierre de touche du patriotisme véritable et rigoureux, c'est le refus de l'occupation du sol de la nation et l'engagement dans la lutte pour lui rendre indépendance et souveraineté.

Ce patriotisme-là, il ne se calcule pas, il est instinctif.

L'ennemi occupe la France, il faut l'en chasser. C'est nécessaire. Donc il faut engager le combat.

Dès juin 1940, de jeunes officiers (Messmer), des fonctionnaires (Jean Moulin), des anonymes, des chrétiens (Edmond Michelet), des philosophes (Cavaillès) refusent de cesser le combat, rejettent l'armistice. Ils gagnent Londres, puisque là-bas on continue la lutte.

Ils éditent des tracts, des journaux clandestins qui appellent à la résistance, et certains effectuent pour les Anglais des missions de renseignement.

Ainsi, la défaite fait coexister plusieurs France durant les deux premières années (1940-novembre 1942) de l'Occupation.

Il y a les départements qui échappent à toute autorité française : annexés à l'Allemagne, ou rattachés à la Belgique, ou constituant une zone interdite.

Il y a la zone occupée, de la frontière des Pyrénées à Chambéry en passant par Moulins.

Il y a la « zone libre », l'État français, dont la capitale est Vichy.

Et puis il y a la France libre de Charles de Gaulle, qui, à partir de juillet 1942, s'intitulera France combattante. Elle a commencé à rassembler autour d'elle la France de la Résistance intérieure.

De nombreux mouvements clandestins se sont en effet constitués : Combat, Libération, Franc-Tireur, Défense de la France.

À compter du 22 juin 1941, jour de l'attaque allemande contre l'URSS, les communistes se lancent enfin à leur tour dans la Résistance et en deviennent l'une des principales composantes, engageant leurs militants dans l'action armée – attentats, attaques de militaires allemands, etc.

Le STO, à partir de l'année 1943, provoquera la création de maquis, l'apparition d'une autre France, celle des réfractaires.

Mais les divisions idéologiques, les divergences portant sur les modes d'action, les rivalités personnelles ou de groupe, caractérisent aussi bien cette Résistance que la France libre, les zones occupées ou l'État de Vichy.

La défaite a encore aggravé la fragmentation politique, les oppositions, comme si la France était plus que jamais incapable de se rassembler, comme si la division, cette maladie endémique de l'histoire nationale, était devenue plus aiguë que jamais, symptôme de la gravité du traumatisme subi par la nation.

À Londres, de Gaulle ne regroupe durant les premiers mois que quelques milliers d'hommes. Et il y a déjà, au sein de la France libre, des « antigaullistes ».

Lorsqu'il tente la reconquête des colonies d'Afrique noire, les Français vichystes de Dakar font échouer l'entreprise (septembre-octobre 1940). Elle réussit en Afrique-Équatoriale avec Leclerc de Hauteclocque. Peu à peu se constituent des Forces françaises libres, qui compteront, en 1942, près de soixante-dix mille hommes.

Mais la « guerre civile » menace toujours : en Syrie, en 1941, les troupes fidèles à Vichy affrontent les « gaullistes ».

À Vichy, autour du Maréchal – dont l'esprit, dit-on, n'est éveillé, et la lucidité, réelle, qu'une heure par jour ! –, les querelles et les ambitions s'ajoutent aux choix politiques différents.

Pierre Laval, président du Conseil, est renvoyé par Pétain en décembre 1940, puis son retour est imposé (en avril 1942) par les Allemands, qui, en fait, sont les maîtres. Peut-être pour s'assurer encore mieux de leur soutien, Laval déclare : « Je souhaite la victoire de l'Allemagne. »

À Paris, Marcel Déat et Jacques Doriot dirigent, l'un le Rassemblement national populaire, l'autre, le Parti populaire français.

Ils incarnent une collaboration idéologique qui critique la « modération » de Vichy et souhaite une « fascisation du régime ».

Une partie de la pègre, contrôlée par les Allemands, s'est mise au service des nazis pour traquer les résistants, les torturer, dénoncer et spolier les Juifs. Elle bénéficie d'une totale impunité, associant vol, trafic, marché noir, pillage et répression.

La collaboration a ce visage d'assassins.

Mais la Résistance est elle aussi divisée sur les modalités d'action comme sur les projets politiques.

L'entrée des communistes et leur volonté de « tuer » l'ennemi sans se soucier des exécutions d'otages sont critiquées par certains mouvements de résistance, et même par le général de Gaulle.

On s'oppose aussi sur les rapports entre la Résistance intérieure et la France libre. De Gaulle n'aurait-il pas les ambitions d'un « dictateur » ?

D'autres sont hostiles à la représentation des partis politiques au sein de la Résistance, puisque ces partis sont estimés responsables de la défaite par nombre de résistants, alors même que Vichy a fait arrêter, afin de les juger, Blum, Daladier et Reynaud. Mais le procès, amorcé à Riom, tourne à la confusion de Vichy et sera donc interrompu.

On s'interroge même sur les relations qu'il convient d'avoir avec Vichy et avec l'armée de l'armistice. Certains résistants nouent là des liens ambigus, sensibles qu'ils sont à l'idéologie de l'État français.

Ainsi, les cadres de Vichy formés dans l'école d'Uriage sont à la fois des partisans de la Révolution nationale et des patriotes antiallemands.

C'est en fait la question du futur régime de la nation, une fois qu'elle aura été libérée, qui est déjà posée.

On craint une prise de pouvoir par les communistes, ou le retour aux jeux politiciens de la IIIe République, ou le pouvoir personnel de De Gaulle ; on espère une « rénovation » des institutions, des avancées démocratiques et sociales prenant parfois la forme d'une authentique révolution.

Mais ces oppositions, ces conflits, cette guerre civile larvée, ne concernent en fait qu'une minorité de Français.

Le peuple survit et souffre, « s'arrange » avec les cartes de rationnement, le « marché noir », les restrictions de toute sorte.

Il continue de penser – surtout en zone libre – que Pétain le protège du pire.

L'entrée en guerre de l'URSS (22 juin 1941), puis des États-Unis (7 décembre 1941), la résistance anglaise, l'échec allemand devant Moscou (décembre 1941), le confirment dans l'idée que le IIIe Reich ne peut gagner la guerre.

Qu'un jour, donc, la France sera libérée.

On commence à souffrir à partir de 1942 des bombardements anglais et américains (qui deviendront presque quotidiens en 1944). Ils provoquent des milliers de victimes, mais on est favorable aux Alliés. On attend leur « débarquement ». On écoute la radio anglaise et de Gaulle.

On imagine même qu'entre la France libre et la France de Vichy il y aurait un partage des tâches : Pétain protège, de Gaulle combat.

La figure de De Gaulle conquiert ainsi, au fil de ces mois, une dimension héroïque et presque mythologique.

Les exploits des Forces françaises libres – Bir Hakeim, en mai 1942 – sont connus. On ignore en revanche les conflits qui opposent les Américains à de Gaulle.

On désire l'unité de la nation.

Et de Gaulle comprend que, s'il veut s'imposer aux Anglo-Américains, il lui faut rassembler autour de lui toute la Résistance intérieure, unir les Forces françaises libres et les résistants.

La tâche qu'il confie à Jean Moulin est donc décisive : il s'agit d'unifier la Résistance et de lui faire reconnaître l'autorité de De Gaulle. Ce qui assurera, face aux Alliés, la représentativité et la prééminence du Général, adoubé par toutes les forces françaises combattantes, qu'elles soient à l'intérieur ou à l'extérieur de la France.

Mais, à la fin de 1942, si l'Allemagne engagée dans la bataille de Stalingrad a potentiellement perdu la guerre, rien n'est joué pour la France.

Réussira-t-elle à recouvrer sa souveraineté et son indépendance, donc sa puissance, sa place en Europe et dans le monde ?

Tel a été, dès juillet 1940, le projet de De Gaulle, qui s'est fixé pour objectif de faire asseoir la France « à la table des vainqueurs ».

Mais les États-Unis de Roosevelt ne le souhaitent pas.

De Gaulle est pour eux un personnage incontrôlable, parce que trop indépendant. Or, selon leurs plans, la France cesse d'être une grande puissance. Ils envisagent même de la démembrer et de lui arracher son empire colonial.

Ils n'ont pas même prévenu de Gaulle de leur débarquement en Afrique du Nord française, le 8 novembre 1942.

Ils veulent l'éliminer de l'avenir politique français.

Une nouvelle partie décisive vient de s'engager pour de Gaulle, et donc pour la France.

63.

En ce début du mois de novembre 1942, alors que les barges de débarquement américaines s'approchent des côtes de l'Algérie et du Maroc, le sort de la France est sur le fil du rasoir.

Quel sera son régime alors que la victoire des Alliés sur l'Allemagne est annoncée, même si personne ne peut encore savoir quand elle interviendra ?

Cette incertitude planant sur l'avenir de la nation ne sera pas levée avant le mois d'août 1944, quand Paris prendra les armes, dressera ses barricades, retrouvant le fil de l'histoire, associant les élans et les formes révolutionnaires à l'insurrection nationale.

Mais, jusque-là, tout demeure possible.

La donne internationale change.

Les États-Unis ont pris le pas sur le Royaume-Uni, Roosevelt, sur Churchill.

« De Gaulle est peut-être un honnête homme, écrira le 8 mai 1943 le président des États-Unis au Premier ministre britannique, mais il est en proie au complexe messianique... Je ne sais qu'en faire. Peut-être voudriez-vous le nommer gouverneur de Madagascar ? »

En fait, c'est aux rapports de forces en Europe que pensent Roosevelt et Churchill, et, au fur et à mesure que la menace nazie s'affaiblit – bientôt, on le sait, elle disparaîtra –, au danger croissant que représente l'URSS.

La confrontation avec le communisme a été cachée sous la grande alliance contre l'Allemagne. Mieux valait s'allier avec Staline que se soumettre à Hitler. Mais l'opposition entre les démocraties et l'Union soviétique refait surface et commence même à envahir les esprits à la fin de 1942.

Dans cette perspective, peut-on faire confiance à de Gaulle ?

L'URSS a été parmi les premiers États à reconnaître la France libre.

De plus, le Parti communiste français et ses Francs-tireurs et partisans (FTP), ou encore la Main-d'œuvre immigrée (MOI), auteur des attentats les plus spectaculaires, jouent un rôle majeur dans la Résistance intérieure que de Gaulle entend rassembler autour de lui.

L'ancien préfet Jean Moulin, qu'il a chargé de cette tâche, est soupçonné par certains d'être un agent communiste.

Plus fondamentalement, il y a la tradition française d'alliance avec la Russie comme moyen d'accroître le poids de la France en Europe. Or cela n'apparaît souhaitable ni aux Américains ni aux Anglais.

Dès lors, ce qui s'esquisse en novembre 1942 – puis tout au long de l'année 1943 –, c'est une politique qui favoriserait le passage du gouvernement de Vichy de la collaboration avec l'Allemagne à l'acceptation du tutorat américain.

La continuité de l'État serait ainsi assurée, écartant les risques de troubles, de prise du pouvoir par les communistes et/ou de Gaulle.

Cette politique se met en place à l'occasion du débarquement américain en Afrique du Nord.

L'amiral Darlan – qui, en 1941, a ouvert aux Allemands les aéroports de Syrie, et qui est le numéro un du gouvernement après le renvoi de Laval – se trouve à Alger.

Les Américains le reconnaissent comme président, chef du Comité impérial français : mutation réussie d'un « collaborateur » de haut rang en rallié aux Américains.

« Ce qui se passe en Afrique du Nord du fait de Roosevelt est une ignominie, dira de Gaulle. L'effet sur la Résistance en France est désastreux. »

Les Américains poussent aussi le général Giraud à jouer les premiers rôles – en tant que rival de De Gaulle. Giraud s'est évadé d'Allemagne, c'est à la fois un adepte de la Révolution nationale, un fervent de Pétain et un anti-allemand.

Mais cet « arrangement », qui évite toute rupture politique entre l'occupation et la libération, et ferait de Vichy le gouvernement de la transition, la France changeant simplement de « maîtres », va échouer.

D'abord parce que les hommes de Vichy ne sont pas à la hauteur de ce dessein.

Au lieu de rejoindre Alger – il en aurait eu l'intention –, Pétain reste à Vichy alors même que la zone libre est occupée par les troupes allemandes le 11 novembre 1942.

L'armée de l'armistice n'ébauche pas même un simulacre de résistance.

La flotte – joyau de Vichy – se saborde à Toulon le 27 novembre. Cet acte est le symbole de l'impuissance de Vichy.

Darlan est assassiné le 24 décembre par un jeune monarchiste lié à certains gaullistes, Fernand Bonnier de La Chapelle. Et Giraud, soldat valeureux mais piètre politique, ne peut rivaliser avec de Gaulle, en dépit du soutien américain.

En fait, c'est l'âme de la France qui s'est rebellée contre cette tentative de la soumettre à une nouvelle sujétion.

Le patriotisme, la volonté de voir la nation recouvrer son indépendance et sa souveraineté, de retrouver sa fierté par le combat libérateur, le sentiment que l'histoire de la France lui dicte une conduite à la hauteur de son passé, qu'il faut effacer cette « étrange défaite », ce 1940 qui est un écho de 1815 et de 1870 – Pétain en Bazaine, et non plus le « chef vénéré » –, ont peu à peu gagné l'ensemble du pays.

Cela ne se traduit pas par un soulèvement général.

La Résistance représente à peine plus de 2 % de la population.

Mais ces FFI, ces FTPF, ces réfractaires, ces maquisards, ces « terroristes », ne sont pas seulement de plus en plus nombreux

– le risque du travail obligatoire en Allemagne pousse les jeunes vers la clandestinité dans les villages, les maquis : leurs actions sont approuvées.

Les Allemands (la Gestapo) et les miliciens mènent des opérations de répression efficaces, mais, même s'ils remportent des succès – en juin 1943, arrestation à Calluire des chefs de la Résistance, dont Jean Moulin –, ils ne peuvent étouffer ce mouvement qui vient des profondeurs du pays.

Ce désir de voir renaître la France est si fort que, le 27 mai 1943, les représentants des différents mouvements et partis politiques créent – grâce à la ténacité de Jean Moulin, l'« unificateur » – le Conseil national de la Résistance.

Le CNR élabore un programme politique, économique et social qui le situe dans le droit fil de la République sociale et du Front populaire, par opposition aux principes de la Révolution nationale.

Le CNR reconnaît l'autorité du général de Gaulle, chef de la France combattante.

Dès lors, de Gaulle ne peut que l'emporter face à Giraud.

Il deviendra le président du Comité français de Libération nationale, créé le 3 juin 1943. Une Assemblée consultative provisoire est mise en place le 17 septembre 1943.

« C'est le début de la résurrection des institutions représentatives françaises », dit de Gaulle.

Une armée est reconstituée. Elle libérera la Corse en septembre 1943 – après la capitulation italienne du 8 septembre. Cent trente mille soldats (Algériens, Marocains, Européens d'Algérie) combattront en Italie. L'armée française comptera bientôt 500 000 hommes.

Pétain, Laval et leur gouvernement, dans une France entièrement occupée, ne sont plus que des ombres avec lesquelles jouent les Allemands.

Lorsqu'il tente de justifier sa politique, Laval déclare le 13 décembre 1942 : « C'est une guerre de religion que celle-ci. La victoire de l'Allemagne empêchera notre civilisation de sombrer dans le communisme. La victoire des Américains serait le triomphe des Juifs et du communisme. Quant à moi, j'ai choisi... Je renverserai impitoyablement tout ce qui, sur ma route, m'empêchera de sauver la France. »

Mais sa parole – sans doute sincère – ne peut être entendue. Elle se heurte à la réalité d'une occupation qui devient impitoyable.

Le 26 décembre, vingt-cinq Français sont exécutés à Rennes pour avoir fait sauter le siège de la Légion des volontaires français contre le bolchevisme et le bureau de recrutement de travailleurs français pour l'Allemagne.

Qui peut croire au patriotisme de Laval ?

De Gaulle, au contraire, incarne la France qui a soif de renouveau, d'une République sociale, mais aussi l'ordre, le sens de l'État, le patriotisme qui rassemble toutes les tendances françaises.

Il est le symbole de l'union sacrée.

Cette réussite est due à la conjugaison d'un homme d'État exceptionnel, comme la nation en suscite quand elle est au fond de l'abîme, et du soutien des plus courageux des Français, sachant dépasser leurs divisions et leurs querelles gauloises.

Lui, de Gaulle, a foi en la France, porte un projet pour elle, fait preuve d'une volonté et d'une lucidité hors pair. Il est l'égal des plus grands dont les noms jalonnent l'histoire nationale. Eux, pour le temps du combat salvateur, le soutiennent. Et parce qu'ils sont ensemble, le chef charismatique et les citoyens dévoués à la patrie, rien ne peut leur résister.

Cependant, les Américains s'obstinent.

De Gaulle, chef légitime du Gouvernement provisoire de la République, n'est pas averti de la date et du jour du débarquement en France.

Des dispositions sont prises par les Alliés pour traiter la France en pays « occupé », administré par les autorités militaires. Sa monnaie est déjà imprimée par les Alliés.

La France « libérée » ne pourra recouvrer ni son indépendance ni sa souveraineté.

De Gaulle n'est autorisé à prendre pied en France que huit jours après le débarquement du 6 juin 1944.

Mais la France alors se soulève, payant cher le prix de cet élan (le Vercors, les Glières, tant d'autres combats et tant d'autres villes où sont exécutés des otages : pendus de Tulle, population massacrée d'Oradour-sur-Glane, etc.).

De Gaulle, le 6 juin, a lancé : « C'est la bataille de France, c'est la bataille de la France », et, replaçant ce moment dans la trajectoire nationale, il ajoute : « Derrière le nuage si lourd de notre sang et de nos larmes, voici que reparaît le soleil de notre grandeur ! »

Paris s'insurge le 19 août 1944.

Acte symbolique majeur : « Paris outragé, Paris martyrisé, mais Paris libéré, libéré par lui-même avec le concours des armées de la France. »

La population a dressé des barricades – tradition des journées révolutionnaires.

Les combats sont sévères (3 000 tués, 7 000 blessés). Les chars de la 2e division blindée du général Leclerc – de Gaulle a dû arracher au commandement allié l'autorisation d'avancer vers Paris – et la démoralisation allemande permettent, le 25 août, d'obtenir la reddition de l'occupant.

Forces françaises de l'intérieur et Forces françaises libres sont donc associées dans cette « insurrection » victorieuse.

Les millions de Parisiens rassemblés le 26 août de l'Arc de triomphe à Notre-Dame, qui acclament de Gaulle, expriment l'âme de la France, lavée de la souillure de la défaite et des compromissions comme si elle voulait faire oublier ses lâchetés, sa passivité, son attentisme.

Ainsi le passé héroïque de Paris et de la nation est-il ressuscité par ces journées de combats.

« L'histoire ramassée dans ces pierres et dans ces places, dit de Gaulle, on dirait qu'elle nous sourit. »

Un témoin ajoute que de Gaulle, ce jour-là, semblait « sorti de la tapisserie de Bayeux ».

Quatre années noires, commencées en mai 1940, s'achèvent en ce mois d'août 1944.

Elles ont condensé dans toutes leurs oppositions, et même leurs haines, les tendances contradictoires de l'histoire de la France. Chaque Français, engagé dans les combats de ces années-là, les a vécus comme la continuation d'autres affrontements enfouis dans le tréfonds de la nation.

La Révolution nationale aura été une tentative, à l'occasion de la défaite, de revenir sur les choix que la nation avait faits avec Voltaire, puis la Révolution française. Il s'agissait de retrouver la « tradition » en l'adaptant aux circonstances du XXe siècle, en s'inspirant de Salazar, le dictateur portugais, de Franco et de Mussolini plus que de Hitler.

Mais c'était nier le cours majeur de l'histoire nationale, la spécificité de la France.

Et aussi la singularité de De Gaulle, homme de tradition, mais ouverte, celle-ci, et unifiant toute la nation, ne la divisant pas.

C'est parce que ce choix et ce projet correspondent à l'âme de la France qu'ils s'imposent en août 1944.

3

L'IMPUISSANCE RÉPUBLICAINE

1944-1958

64.

Combien de temps ceux qui parlent au nom de la France – de Gaulle, les représentants des partis politiques et des mouvements de résistance – resteront-ils unis ?

Dès août 1944, le regard qu'ils portent sur les « années noires » les oppose déjà.

Chacun veut s'approprier la gloire et l'héroïsme de la Résistance, masquer ainsi ses calculs, ses ambiguïtés, ses lâchetés et même ses trahisons.

Les communistes du PCF font silence sur la période août 1939-22 juin 1941, quand ils essayaient d'obtenir des autorités d'occupation le droit de faire reparaître leur journal *L'Humanité*. N'étaient-ils pas alors les fidèles servants de l'URSS, partenaire des nazis ?

En 1944-1945, alors que la guerre continue (Strasbourg sera libéré le 23 novembre 1944, les troupes de Leclerc entrent à Berchtesgaden le 4 mai 1945, la capitulation allemande intervient le 8 mai et le général de Lattre de Tassigny est présent aux côtés des Américains, des Russes et des Anglais : victoire diplomatique à forte charge symbolique), les communistes se proclament le « parti des fusillés » – 75 000 héros de la Résistance, précise

Maurice Thorez, déserteur rentré amnistié de Moscou et bientôt ministre d'État.

Le tribunal de Nuremberg dénombrera 30 000 exécutés.

Ce qui se joue, c'est la place des forces politiques dans la France qui recouvre son indépendance. Le comportement des hommes et des partis durant l'Occupation sert de discriminant. On réclame l'épuration et la condamnation des traîtres, des « collabos », avec d'autant plus d'acharnement qu'on ne s'est soi-même engagé dans la Résistance que tardivement.

La magistrature, qui a tout entière – à un juge près ! – prêté serment à Pétain et poursuivi les résistants, condamne maintenant les « collabos ».

On fusille (Laval), on commue la peine de mort de Pétain en prison à vie. Il y a, durant quelques semaines, l'esquisse d'une justice populaire, expéditive, comme l'écho très atténué des jours de violence qui marquèrent jadis les guerres de Religion ou la Révolution, qui tachent de sang l'histoire nationale. Les passions françaises resurgissent.

En 1944, vingt mille femmes, dénoncées, accusées de complaisances envers l'ennemi, sont tondues, promenées nues, insultées, battues, maculées.

Des miliciens et des « collabos » sont fusillés sans jugement. On dénombre peut-être dix mille victimes de ces exécutions sommaires.

Dans le milieu littéraire, le Comité national des écrivains met à l'index, épure, sous la houlette d'Aragon.

Robert Brasillach est condamné à mort et de Gaulle refuse de le gracier malgré les appels à la clémence de François Mauriac.

Drieu la Rochelle se suicidera, prenant acte de la défaite de ses idées, de l'échec de ses engagements.

Jean Paulhan – un résistant – critiquera, dans sa *Lettre aux directeurs de la Résistance*, ces communistes devenus épurateurs, qui n'étaient que des « collaborateurs » d'une espèce différente : « Ils avaient fait choix d'une autre collaboration. Ils ne voulaient pas du tout s'entendre avec l'Allemagne, non, ils voulaient s'entendre avec la Russie. »

C'est bien la question de la Russie soviétique et des communistes qui, en fait, domine la scène française.

Ceux-ci représentent en 1945 près de 27 % des voix, et vont encore progresser.

Avec les socialistes (SFIO) – 24 % des voix –, ils disposent de la majorité absolue à l'Assemblée constituante élue le 21 octobre 1945.

Mais les socialistes préfèrent associer au gouvernement le Mouvement républicain populaire (MRP, 25,6 % des voix), issu de la Résistance et d'inspiration démocrate-chrétienne.

Ainsi se met en place un « gouvernement des partis » : d'abord tripartisme (MRP, SFIO, PCF) puis « Troisième Force » quand le PCF sera écarté du pouvoir à partir de 1947.

En 1944-1945, c'est encore l'union, mais déjà pleine de tensions.

De la résistance victorieuse, passera-t-on à la révolution ?

En août 1944, un Albert Camus le souhaitera. Mais la révolution, est-ce abandonner le pouvoir aux mains des communistes ?

Le risque existe : des milices patriotiques en armes, contrôlées par ces derniers, sont présentes dans de nombreux départements.

Le Front national, le Mouvement de libération nationale, sont des « organisations de masse » dépendantes en fait du PCF.

On peut craindre une subversion, voire une guerre civile, en tout cas une paralysie de l'État républicain soumis au chantage communiste.

La première bataille à conduire doit donc avoir pour but d'affirmer la continuité de la République et de l'État.

De Gaulle s'y emploie en déclarant aux membres du CNR qui lui demandent de proclamer la République, le 26 août 1944 : « La République n'a jamais cessé d'être... Vichy fut toujours nul et non avenu. Moi-même, je suis président du gouvernement de la République. Pourquoi vais-je la proclamer ? »

Attitude radicale et lourde de sens.

Si Vichy a « été nul et non avenu », sans légitimité, les lois qu'il a promulguées, les actes qu'il a exécutés, n'ont aucune valeur légale. Ils n'engagent en rien la France.

Les lois antisémites, la rafle des 16 et 17 juillet 1942, ne peuvent être imputées à la nation.

La France n'a pas à faire repentance. Ce sont des individus – Pétain, Laval, Darnand, Bousquet... – qui doivent répondre de leurs actes criminels, et non la France.

La France et la République étaient incarnées par de Gaulle, la France libre et le Conseil national de la Résistance.

Les vilenies, les lâchetés et les trahisons sont rapportées à des individus, non à la nation.

L'âme de la France ne saurait être entachée par les crimes de Vichy.

Pirouette hypocrite ?

Décision raisonnée pour que le socle sur lequel est bâtie la nation, qui doit beaucoup au regard que l'on porte sur son histoire, ne soit pas fissuré, brisé, corrodé.

Mais, dans cette France dont l'histoire ne saurait être ternie, en sorte qu'on puisse continuer à l'aimer et donc à se battre pour elle, à assurer son avenir, l'État ne peut être affaibli.

Or la principale menace vient des communistes, adossés à l'URSS, dont l'ombre s'étend sur l'Europe.

Ils sont forts de leur engagement dans la Résistance – fût-il tardif et plein d'arrière-pensées –, des « organisations de masse » qu'ils contrôlent et de leur poids électoral. De Gaulle, dont la personnalité et l'action, en 1944, ne peuvent être contestées, exige et obtient le désarmement des milices patriotiques, l'enrôlement des résistants dans l'armée régulière, le rétablissement des autorités étatiques (préfets, etc.). Il refuse aux communistes les postes gouvernementaux clés – Affaires étrangères, Intérieur, Armées – et met sa démission en jeu pour imposer cette décision.

En même temps, il applique le programme économique et social du CNR, et répète que « l'intérêt privé doit céder à l'intérêt général ».

Les nationalisations – des houillères, de l'électricité, des banques –, la création des comités d'entreprise, sont les bases d'une « République sociale » dans le droit fil des mesures prises par le gouvernement de Front populaire, mais en même temps relèvent de la tradition interventionniste de l'État dans la vie économique, inscrite dans la longue durée de l'histoire nationale, de François Ier à Louis XIV, de la Révolution aux premier et second Empires.

La France de 1944-1946 retrouve ainsi les éléments de son histoire que la collaboration avait – mais non sur tous les plans – voulu effacer, s'affirmant comme l'expression d'une autre tradition : non pas 1936, mais 1934, non plus l'édit de Nantes, mais la Saint-Barthélemy ; non plus la Ligue des droits de l'homme et les dreyfusards, mais la Ligue des patriotes et les antidreyfusards.

Cette « restauration » de l'État centralisé, issu de la monarchie absolue, mais aussi des Jacobins et des Empires napoléoniens, se retrouve dans la politique extérieure.

Il s'agit d'assurer à la France sa place dans le concert des Grands.

De Gaulle a réussi à imposer la présence d'un général français à la signature de l'acte de capitulation allemande.

Il obtient une zone d'occupation française en Allemagne, à l'égal de la Grande-Bretagne, des États-Unis et de l'URSS.

Avec cette dernière, il a signé un traité d'amitié (décembre 1944), manière d'affirmer l'indépendance diplomatique de la France alors que s'annonce la politique des blocs.

En même temps, la France reçoit un siège permanent – avec droit de veto – au Conseil de sécurité de l'Organisation des nations unies. Paris est choisi comme siège de l'Unesco. La France a ainsi retrouvé son rang de grande puissance, et quand on se remémore l'effondrement total de 1940 on mesure l'exceptionnel redressement accompli.

Le fait que la France ait été capable, dans la dernière année de la guerre, de mobiliser plusieurs centaines de milliers d'hommes (500 000) engagés dans les combats en Italie et sur le Rhin, puis en Allemagne, a été la preuve de la reconstitution rapide de l'État national et a favorisé la réadmission de la France parmi les grandes puissances.

Elle est l'un des vainqueurs.

Le plus faible, certes, le plus blessé en profondeur, celui qui commence déjà à subir en Indochine et en Algérie – à Sétif, le

8 mai 1945 – les revendications d'indépendance des nationalistes des colonies.

Mais elle peut à nouveau faire entendre sa voix, envisager une entente avec l'Allemagne.

Depuis 1870, entre les deux nations, c'est une alternance de défaites et de revanches : 1870, effacé par la victoire de 1918 ; celle-ci gommée par l'étrange défaite de 1940, annulée à son tour par la capitulation allemande de 1945. Se rendant cette année-là à Mayence, de Gaulle, face à cet affrontement toujours renouvelé et stérile entre « Germains et Gaulois », peut dire :

« Ici, tant que nous sommes, nous sortons de la même race. Vous êtes, comme nous, des enfants de l'Occident et de l'Europe. »

Ces constats ne peuvent devenir les fondations d'une politique étrangère nouvelle que si le régime échappe aux faiblesses institutionnelles qui ont caractérisé la IIIᵉ République.

Ainsi se pose à la France, dès la fin de 1944, la question de sa Constitution.

De Gaulle a obtenu par référendum, contre tous les partis, que l'Assemblée élue le 21 octobre 1944 soit constituante.

Mais, dès les premiers débats, les partis politiques choisissent de soumettre le pouvoir exécutif au pouvoir parlementaire, le président de la République se trouvant ainsi réduit à une fonction de représentation.

On peut prévoir que les maux de la IIIᵉ République – instabilité gouvernementale, jeux des partis, méfiance à l'égard de la consultation directe des électeurs par référendum – paralyseront de nouveau le régime, le réduisant à l'impuissance.

De Gaulle tire la conséquence de cet état de fait et démissionne le 20 janvier 1946 en demandant « aux partis d'assumer leurs responsabilités ».

C'est la fin de l'unité nationale issue de la Résistance. Dès le 16 juin 1946, le Général se présente comme le « recours » contre la trop prévisible impotence de la IVᵉ République qui commence.

La France unie a donc été capable de restaurer l'État, de reprendre sa place dans le monde. Mais les facteurs de division issus de son histoire, avivés par la conjoncture internationale (la guerre froide s'annonce, isolant les communistes, liés *perinde ac cadaver* à l'URSS), font éclater l'union fragile des forces politiques. Les partis veulent être maîtres du jeu comme sous la IIIᵉ République. L'exécutif leur est soumis. Il ne peut prendre les décisions qui s'imposent alors que, dans l'empire colonial, se lèvent les orages.

65.

De 1946 à 1958, durant la courte durée de vie de la IVᵉ République, la France change en profondeur. Mais le visage politique du pays s'est à peine modifié. Le président du Conseil subit la loi implacable de l'Assemblée nationale. Il lui faut obtenir une investiture personnelle, puis, une fois le gouvernement constitué, il doit solliciter à nouveau un vote de confiance des députés.

L'Assemblée est donc toute-puissante, et le Conseil de la République (la deuxième chambre, qui a remplacé le Sénat) n'émet qu'un vote consultatif.

Dès lors, comme dans les années 30, l'instabilité gouvernementale est la règle. Chaque député influent espère chevaucher le manège ministériel. Mais ce sont le plus souvent les mêmes hommes qui se succèdent, changeant de portefeuilles.

Ces gouvernements, composés conformément aux règles constitutionnelles, sont parfaitement légaux. Mais, question cardinale, sont-ils légitimes ? Quel est le rapport entre le « pays légal » et le « pays réel » ?

Il n'est pas nécessaire d'être un disciple de Maurras pour constater le fossé qui se creuse entre les élites politiques et le peuple qu'elles sont censées représenter et au nom duquel elles gouvernent.

Cette fracture, si souvent constatée dans l'histoire nationale, s'élargit jour après jour, crise après crise, entre 1946 et 1954, année qui représentera, avec le début de l'insurrection en Algérie, un tournant aigu après lequel tout s'accélère jusqu'à l'effondrement du régime, en mai 1958.

La discordance entre gouvernants et gouvernés est d'autant plus nette que le pays et le monde ont, pendant cette décennie, été bouleversés par des changements politiques, technologiques, économiques et sociaux.

À partir de 1947, la guerre froide a coupé l'Europe en deux blocs. Les nations de l'Est sont sous la botte russe.

Le « coup de Prague » en 1948, le blocus de Berlin par les Russes, la division de l'Allemagne en deux États, la guerre de Corée en 1950, la création du Kominform en 1947, de l'OTAN en 1949, auquel répondra le pacte de Varsovie, le triomphe des communistes chinois (1949), tous ces événements ont des conséquences majeures sur la vie politique française.

Le 4 mai 1947, les communistes sont chassés du gouvernement. L'anticommunisme devient le ciment des majorités qui se constituent et n'existent que grâce à une modification de la loi électorale qui, par le jeu des « apparentements », rogne la représentation parlementaire communiste.

Le PCF ne perd pas de voix, au contraire, mais il perd des sièges. En 1951, avec 26 % des voix, il a le même nombre de députés que les socialistes, qui n'en rassemblent que 15 % !

La « troisième force » (SFIO, MRP et députés indépendants à droite) est évidemment légale, mais non représentative du pays.

Elle l'est d'autant moins qu'autour du général de Gaulle s'est créé en 1947 le Rassemblement du peuple français (RPF), qui va obtenir jusqu'à 36 % des voix.

De Gaulle conteste les institutions de la IVe République, « un système absurde et périmé » qui entretient la division du pays alors qu'il faudrait retrouver « les fécondes grandeurs d'une nation libre sous l'égide d'un État fort ».

Même s'il dénonce les communistes, qui « ont fait vœu d'obéissance aux ordres d'une entreprise étrangère de domination », de Gaulle est considéré par les partis de la « troisième force » comme un « général factieux », et Blum dira : « L'entreprise gaulliste n'a plus rien de républicain. »

En fait, l'opposition entre les partis de la « troisième force » et le mouvement gaulliste va bien au-delà de la question institutionnelle. Certes, inscrites dans la tradition républicaine, il y a le refus et la crainte du « pouvoir personnel », le souvenir des Bonaparte, du maréchal de Mac-Mahon, et même du général Boulanger, la condamnation de l'idée d'« État fort ». L'épisode récent du gouvernement Pétain – encore un militaire ! – a renforcé cette allergie.

La République, ce sont les partis démocratiques qui la font vivre. L'autorité d'un président de la République disposant d'un vrai pouvoir est, selon eux, antinomique avec le fonctionnement républicain.

Mais, en outre, le « gaullisme » est ressenti comme une forme de nationalisme qui conduit au jeu libre et indépendant d'une France souveraine.

Or, la « troisième force », c'est la mise en œuvre de limitations apportées à la souveraineté nationale, la construction d'une Europe libre sous protection américaine (l'OTAN).

La Communauté européenne du charbon et de l'acier (CECA) est constituée en 1951. Elle doit être le noyau d'une Europe politique de six États membres, et doit déboucher sur une Communauté européenne de défense (CED) dans laquelle l'Allemagne sera présente et donc réarmée.

L'homme qui, par ses idées, sa détermination, son entregent et son activisme diplomatique, est la cheville ouvrière de cette politique européenne a nom Jean Monnet.

Dès 1940, il s'est opposé au général de Gaulle. À chaque étape de l'histoire de la France libre, il a tenté de faire prévaloir les points de vue américains, pesant à Washington pour qu'on écarte de Gaulle et nouant des intrigues à Alger, en 1942-1943, pour parvenir à ce but.

Or il est le grand ordonnateur de cette politique européenne qui trouve sa source dans la volonté d'en finir avec les guerres

« civiles » européennes – et donc de parvenir à la réconciliation franco-allemande –, mais ambitionne d'être ainsi un élément de la politique américaine de *containment* de l'Union soviétique, ce qui implique la soumission des États nationaux fondus dans une structure européenne orientée par les États-Unis.

Sur ce point capital, la « troisième force » dénonce la convergence entre communistes et gaullistes hostiles à l'Europe supranationale. Elle se présente comme l'expression d'une politique démocratique opposée aux « extrêmes » qu'elle combat.

Le général de Gaulle se trouve ainsi censuré, puisqu'il est devenu le chef du RPF.

Quant aux communistes et au syndicat CGT qu'ils contrôlent, leurs manifestations sont souvent interdites, dispersées, suivies d'arrestations.

Les grèves du printemps 1947 – prétexte à l'éviction des communistes du gouvernement –, puis celles, quasi insurrectionnelles, de 1948 sont brisées par un ministre de l'Intérieur socialiste, Jules Moch, qui n'hésite pas à faire appel à l'armée.

En 1952, les manifestations antiaméricaines du 28 mai pour protester contre la nomination à la tête de l'OTAN du général Ridgway, qui a commandé en Corée, donnent lieu à de violents affrontements ; des dirigeants communistes sont arrêtés.

Mais, face à ces ennemis « de l'intérieur », le système politique tient. En 1953, le RPF ne recueille plus que 15 % des voix. Ses députés sont attirés par le manège ministériel, et de Gaulle continue sa « traversée du désert » en rédigeant ses Mémoires à la Boisserie, sa demeure de Colombey-les-Deux-Églises.

Si les oppositions au « système » ne réussissent pas à le renverser, c'est que, de 1946 à 1954, le fait qu'il soit « absurde et périmé » (selon de Gaulle) ne perturbe pas le mouvement de la société.

Car si la vie politique ressemble de plus en plus à celle des années 30 et 40 – instabilité gouvernementale, scandales, « manège ministériel » –, le pays, lui, subit des bouleversements profonds que le système politique ne freine pas, mais tend même à favoriser.

C'est la période des « Trente Glorieuses », de la modernisation économique du pays, de la révolution agricole, qui transforme la société française par la multiplication des activités industrielles et du nombre des ouvriers, l'exode rural, la croissance de la population urbaine.

Cette période est certes traversée de mouvements sociaux – grèves en 1953, par exemple, dans la fonction publique pour les salaires –, du mécontentement de catégories que l'évolution marginalise – artisans, petits commerçants –, sensibles aux discours antiparlementaires d'un Pierre Poujade.

On proteste contre le poids des impôts. Mais, dans le même temps, Antoine Pinay, président du Conseil et ministre des Finances, rassure par sa politique budgétaire, la stabilisation du franc. Le niveau de vie des Français croît.

La voiture, l'électroménager, la vie urbaine, modifient les comportements. Une France différente apparaît. Les mœurs changent. Les femmes ont le droit de vote, elles travaillent. Et un véritable baby-boom – préparé par les mesures natalistes de Paul Reynaud en 1938, puis de Vichy – marque ces années 1946-1954 et confirme la vitalité de la nation. L'« étrange défaite » ne l'a pas terrassée.

Cet après-guerre illustre ainsi la capacité qu'à toujours eue la France, au long de son histoire, à basculer dans les abîmes, à connaître les débâcles, à sembler définitivement perdue parce que divisée, dressée contre elle-même, envahie, « outragée », puis à se ressaisir, renaître tout à coup et reprendre sa place parmi les plus grands.

Autre caractéristique de l'histoire nationale : les crises qui mettent en cause l'âme du pays sont celles qui associent les maladies internes du système politique et les traumatismes nés de la confrontation avec le monde extérieur.

C'est presque toujours dans ses rapports avec les « autres » que la France risque de se briser. Comme si, trop narcissique, trop enfermée dans son hexagone, trop persuadée de sa prééminence, elle pensait depuis toujours qu'elle l'emporterait sur ceux qui osent la défier.

Simplement parce qu'elle est la France.

Cette France « que la Providence a créée pour des succès achevés ou des malheurs exemplaires [...] n'est réellement elle-même qu'au premier rang... La France ne peut être la France sans la grandeur » (de Gaulle).

Elle ne « voit » pas les autres tels qu'ils sont, y compris ceux qui participent, quoique différents et éloignés de la métropole, à l'Union française, nom donné par la IVe République à l'empire colonial.

C'est sur ce terrain que le système politique va affronter les crises les plus graves.

Le jeu politicien, qui peut être le moyen de régler avec habileté une crise sociale – on élargit sa majorité, on renverse un président du Conseil, on accorde quelques satisfactions aux syndicats –, ne suffit plus.

C'est d'insurrection nationale – et communiste – qu'il s'agit, en 1946, en Indochine. Paris a réagi en faisant bombarder Haiphong.

L'année suivante, la rébellion de Madagascar est noyée dans le sang, comme l'a été, le 8 mai 1945, l'émeute algérienne de Sétif.

Or ces répressions ne résolvent pas le problème posé.

Et le système, prisonnier de ses indécisions, va conduire, de 1946 à 1954, une « sale guerre » en Indochine, ponctuée de défaites, de scandales, de protestations – « Paix en Indochine ! » crieront les communistes.

Des milliers de soldats et d'officiers tombent dans les rizières.

À partir de 1949, la victoire communiste en Chine apporte au Viêt-minh une aide en matériel qui rend encore plus précaire la situation des troupes françaises.

Les chefs militaires jugent que le « système » refuse de leur donner les moyens de vaincre. Le 7 mai 1954, lorsqu'il sont défaits à Diên Biên Phu, dans une bataille « classique », ils le ressentent douloureusement et mettent en cause le régime. Cette défaite ébranle la IVe République.

Pierre Mendès France, combattant de la France libre, radical courageux, est investi le 18 juin 1954. Président du Conseil, il veut incarner, porté par un mouvement d'opinion, une « République moderne » apte à rénover le pays et dont le chef soit capable de prendre des décisions.

C'est un nouveau style politique qui apparaît avec « PMF ».

Il cherche le contact direct avec l'opinion. Un journal est lancé – L'Express – pour le soutenir.

L'homme, vertueux, récuse le soutien des députés communistes. Il ne veut pas des voix des « séparatistes ».

Le 20 juillet 1954, il signe un accord de paix avec le Viêt-minh sur la base de la division provisoire de l'Indochine à hauteur du 17e parallèle. Après ce succès, Mendès France évoque à Carthage un nouveau statut pour la Tunisie.

Pour les uns, la « droite conservatrice », il est celui qui « brade » l'empire.

Pour les autres, la gauche réformatrice et certains gaullistes, il est l'homme politique qui peut rénover la République.

Mais, dans le cadre des institutions existantes, il est à la merci d'un changement de majorité, de la défection de quelques députés.

On lui reproche de ne pas s'être engagé dans la bataille à propos de la Communauté européenne de défense contre laquelle se sont ligués communistes, gaullistes et tous ceux qui sont hostiles au réarmement allemand.

La France rejette la CED le 30 août 1954. Une majorité de l'opinion a refusé d'entamer la souveraineté nationale en matière de défense.

La position de Pierre Mendès France est en outre fragilisée par les attentats qui se produisent en Algérie le 1er novembre 1954, et qui, par leur nombre, annoncent, quelques mois après la défaite de Diên Biên Phu, qu'un nouveau front s'est ouvert.

PMF déclare : « Les départements d'Algérie constituent une partie de la République française. Ils sont français depuis longtemps, et d'une manière irrévocable. »

Et son ministre François Mitterrand de préciser : « L'Algérie c'est la France ! »

Malgré ces déclarations martiales, Pierre Mendès France est renversé le 5 février 1955.

Au-delà même des désaccords politiques qu'on peut avoir avec le président du Conseil, il est dans la logique même du système de ne pas tolérer, à la tête de l'exécutif, une personnalité politique qui s'appuie sur l'opinion et peut ainsi contourner les députés. Le régime d'assemblée peut laisser un chef de gouvernement tenter de régler à ses risques et périls un problème brûlant, la guerre d'Indochine. Mais sa réussite même implique qu'il soit renvoyé pour ne pas attenter, par son autorité et son prestige, aux pouvoirs du Parlement.

Ce régime a besoin de médiocres. Il se défait des gouvernants trop populaires.

Or Pierre Mendès France l'était.

Mais ce système ne peut fonctionner et durer que si les crises qu'il affronte sont aussi « médiocres » que les hommes qu'il promeut. Or, le 1er novembre 1954, l'Algérie et la France ont commencé de vivre une tragédie.

66.

En une dizaine d'années, de 1945 à 1955, la France a repris le visage et la place d'une grande nation.

L'abîme de 1940 semble loin derrière elle, mais, sous ses pas qui se croient assurés, le sol s'ouvre à nouveau.

L'armée est humiliée après Diên Biên Phu.

Et voici qu'on s'apprête à abandonner Bizerte, la grande base militaire de la Méditerranée, parce qu'on accorde l'indépendance à la Tunisie.

On a agi de même au Maroc.

Or on commence déjà à égorger en Algérie. Un Front de libération nationale (FLN) s'est constitué. En août 1955, dans le Constantinois, il multiplie les attentats, les assassinats.

Va-t-on abandonner à son tour l'Algérie ?

Elle est composée de départements. On y dénombre, face à 8 400 000 musulmans, 980 000 Européens.

Les officiers, vaincus en Indochine, soupçonnent le pouvoir politique d'être prêt à une nouvelle capitulation, bien qu'il répète : « L'Algérie c'est la France. »

Le chef d'état-major des armées fera savoir au président de la République, René Coty, que « l'armée, d'une manière unanime, ressentirait comme un outrage l'abandon de ce patrimoine national. On ne saurait préjuger de sa réaction de désespoir. »

Ce message émane, au mois de mai 1958, du général Salan, commandant en chef en Algérie.

Si ce mois de mai 1958 marque le paroxysme de la crise, en fait, dès janvier 1955, tout est en place pour la tragédie algérienne.

Lorsqu'il publie un essai sous ce titre, en juin 1957, Raymond Aron a clairement identifié les termes du problème : la France ne dispose pas des moyens politiques, diplomatiques et moraux pour faire face victorieusement aux revendications nationalistes.

L'attitude de l'armée, l'angoisse des Français d'Algérie – les « pieds-noirs » –, l'impuissance du régime et le contexte international sont les ressorts de cette tragédie.

De Gaulle – toujours retiré à Colombey-les-Deux-Églises, mais l'immense succès du premier tome de ses Mémoires (*L'Appel*, 1954) montre bien que son prestige est inentamé – confie en 1957 :

« Notre pays ne supporte plus la faiblesse de ceux qui le dirigent. Le drame d'Algérie sera sans doute la cause d'un sursaut des meilleurs des Français. Il ne se passera pas longtemps avant qu'ils soient obligés de venir me chercher. »

Seuls quelques gaullistes engagés dans les jeux du pouvoir – Chaban-Delmas sera ministre de la Défense, Jacques Soustelle a été nommé par Pierre Mendès France, en janvier 1955, gouverneur général de l'Algérie – espèrent ce retour de De Gaulle et vont habilement en créer les conditions.

Mais la quasi-totalité des hommes politiques y sont, en 1955, résolument hostiles, persuadés qu'ils vont pouvoir faire face à la crise algérienne. Ils ne perçoivent ni sa gravité, ni l'usure du système, ni le mépris dans lequel les Français tiennent ce régime.

Il a fallu treize tours de scrutin pour que députés et sénateurs élisent le nouveau président de la République, René Coty !

Aux élections anticipées de janvier 1956, le Front républicain conduit par Pierre Mendès France l'emporte, mais c'est le leader de la SFIO, Guy Mollet, qui est investi comme président du Conseil.

Déception des électeurs, qui ont le sentiment d'avoir été privés de leur victoire. D'autant que Guy Mollet, qui se rend à Alger le 6 février 1958 afin d'y installer un nouveau gouverneur général – Soustelle a démissionné –, est l'objet de violentes manifestations européennes, et que le général Catroux, gouverneur désigné, renonce.

Cette capitulation du pouvoir politique devant l'émeute algéroise – soutenue à l'arrière-plan par les autorités militaires et administratives, et par tous ceux qui sont partisans de l'Algérie française – ferme la voie à toute négociation.

Elle ne laisse place qu'à l'emploi de la force armée contre des « rebelles » prêts à toutes les exactions au nom de la légitimité de leur combat.

Des populations qui ne rallient pas le FLN sont massacrées, des soldats français prisonniers, suppliciés et exécutés.

Ainsi l'engrenage de la cruauté se met-il en branle, et derrière le mot de « pacification » se cache une guerre sale : camps de regroupement, tortures afin de faire parler les détenus et de gagner la « bataille d'Alger » – printemps-été 1957 – par n'importe quel moyen et d'enrayer la vague d'attentats déclenchés par le FLN. Et « corvées de bois » – liquidation des prisonniers. On peut aussi administrer la mort dans les formes légales en guillotinant les « rebelles ».

C'est une plaie profonde, une sorte de gangrène qui atteint l'âme de la France.

Des écrivains – Mauriac, Malraux, Sartre, Pierre-Henri Simon –, des professeurs (Pierre Vidal-Naquet, Jean-Pierre Vernant, Henri-Irénée Marrou) s'élèvent contre la pratique de la torture par l'armée française.

On les censure, on les poursuit, on les révoque.

Face à eux se dressent d'autres intellectuels, des officiers qui n'entendent pas subir une nouvelle défaite. Ils estiment qu'il faut, dans ce type d'affrontement, pratiquer une « guerre révolutionnaire » inéluctable si l'on veut éradiquer une guérilla, neutraliser les terroristes.

Le débat touche toute la nation à partir de 1956.

Le gouvernement Guy Mollet – qui obtient les pleins pouvoirs – rappelle plusieurs classes d'âge sous les drapeaux, envoie le contingent en Algérie, prolonge de fait le service militaire jusqu'à vingt-neuf mois. Deux millions de jeunes Français ont ainsi participé à cette guerre.

Des manifestations de « rappelés » tentent de bloquer les voies ferrées pour arrêter les trains qui les conduisent dans les ports d'embarquement.

Des écrivains se rassemblent dans un « Manifeste des 121 » pour appuyer le « droit à l'insoumission » (Claude Simon, Michel Butor, Claude Sarraute, Jean-François Revel, Jean-Paul Sartre) en septembre 1960.

Mendès France, ministre d'État, démissionne le 23 mai 1956 du gouvernement Guy Mollet afin de marquer son opposition à cette politique algérienne.

La France vit ainsi de manière de plus en plus aiguë, à partir de 1956, un moment de tensions et de divisions qui fait écho aux dissensions qui l'ont partagée tout au long de son histoire.

On évoque l'affaire Dreyfus. On recueille, à la manière de Jaurès, des preuves pour établir les faits, identifier les tortionnaires, condamner ce pouvoir politique qui a remis aux militaires – le général Massu à Alger – les fonctions du maintien de l'ordre en laissant l'armée agir à sa guise, choisir les moyens qu'elle juge nécessaires à l'accomplissement de sa mission.

La « gangrène » corrompt ainsi le pouvoir politique et certaines unités de l'armée dans une sorte de patriotisme dévoyé.

Certains officiers s'insurgent contre cette guerre qui viole le droit : ainsi le général Pâris de Bollardière, héros de la France libre. D'autres tentent de faire la part des choses afin de conjuguer honneur et efficacité.

Le responsable de ce chaos moral est à l'évidence un pouvoir politique hésitant, instable et impuissant.

En 1956, outre l'envoi du contingent en Algérie – choix d'une solution militaire à laquelle on accorde tous les moyens, et les pleins pouvoirs sur le terrain –, il a tenté de remporter une victoire politique.

Violant le droit international, le gouvernement a détourné un avion de ligne et arrêté les chefs du FLN.

Puis, en octobre-novembre 1956, en accord avec le Royaume-Uni et l'État d'Israël, la France participe à une expédition militaire en Égypte afin de riposter à la nationalisation du canal de Suez décidée par les Égyptiens. Mais, pour Guy Mollet, s'y ajoute l'intention de frapper les soutiens internationaux du FLN en abattant au Caire le régime nationaliste du colonel Nasser.

Le moment paraît bien choisi : les Russes font face à une révolution patriotique en Hongrie.

Les États-Unis sont à la veille d'une élection présidentielle.

Guy Mollet espère aussi obtenir un regain de popularité dans l'opinion, satisfaite d'une opération militaire réussie – et qu'on exalte –, et favorable au soutien à Israël.

Mais Russes et Américains vont dénoncer conjointement cette initiative militaire, et les troupes franco-britanniques seront rapatriées.

Cet échec scelle une nouvelle étape dans la décomposition de la IVe République et annonce celle du Parti socialiste.

Il confirme que la « tragédie algérienne » domine la politique française.

Des événements lourds de conséquences – le traité de Rome, qui crée la Communauté économique européenne et Euratom en 1957, la loi-cadre de Gaston Defferre pour l'Union française, ou même l'attribution d'une troisième semaine de congés payés – sont éclipsés par les graves tensions que crée la guerre d'Algérie.

Le sort de la IVe République est bien déterminé par elle.

Il est scellé au mois de mai 1958, en quelques jours.

Paris et Alger sont les deux pôles de l'action.

À Paris, le 13 mai, Pierre Pflimlin, député MRP, est investi à une très large majorité (473 voix contre 93, les communistes lui ayant apporté leurs suffrages). Président du Conseil, on le soupçonne d'être un partisan de la négociation avec le FLN.

À Alger, depuis plusieurs mois, des gaullistes veulent se servir des complots que trament les « activistes », décidés à maintenir l'Algérie française avec l'appui de l'armée, pour favoriser un retour du général de Gaulle.

Le 13 mai, des manifestants envahissent les bâtiments publics – le siège du Gouvernement général – et les mettent à sac.

Le général Massu prend la tête d'un « Comité de salut public » qui réclame au président de la République la constitution d'un « gouvernement de salut public ».

En même temps, des éléments de l'armée préparent une opération « Résurrection » dont le but est d'envoyer en métropole des unités de parachutistes.

La perspective d'un coup d'État militaire est utilisée par les gaullistes pour lancer l'idée d'un recours au général de Gaulle, seul capable d'empêcher le *pronunciamiento*.

À Paris, de Gaulle, le 19 mai, au cours d'une conférence de presse, se montre disponible. Tout en n'approuvant pas le projet de coup d'État – qu'il ne désavoue cependant pas –, il affirme qu'il veut rester dans le cadre de la légalité en se présentant en candidat à la direction du pays.

Ce double jeu réussit, avec la complicité du président Coty, qui entre en contact avec le Général et le désigne en fait pour assurer la charge suprême.

Pflimlin démissionne le 27 mai.

La gauche manifeste le 28, dénonçant la manœuvre, répétant que « le fascisme ne passera pas », marchant derrière Mitterrand, Mendès France, Daladier et le communiste Waldeck Rochet.

Mais les jeux sont faits : un accord a été passé avec Guy Mollet et les chefs des groupes parlementaires. Mitterrand seul l'a refusé.

Le 1er juin, la manœuvre gaulliste, utilisant la menace de coup d'État mais demeurant formellement dans le cadre de la légalité, a abouti : devant l'Assemblée nationale, de Gaulle obtient 329 voix contre 224.

Il dispose des pleins pouvoirs.

Le gouvernement – qui comprend notamment André Malraux, Michel Debré, Guy Mollet, Pierre Pflimlin – est chargé de préparer une Constitution.

Le 4 juin, de Gaulle se rend en Algérie. Il est acclamé et lance : « Je vous ai compris » et « Vive l'Algérie française ! »

L'ambiguïté demeure : de Gaulle a été appelé pour résoudre le problème algérien. Par la négociation ou par une guerre victorieuse ? En satisfaisant les partisans de l'Algérie française, ou en inventant un nouveau statut pour l'Algérie, voire en lui accordant l'autodétermination et l'indépendance ?

De Gaulle a les moyens d'agir.

La Constitution, qui est à la fois présidentielle et parlementaire, mais donne de larges pouvoirs au président élu par un collège de 80 000 « notables », permet à l'exécutif d'échapper aux jeux parlementaires, même si le gouvernement doit obtenir la confiance des députés.

Avec l'article 16, le président dispose en outre d'un moyen légal d'assumer tous les pouvoirs et de placer *de facto* le pays en état de siège.

Le 28 septembre 1958, par référendum, 79,2 % des votants approuvent la Constitution.

La IVᵉ République est morte. La Vᵉ vient de naître.

Le 21 décembre, de Gaulle est élu président de la République par 78,5 % des voix du collège des « grands électeurs », où les élus locaux écrasent par leur nombre les parlementaires.

Le 9 janvier, Michel Debré est nommé Premier ministre.

L'impuissance de la IVᵉ République a donc conduit à sa perte.

La crise, qui pouvait déboucher sur une guerre civile, s'est dénouée dans le respect formel des règles et des procédures républicaines. Mais le passage d'une République à l'autre s'est déroulé sous la menace – le chantage ? – d'un coup d'État.

Aux yeux de certains (Pierre Mendès France avec sincérité, Mitterrand en habile politicien), là est le péché originel de la Vᵉ République. Selon eux, la Constitution gaulliste ne pourrait donner naissance qu'à un régime de « coup d'État permanent ».

En fait, le pays apaisé a choisi l'homme dont il pense qu'il peut en finir avec la tragédie algérienne.

Mais de Gaulle voit plus loin :

« L'appel qui m'est adressé par le pays exprime son instinct de salut. S'il me charge de le conduire, c'est parce qu'il veut aller non certes à la facilité, mais à l'effort et au renouveau. En vérité, il était temps ! »

Est-ce, en germe, la manifestation d'un malentendu ?

Le pays et les hommes politiques appellent ou acceptent de Gaulle pour régler un problème précis. De Gaulle, lui, est porté par une ambition nationale de grande ampleur.

Quoi qu'il en soit, la IVᵉ République était condamnée :

« Quand les hommes ne choisissent pas, écrit Raymond Aron en 1959, les événements choisissent pour eux. La fréquence des crises ministérielles discréditait le régime aux yeux des Français et des étrangers. À la longue, un pays ne peut obéir à ceux qu'il méprise. »

Surtout si ce pays a l'âme de la France.

4

L'EFFORT ET L'ESPOIR GAULLIENS

1958-1969

67.

Durant plus de dix ans, de juin 1958 à avril 1969, la France a choisi de Gaulle.

Au cours de cette décennie, le peuple, consulté à plusieurs reprises par voie de référendum, à l'occasion d'élections législatives ou dans le cadre d'une élection présidentielle au suffrage universel (1965), s'est clairement exprimé.

Jamais, au cours des précédentes Républiques – notamment la IIIe et la IVe –, le pouvoir politique n'a été autant légitimé par le suffrage universel direct. Jamais donc le « pays légal » n'a autant coïncidé avec le « pays réel ».

Si bien que cette pratique politique – usage du référendum, élection du président de la République au suffrage universel direct après la modification constitutionnelle de 1962 – a créé une profonde rupture avec la IVe République, qui avait prorogé toutes les dérives et les impuissances de la IIIe.

La Ve République est bien un régime radicalement nouveau, né de la réflexion du général de Gaulle amorcée avant 1940.

C'est un régime rigoureusement démocratique, même si les conditions de son instauration, on l'a vu, sont exceptionnelles.

Ceux qui, comme Mitterand, ont ressassé que ce régime était celui du « coup d'État permanent » et que de Gaulle n'était qu'une sorte de Franco, un dictateur, ont été – quel qu'ait été l'écho de leurs propos dans certains milieux, notamment la presse et le monde des politiciens – démentis par les faits, le résultat des scrutins venant souvent contredire les éclats de voix et de plume des commentateurs, voire l'ampleur des manifestations de rue.

Lorsque, en avril 1969, de Gaulle propose par voie de référendum une réforme portant sur l'organisation des pouvoirs régionaux, il avertit solennellement le pays :

« Votre réponse va engager le destin de la France, parce que si je suis désavoué par une majorité d'entre vous..., ma tâche actuelle de chef de l'État deviendra évidemment impossible et je cesserai aussitôt d'exercer mes fonctions. »

Ce que les opposants du général de Gaulle qualifient de stratégie du « Moi ou le chaos » n'est que la volonté de placer le débat en toute clarté, à son plus haut niveau de responsabilités.

Battu par 53,18 % des voix au référendum du 27 avril 1969, de Gaulle quitte immédiatement ses fonctions.

Cette leçon de morale politique est l'un des legs de ces dix années gaulliennes.

Elle exprime une conception vertueuse de la politique, tranchant sur celles des politiciens opportunistes qui ont peuplé les palais gouvernementaux avant et après de Gaulle.

Elle reste inscrite dans l'âme de la France. De Gaulle lui doit beaucoup de son aura, de son autorité et du respect qu'il inspire encore.

Pour cela, il est l'une des références majeures de l'histoire nationale.

On en oublie même que sa présidence a d'abord été tout entière dominée par la tragédie algérienne, qui ne trouve sa fin, dans la douleur, l'amertume, la colère, parfois la honte, le remords et le sang, qu'en 1962.

De Gaulle ne peut déployer son projet pour la France qu'après avoir arraché le pays au guêpier algérien. Mais il a consacré à cette tâche plus de quatre années, et il ne lui en reste que cinq

– de 1963 à 1968 – pour ouvrir et conduire des chantiers vitaux pour la nation, avant les manifestations de mai 1968.

Ces dernières le conduisent à s'assurer en 1969 que le « pays réel » lui accorde toujours sa confiance.

Au vu de la réponse, il se retire.

D'ailleurs, dès 1958, et tout au long des étapes qui marquent sa politique algérienne, de Gaulle a procédé, de même, à des « vérifications » électorales par consultation des députés ou le plus souvent par référendum.

Il fait ainsi légitimer – par le peuple directement, indirectement par les élus – les initiatives qu'il prend.

En septembre 1959, les députés approuvent sa politique d'autodétermination par 441 voix contre 23.

« Le sort des Algériens, dit-il, appartient aux Algériens non point comme le leur imposerait le couteau et la mitraillette, mais suivant la volonté qu'ils exprimeront par le suffrage universel. »

Ce qui suscite une émeute à Alger chez les partisans de l'Algérie française : cette « journée des barricades » (24 janvier 1960) provoque la mort de 14 gendarmes auxquels les parachutistes n'ont pas apporté le soutien prévu.

Ainsi se dessine un péril qu'aucune République française n'a jamais réellement affronté : celui d'un coup d'État militaire, bien plus grave que la tentative personnelle d'un général cherchant l'appui de l'armée.

Quand, le 14 novembre 1960, de Gaulle déclare : « L'Algérie algérienne existera un jour », il fait approuver ce « saut » vers l'indépendance algérienne par voie de référendum.

Il obtient un « oui franc et massif » : 75,26 % des voix.

Mais une Organisation armée secrète (OAS) s'est créée, qui va multiplier les attentats, les assassinats.

Pis : un « putsch des généraux » s'empare du pouvoir à Alger (21 avril 1961). Il vise à renverser le régime.

Cette rébellion, fait unique dans l'histoire des républiques, souligne la profondeur de la crise, le traumatisme qui secoue l'âme de la France.

La nation mesure qu'elle vit un tournant de son histoire, la fin, dans la souffrance, d'une époque impériale – quel sort pour les Français d'Algérie, ce territoire si profondément inséré dans la République, celui dont tous les gouvernements ont assuré qu'il était la France, unie « de Dunkerque à Tamanrasset » ?

De Gaulle condamne le « pouvoir insurrectionnel établi en Algérie par un *pronunciamiento* militaire ». Il stigmatise ce « quarteron de généraux » en retraite (Salan, Challe, Jouhaud, Zeller) qu'inspirent des « officiers fanatiques ».

Cette tentative, en rupture avec toutes les traditions nationales, va échouer, le pouvoir légitime de De Gaulle recevant l'appui de l'ensemble des soldats du contingent et d'une majorité d'officiers.

Dès lors, en dépit des attentats perpétrés par l'OAS, des manifestations de la population algéroise (la troupe tire sur les pieds-noirs, rue de l'Isly et dans certains quartiers d'Alger, faisant plus de cinquante morts), un accord de cessez-le-feu est conclu à Évian le 18 mars 1962.

Il est approuvé par près de 90 % des Français consultés par référendum le 19 avril.

Fin de la guerre commencée il y a plus de sept années, le 1er novembre 1954.

Mais, pour des centaines de milliers de personnes, ce cessez-le-feu, cette reconnaissance de l'unité du peuple algérien, de sa souveraineté sur le Sahara – dont de Gaulle avait espéré conserver la maîtrise –, est la dernière et la plus douloureuse station d'un calvaire.

Européens d'Oran enlevés, assassinés.

Musulmans tués par des commandos de l'OAS qui veulent créer le chaos.

Dizaines de milliers de « supplétifs » de l'armée française – les harkis – abandonnés, donc livrés aux tueurs, aux tortionnaires.

Horreur partout.

Désespoir des pieds-noirs qui n'ont le choix qu'« entre la valise et le cercueil ».

Seule une minorité de quelques milliers d'Européens restera en Algérie, malgré les menaces et les assassinats perpétrés par les tueurs du FLN en réponse à ceux de l'OAS.

L'été 1962 est ainsi une période sinistre dont les Français de métropole n'ont pas une conscience aiguë.

C'est l'un des traits de l'histoire nationale que de vouloir « oublier » la crise et les drames que l'on vient de vivre.

On est heureux du retour des soldats du contingent, même si près de 30 000 sont morts ou ont disparu.

Qui se soucie des 100 000 harkis assassinés ou des centaines de milliers de victimes algériennes (500 000 ?) ?

On veut aussi oublier les dizaines d'Algériens tués à Paris le 17 octobre 1961 alors qu'ils manifestaient pacifiquement.

On oublie les 8 morts du métro Charonne qui protestaient contre l'OAS.

On veut refouler cette période tragique.

Un nouveau Premier ministre, Georges Pompidou, a été nommé dès le 14 avril 1962 en remplacement de Michel Debré.

Une autre séquence politique commence. On veut pouvoir entrer dans le monde de la consommation – télévision, réfrigérateur, machine à laver, voiture – qui rythme le nouveau mode de vie. Les « colonies » appartiennent au passé. La guerre d'Algérie est perçue comme une incongruité, un archaïsme à oublier. On détourne la tête pour ne pas voir les « rapatriés ». Quant aux soldats rentrés d'Algérie, ils se taisent et étouffent leurs souvenirs, leurs remords, rêvant à leur tour d'acheter une voiture, Dauphine ou Deux-Chevaux.

Dans ce contexte, l'attentat perpétré contre de Gaulle au Petit-Clamart, le 22 août 1962, par le colonel Bastien-Thiry – arrêté en septembre, condamné à mort, exécuté après le rejet de sa grâce – révolte, tout comme avaient scandalisé les attentats de l'OAS commis à Paris contre certaines personnalités – et qui avaient blessé de leurs voisins : ainsi une enfant aveuglée lors de l'attentat contre Malraux.

De Gaulle, sorti indemne de la fusillade du Petit-Clamart qui crible de balles sa voiture, va tirer parti de l'événement.

Il décide de soumettre à référendum une révision de la Constitution. Le président de la République sera désormais élu au suffrage universel direct. Toute la classe politique – hormis les gaullistes – s'élève contre ce projet censé conforter le « pouvoir personnel » et qu'on identifie à une procédure plébiscitaire.

Pour de Gaulle, c'est la clé de voûte des institutions républicaines : « L'accord direct entre le peuple et celui qui a la charge de le conduire est devenu, dans les temps modernes, essentiel à la République. »

La presse se déchaîne, à la suite des hommes politiques, faisant campagne contre de Gaulle. Le président du Sénat, Gaston Monnerville, parle de forfaiture. Une motion de censure est votée à l'Assemblée.

Mais 61,75 % des votants répondent oui lors du référendum du 28 octobre 1962. Et, aux élections législatives du 25 novembre, le parti gaulliste frôle la majorité absolue. De Gaulle a remporté une double victoire sur les partis.

La Vᵉ République prend ainsi sa forme définitive.

De Gaulle, en stratège, s'est appuyé sur la tragédie algérienne pour retrouver le pouvoir et lui donner une Constitution conforme à ses vues.

Ayant tranché le nœud gordien algérien, il peut enfin déployer ses projets pour la France.

La nation le suivra-t-elle alors qu'elle aspire à la consommation ?

« Nous vivons, dit de Gaulle, évoquant cette année 1962, un précipité d'histoire. »

De fait, la France est devenue autre.

68.

De 1963 à 1968, la France se déploie.

C'est comme si la sève nationale, détournée ou contenue et accumulée depuis plus d'une décennie, jaillissait, maintenant que le verrou « algérien » a sauté, et irriguait le corps entier du pays.

Et de Gaulle, dans tous les domaines, pousse la nation en avant puisque, pour lui, « la France ne peut être la France sans la grandeur ».

Rien, dans la Constitution de la Ve République, ne peut, après 1962, l'entraver. Il bénéficie d'un domaine réservé, la politique étrangère, et n'est pas responsable devant le Parlement, où il dispose d'ailleurs d'une majorité disciplinée.

Les alliés de l'UNR (le parti gaulliste) que sont les héritiers des familles modérée et démocrate-chrétienne – le « centre » et, à partir de 1966-1967, les Républicains indépendants de Valéry Giscard d'Estaing – ne deviendront des partenaires critiques (« Oui... mais ») qu'au moment où le soutien populaire au Général s'effritera.

Car de Gaulle, qui dispose de la liberté d'agir d'un monarque, est un républicain intransigeant qui, s'il conteste le jeu des partis politiques et exige des députés qu'ils approuvent sa politique, n'avance que s'il est assuré de l'approbation populaire.

On l'a vu à chaque étape du règlement de la tragédie algérienne.

On le vérifie après 1963 : non seulement il accepte et suscite le
verdict électoral, mais il multiplie les rencontres avec le peuple.

Le Verbe et le Corps du monarque républicain deviennent
ainsi des éléments importants du fonctionnement politique.

Les conférences de presse – télévisées, radiodiffusées –, les
voyages nombreux dans tous les départements, ce Corps et ce
Verbe présents, les contacts lors des « bains de foule », participent de cette recherche d'une communication directe avec le
peuple, presque d'une communion.

L'élection présidentielle au suffrage universel direct est une
sorte de sacre démocratique et laïque du président.

La première a lieu les 5 et 19 décembre 1965.

Décisive, elle l'est d'abord par le nouveau paysage politique
qu'elle met en place.

Aux côtés du candidat du centre, Jean Lecanuet, la gauche
présente François Mitterrand, qui a obtenu le soutien des
communistes.

Venu de la droite, celui-ci – contrairement à une partie de la
gauche, et notamment Pierre Mendès France – a compris que
l'élection présidentielle conduisait à la bipolarisation. Il a donc
eu le courage politique de commettre la transgression majeure :
s'allier aux communistes.

Grâce à la présence de Lecanuet – 15,57 % des voix – qui
draine les voix du centre hostile à de Gaulle, considéré comme
un nationaliste antieuropéen, Mitterrand réussit, avec 32 % des
voix, à mettre de Gaulle en ballottage.

La signification de ce premier tour est claire : les partis politiques et, derrière eux, un nombre important de Français ne
jugent plus nécessaire, puisque la crise algérienne est dénouée,
la présence au pouvoir de De Gaulle.

Les politiciens ont hâte de retrouver une pratique constitutionnelle qui leur permette de se livrer à leurs jeux, censés exprimer
la démocratie parlementaire.

Et le « peuple », plutôt que d'entendre évoquer la grandeur de la France, souhaiterait que sa vie quotidienne soit améliorée par une hausse des salaires.

Une longue grève des mineurs – mars 1963 – a montré la profondeur des insatisfactions ouvrières.

C'est que la France change vite, et cette mutation crée des inquiétudes, des déracinements.

Des villes nouvelles sortent de terre. Les premiers hyper-marchés ouvrent. Un collège nouveau est inauguré chaque jour. Télévision, radio (Europe n° 1), nouvelles émissions, nouvelles mœurs, nouveaux « news magazines », modifient les manières de penser des couches populaires, mais aussi des nouveaux salariés du « tertiaire », employés et cadres urbanisés.

Ceux qui sont nés pendant la guerre ou lors du baby-boom des années 1946-1950 n'ont pas pour repères la Résistance ou la collaboration, de Gaulle ou Pétain. Quand on les interroge, ils répondent : « Hitler ? Connais pas. »

Les plus jeunes – les adolescents d'une quinzaine d'années en 1963 – sont encore plus « décalés » par rapport à ce que représentent de Gaulle et le gaullisme, ou même la classe politique issue le plus souvent de la Résistance et de la guerre.

Mitterrand était à Vichy, puis dans la Résistance, Giscard d'Estaing a fait la campagne d'Allemagne en 1945, Chaban-Delmas a participé à la libération de Paris comme jeune général délégué de De Gaulle, Messmer a été un héroïque officier de la France libre.

Les jeunes gens qui écoutent l'émission « Salut les copains » sur Europe n° 1, acclament Johnny Hallyday et se retrouvent à plus de cent cinquante mille, place de la Nation, le 22 juin 1963, sont le visage d'une nouvelle France qui se sent séparée de la France officielle.

La guerre d'Algérie qui vient à peine de s'achever lui est aussi étrangère que la Seconde Guerre mondiale. Elle ne cherche pas à les connaître.

Si peu de films ou de livres évoquent la guerre d'Algérie, c'est parce que ce nouveau public s'intéresse davantage à la mode « yé-yé » qu'à l'histoire récente.

Quant aux cadres un peu plus âgés, soucieux de carrière et de gestion, ils lisent *L'Expansion* – qui vient d'être lancé par Jean-Louis Servan-Schreiber, frère de Jean-Jacques, créateur de *L'Express.*

Qui, dans ces nouvelles générations, peut vibrer aux discours de Malraux – inamovible ministre des Affaires culturelles –, qui, en 1964 lors du transfert des cendres de Jean Moulin au Panthéon – comme s'il avait l'intuition du fossé culturel séparant la génération de « Salut les copains » des valeurs patriotiques d'un Jean Moulin et de la différence d'expérience vécue entre les contemporains de Johnny Hallyday et ceux de la Gestapo – déclare : « Aujourd'hui, jeunesse, puisses-tu penser à cet homme comme tu aurais approché tes mains de sa pauvre face informe du dernier jour, de ses lèvres qui n'avaient pas parlé : ce jour-là, elle était le visage de la France ! »

Cette fracture entre les générations, l'élection présidentielle de 1965 la reflète aussi.

De Gaulle a soixante-quinze ans, Mitterrand et Lecanuet insistent sur leur jeunesse (relative) et sur la relève nécessaire. Ils veulent rejeter de Gaulle dans le passé, et Mitterrand cherche à en faire le candidat de la droite. Lui-même sait qu'il doit incarner la gauche et que, dans cette élection, dès lors qu'il met de Gaulle en ballottage, il devient – quelles que soient les péripéties à venir – le futur candidat à la présidence des gauches unies.

Même si, lors de ce second tour de 1965, Mitterrand rassemble tous les antigaullistes, de l'extrême droite collaborationniste aux partisans de l'OAS et de l'Algérie française, en sus, naturellement, des socialistes et des communistes...

De Gaulle dénonce dans cette candidature le retour des partis et des politiciens. C'est, pour lui, « un scrutin historique qui marquera le succès ou le renoncement de la France vis-à-vis d'elle-même »...

Il précise que le candidat à la présidence de la République doit se situer au-dessus des partis : « Je suis pour la France, dit-il. La France, c'est tout à la fois, c'est tous les Français. Ce n'est pas la gauche, la France ! Ce n'est pas la droite, la France ! » Et il ajoute : « Prétendre représenter la France au nom d'une fraction, c'est une erreur nationale impardonnable. »

De Gaulle est élu le 9 décembre 1965 avec 54,5 % des voix.

Pourcentage élevé, mais ce ballottage – lourde déception pour l'homme du 18 juin – indique que les clivages politiques traditionnels ont repris de leur vigueur.

L'âme de la France n'oublie ses divisions qu'au fond de l'abîme.

Elle sacre alors un personnage exceptionnel, mais s'en éloigne dès qu'elle reprend pied.

Cette élection de 1965 donne en principe sept années à de Gaulle pour ancrer la France à la place qui correspond à sa « grandeur ».

Mais ce projet par lui-même suscite des réserves et des sarcasmes.

Et il est vrai qu'il y a un style gaullien dont on se plaît à caricaturer l'emphase. On met en scène un de Gaulle en nouveau Louis XIV entouré de sa cour. On en critique les réalisations, du paquebot *France* à l'avion supersonique Concorde.

On sent que derrière ces réticences s'exprime une autre vision de la France, puissance devenue moyenne, qui doit se fondre dans une Europe politique, renoncer à une diplomatie autonome, être un bon soldat de l'OTAN, ne pas chercher à bâtir une force nucléaire indépendante – la « bombinette », comme l'appellent les humoristes.

Mais ils critiquent, du même point de vue, la volonté de Malraux de réussir dans le domaine de la culture ce que Jules Ferry a réussi pour l'instruction. Et, malgré les sarcasmes, des maisons de la culture surgissent dans les régions, deviennent des centres de création, mais aussi des lieux de contestation politique.

Avec le recul, on mesure que c'est dans cette décennie gaullienne que la France de la fin du XXe siècle s'est dessinée : villes nouvelles, effort dans le domaine de l'enseignement et de la recherche, création d'universités (Nanterre, par exemple), d'instituts universitaires de technologie.

C'est le temps où la France glane des prix Nobel (en médecine : Lwoff, Jacob, Monod ; en physique : Alfred Kastler), et même des médailles olympiques (jeux Olympiques d'hiver à Grenoble en 1968).

Certes, ces résultats sont issus des semailles effectuées pendant le IVe République. Ces transformations participent des Trente Glorieuses qui, sur le plan économique et social, bouleversent en profondeur la nation. Mais, grâce aux impulsions données par l'État, le mouvement est maintenu, accéléré, soutenu.

Le Plan est une « ardente obligation » ; la DATAR veille à l'aménagement du territoire.

Il y a un esprit, un espoir, un effort gaulliens. Ils affirment que la France a la capacité de demeurer l'une des grandes nations.

D'ailleurs, ne devient-elle pas la quatrième puissance économique ?

Elle peut, dans le domaine scientifique, développer une recherche de pointe qui lui permet, en aéronautique ou dans le secteur nucléaire, de maintenir des industries compétitives. L'industrie nucléaire est capitale pour assurer une défense – donc une diplomatie – indépendante, et garantir l'autonomie énergétique au moyen des centrales nucléaires.

Quarante années plus tard, malgré le renoncement de fait aux ambitions gaulliennes pratiqué par les successeurs du Général, les directions choisies par de Gaulle sont encore visibles, même si elles commencent à s'effacer, en ce début du XXIe siècle, et si l'on s'interroge pour savoir s'il convient de les prolonger.

La persistance – la résistance – des choix gaulliens, malgré leur remise en cause, est encore plus nette en politique extérieure.

La cohérence du projet gaullien en ce domaine s'appuie d'abord sur une lecture de l'âme de la France.

« Notre pays, dit de Gaulle, tel qu'il est parmi les autres tels qu'ils sont, doit, sous peine de danger mortel, viser haut et se tenir droit. »

Ce qui se traduit en politique extérieure par l'affirmation de l'indépendance et de la souveraineté.

Cela ne signifie pas le refus des alliances et de la solidarité à l'égard des nations amies. Ainsi, en 1962, de Gaulle a manifesté aux États-Unis de Kennedy, engagés dans une confrontation dangereuse avec l'URSS à propos de missiles installés à Cuba, un soutien sans équivoque.

Il a de même affirmé, par le traité de l'Élysée signé en 1963, sa volonté de bâtir avec l'Allemagne une relation privilégiée et déterminante pour l'avenir de l'Europe.

Il n'envisage pas l'Europe seulement dans le cadre de la Communauté européenne. Il veut une « Europe européenne » « de l'Atlantique à l'Oural », c'est-à-dire qu'il se place au-dessus du « rideau de fer » idéologique, politique et militaire qui sépare une Europe démocratique sous protection et domination américaines d'une Europe colonisée par les Soviétiques.

De Gaulle veut que la France soit à l'initiative du dégel. Pour cela, elle doit ne pas dépendre des États-Unis, et s'il refuse l'entrée du Royaume-Uni dans la CEE, c'est qu'il estime que Londres est soumis à Washington et son agent en Europe.

Il faut donc que la France brise tout ce qui crée une sujétion à l'égard des États-Unis.

En 1964, premier État occidental à oser le faire, de Gaulle reconnaît la Chine communiste.

La même année, il effectue une tournée en Amérique latine, invitant les nations de ce continent à s'émanciper de la tutelle américaine – « *Marchamos la mano en la mano* », dit-il à Mexico.

En 1966, il renforce la coopération avec Moscou. Mais c'est « la France de toujours qui rencontre la Russie de toujours ». Il visitera la Pologne, et plus tard la Roumanie.

Nation souveraine, la France estime que les idéologies glissent sur les histoires nationales et que celles-ci ne peuvent être effacées.

La nation est plus forte que l'idéologie.

Mais l'acte décisif, qui change la place de la France sur l'échiquier international – et pour longtemps –, est accompli le 7 mars 1966 quand de Gaulle quitte le commandement intégré de l'OTAN, exige le départ des troupes de l'OTAN qui séjournent en France et le démantèlement de leurs bases.

La France vient d'affirmer avec force sa souveraineté. Elle dispose de l'arme atomique. Elle construit des sous-marins nucléaires lance-engins ; elle est donc indépendante. Elle retrouve, selon de Gaulle, le fil de la grande histoire.

Preuve de son autonomie diplomatique au-dessus des blocs : il se rend à Phnom Penh, et, dans un grand discours, invite les États-Unis à mettre fin à leur intervention militaire au Viêt Nam.

Ces prises de position scandalisent : les uns hurlent de colère, les autres ricanent, affirment que la France n'a qu'une diplomatie de la parole et du simulacre.

Les centristes (Jean Lecanuet) et les indépendants critiquent cette politique extérieure qui fait naviguer la France entre les deux icebergs de la guerre froide. Ces formations politiques s'apprêtent à assortir leur soutien à de Gaulle de profondes réserves. Ce sera, en 1967, le « Oui... mais » de Giscard d'Estaing, qui ainsi prend déjà date pour l'après-de Gaulle.

La gauche et l'extrême gauche, où l'antiaméricanisme est répandu et où l'on crée des comités Viêt Nam, n'appuient pas pour autant de Gaulle, à la fois pour des raisons politiciennes – il est « la droite » – et parce que l'idée de nation souveraine leur est étrangère.

En outre, en se rassemblant et en élaborant un programme – Mendès France et Michel Rocard en discutent lors de divers colloques, notamment à Grenoble en 1966 –, la gauche devient attirante, « moderne ».

La base électorale du gaullisme se réduit d'autant. Les élections législatives de 1967 confirment à la fois le succès de la gauche et l'érosion du parti gaulliste, de plus en plus dépendant de ses alliés du centre et de la droite traditionnelle, qui sont, eux, de plus en plus réticents.

Les propos que tient de Gaulle à Montréal, le 24 juillet 1967, saluant d'un « Vive le Québec libre ! » la foule qui l'acclame, scandalisent un peu plus. De Gaulle perdrait-il la raison ?

Ceux du 27 novembre 1967, lors d'une conférence de presse consacrée au Moyen-Orient, et qui qualifient le peuple juif de « peuple d'élite, sûr de lui-même et dominateur », le mettant en garde contre les actions de guerre et de conquête qui l'entraîneraient dans une confrontation sans fin avec les États voisins, suscitent indignation, condamnation, incompréhension.

Certains évoquent le vieil antisémitisme maurrassien. Mais l'excès même de ces accusations inexactes portées contre de Gaulle montre que celui-ci ne fait plus l'unanimité, pis : qu'il n'est même plus respecté, qu'il exaspère, que de larges secteurs du pays, en cette fin d'année 1967, ne le comprennent plus. Et que, pour d'autres, il appartient à un monde révolu.

Il aura soixante-dix-huit ans en cette année 1968 qui commence.

À Caen, de jeunes ouvriers en grève affrontent violemment les forces de l'ordre le 26 janvier.

À Paris, des étudiants, membres du Comité Viêt Nam national, brisent les vitres de l'American Express ; certains sont arrêtés. Et le 22 mars, à Nanterre, la salle du conseil de l'université est occupée.

Un étudiant franco-allemand, Cohn-Bendit, crée le Mouvement du 22 mars. La « nouvelle France », celle des jeunes qui ont autour de vingt ans, apparaît sur le terrain politique et social ; elle annonce une nouvelle séquence historique. Cette génération s'interroge sur le sens d'une société dont elle ne partage pas les valeurs officielles.

L'un de ces nouveaux jeunes acteurs de la vie intellectuelle et sociale, Raoul Vaneigem, qui se définit comme *situationniste*, écrit en ce mois de mars 1968 : « Nous ne voulons pas d'un monde où la garantie de ne pas mourir de faim s'échange contre celle de mourir d'ennui. »

Le flux inéluctable des générations entraîne et modifie l'âme de la France.

69.

Mai 1968-juin 1969 : c'est l'année paradoxale de la France.

En mai 1968, le pays est en « révolution ». Le gouvernement semble impuissant. Pierre Mendès France et François Mitterrand se disent prêts à prendre un pouvoir qui paraît à la dérive.

Un mois plus tard, le 30 juin, la France élit dans le calme l'Assemblée nationale la plus à droite depuis 1945. Rejetés en mai, les gaullistes y détiennent la majorité absolue pour la première fois depuis le début de la Vᵉ République.

Mais, le 28 avril 1969, au référendum proposé par de Gaulle, le non l'emporte avec 53,18 % des voix. Conformément aux engagements qu'il a pris, de Gaulle « cesse d'exercer ses fonctions ».

Un mois et demi plus tard, le 15 juin 1969, l'ancien Premier ministre du général de Gaulle, Georges Pompidou, est élu président de la République avec 57,8 % des suffrages exprimés !

Cette année jalonnée de surprises et de paradoxes est un condensé d'histoire nationale, une mise à nu et une mise à jour de l'âme de la France.

Le spectacle commence dans la nuit du 10 au 11 mai 1968, quand le Quartier latin, à Paris, se couvre de barricades pour protester contre l'arrestation d'étudiants, l'occupation et la fermeture de la Sorbonne par la police qui les en a délogés.

C'est comme si les étudiants, dépavant les rues, rejouaient les journées révolutionnaires, retrouvant les gestes des insurgés du XIXᵉ siècle, ceux de 1830 ou de 1832, de 1848 ou de 1871, mais aussi ceux des combats de la Libération, en août 1944.

C'est un théâtre de rue : pavés, arbres sciés, voitures incendiées, charges des CRS accueillies aux cris de « CRS, SS », effet de la mémoire détournée qui devient mensongère.

Dans ces affrontements, en brandissant le drapeau rouge, on joue aussi des épisodes de la lutte des classes mondiale : on invoque Marx, Lénine, Trotsky, Mao, Che Guevara, le Viêtcong, et on dénonce l'impérialisme américain.

En cette première quinzaine de mai 1968, Paris marie la tradition nationale et l'idéologie gauchiste qui se réclame du marxisme, du trotskisme, du castrisme et du maoïsme.

En fait, comme en de nombreux autres pays (États-Unis, Allemagne, Italie, Japon, par exemple), la jeunesse issue du baby-boom d'après guerre entre en scène.

En France – particularité de l'âme de la nation –, elle interprète un simulacre de révolution.

La genèse en a été la protestation de quelques étudiants organisés dans des mouvements minoritaires, celui du 22 mars ou ceux relevant de la mouvance trotskiste.

Ils sont le détonateur qui embrase la jeunesse, les « copains » qui, depuis les années 60, investissent peu à peu l'espace social et culturel. Cette génération entre dans le théâtre politique français, où le décor, les textes, la mémoire et les postures sont révolutionnaires.

Surpris – le Premier ministre, Pompidou, et le président de la République sont en voyage officiel à l'étranger –, le pouvoir politique s'interroge.

Il contrôle remarquablement la répression : grâce au préfet de police Grimaud, la nuit des barricades sera certes violente, avec de nombreux blessés, mais restera un simulacre de révolution.

Exception française : la « révolution » étudiante déclenche une crise sociale et politique.

La France est bien ce pays d'exception, centralisé, où la symbolique historique joue un rôle majeur et où ce qui se passe sur la scène parisienne prend la profondeur de champ d'un événement historique.

Longtemps contenues, les revendications ouvrières explosent face à un régime affaibli. Les grèves éclatent, mobilisent bientôt plus de dix millions de grévistes – un sommet historique.

Au gouvernement, certains craignent une « subversion communiste », puisque la CGT est liée au Parti communiste.

Et ce n'est plus seulement Paris qui est concerné. Toute la nation est paralysée.

Les villes de province sont parcourues par des cortèges à l'ampleur exceptionnelle.

Les amphithéâtres de toutes les universités, les théâtres – à Paris, celui de l'Odéon –, les écoles – celle des Beaux-Arts –, les rues, les places, deviennent des lieux de débat. Des assemblées tumultueuses écoutent des anonymes, des militants, des écrivains célèbres (Sartre, Aragon). On applaudit, on conteste.

C'est la « prise de parole », le rejet des institutions. Les communistes sont débordés par les gauchistes, les maoïstes, les trotskistes.

Et l'on crie : « Adieu, de Gaulle, Adieu ! » ou encore : « Dix ans, ça suffit ! »

Ainsi, à la fin du mois de mai, la « révolution » étudiante est devenue radicalement politique.

C'est comme un condensé d'histoire. Les multiples réunions font penser par leur nombre, les participations massives, la diversité des problèmes soulevés par une foule d'intervenants, aux assemblées préparatoires aux états généraux élaborant leurs cahiers de doléances. Déjà on semble à la veille d'un 14 juillet 1789.

Dans les cortèges, certains souhaitent qu'on prenne une Bastille qui ferait tomber le pouvoir du vieux monarque. On lance : « De Gaulle au musée ! »

Tout se joue dans les quatre derniers jours de mai.

D'abord, Pompidou réunit les syndicats. Il aboutit le 27 mai aux accords de Grenelle avec la CGT. Il retire ainsi du mordant au mouvement social et stoppe sa propagation.

En outre, l'indication politique est précieuse : les communistes ne veulent pas – lucidité ou calcul lié à la politique extérieure de De Gaulle ? – d'un affrontement, aux marges de la légalité, avec le pouvoir.

Dès lors, l'acte de candidature de François Mitterrand et de Pierre Mendès France – alliés et concurrents –, se déclarant le 27 mai prêts à gouverner alors que le pouvoir n'est pas vacant, apparaît comme le choix de pousser le pays dans l'« aventure ».

Celui-ci ne le désire pas.

Il suffit d'un appel radiodiffusé du Général, le 30 mai, pour renverser la situation.

De Gaulle s'est rendu la veille auprès du général Massu, commandant les forces françaises en Allemagne, stratagème créant l'angoisse et l'attente, habile dramatisation bien plus que démarche d'un président ébranlé cherchant l'appui de l'armée. À la radio, il annonce la dissolution de l'Assemblée et des élections législatives.

La volonté du pays de mettre fin à la « révolution » s'exprime aussitôt : manifestation d'un million de personnes sur les Champs-Élysées, le 30 mai ; aux élections des 23 et 30 juin, triomphe des gaullistes de l'UDR (gain de 93 sièges) des indépendants (gain de 10 sièges), et échec communiste (perte de 39 sièges) et des gauches de la FGDS (perte de 64 sièges).

Derrière le simulacre de révolution à quoi s'était complue l'âme de la France se manifeste l'aspiration à la paix civile et au respect des procédures constitutionnelles.

L'âme de la France apparaît ainsi ouverte au débat, mais seule une minorité infime désire réellement la révolution. Son discours et ses postures ne suscitent pas de prime abord le rejet : on les entend, on les regarde, on les approuve, on les suit même comme s'il s'agissait de revivre – de rejouer – des scènes de l'histoire nationale auxquelles on est affectivement – et même idéologiquement – attaché. Tout ce simulacre fait partie de l'âme de la

France. Mais on ne veut pas se laisser entraîner à brûler le théâtre parce que, sur la scène, quelques acteurs, qu'on peut applaudir, dressent des barricades et déclament des tirades incendiaires.

D'ailleurs, ces acteurs eux-mêmes – trotskistes, maoïstes, gauchistes de toutes observances – se refusent à mettre le feu à la France.

Les plus engagés d'entre eux – maoïstes regroupés dans la Gauche prolétarienne – n'auront jamais versé – à l'exception de quelques rares individualités – dans la « lutte armée », comme cela se produira en Allemagne et surtout en Italie.

Comme si, dans la culture politique nationale, cette séquence de l'« action directe » de petits groupes prêts à l'attentat et à l'assassinat ne trouvait pas d'écho favorable, mais une condamnation ferme.

Comme si l'action politique « de masse », accompagnée de controverses idéologiques ouvertes plutôt que d'une culture de secte, l'emportait toujours.

Comme si les « militants révolutionnaires » avaient la conviction que le « peuple français », celui de 1789, de 1830, de 1848, de 1871, de 1944, pouvait les écouter, les comprendre et les suivre. Comme si, finalement, l'action armée, groupusculaire, terroriste, était la marque de nations qui n'avaient pas connu « la » Révolution, mais dont les peuples, au contraire, s'étaient laissé enrégimenter par la « réaction », le fascisme, le nazisme... et le stalinisme.

Le refus du gauchisme de passer à la lutte armée est ainsi le résultat moins d'une impossibilité « technique » (petit nombre de militants décidés à agir) que du poids d'une histoire nationale dans laquelle la société – le peuple – a joué le rôle déterminant à toutes les époques, de la monarchie à la république.

Et, en effet, c'est par la société et en son sein que les « révolutionnaires » de Mai 68 l'emportent.

Ils s'y insèrent, y conquièrent des postes d'influence dans ces nouveaux pouvoirs que sont les médias.

Ils constituent une « génération » solidaire qui transforme le simulacre de révolution en vraie mythologie révolutionnaire.

Ils exaltent les épisodes estudiantins – les barricades à résonance historique – et effacent des mémoires la plus puissante grève ouvrière qu'ait connue la France.

Une reconstruction idéologique de Mai 68 est ainsi réalisée par les acteurs eux-mêmes, avec l'assentiment de tous les pouvoirs.

Cette révolution de Mai est aussi une déconstruction de l'ordre républicain et de ses valeurs, points d'appui des mouvements sociaux. La République, c'était l'exception française, manière de s'opposer à la « normalisation économique ».

La révolution de Mai, au contraire, est en phase avec la nouvelle culture qui envahit le monde à partir des années 60. Elle est permissive sur le plan des mœurs (culture gay et lesbienne, avortement, usage du cannabis, etc.), féministe et antiraciste.

Elle refuse les hiérarchies, les structures jugées autoritaires. Elle valorise et exalte l'individu, l'enfant. Elle provoque un changement des méthodes d'enseignement.

Cette révolution culturelle, portée par la diffusion des médias audiovisuels, condamne l'idée de nation. Elle la soupçonne de perpétuer une vision archaïque, autoritaire, hostile à la jouissance, à la consommation libertaire adaptée à l'économie de marché.

L'héroïsme national, l'idée de grandeur, l'idée même de France – et de son rôle exceptionnel dans l'histoire –, sont refoulés.

L'âme de la France se trouve ainsi déformée, amputée.

Dans ce climat, de Gaulle et les valeurs qu'il représente sont condamnés.

« Adieu de Gaulle, adieu », « De Gaulle au musée » : ces slogans des manifestants rendent compte en négatif des aspirations des nouvelles générations.

Le nouveau Premier ministre (Maurice Couve de Murville a remplacé Georges Pompidou, qui a efficacement fait face aux événements de Mai, mais qui apparaît comme un candidat possible à la présidence de la République) incarne plus caricaturalement que de Gaulle les valeurs de cette histoire française que la révolution de Mai a dévalorisées.

De Gaulle est parfaitement conscient du changement intervenu, du « désir général de participer... Tout le monde en veut plus et tout le monde veut s'en mêler. » Mais le référendum qu'il propose le 28 avril 1969, visant à modifier le rôle et la composition du Sénat et à changer l'organisation des collectivités territoriales, ne peut répondre à l'attente qui traverse la société.

En somme, de Gaulle est devenu le vivant symbole du passé.

Sa place est en effet, au musée, dans l'histoire révolue.

Et l'on voit déjà se profiler derrière lui un homme d'État moderne : Georges Pompidou. L'ancien Premier ministre, s'est contenté, pendant la guerre, d'enseigner. Il a « vécu », a été banquier chez Rothschild. Il aime l'art contemporain, est photographié avec un pull noué sur les épaules. Des rumeurs tentent de le compromettre avec le monde de la nuit et de la débauche. Il s'agit d'une tentative visant à l'abattre. Mais peut-être qu'au contraire cette calomnie a plaidé en sa faveur.

Ce n'est plus un héros quasi mythologique que la France désire. Elle veut un homme non pas quelconque, mais plus proche.

Le non l'emporte au référendum du 28 avril 1969.

« Je cesse d'exercer mes fonctions de président de la République. Cette décision prend effet aujourd'hui à midi », communique de Gaulle à 0 h 10, le 29 avril.

Georges Pompidou est élu président de la République le 15 juin 1969 avec 57,8 % des suffrages exprimés, contre 42,25 % à Alain Poher, modéré, président du Sénat.

Au premier tour, les candidats de la gauche socialiste (Defferre, Rocard) obtiennent respectivement 5,1 et 3,61 % des voix).

Mitterrand, prudent et lucide, n'a pas été candidat.

Le communiste Duclos a rassemblé 21,5 % des voix.

Le trotskiste Krivine, 1,05 %.

Tel est le visage électoral de la France un an après la « révolution » de Mai.

La gauche n'est pas présente au second tour du scrutin, alors qu'en 1965 Mitterrand avait mis de Gaulle en ballottage.

Pourtant, malgré la victoire de Georges Pompidou, la République gaullienne est morte.

De Gaulle n'y survivra pas longtemps.

Il meurt le 9 novembre 1970.

Refusant tous les hommages officiels, il avait souhaité être enterré sans apparat à Colombey-les-Deux-Églises.

Il avait écrit, dédicaçant un tome de ses Mémoires à l'ambassadeur de France en Irlande, quelques semaines après son départ du pouvoir, une pensée de Nietzsche :

> *Rien ne vaut rien*
> *Il ne se passe rien*
> *Et cependant tout arrive*
> *Et c'est indifférent.*

5

LA FRANCE INCERTAINE

1969-2007

70.

En 1969, comme si souvent au cours de son histoire, la France entre dans le temps des incertitudes.

Elle avait choisi durant une décennie de s'en remettre au « héros » qui, une première fois, l'avait arrachée aux traîtres, aux médiocres et aux petits arrangements d'une « étrange défaite ».

Respectant le contrat implicite que le pays avait passé avec lui, de Gaulle avait mis fin à la tragédie algérienne.

La France pouvait donc – le moment, l'occasion, les modalités, seraient affaire de circonstances – renvoyer le héros au « musée » de ses souvenirs.

De Gaulle parti, la France est incertaine.

Les successeurs – Georges Pompidou (1969-1974), Valéry Giscard d'Estaing (1974-1981), François Mitterrand (1981-1995), Jacques Chirac (1995-2007) – ne sont, chacun avec son rapport singulier à la France, au monde, à la vie, que des hommes politiques.

Ils ne gravissent plus les pentes de l'Olympe, mais les modestes sommets d'une gloire politicienne, même si l'avant-dernier, qu'animait une jalousie rancie à l'égard de De Gaulle, rencontré pour la première fois en 1943, a tenté – on a l'Olympe qu'on peut – de construire sa mythologie en conviant ses courtisans et les caméras à l'ascension, devenue rituelle, de la roche de Solutré, son site préhistorique.

Mais, derrière la succession apaisée des présidents de la République, dont aucune crise de régime ne vient interrompre un mandat que seule la maladie peut écourter (mort de Pompidou en 1974), les enjeux sont majeurs pour la nation.

Le projet du « héros » était clair, simple mais exigeant : indépendance, souveraineté, fidélité à l'âme de la France, et donc grandeur.

L'exception française devait être maintenue à la fois dans l'organisation économique, sociale et politique – un État fort animant et canalisant la vie économique, instituant la « participation » – et dans les relations internationales – la France n'est d'aucun bloc, elle reconnaît les nations comme des entités souveraines, libres de vivre à l'intérieur de leurs frontières comme elles l'entendent. Ni droit ni devoir d'ingérence.

La révolution culturelle de Mai – réplique de la domination mondiale des images de la société américaine, elle-même modelée par son histoire, son mode d'organisation économique – a contesté le projet gaullien.

Mais le « nouveau modèle culturel » a-t-il réellement pénétré, et jusqu'à quelles profondeurs, la société française ? A-t-il vaincu, balayé tous les aspects du projet gaullien ?

Entre le nouveau et l'ancien, quelle combinaison, quel équilibre peut-on réaliser ? Et comment les présidents successifs – et les forces politiques qui les soutiennent – vont-ils se situer par rapport à cette question majeure ?

Vont-ils s'appuyer sur les aspirations nouvelles, les reconnaître, et, à partir d'elles, « modifier l'âme de la France », ou tenter au contraire de les contenir, de les refouler, ou encore, pragmatiquement, en fonction de leurs intérêts électoraux, tenter de concilier l'ancien et le nouveau ?

Il s'agit en somme de savoir qui va assumer, et comment, l'héritage de la « révolution » de Mai 68. Quelle part on en retiendra, ce qu'on refusera, et vers quelles formations politiques se porteront les acteurs de Mai.

À l'évidence, ils ont inquiété les électeurs de juin 1968, qui ont élu une majorité absolue de députés gaullistes, et ceux de juin 1969, qui ont choisi Georges Pompidou et écarté la gauche et l'extrême gauche.

Pompidou, qui par ailleurs bénéficie d'une conjoncture économique favorable, dispose d'une large assise électorale exprimant la réaction du pays devant le risque « révolutionnaire » et son attachement conservateur au modèle ancien.

Cependant, la société est travaillée par l'« esprit de Mai ».

Au fil des années, tout au long de la présidence de Georges Pompidou (1969-1974), il se manifeste souvent. Les gauchistes sont présents.

La tentation de créer un « parti armé » est réelle, même si – nous l'avons noté – elle ne se réalisera pas. La mort d'un militant – Pierre Overney, en 1972 – et ses obsèques sont symboliquement la dernière grande manifestation gauchiste à traverser les quartiers de l'Est parisien, traditionnellement « révolutionnaires ».

Il y a l'émergence du Mouvement de libération des femmes (MLF) ; la déclaration, en 1971, de 343 femmes reconnaissant avoir eu recours à l'avortement.

Tel ou tel fait divers (le suicide d'un professeur, Gabrielle Russier, qui a pour amant un élève mineur de dix-huit ans, et Pompidou saura, citant Paul Éluard, trouver les mots de la compassion vis-à-vis de « la malheureuse qui resta sur le pavé... »), illustre les tensions, les conflits entre les nouvelles aspirations et la loi.

C'est un travail de déconstruction qui se poursuit.

Il modifie le regard qu'on porte sur deux périodes clés de l'histoire nationale, fondatrices de l'héroïsme national et de sa mythologie.

D'abord, la Révolution française, qu'un historien comme François Furet commence à repenser à la lumière de ce qu'on a appris du régime soviétique. Ce n'est plus de la liberté qu'on crédite la Révolution, mais du totalitarisme. Robespierre est l'ancêtre de Lénine et de Staline, et ceux-ci sont les créateurs de l'archipel du goulag (les trois volumes de Soljenitsyne sont publiés en russe à Paris en décembre 1973, en français en 1974-1975).

L'autre révision porte sur la France de Vichy (titre d'un livre de l'historien américain Robert Paxton). Sur la geste gaulliste qui affirme que Vichy « est nul et non avenu » et que la nation a le visage de la Résistance et de la France libre – sorte de tapisserie où ne figurent que des héros – vient se superposer une France ambiguë, celle que révèle aussi le film de Max Ophüls, *Le Chagrin et la pitié*.

Au mythe héroïque et patriotique déconstruit succède le mythe d'une lâcheté nationale, d'un attentisme généralisé, voire d'un double jeu – où se reconnaissent un Georges Pompidou, un François Mitterrand – aux antipodes des choix radicaux et clairs pris par certains (de Gaulle, Messmer) dès juin 1940.

Ces révisions de l'histoire nationale participent de l'esprit de Mai.

En choisissant comme Premier ministre Jacques Chaban-Delmas – général gaulliste –, Pompidou, en juin 1969, cherche l'équilibre entre l'ancien et le nouveau, puisque Chaban, lorsqu'il présente son programme à l'Assemblée, déclare : « Il dépend de nous de bâtir patiemment et progressivement une nouvelle société. »

Ce projet de « nouvelle société » a été élaboré par Simon Nora – proche de Mendès France – et Jacques Delors, syndicaliste chrétien.

La « nouvelle société » devient l'idée force et la formule emblématique recouvrant toutes les initiatives du gouvernement Chaban-Delmas.

Par ses attitudes, l'homme veut d'ailleurs incarner un « nouveau » type de personnalité politique. Il est « moderne », svelte, sportif, séducteur, souriant.

Cette apparence peut être à soi seule un manifeste politique.

Il y a d'ailleurs une ressemblance d'allure entre Chaban, Valéry Giscard d'Estaing – ministre de l'Économie et des Finances – et Jean-Jacques Servan-Schreiber, directeur de *l'Express*, désormais président du Parti radical, auteur du programme radical *Ciel et Terre*. À travers eux s'affirme un parallélisme des volontés réformatrices.

Les mots *réforme, réformateur*, peuplent les discours politiques. Ils justifient les mesures prises par le gouvernement.

Les plus commentées concernent la justice, la radio et la télévision publiques (ORTF), qui se voient garantir l'indépendance. L'effet est réel à la télévision où, pour la première fois, certains magazines – « Cinq colonnes à la une » – reflètent la réalité avec ses conflits et ses tensions.

Mais, pour Pompidou comme pour sa majorité, ce style Chaban, ces mesures, sont autant de concessions à la « gauche », qui fragilisent la majorité.

La situation économique se dégrade sous l'effet des mesures monétaires prises par les États-Unis de Richard Nixon (fin de la convertibilité entre le dollar et l'or, chute du dollar, hausse des cours du pétrole : en 1973, le prix du baril est multiplié par quatre). Les conflits sociaux s'aggravent. La gauche progresse, et aux élections de 1973, en pourcentage de votants, elle dépasse même la majorité (42,99 % pour cette dernière, 43,23 % pour la gauche).

Pompidou avait anticipé ce recul, tentant, par le renvoi de Chaban et son remplacement par Pierre Messmer, en juillet 1972, de rassembler sa majorité sur les « valeurs traditionnelles » du modèle ancien.

Ce redressement paraît d'autant plus nécessaire que François Mitterrand – en 1971, au congrès d'Épinay – a pris la tête d'un nouveau Parti socialiste. Celui-ci a signé en 1972 avec le PCF et le Mouvement des radicaux de gauche (MRG) un Programme commun de gouvernement. La gauche a donc resurgi rapidement des décombres de 1969. Et il apparaît, au vu des résultats électoraux de 1973, qu'elle fait jeu égal avec la droite.

C'est ainsi qu'à la mort de Pompidou – 2 avril 1974 –, face à la candidature de Valéry Giscard d'Estaing, représentant des modérés libéraux, les gaullistes se divisent. Chaban-Delmas est candidat, mais une partie des gaullistes, derrière Jacques Chirac, apportent leur soutien à Giscard.

Celui-ci l'emporte sur François Mitterrand, candidat unique de la gauche (49,2 % des voix contre 50,8 %, soit une différence de 425 599 voix).

Le faible écart qui sépare les deux candidats est signe de l'incertitude française.

La gauche est portée par le désir d'alternance, les premières conséquences sociales du choc pétrolier de 1973, le recours à une histoire mythifiée : le Front populaire, l'unité d'action.

Maints acteurs de Mai ont adhéré au PS après le congrès d'Épinay, comme de nombreux militants du syndicalisme chrétien. De nouvelles générations peuplent ainsi la gauche et lui donnent un nouveau dynamisme, renforcé par le fait que le PCF perd de son hégémonie culturelle et politique. Il se dégrade en même temps que l'image de l'URSS.

L'« esprit de Mai » reverdit le vieil arbre socialiste, et, dès le lendemain de la défaite du 19 mai 1974 face à Giscard, chacun, à gauche, estime que la victoire était – sera bientôt – à portée de main.

Pourtant, Giscard d'Estaing est le président le plus décidé à « moderniser » la société française.

Jeune (quarante-huit ans en 1974), il déclare au lendemain de son élection : « De ce jour date une ère nouvelle de la politique française. » Il a choisi Jacques Chirac comme Premier ministre, mais c'est pour neutraliser le parti gaulliste. Son gouvernement comporte des réformateurs (Jean-Jacques Servan-Schreiber, Françoise Giroud), des personnalités indépendantes (Simone Veil).

Mais, surtout, cet homme d'expérience (ministre de l'Économie et des Finances de 1959 à 1966, puis de 1969 à 1974) qui a contribué à la chute de De Gaulle en appelant à voter non au référendum de 1969 a un véritable projet pour la France.

Et il est l'antithèse du projet gaullien.

Il s'agit d'abord de réaliser que la France n'est qu'une puissance moyenne (1 à 2 % de la population mondiale, insiste-t-il). Elle doit abandonner ses rêves de grandeur, se contenter d'être l'ingénieur de la construction européenne, qui est son grand dessein et sa chance.

Giscard est, pour l'Europe, le maître d'œuvre de réformes décisives (élection au suffrage universel du Parlement européen, création du Système monétaire européen, renforcement des liens avec l'Allemagne).

Il est à l'initiative des rencontres des Grands, le G5, pour discuter des affaires du monde.

Il croit à la possibilité de la détente internationale comme à la fin de la « guerre civile froide » que se livrent les forces politiques françaises. Il est partisan de la « décrispation », d'une « démocratie française apaisée », de la possibilité de gouverner au centre, en accord avec le groupe central – les classes moyennes –, et, il l'annonce dès 1980, il acceptera une « cohabitation » avec une majorité législative hostile, et la laissera gouverner.

C'est une négation de l'esprit des institutions tel que de Gaulle l'avait mis en œuvre : à chaque élection, il remettait son mandat en question.

En fait, Giscard exprime la « tradition orléaniste » française, qui accepte une partie de l'héritage révolutionnaire et veut oublier que « l'histoire est tragique », ou à tout le moins qu'elle n'est pas seulement le produit et le reflet de la Raison.

Giscard met ce projet en scène.

Le président est un homme accessible. Il remonte à pied les Champs-Élysées. Il s'invite à dîner chez des Français. Il visite les prisons.

C'est un souverain, mais proche, ouvert. Il joue de l'accordéon et au football.

La « communication » commence à balayer comme un grand vent les traditions compassées de la vie politique.

Il s'agit de changer les mœurs, de prendre en compte l'esprit de Mai.

Majorité et droit de vote à dix-huit ans, loi sur l'interruption volontaire de grossesse, création d'un secrétariat d'État à la Condition féminine et réforme de l'ORTF sont la traduction institutionnelle des revendications *sociétales* apparues en 1968. De même, la multiplication des débats où le président rencontre des lycéens ou des économistes veut montrer que le pouvoir est favorable à la « prise de parole », au dialogue avec les citoyens.

Cependant, ce projet récupérateur, moderne, souvent anticipateur, ne va pas permettre la réélection de Giscard en mai 1981.

D'abord parce que la crise de 1973 fait sentir ses effets : le chômage devient une réalité.

Ensuite, les « gaullistes » s'opposent aux « giscardiens » à partir de 1976, de la démission de Chirac du poste de Premier ministre, puis de son élection – contre un giscardien – à la mairie de Paris. Ils signifient qu'ils sont dans l'« opposition ».

Cette défection est révélatrice.

Les gaullistes – leurs électeurs – sont heurtés par la « déconstruction » active, proclamée, exaltée, du « système français ».

Le patriotisme français – ravivé par de Gaulle – s'irrite de cette volonté giscardienne de gommer les spécificités françaises, de nier l'exception et la grandeur nationales.

On est choqué qu'il ait choisi de s'exprimer en anglais lors de sa première conférence de presse.

L'histoire nationale résiste, l'âme de la France se cabre. Quant à la rigueur du nouveau Premier ministre, Raymond Barre, elle heurte. Ni l'opinion ni les forces politiques ne sont prêtes à entendre le professeur Barre, « meilleur économiste de France », énoncer des vérités déplaisantes sur la réalité sociale et économique du pays. D'une certaine manière, la « modernisation » giscardienne devance l'évolution du pays.

François Mitterrand, au contraire, veille à rassembler à la fois les « modernisateurs » – ainsi, en matière d'information, il est partisan des « radios libres », ou bien il prend explicitement position contre la peine de mort – et les « conservateurs » de la gauche.

Ces derniers, d'ailleurs, souhaitent l'alternance politique à n'importe quel prix.

Mitterrand sait leur parler non de « groupe central », ou de la fin de « la guerre civile froide franco-française ». Il évoque le Front populaire (lui-même porte un grand chapeau à la Blum !), la lutte des classes, le sort d'Allende – le président chilien renversé et mort après un coup d'État militaire soutenu par les États-Unis le 11 septembre 1973.

Les communistes, qui ont rompu avec lui sur le Programme commun en 1977 – ce qui a permis la victoire des giscardiens aux législatives de 1978 –, sont contraints de se rallier à lui au second tour.

Tous les Français – y compris les gaullistes – qu'inquiète la « modernisation » de la France, laquelle n'est à leurs yeux qu'une américanisation, se retrouvent dans l'idée d'une « force tranquille » qui protège, sur les affiches de Mitterrand, un village traditionnel blotti autour de son église.

Image « pétainiste » qui renvoie à la terre, aux traditions, repoussant Giscard dans une modernité sans racines dont on ne veut pas. Transformant le « modernisateur » qu'il est en une sorte d'aristocrate rentré de Coblence, compromis dans une affaire des diamants comme il y eut une affaire du collier de la reine ! La calomnie est, de tradition nationale, une arme politique.

Mitterrand est élu le 10 mai 1981 avec 51,75 % des voix contre 48,24 % à Giscard (15 708 262 voix contre 14 642 306).

En juin 1981, les législatives font écho à ce succès présidentiel : le PS et ses alliés obtiennent la majorité des sièges à l'Assemblée.

C'est moins un fort déplacement de voix que les abstentions des électeurs de droite qui sont à l'origine de ce succès.

L'alternance politique est complète.

Mais, pour vaincre, il a fallu ne pas choisir entre « modernes » et « archaïques », donner des gages aux uns et aux autres tout en privilégiant la phraséologie marxisante pour séduire les plus militants des électeurs.

Cette ambiguïté ne peut qu'être source de déceptions.

Mais il est sûr que la victoire n'a été possible que par le ralliement à la gauche des « révolutionnaires » de mai 1968.

En mai 1981, venus de la Bastille, ils arpentèrent les rues du Quartier latin – du théâtre d'une révolution vraie à celui d'une révolution simulacre – en scandant : « Treize ans déjà, coucou nous revoilà ! »

71.

À compter de 1981 et durant les vingt dernières années du
XXᵉ siècle, la France est déchirée entre illusions et réalité, entre
promesses et nécessités.

Certes, souvent l'âme de la France s'est réfugiée dans les
songes et les mythes glorificateurs ou consolateurs. Ils avaient
aussi la vertu de pousser le peuple à accepter, à conquérir
l'avenir.

Rien de tel depuis l'élection de François Mitterrand à la présidence de la République. C'est comme si la vie politique française
– gauche et droite confondues – n'avait plus pour objet que de
cacher la vérité aux électeurs, de les gruger afin de les convaincre
de voter pour tel ou tel candidat.

Si bien que l'écart n'a jamais été aussi grand entre pro-
grammes et réalisations, entre discours et actes.

Et jamais la déception n'a été aussi profonde dans l'âme de
chaque Français ; le pays entier bascule dans l'amertume, la
colère, le mépris à l'égard de la « classe politique » qui gouverne.

Les abstentionnistes sont de plus en plus nombreux et les partis extrémistes – de droite comme de gauche –, protestataires
exclus de la représentation parlementaire et de l'exécutif, re-
cueillent les « déçus » des partis de gouvernement, Parti socia-

liste et RPR – ce parti qui se prétend gaulliste mais qui n'est qu'au service de « son » candidat, Jacques Chirac.

Le PS comme le RPR ont promis des réformes radicales : les uns faisant miroiter au pays la justice sociale, l'égalité ; les autres, la croissance, l'efficacité, donc la richesse et le profit.

Le programme socialiste de 1981 vise même à « changer la vie » !

Jack Lang, ministre de la Culture inamovible, caractérise l'alternance comme le passage « de la nuit à la lumière ». Il inaugure la première fête de la Musique le 21 juin 1981 – jour du deuxième tour des élections législatives qui vont donner la majorité absolue au PS associé aux radicaux de gauche (MRG), débarrassant ainsi Mitterrand de l'hypothèque et du chantage communistes.

Mais l'avenir ne sera pas une fête.

En 1982, dévorée par l'inflation, la France compte pour la première fois de son histoire plus de deux millions de chômeurs.

Quant à Jacques Chirac, élu à la présidence de la République en 1995 au terme des deux septennats de François Mitterrand, il dénonce dans sa campagne contre Édouard Balladur, issu du RPR, Premier ministre de 1993 à 1995, la « fracture sociale ». Et s'engage à la réduire.

Quelques semaines après sa victoire, plus personne ne croit plus au joueur de flûte qui a guidé les électeurs jusqu'aux urnes.

La déception, la méfiance et, ce qui est peut-être pire, l'indifférence méprisante à l'égard des politiques, qui pénètrent l'opinion, expliquent l'instabilité qui s'installe dans les sommets de l'État.

Il peut paraître paradoxal de parler d'instabilité quand François Mitterrand est président de la République pendant quatorze ans et Jacques Chirac, douze ans (un septennat, un quinquennat, 1995-2002-2007). Mais ces durées ne sont que la manifestation la plus éclatante du mensonge et de la duperie qui se sont nichés au cœur de la République.

Ce trucage, destiné à masquer la déconstruction des institutions de la Vᵉ République, se nomme « cohabitation ». Il ne s'agit pas d'un pouvoir rassemblant autour d'un programme résultant d'un compromis politique, du type « grande coalition » entre démocratie chrétienne et sociaux-démocrates allemands, mais d'une neutralisation – stérilisation et paralysie – du président et du Premier ministre issus de partis opposés et préparant la revanche de leurs camps.

La « cohabitation » est pire que l'instabilité qui naissait de la rotation accélérée du manège ministériel sous les IIIᵉ et IVᵉ Républiques. Car, ici, l'ambiguïté, l'hypocrisie, la « guerre couverte », sont le quotidien de l'exécutif bicéphale dominé par la préparation de l'échéance électorale suivante.

Ce système – annoncé par Giscard d'Estaing – présente certes l'avantage de montrer qu'entre les grandes familles politiques, dans un pays démocratique, les guerres de religion et l'affrontement d'idéologies totalitaires contraires ont cédé la place à des divergences raisonnées à propos des politiques à mettre en œuvre au sein d'une société, d'une économie, d'un monde que plus personne ne veut radicalement changer.

C'est bien la fin de la « guerre civile franco-française », le choix de gouverner en s'appuyant sur un groupe central, souhaités par Giscard, qui se mettent lentement en place.

Mais, de manière parallèle, le mitterrandisme puis le chiraquisme ne sont que des giscardismes masqués, l'un sous les discours de gauche, l'autre, sous les propos volontaristes d'un néogaullisme improbable.

Déçu par les majorités qu'il élit, le peuple, d'une échéance électorale à l'autre, contredit son vote précédent, et aucune majorité gouvernementale ne se succède à elle-même depuis 1981.

En 1986, la droite l'emporte aux législatives et Chirac devient le Premier ministre de François Mitterrand.

Ce dernier, désavoué par la défaite de son camp aux législatives, a « giscardisé » les institutions en ne démissionnant pas, mais en menant, de 1986 à 1988, une guerre souterraine contre Chirac, battu en 1988 par un président malade de soixante-douze ans.

Mitterrand dissout alors l'Assemblée. Une majorité socialiste est élue, et Rocard est investi chef du gouvernement.

En 1993, effondrement socialiste, gouvernement d'Édouard Balladur et présidence de Mitterrand jusqu'en 1995.

Élection de Chirac, qui ne dissoudra l'Assemblée – de droite – qu'en 1997, et début d'une nouvelle cohabitation, puisqu'une Assemblée à majorité socialiste est élue...

Cette rivalité au sommet trouve sa justification dans le recours à des discours qui, au nom du « socialisme » ou du « libéralisme », anathématisent l'autre.

Mais ils ne convainquent plus qu'une frange toujours plus réduite de la population. Les couches populaires sont de moins en moins sensibles à ces invocations idéologisées qui n'empêchent pas la dégradation de leur situation (chômeurs, exclus, bénéficiaires du revenu minimum d'insertion, habitants de « quartiers défavorisés »). Ils ressentent cette « guerre verbale » comme un théâtre qui ne parvient plus à masquer une convergence, des arrangements qu'on ne saurait avouer puisqu'il faut, pour des raisons électorales et de partage du pouvoir, continuer de s'opposer comme à Guignol.

Les changements radicaux intervenus dans la situation mondiale rendent encore plus factices les affrontements entre une gauche qui continue de parler parfois marxiste – à tout le moins « socialiste » – et une droite qui, comme la gauche de gouvernement, applaudit à la construction européenne et aux traités qui l'élèvent : Acte unique, Maastricht, monnaie unique, etc.

On verra sur les mêmes tribunes, en 1992, ministres « socialistes » et chiraquiens ou giscardiens favorables à la ratification du traité de Maastricht, cependant que d'autres socialistes (Chevènement) et d'autres « gaullistes » (Séguin) s'y opposeront, les uns et les autres rejoignant pour l'élection présidentielle de 1995 des cases différentes : Séguin, celle de Chirac, Chevènement, celle de Jospin, les giscardiens et d'autres RPR, celle de Balladur.

En fait, la question européenne est révélatrice de la position des élites politiques – et intellectuelles – à l'égard des questions internationales.

Car Mitterrand ne rejette pas seulement l'esprit et la pratique gaulliens des institutions, il abandonne aussi les fondements de la politique extérieure de De Gaulle.

Comme Giscard, il estime que la France ne peut jouer un rôle qu'au sein de l'Europe : « La France est notre patrie, mais l'Europe est notre avenir », répète-t-il. Il faut donc reprendre sa place dans l'OTAN, suivre les États-Unis dans la guerre du Golfe (1990).

La chute du mur de Berlin – 1989 – et la réunification de l'Allemagne, puis la disparition de l'Union soviétique, confortent la diplomatie mitterrandienne dans l'idée que seule l'Union européenne offre à la France un champ d'action.

Restent les interventions dans le pré carré africain, les discours sur les droits de l'homme qui tentent de redonner à la France une audience mondiale non plus au plan politique, mais par les propos moralisateurs, comme si compassion et assistance étaient la menue monnaie de la vocation universaliste de la France.

Ces prises de position manifestent le ralliement du pouvoir socialiste puis du pouvoir chiraquien à l'idéologie du « droit et du devoir d'ingérence », puis du Tribunal pénal international, qui s'appuie sur la conviction que le temps de la souveraineté des nations est révolu.

Les formes nationales étant obsolètes, il convient de privilégier les communautés, les individus, et de rogner les pouvoirs de l'État.

En ce sens, les gouvernements socialistes sont aussi en rupture avec une « certaine idée de la France ».

Ils retrouvent la veine du pacifisme socialiste de l'entre-deux-guerres. C'est au nom de ce pacifisme qu'on juge la Communauté européenne. Elle est censée avoir instauré la paix entre les nations belliqueuses du Vieux Continent. Cette idéologie « post-nationale » ne permet pas de comprendre qu'il existe une « âme de la France » et que le peuple – dans ses couches les plus humbles – ressent douloureusement qu'on ne s'y réfère plus. Pis : qu'on la nie.

Et rares sont les politiques – à droite comme à gauche – qui prennent conscience du caractère « national » de la révolution démocratique qui secoue et libère l'Europe centrale après la chute du mur de Berlin et la fin de l'URSS.

Cette force du désir d'identité nationale est ignorée. Évoquer la France, a fortiori la patrie ou la nation, est jugé, par la plupart des socialistes, comme l'expression d'un archaïsme réactionnaire.

Durant les deux septennats de François Mitterrand, ce qui a été mis en avant, ce sont les problèmes économiques, sociaux, voire sociétaux.

Certes, réduire la durée du temps de travail à trente-neuf heures, fixer l'âge de la retraite à soixante ans, instituer une cinquième semaine de congés payés, c'est satisfaire les couches salariées.

Mais l'état de grâce, comme au temps du Front populaire, ne dure que quelques mois. Et les mesures prises en 1981, qui rappellent celles décidées en 1936, les « avancées sociales ou les nationalisations », n'empêchent pas le nombre de chômeurs d'augmenter, les déficits, de se creuser.

C'est qu'il y a une liaison intime entre l'insertion au sein de la Communauté européenne, les choix libéraux qui sont faits à Bruxelles et la politique qu'un gouvernement peut suivre. Et, au bout de quelques mois, dès 1982-1983, s'annoncent la « pause » dans les réformes, la « rigueur ».

Ne pas s'engager dans cette voie, choisir une « autre politique », exigerait de prendre ses distances avec l'Europe. Ce serait une rupture révolutionnaire, et Mitterrand, malgré les conseils de quelques-uns de ses proches, ne la veut pas.

Au vrai, la nomination dès 1981 de Jacques Delors – naguère l'un des concepteurs de la « nouvelle société » de Chaban – au poste de ministre de l'Économie et des Finances montre bien que, malgré quelques pas de côté, Mitterrand ne tenait pas à s'éloigner de la piste du bal.

Mais alors tout discours « socialiste » devient mensonger,

puisque la politique économique et budgétaire, et donc la politique sociale engendrée par les choix économiques et financiers, est encadrée par Bruxelles.

Mitterrand peut bien, dans des envolées lyriques, dénoncer « l'argent qui grossit en dormant », son Premier ministre Bérégovoy ouvre la France à la libre circulation des capitaux, met en œuvre une législation favorable à l'expansion de la Bourse, maintient une politique monétaire du franc fort qui provoque la hausse du chômage.

En abandonnant la souveraineté nationale, Mitterrand et les socialistes, aux discours près, acceptent une politique de libéralisation qui est en contradiction avec les mesures économiques et sociales qu'ils ont prises en 1981-1982 ou qu'ils promettent encore. Ce qu'ils développent, face à l'impossibilité de prendre des mesures « socialistes » dans le cadre européen dont ils exaltent par ailleurs la nécessité et la pertinence, c'est une politique sociale d'assistance dont le RMI (Michel Rocard), les « emplois aidés », les allocations de toutes sortes, sont l'expression.

Mais la politique sociale creuse le déficit budgétaire, il faudrait relancer la croissance, donc baisser les impôts pour attirer les investissements et favoriser la consommation, ce qui accroîtrait d'autant les déficits – toutes choses en contradiction avec le traité de Maastricht. Le piège européen est en place, qui condamne toute politique non libérale.

Dès lors, le chômage, résultat de ces contradictions, s'accroît. Mitterrand s'avoue incapable de le réduire (« Nous avons tout essayé »).

Par ailleurs, le nombre des immigrés augmente, résultat de la politique de regroupement familial, d'ouverture des frontières, et de l'attrait qu'exercent la France et l'Europe sur les populations misérables du Sud et de l'Est.

Mais les Français ont le sentiment que l'identité de la nation change au moment même où ils perçoivent que le pays a perdu sa souveraineté politique.

Les élites françaises – celles de gauche au premier chef – persistent à ne pas comprendre cette angoisse et cette souffrance, à propos de la perte de la nation, qu'éprouvent les catégories les plus humbles.

Les réponses « mitterrandiennes » sont sociétales, le plus souvent tactiques et politiciennes.

On suscite la création de mouvements antiracistes, manière de dériver vers une bataille idéologique à faible incidence économique, donc compatible avec les directives européennes, les protestations populaires.

L'émergence, à partir de 1983, d'une formation d'extrême droite, le Front national de Jean-Marie Le Pen, qui se présente comme un mouvement nationaliste et qui atteindra en 1995 plus de 15 % des voix, favorise la stratégie mitterrandienne.

On agite l'épouvantail du Front national pour compromettre la droite si elle songeait à s'allier avec lui, et pour rassembler autour de la gauche les jeunes générations.

On recrée une tension idéologique qui déplace les affrontements sociaux sur le terrain de la menace fasciste, du racisme, de l'antisémitisme, de la xénophobie.

En fait, on abandonne le thème de la souveraineté nationale à cette extrême droite, ce qui, imagine-t-on, va conforter l'européisme.

On oublie que la « nation », la défense de l'identité française, sont des éléments fondamentaux de l'âme de la France.

Or des millions de Français, surtout parmi les couches populaires, ont le sentiment qu'ils ne sont plus pris en compte.

Les défilés populaires du 1er mai sont des rituels qui paraissent désuets, tandis que la Gay Pride occupe les écrans de télévision.

L'âme de la France semble à beaucoup s'évanouir.

On ne se reconnaît plus dans les orientations politiques. Où est la gauche ? Où est la droite ? Qu'est devenue la France ?

La corruption éclabousse tous les milieux politiques.

Le 1er mai 1993 – jour symbolique –, l'ancien Premier ministre Pierre Bérégovoy se suicide.

C'est comme si une gauche, celle qui avait conquis le pouvoir et gouverné avec François Mitterrand, venait de mourir. L'Assemblée nationale est à droite, Édouard Balladur est Premier ministre d'un président de la République rongé par la maladie.

En 1995, Jacques Chirac va être élu avec 52,64 % des voix contre 47,36 % à Lionel Jospin, candidat du Parti socialiste.

Ces chiffres ne donnent pas la mesure de la profondeur des changements qui ont affecté l'âme de la France au cours des deux septennats de François Mitterrand.

Le temps de la « force tranquille », du village immuable de 1981 recueilli autour de son clocher, paraît d'un autre siècle.

En 1995, il est question de mosquées et non d'églises.

Le débat qui avait secoué le pays en 1984 sur la place de l'enseignement privé – catholique – et qui, le 24 juin de cette année-là, avait mobilisé plus d'un million de manifestants défendant la « liberté de l'enseignement » contre l'idée d'un grand service public unifié prôné par les socialistes, a été tranché ; la querelle – qui peut rejouer en telle ou telle circonstance – n'occupe plus le devant de la scène.

Mais la question de la laïcité reste centrale. Et elle s'est posée à la fin du second septennat de Mitterrand à propos de l'autorisation ou de l'interdiction donnée aux jeunes musulmanes de porter en classe un foulard islamique.

Tout comme demeure ouverte la question du rôle de l'État central. Gaston Defferre, le ministre de l'Intérieur de Mitterrand, avait, dès 1981, engagé le pays dans la voie de la décentralisation. Elle s'est élargie pas à pas.

Fallait-il aller jusqu'à l'autonomie, négocier avec les nationalistes corses qui n'hésitent pas à utiliser la violence ?

Ces questions – laïcité, pouvoirs de l'État central –, comme les politiques économiques et budgétaires, se posent dans le cadre de l'Union européenne. Du coup, certains s'interrogent : pourquoi un étage national, dès lors qu'il y a le rez-de-chaussée régional et la terrasse européenne ? La nation n'est-elle pas devenue caduque, inutile ?

Durant les deux septennats mitterrandiens, la place, la puissance, la signification de la nation, qui avaient été les obsessions de De Gaulle, paraissent absentes des préoccupations socialistes.

L'âme de la France, c'est dans les paysages de ses terroirs qu'elle gît désormais. On la rencontre au sommet de la roche de Solutré ou sur le mont Beuvray, site de la ville gauloise de Bibracte où Mitterrand avait songé à se faire inhumer, achetant même à cette fin un carré de cette terre, de cette histoire.

Mais l'indépendance, la souveraineté de la nation, que sont-elles devenues ?

Mitterrand enrichit Paris de monuments. Il croit donc à la pérennité de la capitale de la France.

Mais est-elle pour lui un centre d'impulsion politique au rayonnement mondial, ou seulement un lieu de promenades touristiques et gastronomiques dont ce gourmet de la vie sous toutes ses formes était particulièrement friand ?

L'âme de la France ne doit-elle plus être que cela : une mémoire qu'on visite comme un musée ?

Au fond, durant deux septennats, François Mitterrand a fait à son peuple la « pédagogie du renoncement tranquille ».

Et le peuple, de manière instinctive, en s'abstenant aux élections, en changeant de représentants, en votant pour les « irréguliers », a protesté, s'est débattu comme un homme qui refuse les somnifères et ne veut pas renoncer à son âme.

Et qui s'indigne qu'au moment où toutes les nations renaissent on veuille que l'une des plus anciennes et des plus glorieuses s'assoupisse.

72

De 1995 à 2007, d'un siècle à l'autre, la question de la France est posée.

Comme aux moments les plus cruciaux de son histoire – guerre de Cent Ans ou guerres de Religion, « étrange défaite » de 1940 –, c'est de la survie de son âme qu'il s'agit.

C'est dire que le bilan de la double présidence de Jacques Chirac – 1995-2002-2007 – ou du quinquennat au poste de Premier ministre de Lionel Jospin (1997-2002), dans le cadre de la plus longue période de cohabitation de la Ve République, ne saurait se limiter à évaluer les qualités et les faiblesses des deux chefs de l'exécutif, ou à mesurer l'ampleur des problèmes qu'ils ont été conduits à affronter dans un environnement international qui change totalement de visage et pèse sur la France.

En 1995, on imaginait encore, malgré la guerre du Golfe contre l'Irak, un avenir de paix mondiale patronnée par l'hyperpuissance américaine.

En fait, la guerre sous toutes ses formes a rapidement obscurci l'horizon. Bombardement et destruction de villes européennes (Dubrovnik, Sarajevo, puis Belgrade écrasée sous les attaques aériennes de l'OTAN en 1999). Et la France s'est engagée dans ce conflit des Balkans contre ses alliés traditionnels, les Serbes au nom du « droit d'ingérence ».

Elle est aussi concernée, comme toutes les puissances occidentales, par l'attaque réussie contre les États-Unis (World Trade Center, 11 septembre 2001).

« Nous sommes tous américains », affirme le directeur du *Monde* – et la France s'engage dans la guerre contre l'Afghanistan (2002).

Mais elle conteste l'intervention des États-Unis et de leurs alliés en Irak en 2003.

La posture de Chirac, le discours de son ministre des Affaires étrangères, Villepin, au Conseil de sécurité de l'ONU, semblent réactiver une politique extérieure « gaullienne », la France apparaissant comme le leader des pays qui tentent de conserver un espace de dialogue entre les deux civilisations, musulmane et chrétienne.

Ce n'est néanmoins, dans la politique étrangère française, qu'une séquence, certes majeure, mais contredite par d'autres attitudes. Comme si Chirac, plus opportuniste que déterminé, hésitait à élaborer une voie française.

Il est vrai que son choix a suscité dans les élites françaises des critiques nombreuses. On a dénoncé son « antiaméricanisme ».

Par ailleurs, la radicalisation de la situation mondiale se poursuit : attentats de Madrid et de Londres (2004-2005) ; reprise des violences en Afghanistan ; guerre civile en Irak ; guerre entre Israël et le Hezbollah aux dépens du Liban en 2006 ; ambitions nucléaires de l'Iran ; pourrissement de la question palestinienne.

La France hésite, condamne l'idée d'un choc des civilisations entre l'islamisme et l'Occident.

Chirac craint que cet affrontement ne provoque des tensions – elles existent déjà, mais restent marginales – entre des Français d'origines et de confessions différentes.

La France semble donc incertaine, la situation internationale mettant à l'épreuve sa capacité à résister aux forces extérieures.

L'inquiétude se fait jour de voir renaître des « partis de l'étranger », l'appartenance à telle ou telle communauté apparaissant, pour des raisons religieuses, plus essentielle que la spécificité française.

Ainsi se trouve posée la question de la « communautarisation » de la société nationale.

Or, de 1995 à 1997, de nombreux indices ont montré qu'elle était en cours.

On a vu le Premier ministre Lionel Jospin conclure avec les nationalistes corses des accords de Matignon – un « relevé de conclusions » – sans que ses interlocuteurs aient renoncé à légitimer le recours à la violence et à revendiquer l'indépendance.

En acceptant d'ouvrir des discussions avec eux – pas seulement pour des raisons électorales : la présidentielle de 2002 est proche –, Jospin reconnaît de fait la pertinence de la stratégie nationaliste et la thèse d'une Corse colonisée et exploitée par la France.

Or – toutes les élections le montrent – les nationalistes ne représentent qu'une minorité violente, s'autoproclamant représentative du « peuple corse », tout comme les gauchistes affirmaient naguère qu'ils étaient l'expression de la classe ouvrière.

Cette reconnaissance par le Premier ministre, avec l'assentiment tacite du président de la République, et par toutes les « élites » politiques de ce pays – exception faite de quelques « irréguliers » comme Jean-Pierre Chevènement – est lourde de sens.

Le 6 février 1998, en effet, le préfet de Corse, Claude Érignac, a été tué d'une balle dans la nuque à Ajaccio par des nationalistes.

Toutes les autorités républicaines et la population corse ont condamné ce crime hautement symbolique. Le préfet représente l'État centralisé – napoléonien, mais héritier de la monarchie. L'abattre, c'est, par la lâcheté du crime et par sa signification, atteindre l'État, la France, marquer que l'on veut les « déconstruire ».

Accepter que les porte-parole de ces criminels non repentis négocient à Matignon, c'est capituler, admettre, à terme, la fin de la République une et indivisible.

Ceux qui dirigent l'État entre 1995 et 2007 – qu'ils appartiennent au parti chiraquien ou à la « gauche plurielle » – ont jugé que l'espoir de paix civile valait l'abandon des principes républicains.

D'autres signes jalonnant la marche vers une société française communautarisée se multiplient entre 1995 et 2007.

La création du Conseil français du culte musulman, les nombreuses critiques émises au moment de la loi interdisant le port du voile islamique dans certaines conditions, la création d'associations se définissant par leurs origines (Conseil représentatif des associations noires, Indigènes de la République, etc.) sont, quelles que soient les intentions de leurs initiateurs, la preuve de l'émiettement désiré de l'identité française.

Et déjà surgissent – avivées par la situation internationale – des rivalités entre ces communautés.

C'est bien l'« âme de la France » qui se retrouve ainsi contestée dans l'un de ses aspects essentiels : « l'égalité entre les individus liés personnellement à la nation, sans le "filtre" et la médiation d'une représentation communautaire, éthique ou religieuse ».

Le même processus de « déconstruction nationale » est à l'œuvre dans la plupart des secteurs de la vie politique, économique, sociale et intellectuelle.

Dans le domaine institutionnel, Chirac et Jospin ont, de concert, réduit le mandat présidentiel à cinq ans.

Ils poursuivent ainsi le travail de sape de la Constitution gaullienne entrepris par Mitterrand.

Chirac, comme Mitterrand, choisit la cohabitation comme moyen de survie politique.

Il est en effet confronté, dès les lendemains de sa victoire de 1995, à l'impossibilité de tenir ses promesses électorales.

Les contraintes budgétaires d'origine européenne sont renforcées par les obligations liées au passage à la monnaie unique, l'euro, prévu pour 2002.

Premier ministre, Alain Juppé – né en 1945, pur produit de l'élitisme républicain (ENS-ENA) – applique donc une politique de rigueur qui soulève contre lui, en décembre 1995, une vague de grèves à la SNCF, soutenues par une partie des élites intellectuelles représentée par le sociologue Pierre Bourdieu.

Ce dernier aspect est significatif de la permanence et de la réactivation en France d'un courant critique radical. La mort de Sartre en 1980 n'a pas fait disparaître la posture de l'intellectuel critique. Même si les figures emblématiques sont moins nombreuses – Bourdieu en est alors une –, la multiplication du nombre des enseignants et des étudiants aux conditions de vie difficiles crée une sorte de « parti intellectuel prolétarisé ».

Sans se référer obligatoirement à une idéologie définie, les jeunes professeurs, les étudiants diplômés à la recherche d'un emploi, retrouvent, dans telle ou telle circonstance, un discours radical.

Certains d'entre eux, durant cette période 1995-2007, vont rejoindre les rangs des formations d'extrême gauche qui contestent le Parti socialiste en tant que parti de gouvernement. Ces nouvelles générations, plus instinctives et spontanées que théoriciennes, sans culture historique, philosophique ou révolutionnaire précise, prolongent néanmoins une tradition nationale contestatrice.

Dès lors, en France, la « gauche » gouvernementale, séduite par la « troisième voie » telle que peuvent l'exprimer un Clinton, un Tony Blair, un Schröder (à la conférence des sociaux-démocrates européens réunie à Florence en 1999, Jospin, Premier ministre, est présent aux côtés de Bill Clinton), est électoralement menacée et idéologiquement bloquée par cette extrême gauche.

Quand la social-démocratie explicite et théorise sa ligne politique – Lionel Jospin, né en 1937, de culture trotskiste, s'y essaie –, elle ne peut que dire qu'elle est favorable à l'économie de marché, et hostile à une « société de marché ».

Mais elle est serrée par la mâchoire européenne. Elle ne peut prendre que des mesures sociales, étatiques – réduction de la semaine de travail à trente-cinq heures, création d'emplois aidés, recrutement de fonctionnaires –, qui remettent en cause l'efficacité économique libérale.

Elle est tentée de dépasser ces contradictions en portant le combat contre la droite sur le terrain sociétal : mesures en faveur des immigrés, des homosexuels (PACS, bientôt mariage, droit à l'adoption). Mais elle s'avance prudemment sur le terrain de la flexibilité du travail, compte tenu de cette extrême gauche active qui exerce une sorte de chantage idéologique sur elle.

Ces hésitations du Parti socialiste, ce paysage politique qui se radicalise à l'extrême gauche – et, sur l'autre versant, à l'extrême droite : 15 % de voix pour le Front national à l'élection présidentielle de 1995 –, fragilisent la démocratie représentative.

En décembre 1995, les grévistes font reculer Chirac, qui, pour sortir le gouvernement Juppé de l'impasse, provoque la dissolution de l'Assemblée en 1997.

La gauche l'emporte, et une cohabitation de cinq années commence, avec comme seul objectif, pour Chirac, d'user Jospin afin de le battre à l'élection présidentielle de 2002.

Et Jospin, lui, n'a pour but politique que d'être élu président.

Entre leurs mains politiciennes, les institutions de la Ve République sont devenues une machine à empêcher tout projet à long terme !

Surprise révélatrice de la profondeur de la crise nationale et de la crise de la gauche : pour la première fois depuis 1969, le représentant du Parti socialiste, concurrencé par d'autres candidats se réclamant de la gauche, ne sera pas présent au second tour de l'élection présidentielle de 2002. Jospin, écarté par les électeurs, Le Pen est opposé à Chirac, devenu le candidat « républicain », « antifasciste », « antiraciste », etc.

Débat truqué qui empêche la vraie confrontation entre Chirac et Jospin !

Mais situation exemplaire : les électeurs ne croient plus à la différence entre la gauche et la droite de gouvernement, liées en effet par le carcan européen.

Dès lors, c'est la rue qui décide.

En 2006, une loi votée par le Parlement – sur le contrat première embauche (CPE) – suscite des manifestations importantes.

Jacques Chirac la promulgue puis la retire aussitôt, désavouant et protégeant tout à la fois son Premier ministre.

Cette pirouette juridique et politicienne confirme la déconstruction des institutions et le mensonge mêlé de ridicule où sombre la vie politique.

C'est bien la France et son âme qui sont en question.

C'est que, dans tous les secteurs de la société, la crise nationale grossit depuis plusieurs décennies.

En fait, dès les années 30 du XXe siècle, les élites ont commencé à douter de la capacité de la France à surmonter les problèmes qui se posaient à elle.

Les hommes politiques ne réussissaient pas à donner à leur action un sens qui transcende les circonstances, oriente la nation vers un avenir.

Dans ces conditions, la défaite de 1940, cet affrontement cataclysmique, n'avait rien d'« étrange ».

L'impuissance de la IVe République, après la brève euphorie de la victoire, était inscrite dans l'instabilité gouvernementale et dans la médiocrité des hommes politiques, incapables de faire face aux problèmes posés par la fin de l'empire colonial.

Le gaullisme est une parenthèse constructive mais limitée à quelques années – 1962-1967 –, une fois l'affaire algérienne réglée.

Mais, de Gaulle renvoyé, les problèmes demeurent et se compliquent.

Cette France incertaine qui cherche dans la construction européenne un substitut à sa volonté défaillante débouche sur les années 1995-2007, où la crise nationale ne peut plus être masquée.

Il ne s'agit pas de déclin. Les réussites existent. La France reste l'une des grandes puissances du monde. Des tentatives pour arrêter la déconstruction se manifestent çà et là (ainsi la loi sur le voile islamique et quelques postures en politique étrangère). Mais alors que le peuple continue d'espérer que les élites gouvernementales et intellectuelles lui proposeront une perspective d'avenir pour la nation, on lui présente des réponses fractionnées, destinées à chaque catégorie de Français.

Or une somme de communautés, cela ne fait pas une nation, et un entassement de solutions circonstancielles ne fait pas un projet pour la France.

Le vote qui place le Front national au second tour de l'élection présidentielle du 21 avril 2002 traduit ce déficit de sens.

Et le rejet, le 29 mai 2005, du traité constitutionnel européen signifie que la majorité du peuple – contre les élites – ne croit pas qu'un abandon supplémentaire de souveraineté nationale permettra de combler ce déficit de sens qui est cause de la crise nationale. D'autant moins que, de la persistance d'un chômage élevé aux émeutes dans les banlieues (2005), l'insécurité sociale s'accroît, redoublant les problèmes liés à l'identité nationale.

Car durant ces douze années de la présidence Chirac, ce n'est plus seulement le sens de l'avenir de la France qui est en question, mais aussi son histoire.

Ceux qui ne croient plus en l'avenir de la France ou qui refusent de s'y inscrire déconstruisent son histoire, n'en retiennent que les lâchetés, la face sombre.

Par son discours du 16 juillet 1995, Chirac a reconnu la France – non des individus, non l'État de Vichy – coupable et responsable de la persécution antisémite, contredisant ainsi toute la stratégie mémorielle du général de Gaulle. Selon lui, la France – et pas seulement les Papon, les Bousquet, les Touvier – doit faire repentance et être punie.

L'on a vu ainsi s'ouvrir en 2006 un procès intenté à la SNCF, accusée d'avoir accepté de faire rouler les trains de déportés. Et un tribunal condamner l'entreprise nationale, oubliant les contraintes imposées par l'occupant, le rôle héroïque des cheminots dans la Résistance, cette « bataille du rail » exaltée au lendemain de la Libération !

France coupable, comme si la France libre et la France résistante n'avaient pas existé, donnant sens à la nation.

Mais coupable aussi, et devant se repentir pour la colonisation, pour l'esclavage, la France de Louis XIV et de Napoléon, de Jules Ferry et de De Gaulle.

Si bien que, sous la présidence de Chirac, en 2005, la France participe à la célébration de la victoire anglaise de Trafalgar mais n'ose pas commémorer solennellement Austerlitz !

L'anachronisme, destructeur de la complexité contradictoire de l'histoire nationale, est ainsi à l'œuvre, dessinant le portrait d'une Marianne criminelle au détriment de la vérité historique.

Dans cette vision « post-héroïque » de la France, l'État et la communauté nationale sont des oppresseurs à combattre, à châtier, à détruire. Il faut, dit-on, « dénationaliser la France ».

Restent *des* communautés, chacune avec sa mémoire, s'opposant les unes aux autres, faisant éclater la mémoire collective, la mémoire nationale, ce mythe réputé mensonger.

Et, de 1995 à 2007, l'Assemblée nationale a fixé par la loi cette nouvelle histoire officielle, anachronique, repentante, imposant aux historiens ces nouvelles vérités qu'on ne peut discuter sous peine de procès intentés par les représentants des diverses communautés.

Comment, à partir de cette mémoire émiettée, de cette histoire révisée, reconstruire un sens partagé par toute la nation ?

Comment bâtir avec les citoyens nouveaux qui vivent sur le sol hexagonal un projet pour la France qui rassemblera tous les Français, quelles que soient leurs origines, et faire vivre ainsi l'âme de la France ?

C'est la question qui se pose à la nation à la veille de l'élection présidentielle de 2007, sans doute la plus importante consultation électorale depuis plus d'un demi-siècle.

Avec elle s'ouvre une nouvelle séquence de l'histoire nationale. Elle sera tourmentée. L'élu(e) devra trancher et donc mécontenter et non plus seulement parler, ou séduire et sourire. Les mirages se dissiperont. Après le temps des illusions peut venir celui du ressentiment et de la colère. Certains Français douteront de l'avenir de la nation.

Qu'ils se souviennent alors que, au temps les plus sombres de notre histoire millénaire, dans une *France des cavernes* le poète René Char, combattant de la Résistance, écrivait :

J'ai confectionné avec des déchets de montagnes
des hommes qui embaumeront quelque temps
les glaciers.

Dans ces lignes mystérieuses, bat l'âme de la France.

Décembre 2006.

CHRONOLOGIE V

Vingt dates clés (1920-2007)

1923 : La France occupe la Ruhr

1933 : Après l'accession de Hitler au pouvoir (30 janvier), l'Allemagne quitte la Société des Nations

1936 : Hitler réoccupe la Rhénanie (7 mars) – Front populaire (mai-juin). Guerre d'Espagne (juillet)

1938 : Accords de Munich

14 juin 1940 : Les Allemands entrent dans Paris, ville ouverte

18 juin 1940 : Appel du général de Gaulle à la résistance

10 juillet 1940 : Pleins pouvoirs à Pétain, fin de la IIIe République

1943 : Jean Moulin préside à la création du Conseil national de la Résistance (CNR)

1944 (24 août) : « Paris libéré par lui-même »

Janvier 1946 : De Gaulle démissionne (20 janvier)

1954 : Défaite de Diên Biên Phu (7 mai), attentats en Algérie marquant le début de l'insurrection (1er novembre)

Janvier 1956 : Victoire du Front républicain (Mendès France, Guy Mollet)

Mai-juin 1958 : Retour au pouvoir du général de Gaulle

18 mars 1962 : Fin de la guerre d'Algérie

10 mai 1981 : François Mitterrand élu président de la République. Il le restera jusqu'en 1995 (réélu en 1988)

1995-2007 : Présidences de Jacques Chirac (réélu en 2002)

21 avril 2002 : Le Pen au second tour de l'élection présidentielle

29 mai 2005 : Les Français rejettent le traité constitutionnel européen

2007 : Élections présidentielle et législatives

INDEX

TABLE

DU MÊME AUTEUR

ROMANS

Le Cortège des vainqueurs, Robert Laffont, 1972.
Un pas vers la mer, Robert Laffont, 1973.
L'Oiseau des origines, Robert Laffont, 1974.
Que sont les siècles pour la mer, Robert Laffont, 1977.
Une affaire intime, Robert Laffont, 1979.
France, Grasset, 1980 (et Le Livre de Poche).
Un crime très ordinaire, Grasset, 1982 (et Le Livre de Poche).
La Demeure des puissants, Grasset, 1983 (et Le Livre de Poche).
Le Beau Rivage, Grasset, 1985 (et Le Livre de Poche).
Belle Époque, Grasset, 1986 (et Le Livre de Poche).
La Route Napoléon, Robert Laffont, 1987 (et Le Livre de Poche).
Une affaire publique, Robert Laffont, 1989 (et Le Livre de Poche).
Le Regard des femmes, Robert Laffont, 1991 (et Le Livre de Poche).
Un homme de pouvoir, Fayard, 2002 (et Le Livre de Poche).
Les Fanatiques, Fayard, 2006.

SUITES ROMANESQUES

La Baie des Anges :
  I. *La Baie des Anges*, Robert Laffont, 1975 (et Pocket).
  II. *Le Palais des Fêtes*, Robert Laffont, 1976 (et Pocket).
  III. *La Promenade des Anglais*, Robert Laffont, 1976 (et Pocket).
    (Parue en 1 volume dans la coll. « Bouquins », Robert Laffont, 1998.)

Les hommes naissent tous le même jour :
  I. *Aurore*, Robert Laffont, 1978.
  II. *Crépuscule*, Robert Laffont, 1979.

La Machinerie humaine :
  • *La Fontaine des Innocents*, Fayard, 1992 (et Le Livre de Poche).
  • *L'Amour au temps des solitudes*, Fayard, 1992 (et Le Livre de Poche).
  • *Les Rois sans visage*, Fayard, 1994 (et Le Livre de Poche).
  • *Le Condottiere*, Fayard, 1994 (et Le Livre de Poche).
  • *Le Fils de Klara H.*, Fayard, 1995 (et Le Livre de Poche).
  • *L'Ambitieuse*, Fayard, 1995 (et Le Livre de Poche).
  • *La Part de Dieu*, Fayard, 1996 (et Le Livre de Poche).
  • *Le Faiseur d'or*, Fayard, 1996 (et Le Livre de Poche).
  • *La Femme derrière le miroir*, Fayard, 1997 (et Le Livre de Poche).
  • *Le Jardin des Oliviers*, Fayard, 1999 (et Le Livre de Poche).

Bleu, blanc, rouge :
  I. *Marielle*, Éditions XO, 2000 (et Pocket).
  II. *Mathilde*, Éditions XO, 2000 (et Pocket).
  III. *Sarah*, Éditions XO, 2000 (et Pocket).

Les Patriotes :
  I. *L'Ombre et la Nuit*, Fayard, 2000 (et Le Livre de Poche).
  II. *La flamme ne s'éteindra pas*, Fayard, 2001 (et Le Livre de Poche).
  III. *Le Prix du sang*, Fayard, 2001 (et Le Livre de Poche).
  IV. *Dans l'honneur et par la victoire*, Fayard, 2001 (et Le Livre de Poche).

Les Chrétiens :
  I. *Le Manteau du soldat*, Fayard, 2002 (et Le Livre de Poche).
  II. *Le Baptême du roi*, Fayard, 2002 (et Le Livre de Poche).
  III. *La Croisade du moine*, Fayard, 2002 (et Le Livre de Poche).

Morts pour la France :
  I. *Le Chaudron des sorcières*, Fayard, 2003.
  II. *Le Feu de l'enfer*, Fayard, 2003.
  III. *La Marche noire*, Fayard, 2003.

L'Empire :
  I. *L'Envoûtement*, Fayard, 2004.
  II. *La Possession*, Fayard, 2004.
  III. *Le Désamour*, Fayard, 2004.

La Croix de l'Occident :
  I. *Par ce signe tu vaincras*, Fayard, 2005.
  II. *Paris vaut bien une messe*, Fayard, 2005.

Les Romains :
  I. *Spartacus. La Révolte des esclaves*, Fayard, 2005.
  II. *Néron. Le Règne de l'Antéchrist*, Fayard, 2006.
  III. *Titus. Le Martyre des Juifs*, Fayard, 2006.
  IV. *Marc Aurèle. Le Martyre des Chrétiens*, Fayard, 2006.
  V. *Constantin le Grand. L'Empire du Christ*, Fayard, 2006.

POLITIQUE-FICTION

La Grande Peur de 1989, Robert Laffont, 1966.
Guerre des gangs à Golf-City, Robert Laffont, 1991.

HISTOIRE, ESSAIS

L'Italie de Mussolini, Librairie académique Perrin, 1964, 1982 (et Marabout).
L'Affaire d'Éthiopie, Le Centurion, 1967.
Gauchisme, réformisme et révolution, Robert Laffont, 1968.
Histoire de l'Espagne franquiste, Robert Laffont, 1969.
Cinquième Colonne, 1939-1940, Plon, 1970 et 1980, Complexe, 1984.
Tombeau pour la Commune, Robert Laffont, 1971.
La Nuit des Longs Couteaux, Robert Laffont, 1971 et 2001.
La Mafia, mythe et réalités, Seghers, 1972.
L'Affiche, miroir de l'Histoire, Robert Laffont, 1973 et 1989.
Le Pouvoir à vif, Robert Laffont, 1978.
Le XXe Siècle, Librairie académique Perrin, 1979.
La Troisième Alliance, Fayard, 1984.
Les idées décident de tout, Galilée, 1984.
Lettre ouverte à Robespierre sur les nouveaux Muscadins, Albin Michel, 1986.
Que passe la Justice du Roi, Robert Laffont, 1987.
Manifeste pour une fin de siècle obscure, Odile Jacob, 1989.
La gauche est morte, vive la gauche, Odile Jacob, 1990.
L'Europe contre l'Europe, Le Rocher, 1992.
L'Amour de la France expliqué à mon fils, Le Seuil, 1999.
Histoire du monde de la Révolution française à nos jours en 212 épisodes, Fayard, 2001 (et Le Livre de Poche, mise à jour 2005 sous le titre *Les Clés de l'histoire contemporaine*).
Fier d'être français, Fayard, 2006.

BIOGRAPHIES

Maximilien Robespierre, histoire d'une solitude, Librairie académique Perrin, 1968 (et Pocket).
Garibaldi, la force d'un destin, Fayard, 1982.
Le Grand Jaurès, Robert Laffont, 1984 et 1994 (et Pocket).
Jules Vallès, Robert Laffont, 1988.
Une femme rebelle. Vie et mort de Rosa Luxemburg, Fayard, 2000.
Jè. Histoire modeste et héroïque d'un homme qui croyait aux lendemains qui chantent, Stock, 1994, et Mille et Une Nuits, 2004.

Napoléon :
  I. *Le Chant du départ*, Robert Laffont, 1997 (et Pocket).
  II. *Le Soleil d'Austerlitz*, Robert Laffont, 1997 (et Pocket).
  III. *L'Empereur des rois*, Robert Laffont, 1997 (et Pocket).
  IV. *L'Immortel de Sainte-Hélène*, Robert Laffont, 1997 (et Pocket).

De Gaulle :
  I. *L'Appel du destin*, Robert Laffont, 1998 (et Pocket).
  II. *La Solitude du combattant*, Robert Laffont, 1998 (et Pocket).
  III. *Le Premier des Français*, Robert Laffont, 1998 (et Pocket).
  IV. *La Statue du Commandeur*, Robert Laffont, 1998 (et Pocket).

Victor Hugo :
  I. *Je suis une force qui va !*, Éditions XO, 2001 (et Pocket).
  II. *Je serai celui-là !*, Éditions XO, 2001 (et Pocket).

César Imperator, Éditions XO, 2003 (et Pocket).

CONTE

La Bague magique, Casterman, 1981.

EN COLLABORATION

Au nom de tous les miens, de Martin Gray, Robert Laffont, 1971 (et Pocket).

Vous pouvez consulter le site Internet de Max Gallo sur
www.maxgallo.com